WOLFSKIN

Juliet Marillier

TOR®
fantasy

A TOM DOHERTY ASSOCIATES BOOK
NEW YORK

This is a work of fiction. All the characters and events portrayed in this book are fictitious or are used fictitiously.

WOLFSKIN

Maps by Bronya Marillier

A Tor Book
Published by Tom Doherty Associates, LLC
175 Fifth Avenue
New York, NY 10010

www.tor.com

Tor® is a registered trademark of Tom Doherty Associates, LLC.

ISBN 0-765-34590-0
EAN 978-0765-34590-5

First Tor edition: June 2003
First mass market edition: August 2004

Printed in the United States of America

0 9 8 7 6 5 4 3 2 1

To Elly and Simon,
who set me on the path to Orkney

Acknowledgments

My special thanks go to Sigurd Towrie, historical and folkloric guru and creator of a Web site that is a treasure trove of Orcadian knowledge (www.orkneyjar.com). Sigurd's patience in reading my huge manuscript and his perceptive comments and suggestions were of immeasurable assistance. I also thank Haukur Thorgeirsson, Anna Hansen, and Tarrin Wills for their work on the translation of Somerled's graffiti into Old Norse and then into runes. Bronya Marillier managed, as usual, to convert my inscrutable pencil sketches into wonderful maps. My two editors, Brianne Tunnicliffe in Sydney and Claire Eddy in New York, were a joy to work with. My daughters and sons provided constructive criticism and sustaining cups of tea during the book's gestation. Last but not least, my heartfelt thanks go to Cate Paterson at Pan Macmillan for her continuing support.

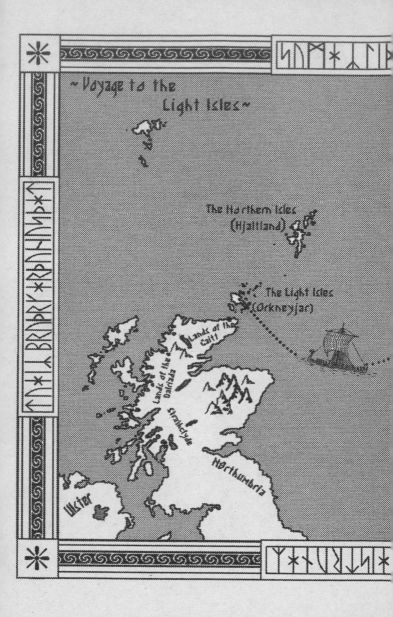

~ Voyage to the
       Light Isles ~

The Northern Isles
(Hjaltland)

The Light Isles
(Orkneyjar)

Lands of the
Caitt

Lands of the
Dalriada

Strathclyde

Northumbria

Ulster

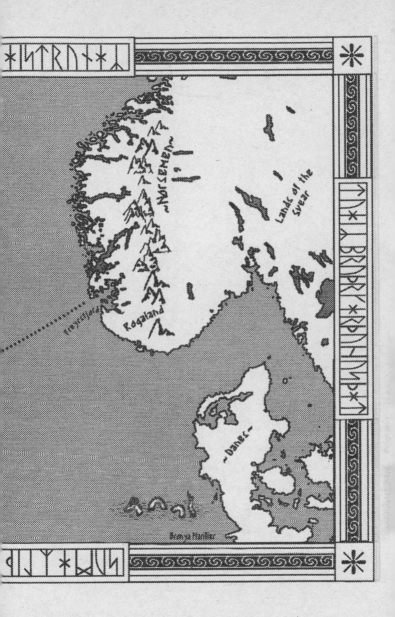

ONE

Winter bites hard in Rogaland. Sodden thatch shudders under its blanket of snow. Within the earthen barns sheep shiver and huddle, their breath small clouds. A man can lose himself in the drifts between byre and longhouse, and not be found again until the spring thaw. The pristine shroud that covers him is deep, but his long sleep is deeper still. In such a season the ice forms black and hard on lake and stream. For some, it is a good time: merchants whip their horses fast along the gleaming surface of the waterways, sledges piled high with pelts of squirrel and winter hare, with sealskins and oil and walrus tusks, with salt fish and fine embroidery. Boys dart across the river on their bone skates, quick as swallows, voices echoing away to lose themselves among the pale twigs of the winter birches.

It was Yuletide, and today there was no skating. The wind screamed around the temple, demanding entry through any chink or cranny its piercing fingers might discover. The timbers creaked and groaned in response, but held firm. So far, the roof had not leaked. Just as well he'd climbed up and shifted some of the weight off the shingles, Eyvind thought. The place would be full to bursting for the midwinter sacrifice.

Folk were already streaming into the valley, coming by sledge and on foot, on skis or skates, old men carried on their sons' backs, old women pulled on hurdles by red-faced children or panting dogs. The wind died down, as if holding its breath in honor of the occasion, but a new storm was coming. Dark clouds built in the west.

Eyvind had been working hard. The temple was on his mother's land, though shared by all in the surrounding district, so the burden of preparation fell squarely on the household at Hammarsby. He'd spent the morning chopping wood, stacking the pungent-smelling logs by the central hearth, making and banking the fire. It was nearly time for the ceremony; he should stir the coals now and put on more fuel. The white goat could be heard outside, bleating plaintively. His sisters had swept the stone floor clean and stripped the cobwebs from the rooftrees, while his mother, Ingi, polished the bronze surfaces of ritual knives and bowls to a bright, sunny sheen. These now lay ready on the altar at the temple's northern end. Cold light pierced the shingled roof above the hearth. From the altar, Thor's image stared down at Eyvind. Bushy browed, full-bearded, the god's wooden features held an expression of ferocious challenge. In his iron-gloved right hand he gripped the war hammer, Mjoll-nir; his left was held across his chest, to signify the making of some vow. Eyvind stared back, meeting Thor's gaze without blinking, and his own hand moved to his breast as if returning a pledge of allegiance. *Till death*, he thought Thor was saying, and he whispered his answer, "Till death and beyond."

The air was crisp and chill, the sacred space clean and quiet in the cold winter light. Later there would be a press of bodies in the temple, and it would be all too warm. As Eyvind used the iron poker to stir the embers to life, there was a sound from the entry behind him. He turned to see a tall, broad figure striding toward him, hair and beard touched to dark gold by the glow of the rekindled fire.

"Well, well, little brother! I swear you've doubled in size since the harvest!"

Eyvind felt a huge grin spreading across his face. "Eirik! You're home! Tell me where you've been, and what you've been doing! I want to hear everything!"

His brother seized him in a brief, hard embrace, then stretched out his hands to warm them before the flames.

"Later, later," he laughed. "Time enough for all that after the sacrifice. We'll have many tales, for I do not come alone."

"Hakon is here too?" Eyvind asked eagerly. He admired Hakon almost as much as he did Eirik himself, for his brother's friend had earned his wolfskin at not quite sixteen, which was generally thought to be some sort of record.

"Hakon, and others," Eirik said, suddenly serious. "The Jarl's kinsman, Ulf, is with us; a fine man, and a friend of ours. He's brought his young brother and several of his household. They're on their way to Jarl Magnus's court. Ulf has a wish for some delicate silverwork, I think to impress a lady. I made it known to him that our sister's husband is skilled in this craft. They will spend some nights here, in any event; the storm looks likely to prevent further travel for a little. The Jarl himself was urgent for home. He has a new son, bred when we came back from the spring viking; he is gone ahead, but we have time before we must join him. He will not set out again before spring's seeding is attended to." He glanced at his brother, and his tone changed. "Eyvind? I've a favor to ask you."

"What?"

There were new sounds from outside now, the rapid approach of many folk, voices raised in greeting.

"Later," Eirik said.

Eyvind asked him no further questions, though it was hard to wait. Eirik was his hero. Eirik was a Wolfskin. That was the most glorious calling in the whole world, for surely nothing could surpass the moment when you heard Thor's call to battle ringing in your ears, pulsing in your blood, filling every corner of your being with a red rage that shut out any thought of fear. To charge forward in pure courage, inspired by the god himself—that bold vision tugged at Eyvind's thoughts by day and filled his dreams by night. What matter if a Wolfskin's life were short? Such a warrior, once fallen, would be carried straight to Thor's right hand. One day he himself would pass the test, and become one of that band to which Eirik and Hakon belonged, as had many of Eyvind's kin in times past. The men of Hammarsby had a noble tradition in the Warfather's service. So Eyvind practiced with the bow and with the axe. He ran and climbed, he skated and swam. He shoveled snow and hunted and grew strong, awaiting that day. Eirik's tales kept his dreams alive. Later, perhaps his brother would tell of the autumn viking, the riches plundered, the battles won.

The folk of the district crowded into the temple, along with the men of Jarl Magnus's houschold, warrior and swineherd side by side. The high seat, its wooden pillars carved with many small creatures, was allocated to Ulf, kinsman of the Jarl, and by him stood the two Wolfskins, gold-bearded Eirik and the taller, hawk-featured Hakon. Each wore his short cloak of shaggy fur, fastened on the shoulder with an ornate silver brooch. Both were well armed: Eirik had the lethal skeggox, or hewing axe, on his back, and Hakon bore a fine sword, its hilt plated with copper

The nobleman, Ulf, was young: not so much older than Eirik himself, Eyvind thought. He had many folk with him, probably housecarls called into service for the autumn viking, with a few richly dressed men who might be part of Jarl Magnus's household elite, or Ulf's own retainers.

Eyvind's eldest brother, Karl, began the ceremony, his solemn features glowing warm in the fire's light. Eyvind was pleased with that fire; the smoke was rising cleanly through the roof opening to disperse in the cold air outside. Karl was no warrior. His choice had been to stay at home and husband the land, his brothers' portions as well as his own. It was a decision that, in hindsight, had been both wise and prudent, for their father, Hallvard Karlsson, had died in his prime, falling nobly in the service of the old Jarl, and leaving Ingi a widow. A young man with a young family of his own, Karl had simply stepped into his father's shoes. Now he and his mother controlled a wide sweep from hilltop to fjord, and commanded great respect in the district. All the same, Eyvind had never understood how his brother could prefer that existence over a life as Thor's warrior. Yet Karl seemed content with what he was.

"Master of storm, tamer of waves, iron-fisted one!" Karl now addressed the god in ringing tones. "Hewer of giants, serpent-slayer, worthiest of warriors! In blood, we honor you! In fire, we salute you! In the shadow time, we seek your protection. May your strong arm guard us on land path and sea path. Smite our enemies and smile on our endeavors."

"Hewer of giants, serpent-slayer, worthiest of warriors!" the assembled folk chanted, and their voices rose with the fire's heat to ring out across the snow-blanketed hills and the dark fir trees, straight to the ears of the god himself. Eyvind joined in the response, his gaze on Thor's staring, formidable eyes. Now Ingi walked slowly around the temple, bearing the ritual armring on a small embroidered cushion. Over many hours a fine smith had wrought there an image of the world tree with its attendant creatures: the serpent Nidhogg at its deepest roots, the noble eagle at its tip, the squirrel Ratatosk scampering between. The pattern went right around the ring; a man could never see the whole of it at one time. They held the sacrifice at first frost, at midwinter and in spring; at all other times, this treasure was well locked away from curious eyes. One hand after another reached out to brush reverently against the gleaming gold: girls' hands still soft and milk-pale, men's hands branded by axe shaft and bowstring, gnarled old hands that knew many winters on the land. All moved to pledge allegiance to the warrior, Thor, and to Odin, who had hung on that selfsame tree in search of wisdom. Even the thralls, clustered like a body of shadows at the far end near the door, stretched out tentative fingers as Ingi passed.

Karl lifted one of the ritual knives from the altar. The goat was struggling, afraid of the crowd and the fire. It seemed to Eyvind that the boy who clutched its neck rope could not hold the creature much longer. If he let go of the rope, the goat would free itself and bolt across the crowded temple in a chaos of hooves and horns. One could not offend the god thus. Eyvind got up and moved forward, relieving the red-faced lad of his charge, soothing the animal with soft words and a careful hand.

"Go on, then," he muttered. Karl raised the sacrificial knife; the firelight shone bright from its bronze blade. Eyvind tightened his grip, forcing the white goat's head back, exposing pink, naked skin where the hair on the throat grew more sparsely. Perhaps sensing the inevitable, the creature made one last desperate surge for freedom. But Eyvind's hands were strong. "Hurry up!" he hissed.

The knife came down, swept across. It should have been easy. Karl was a farmer; slaughtering stock was a routine task for him. But at the vital moment, a bird shrieked harshly above the smoke hole, and somehow the knife slipped sideways, so the blood did not spurt free and scarlet, but only seeped dark against the pure white hair. The goat screamed, and went on screaming. The god was displeased. Karl stood frozen, knowing the omen was bad for them. Thor's eyes were fierce and angry on his back.

"Here," said Eyvind. He took the knife from his brother's fingers, holding the bleeding goat with one hand, fingers twisted in the rope. His legs were on either side of the creature, forcing its agonized form still. This must be done well, now, or there would be failed crops, and sick beasts, and death and defeat on the field of war.

"Iron glove guide my blade," Eyvind said, fixing the god's wooden eyes with his own. "In your name, great battle god!"

There was only one way to do such things: hard and swift, straight across, near severing the neck. Fast, accurate, and merciful. How else could a clean kill be made? The screaming ceased. The white goat went limp. Eyvind's sisters held the bronze bowls to catch the blood. There was no telling what Thor thought of the manner of it, but at least Eyvind had done his best. He turned to face the folk, helping Karl to lift the slaughtered goat high so the blood could flow into the bowls. Drops spattered hands, faces, tunics. The altar bore a pattern of red spots; a bloody tear trickled down the face of the god.

I will kill cleanly for you, Eyvind told Thor, but not aloud. *Let me be a Wolfskin, and I will be your bravest warrior. Braver than Hakon; braver even than Eirik. All that I am, I will give you.* He looked down the temple toward the great assembly of folk, and straight into a pair of eyes so dark, so piercingly intense that his heart seemed to grow still a moment, then lurch painfully back into life. His mind had been on Thor, and blood, and sacrifice, and for a moment he had thought—but no, this was only a boy, a lad of his own age or maybe younger, who stood among the richly dressed entourage of the nobleman, Ulf. But how he stared. He looked at Eyvind as a starving wolf gazes at a man across the wayside fire, wary, fascinated, dangerous. The boy was pale and thin, his brown hair straggling unplaited, his mouth a line. His features were unremarkable save for those feral eyes. Eyvind blinked and looked away.

The girls bore the brimming bowls down the temple, white fingers dipping the blood twigs in, splashing bright crimson on floor and wall, anointing pillar and hearth and door frame, marking each man and woman with the sacrifice. When the bowls were empty, Karl laid them on the altar beside the knives, and the goat was dragged outside to be gutted and prepared for cooking.

"Warfather, we toast you this day of Yule!" Karl raised his great drinking horn. Ingi had passed between the men, pouring the ale with care: one would not wish to offend Thor by spilling any before the toasts were complete. "All hail, great battle leader!" Karl called. They drank.

"All hail mighty Thor, smiter of serpents!" Ulf cried, rising to his feet and lifting his own horn, a fine piece banded in silver. The men echoed his ringing tones and drank again.

"We salute you, crusher of giants!" Eirik's voice was as fierce as his weathered countenance. So the toasts continued, and as they did the patch of sky darkened above the roof aperture, and the inside of the temple glowed strangely in the fire's light. The boy was still staring; now the flames made twin points of brightness in his night-dark eyes. Thunder cracked in the sky above; sudden lightning speared the sky. The storm was on its way.

"Thor is well satisfied," said Eirik. "He calls his greeting to our small assembly; it is a hearty war song. Come, let us move close to the fire, and pass the day with good drink and feasting and tales. A long season we spent on the whale's way, with the wind biting cold through our tunics and never a drop of ale nor a woman's soft form in our sight. We thank the god for guiding us home safely once more. We thank him for our glorious victories, and for the rich spoils we carry. In the growing season, we shall sail forth again to honor him in deeds of courage, but for now, it is good to be home. Let him look kindly on our celebration."

There were many tales told that day, and the more the ale flowed, the more eloquent the telling. There were tales of Thor's valor and Odin's cunning, tales of dragons and heroes. Eyvind sat close to his brother, Eirik, savoring every moment. Of such stuff are dreams made. He wanted Eirik to tell them about the autumn viking: where they had been, what battles they had fought and what plunder they had brought home. But he did not ask. It was enough, for now, that Eirik was here.

That boy was still watching him. Perhaps he was simple in the head. Eyvind tried staring back; the boy met his gaze without blinking. His expression did not change. Eyvind tried smiling politely, though in fact he found the constant scrutiny unsettling. The boy gave a little nod, no more than a tight jerk of the head. He did not smile.

At length, the fire burned lower. The smell of roasted goat flesh lingered. Bellies were comfortably full of the rich meat, and of Ingi's finest oatcakes. The temple was warm with good fellowship. Thor, it seemed, had overlooked the imperfect manner of the ritual, and chosen to smile on them.

Hakon spoke. "I have a tale," he said, "a tale both sorrowful and inspiring, and well suited for Thor's ears, since it tells of a loyalty which transcended all. It concerns a man named Niall, who fell among cutthroats one night when traveling home from the drinking hall. Niall had on him a purse of silver, with which he planned to buy a fine horse, and ride away to present himself to the Jarl's court. He was not eager to give up his small hoard and his chance to make something of himself, for Niall, like many another young farmer's son, was not rich in lands or worldly possessions. He had worked hard for his silver. So he fought with hands and feet and the small knife that was the only weapon he bore; he fought with all his strength and all his will, and he called on Thor for help from the bottom of his lungs. It was a one-sided struggle, for there were six attackers armed with clubs and sharpened stakes. Niall felt his ribs crack under boot thrusts and his skull ring with blow on blow; his sight grew dim, he saw the night world through a red haze. It occurred to him, through a rising tide of unconsciousness, that this was not a good way to die, snuffed out by scum for a prize they would squabble over and waste and forget, as he himself would be forgotten soon enough. Still he struggled against them, for the will to live burned in him like a small, bright flame.

"Then, abruptly, the kicking stopped. The hands that had gripped his throat, squeezing without mercy, slackened and dropped away. There was a sound of furious activity around him, grunts and oaths, scuffling and a sudden shriek of pain, then retreating footsteps, and silence.

"An arm lifted him up. Odin's bones, every part of his body ached. But he was alive. After all, the gods had not forgotten him.

" 'Slowly, slowly, man,' the voice of his rescuer said. 'Here, lean on me. We'd best make our way back to the drinking hall; you're in no fit state to go farther.'

"The man who had saved Niall's life was young, broad, and big-fisted. Still, there was only one of him.

" 'How did you do that?' Niall gasped. 'How did you—'

"The stranger chuckled. 'I'm a warrior, friend, and I keep a weapon or two about me. Thor calls; I answer. Just as well he called tonight, or your last breath would be gone from your body by now. My name's Brynjolf. Who are you?'

"Niall told him, and later, when his wounds were dressed and the two men were sharing a jug of good ale by the fire, he explained to Brynjolf his plans to present himself to the Jarl, and seek a place in his household.

"'But my money is gone,' Niall said ruefully. 'My silver, all that I had saved—those ruffians took it. Now I have nothing.'

"'You have a friend,' Brynjolf grinned. 'And—let me see—perhaps not all is lost.' He made a play of hunting here and there, in his pockets, in his small knapsack, in the folds of his cloak, until at length, 'Ah,' he exclaimed, and drew out the goatskin pouch that held Niall's carefully hoarded silver. Brynjolf shook it, and it jingled. 'This is yours, I think.'

"Niall took the pouch wordlessly. He did not look inside, or count the money.

"'You wonder why I did not simply keep this?' Brynjolf queried. 'When I said you had a friend, I spoke the truth. Let us travel on together. I will teach you a trick or two, for a man with such scant resources will not get far beyond the safe boundaries of the home farm, unless he learns to defend himself.'

"So Niall and Brynjolf became the best of comrades, and on the way to the Jarl's court they shared many adventures. And they swore an oath, an oath deep and solemn, for each scored his arm with a knife until the blood ran forth, dripping on the earth, and they set their forearms together and swore on their mingled blood that they would be as brothers from that day on. They vowed they would put this bond before all other loyalties, to support one another, to stand against the other's enemies even until death. This oath they swore in Thor's name, and the god smiled on them.

"The years passed. Brynjolf joined the Jarl's personal guard, and acquitted himself with great valor. Niall learned to use the sword and the axe, but he was not cut out to be a warrior. In time, he discovered he had a talent for making verses, and this pleased the Jarl mightily, for men of power love to hear the tales of their own great deeds told in fine, clever words. So, remarkably, Niall became a skald, and told his tales at gatherings of influential men, while his friend journeyed forth with the Jarl's fleet in spring and in autumn, to raid along the coast of Friesland and Saxony. When Brynjolf returned, they would drink together, and laugh, and tell their tales, and they would pledge their brotherhood anew, this time in strong ale.

"One summer Brynjolf came home with shadowed eyes and gaunt features. Late one night he told Niall a terrible story. While Brynjolf had been away, his family had perished in a hall-burning: father, mother, sister, and young brothers. A dispute had festered over boundaries; this had grown to skirmishes, and then to killing. Late one night, when all the household slept, the neighbor's men had surrounded the longhouse of Brynjolf's father, and torched it. In the morning, walking among the blackened ruins of the place, folk swore they could still hear screaming, though all were dead, even the babies. All this, while Brynjolf himself was far away on the sea, not knowing. When he set foot on shore, they told him, and saw his amiable face become a mask of hate.

"Niall could think of nothing to say.

"'I will find the man who did this,' Brynjolf muttered, cold-eyed, 'and he will pay in kind. Such an evil deed invites no less. He is far north in Frosta, and I am bound southward this summer, but he and his are marked for death at my hand.'

"Niall nodded and said nothing, and before seven days had passed, his friend was off again on the Jarl's business. Niall put the terrible tale in the back of his mind.

"It was a mild summer and the earth wore her loveliest gown. Flowers filled the meadows with soft color and sweet perfume, crops grew thick and healthy, fruit ripened on the bushes. And Niall fell in love. There were many visitors to the court: noblemen, dignitaries, emissaries from far countries, landowners seeking favors. There was a man called Hrolf, who had come there to speak of trading matters, bringing his daughter. Every evening, folk gathered in the hall, and in the firelight Niall told his tales and sang his verses. The girl sat among the women of the household, and he thought her a shining pearl among plain stones, a sweet dove among barnyard chickens. Her name was Thora, and Niall's heart was quite lost to her snow-pale skin and flax-gold hair, her demure features and warm, blue eyes. As he sang, he knew she watched him, and once or twice he caught a smile.

"Niall was in luck. He was shy, and Thora was shyer. But the Jarl favored his skald, and spoke to Hrolf on Niall's behalf, and at length, her father agreed to consider the possibility of a marriage in a year or so when the girl was sixteen. For now, it would not hurt the young man to wait. They might exchange gifts. Next summer, Niall could visit them in the north. All things in good time.

"The lovers snatched moments together, for all the watchful care of Thora's keepers: kisses in shadowed hallways, one lovely meeting at dusk in the garden, hidden by hedges of flowering thorn. They sang together softly; they taught each other verses of love. Niall told Thora she had a voice like a lark; she giggled and put her arms around him, and he thought he might die of joy and of anticipation. Then summer drew to a close, and Hrolf took his daughter home.

"Brynjolf did not go on the autumn viking that year. He excused himself from court and traveled north, and with him he took his blood brother, Niall the poet. To distant Frosta they journeyed, and by the wayside, they acquired two large, silent companions, men with scarred faces, whose empty eyes filled Niall with dread. There was no need for Brynjolf to tell him where they were going, or for what purpose. It was a quest for vengeance, and Niall's oath bound him to it. He fixed his thoughts on the summer, and on his sweet Thora. Life would be good: the comforts of the Jarl's court, the satisfaction of exercising his craft, the joys of marriage. He must simply do what had to be done here, and put it behind him, for there was a rosy future ahead.

"They moved through deep woodlands by night. At the forest fringe, Brynjolf halted them with a hand. Not far below them lay a darkened longhouse, a thread of smoke still rising from the chimney. The folk were abed; a half moon touched the roof thatch with silver and glinted on a bucket set neatly by the well.

"'Draw your swords,' whispered Brynjolf. 'Not one must escape: not man, woman nor child. Go in quickly. There may be dogs.'

"Then they lit torches from the one Brynjolf had carried, and with naked sword in hand, each ran to a different side of the building. Niall's was the north. He saw the flare of dry wattles catching to east and west; so far, the dogs were silent. But it seemed not all there slept. From within the darkened house, close to the place where he stood frozen, clutching his flaming brand, came the sound of a girl singing. She sang very softly, in a voice like a lark's, a little song known only to a pair of lovers who had crafted it one summer's eve in a sheltered garden."

As Hakon recounted his tale, there was a deathly silence in

the temple. Some of his audience had seen this coming, knowing the way of such tales, yet still the horror of it gripped them.

"What could he do?" asked Hakon. "Thora was there, in the house, and already flames rose on three sides of the building, hungry for wattles and timber and human flesh. She was the daughter of Brynjolf's enemy, the man who had cruelly slaughtered his friend's entire family. Niall loved her. And he had sworn a blood oath to the man who had saved his life. 'Let me die this day for what I do,' muttered Niall. 'Let my eyes be blind and my ears deaf. Let my heart break now, and my body be consumed in this conflagration.' And he reached out with his flaming torch, and set fire to the wattles on the northern side.

"It was a vengeance full and complete. The flames consumed all; there was no need for swords. When it was over, Brynjolf paid off the hired men, and he and Niall went homeward. Brynjolf thought Niall a little silent, a little withdrawn. Still, reasoned the warrior, the skald led a protected life. He was not accustomed to acts of violence, to the daily witnessing of sudden death. Indeed, if it had not been for Brynjolf's own intervention, Niall would not have survived to journey forth from the home farm and become a man of wealth and status.

"They returned to the Jarl's court. For a long time, Niall made no more poems. He pleaded illness; the Jarl allowed him time. Brynjolf was somewhat concerned. Once or twice he asked Niall what was wrong, and Niall replied, nothing. Brynjolf concluded there was a girl in it somewhere. Folk had suggested that Niall had a sweetheart, and had planned to marry, but now there was no talk of that. Perhaps she had rejected him. That would explain his pallor, and his silence.

"Winter passed. Brynjolf went away on the spring viking, and Niall made verses again. Over the years, and he had a very long life, he made many verses. He never married; they said he was wed to his craft. But after that summer, his poems changed. There was a darkness in them, a deep sorrow that shadowed even the boldest and most heroic tale of war, that lingered in the heartiest tale of good fellowship. Niall's stories made folk shiver; they made folk weep.

"A young skald asked him once why he told always of sadness, of terrible choices, of errors and waste. And Niall replied,

'A lifetime is not sufficient to sing a man's grief. You will learn that, before you are old.' Yet, when Niall died as a bearded ancient, Thor had him carried straight to Valhöll, as if he were a dauntless warrior. The god honors the faithful. And who is more true than a man who keeps his oath, though it breaks his heart?"

After Hakon had finished speaking, nobody said anything for a long while. Then one of the older warriors spoke quietly.

"You tell this story well, Wolfskin. And it is indeed apt: a tale well suited for this ritual day. Which of us, I wonder, would have the strength to act as this man did? And yet, undoubtedly, he did as Thor would wish. There is no bond that can transcend an oath between men, sworn in blood, save a vow to the god himself."

There was a general murmur of agreement. Glancing at his mother, Eyvind thought she was about to speak, but she closed her mouth again without uttering a word.

"It is a fine and sobering tale," Karl said, "and reminds us that an oath must not be sworn lightly. Such a tale sets a tear in the eye of a strong man. My friends, the light will be fading soon, and some have far to travel."

"Indeed," said Eirik, rising to his feet. "It grows late and we must depart. I and my companions have journeyed far this day; we return now to my mother's home, to rest there awhile. You'd best be on your way while it is still light, for the storm is close at hand. There will be fresh snow by morning."

It was as well the longhouse at Hammarsby was spacious and comfortably appointed. A large party made its way there, arriving just before the wind began to howl in earnest, and the first swirling eddies of snow to descend. The nobleman Ulf and his richly dressed companions, the two Wolfskins and a number of other folk of the Jarl's household gathered at Ingi's home. The wind chased Eyvind in the small back doorway; he had arrived somewhat later than the others, after staying behind to make sure the fire was safely quenched and the temple shuttered against the storm. The instant he came inside he saw the boy standing in the shadows by the wall, arms folded around himself. There was nobody else in sight; they would all be gathered close to the hearth's warmth. Eyvind spoke politely, since he could hardly pretend the strange lad was not there.

"Thor's hammer, what a wind! My name's Eyvind. You're welcome here."

The boy gave a stiff nod.

Eyvind tried again. "Looks like you'll be staying with us a few days. There'll be heavy snow tonight; you'd never get out, even on skis."

There was a short pause. Then the boy said, "Why did it scream?"

Now it was Eyvind's turn to stare. "What?" he asked after a moment.

"The goat. Why did it scream?"

What sort of question was that? "I—because the sacrifice wasn't done properly," Eyvind said. "It screamed because the knife slipped. It was hurt and frightened."

The boy nodded gravely. "I see," he said.

Eyvind drew a deep breath. "Come on," he said, "it's warmer by the fire, and the others are there, my brother and Hakon, and the guests. My brother is Eirik. He's a Wolfskin." There was a satisfaction in telling people this.

"I know," said the boy. "Eirik Hallvardsson. And there's another brother, Karl, who is not a Wolfskin. Your mother is Ingi, a widow. Your father died in battle."

Eyvind looked at him. "How do you know that?" he asked.

"If I'm to stay here until the summer, I must be well prepared," the boy said flatly. "It's foolish not to find out all you can."

Eyvind was mute.

"Your brother didn't tell you," said the boy. "I see that. I have a brother too, one who has an inclination to build ships and sail off to islands full of savages. He doesn't want me. I'm to stay here and learn what other boys do with their time. You're supposed to teach me."

Eyvind gaped. If this was the favor his brother had spoken of, it was pretty one-sided. The boy was pale and scrawny; he looked as if he'd never held a sword or a bow in his life, he spoke so strangely you could hardly understand what he meant, and he stared all the time. What was Eirik thinking?

"I'm not going to say sorry." The boy was looking at the floor now, his voice a little uneven. "It wasn't my idea."

There was a brief silence. "It's all right," Eyvind said with an effort. "It's rather a surprise, that's all. Do you know how to fight?"

The boy shook his head. "Not the sort of fight you mean, with knives or fists."

"What other kind is there?" Eyvind asked, puzzled.

There was the faintest trace of a smile on the boy's thin lips. "Maybe that's what I'm supposed to teach you," he said.

False courage, thought Eyvind. It must be very hard, frightening even, if you were a weakling and a bit simple in the head, and had no sort of skills at all, to be dumped in a strange household with the kinsfolk of a Wolfskin. No wonder the lad pretended to some sort of secret knowledge; no wonder he tried to look superior.

"Don't worry," Eyvind said magnanimously. "I'll look after you. Don't worry about anything." He put out a hand, and the boy clasped it for an instant and let go. He wasn't smiling, not exactly, but at least that blank stare was gone. His hand was cold as a frozen fish.

"Come on," Eyvind urged. "I'm for a warm fire and a drink of ale." He led the way past the sleeping quarters, which opened to left and right of the central passageway. Though it was growing dark, none of the household was yet abed. The days were short, the time after sundown spent in tales by the hearth, and in what crafts could be plied indoors by the light of seal-oil lamps. Ingi and her daughters were noted for their embroidery; Karl carved goblets and candleholders and cunning small creatures from pale soapstone. Solveig's husband Bjarni was scratching away on his pattern board, making designs which by daylight he would transform into clasps and rings and brooches of intricate silverwork. Helga's husband was away, for the hard winter meant a swift passage by ice roads to the great trading fairs in Kaupang and far-off Birka. In summer, he would take ship for ports still more distant, traveling far east. At Novgorod you could get spices and silks from the hot southern lands, fine honey, Arab silver, and slaves. Ingi herself had a thrall-woman with jutting cheekbones and dark, slanting eyes, who shivered through the winter, wrapped in heavy shawls. This exotic slave had two small children; curiously, neither resembled Oksana herself. Indeed, with their wide blue eyes and golden hair, these infants could have been part of Ingi's own family.

Faces turned toward the boys as they emerged from the hallway, Eyvind leading, the other behind like a smaller shadow.

"Ah," said Eirik with a look in his eyes that mingled relief and apology, "you found Somerled, then."

Eyvind nodded, and went to sit on the worn sheepskins that covered the floor by the hearth. The boy hovered, hesitant. Somerled. So that was his name. Eyvind glanced up, jerked his head a little. Noiselessly, the boy moved to settle cross-legged at his side.

"Good," whispered Eyvind. "There's nothing to be afraid of."

Ulf had told no tales at the feasting. He seemed a cautious sort of man, dark-bearded, neat-featured, and watchful. But in the quiet of the home hearth, as the family sat about the fire with ale cups in hand, he seemed to relax, and began to talk. It then became evident that Ulf was a man with a mission. He wanted to build a ship: not an ordinary longship, but a vessel such as no man had seen before in all of Norway. And in it he intended to journey where no man of Norway had yet traveled; he would sail to a place that might be real, or that might be no more than fable. With his soft voice and the glow in his dark eyes, he drew them all into his dream.

"There is a land out in the western sea," he told them, "a land my father heard tell of from a man he met at the markets in Birka, beyond the eastern mountains in the land of the Svear. This fellow had traveled far, from wild Pictland southward through Britain, by sea to the Frankish realms and north to Saxony. From there he took ship to the Baltic markets with his precious cargo: boards set with jewels and fine enamelwork, which once housed books in a temple of the Christian faith. The books themselves were discarded, but the bindings were indeed things of wonder, and would make this man rich if he were not slaughtered in the darkness first for what he carried. He had made a long journey. Pictland is a bleak territory, inhabited by wild people. But from its northern shores, said this traveler, far out in the trackless ocean, can be reached a place of warm sea currents, of verdant islands and sheltered waterways, a realm of peaceful bays and gentle grazing lands. The crossing is dangerous from those parts in the vessels they use, simple skin curraghs for the most part. It is a longer path from Rogaland, but not so long that it could not be done, if a ship were built strongly enough to withstand the journey. The news of such a place inspired my father. He yearned to travel there. That he was prevented from pursuing it is a lifelong regret for him."

"You plan to undertake an expedition to those parts yourself, my lord?" Karl asked politely.

Ulf gave a rueful smile. "I make it plain enough, I suppose, that I have inherited my father's obsession. Such a venture would be fraught with risk. But one day I will do it."

"You'd need a fine boat," Eyvind said, hoping he did not speak out of turn. "If it's a rough crossing from that southern shore, it could be a rougher one from Rogaland, all the way. It's a brave man who would voyage beyond the skerry-guard, straight out into open seas: into the unknown."

The Jarl's kinsman looked at him with sudden interest. "I'll build a boat, lad," he said quietly. "She'll be a queen among vessels, sleek, graceful, the equal of any of our shore-raiding ships for speed and maneuverability, but strong enough for a long voyage in open water. I'll gather the best shipwrights in all Norway to work for me, and when the boat is ready, the finest warriors in all Norway will travel with me. I'll see that land while I'm still young, and if it pleases me, I'll take a piece of it in my father's name."

The eyes of every man in the hall had kindled with enthusiasm, for when Ulf spoke of this dream there was something in his face, his voice, his bearing that seized the spirit and quickened the heart. It was plain this soft-spoken, reserved man was that rare phenomenon: a true leader.

"It'd cost you an arm and a leg," Eirik observed. "Ships, crew, supplies."

"You doubt my ability to carry this out?" Ulf's expression was suddenly grim.

"Indeed no," Eirik said calmly. "I do not. But even a Wolfskin likes to know what he's getting into."

Ulf smiled. "Ah," he said, "I have one taker, then."

"Two." Hakon spoke from his place on the nobleman's other side. "You are a man of vision, my lord. A new horizon, an un-

known land: what warrior could fail to be drawn by that? I will
go, if you'll have me."

Ulf nodded. "I hope Magnus may be prepared to support us,
and to release you both. It won't be tomorrow, my friends, or
next season. As you say, there must be resources for such an undertaking. I need time. Still, I see the great ship in my mind, her
sails full-bellied in the east wind, her prow dragon-crested; I
taste the salt air of that place even now."

"The expedition is a fine prospect and stirring to the spirit,"
Eirik said. "Good farming land is scarce enough here; a man
with many sons leaves scant portions. There's more than one
likely lad who would jump at the chance to settle in such a
place, if it's indeed as verdant and sheltered as you say. You'll
find plenty of takers before you go, I think."

"As to that," said Ulf, "I winnow my wheat once, twice, three
times before I make my bread, for I am slow to trust. I will not
sink all my resources in such a venture to have it end with a
knife in the back."

"Wisely spoken." To everyone's surprise, it was the boy
Somerled who spoke. "My brother is a man with a curse on
him; he needs to be rather more cautious than most."

Ulf was regarding his brother with a look of distaste.
"Enough, Somerled," he said. "We will not speak of that here at
this peaceful hearth."

"It's a good curse." The boy went on as if Ulf had not spoken. "A kind of riddle. I like riddles. It goes like this:

"Pinioned in flowers of straw
Cloaked in a mackerel's shroud
His dirge a seabird's cry
Neither on land or water does he perish
Ulf, far-seeker, dreamer of dreams
Yet tastes the salt sea, watches the wild sky
By neither friend nor foe
Slain with his hope before his eyes."

There was silence. It was plain to all that Ulf had not wanted
this spoken aloud.

"A strange verse indeed," Karl said after a little. "What does
it mean?"

"As to that," Ulf said soberly, rising to his feet, "it seems nonsense. If a man is neither on land nor water, where can he be? Flying like an albatross? An old woman spoke such a verse over me when I was in the cradle, that is all. Folk make much of it, but it seems to me a man must live his life without always looking over his shoulder. If some strange fate overtakes me and proves these words true, so be it. I will not live in fear of them. Indeed, I would prefer to forget them." He frowned at Somerled.

After that, the talk turned to safer matters, and soon enough it was bedtime. Because Somerled was a nobleman's brother, and a visitor, the two lads who shared Eyvind's small sleeping area had to move, and Somerled was given their space. It meant there was more room, which Eyvind appreciated. He was growing taller; his toes were making holes in his boots and his wrists stuck out of his shirtsleeves. Somerled was small, and slept neatly, rolled tight in a blanket, still as if dead. On the other hand, he had a gift for banishing other people's sleep. That first night, just as Eyvind, comfortably tired from the long day's work and warmed by the strong ale, hovered on the verge of slumber, Somerled asked another question.

"Do you think she screamed?" he inquired.

Eyvind's eyes snapped open. "What? Who?" he asked testily.

"You know. That girl, Thora. Do you think she screamed, when she started to burn?"

"Leave it, will you?" growled Eyvind, too annoyed to think of good manners. He had almost managed to forget the story of Niall and Brynjolf in the warmth and fellowship of the longhouse. Now it came back to him in all its painful and confusing detail.

"I should think she did," Somerled said tranquilly, answering his own question. "I wonder what Niall felt when he heard the singing change. I wonder how it takes you, that moment when everything turns to shadows."

Eyvind pulled his blanket over his head and stuck his fingers in his ears. But Somerled was finished; before you could count to fifty he was snoring peacefully. It was Eyvind who tossed and turned, his mind flooded with dark images.

* * *

Eirik did offer his brother a kind of apology before he left, and an explanation. Ulf had been concerned about Somerled, Eirik said. The boy had never been quite the same since he witnessed his own mother's death. His father was old and bitter and had not been kind to this young son, and the household had taken its lead from the master. Ulf had been away a long time, and had returned to a home on the brink of self-destruction. Powerful chieftains gathered close, hovering as scavengers do, awaiting the moment of death. There was a need to take control quickly, to undo the ill his father's mismanagement had created before lands and status were quite lost. But Ulf wanted his half-brother—Somerled was the child of a second marriage—out of the place first. The boy had seen too much already, and was behaving very strangely. He spent all his time alone, he didn't seem to trust anyone, and he never wanted to play games, or ride, or wrestle, as a boy should. Indeed, Ulf scarcely knew what to do with him, and Somerled had made it no easier by refusing to talk. The boy was as tightly closed as a limpet.

So Ulf had brought Somerled back to the south, and sought out his friend, Eirik the Wolfskin, a man known to have a great deal of common sense. Eirik heard Ulf's tale and made an offer. He had a brother of about Somerled's age. He thought his mother would not object to another lad around the house. Why didn't Ulf leave the boy with them, at least until the summer?

"I must confess," Eirik told Eyvind with a half-smile, "I welcomed the chance this gave me to return here for a little. And Ulf thought it an excellent idea. Somerled has not had the company of other children, and it shows in his demeanor. He seems unnaturally shy; I've hardly heard him utter a word."

Eyvind grimaced. "He talks to me," he said.

"Good," said Eirik. "That's a start. I've a great deal of respect for Ulf; he's a man of vision and balance. I was glad to be able to help him."

"Eirik?"

"What?"

"When can I do the trial? How much longer? I'm nearly twelve now, and I've been practicing hard. I can take a hare neatly at two hundred paces, and swim across the Serpent's Neck underwater without coming up for air. How long must I wait?"

"A while yet," said Eirik. "Four more summers at least, I think."

Eyvind's heart plummeted. He would not speak his disappointment, for Thor did not look favorably on such signs of weakness.

"But maybe not so long," his brother added, smiling. "You are almost a man. What boy has such great hands and feet? And you're nearly as tall as I am, for all I have six years' advantage. Perhaps only three summers."

That was good news and bad news. Eirik thought him nearly grown up; that made his cheeks flush with pride. But three years, three whole years before he got the chance to prove himself? How could he bear to wait so long? How could he endure such an endless time and not go crazy with frustration?

The weather had eased long enough for Ulf and his companions to be away, and both Eirik and Hakon went with them. As if only waiting for their departure, the snow set in again, and Eyvind found his days full of digging, clearing paths to wood store and barn, endlessly shovelling the thick blanket from the thatch. Somerled followed him out, watching gravely as he swung up onto a barrel and clambered to the rooftop. From up there, the boy looked like a little shadow in the white.

"Go back inside!" Eyvind called down to him. "This is not a job for you!"

But Somerled began to climb up, slipped, cursed, climbed again; on tiptoes, balanced precariously on the barrel, he could just reach the eaves with his upstretched arms.

"You can't—" Eyvind began, looking over, and then stopped at the look in Somerled's eyes. He reached down and hauled the other boy up bodily by the arms. "Didn't bring a shovel, did you?" he observed mildly. "Watch me first, then you can take a turn. Next time bring your own; they're in the back near the stock pens. You need to keep moving or you'll freeze up and be no use to anyone."

He didn't expect Somerled to last long. It was bitterly cold, the shovel was large and heavy and the task backbreaking, even when you were as strong as Eyvind was. He worked a while, and then Somerled tried it, sliding about, losing his balance, teetering, and recovering. He managed to clear a small patch. His face grew white with cold, his eyes narrow and fierce.

"All right, my turn," Eyvind told him, finding it hard to stand idle when he knew he could do the job in half the time.

"I haven't d–done my share. I c–can go on."

"Rest first, then have another try," said Eyvind, taking the shovel out of Somerled's hands. "You'll get blisters. If I'm supposed to be teaching you, then you'd better learn to listen."

They did the job in turns. It took a while. He glanced at Somerled from time to time. The lad looked fit to drop, but something in his face suggested it would not be a good idea to tell him to go indoors and let Eyvind finish. So he endured Somerled's assistance, and at length the roof was cleared. When they went back inside, Ingi exclaimed over Somerled's chattering teeth, and his poor hands where lines of livid blisters were forming across the palms, and she chided Eyvind for pushing the boy so. Didn't he know Somerled was not used to such hard work? He should be easier on the lad. Eyvind muttered an apology, glancing sideways at his companion. Somerled shivered, and drank his broth, and said not a word. Maybe both of them were learning.

Several boys lived at Hammarsby. Some were the sons of housecarls, folk who had worked for Ingi so long they were almost family. Somerled did not exactly go out of his way to make friends, and in the confines of the snowbound longhouse it did not take long for others to notice this, and to set him small trials as befitted any newcomer. Someone slipped a dead rat between his blankets, to be discovered suddenly when he went weary to bed in the darkness. The next day, Eyvind spoke to the lads of the household, saying Somerled was not used to such pranks, having grown up without brothers or sisters, and that it was not to happen again. Nobody actually confessed. The morning after that, Ingi inquired what was wrong with the porridge, to make all the boys look so green in the face? Good food should never be wasted, especially in the cold season. But the only two eating were Eyvind and Somerled, and Somerled wore a little smile.

Later, Eyvind discovered the lads' gift had been returned to them in kind. Since there was no knowing who had planted the rat, Somerled had been scrupulously fair, and shared it among them in precisely cut portions. An ear and an eye. A nose with whiskers. A length of gut. He had, it seemed, his very own way of solving problems.

Eyvind did not ask Somerled about his past. He did wonder, sometimes. There were so many things the boy did not know about, or just could not do. He had surely never looked after animals, for he seemed quite ignorant of how to treat them. He did not understand, until Eyvind explained it to him, that when a dog lowered its head and growled at you with flattened ears, you did not growl back or give it a kick. You must speak to it kindly, Eyvind told Somerled. You should not look it in the eye, just stay close and move slowly. You had to let the dog get used to you, and learn you could be trusted. Somerled had thought about this for a little, and then he had asked, "Why?" So, shaggy-coated Grip continued to growl and snap every time the boy went past, though the old dog let little children climb over his back and tug his rough coat with never a bark from him.

Somerled did not like snow games. Sometimes, when all their tasks were done to Ingi's satisfaction, the boys and girls of the household would venture out onto the hillside to hurtle down the slopes on wooden sleds or pieces of birch bark. There were clear, bright days when the world seemed made anew in winter shades of twig gray and snowdrift white under a sky as blue as a duck egg. Eyvind longed for the freedom of summer, but he loved this time as well. There was no feeling like speeding across the ice with the bone skates strapped to his boots, the sheer thrill of the air whipping by, the pounding of the heart, the fierce joy of pushing himself to the limit and knowing he was invincible. This was what it would be like when he became a Wolfskin and rode the prow of the longship: the same feeling, but a hundred times stronger.

He could not understand why Somerled would not join in these games. The other boys jeered at the newcomer and exchanged theories behind his back. Eyvind had tried to stop this, but he would not report it to Ingi; one did not tattle-tale. Besides, the boys were right. Somerled was a very odd child. What if he did fall off the sled, or land on his bottom on the ice? That had happened to all of them. People might laugh, but it would be a laughter of understanding, not of scorn. Yet Somerled would not even try. He stood in the darkness under the trees and watched them, stone-faced, and if anyone asked him why he did not join in, he would either ignore the question completely, or say he did not see any point in it.

Part of Eyvind wanted to forget that fierce-eyed small presence under the trees. Somerled made his own difficulties; let him deal with the consequences. Part of Eyvind wanted to skate away over the dark mirror of the frozen river, to join the others in wild races down the hillside, to build forts of snow or to venture out into the woods alone, spear in hand, seeking fresh meat for his mother's pot. But he'd promised Eirik. So, with decidedly mixed feelings, Eyvind devoted several lamplit evenings to fashioning a pair of skates from a piece of well-dried oak wood, iron-strong, with thongs of deerhide to fasten them to the boot soles. Somerled watched without comment.

Acting on an instinct he could not have explained, Eyvind got up very early, shrugging on his shirt and trousers, his tunic, his sheepskin coat and hat of felted wool as quickly as he could, for the cold seemed to seep into every corner of the longhouse. The place was quiet, the household still sleeping. He took his own skates and the new pair, and turned to wake Somerled. But, quiet as a shadow, the boy had risen from the wooden shelf where they slept, and was putting on his own clothes, as if he did not need to be told. It seemed Eyvind's instinct had served him well.

Ancient as he was, the dog Grip was ever keen to accompany the children on any expedition out of doors, as companion and protector. But today he seemed wary, growling softly as the two of them tiptoed into the hallway and out to the back door. Eyvind gave him a pat and pointed him back inside. Such an old dog was best resting by the embers of last night's fire, for the cold was enough to freeze the bollocks off you. He must be mad, taking Somerled out so early. Still, the boy followed willingly enough, asking not a single question.

Down by the frozen river, in a morning darkness where the snow seemed blue and the sky red, where bushes and trees stretched out twigs like skinny fingers, frost-silvered, into the strange winter light, Somerled strapped on the new skates with no hesitation at all, stood up, slipped on the ice, fell flat on his back, got up again and, arms gripped firmly by Eyvind's powerful hands, began to move forward step by sliding step. That was how simple it was. All that was needed was that nobody else should be there.

That astonished Eyvind. He himself was always first in any endeavor—not reckless exactly, just blithely confident of his own strength. He did get hurt from time to time, but thought little of it. It did not worry him if folk laughed at him, not that they often did, since he tended to get things right the first time. And he was bigger than other people, which did help. He understood danger and guarded against it; he used his skis and his bow and his axe in the right way, cleanly and capably. Somerled's need for privacy confused him. If others' opinions mattered so much, why should Somerled trust *him?* He was, after all, the brother of a Wolfskin. That might be expected to engender fear rather than trust in a scrap of a boy like this.

As time passed, it became apparent to Eyvind that Somerled was attempting a kind of repayment, in the limited ways available to him. Eyvind would fall into bed exhausted after a long day's work on the farm, and when he got up in the morning his boots would be cleaned of mud, dried, and waiting for him. Ingi would send her son out to the woodshed on a chill afternoon, and he would find Somerled there before him, frowning with effort as he loaded the logs onto the sledge. A choice cut of meat, served to their small visitor, would make its way unobtrusively to Eyvind's own platter. Eyvind learned quickly that one did not thank Somerled for these small kindnesses. Any attempt to do so would be greeted either by a blank stare, or a furious denial that any favor was intended. So he learned merely to accept, and was rewarded, occasionally, with a tentative half-smile, so fleeting he wondered, afterward, if he had only imagined it.

Winter slowly mellowed into spring, and Eyvind learned a lesson in patience. Before the ice melted, Somerled could skate; before the snow turned to slush, he could move about on skis without falling. He did not play games, but it was apparent that this was through choice rather than lack of ability. The other boys' eyes were more wary than scornful now as they passed over his small, dark figure. He made no new friends.

The milder weather brought fresh pastimes. It was easier to teach Somerled things now, because spring was a time for expeditions, and Eyvind was accustomed to going alone. Now, wherever Eyvind led, Somerled followed, and there were no others to watch and make fun of the boy's errors. Accepting that this season's ventures must be shorter and their pace slower, Eyvind set about ensuring his companion understood the essential rules of safety, and the basic skills of hunting and trapping. Somerled learned to start a fire with no more than a scrap of flint and a handful of dry grass. He learned to build a shelter from fallen branches and strips of bark. He tried spear and bow and struggled with both, for he had little strength in the arms and shoulders, though his eye was keen. Eyvind set easy targets, and praised each small success. They set snares for rabbits and brought home a steady supply. Somerled had a neat hand for gutting and skinning.

Eyvind was uneasy sometimes. He could see Somerled was trying hard, and it was plain to all that the lad was growing stronger and healthier, thanks to fresh air and exercise and good feeding. But he remained very quiet, and had not lost his habit of blurting out strange remarks. Once, by the fire, they had listened to Ingi's tale of three brothers going to seek their fortunes, and had spoken of what the future might hold for themselves, and what they aspired to. One lad was eager to be a craftsman; he hoped to persuade Bjarni the silversmith to take him on. Another wanted to voyage far away to the lands in the south, where all the folk had skin as black as night. A third dreamed of catching the biggest fish that ever slipped in through the skerry-guard.

"No need to ask Eyvind what he's going to do," grinned red-headed Sigurd, son of Ingi's senior housecarl. "We all know that."

"If Thor accepts me, I'll be the bravest Wolfskin that ever gave service," Eyvind said quietly, his gaze intent on the hearth fire. "First in attack, heedless of peril, fierce and unassailable. That's the only thing I want to do."

There was a little silence. Not one of them doubted that this wish would come true. It seemed to have been understood among them since Eyvind was little more than a baby.

"I'm going to marry Ragna and have ten children," Sigurd joked, and pigtailed Ragna cuffed him, blushing scarlet.

"What about you, Somerled?" Ingi asked kindly, perhaps

feeling their young visitor had been overlooked. "What do you think you will become, when you are a man?"

Somerled looked up at her, his dark eyes opaque. "A king," he said.

There were snorts of ridicule. The boys rolled their eyes at one another; the girls giggled with embarrassment.

"I don't think you can just *be* a king," Eyvind said gently. "I mean, a king is even more important than a Jarl. You'd have to be . . . well . . ." He hesitated. It was not possible to say, *You'd have to be strong, brave, respected*—all the things Somerled was not.

"You doubt me?" Somerled snapped. His small face all at once had the appearance of a savage creature at bay, the nostrils pinched, the eyes furious.

"Oh, come on, Somerled," said Sigurd. "You know you'll never be a king, that sort of thing's only in stories. It's a stupid thing to say."

Ingi opened her mouth, perhaps to announce that it was bedtime, but Somerled spoke first.

"A man can be anything he wants to be," he said, fixing Sigurd with a withering look. "You have still that lesson to learn. But you will not learn it, because you set your sights too low. One day you'll be a bitter old man, looking back on a life wasted. Worse, you won't even have the wit to recognize what you might have been. One day I will be a king, and you will still be a housecarl."

Sigurd muttered something and made a gesture with his fingers. Then Ingi ordered them briskly off to bed, and the strange conversation was over.

Lying awake, Eyvind stared up at the thatch, where small creatures stirred with furtive rustling movements. After a while he said, "I didn't mean it to sound like that. As if I thought you were lying. That wasn't what I meant. I was just trying to be . . ."

"Helpful?" put in Somerled.

"Well, yes. I thought maybe you didn't understand how hard it would be to—to do what you said. Almost impossible, I should think."

Somerled sat up, his blankets held around him. "Nothing is

impossible, Eyvind," he said in his small, precise voice. "Not if a man wants it enough. How badly do you wish to be a Wolfskin?"

"More than anything in the world," Eyvind said. "You know that; everyone does."

"Exactly," said Somerled. "So, you will be a Wolfskin, because you cannot see a future in which that does not occur. It is the same for me. I don't expect to achieve what I want without hard work and careful strategy, of course."

Eyvind was silenced. Somerled sounded extremely sure; so sure there was no challenging him.

"You must not doubt me." There was an intensity in that statement that was almost frightening.

"I don't, Somerled," said Eyvind quietly and, to his own surprise, he found that he meant it.

The weather grew warmer, and Eyvind taught Somerled to swim. The boy practiced this new skill as he did all the others: doggedly, methodically, with no sign of enjoyment. He splashed about, making a gradual, floundering progress through the chilly waters of the fjord, while Eyvind swam and dived and practiced holding his breath under water. It seemed Somerled learned things not because he wanted to, but because he believed he must.

There was one exception, and it unsettled Eyvind. They set snares for rabbit or hare, clever nooses of cord placed so the quarry would wander in unawares and be caught by neck or limb, unable to free itself from the constricting loop. Usually the creatures would be dead by the time the boys checked the snare, but sometimes they were still alive, straining wild-eyed against the cord, or hunched, staring at their captors with a knowledge of death on their small faces. Eyvind preferred it when they were dead; it was better if the snare went around the neck. But he bore a short, heavy club and used it efficiently when he needed to. Somerled would not employ the club. He checked his own snares, and Eyvind came across him sitting there quite still, watching with grave interest the small, struggling animal, whose frantic efforts to free itself had worn the flesh of its trapped leg almost to the bone. Perhaps Somerled was waiting for that moment he had once spoken of: a turning point, when it all went dark. Eyvind shivered, and then reached across and administered the merciful stroke of death. And Somerled was suddenly very angry indeed.

"Why did you do that? This one's mine!"

Eyvind looked into the dark, fierce eyes and swallowed. "There's no need to keep them alive," he ventured cautiously. "It hurts them, you know, being strung up. This is the way it's done. It's the way I always do it."

"And this is the way I do it," said Somerled coldly. "Tend to your own snares."

"Suit yourself," said Eyvind, and then bent toward the limp bundle of gray fur, peering more closely. "What knot did you use?" he asked.

"Ah," said Somerled, "you noticed. Want me to show you?" Deftly, his fingers moved on the hempen cord, flicking under, teasing out the bloodied ends until the complex rosette that formed the knot was unmade. "I invented this. You'll find it quite useful, I think. It tightens swiftly at first, and then more gradually, and it's very hard indeed to undo unless you know the trick. Here, watch me."

It was a clever knot, and decorative. Eyvind practiced it several times, until he could remember the cunning sequence of under, over, across, through and around, which formed the flowerlike result. It would have its uses, certainly, but . . .

"I prefer the old one, for a snare," he commented. "Quicker and cleaner."

"Maybe." Somerled glanced at him sideways. "But this is much more interesting."

The season moved on, and a message came to Hammarsby that visitors were on the way: Eirik and Hakon, traveling from the north back to the Jarl's court at Freyrsfjord. They'd be home for only one night. Ingi ordered a sheep slaughtered, and set her housecarls to baking.

Eyvind was saddling a horse, getting ready to ride out to meet his brother. In his mind was a joyful reunion on the track that skirted the fjord, a companionable ride back up the hillside while the two Wolfskins gave him all the news, then an evening's feasting and tales. He could hardly keep the grin off his face. Somerled stood silent in the stable doorway, watching him intently. Eyvind had gotten used to Somerled being always there, a still shadow, eyes following his every move. At first, this had been deeply unsettling; now, he was so accustomed to it that he thought he might almost miss the other boy if he were not constantly present.

"I shouldn't be long," Eyvind said a little awkwardly.

"It's all right." Somerled's voice was level, self-contained. "I know your brother means a lot to you. He is a Wolfskin; you aspire to be just like him. I can understand that."

"I'm sorry . . ." Eyvind fell silent, not at all sure how to finish.

"Off you go," Somerled said. "I can see every moment's delay chafes you. Go on."

"I'll see you later, then." Eyvind swung up onto the horse, the prospect of a gallop down the broad path under the firs already driving Somerled from his thoughts.

"Eyvind!" It was his mother's voice, and a moment later Ingi appeared from the longhouse, drying her hands on her apron.

"What is it, Mother?"

"I'm sorry, son, I know you wanted to ride down to the fjord and meet them, but I need you to go over to Snorri Erlandsson's. I've two milch cows ailing now, and I need him to have a look at them before another night passes. If we don't nip this in the bud, the whole herd will be at risk. I'm sorry, Eyvind." Ingi had seen the expression on her son's face. "All the other boys are out helping with plowing and I just can't spare anyone else."

"It's all right, Mother, of course I'll go," Eyvind said, swallowing his disappointment. The dairy herd was a substantial part of their livelihood; a chance to greet the Wolfskins on his own was nothing to this. He tried hard not to look as if it mattered to him.

"I'll go."

Ingi and Eyvind turned equally surprised faces toward Somerled. He had never ridden so far on his own; more significantly, he had never before volunteered for a task, though, when asked, he performed them in acquiescent, expressionless silence.

"I don't think—" Ingi began.

"It's too far—" Eyvind spoke at the same time.

Somerled looked at them, and they fell silent at the implacable darkness of those eyes in the small, pale face.

"I said, I'll go. I know the way. I think I can be relied upon to deliver a simple message about some cows."

Ingi glanced at Eyvind, brows raised. "Better if you go, Eyvind," she said. "It's a long way and not an easy ride."

"No," said Somerled. "I will go. Eyvind will ride down to meet his brother. Should I take the black mare or the gray pony?"

"I don't know if—" Ingi began, clearly taken aback. Her word was law throughout Hammarsby.

"Take the gray," Eyvind said, "she's more reliable. And go by the upper track, it's quicker in dry weather." He looked at his mother. "You can trust Somerled," he added.

"What is this, a conspiracy?" Ingi glanced from one boy to the other, a little frown on her brow. "Very well then, off you go. Somerled, are you sure you know the cattle doctor's house? You must cross right over to the southernmost grazing fields, and then—you do? Good. You can ride back with Snorri; you should be home in time for supper. And you," she addressed her youngest son, "straight there and straight back, and be glad you have such a loyal friend."

"I am," Eyvind said, and winked at Somerled. Somerled's blank expression did not change. He turned his back and went to fetch the pony's blanket saddle. Eyvind rode off down the hill, eager for Wolfskin talk and Wolfskin news.

News there was plenty. Eirik and Hakon told some on the ride up the hill to Hammarsby, and more that evening over the fine supper Ingi's household had prepared for them. Karl was there, and Snorri the cattle doctor, who had administered a dose to the breeding cows and pronounced himself satisfied with their general health. Somerled sat at table, neat and quiet, eating little, speaking little, listening, always listening. When he'd ridden in with Snorri, Eyvind had gone out to thank him, but Somerled had simply raised his brows and asked, "For what?" Sometimes there was no understanding the boy; his mind just didn't seem to work like other people's.

Eirik was telling the household how the two Wolfskins had traveled north to assist Ulf with some delicate business, and were now headed back to Jarl Magnus's court, and then away on the spring viking. This season, Ulf planned to take one of

Magnus's ships far south, into a territory more frequently raided by the men of Jutland. There would be competition: things were likely to get interesting, Eirik said with some relish. Ulf would be at Hammarsby by the next full moon, to collect Somerled and take him to court before setting off on the voyage. Ulf would surely be grateful to Ingi and Eyvind, for Somerled was looking very well indeed. Maybe they'd make a Wolfskin out of him too, Eirik added with a grin. But Somerled was not smiling. Like a small creature of the shadows, he slipped away from the room without a word, and when Eyvind went out later to find him, the boy was lying in bed, curled up tightly with the blanket over his face.

"Somerled?"

There was no response.

"Somerled! I know you're not asleep. What's wrong?"

"Nothing." The voice was muffled. "Why would anything be wrong?"

"I just thought—"

"Go away, Eyvind. I'm trying to sleep."

It would have been far easier to obey and go back out to the hall where his family and their guests still sat over ale and good talk. Somehow, Eyvind found he could not do that.

"We don't have to talk about it, if you don't want to," he said quietly, sitting down on the sleeping platform next to Somerled. "But I'll stay here, anyway."

There was a long silence.

"You don't have to." Somerled's voice was a whisper.

"I know," Eyvind said. "Friends don't help each other because they have to. They do it because they want to."

After a while, Somerled spoke again. Eyvind could tell he was trying hard not to cry.

"Eyvind?"

"Mmm?"

"This is something you can't fix. Nobody can."

Eyvind could think of nothing to say; the hopeless finality of the boy's tone silenced him.

"I know you mean well," said Somerled thinly. It was the closest he had ever come to a thank you.

* * *

The time passed swiftly. Still they swam and explored and hunted, but something had changed. Somerled was pushing himself harder, doing his best to keep up and to get everything right, as if to master as much as he could before he must leave. But he had gone quiet again, and that strange darkness was back in his eyes. It was not possible to talk to him about it, for every attempt was cut off by a furious denial of any problem. So Eyvind kept quiet and concentrated on teaching, since learning things was the purpose of Somerled's visit.

When it was close to full moon and the weather set fair, they journeyed far into the woods and built a shelter. They stayed there three days. On the third day, they armed themselves with spears and tracked a wild boar, and at dusk they cornered and killed it. It was Eyvind's throw that pierced the creature's heart, but Somerled's spear had taken it in the belly and slowed it for the final stroke. They had done it together.

That night they sat by their small fire in a clearing encircled by dark firs tall as star-crowned giants. They roasted a little of the meat; the rest, neatly butchered, they would carry home tomorrow in their packs.

"You did well," Eyvind said.

Somerled chewed on his strip of meat, saying nothing.

"I mean it. When you first came here, you could never have done that. Most of the boys couldn't do it. They'd be scared of the dark, of wolves, of trolls. Scared the spear might miss. But you did it."

"Stop trying to make me feel better," Somerled muttered.

There was a considerable silence while Eyvind thought about this remark.

"I wish you'd tell me what's wrong," he said eventually.

"That's the trouble with you." Somerled's voice was uneven. "You're so good at everything, and yet you're stupid. You're so stupid you don't even know how stupid you are."

"Right," said Eyvind after a moment. He threw the rest of his meat on the fire, pulled his blanket around him and lay down to sleep. With Somerled, sometimes there seemed to be no point in trying to understand. There was silence for a while, and he began to feel drowsy after the long day. His limbs ached with weariness, but it was a good feeling, the sort of feeling that went with the cool, clean air of the woodland, and the smell of smoke from the campfire, and the sight of the dark, jeweled sky far above them. He imagined his mother's smile in the morning, when they returned home with their trophy.

"Nobody cares." Somerled's voice came out of the darkness like the whisper of a small, restless ghost. "Nobody cares what happens to me."

"What?" Eyvind rolled over sleepily.

"My brother left me here to punish me. Now he's taking me away to punish me."

"But . . ." Eyvind struggled to get his thoughts in order. "Isn't going to court good, if you want to be . . . you know, what you said?"

There was a silence.

"How could you understand?" asked Somerled bitterly.

"I am trying," said Eyvind, propping himself up on one elbow. He could not see Somerled's face; the boy had his back to him.

"You don't care either," Somerled said in a voice no louder than a rustle of wind in the bushes. "You're just counting the days until I'm gone. Then you'll go out with Sigurd and the others, and have a good laugh about me, and do your swimming and diving and hunting, and be pleased you haven't got me to drag along, slowing you down."

This was true, most of it. Already, in his head, Eyvind had planned a swim across the Serpent's Neck and a run to the top of Setter's Crag, a trip Somerled could never have managed. He spoke carefully.

"You know how much I want to be a Wolfskin. I'm too young now. They won't even let me do the trial until I'm fifteen. It's hard to wait. Three years seems forever. It's been good having you here. You've kept me busy, given me things to do."

"An amusement." Somerled's tone was cold. "A little diversion."

"You know I don't mean that," said Eyvind, sitting up. Still the other boy's face was obstinately turned away. "Have I ever laughed at you, even once? You're my friend, Somerled."

He heard the indrawn breath, and wondered if Somerled were weeping. Then his voice came, harsh and intense.

"Then prove it."

"Prove it? How?" Eyvind was perplexed.

Somerled turned. He had his hunting knife in his hand, and his left sleeve was rolled back. As Eyvind stared transfixed, he scored a neat line in the white skin of the forearm, a wound that flowed with fresh blood from wrist to elbow. Somerled's face was like a war mask, the mouth hard, the eyes fierce with challenge.

"Swear it in blood." His voice rang in Eyvind's ears like the call of a solemn bell or some trumpet of doom, like a sound from an old tale. "Swear we'll be like brothers, forever. Prove to me you're not lying."

And when Eyvind hesitated, staring as the blood began to trickle from Somerled's arm onto the blanket, and descend in runnels to be lost on the forest floor, Somerled's eyes grew chill, his face still tighter.

"I knew you wouldn't," he said. His tone did not mirror his expression. It was the voice of a lonely child who fights to hold back tears.

Eyvind got up and took the knife from Somerled's hands. Not allowing himself to think too hard, he bared his own left arm, took a breath, and cut neatly: not too deep, or it would be hard to explain; but deep enough so the blood would flow freely. It hurt, but he knew how to deal with pain. He lifted his arm and laid it against Somerled's, and they clasped hands as their blood mingled and dripped in the glow of the fire.

"Now swear," Somerled whispered. It seemed to Eyvind that the sound of Somerled's voice was echoed in the rustle of the undergrowth around them, and the restless sigh of the wind in the high branches of the firs.

"What do I say?" hissed Eyvind, though there was indeed no need for hush, since they were quite alone.

"Say what I say. Say, I swear an oath that you are my brother from this day on; my brother in the blood that we share."

"I swear . . ." Eyvind repeated the strange, solemn words, wondering why his heart was pounding thus, and his skin breaking out in a cold sweat. After all, he was only reassuring the poor lad that he was not quite friendless. That was all this was.

"... faithful to each other above all other earthly vows; loyal to each other before all other earthly allegiances, even until death."

"... even until death."

They let go. The blood was a sticky mess, and Eyvind rummaged in his pack for scraps of linen to use as a binding. Wounds of one kind or another were common enough when hunting, and he always came well prepared.

"Here," he said, passing an old cloth to Somerled. "Tear it up, wrap it around."

Somerled bandaged his own arm neatly, finishing it off one-handed with a little knot that resembled a flower.

"I know what you want to be," he said, his voice quite calm now. "That's why I put in that part, 'earthly vows.' I understand your first promise must be to Thor. But your next is to me. When I am a king, you will be first among my Wolfskins, my war leader and principal bodyguard. There will always be a place for you, if you are loyal."

"Thank you," said Eyvind, trying to conceal his surprise. The whole thing had confused him. He would not think of the story of Niall and Brynjolf, which he had hated so much. This was a gesture of good will, no more. Somerled was lonely. He could hardly let the boy go away thinking he hadn't a single ally. When Somerled grew a bit older, he'd realize his grand plans were foolish, something that was all in his head and nothing to do with the real world. In the meantime, the lad may as well dream his dreams. "Good night, Somerled," Eyvind said.

"Good night." The small, serious voice came back through the darkness. Eyvind lay down again and, for all the throbbing of his arm, he was soon overtaken by the exhaustion of a day spent stretching his body to the full, and fell asleep. But Somerled sat a long while by the fire, his dark eyes fixed on a place far beyond the farthest margin of clearing or forest or wide hillside, a place that only he could see. He held his bandaged arm against his chest as if it gave him some comfort. Only the gods heard the words he whispered into the darkness.

TWO

Somerled departed with no sign of anger and no trace of tears. He thanked Ingi in tight, formal words. He glanced at Eyvind and touched his right hand briefly to the inside of his left forearm as if to say, *Don't forget*. Then, as abruptly as he had arrived, Somerled was gone.

A vow was a vow. But it was easy to forget when the days were warm and bright, and there were so many things to do: wrestling, or swimming, or playing a game they called Battlefield, which involved a very hard ball of straw-packed oxhide and ashwood paddles. Battlefield led to bruises and fierce rivalries and, on occasion, broken bones. When Eyvind went hunting, he took Sigurd or Knut or one of the other boys with him, and they did well. He swam across the Serpent's Neck and back again without coming up for breath. In the evenings, he worked with knife and wood, and made a little weaving tablet with a border of dogs on it. He thought he might give this to Ragna, who did not have one of her own. But he remembered Sigurd's joke about the ten children, and he noticed the way Sigurd had stopped pulling Ragna's pigtails, and now made chains of flowers for her instead, and he slipped the small carving away in his pocket.

Three years had seemed forever when Eyvind was not quite twelve, but the seasons passed quickly enough. Sometimes Eirik would visit, and now, as Eyvind grew closer to being a man, his brother began to teach him new skills. There were some techniques you could not practice on a friend, in case you took it too far and maimed or killed him: a little twist of the neck, a thumb applied very specifically, a particular jab to the lower back, or a squeeze to the groin.

And there were refinements in the use of weapons. A Wolf-skin had to be able to be two men, Eirik told him as they rehearsed axe flights against the bole of a great pine in the forest, well out of sight of the house. One was the warrior who leaped first from the longship's prow, screaming Thor's name, so fearsome of aspect, so wild of manner that none dared stand against him. That was the crazy man all feared, the frenzied fighter reputed to chew holes in his own shield, so fierce was his rage for battle. That was one man, and one side of it. But a Wolfskin could not be all raw courage and no skill. His life was likely to be short enough; there was no need to let pure stupidity make it any shorter. In between the viking seasons were times when other qualities came into use: the ability to guard one's nobleman and patron, to fight his feuds on land, and to play hard as well, for a Jarl liked to see his chosen band of elite warriors in demonstrations of skill, be it in horse racing, or wrestling, or challenges of other kinds. So, said Eirik, Eyvind had better polish up his swordplay and his mastery of staves, and try unarmed combat with someone closer to his own size and strength than those puny lads down at the farm. The two brothers pitted themselves one against the other, and Eirik won every time, which was only to be expected. Still, he tended to be a touch breathless at the end of a bout, and he watched his younger brother with the trace of a smile, as if something long suspected were being proven true.

In the autumn, the dark thrall-woman, Oksana, had another fair-haired babe at the breast. In the following spring, Somerled came back. This time he was visiting at his own request, until his brother should return from another expedition southward toward the kingdom of the Franks. If Ulf did well, the silver he brought home would buy the services of fine boatbuilders and bring his oceangoing longship closer to completion. He might lay aside enough to purchase the skills of a master navigator; he might even begin assembling his own force of Wolfskins. A good share of the season's booty would go to the Jarl in tribute, of course, but that was part of the whole process, Somerled explained. One must keep the Jarl content, if one might need his support in future. Such a venture required long and careful planning.

So, Somerled was back, taller, paler, still unsmiling. His clothes were finer. He wore a woollen tunic whose border was pricked out with glinting metallic threads, and his cloak was fastened by a heavy silver brooch in the shape of a dragon's head. His dark hair was neatly combed and held back by a band of the same metallic braid; he watched much and spoke little. As soon as he arrived, the other lads stopped asking Eyvind if he would play Battlefield, or take them through the forest for deer. It was assumed, with not a word spoken, that for the duration of his stay Somerled would be Eyvind's only companion.

Somerled had changed. It was apparent he had not been wasting his time at court, reluctant as he had been to go there. The Jarl had a thrall in his household who had been a scholar far off in hot eastern lands, and from this man Somerled was learning to draw charts and interpret the stars, to fashion verses and to play games. At Hammarsby, he found a willing partner in Eyvind's eldest brother. Karl loved games—not the Battlefield kind, but the sort one played with a small, square board and a set of finely carven pieces. His opponent was usually one of the senior housecarls, who had a shrewd eye for such pastimes. Karl had tried to teach Eyvind the knack of it over the long evenings of several winters, but somehow Eyvind could not get his mind around the intricacies of the strategy; he did not know how Karl could see three, four, seven moves ahead and plan cunning attack and counterattack. In the end Karl gave up, telling his brother with a grin that he'd never learn because he thought like a Wolfskin, his only tactic being to charge straight in, axe whirling, and mow down the opposition. This remark was probably intended as criticism, but to Eyvind it seemed like praise.

Karl was delighted, then, when Somerled expressed a willingness to play. They started with the game that had pegs in little holes, seven by seven, and before long Karl was maneuvered off the board. They played the one with pieces in black and in green; Karl had the sixteen small soldiers, and Somerled the eight, lined up behind a tiny king in gleaming soapstone. That game took longer; at first Karl grinned and joked, then he frowned and mopped his brow. Later he drank ale, cursing, and finally he admitted defeat. Somerled did none of those things. He played games as he did everything else: silently, watchfully, his dark eyes giving nothing away. At the end, he gathered up the pieces neatly, putting them back in their small calfskin bag. He nodded at Karl, unsmiling.

"You play well, for a farmer," said Somerled.

They went hunting, they set snares, they swam in the river or in the cold waters of the fjord. Somerled had not forgotten what Eyvind had taught him, and he learned more. He would never be a warrior, that much was clear. With his new tricks learned from Eirik, and his superior size and strength, Eyvind was as far beyond his friend in physical skills as a master craftsman is beyond the rawest apprentice. But at least, under his tutelage, Somerled learned to defend himself. If he ever had to live rough, he would be able to find his own food and shelter. They built a platform together in the upper branches of a sturdy oak, a secret refuge that could be reached only by means of a knotted rope. The floor was of lashed poles, the walls of wattles, the roof open to the stars. It was very high. Once, during the construction, Somerled had slipped and nearly fallen; he clung by one hand, his fingers all that prevented a rapid descent to instant oblivion on the forest floor. Eyvind had managed to grip his arms and haul him to safety. Near sunset, as they sat on their high perch listening to the cries of homing birds, Eyvind saw Somerled scratching something on the bark with his hunting knife.

"What are you doing?" he asked. "You'll blunt the edge."

Somerled did not answer. The knife was making a neat, irregular pattern of vertical lines and slanting cross-strokes, like a row of little trees, each with one or two or three branches.

"Somerled? What is that?"

The steady movement of the knife continued. Somerled spoke without turning.

"It says here, *Two brothers made this house. Somerled carved these runes.*"

Eyvind's jaw dropped. "You mean, you can write?" he breathed in astonishment.

"I haven't been wasting my time," Somerled said casually, incising a neat pair of parallel lines against one small upstroke. "A man needs certain skills to advance in life. This is one of them. I can read, too. But this is not everyday writing, Eyvind. Here, let me show you."

Patiently he went along the line of tidy markings, explaining what each meant, and why. "They are not ordinary runes, you understand, but another kind, a secret kind. Even among scholars, few understand them. The branches are the clue, a sort of pointer . . ."

His explanation was careful and slow, but after a while he stopped. Looking at Eyvind, he did not smile, exactly; a real smile from Somerled was a rare event. But his expression softened.

"I'm sorry," confessed Eyvind ruefully. "I just don't understand." It was beginning to come to him that perhaps his friend was very clever indeed, so clever that Eyvind might never quite comprehend him.

"It's all right, Eyvind," said Somerled. "You don't need to know these things. It's different for me. To be what I must be, I have to learn everything. Reading, writing and games, archery, rowing and skiing, probably even smithcraft. And I must not forget music and the fashioning of verses. Without the mastery of these, a man cannot call himself a leader. And I don't have long."

Eyvind sat back, round-eyed. He said nothing.

"You don't believe I can do it," Somerled said flatly.

"On the contrary." Eyvind spoke in tones of awe. "I'm beginning to believe you can do anything you put your mind to." He watched as his friend carved the last rune and lowered the knife. "It looks very fine," he added.

Something in his tone caught Somerled's attention.

"What is it?"

"I—" Eyvind was unusually hesitant. "I'm wondering if—"

"What? You want to make your mark here too? You should, brother, for this belongs to the two of us. Our secret."

"I would like to learn how to make my name. Properly, in these signs, not just a cross. It looks difficult. I'm not sure if I could do it."

"We'll practice it here, on the boards, until you have it. Then on the tree. Get your own knife and copy me."

Eyvind was to remember, in later years, how patient Somerled was with him that day, talking him through each upright, each cross-stroke, letting him try it slowly, correcting each error with kindness, until Eyvind could inscribe a passable version of the runes that made his name on the bole of the great tree. For the space of that lesson, it seemed to Eyvind that Somerled became a different boy, one who could find joy in sharing what he knew, one who could give as well as take. It was a brief enough time, but Eyvind never forgot it.

Much later, after Somerled had returned to the south, Eyvind would climb up to the tree house sometimes and study the inscription in the bark. He would run his finger over the signs, just the part of it he knew said *Eyvind*, for the rest of it he was not able to decipher. It seemed to him a proud thing for a man to be able to write his name. As for the other part, that stood as a reminder of the vow he had sworn, for in those runes Somerled had set down the pact between them: two brothers.

That same summer, Eyvind and Somerled visited the cat woman in her strange small hut above the tree line, near the top of Bleak Hill. The seer had another name, but folk always called her the cat woman, as if she were only part human. The old woman's powers were both feared and respected. She received visitors only when she chose. Karl went up sometimes to chop wood and deliver a sack of grain or a round of cheese. Occasionally, the woman ventured down the mountain for some festival or gathering, and they said if she was given enough ale, she would chant to the spirits until her eyes rolled back in her head, and she'd speak in a strange voice, and tell of what the future held. Men liked to hear of their destinies; farmers were eager for tidings of seasons to come, fishermen wanted advance notice of storms, merchants were keen for predictions of where the best bargains might be sealed. The cat woman did not always tell good news, but her warnings were useful, and she was received with great respect, and gifts.

Eyvind would have preferred to spend the day hunting, but when Somerled heard about the seer, there was no stopping him. He must go there before Ulf came for him again; he must know what she had to tell. Besides, it was an adventure.

Ingi gave them a little tub of sweet butter to take, and eggs nestled in a bag of down. The weather was fair and bright but chill for the season. It was a long journey, a full day there and back. They made their way up beyond the tree line and out onto the rocky hillside. Eyvind slowed his pace to accommodate Somerled, but not as much as he would once have done. They saw deer moving silently down in the woods, and an eagle overhead, but there was no hunting; this expedition sought only knowledge. From the narrowed intensity of Somerled's eyes, Eyvind thought he knew what it was his friend wanted to hear. But he held his tongue. One did not question Somerled at such times, unless one wanted a response that stung like a whip.

The cat woman's hut was turf-covered, set low, almost as if the earth had chosen to grow up around it. A small goat grazed on the roof; from the wood pile, a monstrous, thick-necked cat watched them through slanting yellow eyes. Black chickens scattered, squawking. She wouldn't be needing the eggs, then. From a hole in the turf a thin plume of smoke arose. Eyvind called out politely, then stooped to go in; the doorway was hung with a strip of coarse cloth, no more.

Inside, the place was dark and small, and crammed with objects strange and wonderful, bizarre and magical. Masks hung on the walls: faces that were beautiful, wild, blank-eyed, dangerous. The bones of a long, thin creature were laid out neatly on a stone shelf; an iron pot steamed on the central hearth. There was an odd, pungent smell—not unpleasant exactly, just the sort of odor that renders one suddenly, sharply awake. Somerled came in behind him, and stopped.

"We've brought some butter and a few eggs," Eyvind said politely. "My mother sent them. Ingi, that is."

In the shadows beyond the fire, the cat woman stirred. She rose to her feet and moved forward until the light from the smoke hole fell on her face, a face remarkably unlined for one so old. Her skin was very white, as white as the long hair that fell unbound below the strange cap she wore, which seemed made of dark skin on the outside and pale fur inside. Her eyes were like fine blue glass; around her neck she had a string of beads that almost matched them. As she moved, her gown made a faint tinkling sound, as if it were hung with tiny bells.

"Perhaps you don't want the eggs, though," Eyvind added. "I see you have your own chickens."

"Gifts are welcome," said the cat woman, motioning to a dresser of stone slabs by the far wall. "You can set them there, if you will. Your mother is a kind woman. Your brothers came here. I remember them."

Eyvind smiled, hoping he did not appear too nervous.

"I hear you tell fortunes. I want you to tell mine," Somerled said abruptly. "I hope you do not lie, or invent tales when your skills desert you. It is a calling that attracts cheats."

"Somerled—" Eyvind hissed, seeing the change come over the old woman's features. One did not offend a seer. Surely even Somerled knew that.

"I do not perform at folk's beck and call, like some fairground creature," said the cat woman quietly. She turned to Eyvind. "This is no brother," she observed.

"I'm sorry. His name is Somerled. He is my friend, who comes to stay with us sometimes. We were hoping . . . that is—"

The cat woman gave a faint smile. "I have told their future, the warrior and the farmer, and I will do no less for you. But I owe your friend nothing."

Out of the corner of his eye, Eyvind saw Somerled's mouth tighten.

"I have another gift, if you'll accept it," Eyvind said quickly, before Somerled could speak again and make matters worse. "I made this. Perhaps you might like it." From his pocket he drew out the weaving tablet he had carved. Now that he looked at it, he could see that the little dogs were not as regular as they should be, some of their expressions more comic than noble. He hoped she would not be offended. "It's not a bribe, or a payment," he added hastily. "I know such knowledge can never be paid for. But you can have it, if you want."

The cat woman sighed; an odd sort of sigh, as if she bore a burden too heavy for her. Then she took the small thing from his hands, touching the pattern with a finger, lightly.

"Send your friend outside," she said.

Somerled glowered.

"Send him outside. Such tellings are private. You know that. You first, then the other."

In an instant, Somerled was gone. There was nothing there but a sort of angry vibration where he had stood. The cat woman did not chant, or roll her eyes, or call on the spirits. She sat by the fire, and bade Eyvind sit by her.

"Give me your hand, Eyvind. You are grown as tall as your brothers: like a strong young tree. What is it you want to hear so badly? Let us light the candles, one on this side, one on the other. And throw a pinch of this on the fire—ah, that's better. Now, let me see you in the light. A fine young man. There's a great gift for kindness in you, I see it in your eyes. A rare gift. And yet, your path will take you far from such ways. What do you want to know, Eyvind?"

"Will I be a Wolfskin? Will I pass Thor's test?" His words tumbled over each other in their eagerness to get out. "And when? How long must I wait?"

He thought she would not speak at all, so long she took to answer. She gazed at his palm, and into his eyes, and then at the candle flame, and the look on her face was almost pity. His heart shrank. She had seen that he would fail, and was not prepared to speak it.

"Tell me!" he blurted out finally. "Tell me, whatever it is!"

The cat woman sighed again, and blinked, as if returning from a far place. "Oh, yes, you'll swing your axe in the very forefront of it, lad. A cleaver of skulls, a smiter of the strongest, fearless and proud. The best among them, you'll be. And soon; more than one year, less than two, I think. Thor has his mark on you; he had from the first."

Eyvind could feel the grin stretching across his face, and the proud beating of his heart. "Thank you! Oh, thank you."

"That's not all."

"It's all that matters to me. It's all I want: all I ever wanted."

The cat woman frowned. Her long fingers were turning his hand over, turning it back, touching the scar that began above the wrist and disappeared under his shirtsleeve. "You should hear what is to be told, all the same. For it is not solely your own future I tell here, but that of others, those whose lives may be touched by your choices. You have a long and strange path ahead of you, Eyvind; you see only the glory of your existence as Thor's right hand, but that is by no means the sum of it."

"What could be better than that? What could be more important?"

"There are lessons to learn: secret knowledge to be found where least expected. There is a deep well of treachery, and a bright beacon of love, and the path between them is narrow indeed. There's the rarest of treasures laid by for you, son. Make sure you don't let it go."

"Treasure? I suppose I'll see some of that, when I'm a Wolfskin."

"I suppose you will," said the cat woman gravely. "But that is not the kind of treasure I mean. Now go, son. Do not lose sight of yourself, in the midst of it all."

"Thank you. I won't," said Eyvind, but he did not understand her words, nor did he care, for he had received the answer he wanted and his heart was aflame with joy.

He waited outside for Somerled, and tried not to overhear. He stroked the cat; it sat quiet, purring, but he could feel the bunched muscle in it, and see its knife-sharp claws. It was a wonder there were any chickens left.

It was hard not to hear them. Somerled's voice was crisp and clear, the old woman's soft, measured; and yet it came to Eyvind's ears as if she intended her words to reach him. He would have moved away, but the cat had its claws in his sleeve now and a look in its feral eye that said, *You'd better keep scratching my ear or I'll show you what I really am.*

"Tell me the truth," said Somerled.

There was a little pause. "Is it the truth you seek, or merely the confirmation of what you have already decided will be so?" asked the cat woman.

"It does not become an old crone to play games with words," Somerled snapped. "I seek the truth, of course. Why else would I come here? But perhaps you are a fraud. Perhaps you tell only fabrications, to fill folk's heads with impossible hopes."

"What if I tell the truth and it does not please you?" she asked softly. "What then? I cannot always give good news. The world is a harsh place, Somerled. You've good cause to know it."

"What does that mean?" Somerled sounded angry, and yet she had not even begun her foretelling.

"You know what it means. Your path has not been an easy one. As it began, so it will continue. Show me your arm."

A short silence.

"You did your friend no favors," said the cat woman, "in binding him to you thus."

"Is it foretold, then, that I should proceed on this uneasy path quite alone? With no friend at all by my side?"

"I did not say that. Eyvind will sacrifice much to adhere to his promises."

"And what future have you foretold for him? A short but glorious life wielding the axe for Thor? My friend is a simple fellow with simple dreams. If you see that for him, he will be well content."

"If you would know, you must ask Eyvind. Here, it is your future we examine."

"Come on then, out with it! What do you see?"

"Take a pinch of this; throw it on the fire. Now look at me."

Then there was nothing for a long time, so long that Eyvind wondered if the cat woman could not see any future for Somerled, or perhaps a future she was reluctant to tell. When at last she did speak, it was slowly, as if she chose each word with caution.

"Blood and passion, treachery and death. Beyond that, there is . . . there is . . ."

"What? What?" hissed Somerled.

"It is not clear. There are two ways here, and it cannot be told which you will choose. In each there is a journey. One way holds power and influence. I see a man there who is a king; many follow him. The other way . . . that is a strange way indeed, through waters uncharted, with gulls and seals for companions."

"It is enough." Somerled's voice had changed. The edge was gone; he sounded, if anything, relieved. "You speak truth, I see that. There is no doubt which of these paths is to be mine. What recompense do you require for this telling?"

"I want none from you," said the seer. "Your friend's gift is enough."

"That? What use is a trifle like that? Why don't you ask for silver, or fine amber, or a sheep or two? You'll never get out of this hovel that way."

"You have much to learn. Now, it is time for you to go. Your friend waits."

The cat withdrew its claws, and Eyvind watched Somerled come out of the hut, his face impassive, though the eyes were bright.

"What did she tell you?" Eyvind asked as they made their way homeward down the rocky hillside. He could not tell Somerled he had overheard; there had been certain things said that were surely not for his ears.

"What I expected," Somerled said. "That I will be a man of power and influence. Not here, but somewhere far away. I am well pleased. The old woman speaks true. What did she tell you?"

But Eyvind did not reply, for he was thinking. He went over in his head the seer's words to Somerled. They had been carefully chosen, no doubt of that. But they had seemed to him somewhat less certain than Somerled believed. Still, Somerled was never wrong, and he himself did tend to muddle things sometimes. He decided to say nothing about it.

"Eyvind?"

"Oh. She told me I will be a Wolfskin, and soon. She seemed quite sure."

Somerled lifted his brows. "Everyone knows that," he said dryly. "It's written all over you. If every fortune were as easy to tell as yours, my friend, we'd all be seers."

They did not speak further of these matters. But as they came down the steep slopes above the forest, Eyvind's mind was still turning over what each of them had been told and what it might mean, and perhaps that was why the accident happened. He had always been a careful hunter. He looked after his weapons well and used them correctly; he observed rules for his own safety and taught them to those who went with him after boar or deer. When he hurt himself, which was not often, he knew what to do about it. They were still close to the northern limits of Hammarsby land, nearly a half-day's walk from the longhouse, but well down the mountainside from the seer's hut. This was a place where few men passed, a track through the forest known only to the most persistent of hunters. It was a quick way down, but difficult. The ledge they traversed was narrow, with a long drop on one side and a rock wall on the other. Eyvind went ahead, Somerled followed a few steps behind. It was extremely cold; one would not have believed it could still be summer, for even here, in the shelter of the great trees, the air cut like a knife. Above them the dark tops of tall pines blocked out the sunlight, leaving them in a deep world of shadowed gray-green.

It was quick. One instant Eyvind was moving with surefooted confidence along the ledge, the next the ground had crumbled under his feet and he was falling, helpless to stop himself, the tree branches dancing crazily above him, the air whistling chill around him, and with a sickening crunch he hit the earth far below the ledge. For a moment all went dark; he

drew a single shuddering breath, and then there was the pain,
savage, spearing pain through his thigh, and he ground his teeth
hard together so as not to scream. Dimly he registered the frantic, scrabbling sounds of Somerled's rapid descent down the
hill to his side, the gasp of the other boy's breathing. *Don't
scream*, Eyvind ordered himself. *Thor watches you. It is a test.*
He opened his eyes and looked down at his right leg. It did not
show much beyond a huge purple mark, which spread all up
and down the inner thigh; not much beyond a certain swelling;
little enough, for such pain. But Eyvind was a hunter. Through
the mist of rising unconsciousness, through the dizzy blurring
of his vision and the tremors of chill that began to course
through his body despite his best efforts to still them, Eyvind
recognized that the leg was broken and bleeding within, where
it could not be seen. His mind put the pieces together: himself
unable to walk, the cold, the loss of blood, and small, puny
Somerled the only aid at hand. He might die. Far worse than
that, he might survive and be crippled. A Wolfskin must be
whole, and strong.

"Somerled?" he whispered as the darkness came closer.

"Shh, don't try to talk." Somerled's voice was strange, coming and going; his sheet-pale face kept blurring as if this were a
dream. "I'll go for help. Where does it hurt? Here?"

Eyvind did scream then, as Somerled's careful fingers gingerly made contact with the wounded limb. And when Somerled ripped off his shirt and bound the leg as straight as he could,
with strips of stiff bark on either side, Eyvind's howl of agony
echoed through the empty woods until he clenched his teeth
hard to still the sound, for he could see the fear in the other
boy's eyes. The splinting done, Somerled rose to his feet, slung
his small pack on his back and looked down at the shivering
Eyvind, frowning.

"Cold," Eyvind managed. "Bleeding. Bonesetter. Karl . . ."

"I can run all the way," said Somerled. "There and back. I'll
leave you my cloak."

Eyvind looked up at his friend's small, intense face; it was
wavering, blurring, going dark. He tried to tell him; tried to explain that he would die of shock and cold before help could
come, but his voice didn't seem to be working anymore. All
that came out was a sort of grating noise.

"No good?" Somerled asked.

"Cold," Eyvind managed. "Too long . . ."

"Right," said Somerled. "You'll have to help me, then. As far as we can go, walking. Then I suppose I'll manage somehow. Never thought I'd have reason to thank you for those endless lessons about survival in the wild. Come on."

Eyvind could not remember much after that, except the pain, a pain so terrible he put his teeth through his lip, struggling to remain strong. He seemed to have a picture of himself leaning heavily on Somerled, and staggering, hobbling, weaving impossibly down the steep paths through the forest, and Somerled's voice coaxing, encouraging, sharply ordering him to go on. He thought he could recall collapsing part-way down in the shadow under tall trees, the pungent scent and prickling touch of pine needles under his cheek, and his friend's dark eyes staring at him from a face ghost-white with exhaustion. He remembered the familiar set of Somerled's mouth, a look which said that giving up simply wasn't an option. From what they told him later, he knew that here and there Somerled had stopped to adjust the makeshift splint, to prod him awake and force him onward. When Eyvind had eventually lost consciousness, Somerled had improvised a sort of sled from branches and bark, using the rope they carried, and dragged the other boy down to open ground. The man who doctored Eyvind said that if he'd been left up on the mountain while Somerled had gone for help, he'd surely have died before aid could come.

There was no more hunting that summer. Eyvind spent the rest of the season flat on his back in bed, the broken leg held up by a strong hempen rope, which the bonesetter had passed over a high beam; from the rope's other end hung a heavy stone like a roofweight, which dangled in the air beyond the foot of the bed, stretching the limb straight. Eyvind's skin itched and his leg ached and he could not sleep, and the days seemed endless. As the season passed with infinite slowness, he begged the gods that the limb would mend straight, and that he would be strong again. A man who could not run or march or stand fast on the deck of a longship in stormy seas could never be Thor's warrior. A lame man could not be a Wolfskin. So he lay quiet and prayed, and let Somerled try to teach him board games, and recite to him passages of law and wickedly clever verses he had made up about everyone in the household, and at length the summer was over. The weight was removed, and the bonesetter pronounced himself well pleased. The limb had mended straight and clean. Karl presented Eyvind with a fine walking stick fashioned from oak, but Eyvind did not use it. The sooner his leg learned to do its job again, he reasoned, the sooner he might be ready for Thor's trial.

Ulf sent an escort to bring his young brother back to court. Ingi had been furious with the two boys, saying no more expeditions up there until they were at least sixteen. Now she kissed Somerled on both cheeks, and Karl shook his hand. As for Eyvind, he felt somewhere inside him a change that was bigger, deeper, more monumental than any that had ever occurred in his life. When he had made his vow to Somerled, he had done so because the boy was lonely and sad, and it had seemed to Eyvind that everyone in the world deserved at least one friend whom they could depend on. He still believed that, but over the summer of lying on his bed, while Somerled, with infinite patience, sat by his side devising one small entertainment after another to while away the tedious time of healing, Eyvind had come to realize the bond between them was far more than simple friendship. It was no lightly made promise, to be discarded or forgotten once the season was over. It was deep and binding, solemn and lifelong: an oath between men, the men they would someday become.

Another year, they went up to the shieling, the summer pasture high in the hills, where small huts allowed a lucky few to stay the season out, tending the herds and flocks. There were six boys and three girls, with a couple of shepherds and Oksana the thrall-woman, her small fair children in tow. Some guarded the animals they had driven up the hillside, and some milked sheep and cows and made cheese and sweet butter. Eyvind's job was to provide a steady supply of game for the pot. Long hours out of doors give folk hearty appetites. Ingi had warned them that summers at the shieling were no holiday. All must do their share.

The days were indeed full of hard work, but it was a good time. The weather stayed fine; they found time to swim in the stream, and they made a rope swing, and ate their supper out of doors under the pale sky of long summer evenings. Winter-white skin turned golden brown under the sun's warm touch. Sigurd put flowers in Ragna's fair hair, and she blushed a delicate pink and did not scold him at all. Oksana kept her babe close by her, watched over by one of the girls, but the other children rode here and there on the shoulders of obliging lads, and learned to catch a ball, and fell asleep the instant they'd finished their supper. It was a happy time.

There were two huts on the mountainside, one for the girls and one for the boys. The boys' hut was bigger, with a central hearth for cooking. The shepherds slept here by the fire, with the lads at either end of the hut on shelf beds built against the walls. The place had not the privacy of Ingi's longhouse, where wooden partitions divided the sleeping areas. Oksana supervised the girls' hut. This was not so surprising, although she was a thrall, for it was known that Ingi had given her the chance to earn her freedom. This summer's responsibility was part of that. Ingi had made it quite clear to them, before they left home, that the girls' hut was out of bounds to the boys. Anyone who broke that rule would never be allowed up to the shieling again. Eyvind was surprised his mother thought it necessary to warn them thus. Surely it was the sort of rule people understood without being told.

They talked about it one night, lying on their shelf beds: Eyvind and Somerled and the two other lads who slept at the south end, Ranulf and Knut.

"Which one do you think's best?" Knut asked in an undertone. "Halla or Thorgerd?"

Nobody answered; it was late, and they were tired.

"I think Thorgerd," Knut said. "I like the way she walks. And her laugh." In conversations of this kind, nobody ever mentioned Ragna, who was without doubt the prettiest of the three girls. She might be only thirteen, but Sigurd had established a sort of unspoken ownership, which all understood well. And Sigurd slept not so very far away at the other end of the hut.

"Bet I've seen something you haven't seen," Ranulf whispered to Knut.

"Bet you haven't. What?"

Ranulf whispered again. Knut snorted in disbelief.

"Shut up, will you?" said Eyvind. "Some of us want to get to sleep."

"What have you seen?" Somerled's crisp voice challenged.

"I've seen Halla with her gown down to her waist; I've seen a pair of rosy apples that'd be sweet to taste. The girls leave their candle burning when they undress. You can see right in through the window at the back; there's a crack in the shutters."

There was a brief silence. Eyvind knew he should say something; there was no doubt what his mother would think of such talk. But his mind was showing him an image of glossy-haired Halla, brown locks drifting over pale skin in the flickering candlelight, and the involuntary stirring of his body silenced him.

"That's nothing," said Somerled.

"What do you mean?" Knut hissed.

There was another silence.

"Never had a girl, did you?" Somerled asked casually.

Eyvind's jaw dropped. The others stared round-eyed. Then Ranulf found his voice.

"You mean . . . ? Don't be stupid, Somerled. Of course we haven't, and I bet you haven't either."

"Ah," said Somerled. "But I'm not a farm boy, am I? Things are rather different at court. Don't believe me? I'll tell you all about it, if you want."

One of the shepherds rolled over in his sleep, muttering something about keeping quiet or he'd give them what for.

"Go on, then," whispered Knut, edging closer. And Somerled did, in considerable detail. By the end of it, Eyvind was feeling very uncomfortable in more ways than one. There was the hardening of his body, something that did happen to him sometimes, now he had passed his fourteenth birthday. There was a thing you could do to make that go away, but he could hardly do it now, with the rest of them there. And he felt a growing unease, for although Somerled's tale had the ring of truth, there was a wrongness about it that troubled him.

"Somerled?" he whispered, when it seemed the account was finished.

"Mmm?"

"What if the girl went and told her family? What if you got her with child? There would be compensation to pay. That sort of thing can be the start of a blood feud if you're not careful."

"Oh, dear, Eyvind. So serious. It doesn't take much to secure a girl's silence, believe me. I cover my tracks very well. You should know that. After all, it was you who taught me about hunting."

Eyvind lay thinking. In a way, he was impressed. It did appear Somerled had done what none of them expected to try before they were fifteen at least. But Somerled's account had troubled him.

"Somerled?" he murmured. The others seemed to have fallen asleep.

"Mmm?"

"The way you said it, about the girl struggling and—well, it sounded as if she didn't want to . . . to . . . you know."

"So?"

"Then you did something wrong."

Somerled gave a weary sigh. "If a fellow held back because of that, the race of mankind would come to an end, Eyvind. It's a fact of life."

"What do you mean?"

"You'll learn in time. Women aren't made like men. They simply don't enjoy it, not the way we do. They only submit because they've got no choice."

"But—"

"But what, Eyvind?" Somerled was starting to sound a little testy.

"What you said—that doesn't make it all right to force a girl. To do that is . . . it is lacking in honor."

"Odin's bones, Eyvind, where do you think you're living, in some hero tale? That's not the way life is in the real world, my friend. It's high time you traveled beyond the farm and broadened your horizons a little."

"What you did was wrong," Eyvind said doggedly. The more he thought about Somerled's tale, the more it worried him.

"I wouldn't lose any sleep over it if I were you," Somerled advised, his voice a murmur in the strange, cold light of the summer night. "I'm sure Eirik doesn't."

The next day, Eyvind offered to check and mend the shutters on both the huts, part of the summer maintenance of the buildings, and Knut and Ranulf called him a spoilsport, but he did the work anyway. That night he moved down the other end where Sigurd and Sam slept, and Somerled narrowed his eyes at him but said nothing.

Somerled was supposed to help with hunting, but he had wrenched his ankle and was confined to camp until it mended. Eyvind was pleased to be on his own, and took to spending all day away, returning with his spoils only in time for meat to be prepared for the pot. That way he could put his skills to the test, stretching his body, challenging his senses, listening, in the silence of the forest, for the voice of Thor whispering in his ear, *Be strong, be ready, so you can endure the trial.*

One evening when he came back, Oksana seemed edgy and cross, and Ragna was absent from supper; she was sick, and abed early, the other girls said. The next day, the three girls were very quiet at breakfast. Halla chewed her lip, and Thorgerd would not look up from her platter. Ragna sat between them like a pale ghost, her blue eyes ringed with dark shadows. Oksana was grim and silent, ladling the porridge. When Eyvind came home at the end of the day under a rosy sky, with a hare and three rabbits slung over his shoulder, the first person he saw was redheaded Sigurd, chopping wood for the fire. Only Sigurd was not chopping, exactly; he halved the log with a single savage blow, and quartered it, and then instead of throwing the pieces on the wood pile and starting another, he smashed the axe into the chopping block, and wrenched it out, and smashed it in again, and Eyvind could see that his amiable, broad face was blotched, and his eyes wet with furious tears.

"Sigurd?"

He had to say it three times before the other boy heard him.

"What's wrong? The way you're going, there'll be nothing but splinters to put on the hearth. What's happened?"

Sigurd scrubbed a hand across his face and turned away. "Nothing," he growled.

"It's not nothing," Eyvind insisted. "What are you so angry about? What's happened?"

"I'm not the one you should ask," snapped Sigurd. Then he seized another log and began to swing the axe again with such ferocity that Eyvind was forced to retreat to avoid injury.

When he came up to the huts, he saw that there were horses there, and the other boys were sitting on the rocks outside, quite silent. There was no sign of Oksana or the children, or of the

girls. A moment later his brother, Karl, appeared in the doorway, his expression very grim indeed. Karl was armed with
sword and axe; his shoulders were set squarely and his voice
cut like a well-honed blade. "Eyvind, come inside."

He faced Karl across the space of the hut, both standing.

"What's wrong? What's happened?" The strangeness of it all
had Eyvind on edge. "Is Mother all right? Are we under some
threat? What is it, Karl?"

"Be quiet." His brother was calm and stern; even so did he
look when arbitrating in disputes at the Thing—that great assembly where matters of law were decided—or settling arguments among his workers. Eyvind fell silent.

"I've spoken to all the boys; you're the last. Now I'm going to
ask you some questions, and you're to answer them truthfully."

"Of course."

"Very well then, Eyvind. There are rules for behavior up
here, and you all understand them, I know. I want you to tell me
if you're aware of any of the lads breaking these rules while
you've been up here."

Eyvind shook his head.

"Speak up," said Karl.

"No, I'm not."

"Can you speak thus for yourself? Have you conducted yourself as you should at all times?"

Eyvind felt a twinge of anger. "Of course I have!"

"I accept your word," said Karl gravely. "I did not doubt you.
But this must be fair in all respects. What I ask the others, I
must also ask you. In fact, you are already cleared of any suspicion, for I have several accounts that you spent all day away
hunting yesterday, and could not have been involved in what
has occurred. The quarry you brought back last night proved
that. Now tell me. Has there been any talk among these lads
of—any talk that might suggest someone was thinking of mischief, of breaking the rules in some way?"

Eyvind swallowed. "It would help," he ventured, "if you
could tell me what has happened. Has someone been hurt? In-
sulted? Where are the girls?"

Karl's mouth tightened. "Oksana has taken the girls home.
No more need be said. Now answer the question, Eyvind. If you
know anything, you should tell me."

"No," Eyvind said. "I don't believe anyone would break the rules. Sometimes, at night, we do talk about . . . about girls, and that sort of thing—but all the lads want to stay up here; they wouldn't be stupid enough to try anything that would get them in trouble." He remembered Sigurd, and the fury of those axe strokes. "Karl?"

"It's not a matter for public airing. I've given these lads instructions not to talk about it. Tell me, have you seen any strangers here these last few days, any men who do not belong on our land? Perhaps when you were out hunting? Think carefully, Eyvind."

"Nobody. You know as well as I do, we're the only ones who hunt up here. I wish you would tell me—"

"That would serve no purpose. As I said, you boys are not to discuss this. Now, you'd best bring in what you've caught for the day and make up the fire, for we still have to eat. I have not got to the bottom of this, for you all tell the same tale of innocence, and there's not a shred of evidence. I don't like it; but I've enough work on the farms, and cannot take more time now to delve further for the truth. Call the other lads in, do what you can for supper."

"Are the girls coming back?" Eyvind ventured.

There was a brief silence.

"No," said Karl heavily. "We'll send a couple of women up to do the milking and prepare the cheeses. You'll have a particular job here, Eyvind, one you're well suited to, and that's keeping your friends out of trouble. Some of us will come up before harvest and help you bring the stock down. Perhaps this matter is best left to sort itself out."

They all had an idea what had happened. But as to who had done it, that remained a mystery. The boys obeyed Karl's orders; nobody put the thing into words. Without evidence there is no crime. No man accuses another without witnesses and without proof, for such a charge cannot stand when it is brought before worthy men for consideration. Indeed, if one tried to bring such a charge, one might well attract talk of vexatious litigation. You didn't have to be a law speaker to know that. But the matter that was unspoken hung heavy among them. It was in Sigurd's sudden, violent rages, and in Eyvind's dark dreams. It was in Somerled's crooked smiles and narrowed eyes, and it was there every evening when they sat by the fire and felt the absence of the girls, of shapely Halla and giggling Thorgerd and sweet, blushing Ragna with her hair like ripe corn. One day Eyvind found Sigurd with his hands around Somerled's neck, and the other boy backed against a tree trunk, purple-faced and gasping. Eyvind wrenched them apart, gripping the wild-eyed Sigurd by the arms, forcing him away.

"In Thor's name, what do you think you're doing? You could have killed him!"

"I'm all right," Somerled croaked, fingers gingerly exploring the red collar of bruising on the pale skin of his throat. "Leave it, will you?"

"Leave it? How can I leave it? What if he tries it again? Sigurd, I don't know what's come over you. Now come on, walk with me to the hut and tell me what the trouble is. And promise me you'll leave Somerled alone. He's no warrior, and he's a guest here. Besides, you're twice his size."

Sigurd spat in the dirt at Somerled's feet.

"If you've got something to say, best say it plainly." Eyvind kept his voice calm.

"Huh!" Sigurd snarled. "Blood brothers, aren't you? You'll always be blind to what he is."

After that, Eyvind's misgivings began to plague him so badly that he broke his brother's orders and asked Somerled outright, one morning when the two of them were alone together.

"About Ragna, what was done to her—was it you?" The question was bald; there was no other way to ask such a thing.

Somerled's brows shot up in astonishment. "Me? Hardly. Why would a fellow mess about with children when he could have a real woman? The idea's laughable."

Eyvind did not like his friend's manner, but he accepted his words as truth, and slept a little more easily. Somerled would not lie to him. The oath they had sworn in blood made that impossible.

Sigurd grew more and more aloof as the summer drew to its close. He ceased to help with the sheep, and seemed instead to be practicing axe hurling and spear throws, and sharpening knives. For a boy who had never wanted to be other than a housecarl like his father, this was surprising behavior. Eyvind suggested if he felt the need to strangle somebody, he might try it on him, since a Wolfskin could never have too much combat practice.

The summer passed, still sunny and warm, but no longer bathed in that glorious sense of innocent freedom with which it had begun. They did their work, and the days went by, and at length they drove the flocks and herds back down to the farm, for it was haymaking month. All were pressed into service, even Eirik who was back from the spring viking looking bigger and wilder than ever, his full beard and long plaited hair a match for the bright gold of the corn ripening in its sheltered field behind the longhouse. With some ceremony, they mowed the lush grasses of the homefield, where the best of the season's hay was grown. The homefield boar, sole tenant of this verdant domain, stood in a corner watching, his small eyes thoughtful.

Ulf came, and Somerled went back to court. Whether the events of the summer were discussed, Eyvind did not know, and he did not ask. Ragna was very quiet these days; she stayed close by the other women, solemn and pale, and she no longer spoke to Eyvind or to any of the boys. There were no secrets by the fire, no gifts of flowers or whispered words in quiet corners. Indeed, it seemed to be Sigurd she avoided most of all; she would not even look him in the eye. And Sigurd was still angry. Somerled's departure had, if anything, fueled whatever burned inside him, and he seemed compelled to violent activity, as if his rage must be made into action lest it break him apart. Ingi set him to scything, but it was Eyvind who slaughtered the homefield boar when it was time, for he had the steadiest hand. Nobody liked this job. While they were careful not to give this pampered creature a name, for all knew his destiny was to provide ham and bacon, bristles and soup bones, it was hard not to befriend him over the growing months, with a scratch behind the ear here, and a kind word there. Eyvind understood that drawing the knife across the pig's throat was, in its way, another test. Before long it would be a man who screamed and shuddered thus under his hands, and he must think of it no differently, or he could never do Thor's work. He made the killing an act of mercy: swift, clean and final.

In corn-cutting month, the weather turned foul. They managed to get the crop in, and then rain bucketed down and the stream flooded almost up over the bridge. Somebody left a gate open and the chickens got out. During a lull in the downpour, the girls, cloaked in sacking and wearing their heaviest boots, ventured out to find them and herd them back. Grip, the old dog, followed creakily after. Some time passed, and the rain started again. Eyvind was up to the elbows in blood, cutting up a sheep carcass for salting, when he heard Grip barking. The note of it spoke alarm. Outside, Halla stood shivering in the rain while Thorgerd hustled the last of the bedraggled chickens into their coop and fastened the gate.

Ragna was missing. She had gone down the track toward the stream and they had lost sight of her. They'd called but there had been no reply. Now they were back and so were the chickens, but there was no sign of Ragna.

Sensing disaster, Eyvind shrugged on a cloak and yelled for help. Many went out to search; all the men and boys of the household and some of the women as well. Dark-haired Oksana walked beside Eirik, her face tight-lipped and anxious. Halla and Thorgerd had simply exchanged their wet sacks for dry ones and plunged out into the downpour in search of their friend. Not that there was any reason to think Ragna had not simply sheltered awhile in a cave somewhere, or under the trees, until the rain abated. Perhaps she would appear soon, a small, blond figure making her way back up the muddy track to home and warmth, with a lone chicken tucked under an arm. It would be easy to think that, if not for the dog. Grip would never leave a girl out of doors alone in such a storm. Grip had run home and raised the alarm. Besides, there was the thing that everyone knew, and did not say.

It was some time before she was found. Grip led them first to the bridge, where the water now brimmed over the wooden slats, but Ragna was not there. They made their way downstream on either side, and before dusk they saw her between rocks, lying calm and still with her blue eyes gazing skywards, and the water washing clear and swift over her small face. It was Sigurd who lifted her out and carried her home. His face was ashen, his eyes ferocious. Ragna's mother, widowed early, wept for the loss of her only daughter. Ingi was strong as always, comforting the girls, making arrangements. Eyvind thought Sigurd might weep at last that night. But Sigurd shed no tears. Instead he stood silent, gazing at the still figure laid out in her snowy linen, the flaxen hair now neatly combed and plaited, the features at peace. The only part of Sigurd that moved was his hands; they opened and closed, opened and closed by his sides. He stared at Ragna as if to burn her image into his mind. If he had been angry before, now there was a darkness on his face that boded ill for the future.

An accident: that was what they said. But Eyvind heard Eirik and Oksana talking, late at night, when the household had at last settled into an exhausted sleep. They were in the hallway, and they were whispering, but he could hear parts of it, for Oksana's voice was harsh with weeping.

"It's my fault," she sobbed. "It's all my fault, your mother trusted me! How could I let such a thing happen? And now Ragna's dead!"

"Hush." Eirik's voice was soft; there was a note in it Eyvind had never heard before. "Hush, now. Nobody blames you; you did your best to watch over them."

"She was only little, a child herself. I'm guilty, Eirik."

"It was a man did this evil," Eirik said heavily, "and a man who should bear the blame, and suffer the punishment."

"He will escape both," said Oksana. "Ragna takes that secret to her grave. She would not tell who it was; even her mother could not discover it. This man has threatened her, I think; why else keep silent?"

"In time, the truth might have been plain to see. But this sad accident has removed any chance of proof," Eirik said.

"Accident?" Oksana echoed, and Eyvind felt his heart grow cold.

"You don't think . . . ?" began Eirik.

"That child went out today with no intention of coming home again. She was terrified: so small and so hurt, too young for what was to come. Oh, Eirik, I should have stopped her, I should have—"

"Hush, sweetheart. There now, there now. Come, it's late; you must sleep. Don't weep so."

And they moved away down the passage, until Eyvind could hear them no longer. His astonishment at hearing his brother, a man of such high standing, speaking to a thrall-woman as if she were not only his intimate companion but also his equal, was brief enough. It was what they had said that really shocked him.

Their words forced him to recognize a truth he had tried hard not to see. What had happened up at the shieling had been a sentence of death for Ragna. It had snatched away all chance of the life Sigurd had predicted with blithe confidence in the days of their childhood. And so she had stepped off the bridge and let the storm decide the future for her. A man had done that; a man had started it. But Ragna was the only witness, and Ragna could never tell now. Her short tale was over. And although Eyvind had done nothing wrong, nothing at all, still he felt guilty, as if he were somehow responsible for what had happened.

Not long after, Sigurd went away. He took an axe and a bow and a few provisions, but he did not say where he was going, and nobody asked. Truth to tell, things were much easier on the farm without him, for his behavior had grown quite odd, swinging between sudden bursts of rage and long periods of moody silence. Indeed, he had seemed a different person entirely after what happened, and some said that in itself was a sure sign of guilt.

In the time of the first frost, Eyvind dreamed of blood and of fire. He saw bright eyes in the darkness, watching; he heard the whisper of the god. The next day they came for him.

It is not a sight granted to many, to watch a full team of Wolf-skins ride by. A lesser nobleman such as Ulf, brother of Somerled, might hope to assemble a force of six to spearhead his sea battles and protect him against treachery on land. Jarl Magnus had eleven. Eirik led them; Hakon was by his side, and following grim and silent rode an assembly of warriors who seemed the stuff of some fantastic dream. Their hair was long and wild, or cut to mere stubble on the naked scalp. Their faces were fierce and scarred. Each wore the short cloak of shaggy wolf pelt, fastened at the shoulder with a clasp of bronze or silver. But this garment was no uniform, no sign of a particular allegiance. Each man was himself. At the moment of ultimate test, each went forth alone. And they bore the signs of it; one had an ear missing, and one a deep seam across temple and cheek, where the skin puckered around the old mark of some adversary's blade. This same scarred man had many teeth gone; his grin was an alarming sight, but even more worrying was his shield rim, which was splintered and worn down all around its upper edge. The children whispered as they watched him; maybe the stories they had heard were true. There were no old men among the Wolfskins, no men of middle years. Eyvind's own uncles had died nobly in Thor's service, and it was expected a similar fate awaited any who joined this band. To complete four years or five was considered a remarkable feat of survival. Such a calling was not for a man who wanted a wife and sons and a farm, and to die comfortably in his bed.

Eyvind's heart was drumming as he swung up onto the riderless horse Eirik led. He was not afraid; it was the thrill of anticipation that made his blood run swift in his veins. He had his axe and his broadsword and a knife or two, but no shield. Eirik looked him over swiftly, gave a nod, unsmiling, and in an instant the horsemen wheeled around and set off northward with Eyvind in their midst. Not one of them looked back. The farm was gone, and the longhouse, and the days of childhood. The god summoned them; if Eyvind passed the test, he would not come home again before seeding time.

They rode a great distance that day, farther than Eyvind had traveled before. At dusk they halted deep in the woods, on a high flat stretch of ground circled by tall firs. A fire was made, a ring of torches placed well out toward the trees. With nightfall came a bone-chilling cold that crept into every corner of the body, numbing fingers and toes, freezing nose and ears and making each breath a burden. Eyvind was hungry, for they had not stopped to eat and there was now no sign of supper. He did not ask.

The men sat in a circle around the fire. One or two of them were humming under their breath, a strange, monotonous sort of tune that rose and fell, rose and fell. He could not understand the words. A third man had a little drum, cowhide stretched across a wooden frame, and his fingers tapped in time with the chant. Nobody spoke. Above and around them the forest was still, as if listening. The sound was like a tiny whisper in the vastness of the chill autumn night, no more significant than the chirp of a single cricket in a whole field of corn.

Eyvind sat cross-legged. He wanted to ask, *What must I do? When can I start?* Mindful of Thor's presence, he kept silent. In time, no doubt, the answers would become clear. Still, this was not at all what he had expected. Combat, challenges, hunting: all these things he excelled at. When would they allow him to show his strength?

"Here." Hakon was passing a drinking horn; Eyvind took it and swallowed gratefully. The ale was very cold and very strong. He passed it to the man on his left.

"Eyvind?"

Eirik was giving him something now, a wad of some kind of gum or resin, sticky and pungent-smelling.

"What . . . ?"

"You must chew this. And drink more ale. Pass the horn around again, men."

Eyvind eyed the lump of gray matter dubiously. It seemed more the kind of substance one might use to plug a hole in a bucket, or mend a wall, than an item of foodstuff. He might be hungry, but he wasn't sure he was as hungry as that.

"Chew slowly," Eirik said. "Don't swallow it. The ale should help."

"What's in it?"

Hakon grinned. "It won't poison you. Look." He reached out, pinched off a corner of the insalubrious-looking mess, and put it in his own mouth. "Herbs, mushrooms, pine gum. Harmless. Good for you. Drink some more ale; you're a man now."

Eyvind put the lump in his mouth and chewed. It tasted worse than it smelled; still, they were right, the ale took the worst of the bitterness away, and soon he was feeling much better— quite warm in fact, and at ease in the warriors' company. The drum beat on, keeping time with his heart; the odd little chant ebbed and flowed, ebbed and flowed like his own breath, in and out, in and out. It was dark. Beyond the ring of torches was a profound deep blackness that even the moonlight could not penetrate. It was a darkness of *between:* the instant of nothingness before outward breath becomes inward, the point of balance between life and death. What was it Somerled had once said? The moment . . . the moment when it all turns to shadow.

"You must sleep now." It was his brother's voice, and Eirik's hand easing him down to lie on a blanket near the fire.

"Sleep?" Eyvind was dismayed, though indeed he could not stop the convulsive yawning that suddenly overtook him. "But—"

"Sleep now," said Eirik firmly, and as Eyvind's lids closed over his eyes he seemed to see his brother's image doubled and tripled, a fantastic beast with six, eight, ten blue eyes and a crown of wild golden fur, and beyond it a tumbling mass of jewel-bright stars.

The chant went on; the drum passed from hand to hand with never a beat astray. Eyvind slept in the circle of men, in the ring of fire. The dark firs, the star-filled sky, the earth on which he lay made another circle, encompassing all, and in his sleep he understood this. Then, abruptly, he was more awake than he had ever been before. It was still night, still dark, still cold enough to turn the marrow to ice. There was no song now, no drumming. The torches lit a pathway across the clearing toward the deep blackness of the forest's margin. Beyond the torches there were faces—strange, watchful faces that were neither human nor animal: empty eyes, painted brows, pelts that were not hair nor feathers nor fur, but something between. Beyond the fire there were bodies, shifting, moving, changing. What were they? Surely these were no warriors, but some forest spirits conjured from shadow and moonlight. Perhaps his companions were gone, swallowed up by some evil enchantment.

"It is time."

Eyvind whirled around. Behind him a dark-robed figure stood, perhaps his brother, but maybe not, for the face was masked, the body quite concealed by the long garments.

"Undress. Naked the wolf comes to face you; naked you go in challenge. Fire is your only cloak: your weapons, only those he himself possesses. On equal terms you confront him, for to know him is to defeat him, to defeat him is to become him. I will guide you, but I will not stand by you at the end. This battle is yours alone."

Perhaps the guide was Thor himself. The god wore many guises; even so did he delight in walking among mortals. Eyvind stripped off his clothes, wondering vaguely if he might die of cold before he got anywhere near any wolf. The axe: he would take that, surely Thor would approve—or maybe a spear, for at least that allowed the security of striking from a distance. But no. *Your weapons, only those that he himself possesses.* Teeth; claws. A sharpened stick. A little knife. No choice but to hold one in each hand, since he hadn't even a belt to decorate his nakedness.

By the very edge, beyond the glowing coals, the ashes had lost their heat. *Fire is your only cloak.* He smeared the fine powder on chest and arms, on brow and buttocks. It would mask his scent, if not quite smother it. Then, small weapons in hand and blood racing, he set off up the hill along the line of torches. The robed man followed, silent. And beyond the light, the others came, others that now seemed to move on scampering paw and prancing hoof and slithering belly, that seemed to merge and emerge, part substance, part shadow. Their eyes shone red in the firelight, and yet when he glanced across they seemed no more than holes of blackness in the blank masks of their faces. It was so quiet he could hear the cautious progress of his bare feet on the carpet of needles beneath the firs, beyond the farthest torch now, under the trees, into the darkness.

"Go forward," his guide murmured. "Go onward, Eyvind. A blind man does not fear the setting of the sun. Hear with the creature's ears; scent your prey as he does. Be of the earth; be of the night. You have learned to hunt. Learn now to be hunted."

The path led upward, narrow between great rocks, precipitous and quite without light. *The blind man . . . he does not fear the dark because he knows the dark*, thought Eyvind; *he finds his way not by sight but by hearing, and smell, and something else, the something else that sends a forest creature into hiding before ever the man's foot cracks a twig, or his alien scent is borne across the hillside by the wind*. Step by step Eyvind moved forward, balancing his body to keep safe footing yet maintain silence, counting his breathing to make it slow and quiet, listening in a way he already knew. He had been a hunter many seasons, for all he was but barely a man.

The forest creatures had been silent: not a chirrup, not a rustle. Now, sudden in the dark, an owl hooted and he heard the beat of its wings passing high overhead. And behind it, in the same instant, another cry: a howl, a summons, a challenge surely meant only for his ears. He had never hunted a wolf before. Rabbits and hares were easy prey, deer and boar stronger, yet readily taken if you knew what you were doing. But a wolf was clever. And if he understood right, this was not a hunt, but a kind of combat.

Gripping his simple weapons, Eyvind moved forward up the path. The cry had not come again, but he had fixed its direction and thought he knew its distance: three hundred paces maybe, beyond the tree line, on the rocks to the southeast. It would be lighter there, under the moon: advantage and disadvantage.

The track came to an abrupt end, and it was necessary to use his hands to climb. Very well, stick and knife must be held between clenched teeth, and a careful progress made up over the rock face. He could see the moon now beyond the ridge above, fir branches brushing its cold pale visage. His fingers were growing numb; he hauled himself atop the outcrop, wincing as the stones caught his body unprotected and left their mark. He sat, eyes shut. A blind man in the darkness. No sound: his quarry would not call him forth, not now. He must find him in silence. No sound: no sight. But . . . there it was, he thought he had it . . . no, gone again. He made his breath slower. *Forget the cold, forget the bruises; fill your senses with* him, *with the one you seek.* Yes, there it was, a scent, faint but sharp, the edgy, acrid smell that was not boar, nor deer, nor bear, that was not dog either, but something far more subtle, and far more dangerous. He was there, not far ahead, waiting. Perhaps a whole pack of them waited. And Eyvind was alone. No choice. It was like the moment on the longship's prow, when it locks with the enemy's fleet and you charge forward, be there ten or twenty men against you. You see only victory, you hear only Thor's voice, and in that moment nothing in the whole world can touch you.

The same, but different. A wolf did not think like a man. To defeat him, you must become him. Wolfskin. That was the trick of it. Circle up, softly still, bare feet curling and balancing on the uneven surface, body crouched low, ash-cloak blending gray with a landscape slowly illuminated, chill and bare, under the impassive moon. Slow, so slow. These cold-cramped fingers must be made to obey, to grip and control, or he could never succeed. *I am strong. I am a hunter. And I will see him before he knows I am here.* Under the trees, stooping yet watchful, using the last cover of shadows, Eyvind moved with stealthy purpose. It was the upper rim of the great forest; before him, a jagged mass of tumbled stones rose to high, bare crags, the eerie light turning their ledges and cracks and fissures into a place of mystery and wonder. It was a landscape of gray on gray, encompassing every hue from the pale sheen of a fine pearl to a profound shadow-darkness. Twenty paces before him, a ledge jutted out from the hillside like the prow of a great ocean-going vessel, and there stood the wolf. Eyvind gazed at him and felt the hairs on the back of his neck prickle, and his skin grow clammy with sweat. The creature was huge, surely bigger than any earthly wolf, for he stood three times higher in the shoulder than the farm dog, Grip, and his long, silken pelt lent his form a grandeur that had something kingly in it. Such eyes: golden, shining. They were a savage chieftain's eyes, deep and knowing, yet wholly animal. Staring up at his adversary, Eyvind understood the message of that gaze. *You are come. I sense your presence in the darkness. Who is the hunter here, and who the prey? Come out. If you have the courage, come out and face me, for one of us will die tonight.* Then the great wolf raised his muzzle to the sky and howled again, a cry to freeze the blood and still the heart, a call that rang out over the forest and into the very depths of Eyvind's spirit. *It is time.*

If he had had a spear, if he had had a bow, he knew just how he would have done it. But this was to be a combat on equal footing. Equal. Naked flesh against thick pelt, small knife against many-clawed feet, stick against dagger-teeth: the idea was laughable. Still, he must win. His courage must be enough to tip the balance, for that was all he had.

Eyvind rose to his feet, no longer careful to be silent. The wolf turned its head. Eyvind stepped forward and began to walk up across the rocks toward the vantage point where the creature now stood facing him. There was a deep, low growling, very quiet, a sound that said plainly, *Come no farther. This place is mine.* When he had reached a spot ten paces from the wolf, Eyvind halted. Naked, ash-smothered, he held his head high and his shoulders strong. With the sharpened stick in his right hand and the little knife in his left, he looked the great beast straight in the eye.

Now, said a voice that was not a voice: perhaps his robed guide, though Eyvind had believed himself alone on that journey, perhaps another. Maybe it was his own voice he heard. He would not turn. It seemed to him that as long as he held that glowing, amber gaze with his own the wolf would not attack him. The creature stared back unblinking, and for an instant he thought—no, it couldn't be—it seemed it was a man he saw there, stern-faced, strong-jawed, with eyes as yellow and feral as any forest predator's. *Ware behind you*, said the voice, and he heard a breath, sensed the furtive pad of a foot, and there was no choice now but to break that stare and spin around, arms raised. The creature behind him lunged, jaws snapping, breath rancid in his face; a wolf, a masked man, a demon, he did not know, but he slashed high with the knife and stabbed low with the stick and rolled out of the way as the long claws raked down across his shoulder. He smelled blood; he felt the blow, but no pain. Eyes were watching, a circle of eyes in the moonlight. They were all around him. A wolf does not hunt alone.

Eyvind rose to his feet. He could still hold the knife; that was good. Think like a hunter, not the hunted. This was a challenge, not an ambush. Take the strongest; forget the rest. Oh, for a burning brand, for the weapon of fire. That would buy precious time. *Fire,* muttered Eyvind. *Fire.* And the world spun and steadied and spun again, and he felt the fire within him, growing ever fiercer and hotter until his head burned with it, his breast near burst with its power and he opened his mouth and screamed, a cry that made of his whole being a mighty battle trumpet. Perhaps he called Thor's name, perhaps something far older and darker. He turned in place, once, twice, three times as if to ready himself for a great flight of the war hammer or throwing axe. Tonight, his deadliest weapon was the fire within. Roaring his challenge, Eyvind hurled himself across the open space toward the golden-eyed chieftain of the wolves.

The fear: the shock of it. A man does not attack thus, as if he cares nothing for his own safety. A man does not challenge thus, without cold iron. These eyes are wrong; they seem to welcome death. Why is the man unafraid? Does he think to take my place? Mine? I am not old yet, I am still strong. . . . I will kill him, stinking in his nakedness, I will rend him. . . . And yet, the fear. This is not a man, but another like myself, and he comes to take what is mine. . . .

Knife slashed, fingers gripped long hair, the stick, he had dropped the stick, quickly now, dodge beneath, roll, spring, grab the stick and lunge before those teeth close again, perhaps on the neck or the exposed groin. Quick now. Screaming defiance, Eyvind thrust upward with all his strength. The stake

drove true, and hot blood gushed over his face. The wolf
thrashed and twisted, its gut impaled on the shaft of wood. The
claws scrabbled for purchase on the rock and there was an eldritch whine of agony. The others, silent in their circle, watched
narrow-eyed, shivering. The owl called again, remote and sorrowful. The wolf twisted its head back, snapping at Eyvind's
arm, its eyes fierce with outrage. It was valiant; it fought to
wrench the stake from his grasp, and finish him with its dying
strength.

*Brave . . . yes brave . . . but you will not have what is mine.
Pierce me with your long tooth, would you? I fight on; I fight
you until the moment . . . until the moment when all turns to
shadow. . . .*

The wolf bucked and pulled; the stick slid from Eyvind's
grasp, leaving a palm full of splinters. The creature turned,
dragging the stake under its belly. Its mouth dripped blood, its
bared teeth shone red in the moonlight. Out on the rocks, the
others waited: wolves, or men, or something which was in between, some manifestation of moonlight and blood and darkness. Eyvind's hands were cold, so cold now he could hardly
feel his fingers where they still clutched the little knife that had
once carved a token for a girl. One chance. There was still
enough strength in the beast to finish him. Those eyes did not
speak surrender; but Eyvind would win. He must.

*You are nothing. You have no tribe, no place, you have no
weapon but those you borrow. Your body is as naked and weak
as a cub new-whelped. You are nothing. Do not think to take my
place, for you can never be what I am.*

The wolf growled deep and flattened its ears. Even so had
Grip the dog once looked as the boy, Somerled, walked by him.

Eyvind opened his hand and let the knife fall to the rocks.
The little sound of it echoed away across the hillside into the
night. It seemed all drew breath; and then there was silence.
The wolf gathered its last strength to spring.

"Naked I come and naked I overcome," whispered Eyvind,
raising his hands before him. "Against you, I use no weapon
that you cannot use; equal we do battle, equal under the gaze of
Thor. And if I cannot defeat you thus, I am myself defeated."
Then he sprang forward, and the wolf leaped, and the two of
them rolled together, this way and that, a frenzy of tooth and

claw, of straining limb and screaming, growling, bloody combat. Eyvind could not tell where his own body ended and the creature's began, so close-locked were they. It was pain and blood and darkness; it was a pair of strong hands, holding and squeezing and never letting go as the enemy scratched and gouged and snapped, as the blood flowed and the desperate sounds rang in his ears, and the night became a chaotic jumble of moon and stars and shadow, of rock and treetop and sky, of silent, waiting forms that were not man and were not beast, but Other.

At the end, at the very end, they lay panting, spent, almost like lovers worn out by a night of passion, and Eyvind looked into the wolf's eyes one last time. The creature was still now; the golden gaze grew dim as Eyvind's hands maintained their merciless grip about the neck. The wolf bled from mouth and belly; Eyvind knew his own blood flowed from countless wounds on his body, on his chest, his shoulder, his face, his hands, somewhere in another world. He stared into his adversary's eyes and the truth looked back at him. This was the moment: the moment of changing. There were no words, simply the recognition of place, of tribe, of kingship: the knowledge of being, wild, free, strong. Then the shadow, and the darkness. The wolf shuddered and grew limp. The shining eyes clouded and were blank. Time to draw a single breath, and to begin to sense a weariness bone-deep, a pain in every corner of the body, a cold sudden and fierce that numbed his heart and froze his very blood. An instant only; and then with a rustling and a stirring, the waiting circle of beings rose and moved and closed in around him. The world reeled; the stars began to shift in crazy patterns. Beyond them, he thought he saw a man, a great, tall man like a giant with the mask of a wolf and eyes of brightest gold, and the man said, *Son, well done*. Then for Eyvind, too, came the darkness.

He woke, and for an instant thought he was home in his bed. Then he remembered, and disappointment hit him like a hard fist. A dream; imagination, the whole thing, and all he had done was sleep here by the fire like some lad too young and weak to hold his ale. They had not even let him attempt the trial. He moved, rolling to sit up, and felt pain lance through every part of his body. He rubbed his eyes against the daylight, and when he lowered his hands he saw the crust of dried blood on them. He was naked under the blanket, and on his chest, scored deep in flesh still coated with powdery ash, were four angry red stripes. A drum pounded inside his head; his mouth was dry and foul-tasting.

"Here," said Eirik, appearing at his side with a skin water bottle in his hand, and a big grin on his bearded face. The others were behind him: the toothless one, the earless one, the sharp-featured Hakon, the whole band of Wolfskins, and now they were laughing and congratulating him, and he winced in pain as someone thumped him on the back, and someone else was saying now there were twelve again, and Thor would be glad indeed.

"I—I passed, then?" Eyvind croaked, clutching the water bottle and wondering greatly about a number of things. "That was . . . real?"

Eirik's smile was fierce and proud. "For each of us, it is different," he said. "For each of us, it is real. You passed, yes, and more than passed, I think."

"But I saw—" Eyvind broke off. How could he find the words to tell of such wonders, the strangeness of those figures in the darkness, the way the wolf seemed a part of himself, so he knew its thoughts, and yet how it seemed at the same time to be the embodiment of the god? How he had seen death, and for a moment had understood it? And if he had truly slain a wolf, where was it now?

"You'll be hungry," Hakon said, "and thirsty. Get some clothes on, and fill your belly, for we've a long ride today."

And when he was sitting, water bottle in one hand and strip of roast meat in the other, he looked across the fire and saw the skin. They had scraped it more or less clean; it hung over one of the extinguished torches, a great, shaggy pelt, the silver-gray hair faintly gleaming in the morning sun. The breeze stirred it; there was a movement in it, a ripple of life, as if the spirit of the forest chieftain still lingered in the mantle he had passed to his conqueror.

"There's a man at Magnus's court does a good job of curing and tanning," said the warrior with the scarred face. "He'll make it into a fine cloak for you. A good size of skin, that one, big enough even for a little ox of a fellow like yourself. Fit for a king."

Eyvind nodded, saying nothing. His heart and his mind were too full to allow words. No need to ask; no need to tell. Each of them had passed his own trial; each of them was bound to Thor. That made them a band, a team; yet, in the end, each moved forward alone, for the pacts the god made were as personal as they were unbreakable.

So, in his fifteenth year, Eyvind became a Wolfskin. As one of the twelve, he rode south to Jarl Magnus's court. He left the forest, and yet he did not truly leave, for he was one with the wolf now, and he carried the fire within him, burning bright and steady. While that flame lived, he would serve the god, strong in arm and will, eager for battle, stalwart against all enemies and true to his oath. His life henceforth would follow Thor's path, the viking seasons devoted to voyaging, raiding, battle and plunder, the times between spent at the Jarl's side, guarding his person, escorting him safely on his visits throughout his territories, entertaining him with feats of strength and skill. Visits home to the farm would be few, and at his patron's convenience, not his own. The familiar faces—his mother's, Karl's, those of the household in which he had grown up surrounded by love—would become strange to him. That did not seem to matter. He was made new: a man. He would serve three years, five years, more if he was lucky; then, if the gods willed it, there would be a swift death and a place at Thor's right hand. It was a glorious future.

THREE

Eyvind counted them at first, with little notches on his shield; not around the rim, but inside, near the place where the boss was fastened with iron pins. The wood was crosshatched now, covered with small marks, hundreds of them. None was new;

Eyvind had stopped counting long ago. Thor called; he answered. That was all that really mattered.

The voyages in spring and in autumn were the best part. Before he was eighteen, Eyvind had traveled far: north to the realms of ice and back through Hordaland, where there was a powerful ruler with an eye on Magnus's own territory—they bore him gifts to help maintain their uneasy truce—then south around the coast and across to Jutland, where one might expect savage resistance from the Danes. And farther south yet, skirting the land, slipping into the inland waterways that fringed the fair lands of the Frisians and the Franks. There had been rich booty there, some of which Eyvind got to keep for his own, having soon become one of Jarl Magnus's favorites.

Magnus had three longships, light, shallow-drafted vessels, well suited to the tricks of shore raiding. Two bore fifteen benches, the other twelve; all went swift and nimble under both oar and sail. The *Battlesnake,* on which Eyvind usually traveled, could go far upriver. She was easy to beach and easy to launch, and her crew could carry her some distance across a neck of land to reach a new waterway. The *Sea Princess* and the *Longtooth* were fine vessels too, making up a fleet that demonstrated Magnus's strength and built his reputation. Still, the long times at sea were hardly comfortable. One was usually wet, and the rations did not travel well. Camping on shore overnight had hazards of its own. They learned to sleep sword in hand and wake in an instant.

He'd fought his first sea battle at just fifteen; he remembered that one well. Out in the open waters west of the sheltered Limfjord, they were in risky territory. The longships approached the northwestern shores of Jutland where the major waterway threaded through toward the rich trading centers of the Svear. Mist had settled close about their vessels like a soft shroud. It was late afternoon; they had become aware of another ship nearby, just before this blinding curtain of gray had descended around them. Ulf had command of the *Battlesnake*; he bade the men still their oars, and they sat in silence. In such a mist, ears must become eyes. They waited.

Eyvind, the hunter, heard it first: a tiny creaking, as of the timbers of a longship eased through the water with painful slowness. He gestured to Ulf, *that way*, and Ulf gave the sign.

The Wolfskins edged forward past the oarsmen, hands moving to grip weapons: the hewing axe, the short sword, the stabbing spear, the war hammer.

The crew held the *Battlesnake* still; once in position they would ship their oars, for all were warriors and each must be ready to play his part. They could be facing a single Danish longship, or two, or a whole fleet; there could be attack from all sides. Such sea combat was risky indeed, yet it could reap rich rewards, for an enemy ship, once boarded and its crew subdued, might be taken all the way home to form a fine addition to the Jarl's own fleet, or a significant gift to somebody one needed to impress, such as that dangerous fellow in Hordaland. Today, Magnus himself was in command of the *Sea Princess*, out there in the mist somewhere, and one of his nobles captained the *Longtooth*. But it was the *Battlesnake* that bore the Wolfskins, and so the *Battlesnake* must be first to attack.

They crouched on the small deck in the bow; the mist hung so close, even the gilded serpent's head that thrust up fierce and proud from the ship's prow was veiled in it, the faint gleam of gold on savage eye and forked tongue shadowed by soft, clinging tendrils of damp. Now the creaking could be heard by all, closer and closer still, and with it a little rippling of water, as of the movement of many oars plied subtly by skilled hands. Hakon reached into his pocket and brought out a lump of grayish, pungent matter, which he divided among the twelve of them; their jaws moved in unison. Today there was no singing, no drumming. Thor's voice was a whisper in the limp sail, a murmur in the moving water. *Burn bright for me, my sons . . . Smite hard, kill clean. . . .* The very timbers of the ship shivered with it, and Eyvind felt his heart quicken, its thumping a strong drumbeat, in time with the others, in tune with the voice of the god. They waited, every sinew stretched taut, every breath screaming, *Now! Now!* Yet they held still.

A flash of red through the wispy shawl of moisture, and now more colors, yellow, blue, the figure of a fine woman painted bright, riding bare-breasted toward them, not five paces away and moving fast. He heard Ulf's voice behind him, "Now!," and then the Danish vessel was upon them, the prow within reach, bold lady and savage serpent eye to eye, and Grim and Erlend reached out with iron hooks to grapple the enemy vessel tight to theirs; beyond that painted figurehead, bright metal flashed through the mist.

"Attack!" Ulf commanded, and in his voice was the thunderous voice of Thor, urging them on. The fire came again, hot and urgent in his vitals, in his thudding heart, in his bursting head, and Eyvind charged forward, a scream of challenge on his lips. He had waited for this moment all his life. Behind him, the Wolfskins roared as they sprang across to the bow of the enemy ship, their weapons hungry for human flesh.

There were no Wolfskins among the Danish warriors. Still, the enemy fought bravely, considering the odds. They lost perhaps half their number in that first onslaught. Eyvind knew that he had taken one fellow's head off his shoulders at a single blow. He recalled a stroke that had seemed to glance off another warrior's shield, and the surprise on the Dane's features as he looked down and saw that his arm had been neatly severed. Eyvind had never believed in causing pain when it was unnecessary. He made sure his second blow administered instant death. The deck grew slippery with blood, and one tended to step on things better avoided. The Wolfskins advanced like a dark tide down the ship, the first bench, the second, the third; he heard Hakon screaming behind him somewhere, as if in pain. He saw Eirik turning back, but Eyvind moved on, for his axe was sounding a song all its own, dauntless and unassailable, greeting and farewell.

As he hacked his way forward, the mist began to lift and the dark shape of another vessel loomed up alongside; there was, perhaps, a whole fleet of Danish ships out there, each with its complement of warriors.

"Hold hard!" yelled Ulf, now making his own progress along the slick boards of the deck his strike force had cleared for him. "Ware to the starboard flank!"

But there was no threat. The ship that emerged now between the rags of mist was one of their own, the *Sea Princess*, with Jarl Magnus himself in the bows watching with interest as his youngest and newest Wolfskin whirled and thrust and hacked his way ever forward, leaving a trail of broken men behind him.

Later, they told Eyvind that he had killed nine in this, his first battle. The Jarl had his eye on him from that time on. One expected displays of courage from a Wolfskin, but to lead, to provide a rallying point, and to account for so many in one's first encounter, and that at barely fifteen years of age, was something exceptional. There were rewards when they returned to court. Fine weapons, rich cloaks, horses. For Eyvind that was a strange moment, standing before the Jarl, receiving his thanks.

"Well, my brave one," Magnus said expansively, "you've seen the riches I bestow on your fellow warriors. Nobody could accuse me of being ungenerous. I know how to reward valor. And you are among the most courageous, for all you're still a boy. What gift do you want from me? Speak, and it's yours. What does such a fine fellow as yourself hanker after, I wonder?"

Eyvind found it difficult to know what to say. Glancing around the room for inspiration he caught the eye of Somerled, who sat among the nobles gathered in Magnus's hall for the feast of celebration. Somerled raised his eyebrows and twisted his lip, which was no help at all.

"My lord," Eyvind said, "I want no reward, though I am honored that you should offer me one. I have all that I need: my trusty axe, my good sword, and a place among your lordship's Wolfskins. To answer the call of Thor is all that I ever desired in life. I am well content with what I have."

Magnus stared at him blankly for a moment, then threw back his head and roared with laughter. Taking their lead from him, the assembled nobles of the household, the warriors and ladies, the visiting dignitaries, emissaries, and scholars joined in. Eyvind glanced at Somerled again. Somerled was not laughing.

"Well spoken, son," said the Jarl. "Well said, indeed. You may change your mind as you grow older. So, you will not take silver or gold, or rich garments, or fine weaponry. A slave girl, perhaps? There are many here at court, some no older than yourself, and not lacking in charms, I assure you. A hot-blooded fellow must surely say yes to that."

To his mortification, Eyvind felt himself blushing scarlet at these words. He was a man now, there was no denying that. But he had never forgotten what Somerled once told him, and he hesitated, silent. A ripple of whispers and chuckles passed around the assembled courtiers. Thor help him, they'd think him some kind of a freak if he did not reply soon. What kind of man turns down such an offer?

"Well, boy?" Magnus raised his brows.

"My lord, I have an even better suggestion." Heads turned as Somerled rose to his feet, his voice smoothly confident in the crowded hall. "Surely the very best reward for valor is one that lasts forever, a gift which fixes that moment of bravery in our hearts and minds eternally."

Magnus frowned. "Go on," he said.

"What you need is a poem," said Somerled. "A fine, heroic verse that sets out the bravery of all who took part in this encounter: yourself as leader, my estimable brother and the other commanders, and the whole force of dauntless warriors who ventured forth against the men of Jutland. And if you would reward the newest of your Wolfskins especially, let us capture his youth and courage in this mode. It is a challenge for your skald, to render such a poem by tomorrow night perhaps, and thus ennoble both Eyvind's name and your own."

"Mmm," mused the Jarl, a little smile playing on his lips. It was immediately plain the idea had taken his fancy. "Well said, Somerled." He glanced at Ulf, who sat by him. "Your young brother is a clever fellow, never short of new ideas. A cunning strategist on the game board, too, I understand, and no mean poet himself."

Ulf muttered a response.

"What do you think of this idea, young Wolfskin? Does it please you?" Magnus asked expansively.

Eyvind breathed again. "Yes, my lord," he managed, glancing across at Somerled and trying not to make his relief too obvious. Somerled's mouth quirked up at the corner.

"Very well, then," said Magnus. "A poem it shall be, in heroic style; it will be well fashioned, and we will hear it after supper tomorrow. But I will not ask my own skald, Odd Knife-Tongue, to make such a set of verses. That honor shall fall to you, Somerled Gunnarsson. They call you something of a wordsmith. Make us the tale of your young friend's bold endeavor and of our victory over the Danes. Make it both strong and subtle, stirring and clever. We shall await the result with great anticipation. As for Eyvind here, we shall let him go for now; doubtless it will not be long before he again shines bright among our warriors."

So, Somerled had rescued him. Somerled, once such a pathetic scrap of a boy, now moved among these men of power and influence with confident assurance. He was indeed a consummate player of games. Somerled was no warrior; still, there was no doubt in Eyvind's mind that on this particular field of combat, his blood brother was already a champion. And the poem, once rendered, had been a masterpiece of wording, its allusions so clever even Odd himself was stretched to work them out. Somerled had recited it to tumultuous applause.

As for Eyvind, his own particular problem was soon solved, for on the night of Magnus's offer, Eirik found him in the drinking hall, and announced that he was taking Eyvind on a visit, and that he wouldn't accept no for an answer. That was how Eyvind first met Signe.

Signe's house was one of many that formed the sprawling fortified settlement surrounding Magnus's hall. Many folk lived and worked here, all kinds of crafts were plied, goods made and traded, travelers housed and fortunes told. There were blacksmiths and farriers, tanners and armorers, drunkards and priests. The brothers hurried through the darkened alleys; it was late, though here and there lights still burned, and sounds of revelry or dispute could be heard. Eyvind tried to ask where they were going, but Eirik hushed him. They stopped before a neat, small dwelling whose steps bore red flowers in a pot. Eirik knocked. The house was in darkness; would not the inhabitants, whoever they were, take such an ill-timed visit amiss?

A woman's voice spoke from within: a low, warm sort of voice. Perhaps its owner had been asleep.

"Who is it?"

"Open up, Signe! It's Eirik Hallvardsson, and I've my young brother with me." Eirik was grinning. As the door opened, the grin widened and he stepped inside, enveloping the woman who stood there in his arms and planting a smacking kiss on her lips. Eyvind hovered on the doorstep. This, he thought, was only going to make things worse.

"Come in, sweetheart." Now the woman was looking him up and down, and he stared back. Her form was outlined by the light shining from behind her, inside the dwelling house; her dress, perhaps a nightrobe, was of very fine linen, and the curves of a firm and generous figure were clearly visible: long thighs, rounded belly, full, rose-tipped breasts. Her flaxen hair fanned across her shoulders; her expression was friendly. Eyvind swallowed nervously and took a step backward.

"Come on, dearest, don't be shy now." She reached out a white hand; he took it and was drawn inside. The woman turned to Eirik.

"Off you go now, my fine warrior. I'll look after your little brother, and send him home in time for his breakfast."

"Be kind to him," laughed Eirik, and all at once he was gone, and the door closed behind them.

"I–I don't think . . ." Eyvind could have kicked himself. He knew what this was all about, he knew what he was supposed to do. Indeed, his body seemed to be preparing itself for immediate action as the woman drew him along the hallway and into a chamber where a soft lamp burned beside a large, comfortable pallet whose rumpled blankets showed that they had, indeed, disturbed her sleep.

"Now, sweetheart," the woman said, letting go of his hand and sitting on the edge of the bed. Odin's bones, her skin was as white and pink as meadow flowers, and she smelled so good, a wholesome, milky sort of sweetness that made him long to set his lips *there* and *there* and have a taste of her, but . . .

"Eyvind," she said gently. "That's your name, isn't it? I'm Signe, a friend of your brother's, an old friend and a true one. Eirik tells me all his secrets. Don't be shy, Eyvind. You're a man, I see that: a fine man. Your first time, is it?"

"I–ah–yes, but—"

"Come on, sit here by me and let's talk a little. You can talk to me; I've heard everything, and more. Why don't you put your hand here, like this—ah, that's nice, isn't it—and I'll put mine *here* . . . no wonder they call you the little ox, sweetheart . . . now tell me. Something's worrying you about this, and yet you want it, that's plain as a pikestaff. Tell me now, Eyvind."

Her voice was so kind, and her hand so wondrously exciting, that between those two things he did, at last, manage to blurt out the truth.

"It's just—it's just, I wouldn't want to hurt you, or upset you."

"What? Why would you do that, love? What put such an idea into your head?"

"I thought—I was told—" The movement of her hand was agonizing, so sweet it was a sort of blissful torture, a tantalizing pain. "Well, that women don't like doing this, that they get no pleasure from it, and only agree to it because men make them. And I don't like the sound of that at all. That's why I haven't—why I never—"

Signe had taken her hand away. He thought he might explode with longing, and disgrace himself then and there.

"Who told you that?" she asked him, her eyes round with surprise.

"Just someone. I heard it somewhere. A friend."

Signe sighed and rose to her feet. Now she would send him away, and he would feel even more of a numbskull than he did already, his body on fire and his stupid tongue unable to say yes.

"That was wrong, sweetheart," Signe said gently, and she untied the ribbon at the neck of her gown and let the folds of sheer linen fall to the floor. "It's up to the man to make sure she enjoys it. Here, let me show you."

Over many sweet nights since then, Signe had taught him a woman could indeed take joy in the act of mating, could experience a pleasure as piercingly intense, as blinding in its ferocity as his own. Indeed, he learned that to give enjoyment could be as satisfying as taking it, as she taught him new ways and, later, as his skills improved, they discovered newer ones together. He wondered, at times, about what Somerled had once told him: not a lie, since blood brothers do not lie to one another, but a misapprehension that caused him to think hard about his friend, and what had occurred that terrible summer at the shieling. He would have liked to explain to Somerled that he had got it wrong about women; that if one listened to what they had to tell, and valued what they had to give, and offered them respect, there was a depth of happiness in the congress between man and woman that could not be found elsewhere. But he did not speak of this. Somerled was a courtier, clever, sophisticated, still liable to snap with some cruelty if displeased. Tell him this truth, and it was very possible the only response would be a derisive laugh.

* * *

It wasn't until much later, when Eyvind was a grown man of eighteen, that Signe told him she'd known he was a Wolfskin from the way he'd made love the first few times: charging straight in for the kill, so to speak, with not a hint of subtlety about it. He had the grace to blush a little, remembering how much she had taught him since then.

"I was only a boy," he protested, rolling onto his back to watch her as she dressed by candlelight.

"Oh, yes, and you're such an old man now," smiled Signe, putting on her stockings in a way that made him itch to pull her back into bed once more. But he did not. With Signe, there were certain rules one had to follow. He knew she went with other men, his brother among them. He knew she chose carefully, and that she did not ask for payment, though she received gifts gracefully when offered. He understood the meaning of the pot of flowers, and that it must be respected—it was a sign to show if another shared her bed, or if there might be a place there for him when he needed her. For Eyvind, she usually was free; he knew he was some sort of favorite, and never ceased to be grateful for it. The elegant ladies of the court still alarmed him, even now, with their sidelong glances and clever flirtatious asides. And he would not take a woman as part of the spoils of battle, though some of the others saw that as no more than a Wolfskin's right.

"You're a good boy," Signe told him, fastening her overdress with its twin brooches, and leaning over to kiss him on the tip of his nose. There was a tantalizing waft of her scent, that warm, enveloping smell that was part of her very self. "Not now," she said, evading his searching hand. "You're needed elsewhere today, and so am I. Come on, lazybones, up from that bed and into your clothes before I put you out into the alley stark naked. Not that you'd be left alone there long; there'd be some lonely widow quick enough to get her hands on you, I've no doubt."

With some reluctance, Eyvind dressed and made his way back to court. He looked for Thord or Erlend in the stables, but there was nobody around but a couple of lads forking hay. It began to rain, droplets at first, then a sudden deluge. Eyvind ducked inside the first building he came to, which was a small annex to Magnus's great hall, a place favored for embroidery and music and games, since its shutters could be opened wide to catch the morning light. The place was near empty. A couple of women were seated by the far doorway, chatting and sewing, and two people were sitting over a game board, both of them very still, apparently locked in an intense strategic duel. Today, Somerled had the sixteen small soldiers, and the player with the eight, and the tiny king, was a woman. Eyvind stopped in his tracks. Somerled's opponents were always carefully chosen: visiting nobles, traveling merchants, skalds, or priests: none but the most accomplished and the most devious. He never played with women. And this girl was both young and comely, if not exactly to Eyvind's own tastes. He liked a woman tall and generously built, fair-haired, pale-skinned, soft to touch: in short, a woman just like Signe. But he had to admit, as Somerled caught his eye and the girl rose to her feet, looking him up and down in that way the court ladies had, that this one was not lacking in natural charms. She was of middle height and shapely though slender. Her hair was a dark auburn and elaborately dressed in a coronet of plaits, threaded with some kind of sparkling ribbon; her features were pleasing if a little sharp, the mouth full and red, the eyes dark. Those eyes were very shrewd indeed; Eyvind thought she had assessed him already, and decided he was not worth much.

"Ah, Eyvind," said Somerled, not getting up. "Where have you been? This is the lady Margaret, daughter of Thorvald Strong-Arm. She's come here to marry my brother. But Ulf's mind is much taken up with other things these days: ships, mostly. He hasn't a great deal of time to spare. So, as you see, the lady's having to make do with me. Margaret, this large fellow is my friend, Eyvind Hallvardsson. He is a Wolfskin, and much cherished by the Jarl. We don't see enough of him these days. He does rather tend to be away raiding strongholds, or chopping off heads, or—"

"You talk too much, Somerled," said Margaret crisply, and Somerled fell silent. Eyvind gaped. "Sit here by us, Eyvind," she went on. "This game's going nowhere. Perhaps you can help me."

"Me?" said Eyvind, as Somerled's mouth curved in a derisive half smile. "Hardly. I'm no good at games, not this kind, anyway."

"No? A shame. I'll just have to beat him myself, then." Her

dark brows creased in a frown of concentration; her elegant fingers, long-nailed, ring-bedecked, reached to nudge one of her men forward. "Your move," she said sweetly, looking straight into Somerled's eyes.

It was quite a long game. Eyvind had never understood the rules or the strategies; instead of following the pieces, he watched the players. Sometimes he got up to fetch ale, or to stretch his legs. It was very quiet; the others spoke less and less as the morning wore on and the number of men on the board dwindled. It seemed to Eyvind that there were two games being played here: the one with the small soldiers in black and green, hopping about the inlaid squares in a dance of pursuit and evasion, and another, far more dangerous game whose moves were gestures and glances, a slight shifting of the body, the tone of a murmured word. How long had Margaret been here, a day or two? Perhaps he was imagining things, his senses heightened after the night's activities in Signe's bed. Foolish. This girl was to wed Ulf; that was why she had come. And brothers were always loyal. Look at him and Eirik. No, he was wrong as usual, a numbskull. No wonder Margaret had dismissed him with a single glance.

The game was nearly finished; Somerled had five men left, Margaret her king and two guards.

"You're trapped." Somerled's voice was calmly confident. He reached out toward the board, and quick as lightning Margaret's hand shot out to seize his outstretched fingers before they could touch her king.

"No, I'm not."

Somerled withdrew his hand slowly. The expression on his face was one Eyvind had seen before, and did not much care for.

"What can you mean?" The voice was chilly. "The rules are—"

"I know the rules," Margaret said evenly. "It is you who have made an error. See, my guard reaches the end of the board at this turn, and becomes a Wolfskin. Then he can move in any direction he pleases; and he is in position to take *this* man, and *this* man. Now it is your move again, I think."

It appeared she was right. Somerled, who never made mistakes, had missed something, and Margaret had all but won the game. Eyvind waited for an explosion of temper, a withering remark calculated to provoke tears. Somerled was a master of both.

"Your move," repeated Margaret courteously, lifting her artistically plucked brows.

Somerled stared at her. "I think I've met my match," he said. His eyes were bright with some emotion; there was no telling what it was.

"A gallant loser," said Margaret. "We must do it again some time. Tomorrow, perhaps. I sense you don't concede often, brother-in-law."

"Correct. And perhaps, even this time, I have not entirely lost."

"If you think I'm going to ask you what that means, you think wrong," Margaret replied smoothly. "Now, I find all this hard work has given me a hearty appetite. Eyvind, will you walk to the hall with me in search of some sustenance? I've several charming ladies with me, from home; my father insisted. You might like to meet them."

"I shouldn't think he would, you know," put in Somerled, bringing up the rear. "The one he has already is enough for him, even if he does share her with half the town."

If another man had made such a remark, he would not have remained on his feet and conscious long afterward. Eyvind's jaw tightened; his fists clenched.

"No offense," said Somerled lightly. "Mmm, what's that I smell, apple pie?"

"Keep your comments to yourself," Eyvind growled.

"Indeed," murmured Margaret. "It's clear Somerled has no sisters. If he had, he would have learned by now that women are unimpressed by displays of pointless incivility."

"Oh dear," said Somerled, apparently quite unabashed. "I'm sure the girl's a sweet thing, everyone says so. Don't glower like that, Eyvind, you'll frighten Margaret. We mustn't do that. There's so much to look forward to, after all. So many new games to play."

The wedding had been planned for the next full moon, before the autumn viking. But that was not to be. Before nightfall a messenger rode in from the north. He spoke behind closed doors, first to Ulf and then to Somerled. Their father was dead; pressing matters must be attended to at home. Ulf exchanged the briefest of courtesies with his bride-to-be. There was no time for sleep. He took a crew of Magnus's men and set off at dawn in the *Sea Princess,* which the Jarl had generously made available. It was a long weary way up the coast to Halogaland. Ulf did not ask his brother to accompany him. It was understood that they could not be there in time to see the old man buried. The journey, Somerled told Eyvind coolly, was just another strategic move in Ulf's own game. It was no gesture of filial piety, no sentimental voyage of farewell.

"You're wrong, I'm sure," Eyvind had protested, taken aback by Somerled's calm acceptance of such a loss. "Ulf spoke of your father with great respect, and with affection."

"Typical." Somerled's tone was flat. "You measure others by your own yardstick. Ulf cannot wait to cut himself free. He has the light of far horizons in his eyes, and will let nothing and no one stand in his way."

Eyvind looked at him. "That last part sounds more like you," he observed cautiously.

"He is my brother, after all," Somerled said dryly. "See if I'm right."

Ulf was gone from one full moon to the next, and longer. Margaret's father, Thorvald Strong-Arm, could stay at court no longer, for there had been attacks on his borders. He went home to attend to his affairs, but Margaret did not go. She preferred to remain in the south, she said, and wait for Ulf. Surely he would not be much longer. And she liked court; there was so much good entertainment. Margaret played games; she went riding; she made poems and conversed with visitors. If she was put out by the delay, she gave no sign of it.

Often enough her companion was Somerled. This admirable display of brotherly loyalty did not go unnoticed; folk commented on Somerled's kindness in ensuring his brother's betrothed did not feel neglected in Ulf's absence. As for Eyvind, he thought he saw a certain look in Somerled's eyes, and its reflection in Margaret's, although the two of them were skilled in keeping their thoughts to themselves, one of many qualities they appeared to share. But Eyvind held his tongue. He'd been wrong often enough before, and he was probably wrong again. Nobody else seemed concerned. And it wasn't the sort of thing one could mention to Somerled, since his only response would be to raise his brows and make some withering remark.

Besides, Eyvind was busy. Over the years since he had earned his place among the twelve, they had lost five men: one from a slicing wound received in an encounter with the Frisians, two drowned in a storm off Jutland, one the victim of an ague, a sorry end for a warrior. The fifth was slain in a heroic, solitary stand against a fear-crazed mob. He killed eight men before they finished him with shovel, hay fork, and scythe. Some folk see only the wolfskins and know only the tales. They thought, perhaps, it was some monster they had killed. These five had been replaced by new men, though none was as young as Eyvind. He had been part of the trial as each newcomer won his wolfskin, and each time it was as if his own bond with the god were strengthened, his vow remade. Now, he did not need ale or the herbal gum they chewed, or the singing and drumming. The singing was in his veins, the drumming in his heart; he carried the fire in his head.

Life between voyages was not all games and revelry and sweet nights in Signe's arms. Jarl Magnus had many enemies, powerful men with an eye on his borders and an ear out for others inclined to conspiracy. So, when he was not at sea, Magnus made a progress around the halls of his subjects, staying two nights here, three there, just to make quite sure of their loyalty. He received tribute. When he was pleased, he gave gifts. And because you could never really trust anyone, he took his Wolfskins with him. Two shadowed his every move, guarded his slumber, rode by his side. Four hovered at a distance, watching entries and exits, reading men's eyes and gestures. When all twelve were available, the rest would be deployed more subtly, mingling with the local people, apparently off duty. That way, folk found it harder to set traps.

Eyvind found plenty of opportunity to use the skills he had, being one of Magnus's preferred bodyguards. The year Ulf's father died, the Jarl canceled the autumn viking. A tale of disloyalty had come to his ears, and he decided to teach a certain landowner a lesson that would not be soon forgotten. He rode out with his Wolfskins and with many other men of his household, more than thirty in all, and found the plotters to the east of Freyrsfjord, beyond the hills, where they had gathered a considerable force with a plan to attack one of Magnus's own allies and kinsmen. It was a satisfying encounter. Eyvind spiked one man with the thrusting spear, finding a moment when the fellow's shield swung wide of his body, seizing his opportunity with the same unerring aim that had brought down many a wild boar or fleet stag in the woods. His axe separated heads from shoulders and parted limbs from bodies with hungry ease, though, as it usually was with his kind, at the time he was scarcely aware of what he did. There was nothing in his head but the burning voice of Thor, and nothing in his body but the strong unwavering answer to the god's challenge. Around him, his companions swung axe and wielded sword in the same savage obedience. When it was over, all but one of the miscreants lay dead on that blood-drenched field. Magnus had issued a clear warning: let no man think to challenge his authority again. The young fellow they had spared was sent off home. There was a purpose to that: the telling and retelling of the tale must strengthen Magnus's reputation for swift justice.

After that, the Jarl made further visits in the neighborhood, and all greeted his company with lavish hospitality. Ale flowed like a spring torrent, boards groaned with roast meats, and Eyvind received a number of offers from women, both young and not so young, all of which he refused as courteously as he could. Signe was everything he wanted in a woman. To bed these others seemed somehow wrong to him, though he knew his fellow Wolfskins did not hesitate to avail themselves of the liveliest and prettiest of the local girls. Eyvind slept alone. He would wait for Signe. It made no difference that he was not her only lover. With Signe, there was no pretense, no ridicule, no game playing. There was only honesty, warmth, and kindness. It seemed to Eyvind that what she offered was worth waiting for.

Magnus was well pleased with his Wolfskins, and especially with Eyvind. He made it known that he intended a rich reward for his youngest warrior, and that he would not take no for an answer. He would give Eyvind time to think about what would please him most. Later, back at court, they would speak of it further.

The Jarl conferred with his landowners. There would, no doubt, be charges brought at the next Thing. He would need their support, for the kinsmen of the slain would be eager for compensation. Still, as long as there were men who would speak up about the conspiracy and bear witness to the plotting, the one matter might be set against the other, and the price for these deaths not be beyond what he was prepared to pay.

Such negotiations must be handled carefully, and not rushed. By the time the Jarl returned to court, the *Sea Princess* was beached in Freyrsfjord once more, and Ulf was back.

The wedding had been delayed long enough. Within days, the ceremony took place, the vows were spoken, and the bridal ale was poured and quaffed. In view of Ulf's recent loss, the mood was convivial rather than riotous. Margaret was very quiet, as was often the case with young brides on their wedding day. Probably nervous, Eirik commented. After all, she hardly knew the fellow. Eyvind thought Margaret did not look nervous, sitting neat and self-contained in her green silk overdress and snowy linen, with yellow flowers woven through her sleek auburn hair. No, he thought she looked as Somerled sometimes looked: as if she could see much farther ahead than anyone else, and was already planning some far-distant strategy. He thought Ulf was the one who looked nervous. As for Somerled, he sat by a pillar with his face in shadow. Through the long day he had appeared quite composed and not in the least upset. Eyvind took a mouthful of ale. Soon the bride would be put to bed, and her new husband led to her, and this would all be over. Then he would go to Signe's small house, and tap on her door, and for a while he would forget everything but the warmth of her smile and the magic of her touch.

"Won't be long now before Ulf's up and away," said Eirik with a grin. "He's left it long enough; must be well and truly ready for her."

But Ulf seemed in no hurry for the marriage bed. He had risen to his feet now, and was addressing Jarl Magnus, his dark features more than usually intense.

"My lord, you have done us proud today with feasting and gifts, with music and good hospitality. Indeed, you have at all times been the most noble and generous of patrons, the most loyal of kinsmen, and I hope I have not stinted in expressing my gratitude."

Magnus inclined his head, waiting for more.

"My lord," Ulf said, "I wish to ask a favor. I wish to present to you a proposal: a bold plan that has been much in my thoughts."

"Go on."

"I've spoken before of a far-off land: the land of my father's dreams. Those isles in the western sea are a place of sheltered waterways, of gentle hills and verdant pastures. There, countless birds wheel and dive across the open sky; there, the ocean teems with fish and the great rocks guard shores alive with seals. So travelers tell. It is a land of myriad shades of blue, a realm whose shifting light dazzles the eyes with its loveliness. That place is far beyond the farthest reach of our ships. It is days' sailing across open waters, going as the whale does, by stars and skerries, by currents and tides. I have long wished to journey to that place, which some call Orkneyjar, isles of the seal. I would go there with men and women of like mind, and build a new home in those islands, a place where peace and amity would rule, and folk might live in harmony. I have been sickened by the disputes that poisoned my father's last years, and left him unable to trust those who had been friend, neighbor, or ally. I would make a new community, away from warfare and hatred."

"A noble goal, if somewhat unrealistic," Magnus observed. "If these isles are as fair as you paint them, might not others have settled there before you? You might find these shores, and be slaughtered by naked savages the instant your foot touched land."

Ulf's voice was calm. "I will go in a spirit of friendship, though I plan to take warriors with me. This is no foolish, ill-considered mission, my lord. We must have the capacity to protect our women and children, at least. Still, I would try to avoid conflict. If folk dwell there, they may be persuaded to a common goal. They might be glad of new skills and new blood."

Magnus raised his brows. "You astonish me, kinsman. What is it you believe I can contribute to such a venture?"

"I need your blessing and your support," Ulf said. "This winter I will build a ship, a finer, stronger ship than any seen before in all of Norway. This ship will carry me, with my wife and all those bold enough to join me, across the ocean to the new land. My lord, I would carry out this task of shipbuilding in the safety of your anchorage here at Freyrsfjord, if you permit. And I would ask that you release those of your household who wish to accompany me, the Wolfskins Eirik Hallvardsson and Hakon Hawk-Beak, who may return in the autumn, and others who will stay and help me build my new settlement."

Magnus regarded him gravely. "Well, well," he said, and there was no telling what he thought. "An interesting tale, and not altogether unexpected, kinsman. Still, men and women cannot live on lights and colors. You'll need stock, tools, seed, and thralls. How would you make such a difficult journey with these things?"

"I hope to acquire a sturdy knarr, my lord, for it's true, a longship is not well suited to bear such a cargo. I will purchase a vessel and strengthen her for the journey."

"It seems a wild venture to me, and ill-advised." Thorvald Strong-Arm, returned for his daughter's wedding, had a ferocious frown on his brow. Ulf's mouth tightened.

"My husband is not the sort of man much given to wildness." Margaret's clear voice cut across the hall. Brows were lifted in surprise that she should venture to contribute to such a debate. "I am certain he has planned this with care, and allowed for all eventualities. Let us hear him out."

The Jarl gave a nod in her direction. "You speak well, my dear. Your support of your husband bodes favorably for his success. But tell me, do you not view such a venture with some misgivings? It is a long way from home and from your family, after all: an island far out in open sea, and the need to start all over again from nothing. Most young women but newly wed would fear such a great change."

Margaret looked him straight in the eye.

"In such a place great things may be achieved, my lord," she said. "I would be a poor wife indeed if I could not share my husband's vision."

A flush rose to Ulf's cheeks. "Thank you," he said, glancing at Margaret. For a moment, the intensity of his expression softened a little. It was plain he had not expected her to speak out so boldly on his behalf. He turned back to the Jarl. "I will answer my lord's concerns and yours, father-in-law. My intention is to journey there in spring. I will take with me men and women, stock and tools, all that is needed to establish ourselves. Craftsmen, law speakers, farmers, and fishermen. It will be a new community in a new land. There is a bright future for us on that shore."

"I see." Magnus's eyes were very shrewd. "This is where your account was leading, that is clear. You wish to pick the eyes out of my household, and use my facilities, and sail away never to be seen again. Tell me, what rewards could such a venture possibly hold for me as your patron?"

"Ah. I was coming to that." Ulf leaned forward, his hands flat on the table. "It is true, I would take men from your lordship's household, and some will choose to settle in the islands. But I can offer you something of great value in return. I will leave my shipwrights, my fitters, my sail makers behind when I go. They are expert, my lord: the finest in all Norway. Each vessel they build is better than the last, sleeker, swifter, stronger. That knowledge will be yours to do with what you will. And our settlement will be yours to visit and to use as safe anchorage for any longships you may choose to build. From such a vantage point, a force of warriors might journey with speed and ease to shores they say are rich with plunder: southward to the lands of the Saxon, southwest to isles dotted with Christian temples, whose altars groan with fine silver and jeweled reliquaries. To put it simply, my lord, I'm presenting you with a great opportunity, if you are bold enough to see it. This would give you a unique strategic advantage."

"If I might speak, my lord?" Eirik rose to his feet, golden hair glinting in the lamplight, wolfskin proud on his broad shoulders. "There are those of us who have known of this plan since early days. Your kinsman here is a fine leader, and his vision both noble and stirring. There are many good men who will want to be part of it: more than he can take, in truth. Supporting this venture would bring you great honor. Not to speak of a very handy base in the west."

"Mmm." Magnus was thinking hard.

"And how do you plan to pay for all this?" demanded Thorvald Strong-Arm, scowling at Ulf. "A knarr, a fine longship to be constructed at considerable speed, best breeding stock, the services of expert men? Did you find a hoard of troll silver when you journeyed north?"

Ulf looked at him. "I can pay," he said quietly. "I have made my decision, and I will leave these shores with or without Jarl

Magnus's blessing. My father is dead. To journey to these isles
was his dream, his obsession. On his death, my father's lands
became mine, and I have sold them. I will not return there. It
has been a place of much unrest, of strife and sorrow. Now it
belongs to another man. And so, I can pay."

After that, nobody said anything for a while. Eyvind glanced
across to the place where Somerled sat, but Somerled was no
longer there. Turning back, he caught Margaret's eye. She
looked over to the doorway, back at Eyvind, moved her head a
little. The message was clear enough. *You'd best go after him,
since I cannot.*

Eyvind excused himself politely and made his way out.
Clouds veiled the moon; the yard was in darkness. A dog
sniffed around the doorway, lured by the smell of roast meat. A
stone flew through the air, hitting it squarely on the rump; the
dog squealed and bolted. Following the stone's flight back, and
hoping the next target would not be himself, Eyvind made his
way to the steps that led up to the grain store. Somerled stood
there in the dark, hurling stones at the ground now, hard enough
to make them bounce. He did not stop as Eyvind approached.

"Somerled—"

"Go away."

He'd heard that tone before, long ago, and had learned a lesson: not to ask what was wrong. Instead, he seated himself on
the steps, saying nothing at all, and after a while Somerled ran
out of stones and sat down beside him.

"So," said Somerled after a considerable silence, "what do
you think of this fine Ulf, and his grand plans to build a new
home in the fair realms of light? Does it inspire you?"

"It seemed not unreasonable, the way he explained it," Eyvind
said cautiously. "A good place, with opportunities. But—"

"But, ever so slightly regrettable that he has sold my
birthright to fund his dreams? Oh well, never mind. My mother
was no more than a concubine, and my father treated her like
dirt. Why should I expect any better?" His voice was not quite
steady. In the dim light from the hall doorway, Eyvind could see
his ashen pallor and his tight-clenched hands.

"Come on, now," Eyvind protested. "Ulf is your brother.
Surely—"

"That's the trouble with you, Eyvind. You don't listen. I've told you before, Ulf despises me. I'm no more than an embarrassment to him; he's never known what to do with me. Well, he's solved that problem now. Sold my father's lands, all of them, no thought of any share for his father's other son, and he's off over the sea where he'll never have to be reminded again that he has a brother. Neat. Tidy. Only one little loose end, really."

"I don't like to hear you talk like this," Eyvind said. "You must be wrong. Have you spoken to Ulf of this? He must have provided for you."

"As I said." Somerled's voice was tighter now, threatening to slip from his hard-won control. "You judge all men by your own measure. Very unwise, Eyvind. It'll cause you grave trouble some day."

Eyvind drew a deep breath. "Somerled?" he ventured.

"What?" The word was like a whip crack.

"Are you sure you're not jumping to conclusions because you are angry with Ulf? I did think . . . I thought perhaps . . . well, with the wedding, you know—"

"Thinking doesn't suit you, Eyvind. You've never had a talent for it. What can you mean? You believe I am jealous?"

At least Somerled was talking, though keeping up the conversation was a little like making one's way across hot coals. It was ever thus when Somerled was upset. His way of dealing with hurts was to lash out, to use his tongue as his weapon. To be his friend, close by in times of trouble, was to invite wounds. Helping Somerled was a special kind of battle.

"It seemed to me you had grown fond of Margaret, and that today's festivities might have upset you."

"Fond." It was a good attempt at a scathing tone.

"It seemed to me you might have preferred her for yourself. She likes you; you have a lot in common. I imagine that makes it hurt more."

"You'd better go on, since you have decided to explain me to myself. What did you think would happen, that I would step up to Margaret and suggest she choose a man who has no better inheritance than his own wits? Ulf is his father's son, the Jarl's kinsman. He's wealthy. He's building a ship. Ulf has hopes and dreams; men speak of him with respect. Fondness is no basis for marriage, Eyvind. I would think less of Margaret if she chose me, for to do so would be the act of a fool."

There was a silence. It was as if years slipped away, and they were alone in the woods again, in the immensity of the dark. *Nobody cares,* Somerled had said. *Nobody cares what happens to me.*

"You had high and noble aspirations," Eyvind said quietly. "You impressed me, so strongly did you believe in yourself. A boy who would be a king. When you first said that, you shocked me. Yet you convinced me it would be so. I still see that strength, and so does Margaret, I believe. Ulf has hurt and angered you. But you still have friends, Somerled, and you still have a path ahead of you. You are clever and able; sometimes it seems to me you move like moonlight, too quick and subtle to follow. You say Ulf has hopes and dreams. What about your own dreams?"

"For my brother, this voyage is a new beginning." Somerled's tone was bleak. "For me, it represents something rather different: my final repudiation by my own kin. Forgive me if I find it somewhat beyond me to summon a mood of confidence in my future." He spat on the ground at their feet.

"We are too solemn, perhaps," Eyvind said wearily. "Will you come to the drinking hall with me? One can at least seek the oblivion of strong ale, when all else fails."

"Spoken like a true Wolfskin," said Somerled. "And what act of friendly generosity comes next? Do you plan to share your whore with me, so I can look for consolation between her open thighs?"

It was all Eyvind could do not to hit him. He sprang to his feet, unable to speak for anger, and strode off toward the settlement. A pox on Somerled; he wasn't worth the trouble.

"Eyvind?"

He halted, but did not turn.

"I was joking, man. Come on, I'll drink with you."

"You try me hard sometimes," Eyvind growled.

"I'm sorry." Somerled scrubbed a hand across his cheek. "You do rather leave yourself open to it. Now let's find some good ale, shall we? That was the best suggestion I've heard all night."

FOUR

▼

It became apparent soon enough that Somerled was at least partly right about his brother. Questioned directly as to what provision had been made for Somerled, Ulf replied curtly that an amount of silver had been set aside, sufficient to help the boy get on his feet, so to speak. Asked further, would his brother be included in the expedition, Ulf replied no. Somerled was not a creature of voyages and forays, of hardships and challenges. He had always preferred the court; he would rather make runes and poems than journey across the ocean to carve out new territory. Let him remain at court, then, and make a living as skald or law speaker, since he was apt for either calling. And, if he tired of Rogaland, the funds available to him would allow travel, to a limited extent. Did not the Jarls and chieftains of the north welcome men of learning? Somerled would do well enough. With that, Ulf made it clear the subject was closed, and turned to what was foremost in his mind: the building of a ship.

Jarl Magnus had quickly seen the wisdom in Ulf's offer of a safe harbor out to seaward, and had given his full approval for his kinsman's bold venture. Perhaps he saw no other alternative: Ulf's vision had captured the imagination of men from all parts of Rogaland, far more than the expedition could reasonably include. Magnus was heard to comment that Ulf's grasp of strategy was impressive, and his ability to make his dream a reality truly inspiring. The fleet would sail with both Magnus's personal blessing and his financial backing, as well as carrying a number of his own close retainers among its complement of fighting men.

The work began. Timber came from the north, great lengths of it already well prepared, reflecting Ulf's talent for taking calculated risks. Only the oldest oaks could provide the massive pieces required for the vessel's keel and mast blocks. The wood was well seasoned, and supple from storage in marsh water. In addition to these forest giants there were many trunks of smaller size, and as soon as these were unloaded Ulf's shipwrights began to instruct a veritable army of workers, both freemen and thralls, in the delicate use of axe and adze to shape sweetly curved strakes and strong, resilient ribs. The floorboards were fashioned from pine: these would not be nailed down, but left free to be lifted as required for bailing or storage. Men wove caulkings from wool and horsehair; others worked on the oars, the pale pine wood shaped to a graceful taper, the lengths graded so they would strike the water as one, for all the curve of the ship's side. It was a full winter's work. Sails were woven in bold stripes of white and red, and a master woodcarver labored long hours over a great piece of oak heart, fashioning the dragon's head that would adorn the prow. The carver's apprentices worked a fine eagle mask on the tiller.

As the great task unfolded, even the most skeptical members of Jarl Magnus's court were captivated. The vessel surpassed any they had seen before. She was massive as a great whale, yet sleek as an otter. Ulf named her the *Golden Dragon*.

There were fifteen benches; a crew of thirty oarsmen would be required, and five or six more to perform the multiplicity of other tasks: bailing, handling the sails, fending off attackers. And they'd need a crew for the knarr, which would bear the women and children, the thralls, the stock, and the best part of the supplies. Ulf watched the longship grow, strake overlapping delicately curved strake, oar ports neatly covered with little round shutters, each carven with its own small motif, for the pair of fellows who specialized in this field of work liked to add their own touch. Some were runic; such a vessel should bear an acknowledgment to the gods on whom her safety in open seas must depend. But there were little creatures too: a dog, an owl, a beaver; and one or two carvings of men and women who were—how could one put it?—at play, one might say. One hoped these would not prove too much of a distraction for the oarsmen.

There was work for many folk that winter, from the smiths who turned out rivets and nails to the women who wove the spruce-root lashings to fasten the hull's planking to the ribs. This ship would move under the ocean's hard caress, she would shudder and yield and remain whole under the fiercest embrace of the storm. Above the waterline, they used nails.

There came a time when the *Golden Dragon* was close to ready. Now a team of men came with bright paints, and turned the savage figurehead into a masterpiece of red and yellow, the crest and eyes picked out in gold leaf; the tiller received a similar decoration, and a handsome set of shields was prepared to match, though these would adorn the rim-rail only when the ship was at rest; while she crossed open sea, they would be stored away for safety. Ulf sent a man to arrange supplies of dried fish, casks of cheese, flasks of oil, and sacks of nuts and apples. There was a constant smell of bread baking, hard bread that would store a while. Ulf sent another man to check on the stock he had bought. It was hard to believe, but spring was almost here, and soon the expedition would be ready to depart.

The knarr arrived, an ungainly, blockish sort of craft, built principally for strength. She could travel long distances under sail alone, her master told Ulf as they inspected the vessel where she lay at anchor in Freyrsfjord. She required only a small crew, and this he had already, for all his men had volunteered for the voyage, provided the pay was good enough. He'd best take crew and boat together, the master advised Ulf, since the men knew the knarr better than a husband knows his wife. Women and children? Yes, he could carry them as well, though it wouldn't be comfortable. Cattle? They'd need to talk about that. Now, about the pay again . . .

Eyvind was down by the water, helping haul the new ship's mast blocks into place. The crew of the knarr had come ashore; they would find lodgings in the settlement. Among them was a fellow who seemed somehow familiar, though Eyvind could not quite place him. He was broad-cheeked, and sported a beard as red as his hair; he had a hard, brooding sort of look about him, the look of a man all too ready to find new enemies. And yet— and yet Eyvind's memory was of someone open-faced and friendly. He thought—he almost thought . . .

"Sigurd!" Eyvind called, sure now. "Sigurd Gudmundsson! What brings you here to the south?"

The red-haired man turned slowly to look at him. There was no sign of recognition, not a flicker. Still, the more Eyvind looked, the more certain he became.

"Forgotten me already?" he joked. "I'm Eyvind Hallvardsson, the same Eyvind you grew up with. Many's the time we wrestled together, or swam races across the Serpent's Neck. It's good to see you. We didn't know what had become of you after you left my mother's longhouse."

The other man looked back at him, eyes carefully blank. "You've made a mistake," he said, and turned away.

Later, Eyvind asked another of the knarr's crew who the fellow was, for he did not think he had been wrong. The crewman laughed. "Him? Only name he goes by is Firehead, and there's more than one reason for that. You don't want to cross that fellow when he's in his cups. Why do you ask?"

"Nothing," Eyvind said. "He reminds me of someone I once knew, that's all. Someone from home."

"Didn't think Firehead had a home," the man grunted. "Been with us a long while. Two or three years at least. Odd sort of fellow. Good worker, though. Strong."

Eyvind made no further comment, though he thought he was right. Still, if Sigurd did not want to know him, that was Sigurd's business. Meanwhile, there was Somerled to worry about. Somerled was behaving oddly. He appeared to have abandoned gaming and poetry and music, and instead could be seen restlessly pacing the halls. Often he watched his brother, or his brother's wife, with a look in his eye that filled Eyvind with a deep unease.

Before the ships set sail, Eirik went north to Hammarsby to bid his mother farewell. Thinking it was well past time for Somerled to be away from court for a little, Eyvind suggested the two of them go too, and Somerled agreed in the manner of a man who cares very little about anything.

The farm seemed different, smaller. His mother had white streaks in her blond hair. And Eirik greeted the thrall-woman, Oksana, with a kiss on the lips, in front of everyone, and went indoors with one towheaded child on his shoulders and two others holding his hands, while Oksana carried the newest baby. Many things had changed. Halla was married and gone. Thorgerd was still there, quite fat now, bustling about with cooking pots and glancing at Eyvind under her lashes.

They did not stay long. On the last day, Eyvind and Somerled went up into the woods under lowering skies, and found the tree house they had made one summer's day long ago. It was still sturdy enough, though something had nested in one of the corners, and the ropes had begun to rot. On the bole of the great oak, the runes Somerled had carved were as clear as the day he made them.

"*Two brothers made this house*," said Eyvind. "See, I remember. *Somerled carved these runes*. And here below, my own name: *Eyvind*."

Somerled nodded. "Would you be content," he asked, "if this were all you left behind you for folk to remember? A few markings high on a tree, the only sign that you lived your span in the world?"

Eyvind stared at him, not sure he understood. "No, of course not," he said. "I hope I will be remembered, for a little at least, as a brave man, one who served Thor and fought for the Jarl with as much courage and skill as he could. I would like to be remembered for that. What about you?"

Somerled said nothing. He stared ahead of him, his expression unreadable.

Suddenly Eyvind was impatient. "Odin's bones, Somerled," he said, "what is it you want? To please your brother? To go on this voyage with him? To forget him and go your own way? One thing is certain: you have lost the strong will you showed as a boy, when first we sat here together, and you helped me make my name on the wood. I thought then you were a man who could do whatever he wanted, and you made it clear what you would be. But now, you seem to me—lost." The flow of words ceased. Eyvind waited for the scathing response. No doubt Somerled would tell him to stop trying to think, since he was so bad at it. But Somerled remained silent.

"Somerled?" Eyvind ventured after a while. "I hope I didn't offend you. I want to help, if I can."

"You can't help. Nobody can. Shall I explain it to you? Ulf doesn't want me to go. He wishes to be rid of me. And he's right. I dislike voyages of discovery, I don't enjoy getting cold and wet, the idea of living in some outpost surrounded by savages doesn't appeal at all. But my brother's voyage was purchased with what was mine. I should go. He owes it to me to let me go."

"I doubt if he's even aware you want to," Eyvind said carefully. "Have you asked him?"

"I don't need to ask. He will not take me."

Eyvind thought for a moment. "What about Margaret?" he ventured. "Couldn't she speak to him on your behalf—"

"I've not yet fallen so low that I need some woman to plead my case," Somerled snapped. "Besides, it's pointless. Ulf makes it clear I am to remain behind. The ties of kinship are nothing to him."

He was scratching on the tree trunk with his knife blade again. The image of a small ship appeared below the runes: striped sail bellying in the wind, oars moving as one. Eyvind watched and said nothing.

In the morning they left Hammarsby and rode back to court. Eirik was not his cheerful self, and Eyvind asked his brother what ailed him.

"I may as well tell you, I suppose," Eirik said as their horses moved along a broad track under pines. "I hoped to persuade Oksana to come with me to the islands and to stay. Her and the children."

"Persuade her?" echoed Somerled. "Why didn't you just tell her? She's a thrall, isn't she?"

Eirik's mouth tightened. "Such words reflect a narrow vision," he said. "A man or woman becomes a thrall simply by being in the wrong place at the wrong time. A moment of bad luck, that's all it takes. Back home in Novgorod, Oksana is a nobleman's daughter. She has my offer of marriage, these four years past."

Eyvind stared at him. "Marriage?" he queried. "Then why—?"

"Oksana's a proud woman. She's determined to do this her way or not at all. First she'll earn her freedom with her own work: no concessions, she's made that clear both to Mother and to me. Only then will she agree to marriage. After that, she says, if I want to take her off voyaging, it's up to me. The fact is, she likes it on the farm, and Mother would miss her now; she's more like a daughter than a slave. There it is."

"So, she won't wed you," Somerled mused aloud. "That hardly matters, surely. She seems ready enough to welcome you into her bed, judging by that mob of small warriors that ran out to greet you. Why tie yourself down when you can have what you want with no obligations whatever?"

Eirik set his jaw, hunched his shoulders under the wolfskin, and rode on. "I'm coming to understand why Ulf can't stand the sight of you," he said.

Eyvind changed the subject quickly. "The Jarl won't be well pleased to see so many of his warriors go, perhaps for good," he observed. "They say Thord won't be coming back; even Grim's talking about staying on over there. And there's Hakon. But that's different."

Eirik did not reply. It was common knowledge that Hakon's hearing was not what it had been, not since the stunning blow to the head he had suffered in that encounter with the men of Jutland, more than three years ago. He still fought well; he played his part in every encounter, steadfast in his obedience to Thor. Nobody, not even Jarl Magnus, knew the extent to which the others covered for him, as his ears gradually lost their acuity and his confidence began to wane. All of them were glad Ulf's venture had offered Hakon a chance to leave with dignity. Perhaps Thor himself had made this possible, as a reward for faithful service.

"A comfortable young wife, a farm, a squalling infant or two," mused Eirik. "It's not such a bad prospect."

"To me it sounds like a living death," Somerled observed. "Tedium incarnate. What sort of a man chooses to waste his life so?"

Eirik glanced at him. "Hakon is a stalwart warrior," he said grimly, "and a true friend. His choice has not been an easy one, but he's taking a wise course. Don't underestimate those of us you think simple, Somerled. Someday that could get you into trouble."

Somerled narrowed his eyes at him, but said nothing. Perhaps even he understood that it was not a good idea to pick a fight with Wolfskins.

The supplies came and were loaded into the knarr. The stock arrived: a ram and two ewes, a coop of chickens, another of geese, which kept up a continuous honking chorus and deprived all of sleep. There was also a fine young bull, long-horned, chestnut-coated, and a pair of dreamy-eyed heifers. These they would not load until the day of sailing. Men came back from farms with their wives and children and their selected thralls; the settlement was full to bursting. All in all, it was a fine company.

The day came when the last bright shield was hung on the *Golden Dragon*'s side, and they launched her into Freyrsfjord for her first real trial. Her oars sang through the water; she moved before the wind, swift and graceful as a great seabird in flight. Ulf pronounced himself well pleased, and failed utterly to keep a grin of satisfaction from his usually sober features. Then Jarl Magnus held a feast to acknowledge the work that had been done, and to wish his kinsman well. In the afternoon there were games: horse fighting, wrestling, running races, and even a bout of Battlefield, in which Eyvind led one team and Eirik the other. It was difficult to play properly when one had to avoid causing the opposition serious injury. Several men from each side were to join the expedition, after all, and they could hardly do so with a split skull, a broken jaw, or a shattered ankle. By dint of some quick prematch negotiation, Eirik and Eyvind guided their teams through a bout which was more spectacular than bloody. They made sure there were plenty of close calls, since the crowd must be entertained. There was a great deal of leaping and dodging, a somersault or two, and lethal blows calculated to miss by a hair's breadth. Women screamed; children squealed; men yelled helpful instructions. Eyvind's team was pronounced by the crowd to have won. Wiping the sweat from his face, he glimpsed Signe there, clapping and cheering with the rest, and gave a little bow in her direction. By the time he had straightened up, she was gone from sight.

Before the sun set, Jarl Magnus's priest performed the ritual for the fleet's safety. By the water, where the knarr lay at anchor and the great longship was drawn up on the shore, a white ox was slaughtered. The blood filled many bowls. The priest was an old man, and moved stiffly in his long woolen robe, but his hands were supple enough, dipping the blood twigs, sprinkling the libation from bow to stern, from keel to rim-rail of each proud vessel. Herbs were burned, and a wreath of oak leaves placed around the neck of the great creature that adorned the *Golden Dragon*'s prow. Eyvind felt a thrill of excitement as the priest gazed up into the darkening sky. The old man's eyes were filmy with age, and yet he seemed to see a great distance.

"Mighty Thor! Storm god, battle god, sky god, we greet you! Let fair weather and calm seas welcome these voyagers, may a sweet wind breathe them safely across the ocean. Thor, strongest of fishermen, let no sea monster threaten our vessels, our folk, or our possessions. We ask your blessing, slayer of serpents!"

There was no answering roar of thunder; no spike of lightning split the sky. There was only the gentle wash of water on the pebbles, and the plaintive bellowing of the cattle, which were tethered not far away, awaiting loading into the knarr. Still, the priest appeared satisfied. He reached out a gnarled hand and ran his fingers along the strakes of the new ship's side, pausing as he touched the point where the keel swept upward toward the prow. Here, runes were carved, a band of them swirling snakewise up the fine oak, and between them were tiny images of men and gods and creatures.

"She goes with Thor's blessing, and Odin's, and Freyr's," the old man said, "for she goes to a fair land, over sea, and the men who travel in her must perforce be sailors, and warriors, and farmers too. May Thor carry you safe through the perils of the deep. Odin smite your enemies and give your leaders wisdom. Freyr smile on your crops and cattle, and grant you times of plenty. Fair Freya, his sister, grant your women peaceful hearths and healthy children. Go forth with courage into your new world."

With that, the fleet was ready. Cattle and sheep, chickens and ducks, men, women, and children would board in the morning, and by the time the sun was high in the sky, the vessels would be slipping out between the small islands that formed the skerry-guard, and into open sea.

A great crowd of folk had watched the ritual. Margaret stood by Ulf's side, the picture of a good wife, her dark eyes watchful. She spoke to her husband once or twice, and he bent his head courteously to listen. And Eyvind saw that fellow again, the one they called Firehead, standing among the crew of the knarr. They were a rough-looking group of men, but folk said

they were the best, tried and tested in all conditions. He was
sure it was Sigurd; now the fellow was looking across at
Somerled, who stood tight-lipped and pale at the back of the
Jarl's household. There was an expression on Firehead's face
that Eyvind fancied he had seen before, in the hills above his
mother's longhouse, when Sigurd had chopped wood as if met-
ing out deadly punishment. Somerled glanced across, and suddenly Firehead was talking to one of the other crewmen, and
not looking their way at all. The smallest trace of a smile flickered across Somerled's face, and was gone.

That night the feasting was long and hearty, and Jarl Magnus
was generous with his praises and his gifts. Reluctantly, he
granted Hakon formal release from his service. He gave his
warrior a fine cloak of beaver pelt, and a sword whose blade
flickered in the light with a pattern like sun on a fair waterfall.
There were others who intended to stay on in the Light Isles,
and all received rich gifts: robes, cloaks, daggers, or axes. He
gave Ulf a pair of great hunting dogs. Behind the Jarl's back,
the knarr's crew exchanged glances and grimaces: more live-
stock to carry. Thord, who had served five years as a Wolfskin
and wore a great seam across his face to prove it, was presented
with a comely dark-skinned slave girl with long hair to her
waist, and midnight-black eyes. Thord could not keep the grin
from his scarred features, and the girl did not appear at all put
out by the prospect of a long ocean voyage, or the company of
a man with so many teeth missing. It is in such ventures to new
lands that slaves become wives; that serfs become free men and
women. Perhaps she sensed that, for her dark eyes snapped
with excitement as she made her way to the Wolfskin's side. It
was well known that Thord intended to size the new place up,
and stay on if it took his fancy.

Margaret received a length of best linen, a double string of
amber beads, and a set of game pieces cunningly carved in
whalebone, with a silver inlaid board. She smiled politely, inclined her head respectfully, and thanked the Jarl in economical
words. Eyvind could see the small frown on her brow; he
watched as her eyes flicked across to Somerled, who sat silent
in his usual place, shadowed by a pillar. Then she sat down
again by her husband, her hands in her lap.

"Now," said Magnus expansively, "I have been well entertained today, with excellent sport, and I have had cause yet again to observe how my youngest Wolfskin acquits himself as strongly and ably in the arena of games as on the field of war. I made the lad a promise some time since, and I intend to honor it today. Come forward, Eyvind, let's see you."

Eyvind remembered now something about a reward, and he'd been supposed to think about what he wanted, but it had entirely slipped his mind what with one thing and another. He'd have to come up with something quickly or the Jarl would be offended. He got up and walked forward to stand before Magnus, wishing he did not always feel so awkward on such occasions, as if the fine folk of the court were judging him in some way. He might be able to charge into an attack and kill many men; he might be able to win games of Battlefield, and hunt stag and boar and wolf, but he had never mastered the art of finding ready words at times like this.

"My lord."

"Well, Eyvind. You've acquitted yourself splendidly today, as indeed has your brother. I have a gift for you, a reward for this afternoon's victory."

"Thank you, my lord." Eyvind was much relieved; it seemed the gift was already chosen, and all he had to do was accept politely, then sit down again.

"Wear this in your next battle," Magnus was saying, and his senior housecarl brought out a wondrously wrought helmet, its broad headband decorated with figures of horses and warriors, its triangular panels rising to a short spike on the top. Eyvind could imagine already how he might use that in close combat. The eye guards were well shaped and strong. Most remarkable of all, from the headband a fine curtain of woven links, fashioned from beaten metal, hung down to shield face, ears, and neck. This was a helm of superior make even to the Jarl's own.

"You are a Wolfskin," Magnus said with a smile, "and a Wolfskin needs no armor. He goes into battle clothed in the breath of the gods, and shielded by their hands. Still, I want you to wear this. Your kind are not entirely immune to injury, and you in particular are over-fond of risk. Let this gift grant us a few more seasons of your company, young Eyvind."

"Thank you, my lord. It is indeed a generous gift." Good, it was over; he need say no more, but could return to his seat by Eirik.

"Not so fast, my friend."

Eyvind halted.

"The helm is your reward for today's sport. But we have a little unfinished business, I think. Have you forgotten the battle we fought, and the courage you showed against the plotters whom we overthrew east of Freyrsfjord? I promised you a reward then, and you shall have one."

"My lord—there's no need—"

"Ah—don't tell me the helmet is sufficient, lad, I won't have it. Let not the tale be spread abroad that Magnus fails to give due recompense for loyalty, or does not keep his promises. I said then you could name your own reward; you must do so now."

To his annoyance, Eyvind felt himself blushing. He could see Eirik grinning at his discomfort, and Margaret looking at him very intently indeed, as if trying to convey some message. Somewhere behind him, in the shadows, sat Somerled; Somerled who, it seemed, had been cast out by his family not once, but twice, who had no home to return to, no brother to drink with, no woman to welcome him with her arms and listen to his secrets. And now, the words he needed came to Eyvind with no difficulty at all.

"My lord Jarl, I have considered this as you bade me. You are the most generous of leaders, and I hope you will not think my request odd or inappropriate. I know you may expect me to ask for a horse, or a weapon, or a fine cloak of fur, perhaps even for a handsome slave woman such as the one who has put such a twinkle in my friend Thord's eye."

This was greeted with general laughter.

"But?" Magnus asked, his eyes thoughtful.

"My lord, I wish to request something not for myself, but for my friend Somerled, your young kinsman."

Magnus's expression did not change, but Eyvind saw Ulf stiffen, as if he knew what was coming, and Margaret's eyes narrowed.

"My lord," Eyvind continued, "Somerled is a proud man and will not ask this for himself. He has always vowed to make his own way without patronage or favor, and indeed, he is a clever fellow who will do so whatever your answer. But Somerled wishes for nothing more than a place on board the longship his brother has built, and a chance to accompany this expedition to new shores. In these isles of the west, such a promising scholar will find much work to exercise his talents, and is sure to make his mark. He will bring nothing but honor to his patron in Rogaland. I would ask that you influence your kinsman, Ulf, to include his brother among the folk who depart on this voyage. I am certain Ulf will not have cause to regret such a decision, for Somerled has much to offer."

There was a little silence. The Jarl did not seem taken aback. He studied Eyvind's face as if to read his intentions, and was apparently satisfied.

"Well spoken, young Wolfskin," he said at last. "You have a generous spirit. A man should be grateful indeed for such a loyal friend. And I must grant this request, for I have already given my word. What do you say, kinsman Ulf?"

Ulf had gone extremely pale. One did not refuse to do the Jarl's bidding, especially when one's expedition was largely dependent on his patronage.

"I will do as your lordship pleases, of course," he said, his expression belying the polite words, for he had the look of a man facing the point of his enemy's sword. "This comes as a surprise to me. I had no inkling of my brother's wishes, or that he believed he might have anything of value to contribute to such a venture."

"Any new settlement needs men of learning." There was a note of mild reproof in Magnus's tone. "Go on, take the boy with you. It could be the making of him."

Ulf gave a tight nod. Margaret's lips curved in a tiny smile. Eyvind bowed to the Jarl, and returned to his place by his brother.

"What did you do that for, you fool?" Eirik hissed, the moment he sat down.

"What do you mean?" Eyvind whispered.

"You know Ulf doesn't want him there. The boy's a millstone around his neck." Eirik wasn't joking; his expression was grim.

"All he needs is a chance," Eyvind hissed back. "To know

someone cares about him. If—" He fell silent as the Jarl began to speak again.

"Stand up, young Somerled," Magnus commanded, and by the pillar Somerled rose to his feet, silent. "Your friend is generous, and so am I in granting him this selfless gift, instead of the riches I wished to lavish on him for his many acts of courage. You'll wish to thank him, no doubt."

"And yourself, my lord," Somerled said smoothly. If he felt any pleasure or surprise at what had just happened, he hid it expertly. "I am aware that my future is dependent on your lordship's generosity, and I am grateful for that, though Eyvind is right; if men remember me, I hope it will be as one who succeeded on his own talents, and did not ride to victory on the shoulders of others. I can assure you that I will not waste the opportunity you have given me today. I will use it to the full extent of my ability. And I wish to thank my friend in kind. Eyvind does not accept gifts readily, your lordship is already aware of that. He's a modest fellow, more ready to see his own shortcomings in matters of intellect than he is to value his strengths in other spheres. My lord, let us reward Eyvind in a manner fitting his own generosity of character. Allow him to come with us. Oh, not for good," he hastened to add, as Magnus's brows drew together in an ominous frown, and Eyvind choked back a shocked protest, "not for good, for I know this youngest Wolfskin is dear to you, and a vital part of your strike force. Release him for a season only. He has proved a loyal warrior to you, and a faithful friend to me. He has not asked for any special favors or particular recognition. Set him free from your service for a little, and let him go forth with this venture, boldly across the sea, and support the men of Rogaland against whatever enemies they may encounter. Before the storms of summer's turning, he can return to your side; he will most certainly be back in time for your autumn viking. And what a fine tale he will have to tell you."

Magnus made a rumbling sound which seemed to denote disapproval. "I don't know about this," he said. "I don't owe you any favors, Somerled. Besides, I'm losing half my Wolfskins for the summer, and not all of them will be coming back, I suspect. Generous I may be, but I'm not a fool."

"Indeed not, my lord," Somerled agreed. "Still, young men should be offered such experiences, I think. A little exposure to far places and alien people can but strengthen their attachment to home, their loyalty to their own."

Eyvind could not make himself speak. His heart still thumped with shock. He bit his lip, willing Jarl Magnus to say no. He had not the least wish to sail over the sea to some god-forsaken island, nor to linger there, tilling fields and feeding chickens. He was a warrior; his job was here, fighting the Jarl's battles and keeping him safe. How would Thor find him, so far away? And what on earth had got into Somerled to ask such a thing? It was just as well Eyvind was the Jarl's favorite, or he might end up not seeing Signe again for a whole summer.

"My lord Jarl."

Eyvind blinked. His brother Eirik had risen to his feet and was speaking now.

"This suggestion is clearly not to your liking, and I understand the reasons for that. But it's a good notion. After the battle in the east, where my brother acquitted himself so well, your borders are very secure in that quarter. Your new alliance with Thorvald Strong-Arm here reinforces your support in the north. It seems unlikely you will face any real threat before summer's end. Enough of your Wolfskins remain to guard you and deal with anything that might arise. Don't forget the three young men we've trained, who are all too eager to put their skills on display. The best of them will be chosen to take Hakon's place, when we return. I think you could spare my brother until harvest month. The change would be good for him, and I'll undertake to look after him, and bring him back safe. I've no intention of staying on in those parts myself."

Eyvind glared at him but Eirik would not meet his eye.

"Hmm," said Magnus. "We must let the young warrior choose for himself, I suppose. Let it not be said that I held him back. What do you say, Eyvind?"

One could not give a plain answer to this type of question. "My lord, you know I want nothing more than to serve you with axe and sword, and to follow the will of Thor. I will do whatever your lordship wishes." This was as close as Eyvind might come to saying he did not want to go.

"Have you room for another on your longship, Ulf?" Magnus asked with a smile.

Ulf was not smiling. "Eyvind is a valiant warrior, another like his brother," he said. "Him, I have no objection to, though he has surprised me today."

"Very well," Magnus said. "There is nothing touches the heart so much as a fine display of loyalty between friends. These two young men have impressed me: so different in appearance, in talents, and in bearing, and yet so thoughtful for each other that they might almost be brothers. Both shall go; but, Eyvind, I need your promise that you will stay a season only. We'll have work for you here as soon as the nights begin to lengthen."

"Yes, my lord." Eyvind's heart felt like lead. A whole summer with no raids, no battles, a whole summer with no Signe. A pox on Somerled, and a pox on Eirik. When had he ever said he wanted to go voyaging?

"No settling down and setting up house with some buxom native girl, now," the Jarl grinned.

"No, my lord."

Folk began to talk again, and Eyvind spoke to his brother in a furious undertone.

"Why did you say that? You must know I don't want to go. I don't know why Somerled asked, everyone knows I want to stay here."

Eirik smiled without mirth. "Look at Ulf," he said flatly. "There's your answer. You're the one who got Somerled invited on this, when his own brother was afraid to take him. If he's coming, you're coming. I've got a job for you, one you've done before."

"What job?" Eyvind watched Ulf; perhaps that pinched look on his features really was fear, though he couldn't imagine why.

"Keeping your friend out of trouble," said Eirik. "Off you go, then. We sail at dawn; you'd better go and say good-bye to a certain lady. It's a long time till harvest."

Voyages were nothing new to Eyvind. He was not troubled by the movement of the ship under his feet, or the way the sea somehow got into every corner, including boots and leggings, tunics and cloaks and hoods, so that being wet became constant. He was used to the way the skin chafed and itched, and the constant stink about the place. He did not mind having to row; the winds were fickle within the sheltered waters of Freyrsfjord, and progress was slow under sail. What made this voyage different was what came next. Beyond the skerry-guard, one could no longer hug the coastline, putting in at night to camp on shore, make a fire, and sleep tolerably warm and dry in a tent. Instead, the ships were heading out into open ocean, toward a realm whose existence was more legend than known reality, more story than substance. Navigation must be guided by intuition, not visible markers; the very lives of the entire complement of passengers, crew, and stock were dependent on Ulf's ability to weigh unknown risks and find the right decisions. A storm, or contrary winds, or unexpected attack would soon set them off course, and if they missed their destination, who knew what lay between those regions and the very edge of the world? It came to Eyvind that Ulf was indeed a man of great courage, and of vision, for he sailed forth with little more than a dream to guide him. Eyvind admired that greatly, though he took care not to express his opinion in Somerled's hearing. Still, when Ulf told him both he and Somerled would be traveling on the knarr, Eyvind put up no argument. There was stock to convey, after all, and Eyvind was good with animals, being farm-bred. Besides, with eight oars on the knarr and a crew of only ten, it was evident that he would be able to make himself useful.

Many folk lined the shore to salute their departure, but Signe did not come down. Her farewell to Eyvind had been tender and secret, its message conveyed more by touch than by words. It had been strange; it almost seemed to Eyvind like a good-bye that was forever, though he'd assured Signe he would be back in the autumn. Hadn't he given his word to the Jarl?

Even before the sheltered coastal waters gave way to open seas, the folk they carried grew sick. Women staggered to the side to heave their breakfast up; children failed to do so, and spewed forth on whatever was nearest. The crew ignored them completely, save for curt commands to get out of the way when necessary. It was their job to convey the cargo to the islands,

not act as nursemaids. The folk huddled in the bows of the
knarr, their small bundles by them. The stock were closer to the
stern, tethered to iron rings set in the decking. Ulf's dogs had
traveled on the longship, a small mercy. The cargo was loaded
below, and beneath it the knarr bore a ballast of smooth river
rocks. For all that, she rode higher in the water than the *Golden
Dragon* with its smooth lines and great bank of oars. Eyvind
had never traveled in a cargo boat, and wondered how they
would manage to keep up, burdened with their whey-faced
complement of nonsailors. But the knarr surprised him. In open
sea, with a following wind, she moved swift and steady as a
small, neat bird, the square sail carrying her on an easy, stable
course. At most, they needed four oars, and generally none. The
Golden Dragon, by contrast, seemed to be employing both oars
and sail to make progress, and it became a challenge not to go
too far ahead and lose sight of her. This crew was experienced.
They had sailed much farther south than Eyvind had ever traveled on Magnus's raids; they had taken a load of walrus tusks
and fine furs westward from the Frankish coast across to a trading center called Lundenwic, a full day's journey. Still, this
voyage was daunting even for them. Nobody liked the idea of
nights at sea, and a ship full of puking infants, shivering women
and useless thralls did nothing to improve the prospect.

The sounds made a pattern; the ship's timbers creaked as the
ocean tested her strength, the water slapped against her sides,
the crew sang ribald ditties as they bailed or rowed or worked
yard or tiller or whisker-pole at the master's shouted commands, cries as harsh and strange as some great seabird's call:
Aaar-dup! Aaar-dan! Eee-way! All learned to duck and dodge
when they heard that, or they might find themselves engulfed in
a rolling expanse of wet canvas. And one must stay well clear of
the whisker-pole, which was used to change the set of the sail in
order to take advantage of even the most contrary wind. As in
the longship, the knarr's tiller was on the starboard side; the
tillerman had arms like a blacksmith's and needed all his
strength, for the thing could buck and jerk under the sea's violent surges like some wild creature. The man they called Firehead, who spoke to nobody but his crewmates, appeared to be
much valued among these hard-bitten seamen. It was he who
assumed control while the ship's master snatched a brief rest.

At times he took his own turn on the tiller, and those were the only times when Eyvind saw something resembling peace on the fellow's brooding features. Gazing ahead into the dark surge of the swell as he kept the knarr on her steady course, Firehead's eyes lost their dangerous look and seemed instead to be seeing something else entirely, something that was not on the ship or in the ocean but far away in a place only he could catch sight of.

While Eyvind took a turn on an oar, and helped calm the frightened stock, and even shared out hard bread and apples among the passengers huddled together on the forward deck, Somerled also was far from idle. It was not long before one and then another of the crew commented that the lord Ulf's brother was no mean hand with a line, and could tie a knot as well as any of them, and that it wasn't every nobleman's son who would step up and give a hand, especially when he'd just been sick as a dog over the port railing into the sea. Firehead made no comment at all. When the crewmen rested, in turns, Somerled sat among them, listening to their tales of exotic ports and even more exotic women, laughing appreciatively, and putting in a few stories of his own that soon had the men in stitches with laughter. It was a side of Somerled that Eyvind had never seen, and it seemed to him something of a miracle, for his friend had ever been aloof and disdainful among working folk.

The winds died down before nightfall, which pleased everyone. The sail was lowered, the oars stilled; they dragged an anchor, for here even the longest line could not find the sea's floor. Lanterns were lit at bow and stern, and the men put up a makeshift tent for shelter. Not far off in the fading light, the long, dark form of the *Golden Dragon* could be seen riding low in the water, her own lamps tiny points of light which moved crazily against the mysterious, breathing darkness of the ocean. Eyvind stood watching as stars emerged in the night sky, one, then two, then a whole great pattern of them from edge to edge of the world. He felt the immensity of that black expanse of water around them, a sea so vast that no land could be sighted in any direction, not by the man with the best eyes in all of Norway. These ships were so small, so fragile, though they had seemed strong and dauntless on the safe shores of Freyrsfjord.

Would not the coming of dawn snuff out each one of those tiny stars that now shone so splendidly in the inky sky above him? Perhaps the same dawn would see the frail craft of Ulf's venture extinguished as well, sunk by a freak wave, overturned by the sudden breaching of a whale, or driven off course by spring gales to splinter on some half-submerged reef. Perhaps their human cargo—leader, warrior, crewman, innocent woman, and infant—would perish one and all, gone as quickly as those small stars that faded in the coming of the light. *We think ourselves so grand,* thought Eyvind, *so brave and strong. But before this, we are like chaff in the wind, like bubbles on the stream.* The thought did not frighten him. He felt only a great sense of calm and of quiet, and he stood there long, gazing out into the deepening night as crew and passengers settled to sleep as best they could, and two men stood watch.

The second day brought a thick blanket of cloud. On the *Golden Dragon,* Ulf could be seen squinting at his sunstones, trying to fix his course. As long as there was the smallest patch of blue somewhere in the sky, a man who had the right skill could catch the sun's light in the crystalline depths of these stones and use it to help find his way. Ulf had brought ravens, as well, but he would not release them yet, for the fleet had not journeyed far enough from Rogaland; the birds would simply turn and fly straight for home. The true test would come in a day or two, if the wind stood fair.

Some of the passengers had begun to get their sea legs, and among these was a lively infant of perhaps three years old, a sturdy little fellow with a dangerous bent for exploration. His mother was prostrate, retching and moaning; the other folk tried to curb the child, but what with the rocking of the boat, and the need to keep out of the crew's way and tend to those who were sick, it was no easy matter. There was a girl, the boy's sister, a fair-haired lass of about fourteen, sweet-featured and quiet; she hauled the infant back from trouble time after time with soft-voiced reprimands, but it was a bit like ordering the wind not to blow, or the tide not to come in. This was a boy who would make a fine sort of man, if the gods let him get that far.

Toward midday, the girl was busy tending to her mother, and most of the others were rolled miserably in their damp blankets trying to shut out a world that had grown suddenly too difficult.

Eyvind was coaxing the restless cattle into sampling grain from a bucket when he spotted the small lad scaling the knarr's side to perch precariously astride the rail, a hair's breadth from tumbling over and down to the chill surge of the sea. There was nobody near the boy; the crew were rowing, or steering, or sleeping, and Firehead was in the stern keeping an eye on the other boat and shouting orders as necessary in that strange seaman's tongue: *Aaar-dup! Eee-way!* The child teetered; the swell rose; two crewmen moved into position to swing the whisker-pole. As soon as they did that, the whole vessel would shudder and shift, and even those lying on deck would need to hold on, not to be tumbled hither and thither. Eyvind opened his mouth to shout a warning, but the crewmen moved too fast, the whisker-pole swung across, shifting the great crackling sail, and the knarr juddered and swung after it, obedient to the wind. The boy toppled and fell, and quick as a flash, a man who had been hidden from view because he was leaning over the side, retching the last drops of bile out of his tortured gut, reached to grab one small arm, hooked his own foot under the ledge that skirted the oar ports, strained to haul in his shrieking catch before the wind and the waves snatched the two of them off the boat into a last cold embrace. Eyvind sprinted across the slanting, slippery deck, and now others too saw Somerled hanging there, his foot, jammed under the railing, the only thing that kept him and the boy from the ocean's icy grasp. The wind rose, bearing the child's screams away from his lips as if they were of no account whatever. Somerled's face was the color of fresh cheese, his jaw was set grim, his hands gripped white-knuckled around the child's arm. He did not have enough purchase to pull the lad to safety, and his foot was beginning to slip now, the boot leather tearing under the strain.

"Help me, will you?" he hissed through tight-clenched teeth as at last Eyvind reached his side. Both taller and stronger than Somerled, he had no trouble reaching down to seize the child under the arms and lift him to safety. The boy's screams subsided to hiccupping sobs; his sister, ashen-faced, took him in trembling arms and proceeded to scold him roundly, with tears of fright glinting in her blue eyes.

"All right?" Eyvind inquired as Somerled eased his cramped

arms, and unhooked his foot with extreme caution, as if it might be hurting quite a lot.

"Yes," said Somerled faintly, "or maybe no. Excuse me," and he leaned back over the rail, his stomach heaving anew in protest at the knarr's relentless movement. It took a while. "Perhaps that's all, until next time," Somerled observed, straightening up and wiping his mouth with his sleeve. "My brother must be crazy. Who'd do this by choice?" Then he looked up and saw the girl standing before him with the child, now quiet, in her arms.

"Thank you," she said, looking at him under her lashes. "You saved his life. Thank you so much."

Somerled appeared quite taken aback, as if he did not think what he had done was in any way remarkable. "It's nothing," he said, reaching out to pat the child rather awkwardly on the arm. "Don't mention it."

"It didn't seem like nothing to me," the girl ventured, her cheeks turning a delicate pink. "And thank you, too." She glanced at Eyvind and quickly away, as folk sometimes did with his kind. "My brother's always getting into trouble," she went on shyly. "I'll try to look after him better. And I'm sorry you're so sick."

Somerled did not reply, but he watched the girl as she made her way back to her mother's side and settled her small brother with bribes of salt fish and wrinkled apples. Then one after another of the crew came forward to clap Somerled on the back and congratulate him for his quick thinking, and comment that they'd like to share an ale with him, only it would hardly be worth it since he'd be lucky to keep it in his belly long enough to enjoy it. Somerled had become a sort of hero.

Firehead did not shake his hand and grin and make friendly jokes. Firehead had not moved from where he stood in the stern of the knarr, alone. But he watched with narrowed eyes, and Eyvind read the look on his hard features and was uneasy. It was unfortunate, he thought, that Somerled had traveled on the very same craft as this taciturn fellow who might or might not have once gone by the name Sigurd. Yet, if Somerled had been on the *Golden Dragon* with Ulf and Margaret, that lad would have fallen overboard and drowned. You could never second-guess the gods. Still, Eyvind would be glad when they reached their destination and could pay off the knarr's crew and get on with things. Maybe Somerled's newfound popularity would set him in better stead with his brother. One could always hope.

The weather got rougher, so rough they could not go under sail. They used the oars as best they could to keep within sight of the longship. The passengers grew quieter and the stock noisier. A crewman was heard threatening to wring the gander's neck if it didn't leave off that wretched honking. Eyvind shoveled cattle dung over the side and tried to ration the grain. He did notice, once or twice, that the fair-haired girl was talking to Somerled quite a bit, and he wondered what the two of them could possibly have in common. Since Somerled was still spending half his time leaning over the sea retching, he was surely less than an ideal companion. Once, Eyvind saw the girl slip as a wave caught the knarr, lifting the bows high, and Somerled's arm come out quickly to steady her. If anything, Eyvind was pleased by this development. She was a little young, certainly, but if she took Somerled's mind off his brother's wife, that surely had to be good.

On the fourth day, Ulf released one of his ravens. The bird circled the fleet and flew off westward. They waited. By nightfall the creature had not returned, and Ulf conveyed to the other ship by shouts and signs that he was well pleased. It seemed their course was true.

Eyvind had had little sleep, but he was used to that. A warrior is trained to endure far worse hardships. That night he slumbered lightly, for all his weariness, and woke abruptly while it was still pitch dark. He could not identify what he had heard. He only knew it meant danger. Not the boat: it was moving steadily and slowly, sail reefed, anchor trailing. The folk slept safe under the awning, the stock were mercifully quiet. He could see the fellow on watch in the bow, up beyond the sleeping area. All seemed well. But he had heard it. Eyvind got quietly to his feet, and there it was again: not creaking timbers nor snore of man or woman, not moving water nor cry of sea creature, but something wrong, something out of place. A hissing gasp, a wheeze of expiring air, a sound born of pain. He moved. A hunter has sharp eyes and sharper ears. Something dark by the rail on the port side: perhaps only Somerled being sick again? No, there were two men here, and the one bent over the rail was held there forcibly, pinned down by the other. The red-headed man had a grip on Somerled's hair and was pushing his head downward, crushing his neck against the rail. Somerled's left arm flailed helplessly, his right was twisted up behind his back at an impossible angle. It was his gasp Eyvind had heard, the sound a man makes when he has not quite enough time to breathe before his throat is constricted once more. And Firehead's fierce whisper, "That's for today . . . and that's for yesterday . . . and that's for what you did before . . ."

Eyvind was there in two great strides, grabbing Firehead by the arms. The fellow was strong; his fingers were most reluctant to give up their deathlike grip on Somerled's hair. Eyvind applied a well-practiced technique involving a knee to a particular point in the back, and Firehead gave a grunt of pain and released his hold. Somerled crumpled to the deck, sucking in a strangled, croaking breath. Eyvind backed Firehead against the knarr's rail, holding him fast with a cunning grip on the neck. Firehead had stopped struggling, realizing, perhaps, that it was pointless when the man who held you was a Wolfskin.

"You can let me go," he muttered. "I've no quarrel with you."

"What sort of fool are you?" hissed Eyvind. "You nearly killed him! Your job's to sail this thing and follow Lord Ulf's orders, not strangle his family! What am I supposed to do with you?" Cautiously he released his grasp. Firehead stared back at him, his face reduced to a mask of moonlight and shadow in the rocking dark. Beside them, Somerled was getting slowly to his feet. His breathing sounded tight and painful.

Firehead spat on the deck. "I've told you," he said flatly. "But you wouldn't hear me. He's at it again; he'll never change. Haven't you seen him with that girl, the one with the young brother? But no, you wouldn't notice, you're blinded by the promise you made. You should have let me finish this now."

It was as good as telling them who he was; who he had once been.

"We thought you might be able to put that behind you," Eyvind said quietly. "Not let it poison your whole life. My mother thought you might have come back. There's always been a place for you at Hammarsby. It's your home as much as it is mine and Eirik's."

"There's no going back." Firehead's tone was bleak. He turned and walked away, down to his watch in the stern, and the darkness swallowed him.

"Are you all right?" Eyvind whispered to Somerled, who was touching his throat gingerly. "We'll have to report this to the ship's master; he nearly killed you."

"No need," Somerled croaked.

"But—"

"Leave it, Eyvind. This will work itself out. Trust me."

"But, Somerled—"

"Leave it, will you?"

The next morning Ulf released a second raven, and they observed its direction before hoisting sails and following after. The wind was strong from the north, there was a relentless swell, and progress was both fast and uncomfortable. All longed for the voyage to be over.

As for what had happened the night before, both Firehead and Somerled appeared to have forgotten it. Each behaved as usual, the one occupied with sailing the ship, the other still spending most of his time doubled over the rail. Somerled was no seafarer. Eyvind was beginning to relax, thinking that there was not so far to go now, and perhaps they might get there without further trouble, when there was a sudden bellow from the stern of the knarr, followed by a chorus of shrieks from the passengers. The bull, which had been growing increasingly restless as the days of close confinement and lurching movement went on, had begun to jerk its head about with some violence, snorting and stamping. Two stout ropes tethered the creature to iron rings set in the decking, but it was not hobbled. Such fetters would pose too great a risk of breaking a limb if the ship's movement caused a fall, and this fine animal was to be the foundation of Ulf's breeding herd. Now its angry struggles had broken one of its tethers, leaving only a single length of rope to restrain it. Sensing freedom close, it continued to buck and twist and pull at this last bond, roaring its anger. The heifers raised their voices in support; the sheep, chickens, and geese joined in hysterically, driving the bull to more strenuous efforts.

And suddenly, amidst the cacophony of animal noises, there was a sound of splitting timber as the pine decking started to give beneath the onslaught of the creature's hooves. The crewmen backed away, oars abandoned. The women screamed, gathering children in close. Little imagination was required to picture what damage a beast of that size, with those horns, could do to vessel and passengers before it might be checked or leap overboard in its frenzy. The head jerked anew, the horns scythed through the air. Folk cringed. Who could get anywhere near, even supposing anyone were foolish enough to try?

They say a Wolfskin does not know fear, not as a normal man does. It did not occur to Eyvind to stand back. Arming himself with a looped length of rope, he moved in on the crazed bull, holding the tether unobtrusively by his side. He made his progress slow and quiet, balancing each step against the knarr's movement. On the other side, Firehead was edging in behind the thrashing animal. He had seized a short pole with an iron hook on one end. Because they had done this sort of thing before, catching stock for branding or gelding, there was no need for either man to speak; each knew his part. Firehead would try to get a purchase on the remaining tether, or the horns, while Eyvind moved in to loop the rope on and secure it. They'd need to be quick; the single restraint was starting to give, and the boards beneath the bull's hooves were cracking and splitting. The animal was kicking at random, and the swinging of its head grew ever wilder.

Firehead moved closer; he lifted his hook. Eyvind stood still, noose now ready in his hand, awaiting the single moment when it might be slipped on safely. The hook would not hold the bull for long. The creature's small eyes moved from one man to the other and back again. Eyvind glanced at Firehead, and Firehead gave a little nod, *Now*.

"Why don't you use a spear and kill the creature?" The voice was Somerled's, clear and logical. "That way you can keep your distance, and we all stay safe."

"Get out of the way, you fool!" Eyvind snapped, alarmed that his friend had been foolish enough to come so close; he stood on the opposite side, barely out of reach of those flying hooves. Somerled didn't know a thing about handling stock. "Let Sigurd get in there, he has to hold the head still while I put this on. If you think I'm stupid enough to slaughter Ulf's stud bull you're mistaken. Now shut up and let us get on with this."

The creature's eyes narrowed; it lowered its head as if to charge.

"Hoo now, hoo now," Eyvind repeated softly, knowing this creature was beyond being reassured thus, but saying it anyway, for at least it kept the bull's attention on him and off the others. "Hoo now, bonny one." That fraying rope was the only thing stopping the bull from coming straight at him; there was blind terror in those crazy eyes. "Hoo now, my bold one." For an instant, the creature held still; this was the moment. Firehead stretched out with the hook. Eyvind had the noose in place to slip over the horns. Then everything went mad. There was a furious bellow and a whirl of chaotic movement. Hooves flew, wood splintered, the bull's head swung to the side in a violent jerk that snapped the last tether, and it was free. The great horns swept across this way, that way, and entered Firehead's chest as easily as a knife pierces a ripe pear. Eyvind stood frozen in shock as the creature lifted Firehead bodily from the deck, cruelly suspended on that spear of horn. Then, in a single great swing of its head, the bull set its burden free, tossing the red-haired man clean over the knarr's side and out into the heaving swell of the ocean. Firehead had made no sound at all, save for a grunt of surprise as the horn took him; death had granted him no chance to tell his story, or call on his gods. He was gone in an eye-blink. The bull pawed the deck and lowered its head again; its horns were stained bright red. But Eyvind's axe was already in his hand. There was no choice now. His single blow struck true, cleaving the skull between the small, furious eyes, and Ulf's best breeding bull fell lifeless on the splintered deck. Its end was as quick as the man's. If Eyvind knew anything, it was how to kill cleanly.

Once people accepted the bull was really dead, they ran to help. It was too late for Firehead. No man could survive such an injury, even supposing it might be possible to find him in that surging expanse of icy water. While the ship's master maneuvered her close enough to the *Golden Dragon* so they could shout across to Ulf, Eyvind knelt by the bull's still-warm body and carefully extricated his axe from where it was lodged deep in the skull. Biter was a fine weapon; he never let it rust or lose its edge. The axe had saved many lives today. He wished it could have saved Sigurd's—Firehead's—as well. Why had the bull suddenly gone mad like that? He was sure they'd had enough time, certain they could have tethered it safely, between the two of them. Now all the creature was fit for was roasting on a spit and being served up for supper, and Eyvind would never learn the tale behind Firehead's haunted eyes. He got to his feet, studying the great, limp body and thinking that the open deck of a knarr, with rain beginning to slant in, was scarcely the ideal spot for cutting joints of meat. He bent over again, looking more closely. He squatted down by the creature's rump. What was this? There was blood here, not Sigurd's blood, for that was all on the horns and the rail and sprayed over the inner surface of the strakes. This blood dripped down the inside of the bull's rear legs, and pooled now on the deck beneath its tail. There was a fresh wound there, a slit to the animal's testicles, and it was from this the blood still ran, though that would stop soon enough. How could such a tidy cut have been inflicted in such a place? Perhaps the bull had damaged itself in its frenzy, maybe it had gashed the testes on something: a jutting piece of wood, a food trough, anything. What else could this be? Yet the cut was so neat, like a surgeon's incision, and there was no barrel, no protrusion; the stock area was always kept as clear as possible. This was like a knife wound, precise and true. But that could not be. There had been nobody close enough, nobody with the opportunity. Almost nobody. In the back of his mind, Eyvind put two things together. A painful jab to the privates. A sudden enraged lunge, breaking the last rope and impaling a man all at once. He knelt by the bull, thinking. Firehead had died. But it might just as easily have been himself or even Somerled. Nobody could have known which way the bull would turn. A risky game indeed.

The ship's master was calling; Ulf was responding. He wanted the bull thrown into the sea: an offering for Freyr. They could not afford to have the ill omen of Firehead's death over this voyage. Eyvind decided he must be imagining things, for there was no sense to what his mind was telling him. He rose to his feet; there was work to be done.

"Oh, dear," said Somerled. He stood quietly at a little distance, his face gravely composed. "He seemed quite a useful fellow, too. Still, I expect they'll manage to sail this tub without him. And if these islands provide the lush grazing my brother praises so lavishly, no doubt there will be wild cattle there for the taking."

"He was a friend of mine once," Eyvind said, frowning. It unsettled him when Somerled spoke like this. It was as if he thought nothing in the world of very much account.

"You're a strange creature, Eyvind," said Somerled. "Death should be nothing to you. Don't you deliver it a hundredfold as your daily business? What does it matter if this fellow got his chest split open? He was nobody. He was no different from the Jutes and Franks you take with your trusty axe when you're out impressing Magnus on his raids."

"It is different." Eyvind was watching the crew as they began to drag the bull's bloody carcass forward to the place where they could most easily lift it over the side of the knarr. "This was a friend. At heart, a good man. And it seemed to me that we—I—owed him something. Because of that business with Ragna."

"Who?" asked Somerled blankly.

Eyvind looked at him, and looked away. "Forget it," he said. There was a doubt in his mind, a terrible, dark doubt, that stretched not just over today's shocking events but back into the distant past. His fingers touched the scar on his forearm, mark of an oath deep and binding, a promise of lifetime loyalty. He closed his eyes a moment, and sent up a silent prayer to Thor. *Let this not be true. Let me be wrong about him.* They cast the bull's body into the water, but Freyr was not pleased. The wind changed; the rain began to descend in icy sheets, plastering the men's clothing to their skin and scouring the deck clean of blood. Ulf's intended course had been toward the setting sun, but it now became clear the god's angry breath was driving both vessels away from their true path toward a region trackless and empty, where the dark waters held only the lurking terror of sea monsters and the sudden sharp grip of low-lying skerries. On the knarr, they manned the oars, but the current pulled so hard it threatened to rip the lengths of heavy pine from their hands, and the vessel plunged ahead on her own wild course. The passengers clung to ropes, to rails, to one another, to whatever they could find, shocked into a white-faced silence. Ahead of them in the gloom of driving rain and ocean spray, the dark form of the *Golden Dragon* was barely visible above the turmoil of surging water.

Eyvind narrowed his eyes; he could scarcely see a ship-length beyond the knarr's prow. If Ulf had been right in his calculations, they must surely even now be passing their intended safe harbor, swept beyond it by the elements' fury. It was as if day had become night; the storm had turned the world to darkness. He closed his eyes. *Thor!* He spoke in silence, in the depths of the heart. *Thor, I am your loyal son. I have served you with all my strength. Help us now, best of sailors. Show us the way.*

"Land!" someone shouted. "I see land! Look, there to the south!"

"And there to the north!" yelled another man.

Eyvind's eyes snapped open. It was true. Now, dimly showing between the curtains of rain, a low, dark mass could be discerned. It was not so very far off, and yet it might have been at the other end of the world, so little chance there seemed of changing course to reach it. The ship followed her own will now. Another shape loomed farther away, and more again, small islands, bigger islands, like a pod of whales rising in stately convoy from the ocean depths.

The crew shouted to Ulf, "Land! Land!," but the gale snatched away their voices. They hauled on the oars anew; they wrestled with the sail. The angry waters were full of white spray, and the knarr pitched and tossed, timbers groaning in protest. The *Golden Dragon* was a distant shadow in the gray ocean.

Eyvind gripped his oar, knuckles white. He looked up into the storm-split sky, and the rain fell hard and punishing onto his face. *I did not want to come here, Thor.* Surely the god must hear his warrior, even in this desolate corner of the world. *You know how it is for a fighting man. I obeyed my chieftain; I went where I was bid to go. But I am loyal. Guide us safely to shore, Warfather! Let us not come to grief on these skerries, nor be wrecked against these rocks. Bring us whole to landfall. We are your Wolfskins, and will serve you while we have breath in our bodies. Save us for a noble death in battle, not a futile end, adrift without purpose. Thor, aid your sons!*

He waited. If Thor did not help, he thought, then no god would. Odin was a trickster, clever and unpredictable; he was difficult to please and his games were only for men who thrived on risks. Freyr had a temper. If one offended him, cataclysmic events might ensue: tempest, flood, drought, sudden maladies striking crops or men. With his power over the elements and seasons, Freyr could bestow plenty or famine. He appreciated a sacrifice, but even a fine bull might not be enough to calm his rage. Thor was different. Thor thought in terms any man could understand: life and death, friend and foe, courage and cowardice. He rewarded loyalty and despised treachery. Thor understood a warrior's heart.

The wind changed. Still it blew fiercely, sending the boats fleeing before it like specks of foam on a flood-swollen stream, yet now there seemed an eerie purpose behind it, for they were driven on a course that veered past small, flat islands and skirted the shores of larger ones where signs of settlement showed in wandering sheep and the smoke from cottage fires. North they were driven, then south, then westward again, and the rain cleared, and it became apparent that this strange intervention of the gods had carried them through broad ocean firths into the very heart of this group of grass-clad isles; they had indeed reached the destination Ulf had intended for them, and now sailed westward into a sheltered bay in whose waters two small islands lifted low, grassy forms above the sea. These islets were fringed by spreading rock shelves, and here rested many seals, watching the visitors with mild, dark eyes. The land beyond the bay was gently sloping, green-clad, and entirely without trees; this was perhaps the biggest island in the group. To the southwest, beyond the rolling hills, there was another isle where twin dark, mysterious peaks loomed in forbidding grandeur. The crew rowed into the bay, the oars obeying them now, and dropped anchor. The *Golden Dragon* was beached on a narrow strip of pebbly shore; Ulf was the first to spring over the side. He fell to his knees on the wet ground and gave thanks to Odin, and Freyr, and Thor for their safe deliverance.

It was a wondrous place. The waterway across which they had been driven was serene and bright now, and all marveled at the changing colors of sky and sea, the cool, clear light that bathed these low, green hills, the shimmering, pearly water. Birds circled their battered craft, perhaps hoping for fish.

There were dwellings here, low houses of stone with heather-thatch roofs, but if any folk dwelt in them, they had fled at the sight of the two ships coming in to shore. Supplies were unloaded, enough to last a few days, and the women and children settled as comfortably as possible. Ulf left guards; he instructed them that Lady Margaret was in charge. Then he set off inland with his men by him, to determine what kind of place this was, and who might hold sway here.

It was indeed a fair land, with broad lakes and inlets and fine grazing pasture. Someone ran sheep and cattle; to Eyvind's eye, the beasts looked well-tended and strong, though somewhat stocky in build. There were modest dwellings tucked here and there; plumes of smoke rose from household fires. A good place, though curiously devoid of trees. The few they saw were clustered in sheltered folds of the land like refugees of conflict. They speculated on this. There had been giants, maybe, who ripped them up like twigs, or fierce-toothed creatures that crunched them as easily as stalks of wheat. Perhaps the island had suffered a great fire. Or maybe it was simply too windy; those small birches and willows that clung here and there did have a somewhat prostrate look to them, as if accustomed to bow before some powerful force of nature.

"If I were to offer a gift to these people," Ulf remarked, "it would be timber for building, for they surely have a sore lack of it."

They came to a place of standing stones, set on a heather-cloaked rise by a neck of land which separated two wide expanses of bright water. In that place, all fell silent. The stones were tall; even Eyvind was dwarfed by them. And they were many. Holgar tried to count them, but he ran out of numbers before he came around that great circle. More than fifty, Ulf reckoned, and beyond them mounds in the earth, burial chambers perhaps, sealed by a blanket of turf. Somerled remarked that such hidden places might just as readily conceal gold or silver than men's bones, and it was a shame there was no advantage to be had, in such a desolate corner of the world, from the sudden acquisition of such treasures. They did not stay long in that

place. No priest had traveled with them, and there was no saying what ancient gods lingered there, or what they thought of
unexpected visitors.

They walked a long way, and never a living thing in sight but
cows and sheep and a chicken or two. The wind got up and they
began to feel the bite of it through cloaks and tunics still damp
from the hard voyage.

"What are these people, some kind of ghosts, that they let us
cross their land unchecked, and themselves remain unseen?"
Hakon commented as they came up over a rise in the land and
looked northward. "We should return, perhaps, and stay by our
womenfolk until we learn more."

"I think not," said Ulf in a strange tone, and there, striding
toward them across the grassy hillside with grim purpose was a
group of men in tunics dyed blue or green or red, men of small
stature, dark-haired and armed with bows and staves.

"Well, well," observed Somerled under his breath. "Genuine
barbarians. I wonder if they'll introduce themselves before they
start shooting. What tongue might we try, do you think? Latin?
Frankish?"

But his brother ignored him. Stepping forward and raising
his hands in a gesture that clearly denoted the wish to talk
rather than fight, Ulf set about making his new world.

FIVE

If there was one day Nessa remembered from her childhood, it
was the day when she found the tower in the earth. If she
hadn't argued with Kinart and gone off in a huff, it might never
have happened, and her life might have been quite different.
She'd been a very small girl then. Kinart had made her so cross
that she'd forgotten to be careful, and she'd wandered into a
forbidden place, a place nobody walked across because it was
brimful of magic. She'd gone without thinking, and suddenly
there it was, a hole in the ground, hidden among the rocks be-

yond the low line of grass-crested dunes. If she hadn't been the sort of girl she was, one who liked adventures, she'd have been too scared to scrape away the earth and look in, for there was no doubt it was a spirit-place, a place a good child would do well to keep clear of. Kinart was down by the shore gutting their catch; gulls squabbled all around him, fighting for the scraps. The little skin boat was drawn up on the shingle close by. When she'd forgiven him, Nessa would go back.

The strong westerly wind whipped her hair across her face, and she brushed it back impatiently. A little spade would be useful, a shard of bone, anything she could dig with. She scrabbled the earth away with small, capable hands; there was a bigger opening now, and the spring sunlight glanced in over her shoulder to show some sort of chamber there below, large, dry, lined with precisely laid slabs of stone and floored with earth. The hole was too small; she could not see properly. It almost looked as if the subterranean room opened down to another, but peer as she might, Nessa could not quite make it out. And the tide would be turning soon. When you lived in a place like the Whaleback you could not let disagreements delay you too long, or there would be no going home until low water came round again.

Perhaps it would rain. This secret place had been sealed against the weather a long time, until the violent storms of this season's turning had begun to uncover it. She bent to shift a slab of flagstone, to drag it across the opening she had widened. Another time. There was plenty of time. Summer was on the way, and the days were light and long. Maybe she'd tell Kinart, and maybe not. If he stopped teasing her about how she made up names for things, if he stopped saying she'd never find a husband, then she'd show her cousin the place she had discovered. Who wanted a husband anyway? One of her sisters could find one and produce the son required to secure the kingship. Her sisters were older and prettier and quite good at sewing and baking bread. They couldn't fish, and they couldn't row, and they couldn't run or climb or swim as well as Nessa could. Kinart said husbands cared nothing for those sorts of skills. It was other things they wanted. What things? Nessa had asked him. But when he told her, she thought he must be joking.

There were two ways to get home to the Whaleback. When

they had the boat, they could row back to the hidden cove, no more than a slit in the tidal island's rocky southern flank, clamber precariously out and drag their small craft up to a little hollow above high water. Then they'd climb farther, till they reached the curving grassy top of the Whaleback, and run downhill to the houses that clustered low at the eastern end, perched on the level ground overlooking the causeway. If you'd gone over to the mainland on foot, there was but a single way to return, and that was over that same causeway, picking a careful path on the weed-draped stones. They knew the tides as they knew the patterns of their own breath. In summer there was time, before and after the lowest ebb, to walk a fair way up or down the coast or inland across the home farms to check on stock or visit neighbors. A journey farther afield meant a longer stay, for once the rising sea came close to washing over that central pathway, there was no crossing over, not unless you fancied a life among the mackerel and the selkies. In times of winter storm, sometimes there was no way over for days on end, for the winds howled fiercely, and the water whipped sideways through the gap between brough and shore, and there was no corner of the Whaleback left untouched by the icy spray of the western sea. The sky was a lowering cloak of darkness; gulls were tossed helpless on the wind. In winter, a stranger might have wondered that the Folk had named their home the Light Isles. Was not this a realm of endless, freezing darkness, visited by hellish winds, pounded by nightmare seas, a stark, empty place where scarcely a tree dared lift its branches from the earth to soften the bleak landscape?

Then spring would come, and if the stranger had waited, he would understand all at once why those who dwelt here knew it for the loveliest place on earth. Here the sky held more colors than there were blades of grass on the hillsides; here the sea was endlessly changing, moody, bountiful, capricious, a shawl of mystery wrapping these fair islands with its fluid touch. Each stone bore its own story, each shell its own pattern, each flower its enchantment. When you sat on the clifftops in springtime, the air was alive with the calls of birds: puffins and gulls jostled for space on the ledges and spread their wings to the wind, soaring and gliding. Ahead of you was an ocean that had no ending. Behind you the low, sweet hills rolled away to shining lakes. To the south, in the distance, was High Island with its twin mountains, a place of hidden valleys and monstrous rock stacks, a realm best fit for fishermen and priests.

There were old things in the Light Isles. The Folk had dwelt here many generations, but there were others, beings of earth and of ocean, embodiments of light and water, presences of bone and darkness, whose claim was ancient and undeniable. These creatures must be respected if one were to share the land in relative peace. The Folk had always known that. At six years old, Nessa knew it, even as she'd known that to look into their secret places, like the chamber she had discovered under the earth, was to court trouble. So, before she left, she placed a pattern in small stones atop the covering slab, a sign of acknowledgment. She hoped they would understand, whoever they were. The four stones at the corners were for the four quarters; in the middle, pebbles made a wavy line, that was the sea, and above it, round sun, crescent moon. Thus she told them she knew what sort of place it was, and held it in respect. If there was anything the Folk understood, it was the importance of signs.

Nessa rose to her feet and turned, and there was the old woman, not three paces away, staring at her with eyes like gray pebbles. Nessa's heart pounded in shock, but she could not run away, for it felt as if her feet had grown sudden roots, holding her there to the earth.

"Come closer, child," the old woman said. "My sight is not what it was."

Now the ground released its grip and she could move. She stepped toward the ragged figure. The woman's gray plait hung down to her waist; her features were seamed and creviced like old stone. And Nessa knew who she was, because Nessa had always loved stories.

"Rona," she whispered. "The wise woman. I told Kinart you were real, but he wouldn't believe me."

The old woman gave a grunt of amusement. "What is real?" she asked. "Is music real? Is shadow real? Your cousin is a boy; he knows only what he can see, what he can touch. For you and me, it is different."

"You and me?" Nessa was staring. She was not afraid anymore. Rona the priestess, keeper of the mysteries, was another tale like the Seal Tribe and the Hidden Tribe, as much part of the islands as the tides and the wind, the rocks and the heather. It seemed entirely unsurprising that she had appeared here, by the secret chamber in the earth.

"I've been waiting for you," Rona said.

"Waiting?"

"Waiting for you to be ready." The old woman glanced at the sign Nessa had made on the slab of stone. "I see that you are ready now."

It came to Nessa then that she did not need to ask, *Ready for what?* She knew the answer without being told.

"Every day," Rona said. "There's a great deal for you to learn. Every day at low tide. You can go home in between."

"I'll have to ask Uncle Engus's permission," Nessa told her. "And my mother's."

The old woman smiled. "You're the youngest of three, aren't you? Engus doesn't need you to wed and breed. And your uncle's no fool, for all he's a man. He knows the importance of the ancestors. He understands the need for the rituals to be performed properly, after I'm gone. Tell him what I've said. He will let you come and learn."

Nessa nodded. "I'd better go now," she said. "The tide's on the turn, and Kinart will be looking for me."

"Tomorrow," said Rona gravely. "Your cousin must learn to fish alone now."

That day had been her turning point, Nessa thought, as she picked her way across the narrow path of tumbled stones to the safety of the Whaleback on a fine, gusty spring day. If she had not run without caution into the dunes all those years ago, she might by now have been betrothed to some chieftain of the Caitt: married, even. Uncle Engus was cautiously negotiating good matches for her sisters. But she'd escaped that, thanks to Rona. Her path would be different. For ten years now, she had learned what the wise woman had to teach; for ten years she had practiced and perfected the rituals of sun and moon, earth and ocean. She had grown up in the knowledge of things seen and unseen, in the reverence and understanding of the old ways. These patterns were eternal; without them, the Folk could not survive. Soon she would leave the Whaleback and King Engus's household, and dwell alone in the place of the mysteries, as Rona did. Folk would see her from time to time, for on certain days of the year, the women of the island gathered to reverence the earth and the moon, and on other days, the men acknowledged the life-giving force of the sun, the power of the ocean. It would be her part, in time, to make sure these rituals were conducted properly. When that happened, she would become like Rona herself, a being regarded as not quite real, poised between flesh and spirit, woman and wraith. That would be strange indeed.

Nessa came up the bank to the level, grassy ground of the settlement. The household was much reduced in numbers, for Uncle Engus had gone away with many of his men. There had been a report of strange vessels sailing into Silver Bay, and folk with hair the color of ripe barley coming ashore armed with many weapons. Engus had taken a party of warriors and traveled south. Perhaps the unexpected arrivals hailed from the land of the Caitt, and would demand some token of fealty. Engus was used to that, since it happened every few years. What one did, Nessa had learned, was to give a few gifts and pass a few compliments, and they'd go away again thinking you'd agreed to something. Most likely this was the same business again. Yet the description of the strangers' ships did not match anything seen before in these waters. Engus would surely have a tale to tell on his return.

It was quiet with the men gone. Still, the evening would not be without entertainment, for Brother Tadhg was here. Everyone remembered the boat that *he* had arrived in with three others of his kind, all the way from some distant place called Ulster. Nobody believed, at first, that a tiny craft of wattles and skins, with the merest scrap of sail, could carry men safely across the sea to land them, ragged, thirsty, and windblown, on the sandy beach at South Bay. Fishermen there said the brothers had knelt down on the shore with the wavelets lapping around their long robes, and uttered some sort of prayer, and then had walked calmly over and introduced themselves. Not that anyone there had understood their speech; that came later. Nessa had asked Brother Tadhg about the voyage, and he'd told her God's hand had guarded the boat, and held back the waves and the storms and the sea serpents, to bring his children to safe haven.

They were crazy men, but harmless. Their madness showed not only in the folly of their voyage and the blind trust that inspired it, but in the home they chose once they arrived. Engus had offered them a house and a patch of land well sheltered from the wind and bordered by sweet pasture. But they chose a spot long uninhabited by humankind, an isle whipped on either side by a violent tide race, a low-lying, windswept place. There were enough tales about that island to keep any man in his right mind well away: disappearances, strange lights, mists, and shadows. Everyone knew the place belonged to the Seal Tribe, a race ancient, elusive, and deeply dangerous. The brothers sailed their rickety boat across and began to build a dwelling house, a prayer house, a sheep pen, a chicken coop. From that day on, the Folk began to call it Holy Island.

The brothers did not beg; they did not ask for help. Their small community grew slowly, one or two more drifting in to the shore as the first had done, in scrappy boats hardly fit for lakeshore fishing. A couple of the local lads had gone over to Holy Island to offer help with shifting stones or shearing sheep, and stayed to work and to learn. In time, there were eight on the island, and seven of them kept to themselves. The exception was Tadhg. He had learned the tongue of the Folk with remarkable speed, and was now a frequent visitor in most parts of the islands. Indeed, he knew many languages, having traveled widely as a younger man and lived among many kinds of folk. He delighted in teaching what he knew. Nessa, an eager student, could now keep up a passable conversation in basic Latin and a better one in Norse. Others of her people dismissed such knowledge: when were they ever likely to need it? But Nessa said, all knowledge is precious, and Tadhg agreed with her.

Everyone made Tadhg welcome, for he told wonderful stories. And while the brother never asked for food or fishing line or a length of woolen cloth, he never went home without a full satchel, for folk had not forgotten his feat of navigation. They admired his courage even as they recognized the folly of his voyage.

When he came to the Whaleback, Tadhg would sit in his usual place on a bench near the fire, his half-shaven head shining pink in the glow of the flames. All the brothers adopted the same odd style, with the front part of the skull bald as an egg.

This tonsure was the way of their brotherhood, Tadhg had explained, though there was another kind, where just a circle on top of the head was shaved. It had been the cause of much dispute among the adherents to their faith, almost as much as the method of calculating the right day of the year for the holy feast of spring, which he called Easter. There had been great unrest over that issue in his own country. Nessa thought perhaps that was why Brother Tadhg and the others had voyaged so far across the sea: simply for peace and quiet.

When she was smaller, Nessa used to beg Tadhg for stories. Most of them she had loved. There was one about a boy who defeated a giant. There was one about a man who lived inside a whale. There was one about a great flood, and another about a magical coat. Those were good tales, and easy to understand. It was the stories about that fellow called Jesus Christ, who was both man and god, that she'd found difficult. Nobody in the household really followed those. After all, Jesus' disciples had been sturdy fishermen and farmers, and the ordinary people had followed and supported him. Why hadn't he fought back, in the end? What sort of man lets himself be captured, tortured, and strung up to die? A sacrifice, Tadhg had explained gravely. To save mankind from wickedness. But there still is wickedness, someone said. Whatever it was meant to do, it didn't work. Then came the catch: if they wanted it to work, they must lay down their arms and follow this Christ; must put aside the old gods and take the new one, the only one, according to Tadhg. All men must love one another, and if your enemy smite you, turn the other cheek. This was the point at which the audience tended to go off into gales of laughter. If a man acted thus, would not he live a short life indeed? Fail to stand against your foes, and you stood to lose farm and family, stock and land. What about the brothers themselves? Where had this strange faith got them? Adrift on the sea in a vessel more like a child's toy than a real boat, and washed up far from home.

"We are rich in God's blessings," Tadhg would say, smiling.

There were three turnings of the tide before Engus came home to the Whaleback, and when he did, he brought the new arrivals with him. Nessa watched them striding across the causeway, the king of the Folk side by side with a slender, finely dressed man, whose dark hair was drawn back and fastened with a band of ribbon. Engus's warriors, more accustomed these days to plowing and seeding, harvest and hunting than the bearing of arms, nonetheless walked proudly behind their leader. But it was the other man's companions who made Nessa's jaw drop and Brother Tadhg's hand move before him in the sign of a cross. These were big men, fierce men bearing axe and sword, warriors with cloaks of gray fur, thick and shaggy over their massive shoulders. Some wore helms of iron; some were bareheaded, their hair shining fair as wheat under the midday sun. They were, perhaps, a race of giants come to steal her uncle's stock and land, or magical beings from the sea, though they were not of the fearsome Seal Tribe; the iron they carried made that plain. The king did not appear to be ill at ease with them, for he stopped halfway across, pointing, as the man by his side watched attentively. Engus was explaining about the tide, perhaps, how treacherous it might be to those who did not know this shore. Maybe he showed the extent of his own holdings: southward beyond the cliffs to the sandy cove, inland past the lakes, north around the coast, and across the water to Holy Island.

There was one among these warriors who caught Nessa's eye. He seemed young, though he was as tall and broad as the biggest of them; he had hair of butter-yellow that curled around his ears. While the others shifted and moved and fingered their weapons, talking and gesturing, this one stood looking along the shore to the rock shelves where seals basked in the sun, and the great shawls of weed moved purple and green and black in the swell. He was as still as a standing stone, quiet and strong. When Engus walked on, leading his visitors toward the settlement, this man was the last to move, the last to take his eyes from the sea.

"God guard us," muttered Brother Tadhg. "I have lived among men of this kind, long ago. They have little respect for what they cannot understand."

"Who are they?" asked Kinart, who stood beside them, squinting into the sun to watch the travelers approach.

"Killers and spoilers. They follow a barbarous faith. They

are Norsemen from the snow lands, far east. We have scarcely begun to feel the ferocity of their touch."

"They do look fierce," observed Nessa gravely, watching as Engus ushered his visitors up the steps cut in the rock, from causeway to safe ground and the start of the settlement. Then after a moment, she asked, "Aren't you supposed to love your enemy?"

"I am too quick to judge, perhaps," Tadhg said with a sigh. "Come, I think your uncle may need my help here. It would surprise me greatly if these barbarians understand the tongue of the Folk."

But Nessa did not follow them. She slipped away as unobtrusively as she could to join her mother and sisters inside, where rapid preparations were being made to receive guests. Who knew how long these wild-looking men might intend to stay? Blankets must be found, bracken for bedding, clean straw. They'd need eggs, cheeses, more bread. Fortunately, a sheep was already roasting on the spit, and there was a plentiful supply of ale.

Nessa combed and re-plaited her hair, and returned to the cooking hut to make herself useful, perhaps basting the meat or cutting cheese. But her mother would have none of that.

"There are plenty of folk to perform these duties, daughter. Sometimes I think you forget what you are."

Nessa smiled. "I never forget that, Mother. But even a priestess should wash dishes or draw water once in a while, I think. There's wisdom to be found in such tasks. Here, let me carry those. Where do you want them taken?"

"Slip quietly into the hall and put them on the shelf by the door. Don't linger; Engus will call when he wants food. Your uncle will not wish you or your sisters to be seen, not until he knows what these men expect from us."

The king's hall stood proudly on its own. It was for gatherings and celebrations, for observance of ritual and the higher festivals. The people of the Whaleback lived in the other houses, which were like many-lobed leaves with a central chamber for eating and talking and indoor work, and smaller spaces opening off it for sleep and storage. The houses were cozy. The hall was grand, its central pillars tall timbers bleached by long sea journeys, travelers from a far land washed up, like Tadhg, on the sweet shores of the Light Isles. The ribs of a great whale stretched across to support the roof thatch, thick bracken held down by stone-weighted ropes. The walls of this building were of red sandstone, but the inside was softened by skins laid on the floor and across the benches, and there were fine woolen hangings on the walls, embroidered with the symbols of the family: the rod and crescent, the mirror, the eagle and sea-beast which were the signs of the royal line—her own line. The eagle had a noble look to it. The sea-beast was different. When you didn't really know if a creature was a seal or a horse or some sort of monster, it was hard to make it seem real. The one on the hanging was copied from the only model there was, the picture on the Kin Stone, which stood at the top of the Whaleback overlooking their settlement, establishing this tidal island as the heart of the Folk's dominion.

The Kin Stone was ancient. It had stood there since the very first of their kind had dwelt in the Light Isles, and would stand until the day the last of them perished. Three mighty warriors, a king and his sons perhaps, strode across its carven face with noble purpose. Above them were the signs of family, including the sea-beast. That creature looked no less odd than the version in colored wools which stirred now in the draft as Nessa slipped in the doorway of the hall to set her platters ready for later feasting.

It seemed important to know what was being said here. Nessa stood very still; surely if she kept silent nobody would notice her in the shadows by the door. The talk was animated, with two different tongues in use. The chieftain of the giant-people would say something, and Tadhg would translate it for Engus and the men of the household in their own tongue. Then the whole process happened in reverse. It was laborious, and not made any easier by people's tendency to speak all at once. Tadhg was calm. He was always calm; sitting among men he had described as barbarians did not alter the serenity of the mild, gray eyes, the composure of the pale features. The ale was flowing freely. Engus would wish to appear generous, Nessa thought, until he found out just what these visitors wanted. At least it seemed they had not come in war.

The large young man she had noticed before was not joining

in the talk. He stood behind the strangers' leader, and she saw now that he was hung about with weapons: a great gleaming axe, a sheathed sword, more than one knife in the belt. He was some sort of guard, then. His fearsome armory somehow disappointed her; it sat at odds with his quietness. His eyes were very blue: blue as summer speedwell.

"It is not easy to believe," Engus was saying now, his eyes shrewd as they scrutinized the chieftain who sat opposite him, "that your purpose in coming here is solely curiosity: a young man's desire for adventure. You have journeyed a long way; they say your ships are strong, well made for ocean voyages. Forgive me, but a man must be careful. I've heard you bring women and children with you, and yet you are a company of warriors well-mettled. You do not seem to come as the brothers came, driven by the strong tempests of the spirit. What, then, do you seek here among the Folk?"

"Do you speak for all?" asked the leader of the voyagers. "When we deal with you, do we deal with the ruler of these islands?"

"You do, traveler. I am Engus, king of the Light Isles. I have ruled here a long time, and while there are other leaders, for our isles are many, mine is the voice of the Folk. You say you have sailed from Rogaland in the east. What sort of land is that? Are you king there?"

The other man smiled; his companions grinned as these words were translated for them.

"No such thing, nor even a Jarl, which is second to a king in our homeland. But I am a man of standing, close kin to Jarl Magnus of Freyrsfjord, and the ships that bore us here are my own. My wife travels with me, and many worthy men of that far country. A man might indeed question why I made such a journey as this. My father heard tell of these isles once, and dreamed of seeing them one day. This dream he passed to me. I have long wanted to come here and discover if the place matched the telling. A wondrous realm; the fairest in the world, so it was said."

Engus regarded him gravely. "That much is true; the longer a man remains here, the deeper the spell the islands weave over him. Still, we have few visitors." There was a question in his tone.

"I would welcome the opportunity to travel more widely," said the other man. "Perhaps to visit other islands, and to fish and hunt, if that is permitted. We would hope to remain here over the summer. In our homeland, a man must perforce be warrior and farmer, voyager and herdsman. There are those among my company who must be home for harvest."

Engus was stroking his neat, gray beard and furrowing his brow. Nessa recognized those signs well; they meant he was pondering a dilemma. He spoke quietly to the men beside him, and this time Tadhg did not translate.

"Of course," the stranger added hastily, "we would build shelter for ourselves, and not expect to be provisioned from your own supplies, though we have fine goods to trade and can pay well. We would seek your approval to build a hall, at a place of your choosing. We offer an assurance of peace and friendship if your people will give the same."

It sounded harmless, Nessa thought. The man seemed well spoken and well intentioned. It was those giants with the axes who worried her, and it seemed Engus, too, was not altogether convinced.

"This is a serious matter," he said, "and I must have time to consider it. You have come a long way; you'll be hungry. A feast is being prepared even as we speak." He rose to his feet. "Follow me. I will show you the cornerstone of my realm, the foundation of this kingdom; meanwhile let the board be prepared." Engus glanced across to the doorway, but instead of the serving man he doubtless expected, there stood Nessa in her blue tunic and her skirt with the ribboned hem, her hair plaited demurely down her back, observing them in grave silence. "Go, child; bid your mother bring what food is prepared, for these men will have hearty appetites, and we must show them the fine fare our islands can offer. Go on, now."

She lingered long enough to hear one of the strangers inquire, "Your daughter?" and Engus reply curtly that he had no daughters, only nieces, of whom this was the youngest. The man with the axe and the blue eyes was watching his leader, and did not seem to notice her. But the others were looking her up and down in a well-practiced sort of way, and one pale-skinned fellow with sleek dark hair gave her a little smile she did not like at all. As Nessa fled to the cooking hut, her uncle led the party of strangers up the long, grassy slope of the Whaleback to the point where the Kin Stone stood high and proud between isle and ocean. He would explain the symbols, reinforce his own status here, warn them, perhaps, against expecting too much. They had not really said what they wanted. It had to be more than a summer camp and the right to trap a few rabbits. Still, these things took time, gifts, flattery; it was almost like a courtship. She watched them walking up, smaller and smaller against the immense sweep of the brough. A big fellow with a bushy yellow beard looked back over his shoulder and grinned at her. She made no response. You couldn't trust men with so much iron hung around them. Beside these warriors, her uncle's retainers seemed like boys, dark, slight, and small. Nessa frowned. Her uncle was no longer young. She hoped he knew what he was doing.

On Engus's own orders, the girls did not sit at table that night. This suited Nessa very well. One could not expect such men to understand what she was; one could not expect them to refrain from looking at her and making comments to one another, since to them she was just another woman. That did not mean one had to endure such inappropriate behavior. She remained out of sight, and so did her sisters. All the same, as priestess of the Folk she had a certain responsibility. She needed to know what they were saying: to understand why they had really come. There was a significance to their presence that went far beyond what was visible; Nessa had sensed that the moment she saw these men marching across the causeway with such confidence. So she lingered by the entry, half-hidden behind the wall hangings, watching.

It was a good feast, and their guests appeared well pleased. The lack of a common tongue stemmed the flow of conversation somewhat, but it did not stop the travelers from exchanging a smile or a wink with one or other of the women of Engus's household, nor their enjoyment of the excellent food and fine ale on offer. Nessa listened intently and began to learn names. Ulf: that was the leader. There were two frightening-looking men who shadowed him closely: Hakon and Eirik, some sort of bodyguards. A brother, the man who had smiled and made her flesh crawl: Somerled. That was too fair a name for such a man. There were more warriors, Grim, Holgar, Erlend, too many to remember. A fine company. The big, quiet one had an odd little name, she was not sure she had heard it right: Eyvi? There were more of them at Silver Bay, where their ships were now hauled up safe out of the sea's grasp. The leader's wife had been left in charge while he traveled to Engus's court. She must be a woman of some authority.

They had brought gifts taken from their cargo, skins of bear and white fox, beads of glass and of amber, blue and green, sun-yellow and water-clear, and they also had gold: an arm-ring wrought very fair with a pattern of interwoven leaves and fruit, and a fine chain suitable for a lady to wear.

"I thank you," Engus said, unsmiling. "We will return your gesture in due course, and handsomely. I do not know you yet, and so I cannot judge what you may need most."

Ulf nodded, his eyes shrewd. "You are both prudent and generous, my lord," he said. "We, in our turn, may offer you more. And I will not be slow in guessing where your own needs lie."

Engus frowned. The clatter of knives and bowls died suddenly. "You read us so quickly? What are you, a soothsayer? A magician?"

Ulf smiled. "No such thing. But I can observe as well as the next man. If I were the king of a fair land such as this, I would wake every day with a prayer of gratitude on my lips that the gods had set me in this corner of the earth. And if I were such a king, and a voyager offered to bring me gifts, I would ask him for two things."

"Go on." Engus's tone was cool.

"Firstly, a cargo of fine timber for building. These isles are strangely lacking in trees. Such a cargo, a farmer in Rogaland could fell in twice seven days, with men to help him. That is a land of forests. It could be loaded and brought back in next summer's sailing."

"And the second gift?" Despite himself, the king of the Light Isles was showing interest now.

"I'd ask for help in building a ship. Not just any ship, but a fine oceangoing longship, the equal of my own vessel, the *Golden Dragon*. With such a craft, a man could move from isle to isle on the breath of the wind, and he could, I think, reach the coast of his southern neighbors rather quickly, certainly before the local chieftains were ready for him."

Now there was a silence of rapt attention. Such a game is good entertainment, even when each man's speech must be translated before the other understands it. The knowledge of tongues gave great power, Nessa realized, as she watched Tadhg take a deep draft of his ale. His throat would be dry as chaff by now. Great power and great danger: in such an exchange, errors could prove costly indeed.

"There is only one such vessel in all of Norway, and that is mine," Ulf said quietly. "I built her myself; she was two years in the planning, a season in the making. The next will be quicker. In time, there will be many such ships, for men seek to emulate what they admire, and the *Golden Dragon* is not only fair and swift, but also strong enough to withstand the rigors of long journey in open sea. If I were king of these isles, I would ask that the next such ship to be built would be my own. Timber from Rogaland would make that possible; my men's skills would achieve it. This could be completed within two summers, I believe."

Engus only nodded. If there was a question he was meant to ask at that point, he chose to save it. Very wise, Nessa considered, yawning. It was getting late. The tide would be well up over the causeway by now, so the guests would have to stay, whether they wanted to or not.

The beads were lovely; the white fur was soft and pretty. Still, you couldn't wear such a thing without wondering about the creature that had once lived in it. Those men wore fur, the ones who guarded Ulf: great shaggy pelts over their shoulders, like the skin of some mythical dog far bigger than any that lived in this world. It added to their look of wildness. She yawned again, and slipped away outside, shivering in the night chill as she ran across to the little hut she shared with her mother and sisters and a couple of serving girls.

It was a clear sky tonight; a blanket of stars stretched from one edge of the world to the other, piercing bright against the soft blue darkness. The moon was a sliver, not yet as full as the crescent she had shaped from stones atop that subterranean dwelling, all those years ago when she was still small and had not learned the mysteries. She knew every corner of that secret place now: its three long chambers with the niches to the sides, its precipitous, crumbling inner steps, the shelf partway down, which held seven tiny skulls set out in a row, right at eye level. The bottom-most chamber was a place of utter darkness. Back then, when she was still a small girl, Nessa had asked Rona what it was, but even Rona did not know, or would not say. So Nessa, with the confidence of childhood, had told Rona what she thought.

"I don't think it's an underground house at all. It only looks like one. I think it's a tower."

"Interesting," Rona had observed. "A tower in the earth."

"It wasn't always like this," small Nessa had told her, warming to the story. "Once there was a fisherman lived here, a good place, not far from the bay but quite sheltered. It started as a cottage, but he wanted to look out to sea, far out, because he always thought, if he looked hard enough, he'd catch a glimpse of the people of the Seal Tribe swimming and playing in the foam, as the old folk said could happen."

Rona had nodded, saying nothing.

"In those days it really was a tower, high up above the top of the dunes, and there was a little window looking out to the west. That was where he used to stand and watch for them. He was very patient, and in the end he got what he wanted. One moonlit night, the Seal Tribe swam up to the rocks at the north end, and climbed out of the water, and danced there naked as newborn babes, each one of them more beautiful than the last."

"What, even the men?" the wise woman had asked with a gap-toothed grin.

"These were all girls," Nessa had said with six-year-old confidence. "The fisherman crept along the shore and tiptoed across the rocks as the strange creatures sang and chattered and combed their long green locks, and quick as a flash he grabbed one of them around the wrist, and held on as hard as he could, for all her entreaties, until the dawn began to break and the others slipped silently into the sea. The sun rose, and the sea-woman had to go home with him, because once day has arrived, they can't go back anymore. He kept her a while. But it's true what they say about the Seal Tribe. Such a pairing can end only in sorrow. One night her menfolk called to her, and when she came down to the shore, they held up those wee pearly shells to catch the moonlight and guide her back home. She broke the fisherman's heart.

"I think he died alone, here in this house. Perhaps his ghost is still here somewhere, hiding in that bottom chamber by day, wandering the shore alone at night, calling out to her, a call that's never answered. It was a long time ago. Great storms came, and the sands covered up the cottage, and then the bottom of the tower, and at last came up over the window and left it all in darkness. So you see, you can have a tower in the earth. That's what it is."

"What about the skulls?"

Nessa had pondered this for a little. "I suppose the Hidden Tribe come here sometimes," she'd replied. "Maybe they use them for drinking bowls."

"Tell me," the wise woman had said. "Tell me why you sealed the entry so carefully. Are you afraid of the Hidden Tribe?"

"I don't think so," Nessa had answered, considering. "Folk do fear them, but they belong here on the islands just as we do, almost as if they are a kind of ancestor, a rather odd one. What they do is only mischief: stealing a jug of milk, or putting your fire out. It's the Seal Tribe who are dangerous. They're the ones who take your child or steal your spirit; the ones who leave you lonely forever, like that fisherman. Of course I'm careful. Nobody's ever going to do that to me."

"Of course," Rona had observed dryly, "your fisherman could have chosen to forget it and get on with things. He could have married and had children and moved away from the tower. He didn't need to waste his whole life just because he didn't get what he wanted."

Nessa could remember her own grave answer. "The Seal Tribe care nothing for us, only for what we can give them. His mistake was to fall in love, and think she could return his feelings. He gave away his heart. After that, he was no good to anyone, not even himself."

Now, so many seasons after, Nessa recognized the wise woman's patience. Rona had been a kind teacher, as well as a hard one. She had set tests of endurance and tests of will, and had guided her student with strength and love. She had taught Nessa how to dream, how to move into that other place where there were tales as numerous as the stars in the sky, wondrous stories that were patterns of wisdom for the taking, provided

one could hear them. Rona said storytelling was a kind of healing, and that Nessa should remember that in times of trouble. It
was interesting; Brother Tadhg said much the same thing.
There was no doubt in Nessa's mind that his stories of the boy
born in a stable and nailed up to die were learning tales. As she
settled to sleep, she wondered what gods these strange fierce
men from the snow lands followed, or if such folk felt the need
of gods at all.

Engus offered the strangers shelter until the end of summer and
the right to travel across his land. In return, they promised to refrain from any acts of violence, and to respect the local people,
both men and women, and not to take what was not theirs. They
might buy flour and meat and whatever else they needed from
his farmers, but must offer a fair price. Engus even suggested a
trip to High Island later in the season. Hares could be found in
abundance there, and many birds. It was understood, without
needing to be put into words, that this short voyage would allow
the *Golden Dragon* to display the features that made her outstanding among longships: indeed, the first of her kind.

The strangers settled into their new quarters in a tranquil spot
some distance to the southeast of the tidal brough which was
the king's stronghold. Their stone-and-turf dwelling houses
were set close by one of the island's rare groves of trees, on
level ground beside a small, peaceful lake. To the north and east
lay hills and moorlands, to the west, verdant pastures for grazing. One could hardly have chosen a spot better to demonstrate
all the beauties of spring in the Light Isles. The days grew
longer, the air warmer, and the newcomers' hair was bleached
gold-white by the sun. Their fair skins glowed pink; wolfskins
and woolen cloaks were discarded, and well-muscled bodies
applied themselves to fishing or hunting, to mending a roof for
a widow or helping a farmer butcher a steer. Their women were
tall and strong like the men, and seemed just as capable, setting
their hands to baking and brewing and tending chickens.

Ulf was everywhere: inspecting the results of his men's toil,
walking by Engus's side as the king showed him his stables or
his grain stores, and often enough, deep in conversation with
Brother Tadhg, though what the two of them spoke of, nobody

knew. It did not take long for Engus to learn that these men from beyond the sea had a plan, a plan that went much further than a summer of toil in the fields and a journey home at harvest time. They had a mind to settle, Ulf said, to be granted some land for farming, perhaps some corner as yet untouched by the plow, untrodden by oxen. If Engus allowed this, he could expect friendship and cooperation. And another thing: they had among them some of the best fighting men in Rogaland, and many of these wished to remain in the islands, though some would indeed sail home in the autumn. With that kind of support, Engus's own position would be much strengthened. Should his neighbors in the lands of the Caitt or the northern isles take it into their heads to pay an unfriendly visit, he would be more than ready for them.

"And if I do not agree?" Engus had inquired.

"Then all is as before." Ulf's manner was forthright; one could not doubt his honesty. "If you say no, we will return to Rogaland before the autumn gales sweep these hills, and we will not return here. We would not stay where we were unwelcome."

Engus told Ulf he would think about it and give his answer when he was ready. And he watched them. As spring became full summer, as sheep and cattle grew fat on rich grasses and barley ripened in the sun, he watched and listened, assessing what manner of men these were, and how this decision might weigh upon the future of the Folk.

The visitors showed a great capacity for hard work. They also knew how to play. Indeed, they had a passion for sports and games, and on many a day the labor of the fields would be succeeded by contests of various kinds among themselves: running, wrestling, swimming. Sometimes, there was combat with weapons. Occasionally, there were injuries: a black eye, a torn ear, a sprained wrist or ankle. Once a man broke his leg, and Engus's own bonesetter had to doctor him. Nessa stayed away from these activities, wishing neither to see nor be seen by the newcomers, but she could not avoid her sisters' chatter.

At midsummer, Ulf played host to the king's household, offering a feast of sorts on the flat sward by the lakeshore, preceded by an afternoon of games. By that time, a wary sort of trust had replaced folk's initial reservations, and some of the local men had started to form friendships with the foreigners. As for the local women, what dealings they had with these fair-haired giants were their own business, but it had been whispered that by next spring the island's population might be swollen by one or two particularly strapping infants. At Ulf's feast, Engus watched a game called Battlefield, in which each team was made up of both locals and visitors, and in which all participants acquitted themselves with the combination of courage and insanity that the rules of the game seemed to demand. There were no major mishaps, beyond a dispute about which team had actually won that was carried on late into the night over the ale cups. And still the king watched them, assessing.

That season the brothers did not see much of Tadhg on Holy Island. Tadhg was very busy, his services as translator in high demand. For three reasons, Nessa could not assist the cleric in these duties: she was a girl, the king's niece, and a priestess of the Folk. Still, she practiced the Norse tongue whenever she could. She could not see the future, but the unease she felt still lingered, and it seemed to her this knowledge could only give her strength to fight what might come. When Tadhg could spare the time, they would sit on the rocks together, watching the changing patterns of the sea, observing the seals sunning themselves on the haul-ups where reef met water, and they would practice new words and sayings, or exchange stories, or simply be silent as sky and sea moved through their great dance all around them. The Norse tongue was harsher than the lilting language of the Folk. Even the names had a different ring to them. Nessa had always thought she could tell, from a name, what kind of person its owner really was. She did not talk about this much, because it was something people found odd. Brother Tadhg was different. She could tell him anything.

"I mean," she said to him, "what sort of a name is Ulf? I can make sense of your name, Tadhg: that speaks of courage, like a flame burning. And Kinart, there's a meaning in that, too, a quick sort of purpose. But Ulf? It sounds like a dog barking."

Tadhg smiled. "In his own country, I believe it is a suitable choice for a nobleman. I have revised my opinion of the fellow, I must admit. This is a man of balance and fairness, one who speaks his mind and knows how to listen. He has been much interested in what I have to tell. It's hard to believe he means your uncle any ill."

Nessa nodded. She was watching a rock pool. Small creatures like drowned stars clung to its underwater crevices, and
tiny glinting fish darted among fronds of impossibly green
weed. "But you're still worried, aren't you?" she asked him.
"You feel what I feel: a shadow, a danger."

Tadhg sighed. "I can't say, Nessa. I've seen them put aside
the instruments of war, and demonstrate they can work hard
and live in harmony with the folk of the land here, at least while
times are good. There may be many worthy men among them."

"But?"

"It seems to me this is a little like making an agreement with
some wild beast. The creature comes down from the hills and
sits by your door, and you feed him. He behaves like a well-
trained dog. Maybe he even guards your house. Then something changes, some small thing, and suddenly he remembers
what he is. One night he hears the call of his ancestors, the summons of a pagan god. On an instant, this is a savage beast of the
wild again, and you are at his mercy. I've no wish to see that
visited on these islands. Your uncle is a great and wise ruler.
The Folk are not aware, perhaps, of how rich they are in God's
blessings. Maybe they will not recognize what they have until it
is lost."

"Don't say that!" Nessa turned to stare at him, alarmed by
these words. "How can you even think such a thing? It cannot
be lost! Anyway, if your stories are true, then there's supposed
to be good in everyone. Doesn't your god love even sinners?"

Tadhg regarded her gravely. "Indeed. God is in all of us.
Some are clothed in the brightness of the Holy Spirit, and
goodness shines from them, a goodness which has its source
deep within. Such a sweet wellspring never runs dry. No force
of evil can pollute its clear water. But some are weaker vessels,
and that small spark of the divine is hidden far within them. It
takes a brave man or woman, Nessa, to open up his very being
and examine what is there: to lay his soul bare to that burning
light. Such a choice is fearful indeed, for one must recognize
the fear and anguish, the deceit and duplicity, the lust and the
violence, all the wretchedness that mortal man bears in his essential clay. Yet, if a man dare open himself to God's love, his
sins are forgiven and the path made new. That is the wondrous
truth of which our Lord Jesus told. It is the way of light. And

even a savage warrior may be touched by grace. God loves all his creatures, the strong and the weak alike, and rejoices in their difference."

Nessa was silent a long time, gazing at the long gray form of a seal as it rolled lazily, scratching its back on the reef, exposing a pale belly to the sun.

"I like that idea, about being forgiven and able to start again, even if you've done really evil things," she said eventually. "Still, I have never understood why this god of yours resembles a man. There are forces so much more powerful than men and women, binding everything together. That is our faith, to observe the rituals for the turning of the year, to honor the power of moon and sun, the spirits that send rain and warmth to make our barley grow lush and fair and to nurture sweet grasses for cattle and sheep. We respect the forces of earth and ocean, binding and eternal. We open our hearts to the voices of the ancestors. If we do not heed those powers we are nothing, less fit to live on this earth than the wild creatures, who understand this wisdom in their very being. It seems to me there can be no more potent gods than these."

Tadhg was smiling. "Perhaps, at heart, they are the same," he said.

Nessa was ill at ease, and took to spending more and more of her time in the women's place. It was safe here. Here, between the folds of the land, close by the tower in the earth, sweet water welled from the ground, and low bushes grew to fringe the edges of the pool it made. In spring, primrose and celandine brightened the grassy banks; in summer the air was alive with the calls of meadow birds, and in the distance was the great soothing music of the sea. Here Nessa could carry out her work in peace. There were divinations to be performed and signs to be read. There were the times of trance, when one might hear tales. These tales were maps and warnings, lore and guidance. What they told was past and future, the way of the Folk. When the women gathered for the earth feast, at the time when the year turned dark, Rona would tell them of what she had heard, and what the season to come might hold for them. When Rona was gone, this task would be Nessa's.

In the sanctuary of the women's place, she could make the patterns: smooth pebbles, tiny bones, feathers and shells laid out on the smooth-raked earth by the spring. She could chant invocations and sing songs and whisper secrets with only the wild creatures of the island to hear her. There was Rona, of course, but Rona often seemed less a woman than part of the fabric of the place itself. She was increasingly silent these days, not teaching in words or demonstrations, simply sitting, blotched hands folded in her lap, watching and listening as Nessa did what must be done to keep the Light Isles whole and the Folk safe and wise. And when Nessa told her she was worried, for since the men had come from the snow lands there was a shadow on the moon, a darkness in the water, a wrongness in the sigh of the west wind, Rona simply nodded, as if she understood all too well, but there was nothing she could do about it. That made Nessa still more anxious, and she began to fear returning home lest some ill news await her. But Rona would not let her stay in the women's place for good, not yet.

"You're not ready," she said. "You're younger than you think, child. Go on, go home. They still need you there, and I can wait. I'm not so old yet." And, as if to belie her own words, she smiled, awaking myriad wrinkles in her ancient, wise-eyed face.

One day as Nessa walked home along the weed-strewn shore, she saw a man sitting on the rocks, watching the sky. He had his back to her, but his identity was instantly plain from the way he sat. She did not need to see the bright yellow hair or the big axe on his back or the gray pelt he wore on his shoulders to know this. No other man she had ever seen could be so motionless, as if he were part of the very rock that supported him. Nessa passed well behind him, keeping as quiet as she could, but she wondered what he was thinking. He gazed up into the clouds as if he hoped to hear some voice there, or see some vision. He stared as if hungry for answers. It seemed to Nessa that he was not happy. Perhaps he did not like the islands. Maybe he was homesick for a wife or sweetheart. Well, his wait would be over soon enough if her uncle made the sensible choice. Autumn would come, and these men would sail their boats home, and all would be as it had been before. Nessa shivered as she passed him. It was not so, of course. You could never go back. She glanced over her shoulder, expecting to see the fellow still seated on the rocks unmoving. But now he was standing, watching her as she walked away toward the Whaleback. As quiet as she had been, still he had heard her footsteps above the roar of the sea, above the scream of the gulls. The man's ears were as finely tuned as a night owl's. She pulled her hood up over her head and walked on. Closer to the causeway were more of the Norsemen, three big warriors, and two of her uncle's guards talking to them; it was some sort of deputation, maybe. As she scuttled past, one of them gave a piercing whistle of summons, and Nessa sensed, rather than saw, the yellow-haired man move away from the sea and back toward his companions. She fled across the narrow path to the Whaleback, and safety.

Engus invited the strangers to another feast before harvest began. This time the king allowed his nieces to sit at table, but Nessa would not. She hovered in the shadows, an unseen observer. She had spoken to her uncle, and he had listened gravely, but pointed out that her misgivings were not supported by evidence. So he had made his decision. But Nessa would not break bread with these folk; to do so seemed to her dangerous, and she would have no part of it. Tonight, Ulf's wife sat there beside him, a girl with a very straight back and a regal carriage of the head. She was no blond giantess, but shapely, red-haired, and composed in her manner. On her other side sat the one called Somerled, and from the place where Nessa stood she could see how the hands of these two met and clasped beneath the table, out of folk's sight.

"I have observed you over the summer," Engus was saying. "You have worked hard, not stinting your efforts to aid those who needed help, and never transgressing the boundaries we established for good conduct. You have extended the hand of friendship, and shared what you had. Your good will has warmed us. We have welcomed your presence."

Ulf inclined his head courteously.

"Still, such a decision is not lightly made," said Engus. "We hold our land dear; it is a realm of deep beauty, rich in the bounty of earth and ocean. And it is old: old and powerful. We do not share it readily, for to do so is to risk what is beyond any price. It is a measure of the faith I hold in you, Lord Ulf, in your honesty and vision, that I decide thus. You may remain here, keeping the houses I gave you and building more as you require them. I will negotiate the purchase of land where it is owned; I will ensure your holdings can carry stock and yield good crops. I also offer the services of my stud bull, and ten good heifers to add to your own two. I'll take my choice of the calves in spring."

"We are indebted to you, my lord." Ulf could not contain the smile that spread across his usually well-disciplined features. "This is welcome news indeed."

A roar of approval greeted the translation of Engus's words, accompanied by thumping of the table and raising of cups.

"There are certain conditions," Engus went on, and the noise died down. "I require a pledge of peace. Your folk will respect my borders and my people. They will honor the land and its ancient signposts."

"I give you my word," said Ulf solemnly, "and my word is good. I speak for every Norseman here."

"Understand well," Engus went on, "that I am sole king of this land, and that while your kind live here, you will obey the laws of the Folk. I care not what gods you worship, what rituals you observe; that is your own choice, though no doubt Brother Tadhg here will try to change your ways. He works daily on our own recalcitrant minds to little avail. I offer a single warning, but one which must never be forgotten. These islands are full of ancient powers. You have seen the place of standing stones. These markers hold together the very fabric of the Light Isles. They are far older than the Folk; they were set there by hands whose bones were the very bones of the earth herself. There are other such places, other such signs. Interfere with them at your peril."

"I understand," said Ulf. "The stones are indeed wondrous. A man would be a fool not to recognize their importance."

Engus nodded. "Then we are friends and allies from this day onward. Let this treaty be sworn with due ceremony in three days time. We shall meet at the Great Stone of Oaths, and there make our vow of peace and friendship under the eyes of the ancestors. Let all men here be present at that time."

"In our homeland," commented Ulf's adviser, Olaf Sveinsson, with a frown, "such an oath must be ring-sworn; only then is it truly binding. A fine circle of gold, sacred to Odin or to Thor, allows the gods themselves to bear witness to the solemnity of such a promise."

"A ring?" queried Engus. "If that is your custom, what I propose should satisfy you well. The place of our ritual will permit this vow to be doubly sacred, and doubly strong. When we meet for the swearing you will understand my meaning."

Even so was it done. Nessa had the account of it from Kinart, for this oath was between men, and even the priestess of the Folk did not attend at such a swearing. Her cousin told her how, at the appointed time, the men of the islands had gathered around the sacred stone, which stood majestically alone in the fields close by the place of the greater and lesser circles, in that part of the land where lake shone under sky, where cloud lay drowned in water, where wind whistled around the ancient monoliths and sang across the buried chambers. In this place, margins met and blurred; the elements merged, and the ancestors whispered in the ear of any true son of the Folk. A vow made here, on the Great Stone of Oaths, was as binding as any promise might be. No man dared break such an oath.

The men from the snow lands marched up to join the islanders, led by the solemn Ulf and his brother, Somerled. There were the advisers, the men-at-arms, the wolfskin-clad guards. They took their places in the circle, and Ulf and Engus advanced to stand by the tall stone, a veritable giant pierced by a single, round hole: the mark of a god's angry fist, one of the visitors had suggested, but Engus had explained calmly that it was an eye. Swear on this, and the ancestors would be watching you every moment to ensure you kept faith. It was also a passage, a portal between worlds. Thus, to make a promise this way meant you understood what these islands were, how they contained not just the human life that tilled their fields and fished their seas, but a deeper, more secret life, the life of earth, the spirit of the ancestors. Ulf had nodded gravely at Tadhg's translation, saying nothing.

As to the ritual itself, it was quite simple, and all could see clearly how it satisfied the requirements of both Engus's folk and Ulf's. Both ring and stone were here present in one; the treaty would indeed be doubly sworn. Through the hole in the looming monolith, Ulf clasped the king's hand, and each bowed his head. There was a silence, and then Engus's voice rang out:

"Let not sword be raised, nor bow be drawn, nor fist be loosed in anger between my folk and yours!"

And Ulf repeated the vow, pleasing Engus's men mightily by using the tongue of the Folk. He did not yet understand this language, but was learning as quickly as he could, seeing the advantage of it. A flock of small birds flew overhead at the moment he spoke, circling once before they headed westward, and this was generally considered a good omen. A cheer went up from the men, and Engus came around to clasp Ulf by the shoulder, a smile transforming his bearded face. The agreement was made.

The barley was ripening toward harvest time, a fine crop this year. Ulf's people were busy constructing their new dwelling houses, building stone walls, fashioning thatched roofs, coming to terms with the fact that they were staying. Those who were bound home for Rogaland were tending to the ships, getting them ready for another voyage. They had moved the vessels to a bay in the south, finding that place more suited to the mending and rebuilding work required. The local fisherfolk had been generous in the provision of accommodation and supplies. Brother Tadhg took his small satchel and his book of stories and returned to Holy Island, and he took Ulf with him to see the settlement the brothers had made in that unlikely place. Seals formed an escort as his frail craft bobbed away through the tide race.

With scythe and sickle, rake and pitchfork, the Folk began the harvest under fair skies. They had gathered perhaps half of the ripe grain before the sickness came. It crept up on them as subtly as a midsummer dusk, starting as a tickling cough, a dripping nose, a slight fever. First one man had it and recovered, then his brother took sick and worsened. Before seven days were gone he was laid in his grave, stone dead. It began to pass between them like a sudden fire, taking man, woman, and child without discrimination. It was like no plague the Folk had ever seen before, swift and deadly. Many remedies were tried; none worked. The harvest was abandoned, for within one cycle of the moon there were only two occupations for a man or woman not already dead or dying: tending the sick, and digging graves.

Amongst the newcomers, few succumbed and none died. Ulf's wife, Lady Margaret, set her people to helping as best she could. But there was little that could be done in the face of such a scourge, and they had their own folk to tend to. Engus himself remained healthy; his son, Kinart, was briefly ill, but rallied soon. Others of the king's household were not so lucky. Engus sent his men forth among the people to offer what aid they could; his men sickened and died. The farmhouses were shuttered. Within, lonely survivors wept in shadowed rooms. In the fields, sons buried their fathers; by cold hearths, mothers keened for lost children. Ulf's men rescued the barley left standing in the fields and stored it away before rain came. That was a small mercy. He used his hunting dogs to seek out wandering stock, but they could not be everywhere. Sheep fell into gullies and starved; eagles stole autumn lambs.

Nessa knew little of this at the time, for she lay shivering and burning, trapped in feverish visions. She dreamed she was bound up in tight ropes and held near flames; she dreamed she was being chased by slavering monsters, and running through quicksand. She dreamed of skulls with empty eyes, dead husks whose features she recognized. She thought her mother was there, and then gone. The serving girl looked after her a while, and then she, too, was gone, and the only one around was Brother Tadhg, which was odd, because he had gone home. He was sponging her face with a cloth and making her drink water, but she didn't want to, she was tired, she was so tired . . .

She was sick for a long time, and when at last her head came back to itself, the autumn was almost gone. She tried to get out of bed, but her legs gave way under her and she fell in a heap on the floor. There was nobody else in the girls' quarters, nobody at all. And it was quiet: so quiet that for a moment of sheer terror she wondered if she were the only one left, of all of them. Then Tadhg came back and sat her on the bed, blanket-swathed, and made her drink soup. He would not talk to her until she had finished it all. Then, because Nessa refused to let him go without telling her what had happened, he gave her the truth. The sickness had taken almost half the Folk on the home island, and more than half the household on the Whaleback. They did not know about the other islands yet. The old woman, Rona, had survived, and had been venturing out with potions for the sick. Engus was well, and so was Kinart now. Indeed, Kinart had been quite a hero, helping maintain supplies of food to all the farms, and making a trip across to fetch Tadhg and Ulf. The

Christians themselves had not escaped unscathed, for the two local lads who had joined them on Holy Island were both dead now, burned up by the sickness.

The account was as yet incomplete.

"My mother?" whispered Nessa.

A shadow passed over Tadhg's calm features. "She has been gravely ill, my dear," he told her gently. "Near death. She is past the worst now, but much weakened. When you are stronger, I will take you to see her."

There was another silence. Nessa found that this time she did not have the will to ask. She closed her eyes, feeling slow tears begin to well as Tadhg's quiet voice continued its litany of loss.

"Your sisters . . . your two sisters are both gone, Nessa. I'm sorry. I'm so sorry that I must bring you this terrible news. Sometimes God wills it thus; he gathers the innocent and the good to be with him, to pass straight to that heavenly realm where all is light and grace. Now you feel only pain; you cannot see beyond the darkness of your own grief. In time, you will understand that they are in a better place, a place where there is no sadness."

But Nessa pulled the blanket over her face and turned away from him, and would not be comforted. Anger burned like a small flame within her: anger at herself for being so weak and helpless she could not even get out of bed; her sisters had died right here and she had not even known, she hadn't done a single thing to help them. Anger at Tadhg for his words that meant nothing, for his faith that was lies, all lies. Anger at her uncle, too. He had changed the way things were. He had welcomed strangers to the Light Isles, and made a new pattern. Then the sickness had come, and now the Folk were weakened and the cycle unbalanced. If Engus had left things as they were, maybe this would not have happened. No wonder she had felt uneasy, seeing those men with their big axes made welcome at her uncle's table.

There was a little time, brief enough, when she let despair overwhelm her and sat weeping in the dark. But she forced herself to recover, for there was no longer any time to waste. She made herself eat, though all food tasted like sand. She made herself walk, though every part of her body felt limp as a hank of spun wool. She went to see her mother, who sat listless on a bench, hair uncombed, hands idle in her lap, staring out toward the sea. It became immediately apparent that Nessa herself must take some sort of charge here, young as she was. There were few serving folk left. Those who had not perished were away tending their own families in scattered farmhouse or cottage. Engus had gone to assess how many islanders remained, what stock had been let wander, what damage autumn storms had done to ill-guarded homes. Ulf had come with his big guards and made a formal offer of help, though all knew he was already doing as much as he could for them. Kinart was organizing a small group of fishermen to maintain supplies and bring boats up to safety before winter. That left Nessa to keep the pitiful remnant of Engus's household in order, and she did. There was no time for the mysteries, no time for the women's place.

By autumn's end, the sickness had run its course, and the survivors were putting things to rights as best they could. There were one or two, like Nessa's mother, who might never quite get over it. But life had to go on. There had been hard times before: harsh winters, cattle plagues, war with the tribes of the Caitt. The wisdom of the ancestors had enabled the Folk to endure such reversals. They would continue to survive. It was whispered that perhaps it was just as well Ulf and his snow giants had come when they did, since the Folk had lost so many good people this season. At least there would be strong men for plowing, in the spring.

As for Nessa, she was glad to be busy. It stopped her from thinking too much. When she thought, she grew very angry, so angry she had to go away from the settlement and stand alone at the western end of the Whaleback, on the clifftop, letting the wind and the sea spray sting her skin and whip her long hair into a flag of defiance. Sometimes she would find herself screaming like a wild creature into the gale. Sometimes she wept. She never returned to the settlement until the signs of her anguish were quite erased from her features. There was a rain pool up there in which you could see an image of yourself. She knew that person in the water was someone different from the Nessa of last spring, who had walked the cliff paths and bright shores of the island and never dreamed her people's lives could hold such pain. The creature who looked up at her now had the same gray eyes; her hair was still long and brown and wind-tangled. But she was paler and thinner, and her expression was quite changed. There was a sort of shadow in it, as if she had lost something, or perhaps had found something she didn't want, but must keep forever.

Once she came across Tadhg standing quietly by the place where her folk were laid in the earth, so many, her sisters among them. There was a cairn over them, stones layered neatly. In time, a green turf blanket would soften it. Tadhg's lips were moving. His hands held the plain wooden cross that he wore around his neck, and all of a sudden Nessa could not control her feelings.

"Stop it! Stop it!" she screamed, running at him and grabbing his hands so that the cross fell back against his robe, swinging on its rough cord. "They don't want your prayers, they can't hear your words of wisdom! These are lies anyway, all lies! Your faith is a web of falsehoods! If your god is so gentle and forgiving, if he loves the innocent and pure of heart, why did he let my sisters die?"

Tadhg did not reply at once. He stood quietly as she hit him with her two fists; he watched as she stepped away, clutching her arms around herself in an attempt to contain her fury. At last he said, "God is love, Nessa. He gathers your sisters to his heart, and heals all their suffering. They look down on you smiling. God loves all his children."

"It's not true! Everyone died, little babies, old men, hard-working folk, all kinds of people. How can you say everything's all right when it's so wrong? My sisters died before they could grow up and be married and have children, before they could do anything. There's no reason at all for that. Why were my people taken, and the strangers spared? We have not deserved this, it is cruel and unjust. I spit on your god and his false words of love. I despise him."

"Now, Nessa," said Tadhg, "you do not believe me, I know, but this will become easier to bear in time."

"How can it?" Nessa snapped, furious with his patience.

"It will," he said. "You will never forget them, but you will put them away in your memory, and move on. We all do."

There was a silence.

"Tell me," said Tadhg, "do you think if I were not here, and you had never heard of Jesus Christ and his teachings, this plague would not have come?"

"No," she conceded.

"Who would you have blamed then?" asked Tadhg softly. "This is not his doing, and it is not the fault of Ulf's people. They have shown their strength and their kindness during this dark time; my opinion of them is changing. Now come, shall we walk back together? I find prayers helpful. Why not seek answers in your own faith? We must heal our wounds in whatever way we can."

After that, Nessa made time to walk on the shore and look at the patterns on the stones. She went south down the coast to the high cliffs and sat in a hollow looking out to the west, hearing the seabirds squabbling on the ledges below, not so many at this time of year but still enough to set the air alive around her. She stood on the rocks where she had seen the silent warrior, and watched the sea. These journeys were indeed a kind of prayer, her own kind. The hurt did not seem to lessen, not when little things kept reminding her: a bone comb carved with seals, which had been her sister's, left behind in a corner of a shelf; a pair of green felt slippers, which had been her other sister's, and that she had always wanted for herself. Now the slippers sat by her bed, and she could not bear to put them on.

And all the time, Engus's eyes were on her, assessing, appraising. For everything had changed. Her uncle had been proud to see her become Rona's student, proud of what she would be for the Folk. But that was before. Since the sickness, the family was no longer rich in girls. Kinart could not take his father's place. The royal line was the women's line; it had always been thus, for such a manner of succession ensured strong blood and meant disputes between kin were few. In the space of a season's turning, Nessa had become the last princess of the Folk, and it was no longer possible that she devote her life to the mysteries. If the crown were not to pass to the Caitt, Nessa must wed and bear a son: a son who would one day be king of the Light Isles.

SIX

Once he had counted kills. Now he counted days, endless days until they might at last take ship for home. Thor's voice had grown faint as a whisper, so far away he strained to hear it. These islands were no place for a warrior.

Eyvind had hoped Ulf's building plans might include a temple. That way at least the rituals might be observed, the sacrifices made. That way at least Thor might understand this was temporary, an exile imposed purely by a quirk of Somerled's thinking. Soon enough, both longship and knarr would be on the way back to Rogaland, and Eyvind and Eirik would be going home: home to the Jarl's court, home to a life of honor and pride, serving the god with axe and sword. But Ulf had built no temple, and there were no rituals. Eyvind was obliged to call on Thor as best he could from lonely shore or desolate rock or open field. *I am your right hand! Do not forget me!*

Others were of different mind. Hakon had lost no time at all. Perhaps he could not hear so well anymore, but that had not slowed his other faculties. With remarkable promptness, he had moved out of Ulf's settlement and into the isolated cottage of a comely young widow with two small sons. And, Eirik commented with a grin, by the look of the widow's burgeoning figure, another infant was already on the way. Hakon looked as sleek and content as a well-fed cat. They took wagers on who'd be next to move out; Thord was top of the list. His lively slave girl had him wrapped around her little finger, and it was common knowledge that she preferred her man to be close to home, where she could keep an eye on him. It wouldn't be long before this battle-scarred warrior succumbed to her coaxings and put aside his sword in favor of a plow or fishing net.

It shocked Eyvind that a Wolfskin might change thus, as if Thor's call no longer inspired him. The islands had done that.

They had woven a kind of magic that made men forget who they were and what vows they were bound by.

There had been work of a sort. At first, Ulf had maintained a personal guard: two close by him, two more at a slight distance, others carefully placed to observe. But there had been no attacks, no plotting, no threats. There was nothing to see but a summer of cooperation and hard labor on the land. Now Ulf had all but dispensed with his Wolfskins' services, saying he had an agreement with King Engus, and there would be no need for fighting until such time as they might stand side by side with the islanders against some common enemy. He posted Eirik in the south to oversee the maintenance of the ships, and to ensure all was well with those who had remained there. The crew of the knarr had not joined Ulf's settlement, but sat out the summer months among the fisherfolk who dwelt near that peaceful anchorage, which Ulf had named Hafnarvagr, haven bay. In the north, Erlend and Grim and the others were as often found shifting stones or cutting heather for thatch as sharpening their weapons and rehearsing the moves of combat.

With time on his hands, Eyvind observed. He saw that Ulf was much away. At first he was establishing boundaries, planning houses and a hall, negotiating the purchase of stock and supplies. Later, he seemed to spend a great deal of time with Engus's translator, the Christian priest. Tadhg was a slightly built, harmless-looking fellow. Nobody took his ideas seriously; nobody, that is, except Ulf. Ulf found them interesting. Indeed, he found them so interesting he would be gone for days at a time, traveling to that island where the fellow and his followers lived a life of privation and solitude, quite happy to exist on a fish or two, a broth of boiled seaweed, and a day shaped by prayer. Each time Ulf returned from these sojourns he was quieter and more remote. His dark features began to assume the same serenity of expression as one could see in the eyes of the translator. Folk started to talk, and the talk was uneasy. Surely their chieftain would not abandon the old gods? Was it possible that Ulf, whom they so admired and respected, might turn against Odin? It could not be so. Still, the whispers continued.

Somerled had surprised Eyvind. Somerled, accustomed to the clever talk and complex games of court, did not chafe at the restrictions of this new life. He did not long for home as Eyvind did. Somerled, who had ever been a solitary fellow, now had a tight circle of friends and followers, and they were not smooth courtiers such as himself, but tough, working men. Among them were the crewmen from the knarr, and others who were, at best, on the periphery of Ulf's household: a farrier, a smith, one or two who had been housecarls. All were men without families, men who had made the voyage alone. There were no islanders in Somerled's group. They would meet of an evening at the dwelling house that the knarr's crew shared in Hafnarvagr and drink ale together, and Somerled would teach them games with dice and tell tales that made them roar with laughter.

It was at about this time that Somerled acquired another name, and increased his popularity still further into the bargain. Ulf's people lacked horses, and in this land horses were an essential commodity, since the gentle contours and complete lack of forests made riding the most efficient means of getting about. Engus had provided Ulf with some strong, heavy creatures for farm work, and a riding animal for his personal use; any further requirements must be purchased from the local landholders, and not all of them had much need for the silver jewelry or fine furs offered in exchange. This was a frugal country where each animal had its own unique value.

So, when a farmer named Gernard offered to sell a fine young stallion for a bag of scrap silver to whatever man could stay on its back to the count of twenty, there was plenty of interest. The fact that the offer was made in the drinking hall late at night only added to the number of enthusiastic takers. Had Eyvind been present that night, he might himself have acquired a horse and perhaps a name as well, but Eyvind was occupied in the north, and heard it all later from an astonished Thord. They'd gathered at the fellow's farm the morning after the offer had been made, most of them a little the worse for wear, and once they'd seen the stallion with its twitching tail and rolling eyes and its nervous, sidling gait, all of a sudden there were only three men left who really wanted a bargain. One of the three was Somerled.

It was plain the creature was quite mad and scarcely worth even the low price mentioned. They'd barely begun to count before the first fellow was sprawled on the ground, groaning and clutching his side. Broken ribs, possibly: bruised pride, certainly. They hauled him back over the stone wall, and the second man went in. The stallion was tied; it wore a rudimentary halter with a long rope fastened to a hook in the barn wall. Three men had to hold the rope before Einar Long-Nose could get on the horse's back. When they let go, he dug his fists into its mane and clung with his knees, his face turning the color of soft cheese, and before they counted to six he, too, was tossed from his perch, narrowly avoiding cracking his head on the stones that bordered the horse yard.

"Not worth the risk," Einar growled, clambering back to safety as the stallion reared, flailing with its hooves and sending men scattering. "Creature like that'll never be any good to ride. Look at its eyes."

"You think?" Somerled was rolling up his sleeves, frowning a little, dark eyes thoughtful as he regarded the plunging, thrashing animal. "Perhaps it only needs to be shown who's in charge here. Give me a hand, will you?"

There were theories afterward about how Somerled had done it. Some said it was because he was light and agile; some put it down to raw courage. Everyone knew the man was no athlete. There was talk that he used a goad of some kind and terrified the creature into submission. The exact details of it hardly mattered; all present that day agreed that Ulf's brother had indeed managed to stay on the wild horse's back for the allotted time, and in addition, caused the stallion to give up its fight and stand in shivering, trembling submission. Somerled had dismounted and walked calmly over to the owner, Gernard, while reaching into his pouch to pull out the animal's price: a small bag of scrap silver.

"Never underestimate me," Somerled had said, according to Thord's account. "It is only a horse, after all."

That night he had taken them all back to the drinking hall, and amid much laughter and festivity they had given him his second name: they called him Somerled Horse-Master. In a way, the news did not surprise Eyvind. With Somerled, one always expected the unexpected. If his boldness had acquired him a fine animal, albeit a somewhat troublesome one, good luck to him. The name had a certain ring to it. Eyvind was glad he himself had not yet acquired something similar, for he had long feared the choice would be Little Ox, and he did not know how he would explain that to his mother.

* * *

One could not fault Margaret's efforts to be a good wife. When the sickness had come, and cut the islanders down like so many fragile stalks of wheat, it was she who'd dispatched men and women to help, it was she who'd admonished those too fearful to enter a plague-ridden house, and bade them put others first for a change. Many days had passed before Ulf was fetched back from Holy Island. By the time that happened, Margaret had the harvest organized, and men digging graves, and women making soup and tending to motherless infants. Eyvind wondered if she herself were sick, for the elegant girl of Freyrsfjord now looked wan and tired, with a grim set about her mouth, which showed no sign of disappearing when her husband returned to add his own offers of help to those she had already set in place. Ulf thanked his wife before the whole household for what she had done in his absence, but there was a certain stiffness, a formality about it, and Eyvind saw the look of hurt in Margaret's eyes. Privately, he thought Ulf's wife would have greatly preferred her husband just to put his arms around her, hold her close, and tell her he loved her. He wondered if Ulf had thought of this, or whether the passions that compelled him to a new shore, a new faith, had driven the importance of something so simple out of his mind. Perhaps Ulf had forgotten how young his wife was.

When Somerled came back to the north, riding his newly won horse and leading two more, a slight flush appeared on Margaret's pale cheeks and a trace of the old brightness returned to her eyes. It seemed not at all inappropriate for the two of them to go out riding, with Eyvind as their chosen escort. They might travel inland, Ulf suggested, and see what traces of game might be found in the hills there, for the men had been complaining of the constant diet of fish, supplemented only by a hare or two. Eyvind took his axe and a bow, expecting to use neither. It was an insult to Thor, he thought, that he was reduced thus to a token guard, and as soon as he got back to Rogaland he would set that to rights. It could not be long now. Delay much further and they would miss the autumn viking altogether.

Margaret and Somerled rode ahead, Eyvind behind. He could not hear what they said to each other. The day was fair;

later in the afternoon, a mist would roll in from the sea and blanket hill and crag and glittering waterway in a thick veil of damp. There was a pattern to this, which he had learned to recognize. They must not go too far, for to ride home in such a mist was to invite trouble. And they had not journeyed east as Ulf suggested, but far to the southwest, into a wild place, a forbidden place, part of King Engus's own realm.

"Somerled," Eyvind called as they rode farther toward the coast. "We're already across the boundary. You'll find no game here. What about Engus's sentries? We're in breach of your brother's agreement."

Somerled glanced back over his shoulder. "I wouldn't worry yourself with it, Eyvind," he said. "These islanders have scarcely enough folk left to draw water and catch fish for their supper: certainly none to bother with keeping us off their land. Besides, I have something to show Margaret."

With that, he kicked his horse to a canter, and Margaret's mount followed, and there was nothing for it but to go after them, cursing Somerled's propensity for disregarding rules whenever it pleased him.

It was quite a long way. At last they came to a place where the land fell away sharply, and there, far below, the sea smashed in great plumes of white on a jumble of unforgiving rocks. Somerled dismounted and helped Margaret down.

"We need to walk a little farther," he said. "That way, over the rise. It's too dangerous for the horses. You'd best stay here, Eyvind, and watch them. We won't be long."

"But—" Eyvind began.

Somerled's brows rose. "You're a bodyguard, not a nursemaid," he said. "And we're under no threat here, I told you. Why would the islanders attack us? I'm Ulf's brother, after all."

"But—"

"It's all right, Eyvind," Margaret said. "Somerled will look after me."

And when Eyvind looked at the two of them, standing there side by side, he saw that their mouths had the same set, and their eyes the same expression, and it seemed to him that whatever was between them, the working out of it was quite beyond his power to stop.

"Poor Eyvind," Somerled said with a half smile. "Don't

think so hard—it hurts your head and does you no good at all. Enjoy the day. Enjoy the view."

But Eyvind could not. All the time he waited for them to come back, he felt a shadow over himself, and Ulf, and Margaret, and the whole of the crazy endeavor that had brought them to this far corner of the world. He was jumping to conclusions, he told himself. Surely Somerled would not take advantage of his brother's wife? Surely Margaret would not betray a man as transparently good as Ulf? Probably they only wanted a chance to talk in private together. Margaret was unhappy, a blind man could see that. And Somerled had been her friend; they understood one another. Perhaps she only wanted to tell him her troubles. Why, then, did he feel so worried, why did that sense of dread hang over him? Even if his worst suspicions were true, it would not be the first time such a breaking of the marriage vows had happened. It might be over quickly, and Ulf never the wiser.

Eyvind waited while the horses cropped the meager grasses near the clifftop. He watched the birds circling and the clouds gathering to the south. He thought about the sickness, and the people he had helped bury, small infants just days old, young women of Margaret's age, old men laid hastily in earth without due ritual, since there was barely time to attend to one burial before the next must come. They were a strange folk, little and dark. There was something about these people and this land that suggested secrets, mysteries hidden below the surface. The hills here were dotted with ancient mounds, the dunes with half-buried structures of neatly laid slabs. You'd be walking across open ground and come suddenly upon some great standing stone, lichen-crusted, a monumental thing like a huge earth troll, and you could hardly go by without asking its permission. He wondered if the people, too, were not quite what they seemed; he had sensed this. Brother Tadhg, now: who'd have thought such a plain little fellow could wield such influence over a strong leader like Ulf? The rumors were increasing daily in the drinking hall; they whispered that Ulf would be baptised a Christian before Yuletide. It seemed that Tadhg had strengths not visible on the surface. And there was that girl, Eyvind had only seen her once, on the beach down by the tidal island, on a day when misery had sent him farther than he should have gone, to seek Thor in the thunderous expanses of the western sky. Her footsteps had been soft as a wren's, but something had made him turn, and when he saw her, he couldn't tell if she were human or spirit, a waif of a thing with long hair streaming in the wind, and eyes such as he'd never seen before, the palest sea-gray with a darker rim to them. She'd fled, as if by looking he had uncovered something best left untouched. He wondered if she had died with the rest of them.

It was a long wait. When at last Somerled and Margaret returned, it seemed to Eyvind that they had quarrelled. Margaret's lips were set tight, her dark eyes angry.

Somerled wore a mask of nonchalance. "It's a fine spot," he said. "A great rock stack, like a giant standing in the ocean with the waves breaking over its feet. Quite a spectacle. We'll wait, if you want to go and take a look."

"We should head for home before the mist comes in," said Eyvind tightly. "You wouldn't want your new horse to break its leg, would you? And Ulf will be expecting us."

Somerled attempted a laugh. "You think so? For a man of vision, it is surprising how much my brother fails to see. Come on, then, I suppose we must go back some time."

Nobody asked Eyvind about this ride, and he did not speak of it. It was surely wiser to think the best of folk until the truth, whatever it was, became plain. If he spoke of his misgivings, to Eirik for instance, all he'd be doing was spreading rumors. Besides, he'd be going home to Norway soon, and they could work this out for themselves. Eirik might decide to make the trip again next spring, when Ulf would expect his ships to sail back with a cargo of timber and the other things he needed, but Eyvind would not be part of that voyage. It shouldn't be hard to convince the Jarl. He must simply acquit himself so well in this season's viking that he became quite indispensable.

It was around this time that Eyvind began to hear another kind of talk that disquieted him. Eirik knew of it, too; he commented that he could not for the life of him imagine where such notions came from, but his tone suggested he knew all too well. It was put about in Hafnarvagr that Ulf was missing an opportunity, with the islanders much weakened by the sickness. Instead of setting his folk on errands of mercy, people said, a real leader would seize the advantage and establish control while he could. There was fine land for the taking, perhaps even treasure hidden away in Engus's stronghold on the brough. Eyvind heard this sort of thing more than once, and reminded one fellow who said it that Ulf had given his word; there was a treaty. And someone commented that a treaty was only as good as the man who swore it. Everyone knew Ulf was about to put aside the old gods and let Brother Tadhg baptize him as a Christian. Where did that leave the rest of them? If enemies came, Ulf would not be prepared to take up arms, not if he followed a god of peace and forgiveness. If Ulf demanded that his people follow his example, the shoe would indeed be on the other foot. What was to stop Engus's barbarians from coming in the night and killing them all? And if the natives didn't account for them, Odin surely would, once he learned they'd turned their backs on him. Either way, they were doomed. When Eyvind pointed out that this was nonsense, somebody grumbled that if Ulf's own warriors couldn't see what was coming, they'd only have themselves to blame when they were cut to ribbons in their sleep. Treaty or no treaty, you couldn't trust folk who lived in such an outlandish place, full of monstrous stones and underground chambers with who knew what lurking in them.

Tomorrow, thought Eyvind. *Tomorrow, or the next day, or the next we will be gone, and I need never return here.* And it seemed to him Thor's voice grew stronger in his ear, and his heart beat more steadily, as if the drum were not so far beneath the surface. *Come then, my loyal son. Come home and wield your axe for me once more.*

Then Ulf called a Thing, a council to which all his people were summoned. It was the first such assembly in their new home, and Ulf had invited King Engus to attend as his guest, with four men of his household and Brother Tadhg. Ulf required the putting aside of all arms before folk entered the hall. Eyvind oversaw this process, laying the knives and spears of the islanders beside the handsome swords and axes, the hammers and bows of his own people in the anteroom. Some were not so keen to give up their weapons; that was why Eyvind had been given this job. It didn't pay to argue with a Wolfskin.

For the benefit of his guests Ulf explained the formal process. First, a law speaker would recite a portion of the body of legal wisdom, which it was his job to retain in his memory. The usual rule was that one-third was presented at each Thing. This was to keep the laws clear in men's minds. Then the cases would begin, perhaps only one if there were a major dispute over, say, a hall-burning or an ambush with multiple casualties. Respected men would be appointed judges for the case. Evidence would be heard and arguments presented for either party. Then, after deliberation, culpability would be apportioned and penalties determined. It was not uncommon for compensation to be paid up then and there, and the matter neatly concluded. Usually, Ulf explained, the system worked very well, since the parties agreed in advance to accept the decision of the judges as to guilt or innocence, and to abide by whatever punishment was chosen. Sometimes there was wrongdoing on both sides, and each must pay. King Engus nodded, and asked what penalties might be applied beyond the payment of restitution. Banishment, Ulf said, for a year, or three years, or forever. A man who chose to ignore that did so at his peril; he could expect a short life and a surprising death.

"Do you ever impose a punishment of execution?" Engus asked. "What of a man who harms a child, say, or defaces a place of ritual?"

Ulf shook his head. "We are not barbarians," he said. "Such a wrongdoer would be exiled beyond the borders of Rogaland, never to return."

"That's if he ever got as far as a trial," put in Eirik, and Ulf frowned at him. But Tadhg translated this comment faithfully, and King Engus gave a nod.

"So, justice might be done outside the walls of this assembly," he commented. "Here in the Light Isles, there is no need for such measures. For crimes such as those, the ancestors mete out their own punishment. A man who acted thus would certainly perish soon after, weighed down by guilt and crazed with fear."

"Indeed," said Ulf. "And how do you deal with lesser crimes? A family feud, perhaps, where violent deaths occur? A man who steals his neighbor's wife, or beats his own?"

"I am king here," Engus said. "These grievances are brought before me, and I am the sole arbiter. Such ill-doing is rare among my people. In the end, we are all subject to the old powers."

The Thing began. There were but two cases to be heard, and both of them trifling. One of the knarr's crew said another man had stolen a fine woolen cloak, a knife, and a sack of dried beans from his sea chest. They had come to blows over it. The second man accused the first of giving him a black eye and half blinding him; he'd never be the same again, he added piteously. Each had appointed Somerled to speak for him. It was unheard of that one man should represent both parties in a legal dispute, but Somerled did so with a dazzling display of wit and humor. By the end of it, everyone was bent double with laughter, including the two litigants themselves. The judges did not take long to reach a verdict, finding some merit on both sides, and some culpability. In the absence of any wealthy kin, Ulf offered to replace the cloak and knife, but not the beans, and he volunteered the services of his own physician to give the second fellow a look over and cure him if he could. The case was pronounced closed. They paused to take a meal.

Then there was a wrangle over a woman: more tricky, this, since she was one of Engus's folk. Two of the men had taken a fancy to her, and each claimed she'd given a promise of marriage. The judges sought Engus's advice. Engus suggested the girl be packed off home to her father on Sandy Island, and the fellows left to cool their heels awhile. With some reluctance they clasped hands and agreed, and that was the day's business over. But Ulf was not finished. He stood to address the assembled people. Eyvind had not been concentrating. He was keeping an eye on the weapons, making sure none disappeared before their owners came to claim them. Then, suddenly, he realized what Ulf was telling them.

"This plague has tried King Engus's folk very hard. They have lost many good souls, and are ill prepared for the winter. And they say the season here is harsh indeed: the wind a scourge, the seas merciless. The nights are very long. That is why I have decided thus. Our ships will winter over here in the islands. We will not send them back until after spring seeding. For it seems to me the need is great here. If all of us remain, we can support and aid these good folk who have so generously allowed us to make their home our own."

Eyvind's heart seemed to shrink down to a hard chip of ice. He had waited so long, all this time, and now, to be told this—it could not be endured. He had promised Jarl Magnus. He had promised Thor. Signe was expecting him. How could Ulf do this? It was as if he had no control over his own life anymore.

"This is generous indeed," said Engus, "and I thank you from my heart. There is, of course, still the matter of a cargo of timber which was promised me."

"I gave my word," Ulf replied, "and I have not forgotten. In spring my friend Eirik here will take my ships home, and arrange this gift for you. You will have your fine trunks of oak and pine by midsummer."

"It's not in any agreement of ours to stay here over the winter," growled the knarr's captain. The men around him wore heavy frowns. "We're working men, not idle courtiers who can afford to sit around twiddling their thumbs a whole season. We're expected back."

Somerled stepped forward. "You'll be compensated for your time, of course," he said smoothly. "Generously compensated. And I'll have work for you over the winter. You won't be idle."

"Thank you, my lord," the fellow said, somewhat mollified.

"I would remind you, too, that the knarr belongs to me," put in Ulf. "While you stay with her, you're under my command."

"You can buy a boat," the captain muttered, tight-jawed, "but you'll find it's not so easy to buy a man."

"Anyone can be replaced," said Ulf coolly. "Let's see if you are so ready with your comments in the spring."

It was that evening, over supper, that King Engus reminded Ulf of another promise: to sail the *Golden Dragon* across to High Island while the weather was still good enough. He would like to see the longship put through her paces. Besides, he wanted to show Ulf a place of magic there, a center of ritual, where it was customary for the men of the islands to gather once a year to reverence the sun. The significance of this offer was lost on nobody. Engus's words were greeted with a deep hush. By extending this invitation, he was recognizing Ulf as a part of the islands, not merely an ally but almost a kinsman.

"This is the first time," the king said, "that a man who is not of our people has been offered the chance to see this place. The terrain is difficult; we'll be gone a night or two."

Ulf nodded gravely. "I am honored by your trust," he said.

"Not tomorrow, but the next day, if the winds are fair, we shall set out on this short voyage."

"This king must think we are mountain goats, not men," observed Somerled as the *Golden Dragon* came in to shore at around midday. Above them rose the daunting flank of a great, bare hillside, the northern of High Island's two massive peaks. "I never thought I'd be grateful for all that running about in the hills above Hammarsby, but the practice may yet come in useful."

Eyvind grunted in response, watching as the pebbly shore below the dark rise of the land grew closer.

"Poor Eyvind," said Somerled. "So disappointed. You shouldn't be. I've told you, my brother is on a mission here; he cares for nothing but his own path. Maybe winter won't be so bad."

"It'll be long and dark," growled Eyvind, "and, unlike you, I get no pleasure from endless games of dice."

"There'll be work for you," Somerled said quietly.

"What work? Feeding pigs? Cutting turf?"

"We'll find something closer to your heart than that, old friend. Trust me."

They beached the *Golden Dragon* and, carrying their small packs, set off in King Engus's wake up a barely discernible path toward the hills. There was a hidden vale, Engus had said, a fair, sheltered place tucked away between these forbidding peaks, and there they would find an ancient tomb, carven from living stone before ever the Folk walked on this isle. Not all could go close; he would take Ulf to see it, and the others must wait at a distance. Then they would go on to the high cliffs on the island's western margin, for those were a wonder to behold.

They had taken a full complement on the *Golden Dragon*, to show her speed under oars: thirty for the crew, including Eyvind and Eirik, and with them Ulf and his brother. Engus had brought ten of his own warriors, and the indispensable Brother Tadhg.

Ulf was concerned for his ship's security. It seemed to him a high tide and a strong wind might be enough to drive her off the shingle and out to sea, leaving them stranded, but Engus said that would not happen. There would be the usual mist, no more; the ship would be safe, and so would they as long as they made camp while they could still see their noses before them. Best move quickly. Ulf was not convinced. The ship was his jewel, his treasure. So he left a good number of his men by the anchorage, and these were willing enough to stay behind, having seen the way that track went up and up like some pathway to the heavens themselves. They'd make a fire, and catch a few fish, and be ready when the others came back. Two of Engus's men remained with them.

Eyvind enjoyed that day. The pace was brisk, the climb hard. He liked that feeling, once so familiar, of pushing himself until every muscle in his body ached. Besides, the grandeur and beauty of the place were irresistible. For all the barrenness of the slopes, devoid of even the smallest tree, High Island put him in mind of home. This was a wild, dark, secret land, a land where there was not such a distance between man and god. His companions were mercifully silent, saving their flagging energy for the climb. Ulf's seasoned warriors struggled, panting and rubbing their backs, while the islanders seemed tireless. Evidently they were not such weaklings as their stature suggested.

They reached the sacred place, and waited by the track while Engus took Ulf close. It was a great stone, lying on its side like a stranded whale.

"It is a tomb," Brother Tadhg told them. "Hollowed out inside, with chambers and a passageway. Very old: hewed in a time before memory."

"What's it used for?" asked Holgar.

"I'm told it is a place of ritual, a men's place," Tadhg said. "They gather here on the day the year turns to light, and celebrate the sun's rising. It's said to ensure seeds germinate and crops grow lush."

"Looks like the work of giants," Eirik mused, "or maybe hill trolls. Something with great big hands and tools to match."

"How do you know all this?" Somerled challenged the priest. "It's clear you yourself cannot be part of this inner circle; your own faith must scorn such observances. You are an outsider. Do you not think these notions primitive? Sun worship?"

Tadhg smiled. "My adherence to the Christian faith has not

rendered me deaf and blind. There are many paths to wisdom, and they can be more closely aligned than they seem."

"Really?" Somerled's brows lifted. "And what of my brother, the worthy Ulf? Have you brought him around to your way of thinking yet? When can we expect to see him with a cross around his neck, and a penchant for forgiving those who murder his mother, or violate his sister?"

"Somerled!" Eyvind hissed. The other men glanced over, not prepared to speak, but plainly unsettled by this turn of the conversation.

"I can but ask," said Somerled.

"As to that," Tadhg replied, touching the wooden cross that hung around his own neck, "you must seek an answer from your brother. He is his own man: a man who thinks deeply, and does not reach decisions lightly. Our faith is not quite as you describe it. You should let me tell you, sometime."

"Huh," scoffed Somerled. "I need know no more than I do already. You may turn my brother away from the true faith of our homeland, but you'll have no luck with me, nor with a single one of our people. These beliefs are not for a red-blooded man. They are no more than a smokescreen to hide behind, when you lack the valor to defend what is yours with cold iron."

"But," Eyvind said, remembering the wolf, "a true measure of bravery, surely, is to walk toward your enemy with no weapons at all. A real hero wears only the armor of his own courage." He felt a blush of embarrassment rise to his cheeks, and hoped his words had not sounded too foolish.

Somerled laughed. "And you a Wolfskin, Eyvind! Shame on you! Where would you be without your big axe and your fine sword? Don't tell me you, too, are turning soft."

Tadhg seemed unperturbed. "Your friend speaks wisely," he said. "There is more than one kind of courage. I hope it does not take you too long to learn that."

Engus's men prepared a fire; turves of peat had been stored up here for just such a purpose, kept dry in a low stone hut. Eyvind went off with his bow and brought back two hares already starting to grow their white winter coats. Even here it seemed there was no bigger game to be found, no deer, not even the goats Somerled had mentioned. Somebody's sheep wandered on the lower slopes, but one could hardly shoot those.

Ulf was very quiet when he came back, as if what he had seen had set an awe on him that would linger far beyond this day. They ate their meal and walked on. One could not come all the way to High Island, Engus said, without going to the sea cliffs. There was a rock stack there, which surpassed even the stone giant off the coast south of the Whaleback. This was a veritable tower, majestic in its size, an ancient marker of boundaries. It was fitting that they should see it. There would be beds and a fire and roast mutton at the western settlement. In the morning they would return to the anchorage.

The climb had taken its toll. Some of Ulf's men stayed in the valley to make camp and hunt, and some decided to head back to the ship and wait the time out there. Engus sent two of his own men with each group; it was clear he was not prepared to leave any of Ulf's party on High Island unsupervised. It was therefore a much smaller group that made its way westward down to a fair bay then, after a rest that was all too brief, up and up again along the coast to a place lofty as an eagle's nest. The track was treacherous; Eyvind had never seen cliffs so high. Here and there the ground was crumbling; great chunks of it had split away and now stood on their own as if ready to collapse into the raging ocean on the slightest provocation. Birds screamed overhead. There were fissures and cracks in the rock, and the wind caught at hair and cloak, tugging him insistently toward the edge. He was glad he had no fear of heights.

It was nobody's fault that the mist came in early and swiftly. One moment they were striding along, wondering exactly what King Engus meant when he said it wasn't much farther, and the next they were enveloped in a thick, gray blanket and could scarcely see their own feet on the ground, let alone their companions. Eyvind halted. He heard Engus calling, and Tadhg translating, *Stop! Stop here!* They gathered in a hollow; it was quite clear they could not go on in any direction, not until morning. The plan had been to return to the western bay, where a scattering of fisherfolk dwelt, and spend the night there in relative comfort.

"I regret this greatly," Engus told them. "There is no choice but to settle down here and wait for tomorrow's sun to disperse this mist. Are we all accounted for?"

They moved in closer. Eirik was there, with long-legged Holgar and tow-haired Grim. But Ulf was not there, and neither was Somerled. And when King Engus counted his own men, two were missing. They called through the mist: "Ulf! Ulf, where are you? Somerled!" And once or twice, at first, they thought they heard a faint response. After a while, they stopped calling. The mist clung so close, it was no longer safe to attempt to bring a man to your side by sound, not with such treacherous ground to cover.

"With luck they're all together, as we are, and can shelter well enough till morning," Eirik said. "A pity we can't make a fire, they might see that. It'll be a long, cold night."

As Eyvind lay miserably awake, shivering under his wolfskin, the last thing he saw between the shreds of mist before the light faded was the straight-backed figure of Brother Tadhg, sitting with his wooden cross in his hand and his lips moving in prayer.

Morning came, and there was no sign of the others. Eyvind was eager to begin a search, for there was a chill feeling of dread creeping over him that could only be banished by immediate action. Engus made them wait. The mist still lingered, though a faint sun tried to pierce the veil; it was not yet safe to venture forth. Eyvind paced, biting his nails to the quick. Eirik watched him, frowning.

"All may be well," said Brother Tadhg. "If they are as wise as King Engus, they will be sheltering in a place of safety as we are. We may see them approaching as soon as the day clears." But there was a pallor about his features, and his fingers seldom left the cross.

At last the mist began to lift. They divided into four groups, two men in each, one of the islanders and one of Ulf's party. King Engus himself set off with Eirik; Eyvind was paired with a silent, black-bearded fellow, who moved swift and sure on the difficult terrain. The only man left behind was Brother Tadhg. If the others returned before the search parties, he could explain what was happening and so prevent a pointless exercise of tracking in circles.

Eyvind and his partner went northward and inland. The pace was relentless. When they could run, they ran. With what breath they could spare, they shouted the names of the lost men. They could hear the other searchers in the distance calling the same names, but there was no reply. Time passed. They rested briefly, and Eyvind shared the contents of his skin water bottle with the islander. They went on. Rain fell for a time; the rocks underfoot became slippery, and Eyvind was glad they had not taken the clifftop route. Yet perhaps they should have done. A long time ago, he had helped find straying stock and, on occasion, lost children in the mountains above Hammarsby. Maybe what he should do was go back, and look where nobody else was prepared to look. A pox on Somerled. It would be just like him to be sitting there neat and cool when they returned, saying with an air of faint surprise, *Oh dear, Eyvind. It was only a game.*

The sun was at midpoint. They had been searching all morning, and were heading back to the start with nothing to show for themselves.

"Shh," Eyvind hissed suddenly, for he had heard a cry, faint but unmistakable. He cupped his ear and pointed so the islander could understand. There it was again, from higher up the craggy hillside, a sound that was the voice of a man in some distress. They scrambled up together and found one of Engus's warriors lying behind a rock with his leg bent under him in quite an improbable position: broken, no doubt of it. The fellow was gray in the face and sweating hard. They worked quickly. The man screamed as Eyvind splinted the leg with arrow shafts and a binding torn from the other islander's undershirt. There was no asking, *What happened?* The fellow was in too much pain to speak coherently. They carried him down as best they could; it was too far to the bay, where such useful items as a flat board or a flask of strong drink might be found. When they got back to the place where they had slept, there was Somerled, looking pallid and drained, and the other of Engus's men who had been missing was sitting nearby, his expression angry and confused. Neither appeared hurt. There was no sign of Ulf.

"Where's my brother?" Somerled was demanding. "What's happening here? There is surely some mischief at work!"

"It is strange indeed that you were separated thus in the night, and stranger still that we have found all but your brother," King Engus said. He, too, sounded edgy. "But there's a decision to be made now. This man is badly injured. We must get him off the cliffs. And it is already late: not long before the mist closes in again."

"We'll carry him down," Eirik said, "my brother and I, and Holgar and Grim here. We can put together a sort of sling, using our cloaks; he'll be more comfortable that way. It won't take long to get to that settlement in the bay."

The man's breathing was shallow; Eyvind thought he had fallen some way. Perhaps a broken leg was the least of it.

"Very well," Engus was saying. "But—"

"What about my brother?" Somerled's voice was shaking. "We must find Ulf. Perhaps he, too, lies somewhere in these accursed hills with broken bones. We must search again. These men cannot go back."

"My own warriors will remain and search," Engus said, glancing at Somerled. "We've no intention of giving up. We may yet find your brother before nightfall."

Somerled's face was white, his mouth a thin line. "Not good enough," he said coldly. "My brother went missing in company with your own men. They are returned and he is not. How can I trust these same men to bring him back safely?"

Tadhg translated, blank-faced.

"What are you implying?" Engus drew himself up to his full height, brows creased ferociously. "Are you suggesting there has been some foul play here?"

"Somerled," said Eyvind quietly.

"What?" The tone was like a whip crack.

"I will stay and help you search. Both Holgar and I, if you like. King Engus has three fit men left to help carry the sling down the hill."

"I don't—"

"Somerled. We're brothers, remember? Trust me. I'll help you with this."

Tadhg had been translating as well as he could, while at the same time kneeling by the injured man, holding his hand in an attempt to provide comfort. Now he glanced up at Eyvind.

"Brothers?" he queried. "Is it not Eirik here who is your brother?"

Eyvind rolled back a sleeve to show the long scar that still marked his left forearm. "Brothers of another kind," he said.

Tadhg nodded. A small frown appeared on his tranquil brow.

"Pledged to help one another," Eyvind added, not sure why he felt some further explanation was required. "Now we must go and search. Ulf may be lying hurt somewhere, and it's late."

"Go with God," said Tadhg.

There were not many gods in evidence that day, or if there were, they were cruel and savage deities, suited to these wild shores. Engus would not leave the Norsemen to search alone; he insisted one of his own men stay. Tadhg offered to help carry the sling. Holgar remained behind. They split up as before, Holgar with the islander going inland, Eyvind and Somerled tackling the cliff edge.

There was no good reason to suspect they would find Ulf there. Still, something compelled Eyvind that way, a chill in the blood, a darkness in the mind, a feeling whose roots were ancient and shadowy. Like a wolf, he scented evil in the air, but he did not flee from it, as a wild creature might in order to survive. Instead, he made himself hurry toward it, and for the first time in his life he thought he felt fear. It seemed to him they were poised on the edge of another cliff here, a cliff made not of stone and earth but of suspicion and jealousy, fear and hatred. Take a step too far, and all would tumble into darkness.

Eyvind moved cautiously, with what speed he could. It was necessary to allow for Somerled, less fleet of foot, less clever at balancing, less strong in endurance. And Somerled was distressed; his white face and angry eyes attested to that. Perhaps that was not as surprising as it seemed, Eyvind thought, as he made his way gingerly down a crack in the cliff to a place where a ledge allowed better views to north and south. Maybe it only took one fright like this to make a man realize the worth of family. It was possible Somerled's cutting comments about his brother were merely part of another game.

Although the ledge was high above the ocean, still the salt spray stung him. The waves below were huge, smashing the cliff face with unremitting fury. Birds flew by with harsh cries, diving close enough to unsettle his balance. Eyvind made himself breathe slowly, but he could not change the rapid thudding of his heart. "Thor," he whispered. "Help me to see. Help me to hear as the wolf does. Help me to be strong." He hardly understood why he had said this. He was already strong. When there was no fighting to be done, he made sure he ran and swam and shifted stones, he made sure his body would be ready for whatever challenges it must face. Yet the words were on his lips: a prayer. *Help me to be strong.*

Then he looked up and to the north, and he saw something. A scrap of color, blue, white, red, something suspended below the clifftop, an old net, an old sail, moving where the wind caught and lifted it.

"Somerled!" he called. He narrowed his eyes against the sun, and put up a hand to sweep aside his hair, which the wind was blowing insistently across his face. "No, don't come down here, it's not safe. But I can see something, up yonder."

"What?" Somerled yelled from up on the clifftop. "What can you see?"

"I don't know," Eyvind whispered. But he knew. What he had seen, though his mind was refusing to put the pieces together, was a man. That was a man hanging there, somehow dangling between land and water, held cruelly balanced in air. Ulf's blue tunic, Ulf's white face. Ulf's blood.

Heart pounding, Eyvind scrambled back up, forgetting caution. Pieces of rock crumbled and fell, his foot slipped, he snatched at a clinging plant for purchase.

"Slow down!" Somerled was stretching down a hand to help him. "What's wrong, what is it? You look as if you've seen a ghost."

"This way." It seemed to Eyvind that if he did not tell, if he did not put into words what he had seen, then it might still prove to be a mistake, or some bad dream from which he would emerge sweating and relieved. They walked northward until they reached a spot Eyvind judged to be roughly above the place. There were no pathways, no convenient fissures or ledges, merely the clifftop, flat and grass-covered, then a sudden descent to oblivion.

"No wonder they missed it," Eyvind said, trying to keep his voice under control, not to alarm Somerled. "You can't see anything from up here. Maybe I was wrong. Maybe it's nothing."

"What?" demanded Somerled. "What did you see? Tell me!"

"A man, I thought." Now there was no choice but to tell.

"A man down there on the cliff. I don't know how we could reach him, Somerled. It could have been just an old sail or a net. It could have been just a trick of the light." Nonetheless, he was casting about, seeking the smallest chink or crevice where he might climb down somehow, and make sure one way or another. Above them, afternoon clouds were building.

"Ulf!" Somerled shouted, and strode so close to the edge that it seemed he would go straight over with no hesitation whatever. Eyvind grabbed his arm, and they both teetered off balance.

"Don't be stupid," Eyvind gasped, using his full weight to wrench the two of them back to safety. "Holgar's got a rope; we'll use that if we have to. And it'll be me going down there, not you. Take a deep breath and try to stay calm. I told you, I may be wrong."

They called out to the others and heard a faint reply. While they waited, Eyvind lay on his stomach and edged himself closer to the drop while Somerled held him by the ankles. After a little, Eyvind shut his eyes. It was not the sight of the boiling sea far below that chilled his heart and froze the blood in his veins. He wriggled his body back, and for a moment could only sit there on the ground with his hands over his face.

"What? What?" Somerled's tone was frantic.

"Somerled, this is bad news. It looks as if he is down there; certainly, I see a man. But I can't tell if he is alive or dead. He seems to move, but perhaps that is only the wind. There are many gulls squabbling around him, and there's blood."

Somerled grew even whiter. "How can he be there?" he asked. "Is there a ledge, is he somehow wedged in the rocks? If he is dead, why doesn't he fall?"

Eyvind hesitated. "He seems to be . . . to be somehow caught," he said, "though I cannot see clearly. He's held by something, a net perhaps, which has been abandoned here; that's all that keeps him from falling into the sea. He's–he's hanging in the air."

Somerled said nothing. They looked at one another. Between them, unspoken, were the words of the curse that had dogged Ulf since he was a child. *Neither on land or water . . .*

The others came running up, and Holgar did indeed have a rope. After that it was quick. Eyvind tied the rope around his

waist; the others anchored it while he climbed down. He had
seen death before, death in many forms, most of them violent
and bloody, for that is a Wolfskin's very existence. But this
made him tremble to the core, it made his heart quail. There
was a net, as he had thought. The net was hooked on the rocks,
perhaps flung there by some capricious wind, for this was a
place where everything was larger than life, the cliffs tall beyond reckoning, the waves monstrous, the wind a demon's flail.
Perhaps this net had once held a fine catch of juicy cod or shining mackerel. Now it had captured a man: Ulf, dreamer of
dreams. His face was bone-white; there was no blood left in
him. One eye stared blankly seaward. Birds had feasted on the
other, brazen gulls that swooped close to Eyvind's face as he
cursed and swung his arm to fend them off. There was something tied over Ulf's mouth, a strip of stained cloth: a gag.
Eyvind edged closer. His foot slipped, his hands clutched the
rock, slick with the residue of birds. The rope tightened, holding him safe. Thank the gods Engus had let Holgar stay; only a
Wolfskin had the strength for such a task.

"All right, Eyvind?" came a call from above, and he called
back, "Yes," but it was not all right, it was desperately, terrify-
ingly wrong. He reached out a cautious hand. The gag was tight;
behind it, strange, dark stuff blocked Ulf's mouth, spilling out
to stain the stretched cloth green. Seaweed. He would not think
about the curse, Eyvind told himself. His fingers worked the
fabric away from Ulf's bloodless lips and cleared the other
man's teeth and tongue of their choking burden, for this seemed
an obscenity that must be put right, never mind that Ulf was
gone far beyond helping. He would not remember the foretelling. But it was there, all the same. *Tastes the salt sea . . .*

He would have to cut Ulf loose somehow, so he could be
hauled to the top. But he'd need to do it carefully or the dead
man would simply drop, to be smashed by the rocks and the
waves as they played out their hard battle far below. Ulf had
been granted no dignity in the manner of his death; he must at
least be brought from this place and laid to rest with proper ritual. Somerled would expect that. Margaret would expect it.
Who would tell Margaret? He got the last of the weed from
Ulf's gaping mouth and paused, his hand resting on the other

man's neck. *I'm imagining this,* Eyvind told himself. *It's fear and shock and too much time for thinking.* Ulf had been missing since yesterday: a whole day and night, almost. Here on the cliff, where nobody could see him. His mouth plugged so nobody could hear him. Ulf was hideously, indisputably dead. And his body was still warm.

Eyvind could not bring himself to think further; his mind recoiled from the possibilities. Quick, then, he must release Ulf from these bonds, and hold onto him, and get the others to haul them up. No, that wouldn't work. The two of them together would be too great a burden even for Holgar's strength. Eyvind himself was a very big man. That meant he must untie the line that kept him from that final fall, and tie it around the dead man. And then he'd have to hold on somehow, and wait.

He called up to the others, telling them Ulf was here, telling them Ulf was dead. There was no way to soften that blow. They must wait, he yelled, until he tugged twice on the rope, and then they must haul it up.

There was a tiny crevice near the net where he could wedge his toes, the merest illusion of a safe purchase. Letting the rope take his weight, he drew the knife from his belt and began to cut. He must free Ulf as far as he could until it became too perilous to cut more; he must fasten the dead man to the safety rope before he severed those last ties. Odin's bones, the bonds around Ulf's wrists were tight indeed, and the man had fought hard against them. There was blood down his left side, staining the blue tunic scarlet. Eyvind reached to find the strand of net that pinioned that left hand. His fingers encountered something hard and sharp: naked bone. In his desperate struggle to free himself from these bonds, Ulf had flayed the flesh from his wrist; he had nearly severed his own hand. It had not helped him, for it seemed the cords that held him had only grown tighter as he pulled against them. That wound in itself had been enough to kill him; his blood had drained' from his body. How could the strands of a net wind so tightly around a man? What had he been doing, alone on the top of these perilous cliffs? If he had slipped and fallen, surely his natural path would have taken him out beyond this place where the old net hung. And what about the seaweed? *Don't think so hard, Eyvind,* he told himself, hacking at the cord. *It only hurts your head.* And yet the thought he wished most fiercely to banish would not leave his mind, but played itself over and over. *Somerled is so good at knots.* It was not possible, he would not consider it; he had seen his friend's distress, back there on the clifftop.

The rope parted; Ulf's dead arm fell limp by his side, the hand hanging by a thread of skin, a shard of bone. Eyvind gritted his teeth and reached to start on the other wrist. He had to lean across, his body pressed against Ulf's, the staring eye not a hand's breadth from his face. The knife slashed; the bonds were severed. Ulf's body sagged forward, but the net still held.

"Right," Eyvind whispered to himself. "One step at a time." He held the knife in his teeth; it was necessary, now, to find a position in which he could cling on and at the same time use his hands to untie the rope. Impossible. There was no choice but to trust those last shreds of net. He edged across until the tattered web of cords was around his upper body. He leaned back cautiously against it, testing its strength. It seemed to hold, just; the real test would be when he untied the rope from around his waist.

"What are you doing?" Holgar shouted. "Is everything all right? The mist's coming in, you'll have to hurry!"

"Wait!" he called. And told himself, *Don't think, Eyvind, just do it.*

He untied the rope. The net creaked ominously under his weight. He reached to put the rope around Ulf's body. There was something in the way, something caught behind: the buckle of Ulf's belt, twisted around and tangled with his bonds. The knife: he'd have to cut blind. Thor's hammer, this was an embrace to make any right-thinking man recoil, to hold a dead man thus in your arms and look into the socket of an eye picked clean by hungry seabirds; to feel his body pressed to yours and know that within the space of that last desperate search, he had probably still been alive. How long had he hung here, fighting against the encroaching darkness?

Eyvind severed the buckle from the belt, though it was still entangled with a network of knotted cords. It was a fine piece of craftsmanship, intricately wrought in silver; he knew it had been Ulf's father's. Eyvind stuffed it into the pouch at his own belt, cords and all, and slipped the rope around Ulf's waist. A good knot; it would be enough, for Holgar knew what he was doing, and would have this burden up quickly and neatly. A slash here, a cut there, and Ulf was free of the net; the shreds that held Eyvind shivered and trembled.

"Right!" Eyvind shouted. "Hold tight; I'm letting him go now. Haul him up, then send the rope back down. And be quick about it, will you?" He tugged at the rope once, twice, and then he released his hold, and Ulf's body swung free to hang, like some crude effigy of a man, dangling sickeningly high above the sea. The wind snatched at the chieftain's dark hair, and sent the stained wool of his tunic fluttering like a banner. He moved in ghastly semblance of life, and vanished from sight as the men on the clifftop hauled on the rope.

They told Eyvind, later, that he had been very brave: a hero. This was wrong, of course. If he had not done what he did, someone else would have: Eirik, Holgar, any of the others. If he had been a clever man, if he had been good at working things out, he would have looked on the clifftops first, instead of wasting time scouring the hillsides. Perhaps, then, he might have found Ulf still alive. Then he would have been a hero. But he had got it wrong, and all he had rescued was a blood-drained husk of a man, a limp, white thing with one eye gone: the stuff of nightmare. Expert hunter though he was, Eyvind had misread the signs. He had felt a shadow, that day, and had not known what it was. But soon enough he understood. It was not just a premonition of Ulf's death; it was a warning of things to come. For that day ushered in a time of darkness such as he had never known before.

Somerled did not accuse Engus to his face, but all through the grim walk back to the anchorage and the swift voyage home, his eyes and his mouth and the set of his shoulders made his thoughts plain. You'd have to be stupid to believe Ulf's death was an accident. Whose was the voice that had led them astray in the night, calling strange words they could not understand? How was it a net had been conveniently at hand in that out-of-the-way place? Whose were the hands that had crammed Ulf's mouth full of sticky weed, so that he could not cry out for help? What cruel mind had determined that he hang there like a sacrifice, fighting for his life, rather than perish with merciful speed on the rocks below? It was no chance that had led their leader to this terrible end, and it was only Eirik's muttered warnings and Somerled's silence that kept the men from speaking out then and there. Perhaps they had thought these islanders generous, before. Perhaps they had believed they could be friends, in time. Not now. They had seen what kind of people these really were, and it was all they could do to keep their hands off their swords and on the oars, rowing swift for home.

As soon as they got back to Ulf's settlement, Somerled assumed control. The white-faced panic of the clifftop had been replaced by a tight-jawed sternness of manner, and nobody questioned his authority. He broke the news to Margaret. He arranged the burial. He made it clear that the ceremony would be conducted in full accordance with the rites of Odin. Indeed, in his very first speech to the assembled folk of his brother's household, Somerled left no doubt about his own unswerving allegiance to the gods of his homeland, and his repudiation of the tenets of other faiths, such as Christianity.

At home in Rogaland a chieftain of Ulf's status would have been laid to rest in a fine ship of oak, along with those treasures that had aided him in life: his sword, his spear, his gold and silver jewelry, his fine cloak of beaver pelt. Here there was no oak, there was not the smallest pine to be felled in order to make even the semblance of a ship to bear Ulf to the afterlife. Instead they laid rocks, placing them to form the shape of a vessel. Within this, they laid Ulf's body on a platform of flagstones, softened with a layer of heather, and they covered him with his cloak of wool dyed red, which he had worn for feast days. They put his possessions by him, his weapons, his helm, his arm-ring and torc, the silver brooch that had fastened his cloak. Somerled suggested they might sacrifice the hunting dogs and lay them beside their master in his grave, and he sent Eyvind to fetch them from the place where they were kennelled. The hounds heard him coming and pricked up their ears. As he opened the gate to their enclosure, they fixed their eyes on him with soulful dignity, an effect somewhat undermined by the furious wagging of their tails. Eyvind slipped their chains and walked away, leaving the gate ajar. Perhaps understanding Ulf would not be back for them, the hounds departed swiftly and silently across the fields. Eyvind hoped Odin would not be offended; it seemed to him there had been enough bloodshed already. He told Somerled the dogs were nowhere to be found. By then, it was the truth.

Margaret had chosen a place atop a small hill with a distant view of the western sea. It was a peaceful spot, where few would pass save a grazing sheep or two, a meadow pipit, a foraging vole. Here Ulf was buried with what ceremony they could give him, and by dusk that day there was only an earthen mound to show that he had lived, and dreamed, and died. In time, grasses would creep up over it, and it would be just like all those other secret howes that were everywhere on these islands, hinting at the hidden things below the surface. Who knew how many kings, how many queens, how many brave visionaries lay under this fertile soil? It made Eyvind shiver to think of it. So many old bones, so many wandering spirits. You could feel them all around you. These days, he could almost hear their whispers as he passed. For him, spring could not come soon enough.

The days grew shorter. King Engus sent a messenger, accompanied by Brother Tadhg. They had not seen Brother Tadhg since the time of Ulf's death, when he had made the sign of a cross over the body and begun to mutter what was undoubtedly a Christian prayer. Somerled, furious, had grabbed the little man by the shoulders and shaken him hard, shouting what right had he to impose his ridiculous faith, how dared he assume that Ulf would want such nonsense spoken over his deathbed? Eyvind had restrained Somerled before any real harm was done. Tadhg, being what he was, had taken this calmly, but King Engus had been less than pleased.

Engus had requested, politely, that he might attend Ulf's funeral. For obvious reasons, Somerled had refused. At the time, it had occurred to Eyvind that Ulf himself might have wished the islanders to be present, whatever questions still existed over the manner of his death. It would have been in keeping with his vision for the two peoples to stand by his graveside in peace. But he did not say this to Somerled. It was becoming harder and harder to say much to Somerled, for he was a chieftain now, and people jumped to obey him. Those fellows who had crewed the knarr had all moved up from Hafnarvagr to the settlement by the lake, and wandered about armed with cudgels and short swords. They shadowed Somerled wherever he went, and some folk had begun to be afraid of them. As for the Wolfskins, Grim, Holgar, and Erlend did Somerled's bidding without question, as they had done his brother's. That was their job. Thord kept himself to himself; Eirik, too, was very quiet. Soon he would return to the south and wait out the winter close to the boats, just in case of trouble.

Engus's messenger came one evening as they sat at supper. He was clad in a good tunic of green-dyed wool and was armed with a dagger at the belt. Brother Tadhg wore his coarse brown robe, with sandals on his feet. Somerled had guards all around the perimeters of the settlement now, and the visitors entered flanked by two fellows with their swords drawn.

"Well, well," Somerled remarked, raising his brows. "What have we here?"

"My lord," Brother Tadhg began, "this man is called Brude, son of Elpin. He is of the king's household, and he bears you a message. We come in peace; there is no need for naked blades."

"So Engus uses Christian priests as his emissaries now." Somerled's smile was dangerous. "Are these his words, that we should lay down our swords and make you welcome?"

"As you know, my lord, I am no puppet." The little man's gray eyes were perfectly tranquil. "There are many of you and just the two of us, and I am unarmed. You might bid your men sheathe their weapons, at least."

"As to that," Somerled said, "there have been changes here. You'd do well to remember that I am chieftain now, and that I expect matters to be conducted according to my own rules. What is this message? Has the other fellow no tongue in his head, that he keeps silent and leaves it to you to be his mouthpiece?"

Eyvind was taken aback by Somerled's manner, and even more taken aback by the way folk nodded approvingly as he spoke. Certainly, Ulf's death had caused suspicion and distrust toward the islanders, and toward this priest in particular, for the way he had worked on Ulf's mind, subverting his belief in the old gods. Still, it disquieted him that things could turn around so quickly.

The green-clad islander began to speak, and Tadhg rendered his words calmly into their own tongue.

"King Engus sends his respects to the lady Margaret. He regrets greatly what has occurred. The king requests a meeting, my lord. It can be here, or in his own hall on the Whaleback, whatever you prefer. He is anxious to ensure the agreement he made with your brother will be honored."

Somerled raised his brows. "Agreement?" he queried in a voice smooth as silk.

When Tadhg translated this, the islander's jaw tightened. "Yes, my lord." His voice had changed too. "An agreement of peace between our two peoples, sworn on the Great Stone of Oaths, that we would not take up arms against each other, and would respect each other's boundaries. Lord Ulf undertook to assist us over the winter, should there be the need. There was also the matter of a cargo of timber that was promised."

Somerled regarded him levelly. "This agreement has already been broken, and not by us," he said. "Tell Engus that Somerled Horse-Master sees no reason to treat with him. I am affronted that he should expect this so soon after my brother's death. He must know the suspicion that attaches to him concerning that tragic event."

"I see," the man said. His voice was shaking. It seemed to Eyvind that this was not fear, but furious anger. "Am I to tell the king you will not meet with him? That you refuse to discuss these matters?"

Olaf Sveinsson, who had been Ulf's chief adviser, rose to his feet, frowning.

"This translator is a Christian. We know how he tried to influence your brother with his dangerous doctrines. We cannot trust him. We cannot trust any of them, my lord."

"Hear, hear," rumbled Harald Silvertongue, who had been Ulf's law speaker. "Send them packing, that's my advice."

At this point Margaret, who had been sitting tight-lipped and pale at Somerled's side, leaned toward him and spoke quietly.

Then Somerled said, "Lord Ulf's widow is more magnanimous than I. If it were my choice alone, I would say Engus is the last man on earth with whom I would share my salt. Lady Margaret advises a middle road. Inform your master that I will advise a meeting on my own terms, and in my own time. You may go now. Eyvind? Escort these fellows across our boundaries, will you?"

There was a brief silence. Then Eyvind stepped forward from where he had stood behind Somerled's chair, and with a jerk of his head indicated to their two visitors that it was time to go. Brother Tadhg gave a little nod in Margaret's direction; the other man only grimaced. As they went out, talk and laughter and the sounds of eating and drinking began again behind them.

It was pitch dark beyond the environs of the settlement, and bitterly cold. Eyvind had lit a torch from the one that burned in a socket at the hall's entry, wondering how their visitors had expected to find their way back. They walked in silence for a while. It was Brother Tadhg who spoke first.

"I'm sorry that Ulf died. He was a friend to me: a wise man, a good man."

Eyvind nodded, saying nothing.

"It was not Engus's people who killed him," Tadhg said.

"You can't know that." Eyvind was not sure if he should speak; these were dangerous matters.

"Ah, but I can." Tadhg's voice was very soft, very certain. "If there is one thing I understand, it is faith. That clifftop where your chieftain died, it is a sacred place, a place much revered by the Folk. It is heavy with the presence of those they call the ancestors; it is alive with the lore that is the very backbone of these islands. If a man of the Folk wished to murder his enemy, he would choose a spot where there were few local spirits to be offended: the back room of a drinking hall maybe, or the pallet of a faithless lover. To kill a man on those cliffs would be like defacing an altar. It is not possible."

"But . . . someone killed him," Eyvind said hesitantly. "It was no accident."

"Yes," agreed Tadhg gravely. "Someone killed him, and set your people at bitter enmity with the Folk. I ask myself, why?"

The islander made some muttered remark, perhaps asking what they spoke of, and Tadhg replied in reassuring tones.

"I can't talk to you about these things," Eyvind said. "It wouldn't be right."

"Not right to want to know the truth?"

"I'm only a warrior. It's my duty to guard my patron and fight his battles, not to ask questions. I do as Thor commands, or as my chieftain orders. I will not speak of these matters to you."

"Tell me," Tadhg said. "If this Thor told you to go out and kill a man, and you knew that man was a good man and innocent of any wrongdoing, would you do as you were bid?"

"Why are you asking me this? Of course I would," said Eyvind, more than a little irked at this turn of the conversation. "I am a warrior and sworn to Thor, and a warrior keeps his oath, always. It is my duty to do the god's will; it is my life. But that does not mean I killed Ulf."

"No indeed. That was not what I meant. Tell me. Somerled Horse-Master is your chieftain now. Will you kill at his bidding, even if you think it wrong?"

Eyvind scowled. "Somerled is my blood brother. Long ago, we swore loyalty to one another. That must be sufficient answer for you."

"What if he ordered you to kill me?" Tadhg's tone was light.

"He wouldn't," Eyvind said curtly. "You're too useful. But don't think you're any different from another man where I'm concerned. The thing I do best is killing. If Thor bid me cleave your skull with this axe, I would do it, priest or no priest."

"How sad," Tadhg observed.

"Sad? What's sad about it?" Odin's bones, the fellow certainly had a way of getting under your skin and making you feel uncomfortable.

"That your calling prevents you from making your own choices, from being your own man. On Holy Island, we have no axes and swords and fine spears, we have no golden torcs and arm-rings, we have no chieftains. We need none of these things, for we have two gifts of priceless worth."

"What gifts?" Eyvind was intrigued, despite his annoyance.

Tadhg smiled in the torchlight. His words came softly to Eyvind's ears.

"God's love, and the freedom to choose what is right."

Winter came, and there was no meeting between Somerled and the king. The situation went from bad to worse. There was a skirmish on the border between their own land and Engus's farms, and one of the islanders was killed. There was another

encounter in the south, and men on both sides were injured.
Eyvind did not take part in either, for Somerled had sent him
off to check on the security of their easternmost holdings, and
by the time he came back to the settlement, it was all over. But
the first blood had been spilled. It seemed to Eyvind that now
would be a good time to talk to the king, before matters got
completely out of hand. Indeed, he wondered why Somerled
had not arranged this already. He mentioned it, diffidently, to
Harald Silvertongue and to Olaf Sveinsson. Both greeted his
idea with indifference. He asked Holgar what he thought, and
Holgar said, "Aren't you his friend? Speak to him yourself." So
he did, though by now he was beginning to remember things
Somerled had said in the past, about how a Wolfskin should
stick to what he knew best, which was fighting, and leave thinking to those who had the wit for it.

"Somerled?"

"Yes?" Somerled was making a map, his quill moving in
confident strokes on the piece of parchment that lay, its corners
weighted by polished stones, on the table before him. It was a
map of the Light Isles, Eyvind could see that, with little bays
and lakes and here and there words that he could not understand. It covered all the parts where Somerled had so far journeyed. There, in the northwest corner of the largest island, was
the Whaleback sitting in the ocean, and a tiny line joining it to
the land. It was wonderful that a man could make such fine
things, such clever things.

"I wanted to suggest something."

"Mmm?"

"It seems to me . . . I was thinking . . ."

"Come on, Eyvind, I'm not an ogre. Out with it."

"I thought it might be time for that meeting with King Engus.
Before things get any worse. You know what Ulf agreed to,
what he wanted for the islands. I think he would expect that you
make peace with Engus, despite what has happened. That might
be best."

The movement of the quill halted. Somerled looked up.

"Why?" he asked.

"I think . . . it seems to me there could be great losses here, if
you don't do something about it now," Eyvind said, relieved
that Somerled had not dismissed his idea outright. "There is

still a chance of peace and cooperation. But you must move before it's too late. That's what I think."

There was a little pause.

"Finished?" inquired Somerled.

Eyvind said nothing.

"You worry me sometimes." Somerled was drawing again, marking in the cliffs of the west coast, south of Engus's stronghold. "You make things so difficult for yourself, when really they are quite simple. If a man wants something, he should take it. Why worry about anything else?"

"I don't understand," Eyvind said, frowning.

"If I follow the path you suggest and become a man of compromises and treaties like my brother, there'll be nothing to keep you amused over the winter but feeding chickens and mending holes in fishing boats," Somerled replied. "Aren't you itching for a real battle? You're so good at it. Why else did I bring you here, after all?"

"Perhaps because we are friends, and you wanted me here," Eyvind said, wondering why he was suddenly feeling cold, as if the breath of winter had crept into this fire-warmed chamber. "I do not relish the prospect of war with these folk. They are not our equals in fighting; such a conflict would be unfair, one-sided. There is little glory in winning such a combat. Besides—"

"Besides what?"

"There's something more here. Not the folk themselves. We'd defeat them if it came to war, because our skills at fighting are superior, because our weapons are better, because we have Wolfskins. But they have . . . something else. I can't say what it is. Something old. Remember what King Engus said, that first time? They're part of the land, somehow, and the land doesn't give up. Maybe that sounds silly, but you can't ignore it."

Somerled sighed. "It does sound a little silly, Eyvind, but you are my friend, my oldest friend, and I understand your concern. You can rest easy. I will be going to see the king, but not yet. The winter's closing in; this is not the time for major campaigns, it's a time for settling down for some serious planning, so we're ready for whatever comes our way. There's something you must remember. I am not Ulf. I conduct my affairs in my own way, and if folk want to be part of my household, they need to understand that. My brother died. That changed everything here. These people must be punished for what they did. I would be a weak leader indeed if I did not seek retribution for his murder."

"I wondered . . . I did wonder if it was quite fair to blame Engus for what happened. He did say it was not his doing. Others say the same."

"Others?" Somerled's tone was suddenly sharp. "What others?"

"Just people, here and there. I don't remember who."

"You're a bad liar, Eyvind. Of course Engus's folk killed my brother. Of course they did. Who else would have done it?"

This was a question Eyvind could not answer; a question he did not want to think about. In his dreams, he still saw Ulf's blind eye, his open mouth, his shattered wrist. He still felt the dead man's body pressed close to his own. He sensed deep within him that, whatever Somerled said, in the end the islanders could not be defeated. Yet it was perplexing, for Somerled was right as well. The winter would be long and tedious; only the call of Thor and the bright challenge of sword and axe could relieve those dark months until spring. He longed for action. He longed to drown out the memories of that day on the cliffs of High Island with the music of war, the song of blade on naked blade. The helm Jarl Magnus had given him lay hidden in a corner of his storage chest. He had never worn it.

Eyvind did not try to speak to Somerled again on the matter. It was enough that Somerled had promised a meeting would take place. He must wait, and hope all would be well.

They had seen little of Hakon, now settled on his farm with his new wife, his stepsons, and his own small babe. But one evening Hakon came to the settlement. He brought a gift of a fat sheep, and stayed for supper. It was a good reunion. Hakon sat with Eirik and Eyvind, Holgar and Erlend, Thord and Grim, exchanging tales of times past, of battles won and trophies taken. More times like this, Eyvind thought, that was what they needed. Somerled sat at the head of the table, very quiet, watching and listening. Margaret was composed as always, features grave, a neat, demure figure in her black-dyed overdress and white linen.

They say drink makes men bold. The ale had certainly been flowing freely. Perhaps that was why Hakon, normally a reserved sort of man, spoke as he did.

"My lord," he said suddenly, looking at Somerled, and everyone fell quiet. "I have not come here solely to see my old friends, though I welcome the hospitality. I've been hearing rumors that concern me greatly. It's being put about that the treaty Lord Ulf made with Engus has been disregarded, and that fighting is starting to break out on your borders with very little excuse. A fellow died; another lost an ear. People are frightened, my lord. Is it true that you would take up arms against the man who was your brother's ally?"

Somerled gave a slow smile. "You forget," he said, "and that surprises me, for Ulf regarded you as one of his closest friends. I would not accuse Engus personally of my brother's death; indeed I cannot, since his actions are well accounted for during the period in question. But I have no doubt his people killed my brother. Would you have me make peace with a bunch of cutthroats and murderers? If they don't like what is happening, they have only themselves to blame."

"If you believe them responsible," Hakon said doggedly, "why not hold a Thing, so the matter can be settled according to correct practice of law? That would be well accepted, I think, even among Engus's folk. You'd come closer to proving what really happened if it was all brought out into the open."

"Well said," Eirik was heard to mutter. "Well said."

"There's no need for a Thing." Somerled's voice was calm and authoritative. "I am chieftain here, and I will determine how matters are settled. My brother's killing was an outrage, the manner of it barbaric to the point of obscenity. Resolving it goes far beyond empty gestures of reparation. And be warned. You have a wife here, and she is not of our kind. That renders you immediately suspect. It's time for you to make up your mind which side of the border you consider your own: which side of the scales bears your weight. These islanders are sharp little fighters and devious in their ways. They may not take kindly to your visits here, and to your continuing friendship with your old comrades. They are certain to distrust any man of Rogaland who allies himself with one of their own women. You're in a very uncertain position, Wolfskin, and you'd best look to yourself and your own."

"I don't know what you mean," said Hakon, who had turned pale. "Is this a threat?"

"Of course not," said Somerled. "I value my warriors dearly, every one. I simply require a pledge of loyalty, that's all. If I should call on you to fight, you must be prepared to do it, whatever the circumstances, whoever the enemy. It's not so much to ask: no more than a Wolfskin's usual promise to do battle for his patron. Will you swear this?"

There was a lengthy silence. Eyvind could see Eirik's fingers tightening around his ale cup; the other Wolfskins looked down at their boots, or at the wall, or anywhere but at Hakon's white face.

"Well?" challenged Somerled. "Not struck dumb as well as deaf, I hope?" He raised his voice, as if to ensure Hakon could hear him. "What have you to say?"

"I heard you," Hakon said heavily. "And I will not swear. I cannot. My wife is one of these folk: so is my small son. I will not promise blindly to kill, when I cannot know if her brother, her father, her kinsman may face the point of my bloodied sword. For Ulf, I might have made such a vow. But not for you."

And with that, he reached up to unfasten the silver clasp that held his wolfskin around his shoulders and, stepping forward, took off the heavy gray pelt and laid it on the table before Somerled. There was a collective gasp of indrawn breath.

"Very well," Somerled said evenly. "You've made your choice. I wish you luck. You'll be needing it."

Hakon said nothing. He inclined his head toward Margaret, and looked at his old companions once more, and walked out of the hall into the night.

After that, there was some unrest. Eirik was angry, Thord silent, the others saddened but unwilling to put what they felt into words. Eyvind was sure Somerled must be wrong. When Hakon had married the widow, back in summertime when things had been so different, both islanders and men of Rogaland had danced at the wedding, and shared the same ale. But soon enough it was proven that Somerled's misgivings were well founded. There was another border skirmish. This time Grim was in it, and he said that he had broken one fellow's neck and finished another with his war hammer before Engus's men fled into the darkness. Two nights after that, as Eyvind walked from hall to sleeping quarters he saw a fire in the distance to the east. It burned long and hard. In the morning, when they walked out to investigate, they found the widow's cottage burned to the ground, and five sets of bones there among the ashes. You could tell from the way they lay that Hakon had tried to protect his small family, for his arms had been around them, his wife, her little sons, the infant, as if to shield them from the suffocating smoke, the searing heat. His face the color of the ash that still drifted and settled in that place of death, Eirik lifted out the remains, while Thord and Eyvind dug a makeshift grave. They laid their old friend to rest with those who had been his hope of the future. And when it came time to return to the settlement, Eirik said he was not going.

"What?" asked Eyvind, rubbing a hand across his face.

"I can't go back. I just can't do it. Besides, there's a job for me in Hafnarvagr, guarding the ships over winter. Thord's coming with me; his woman's already down there. We'll do well enough."

"What if there's war, after this?" Eyvind was surprised at the alarm Eirik's announcement caused him. "We need you."

"Listen, Eyvind. I'm not going to talk about this openly, not even out here. But you must be careful. You need to watch yourself. Why don't you come to the anchorage with me? There's no reason why we shouldn't both stay there until we can take ship for home."

Eyvind stared at him. "I couldn't do that," he protested. "Somerled needs me. He said once, that when he was . . . when he was a chieftain, I'd be his main bodyguard, his first Wolfskin. I think I have to do that, Eirik, even if . . . I think I have to keep my promise. Only until spring. Then I'll go home."

Eirik looked at him through narrowed eyes. "Be careful, that's all. There's danger all around you, little brother, and you're not very good at seeing it sometimes. Stay awake; be watchful."

"I wish you'd explain—"

"Shh. Some things can't be spoken, not even here. There's nowhere safe. And I'm all for getting home intact." He glanced around the remains of the burned-out cottage, the pitiful heap of soil that now blanketed its inhabitants. "This is a cursed place, Eyvind. I never thought to bury my best friend thus, without dignity. And I'll tell you something. It's one thing to speak out, as he did. But I'd only to see them lying there, and think of Oksana and the boys, and I knew all that matters to me is getting back safe to Hammarsby. You won't be hearing much from me before spring, and neither will your friend Somerled Horse-Master."

The shadow touched Eyvind's thoughts again, a suspicion, a doubt that could not be allowed to clarify itself, for if it were truth, it would open a yawning abyss before his feet. An oath in blood was binding and lifelong. It did not offer any room for doubt.

Thord had been laying sprigs of greenery on the low mound they had made. Now he came over to them, and Eirik fell silent.

"Farewell then," Eyvind said. "The gods guard you."

"You too, little brother," said Eirik. "Farewell until the springtime."

On a windy, dry day not so long after this burning, they sat in the hall before the fire. Somerled and Margaret were playing a game as they had so many times before, though now Margaret moved her pieces listlessly, as if her mind were elsewhere. She had seemed stunned by her husband's death, and showed none of her old vitality. Somerled waited patiently for her move; he made helpful suggestions; he tried to divert her with jokes and tales, and sometimes he coaxed a faint smile to her lips, and a little spot of rose to her wan cheeks. Eyvind stood watching. It was Somerled's choice to keep him close at hand now. The times were growing more dangerous, and it was prudent to take due care, since so many people depended on Somerled's leadership. At the other end of the hall, a group of women sewed, and a group of men tended to their weaponry, sharpening blades, oiling leather, mending worn fastenings on scabbard or quiver. The wind howled outside, setting the fire flickering and hissing.

Thor's breath, Eyvind thought. *Something's changing.* A chill went up his spine; he could not say if it was excitement, or fear, or something else altogether. And then the door slammed open, aided by the fierce wind, and Grim came striding in.

"The islanders are assembling up the valley," he gasped, holding his side, "a body of them, well armed. They didn't see me."

Already every man in the hall was on his feet. Belts were buckled, cloaks fastened, boots laced more tightly.

"Eyvind?" said Somerled. "Deal with this for me, will you?"

Eyvind had not, in fact, taken charge of such a venture before, but it was easy enough. "How many men?" he asked Grim, and was told at least fifteen, perhaps twenty. Very well, ten of their own must go in response. One Wolfskin was generally weighted against five of the opposition, perhaps three in the case of Danes; but the islanders were tricky, and they were on their own terrain, so one should err on the side of caution. Himself, Grim, and Holgar. And seven other men, including five who had crewed the knarr, not seasoned warriors, but known to be dogged fighters with a few of their own tricks up their sleeves. He bade them arm themselves quickly, and fetched his own things from the sleeping quarters. The axe, Biter, was already on his back. He strapped on his sword, and took the fine helm from where it lay in the chest. The rippling metal rings caught the sun from the narrow window, sending a dancing spray of light across the gray stone of the walls. This would be his first battle since leaving Rogaland, so far away now it was almost like another world. It seemed fitting to wear the Jarl's gift, and to remember those times, so that he might demonstrate true courage and lead his small party to a victory worthy of Thor's trust in them. Then the god would look kindly on him, and see him safe home at winter's end.

They moved quietly, keeping to folds of the hills, seeking what sparse cover there was on the open ground. The sun was low; each rugged stone, each tattered bush cast a long shadow as they passed. The wind scoured the face of the land, sending birds hurtling across the sky, ripping at cloaks and setting the fine chains that fringed Eyvind's helm rattling in a wild music of their own.

They came upon the islanders suddenly, in a narrow divide between two low hills, where a boggy stream flowed down. A man with a spear, two more behind him, bows drawn, more at the rear, red, green, blue tunics, fierce dark eyes, leather helms. Eyvind looked at Grim; Grim looked at Holgar. As one they opened their mouths and roared; as one they charged, and the others followed. Thor's voice rang clear and strong in Eyvind's head as he advanced, *Strike hard, my son! Burn bright for me!*

Biter swung and fell, chopped and smote, true and final. Around Eyvind's whirling form men screamed, swords glinted in the light, shields splintered, arrows whistled in air and landed with the dull thud of barb piercing flesh. At such times a Wolfskin knows only the red mist of the god's will. Yet somehow, today was different. Eyvind saw Grim take a man's legs off at the knees, and finish him with the handle of his war hammer. He saw Holgar split one fellow near in half. Every man played his part, even those who had been seamen once, and now fought the only way they knew, hard and dirty. But the islanders battled on. Though plainly outclassed, they showed no signs of retreating. And they had done some damage of their own. One of the men from the knarr lay moaning on his back, both hands pressed tight to his belly. Another had fallen face down into the muddy water underfoot; his neck seemed to be broken. Now there were fewer of the enemy on their feet, a mere handful. *They should cut their losses and run,* Eyvind thought. *Why don't they run?*

The fighting moved away from him; Holgar was engaged with two fellows who alternated sword thrusts, trying to get under his guard. It was clear to Eyvind that the Wolfskin was only playing with them. Grim wrestled with two more, who had been foolish enough to think they might relieve him of his hammer. Farther up the stream, three islanders stood back to back, weapons at the ready, in a last desperate effort at resistance. Eyvind's other men had formed a circle and were closing in around them. The islanders were doomed. *Why hadn't they run away?*

There was a tiny sound behind him. Eyvind spun around, axe in hand. A green-clad warrior stood ten paces away, bow drawn, arrow pointing straight at his heart. *Burn bright for me, son,* sang the voice of Thor in his ear. Eyvind's response was automatic: Biter flew from his hand in a spinning, glinting arc toward the islander's leather-capped head. And, as the axe danced through the air, Eyvind looked into his opponent's face. He saw the blanched cheeks and terrified eyes of a boy, perhaps twelve years old, no more, a lad who had danced at his sister's wedding in summer with a grin on his face and a spring in his step, a boy whose sister had died by fire, with her children in her arms and her man by her side, her man who had been a Wolfskin. He saw the trembling of the youth's hands where they gripped the bow, he saw the furious set of the young mouth, and then Biter found its mark, true as always, and its quarry fell lifeless to the ground. Eyvind had always prided himself on a clean kill.

He stood immobile. Something was wrong. Everything was wrong. Thor had called him, and he had answered, he had answered in his bravery and skill, he had answered by his actions and thought he had done well. But Thor was silent now. The voice, which had roared in his ear, which had guided him forward all these years as a father does his son, as a great leader his warriors, was gone as if it had never existed. Eyvind reached down and pulled Biter from the boy's skull. He wiped the blade on the grass. The broken bodies of the islanders lay all across that hidden glen, and now he could see that many of them were mere lads, and many more were old men, gray-bearded, white-haired. Such children, such ancients had no business making war. It was foolish. It was not right. Farther up the valley, his own men were yelling now, shouting and stabbing and kicking at what lay on the ground in their midst. This was not a battle, but a rout.

Eyvind's head swam. Images rushed before him, old ones, new ones: Ulf's dead eye, a child's fragile skull, a bull's horn piercing living flesh, his own axe rising and falling, rising and falling, only it wasn't the helm of an enemy warrior he split in two but the head of an infant with round, innocent eyes, the head of a fair-haired woman in a clinging nightrobe, and he held in his hand not an axe but a little knife, a knife that scored a set of runes in the white flesh of a boy's forearm, neat twig-runes that spelled out, for everyone to see, his own name, Eyvind. Eyvind made this. This was Eyvind's doing. "Thor," he whispered as a kind of darkness fell on him, "Thor, where are you?" But there was only silence: a silence that was like the stillness after a great door closes, a silence that seemed to him as final as death. He was somewhere new, somewhere he did not want to be, and there was no going back. In their circle, the others still jeered and cursed, smiting their fallen prey. There wouldn't be much left when they were done. Eyvind eased off his fine helm with the fringe of metal rings, and put it under his arm. Without looking back, he began to walk away. Then he began to run, and his heart kept pace with his feet, faster, faster, away, away, farther and still farther. His spirit called, and called again, *Thor! Thor, help me! I have been true. Where are you?* But there was only the silence, and the distant roar of the sea. As he ran, unseeing, blundering up and down hillocks, stumbling over rabbit holes, as rocks bruised his flesh and needle-sharp grasses tore at his skin, something padded soft-footed beside him on the margin of sight: something as long and gray and quiet as a wolf.

SEVEN

The dog had been following her for a while now. It was a big, gray thing, shaggy and wild-looking. She'd walk across from the Whaleback to the shore, and as soon as she reached a certain point, she'd catch a glimpse of it up in the dunes, padding along quietly as if keeping watch on her. Its hair was matted; its ribs showed. The dog did not come within the boundaries of Rona's secret domain. It halted in the same spot every time, crouching very still under a group of low bushes, while she went forward to the sheltered hollow of the women's place. It would wait there while she performed the necessary tasks. When she was ready to head back home, the dog would get up and follow, as if to see her safe on her journey. Lately, Nessa had taken to bringing scraps of food, a little fish, a crust of bread, and leaving them where the dog could reach them while she worked. Sometimes, it would let her come quite close, almost close enough to stroke its rough pelt. For all its fierce looks, it was a shy thing.

She knew whose it was, of course. They'd all seen those two hunting dogs the Norse chieftain had with him; he'd even used them to help find their own lost sheep in the time of the sickness. But Ulf was dead now. Perhaps nobody wanted the hound anymore. Perhaps its mate had died, and it was lonely.

Nessa could understand that. Her heart still ached for the loss of her sisters. Her mother had drifted off into some strange world, where nobody could reach her; her eyes were blank, her words could no longer be understood. And Engus had changed since that fateful trip to High Island. Nessa could read on his face the realization that he had made a terrible mistake. The newcomers struck where and when it suited them; it was no longer safe for the Folk to travel across the island unarmed. What about the widow, Ara, who had married one of the strangers, and died by fire with her bairns in her arms? That had been no accident. It was after that, Nessa thought, that her uncle had begun to recognize what he had unleashed on his people. Ara's kinsmen had gone out to seek vengeance for her killing. The Norsemen had slaughtered every one of them, hacked them to death without a shred of mercy. The little vale of Ramsbeck was a cursed place now, a place of deep sorrow. The Folk would not walk that way again. Nessa could only be glad Kinart had not joined that party as he had wished, or her cousin's body would be lying now under the earth with the broken remains of the others. A whole family of men had perished that day, brothers, father, grandfather, uncles, cousins. Kinart was burning with fury. He had sworn to take a Norseman's head for every one of those killed at Ramsbeck, for all he was not much more than a lad himself. Engus held him back. He held them all back. That heroic, futile attempt at revenge had been undertaken without his knowledge, without his sanction. Only a fool, Engus said, would underestimate the Norsemen's strength. The Folk had no chance against them in open combat. But there was still a possibility of a new treaty. They must not lose hope. All the same, Nessa knew he had summoned men to come from the other islands, and he had doubled his border guards. Engus had trusted Ulf, a good and wise chieftain. Somerled Horse-Master was quite a different matter.

Their own lands in the west were still safe. True, Engus had muttered something about her not going out without Kinart or one of the other young men, just in case, but Nessa had chosen not to hear him. She didn't want a guard trailing after her and getting in the way. She didn't want Kinart hanging about on the fringes of the forbidden place, calling her to hurry up. There was no need for that. The Norsemen knew not to venture over the borders, that had been made very clear to Lord Ulf, and his brother must surely understand it. Besides, she was a priestess, and if the dog did not protect her, the ancestors would.

It seemed more important than ever to make sure the rituals were performed correctly, the right songs sung, the stories remembered in every detail. There was no doubt the Folk were frightened. Those who had warned Engus that inviting the Norsemen to stay was asking for trouble now nodded their heads as if to say, *I told you so*. Some people with family on the outer islands talked about leaving; it would be safer to be well away from this new chieftain, whose men were inclined to use their weapons before they bothered to ask questions. But it was midwinter, and travel between the islands was well nigh impossible. Besides, Engus wanted the men here, near the Whaleback, as many of them as were prepared to make a commitment to their king and to the future of the Folk. Without anything put into words, Nessa understood that her uncle was preparing himself for war.

It was cold today. She wore two cloaks over her tunic and skirt, and her thick woolen stockings and sheepskin boots, and a felt hat jammed down over her ears. The wind tore at her hair and numbed her face and hands as she made her way southward along the path through the dunes. She had been close to abandoning her walk altogether. Even at ebb tide, the wind had whipped ocean spray through the gap between Whaleback and mainland. She must not spend too long over the rituals, for the tide's inward surge across the causeway was powerful in all seasons, and today the narrow path was treacherous indeed. There were huts near the point, where fisherfolk dwelt, but Engus did not like her to stay there overnight. Were it not for the importance of the rituals, she thought he would have sent her away, as far away as he could, until the troubles were over.

As Nessa neared Rona's tiny cottage, the dog, which had been keeping pace with her at its usual cautious distance, began to edge closer. Its dark eyes were fixed on her as if expecting something. She had brought bread today, but it was fastened into the small pack she bore.

"You'll have to wait," Nessa told the hound gravely. "Later. Good boy."

The dog kept looking at her. They passed the bushes where it usually settled to wait. They walked on, down into the hollow where the stream flowed by, down into the women's place. The creature's tail was wagging furiously; it sniffed the ground and barked again, and now there was an answer, another dog barking in greeting, but the sound seemed to come from under the ground, from the tower in the earth.

"Here you are." Rona, well shawled against the cold, was sitting by a small fire, which burned between rocks on a patch of level ground. The stream gurgled by, swollen from autumn rains. There was a pot on the fire, and steam rising, and a fragrant scent of herbs. Rona's hut was not far away, but she could usually be found here, for she liked to watch the many moods of the sky. "You've brought a visitor, I see. But we have a visitor already. And we have a problem."

Nessa put her bag down. The other hound must have wandered in here somehow and sheltered in the ancient cairn. That did not present much of a difficulty as long as the Norsemen did not want them back. Now the first dog was running about and pawing the earth at the cairn's entrance. Nessa walked across. Since that time long ago, when she had first discovered the tower in the earth, she had dug out its true door and its original passageway, always with due respect for the ancestors. It was now possible to walk in, though one had to stoop, and to stand upright in that first chamber. Light could be admitted by shifting the flagstone on the top, where a small Nessa had once made patterns of sun and moon, sea and quarters. There were little oil lamps inside and an old blanket or two. She used the tower for certain rituals, solitary ones. Some powers are best honored in underground places, secret, cradled places such as this.

"Careful," Rona cautioned, but Nessa knew the dogs meant no harm; she had known that from the first moment she saw that creature moving along beside her like a graceful shadow. They might have come all the way from the snow lands, but they belonged here now. All the same, Rona did not utter warnings without good reason. Perhaps the other dog was injured, and might bite. If it was unharmed, why would it remain inside?

Nessa retreated, fetched a lamp from Rona's hut, bent to light the wick from the fire. Rona wasn't saying anything. There wouldn't have been much point, with the racket the two dogs were making. Nessa walked back to the cairn's low entry and

made her way in through the stone-lined passageway that led to
the first chamber. The dog pushed past her, knocking her sideways; she bumped her head and nearly dropped the little lamp.
Ahead, there was an ecstatic chorus of canine greeting.

As soon as she emerged from the tunnel and straightened up,
the two dogs jumped on her, planting large paws on her chest
and arms, tongues licking enthusiastically. Standing thus, they
were as tall as she was. The lamp wobbled dangerously.

"Down!" Nessa commanded sharply. They obeyed, tongues
lolling, dark eyes gleaming expectantly in the shadowy chamber. The second creature was skin and bone, its ear torn, its coat
filthy. It seemed friendly enough. She should be able to coax it
out without much difficulty.

"Come on, then," Nessa said encouragingly. "Good girl.
Come on, then." She backed toward the passageway, clicking
her fingers. The dogs stood still as carven images, watching her.
She'd have to go out and get the bread. "Come on. Good boy."

She took another step back, trod on something, lost her balance and fell to one knee, putting out a hand to steady herself.
Still grasping the flickering lamp, she looked down. There at
her feet was a bundle of old cloth and fur and bits of metal, a
large bundle that didn't belong here, for this was a secret place
where only she and Rona could come, a place where nothing
was left without a purpose. The dogs padded closer, quite silent
now. Nessa looked again. There was an axe. It was a very fine
axe with patterns like shimmering water on the blade and a
handle of oak. She held the lamp nearer, and her heart lurched.
There was a fist clutching the handle. The fist belonged to a
man, a man who lay curled on himself in a ball, knees drawn
up, one arm over his face, the other protective around this great
weapon of death. He clung to it even in what seemed the deepest sleep, a sleep beyond dreams. He was not dead: those
clutching fingers showed that. Perhaps he would wake suddenly
and the arm would come up and the axe would strike her down
where she knelt by him. Perhaps. But the dogs were quiet, sensing no danger. Nessa reached out her hand and, taking a corner
of the woolen cloth that covered his face, peeled it gently back.

She had seen this man before. He was the big one, the silent
one who watched the sky. His eyelids were heavily closed, his
chin rough with a stubble of new-grown beard, his skin pallid

and dry. He had dark shadows around his eyes, and a sunken look to his features. Still, she knew him. His hair gleamed dull gold in the lamplight. He was shivering, she could feel the trembling through the woolen cloak that lay over him. Under his head was the wolfskin he had once worn on his shoulders. Everything was damp; cloak, fur, tunic, hair, everything. He looked as if he'd been a long time without food and water. Rona had been right. They did indeed have a problem.

Nessa set her lamp on a shelf. She took off her thick outer cloak and laid it over the man, tucking it close around his neck and shoulders. She stepped back. The cloak, which came down to her ankles when she wore it, barely covered this man, even in his tightly curled position. His skin was cold to the touch, deathly cold. She fetched the old blankets, wondering that he had not found them himself, wondering that he had not sought out Rona's fire. Now she could cover him right up, so that all she could see was a wisp or two of his bright hair, and the pale skin of his brow.

She went to the passageway, motioning the dogs to follow. They stared at her. Then the second dog, the female, moved back to the fallen warrior and flopped down at his side, muzzle on paws. She might be starving and hurt, but it was clear she was not leaving him. Probably it was her warmth that had kept the young man alive thus far. The other dog followed Nessa outside and down to the fire.

Rona handed Nessa a cup of the steaming, aromatic brew. It was good to feel its warmth thawing the frozen bones of her hands. The wise woman swore by herbal teas for times of confusion, sadness, or just plain cold. She had a brew for every occasion. The dog settled by Rona's feet. For a little, they sat in silence.

"How did he get here?" Nessa asked eventually. "When did he come?"

The old woman sucked her tea between her teeth. "I found him yesterday. He could have been there seven, eight days; it's at least that long since you or I had cause to go in there. Must have found his way in and made himself at home, very quietly indeed. Him and the bitch. Hard to say which is the sorrier specimen."

"Did you give him food? Water? Did he tell you anything?"

Rona turned her pebble-gray eyes on Nessa. "Me? No, child. I bolted out of there the moment I saw him. What is he but a big man with a big axe? His kind knows nothing but killing. He doesn't belong here, no man does, and that sort least of all. As for food and water, he's beyond either. Hound's been out once or twice since I found them, but the fellow hasn't moved a muscle. Curled up like a frightened babe, eyes squeezed shut: past helping, that one. Didn't stop you giving up your cloak, though, did it?"

Nessa shivered. "What do you think we should do?"

"I don't think, I know. I was only waiting for you. This man's nothing but trouble. You must go straight back and tell your uncle. Engus must come in here and take the fellow away. The king won't like walking into this place, he understands what's right and what's not. But we've no choice, and better him than anyone else. Tell him to bring the lad, Kinart. It'll take two to shift the man. It's the only way. Once the fellow's gone from here, they can do what they like with him."

Nessa could imagine. Her uncle might see the strategic advantage of a hostage, a bargaining tool for the new alliance. Kinart would be less magnanimous, with a captive Norseman lying helpless before him.

"They'll kill him," she said, her fingers stroking the dog's rough coat.

"These folk are savages." Rona spat on the earth. "Ignorant of the ways of the spirit, despoilers of land and people. They don't deserve your kindness, Nessa. You heard what happened at Ramsbeck."

There was a lengthy silence.

"Nessa?" asked the old woman after a while. "What is it?"

Nessa twisted her hands together. "What if you were really, really scared," she said, "and you ran away somewhere hidden, somewhere you thought you would be safe, and then it turned out you weren't safe at all, because someone gave you up, handed you over to your enemies? That would be a terrible betrayal."

Rona looked at her. "Him, scared?" she queried. "Did you see the size of him? Of course, he does have such bonny yellow hair. That might make a difference to you, I suppose."

"Of course it doesn't! Such things mean nothing to me. But . . . but I don't think I can do as you bid me."

"Give him up, you said. He's not yours to give, child. There's no betrayal if the fellow's your enemy. That axe still reeks with the blood of those lads who were butchered not eight nights since. A lost man's not the same as a stray dog, Nessa. Now get your cloak on, and off home with you before the fellow decides to wake up and add the two of us to his tally. You know what you have to do. Trust an old woman, will you?"

Nessa unfastened her pack and rummaged for the scraps of bread. She put them on the ground by the dog. The creature sniffed them and wagged his tail. He looked at her. He looked across at the tower in the earth.

"I have to go back in there," Nessa said, "just for a moment. I'll take some water for the other dog. Rona?"

"What is it, child?"

"You've been my teacher these ten years, the wisest mentor, the best of friends. You know I trust your judgment and follow your advice in all things. How else can I learn all I must know? But it's different this time. I am really sure about this. Surer the more I think about it."

"You're wrong," Rona said flatly. "If you don't tell, you act against all that is right and natural. It would be in defiance of the ancestors. The man must go. He has trespassed where he does not belong."

"Rona, I'm asking one favor from you. While I'm in there, I want you to look in the smoke and speak to them, to the ancestors. Ask them about this man. Read the signs. If they say you are right, if they say he's a danger to us, then I promise I'll go and tell my uncle. If not, then give me a little longer. Please?"

"You always did have a stubborn streak," Rona said. She moved closer to the fire, blew the embers to a rosy glow, then threw on a handful of half-dried seaweed from the crock she kept close for this purpose. Much could be seen in such a fire: visions, foretellings, past and present and future mixed and muddled. Only a wise woman could make any sense of it. Smoke rose into the cold air, pungent and thick. Rona closed her eyes and began to chant.

Inside the tower the man had not stirred. Nessa divided the bread between the two hounds. The dog waited until his mate had finished her own share and most of his, then bolted down the scraps she had left for him. The bitch drained the water cup dry. Nessa went out again and fetched a bucket from Rona's cottage. She filled it from the stream. Rona sat on, unseeing, by the fire, rocking to and fro, her chant accompanied by the murmuring of the water. Nessa fetched cloths and another blanket.

Now the hounds were both lying close to the man, and he did seem a little warmer, though the febrile shivering still persisted. His clothing was damp right through; even his boots were soaked. How long had he been wandering without shelter? Didn't these people know how to look after themselves? And he was filthy; he smelled worse than stable muck. But he was so big and heavy, and so deeply unconscious, that she could not even roll him over, let alone get him out of those wet things and into some dry ones. Not that it would be at all appropriate for her to attempt such a task. Still, the man was sick, hurt, perhaps afraid. Nessa remembered how he had stood and watched her on the beach, so still, so quiet. There was a certainty about this that could not be questioned. With the deep knowledge of a seer, she recognized that she had no choice but to help him.

She wet a corner of one cloth and wiped his face. His cheeks were quite sunken, the eye sockets dark with exhaustion. There was something terribly wrong with him. Maybe he would die, and she would never know what it was. Maybe she should be telling his own folk that he was here, so they could come and help him. Perhaps that was what he would want. But they could not come here. If he died, it might be her fault for not fetching help. What was he hiding from? With gentle fingers, Nessa smoothed the hair back from his brow. The sun-gold locks were tangled and matted with dirt and sweat. It would be a battle to get a comb through. She filled the cup, dipped the fresh cloth in, and squeezed a few drops of water onto his cracked lips. There was no way to tell if he could feel it. She tried again, and thought maybe his lips moved just a little. Perhaps he swallowed, perhaps not. The dogs were watching her every move.

After some time had passed, Nessa tucked the blankets close around the warrior once more as if he were a small child she was settling to sleep, and went back out to the fire. One dog shadowed her, one remained behind. Rona's eyes were open now. The smoke had cleared. In place of the pot, a flat pan was on the coals, and two griddle cakes were browning.

"I don't like this," said the wise woman bluntly.

Nessa waited.

"I don't like it. It feels wrong." Rona gnawed at her lip. "But I have to let you go your own way. That's what the signs tell me."

A great tide of relief washed through Nessa.

"So what are you going to do?" Rona asked a little testily.

"Keep him warm. Get him to drink. Find out what's wrong and try to help."

"Uh-huh. You know Engus won't let you stay away. What about when you're not here? What about that?"

"I was hoping you might help me," Nessa said quietly. "Do you think you would?"

She had to coax Uncle Engus into letting her stay with Rona a while, even though he preferred her to be at home. There was a plausible excuse. The days were very short and the weather inclement; there were fewer and fewer times when light and low tide and calm came together, allowing her a safe walk to shore and back before dusk fell. And she must observe the rituals, since Rona was growing old and could not do everything herself. That was an argument no king could ignore. The Folk were in peril. Engus built an army and hoped for a treaty. Nessa told the mysteries, scattered the bones, and listened for the ancestors. Between the two of them, perhaps there was a chance of a future. If Engus saw a life for his niece that was not the solitary one of a wise woman, he did not mention it openly. He muttered sometimes about the chieftains of the Caitt and of Dalriada, and their sons. That was as far as it went, for now.

She arrived with a bigger bundle than usual; Kinart had carried it along the shore for her. Now Kinart was heading back home, spear over his shoulder, dark eyes full of frustration, for Engus kept him close to the Whaleback, not wanting any more pointless losses. They must renegotiate the treaty. Soon the king would call Brother Tadhg back from Holy Island and send him to speak again to that man they were calling Horse-Master. But not quite yet. Even a holy man needs a rest sometimes.

While she tended to the warrior, Nessa practiced the Norse

tongue, preparing for the moment of his waking. She rehearsed possible things to say. *Your axe is not lost, I have put it away safely.* Or maybe, *I am a priestess. I can help you.* That sounded a little pompous. *You are quite safe here; don't be afraid.* That was more like it. Rona asked what she was muttering, and added a few suggestions of her own, such as, *Don't kill me, I'm a good cook,* or, *What pretty yellow hair you have.* Between the two of them, they managed to roll the young man over, and change most of the wet clothes for dry ones. Nessa had brought some of her uncle's old things, the only ones that were anywhere near big enough. She washed the warrior's own garments in the stream and dried them before Rona's cottage hearth. The shaggy skin cloak she wiped down and hung on a line. It was very big: made from the pelt of a single huge animal. The fur caught the light and shimmered as if it were alive. It was a fierce and beautiful thing, a garment she knew held its own magic. *What is this skin? Is it a part of you?*

It had been hard to take away the axe. The mists of unconsciousness wreathed him deep, yet still his fingers clung on, as if that weapon were his only anchor, his last link with what he held dear. Nessa had sat by his side a long time, watched solemnly by the two hounds, and she had stroked the fingers of his clutching fist as she might touch a nervous animal or a fretting child.

"It's all right. You can let go now. Let go, rest now. You are safe here. It's all right." Over and over she repeated such words of reassurance. There was a rightness to this, against all logic; she could feel it. As she sat there, she could sense the power of the place gathering around her, a dark, cradled power that slipped into her breathing and her voice, a healing force that moved her fingers, that flowed there like a soothing balm. It seemed to take forever. The little lamps burned steadily; Rona slipped in with a cup of water for her, and went out again in silence, a shadow woman. At last, the young man's fingers began to loosen their grip, and his hand to relax, and Nessa was able to take the handle of the great axe herself and move it gently out of his grasp. The thing was so heavy she could barely support its weight. Imagine the strength he must have to carry this about and lift it over his head and . . . no, she would not think beyond that. Nessa wrapped the shining weapon in a cloth and laid it carefully in one of the alcoves set in the cairn's inner walls. There were several of these little chambers. Rona said once, in a time before memory, they had held the bones of the ancestors. Nessa inclined her head in respect as she put the axe away, and beside it she laid a pattern of white stones: full moon, deep cave, owl mother, signs of protection. After that, she sat by his side a little longer, holding his hand, moving and stroking the cramped fingers. The warrior had nothing to cling to now, save herself. At last, she put the blankets over him again and went out.

In the cottage, Rona was warming bere gruel over the hearth fire. There were reminders everywhere of their strange visitor: boots near the door, tunic and trousers spread over a bench, the great shining fur hung up in a corner, whispering in the winter draft.

"He drank well today," Nessa said, settling by the fire. "He seems to be able to swallow, for all this heavy sleep that's on him. He just doesn't seem to want to wake up."

"He'll wake up all right, more's the pity," Rona grumbled, dropping a pinch of salt into the iron pot and giving the gruel a brisk stir. "That's when your problems will really start. Still, at least he'll be able to take a hand in cleaning himself, then. I never wanted bairns, too much bother entirely. I didn't think I'd get a big one like this in my old age. Here, lassie, eat up. You look weary to death. Why does this matter so much?"

Nessa shook her head. "I don't know. But it does. All the signs are telling me that. It's the way that must be taken, the way I must go."

"That's what's worrying me," Rona said, dipping a horn spoon into her bowl. "I thought there was a path mapped out for you; I saw it clear from the first day you made your way in here and fashioned your wee pictures in stones. Now it's looking as if maybe I was wrong."

"Nonsense," said Nessa as a shiver went through her. "We'll feed him up and get him moving, and he'll go away back to his own folk. Then it'll be just like it was before."

"Uh-huh." It was plain from Rona's tone that she believed this bold prediction no more than Nessa did herself. As they sat listening to the wind that howled outside, beating against the shutters, setting the roof weights knocking on the walls, both of them knew the future had changed the moment the warrior had stepped into the forbidden place. He had broken a pattern; he had altered not just his own path, but theirs as well.

"If it weren't for the ancestors," Rona said, scraping the last of the gruel from her bowl, "I'd push him out of the nest, and you with him, and be my own woman again. But you can't ignore the signs. What if he wakes at night?"

"The dogs will warn me."

They finished their frugal supper. Nessa cleared the bowls away, wiped out the pot, damped down the fire. As the rising gale tore at the thatch and rattled at the door, they settled themselves for the night. By Nessa's pallet, one dog slept, nose on paws. The other was in the ancient cairn, curled up by the sleeping warrior. It was clear they kept some kind of watch.

That night Nessa dreamed of children, two boys climbing a tall tree, taller far than any of the stunted trees that grew on the islands, a tree such as existed only in stories or visions. She thought the boys were brothers, though one was dark as night, one fair as day. All the way up, one helped the other, stretching out a hand, showing the best place to balance, offering words of encouragement. They reached the top. There was a little platform there, and for a moment they perched side by side like a pair of owls, gazing out over a wide land of fertile fields and fair waterways. Then the dark lad gave the other a push in the back, and the fair one was suddenly hanging, clutching precariously by one hand, his fingers clinging to a slender branch that bent and creaked under his weight. Quick, quick, the other must seize him and haul him up; it was so far to the ground below, to fall was certain death. Now it was Nessa hanging there, and her fingers were slipping, and she was gasping, *Help! Help me!* The dark-haired boy leaned over and reached down, he was going to save her, and then, oh . . . then, she saw the little knife in his hand, and felt the slashing of it into the flesh of her arm, and looked up into a pair of eyes shadow-black, and a face quite devoid of any human feeling save mild curiosity. *Oh, dear,* said the boy, and then her fingers lost their grasp and she was falling, falling away down. . . .

Nessa sat up abruptly. A dream: a terrible dream, that was all it was. Her heart was thumping, her skin clammy. On the far side of the cottage, Rona snored gently under her coverlets. The dog was awake, ears pricked, its eyes on Nessa as she sat there in her nightrobe and woolen shawl. Now. Now was the time. Never mind that it was the middle of the night and there was a storm raging outside. The dream had been a sign. Shivering, she threw on her cloak and lit a lantern from the embers on the hearth.

The moment she stepped outside, the lantern blew out. It was too dark to see the way; she clutched the long hair of the dog's back and let the creature lead her. By the time she reached the tower in the earth and stumbled in through the passageway, her hair was in a wild tangle over her face, and her cloak was slipping off her shoulders. It was not quite dark inside the cairn; the tiny oil lamp she had set in an alcove when she left was still burning, for this earth-guarded place was far more sheltered than the cottage. Had not it stayed secure since the time of the first ancestors? The warrior had chosen his hiding place wisely.

She had known he would be awake. He was sitting up and had drunk some of the water she had left there; he held the cup in his hand. In the lamplight, his strong features looked like a ghost's, all white planes and shadows.

Nessa had practiced what to say often enough. Now she lit her lantern from the lamp, and stood watching him for a moment. The words, when they came out, were not the ones she had prepared.

"I had a—a nightmare. I was frightened. I thought you might be awake."

The man stared at her with his bright blue eyes. He must think she was crazy; she had to assemble her thoughts and try to sound as if she were in control.

"Don't drink too much at first," she went on. "You've been a long time—" what was the word for unconscious, she had forgotten, "—a long time sleeping, not knowing; it is bad to drink too much, too quickly."

The man was still shivering. "Nightmare," he said, and reached out toward her. There seemed no choice but to take the proffered hand and sit down beside him. She did not know if he was referring to himself or to her.

"Yes, a bad one," she agreed, wondering why she seemed unable to say any of the practical, sensible things. "It scared me. I was falling, he cut me and I was falling."

The man nodded. His hand was still around hers, a very big hand, in keeping with the arms that had once wielded that war axe. It seemed he was not going to say any more.

"Eyvi?" Nessa ventured after a while. "That's your name, isn't it?" She hoped she had remembered right. "Are you lost?"

He glanced at her, and quickly away.

Nessa tried again. "Is that your name?"

The man gave a sort of half nod, as if he were not quite sure himself.

"My name is Nessa. You are safe here. I will look after you." There, at least she had got some of it out. This was strange indeed, to be sitting here by his side, letting him hold her hand as if it were she who needed comfort. She had never let a man do that before, and she did not intend to again. The two dogs settled down together in the blankets at the warrior's feet. He had not asked about the axe.

The young man leaned back against the stone wall and closed his eyes. His skin seemed almost transparent, the bones starkly prominent. It was a long time since he had eaten anything: too long.

"You are hungry?" ventured Nessa. "I have bread, fish; I can fetch them. You are very weak. You have been many days without food."

He simply shook his head without opening his eyes; perhaps it was an effort to speak at all.

"In the morning, then," she said. "You must eat. You must get well."

He shook his head again, as if he barely understood. She was sure she had got the words right.

"You want to go home?" she said. "Eat, rest, then go home?"

"No," he whispered, opening his eyes suddenly. "No!" The shivering began again, so violent now that he let go her hand and wrapped his arms around himself as if to try to force himself still. "Sorry," he said through chattering teeth, and then yawned convulsively.

"You must try to sleep," Nessa said, motioning that he should lie down again. "It's cold, I know. We could make a small fire in here tomorrow. Here, put this blanket around you, that's it, and—"

"Wolfskin," he said suddenly. "Where's my wolfskin?"

She did not know *wolf,* but she understood. "Safe," she told him as he lay down once more, eyelids already closing. "It was wet; I'm drying it. You can have it in the morning. A beautiful skin. That must have been a fine animal, a great hunter of some kind."

"Once, maybe," he said. "Not anymore. He can't hear it anymore."

"Hear it? What?"

"The call. Thor's call."

"I'm sorry," she said, not understanding what he meant. "Maybe I can help. But sleep first."

"Cold," he said, sitting up again and grasping her hand as she tried to tuck the blanket over him. "Cold. Lost. I dreamed that, only it was real. What did you dream?"

"I . . ." Nessa hesitated. The nightmare was there in her mind, not so very far away; it could not help him to hear it. "I don't—"

"Tell me." Perhaps he was not so weakened after all, for he drew her down to sit by him again, close enough to share the blanket's warmth, close enough to feel the trembling of his body against hers: too close. "Tell me," he whispered.

"I–I was climbing up, the boys were climbing up the tree, helping each other. It was exciting, it was a big tree, so high, so high, the tallest tree in the world. When they got to the top, they felt like kings. They could see a whole land down there, villages, farms, little cows like dots on the green fields. And then . . . and then . . ."

His arm came up and around her shoulders; curiously, this did not alarm her. She felt safe.

"Go on," he said.

"Then the boy pushed him—pushed me—and I fell down, I couldn't hold on. He was my friend, and he cut me, and I fell down, right down, all the way to the ground. But he was my friend."

Why had she blurted it out like that? The man was a complete stranger, an enemy. Yet here, in the darkness of this little space, there was a strange sense of rightness to it. The usual rules did not seem to apply tonight.

"Nessa," the young man said, trying out her name. "Nessa, why did you dream my dream?"

That shocked her. "I don't know," she said. "Was it the same?"

"One of them." The shivering suddenly grew more violent, great tremors that shook his whole body. Perhaps he had an ague, or some other malady new to her. "Cold," he said again. "Sorry. They come, the dreams, they come over and over. They won't go away. Set me shivering like a . . . like a stupid, weak—"

"It's the ancestors speaking to you," Nessa told him. "When you have a dream you cannot forget, even a bad one, they are trying to tell you something. It's up to you to make sense of it, to work out what it means."

"Ancestors?" His teeth were chattering, bone music, death music. "What ancestors?"

"You might call them gods, or spirits." The blanket slipped down, dislodged by his involuntary shaking. Nessa tucked it around the two of them again. They sat a while in silence, and slowly the trembling subsided, and she could feel the shared warmth seeping into her.

"If they are gods," his voice came haltingly, as if with a great effort, "what are you? Are you not a goddess or spirit? Isn't this part of another dream, a good one this time?"

That explained a certain amount, Nessa thought wryly. "No, Eyvi," she said. "I am a wise woman, a priestess. You stumbled into a forbidden place, a place where men cannot come, not even our kind."

"I saw you," he said. "By the sea. I didn't think you were real. Maybe this is not real either. None of it, none of the dreams, none of the memories, maybe I will wake and Thor will be there as if he had never left me, and . . ." He had begun to shake again for all the warmth, a fierce tremor that was perhaps not cold, but fear. She remembered how he had looked the first time she'd seen him on the path between land and sea, an island of quiet among the others. That tall, still figure had not seemed a man who would be easily frightened.

"It is real, Eyvi," she told him. "Perhaps that's bad for you, I don't know. I don't know what has happened to you. But you are awake, and so am I, and in the morning we will both still be here. And because I am a real woman, I cannot stay here with you tonight. I have another place to sleep, and I must go there. In the morning, I will bring food, and I will make a little fire to keep you warmer."

"No. Please." His words were the merest wisp of sound; his arm tightened around her shoulders. "Cold." And he was right, it was dark and windy outside, and the warmth of his body felt good, as if it would keep away unwelcome thoughts until tomorrow. The dogs slept, a bundle of limbs, tails, whiskery muzzles, a faint sigh of breath.

"Just a bit longer, then."

"Your name is like the sea, like a little wave on the pebbles, or a sigh," the young man said. "Nessa. I never heard that name before."

She heard this as a soft whisper, so soon gone, she decided she had imagined it, for surely a warrior with a big axe would never say such a thing. Surely she was the only person in the world who thought about names that way, as if they could tell you something about their owners. She waited until his breathing quieted, and the shivering stopped altogether, and she thought he was asleep. In a little while, she would slip out from under his arm and creep across to the passageway, and go back through the dark to Rona's cottage. She'd go in just a moment . . .

Old folk need little sleep. It was as well, then, that Nessa woke very early, before the wise woman was stirring. She lay in a tumble of blankets and dogs, and the young man was stretched out behind her with his arm comfortably around her as if it had every right to be there, and his breath gentle against the back of her neck. It was completely inappropriate. She could not believe she had been so foolish as to let herself fall asleep here. Imagine if Rona had come wandering in. As for how good it felt to wake thus, sheltered by his arm and warmed by his body, that she would not even begin to think about. Nessa slipped carefully from under his arm and went out into the dark morning. Today, her dog did not stir, but lay close-folded with his mate in blissful slumber.

By the time Rona rose creakily from her own bed, Nessa had the cottage fire made up and flatcakes cooking in a pan. She sprinkled dried herbs into a cup, added a scoop of honey, filled it with hot water and set it by the wise woman's side.

"Mmm," Rona grunted, easing her joints. "Perhaps it's not so bad having company here after all. Big breakfast. Hungry, are you?"

"He woke up," Nessa said.

"What?"

"He woke up in the night. Some of this is for him. He seems . . . confused. Frightened even. He thought I was a spirit."

Rona's gaze was sharp. "Oh yes? When did all this happen?"

"In the night. I left him sleeping. The dogs are there."

"Oh yes," said Rona, which could have meant anything, and she watched through narrowed eyes as Nessa bore a platter of food and a jug of tea out of the cottage.

Nessa had wondered what the young man would say and how she could reply. It might be a little awkward. As it turned out, he wasn't saying much, not now. He was sitting with his back to the wall, the blankets tossed aside, despite the chill. When she came in, he started and blinked, as if returning to himself from far away. Nessa put the platter down by him, fetched the cup, and filled it from her jug.

"You'll be hungry," she said, dividing a flatcake with her fingers and offering him a piece. It smelled appetizing, warm from the fire and flavored with parsley and dried mushrooms. The young man shook his head; closed his eyes.

"You should eat, Eyvi," Nessa said, settling herself on the ground, not too close this time. The dogs hovered, noses twitching eagerly. "It's good. I made it myself."

There was a noise from outside, the creak of the cottage door as Rona made her way out to the privy. The young man's eyes snapped open. He made an attempt to spring to his feet; his legs buckled under him and he collapsed to the ground, muttering something under his breath.

"Too weak to stand up," Nessa commented. "You see? Now eat your breakfast."

"Who is here?" he hissed. "Who's that outside? Who knows that I am here?"

"Nobody," Nessa said, alarmed at the look in his eyes, which was the dazed expression of a wild creature trapped. "Just my friend, an old woman, a priestess like myself. She is no threat to you. I told you, this is a forbidden place. None of my folk know you are here, save Rona and myself."

This did not seem to be the answer he needed, for he had begun to shake again; Nessa could see how he clutched at the blanket, at the rock wall, in a vain attempt to still the shuddering that ran through his body. She made a guess.

"Nobody knows. Not even your own people. You are safe here. Now do as I say. Start with the tea, the herbs will give you strength. Take the cup in your hand, good. Now drink. Just a little at a time. Then the food. Not too much, a small piece, and chew it properly. I hope I won't have to feed you like an infant."

His hand was shaking so hard that the tea slopped over onto the ground. He managed a sip, grimacing. He took a scrap of flatcake in his other hand. A start, anyway. This could be laborious. Nessa herself was hungry, for it had been a long night. She started on her own breakfast, throwing the dogs a morsel each. The warrior watched her over the rim of the cup, blue eyes wary.

"You don't like my cooking?" she ventured. "It's all you'll be getting while you stay here. Best make the most of it. Why have you come here, Eyvi? What were you running from?"

"Nothing," he growled.

"I want to help you," Nessa said cautiously. "I can tell something is wrong."

"Why would you help?" he muttered. "Your folk are killers, destroyers of the innocent. You break your promises."

Nessa stared at him. "What do you mean?" she asked. "That is not true."

"First Ulf. He made peace, and your people strung him up to die a slow death. I know; I found him. And a woman was burned with her children, just because she wed one of us. Hakon was a good man. He did not deserve that. If you hate us so much, why shelter me? Why not hand me straight over to King Engus?"

Nessa gaped. "How can you say that? That the widow, Ara, was killed by her own folk? We would never do such a thing, it is against all we believe in. It was your people killed her. A savage, cruel murder, like that of your chieftain, Ulf. How dare you accuse us of such deeds? Would we destroy our own children when we have so few left?"

There was a silence.

"I'm sorry," she added, watching the play of expressions on his drawn features. "It is the truth. Our people had no hand in this act of evil."

"You say, then, that it was my kind who lit that fire? I will not believe it."

"I have no reason to lie to you."

"Our people would not murder a Wolfskin, with his family by him. I saw their bodies. I helped to bury them. It cannot be so." There was a note in his voice that belied the words; it came to Nessa that he spoke less to convince her than to deny a truth already known.

"What is this word, Wolfskin?" she asked him. "I don't understand."

"A special kind of warrior; a man such as I am—was. To pass the test, we battle the wolf. We wear his skin. Thor calls; we answer. Hakon, who was burned, he was such a one in times past. A friend. No man deserves such a death, a death without honor."

Nessa frowned. She had finished her flatcake; he had eaten only the smallest fragment of his own. "Surely it is not without honor to die protecting your family," she said. "That was what I heard. It was terrible, but at least they were together. He sheltered them as best he could."

The young man set the cup down abruptly and put his head in his hands. The dogs moved in on the scattered remnants of the food.

"I'm sorry," Nessa said again.

"A Wolfskin lives and dies on the field of battle." His voice was not much more than a whisper. "He is obedient only to Thor's will; that is his sole purpose. If he is slain thus, he is carried straight to the god's right hand, a reward unequalled in life. A Wolfskin charges forward, whatever the odds, armed with his own courage, his own strength of will. If he cannot do that, if he can no longer hear Thor's voice, he is . . ." His voice faded away altogether.

"Lost?" asked Nessa gently, and when there was no response, she got up and busied herself tidying, and opening the roof slab so they could make a fire, and generally trying to give him a little time. She was not sure she had understood all that he said. He hated his weakness, that was plain. The bleak emptiness in his eyes, the flatness of his voice chilled her. If he had not reached out for her last night, she might have thought he had given up. Still, a man who wants to die does not seek shelter. And there were the dogs, keeping close to him, guarding him almost like—almost like family.

"I do not know *wolf*," she said. "Is a wolf like a dog, only bigger?"

"He is very brave. Fierce, wild, loyal to his own. A fine hunter. A leader. Such was the chieftain I killed: a king of wolves."

"Did you kill him with your axe?"

"With my hands."

"Your *hands?*" Nessa thought of that huge skin hanging now in Rona's cottage, a pelt as big as a pony's, almost. She knelt down beside him and turned his hands over, palms up, wondering how even such a large man could manage such a feat. "When did you do this?"

He shook his head. "Long ago, in another land. When I was a boy. In my fifteenth year."

"That is very young. How could you kill such a great creature with your bare hands?"

"I don't know," he said tightly.

"What is this?" Nessa asked him, her fingers moving to touch the scar above his wrist, a long line that scored the forearm deep. She had seen it before, when they changed his clothes, and wondered.

His hands balled themselves into fists. "Nothing," he snapped, trying to pull away from her.

"That is strange," Nessa said. "When I touch this, I see—" She broke off. Before her eyes was last night's dream, the climbing, the vista, the cutting, the falling. She shivered.

"What's wrong?" His voice had changed completely. "What's the matter?" His big hand came up over hers, and now it was she who snatched her fingers away, backing up to leave safe space between them.

"Nothing. I—I just wondered. I'm sorry, it is not my business."

"Why do you ask so many questions? What do you want me to do?"

"I told you, I want to help you. Help you regain your strength, and then . . . and then go wherever you want to go."

"You will not want to do that when I tell you . . . when I tell you . . ." His voice began to shake.

"You should rest again," Nessa said. "Lie down. There."

"It's too much," he muttered. "You're only a girl . . . but I can't, I can't even stand up, I'm good for nothing anymore. . . ."

"If that worries you, there is a simple solution. Eat what I give you, rest when I tell you, and get better quickly so you can look after yourself. Even a . . . even a Wolfskin can't go without food and drink for so many days and expect to be himself. Lie there a while. Do you know Brother Tadhg? The holy man?"

He nodded weakly.

"Tadhg told me something once. He said, no matter what you've done, no matter how terrible it is, as long as you are truly sorry you can be forgiven. That means you can go on, no matter what mistakes you have made. His god is a god of love; he loves all his creatures, no matter what their past may be."

"Are you a Christian, then?" he asked her. "Is that why you tend to a man whose axe bears the lifeblood of your own folk?"

Nessa shuddered. "No, I am of a far more ancient faith, a darker faith. It is not so easy for me to forgive, and the ancestors do not forget. The shadow of ill deeds lingers in the hollows of the land and darkens the waters. It rustles in the leaves; the wind howls the song of sorrow. It cannot be put aside as if it had never been."

"Then why do you keep me safe?"

"Because I know I must. I have known it since I first saw you. The signs tell me."

"Signs? What signs?"

"Shh. You must rest."

"Will you stay here with me?"

"Only until you fall asleep again. And only if you promise to eat, later. Promise me."

But he was overtaken by shivering again, and could not answer her. His sleep, when it came, was fitful, brief snatches of slumber ended by sudden, white-faced waking, as if what he saw in his dreams was too terrible to be endured longer. Later, he attempted to eat what she had prepared, but could not hold even the few mouthfuls he took in his stomach long. When he had retched it up into the bowl she held for him, he turned his face away from her.

"Sorry," he said. "I don't think there's much point, really."

"Are you telling me I can't do this?" Nessa asked him fiercely, overtaken suddenly with feelings she could not explain: frustration, fear, and something perilously like what had been there, for a moment, when she woke that morning in his arms. "You think we should just—give up?"

"You don't know me," he whispered. "Once I was a man, a warrior. Now I am nothing, not worth your efforts, not worth your care. Thor has abandoned me. I disgust him. I disgust myself. Why should you bother with me?"

"You could tell me about it if you want to," Nessa said. "Then I could make up my own mind."

"I would distress you. I would frighten you away."

"I'm a priestess," she reminded him. "I don't frighten so easily. Tomorrow you could tell me. Or the next day. This is a new path; perhaps we must walk it more slowly, until the two of us learn it."

Progress was indeed slow. He nibbled at the food she gave him, eating scarcely enough to keep a vole alive. He drank the teas she brewed. He spoke less and less as the days passed, responding only when she asked him a direct question, and then as briefly as he could. He was wary of Rona, a sentiment the old woman returned.

Because his sleep was fitful and much visited by night terrors, the two women tried to sit with him in turns and keep the little fire going, since the young man seemed to feel the cold so badly.

"That's a chill that's right inside," Rona observed. "The spirit's frozen; no wonder he can't stop shaking, for all the fire and the dogs and the nice warm cloak that should be on your own shoulders, not his. There's a kind of curse on him, a darkness. He'll never get warm until that's lifted. I don't like it, and

I don't like him, child. If you're not careful, this one will take
and take until there's nothing left of you to give."

Nessa only shook her head. Maybe right now this young warrior seemed weak and hopeless, a wreck of a man unable to
help himself. But she had seen him before. She had seen and
recognized what he was. The ancestors knew him. The dogs
had guarded him. It was just a matter of waiting, and taking one
step at a time.

He talked to himself sometimes.

"Cursed islands," Nessa heard him muttering one day as she
watched him pretending to eat the soup she had prepared. The
dogs were growing fatter, sleek and content, but he was like a
pale shadow warrior. "Godforsaken place. There's nothing but
loss here, death and loss."

Nessa put a little more turf on the fire. Outside, the wind
scoured the land, whipping sand into a stinging curtain, driving salt spray far into the dunes, so that everything was damp
and clammy. Rona had stayed in the cottage. Nessa knew the
old woman's joints ached on days like this, though Rona never
said so.

"I hate this," the young man whispered, giving up altogether
and putting the soup bowl on the earthen floor, where the bitch
soon licked it clean. "I hate this place. These islands set frost in
the bones and winter in the heart."

Nessa stared at him. "Oh, no," she said softly. "You see from
your own pain, and so you do not see truly. The Light Isles are a
place of wonder, Eyvi. You need only open your eyes. And you
can do it, I've seen you. I've seen you watching the sea and the
sky. That's how I know . . ." She was not sure how to finish this.

"Know what?"

"Know that you have a part to play here. Know that somehow
you belong here. If not for that, I would have done Rona's bidding and turned you over to King Engus. Believe me, I do not
make a habit of sheltering enemy warriors in this place sacred
to the women's mysteries. I did so because I recognize something in you that you have forgotten, or have not yet seen."

"You say I belong here." He would not look at her, but she
could see the shadow of disbelief in his eyes. "That is not true.
This place has destroyed me."

"You want to go home, then? Back across the ocean? Would that make all well for you?"

He was silent a while; it seemed the effort of maintaining a conversation had exhausted him. "When the wolf becomes too weak to hunt, when he can neither lead nor follow, it is the end for him," he said eventually. "I belong nowhere."

"You could become strong again," Nessa ventured, "if you would eat. This dog came here as weak and damaged as yourself. She's growing well now, see her bright eyes? You could help yourself, Eyvi."

"Grow strong to what purpose? There is no purpose. Grow strong to face my enemy and hear only Thor's silence? Grow well to find I can no longer do what my whole life has prepared me for? I should not have sheltered here. I should have had the courage to end it. Thor did not want me to come to these islands; he punishes me with a shame that is lifelong."

Nessa hated the flat, hopeless tone of his voice. "You're making me angry, Eyvi," she said sternly.

Now he looked at her. "Angry? Why?"

"Because it is such a waste. Unlike the wolf, a man can tread another path. Unlike that wild creature, a man can listen for other calls, can make a choice about his future. I, too, wish winter was over. The time of darkness stretches out; it sets a shadow on every spirit, even the gladdest and most innocent. But we need it. We need it to rest, and reflect, and become open to the mysteries. Waking cannot exist without sleeping."

He seemed to be listening; his eyes were fixed on her face now. He said nothing.

"If it were spring, I would take you up to the high cliffs south of this bay," Nessa said, seeing it as she spoke. "There is a little hollow, a grassy cup just below the clifftop where you can sit and look out far over the western sea, so far it seems you might see the edge of the world itself. The sun warms that small, safe place; the earth holds you in a hand more ancient than the oldest stories of the first ancestors. And yet, sitting there is like being poised on the brink of something new: a fresh beginning, clear and strong as the wind from the sea. There are so many birds there, Eyvi, all kinds, wheeling and gliding, coming in and out with fish for the small ones on the ledges. It is an endless dance of wind and feather, balance and brightness. Their cries make a music, a wild song that sounds above the endless roar of the sea, borne on the breath of the west wind. If you were well, and it were spring, I would take you there. To sit there in stillness, to let it unfold around you, is to know the wonder of this place."

He was silent; his fingers moved to stroke the dog's gray hair behind the ears. Watching Nessa, his eyes were bleak and empty.

"Summer days are long in the Light Isles," she went on. "The best time then is early in the morning, when the sea shows a thousand colors, pearl, dove gray, silver, duck-egg green, sweet soft blue. At such a time, it is easy to hear the voices of the ancestors, whispering words of peace, words of belonging. I walk on the shore at those times, but slowly, because there are so many treasures to find: so many wonders to capture the eye. Each little stone is different, its shape and color all its own; each one is lovely and mysterious. Some have patterns, pale lines in a strange tracery like old, old writing in some language lost from memory. Sometimes I sit and hold one in my hand, and wonder if the message flows into me somehow, making me wise in the ways of the earth. The weed washes in and drapes those stones in a feathery cloak; the sand clings to them, and makes small hills and valleys around their curves. There is so much to discover there: tangled fronds of kelp like a puzzle; delicate, secret shells; tiny crabs like bright jewels; shy, creeping plants; long-legged foraging birds whose feet make their own neat script in the sand. So much to see, if only your eyes are open. When the sun is setting, in springtime, the wet beach shines like fire, and the sky glows with an enchantment of colors. These things are part of us, Eyvi; they are our life, and we are theirs. Because of that, we do not give up hope, even in times of terrible darkness. That's why I wish things were different now, so I could walk that way with you, and show you."

"In a life such as mine there is no place for these things," he said. The dog had laid her head on his lap, and his hand still moved, gently stroking her coat. "It is a different world."

"No, Eyvi," Nessa said. "This is the same world. It is you who are different. Not weak, not useless, not lost: just changed. Perhaps you did not want to come to these islands, but you have come, and the islands have changed you. They have claimed you. Do not curse them for that. The ancestors need you here. They want you here. We need only discover why, I think."

"I am no part of this," he said in a whisper. Nessa made no reply. The signs had made it clear to her that he must stay, but she could not show him the signs; that was forbidden. How could she show him? He could not summon the strength so much as to crawl forth from his hiding place, and a warrior does not see with the eye of the spirit. How could she reach him?

"You are become a part of it," she said. "Perhaps we need only wait, and it will become plain to us what we must do."

The days passed, many days. He was quite weak, unable to walk, and the trembling continued to plague him, despite his furious efforts to control it. He did not talk much, not now, but simply sat watching Nessa as she went about her tasks. The silence between them was not uncomfortable; if one shared the same dreams, Nessa thought, that made a sort of understanding that did not require words. All the same, she blessed those practice sessions with Tadhg, for she must try to break through the barrier the young man held around him so fiercely. The Ulsterman had taught her well, and the language flowed ever more freely, words coming swiftly to her mind when she needed them.

"I do know how it feels to be sad, to feel everything is against you," she told him as she rekindled the small fire one morning. "There was a time not so long ago when I felt like that. I was angry as well. I only had to sit still and open my eyes to the world around me, and the path forward became clear again. I'm sorry it is not springtime, Eyvi. I'm sorry what has happened between your people and mine means I cannot take you to those places I spoke of. I would show you the web of life itself: the wonder that surrounds us, the ancient pattern we are a part of. If you understand that, the mystery and loveliness of it, you can never be quite lost in despair. You just need to open your eyes and look, that's all. Look beyond the axe and the sword."

"The axe and the sword are my world," he said. "For me, there is nothing beyond."

"I don't believe you." Nessa set a small pot of water on the fire. "I see more in you than that, I did from the first."

He said nothing, only watched her. Fluent as she was in the foreign tongue, still she wondered sometimes if he had understood her. If only she could make him see beyond what he thought were his own failings; if only she could make him see beyond the call to battle. It would take time; she must be patient.

There came a day when the wind was calmer, and she wondered if she might persuade him to test his legs enough to venture outside. He was still very weak, but she knew he hated others tending to his body's every need, and if he could at least make his way out to the privy with a little help, he might begin to despise himself less. Rona had the fire lit out in the open; it was the first time this had been possible for many days. Nessa stretched, looking up at the heavy clouds, the low, slanting sunlight trying to break through. It was strange. Within the confines of the tower in the earth, tending to her warrior, she almost forgot there was another world out here. Perhaps some of what Rona had said was right.

There was a call from down on the shore. "Nessa! Nessa, come out if you're there!"

Kinart's voice. Kinart come to bring food or maybe a message. She'd have to go and talk to him, explain that she must stay here a bit longer. It was just as well he was forbidden to come any closer, just as well she had not managed to coax her Norseman out. Nessa made her way along the path through the dunes and down over the tumbled stones to the little shingly beach. From here, the Whaleback was clearly visible to the north, the breaking waves a white shawl fringing its seaward cliffs. The beach was strewn with weed, thick brown stems, delicate green fronds and a tumble of broken shells. Her cousin stood waiting, spear in hand. He did not seem to have brought any supplies.

"You can stop shouting, Kinart, I'm here. What is it?"

"You took your time. You must come home, Nessa. Your mother's taken a turn for the worse. Father needs you there. And he's worried; there's been more trouble on the borders. It's not safe for you anymore out here on your own."

Nessa swallowed. Go home? Not yet, it was much too soon. But Mother sick: Mother dying, perhaps. How could she not go? "I–I have a ritual to perform. It's important. I must remain here a few more days at least. Tell Uncle Engus I'll come back in . . . in, say, four days, five? If the tides are right. What's happened with Mother?"

Kinart's dark brows creased in a frown. "She's bad," he said sternly. "Wandering, distressed. She keeps asking where you are. We tell her, but she doesn't remember. She goes on about losing all her girls, and cries. The women can't cope with it. You should come back with me today, Nessa. Father told me to fetch you."

"Three days," she said, imagining her mother all alone in some sort of madness, thinking her youngest child lost as well. "Tell Mother I'll be there in three days. After that, I'll only visit Rona at low tide, like before. But I can't come today."

"You have to come." Kinart's jaw had a very stubborn set to it; he was looking more of a man and more of a warrior every time she saw him. "This is not safe anymore. And you won't be able to keep coming back here, either. Not until Father has a treaty in place." He spat onto the pebbly ground. "Not that there's much chance of that, the savages. They'd rather pillage and slaughter than make deals. Men like this have no respect for your kind, Nessa. To them, you'd be just another young girl for the taking. You must come home to the Whaleback and stay there where we can protect you."

"What about Rona?" Nessa's voice shook with sudden anger. "I'm supposed to leave her here, am I, to tend to the mysteries alone? An old woman?"

"She could come too, I suppose," Kinart muttered. He had the grace to be a little embarrassed, at least.

"Did Uncle Engus tell you to say all that?" she demanded, folding her arms. "Or was some of it your own idea? Uncle Engus knows we must guard this place. He knows the ancestors must be honored. Now listen, I've said I'll come home in three days. You can walk back here and fetch me if you must, if you think I'm not capable of making my way along the shore alone, though I've done it most days for the past ten years. But that's it. Tell Mother I'll be there. Tell her I love her. I will come back. But I'm not abandoning this place and what belongs here. I have to keep doing this for the sake of the Folk. Without the ancestors, we'll be defeated, Kinart. Your spears and arrows, your anger and courage, those won't be enough if there's outright war."

"You're only a girl," her cousin said, as she had known he would. "We can't put you at risk. These people are capable of anything. Two more men were killed last night, stepped off a boat from High Island and into an ambush, cut to pieces. There's no reason for that save to make trouble. Scum, that's all these folk are, complete scum. I don't know what this Somerled is trying to prove."

A chill ran through Nessa. For a moment she was somewhere else, and she was playing a game, a game with little men of carven stone, black and green; she reached to move a small warrior from one finely inlaid square to the next, and a hand came out and swept the board clean, a whole army laid waste with a single, confident stroke. She looked up and saw that face again, dark-eyed, calm, clever, entirely without feeling. She did not hear him speak, but knew his thoughts. *You can't win if you don't understand the rules. Never mind, old friend. No need to trouble your head with this. I can play well enough for the two of us.*

"What is it?" Kinart asked, staring at her. "What's the matter?"

"Nothing." Nessa blinked, and there was the sea and the shore again, and the gulls pecking at what the waves had scattered. Her cousin peered at her closely, his expression concerned. "Nothing. I know what he's trying to prove. This man, Somerled Horse-Master. He's trying to prove that he's the best. The king. Highest up the tree. He's trying to prove that he always wins. Uncle Engus won't defeat him with an army, not unless the lords of the Caitt arrive in numbers to support him, and why would they do that? It's the islands themselves that will defeat this chieftain. Deep magic: the ancient knowledge. We cannot afford to neglect the rituals. Tell my uncle that. And tell him, three days."

"But—"

"Tell him, Kinart. Now I have to go. You might have brought a bit of fish or a round of cheese. Rona doesn't have much here, only what folk leave for her."

"Hungry, are you? I might have a little something." He retreated to a spot farther along the shore, retrieved a bag he had half-hidden there. "Here. I had a feeling you'd refuse to come. Caught you some fish, keep you and Rona going until I get back. Watch out for yourself, now." He bent to give her a little peck on the cheek, frowning again.

"Goodbye, Kinart. And thanks. See you in three days."

Three days: so short a time. Nessa gave the fish to Rona, and told her.

"Wonderful," the wise woman commented dryly. "So I'm left with the big baby, all on my own. If I'd wanted to be a nursemaid I wouldn't have chosen to follow the path of the spirit all those years ago. The fellow's hopeless, Nessa. There's no fight left in him. He's like a dead man."

But Nessa knew that was wrong. It had to be wrong. The signs did not lie. All he had to do was find his strength again.

"You think you can cure what ails him?" Rona asked. "Say you do. Say you succeed. Then all you'll have done is give these people back another fighting man, as if they hadn't enough already to put our folk to the knife. I can't understand why the signs lead this way. It feels like treachery. Surely the fellow would be more use as a hostage. Why didn't you tell Kinart? How am I supposed to do what must be done and tend to him as well?"

All the time the old woman was grumbling, her hands were occupied with a sharp knife, neatly gutting and scaling the fish for baking on the coals. Gulls appeared around them, gliding, squawking, ready to descend on the spoils. The two dogs came out, sniffing eagerly, tails thrashing in unison. And yes, that sound at the entry to the cairn was the whisper of a man's bare feet on the earth, the dragging of a man's cloak as he crept out from the passageway, the rasp of an indrawn breath as he rose cautiously to stand upright, swaying, one hand groping at the rocks for support, the other shielding his eyes from the sun. His face was linen-pale.

"Couldn't resist the smell of my cooking," said Rona with a grimace, throwing the fish scraps to the two hounds. Nessa was already at the young man's side, offering her shoulder for support, listening carefully for signs of distress, changes of breathing, for if he collapsed out here they would not be able to move him to shelter.

"Well done, Eyvi. This is good, very good indeed. Let's see if you can walk over to the fire; no need to open your eyes yet, lean on me, I'll guide you. Go slowly now. Good, good." His steps were shuffling, his weight on her shoulder almost enough to topple her, but somehow they got to the fireside. His legs folded; he sat down abruptly, blinking, yawning, shivering despite the winter sun.

"Better tell him." Rona glanced at Nessa. "Better break the news that he won't have his bonny wee nursemaid much longer. Fellow'll have to get used to the old crone. And me to him, worse luck. Still, at least he's walking. That's a blessing."

Nessa opened her mouth and shut it again. It was hard to choose the words.

"I'll tell him later."

"What are you saying?" His eyes were open now; she had forgotten how blue they were, summer-sky blue, spring-flower blue. "What is the old woman saying?"

"Tell him now," Rona said sharply. "He's a grown man, not a child, and he's where he doesn't belong."

"Eyvi." Nessa's tone was hesitant. She cleared her throat. "I have to go home in a few days. Three days. I'm needed there, my mother is sick. Rona will look after you."

There was a silence.

"I don't live here all the time," she added. "I have stayed because you came. But I can't stay anymore. Rona is old. She'll help all she can, but you'll have to help too."

"Where?" was all he said.

"Where what?"

"Where is home? Where are you going?"

"Up there." She pointed northward. "Not far. I will come to see you when I can. It depends on the tide and . . . and other things."

Rona was wrapping the fish in seaweed; she laid the neat, tight parcel in the embers. There was a hissing; steam rose.

"You live on the Whaleback?"

Nessa nodded.

"What's that he says?" asked Rona sourly.

"Nothing much. I have told him."

"Tell him he needs to practice walking to the privy and back, and washing his own dishes. That'd be a good start."

"What did she say?"

"She said she will look after you," Nessa told him. "And she is glad you are stronger, because she's an old woman and can't do everything."

"She cannot talk to me as you do, nor I to her," he said quietly. "I must leave here, I see that. I am a burden, fit for nothing. I can walk now. I will go." He set his jaw; she could tell he was trying to still the trembling.

"Where do you want to go?" she asked him. "Back to your friends? Home to the snow lands?"

"It doesn't matter." His voice was flat; his hands were clenched together as he tried to conceal the shaking. "There is nowhere for me to go. Not like this. But I will go from here; it is not safe for you, not safe for her to shelter me."

"Right," Nessa said, giving him a direct sort of look. "In the middle of winter, with your ribs poking out from starvation, and your whole self shivering from cold, and your head full of dark visions, you're going to walk off across the fields to nowhere. You expect me to agree to that, do you?"

"You are . . . angry with me?" he asked, turning the blue eyes straight at her. "I do not mean to offend you. It would be quicker that way, I think. Easier."

Nessa shivered.

"What's he saying?" Rona was breaking up the leftover flat-cakes, poking at the fish with a little knife.

"I think he's telling me, quite politely, that he'll just wander off into the hills and die, and make your life easier."

"Stupid man!" Rona turned on the young warrior, letting flow a torrent of words he could not understand. "How dare you throw this girl's kindness back in her teeth like that? Have you any idea what she's done for you? Can't you see the smudges under her eyes, can't you see how tired she is from running around after you? Shame on you! I don't care what's wrong with you, it matters nothing to me if you live or die, but she matters, she's like a daughter to me and if you hurt her, you'll have me to answer to, young fellow. Nessa's my treasure. And she's a priestess, by the way. Just remember that." She jabbed the knife into the fish; juices sizzled out onto the hot coals.

The warrior was staring open-mouthed. "What is she saying?"

"She's angry with you for giving up."

"There was more than that. Something about you. You and me. Why is she so angry?"

Nessa felt herself blushing. "She reminds you that I am her student, a priestess as she is. She mentions that I am looking a

little tired, and suggests you do as I tell you, so my efforts will
not be wasted. She's not really angry; it's just her way."

He did not reply, but sat looking into the fire a while. Rona
fetched a platter from the cottage, a jug of ale, three cups.

"When will you come back?" he asked, after a long silence.
"How soon?"

"As soon as I can. And we have three days. If the weather
stays fine, we might try walking a little farther. We might talk,
as well. If you are ready."

But he wouldn't talk, and he couldn't walk, not far anyway.
The constant tremor in the body made every movement difficult. He forced himself as far as the privy, as far as the fire, but
each short journey seemed to drain every morsel of strength he
could find in himself. He tried to eat, but managed no more than
a small child's portion; his broad features were skin and bone,
the eyes full of shadows. Nessa saw how he tried to conceal the
trembling, by gripping his cup tightly, by folding his arms, by
leaning against the wall with his hands behind him. Time
passed, and she dreaded the moment when she must leave, for it
seemed impossible that the two of them could manage this
without her, that the warrior would choose to stay, believing
himself a burden, a doomed man: that the wise woman would
tolerate his weakness, his large presence disturbing the peace
and sanctity of her domain.

"Doesn't know how to help himself," Rona sniffed as she went
about her work. "Well, he's a man. What would you expect?"

He must start talking, Nessa thought. Without that, she could
not really help him. There was something about Thor, a god she
had heard of from Tadhg, and something about the wolfskin.
What had he said? That Thor did not call him anymore: that
Thor was disgusted. That was at the root of it. She asked him to
tell about Thor, but he would not. "It doesn't matter." He said
that a lot. So she tried a different approach. *You would not help
me if you knew what I have done.* Very well, he should tell her
that, and see if she shared his opinion. She asked him straight
out, was he at Ramsbeck? Was that what he meant when he
spoke of the axe, and the blood? But he would not answer,
merely closed his eyes and put his hands over them again. And
when she thought about it, these two things did not go together

at all. If you wanted to hear Thor's call, that meant you wanted to be a warrior, to fight battles, to kill. If you had killed, and the memory of it hurt so much you could not even begin to speak of it here, in this safe place, to a . . . to a friend, then . . . then maybe that was your problem. You thought you knew what you wanted, what you wanted more than anything, and suddenly everything got mixed up, and right became wrong, and no wonder you thought you were lost.

And there were the dreams. She knew some of the dreams, but there were more; he saw them before his eyes, even when he was awake and the cold winter sun was shining. Nessa knew that from his face, which she had learned to read well. He had to speak of these things or he would wander in that lonely place forever. If he did not begin to talk before she went home, he might well stumble out of this small haven as he had said he would and end up dying alone, cold and frightened somewhere in the valleys east of the Whaleback, or staggering off some clifftop led by his dark visions. He had talked to her before, that first night, when he had not known if she were woman or spirit. That had been a time apart, somehow outside the ordinary. Was that the key?

Rona would not be happy. It was fortunate, then, that although Rona woke early, she was a sound sleeper. There was a night, a day, a night before Kinart would come back; low tide would be soon after winter's late sunrise.

Her cousin's fresh fish were all gone, so Nessa cooked a barley broth and they drank it by the outside fire. She made a futile attempt to teach each of them a few words in the other's language. Rona snapped that she couldn't be bothered with such things; if the foreigners chose to walk into other people's lands the least they could do was learn to talk properly. The young man looked at Nessa and said nothing at all. He was doing that more and more, and it unsettled her.

They slept, the dogs in the cairn with their warrior, the two women in the cottage. Nessa had instructed herself to wake when night was at its darkest, and she did. Then it was the cloak, the boots, the lantern, the short walk through the night to the tower in the earth. He had better not misunderstand her purpose, or this could be difficult.

His lamp was lit; he sat much as he had the first time, blanket across his knees, arms held around himself, eyes open but, she thought, unseeing. Nessa said nothing. The tiny fire still glowed on the hearth they had built below that opening in the roof; above, a single star twinkled against a scrap of dark sky. She settled herself by the hearth, blew on the remnants of the fire, added a handful of dried bracken, a piece or two of dried cow dung. She waited. This time she would be sparing with her questions.

"You came back," he said, as if he had not seen her since that first night. "I didn't think you would come. Did you dream again?"

Nessa shook her head.

"I have dreams," he went on. "Always the same, but they get mixed up, jumbled. I'm not very clever. I can't understand them."

She nodded, not speaking.

"Nessa, I don't know what to do. I don't know where I can go. Not like this. My brother is here, I trust him. But I could not let him see me thus, so helpless, so useless."

"Where is your brother?" she asked softly.

"In the south. At Hafnarvagr, guarding the ships. He's going home in spring."

She looked for something in his eyes, anything that might tell her which way to go. But they were shadowed, revealing nothing.

"Have you more family, or just the one brother?"

"Two sisters, two brothers. I am the youngest. My father died in battle, long ago. My mother still lives. Back at home."

"Where is home?"

"A place called Hammarsby."

"Is that a settlement? An island?"

"A farm. It's not like here; there are many, many trees, tall trees of different kinds, and mountains which dwarf those on High Island. It can be very cold, but not like this place. The winter snows close the longhouse in; ice hardens the lakes. We had good times there. But . . ."

"But?"

"That was not what we wanted, Eirik and I. We wanted to be Thor's men, and we are. Were. I am not much of a warrior now, as you see. I am no longer fit even to be a farmer like my brother, Karl. I once despised him for making such a choice. Now I am a far lesser man than he is, incapable of such hard labor, handling stock, cutting wood, guarding his family and folk. This . . . this," he held out a hand, watching the way it shivered and trembled, "if this does not stop, I will be fit for nothing at all, Nessa. Why won't it stop?"

"It will stop," she said fiercely. "It must. I can see deeper than that, Eyvi. I see how strong you are. This is just a matter of looking, and finding your way. I think you must understand that it is a different way from the one you expected. I want you to tell me about Thor. How can a god make such terrible demands of his followers? How can he ask you to risk so much for him?"

He frowned. "It is a challenge: a bright banner. What is a man without courage? When the god calls, a Wolfskin changes. His heart beats Thor's song, his eyes see only the red haze of Thor's anger, his body is entirely obedient to Thor's will. It is like a dance. It is like a prayer. It is the true manifestation of bravery. There is nothing else like that. There is no other calling to equal it. We live short lives, and think nothing of it. Our deaths are glorious; Thor rewards us in keeping with our loyalty."

"I see," said Nessa after a little. "But . . ."

"But what?"

"Maybe I have misunderstood. This is very much a man's god, and I am not a man. Still, I don't think what you tell me can be quite right."

He made no answer.

"First, the man Hakon, the one who was burned by your own people. You said he was a Wolfskin like yourself. But he wasn't a warrior, not anymore. He married, he had a child, he was farming Ara's fields. For him, another path opened up, and he chose it willingly."

"That was different. Hakon was sick, his hearing was going. He could not continue."

"Then there is your brother. Eirik, is that his name? Not fighting with your chieftain's men, not taking arms against my—against King Engus, but somewhere in the south, waiting to take ship for home. Yet he, too, is a Wolfskin."

"He has a woman, he has children back in Hammarsby. Eirik surprised me. But perhaps it becomes more difficult to go on, if a man allows himself that."

"What about you, Eyvi? Have you thought that, if Thor has ceased to call you to battle, it may be for a reason?"

"I don't know what you mean. What reason could there be, save that my weakness sickens him?"

His jaw was set very grim; she did not like the look in his eyes. Instead of going on, she filled a little pan with water and set it on the fire, fetched dried herbs from the alcove, sprinkled them in. The axe was still there, laid away. He had never asked for it, nor his fine sword. The water bubbled to a boil; she poured the tea into two cups. This mixture was for calm and clarity.

"I had another dream," she said. "It was a dream about a man who was very good at playing games, a man who was so clever he could make up his own rules as he went along, and nobody else could understand them. A man who always had to be first; who always had to win. Did you have this dream, too?"

He bowed his head.

"I tried to play, but I couldn't," she went on. "And he said something like, "Don't worry if you're not clever enough, I'll play for the two of us." I've wondered about that dream, and the other one, because it seemed as if the boy who pushed me down, and the man, were the same. You don't have another brother, do you?"

He choked on his tea.

"Tell me, Eyvi." She had sworn to herself that she would not sit close, would not touch him this time, but now she moved over to his side and took his hand in hers. "Tell me." She could feel the place above his wrist where that long scar began, scoring his arm like a brand of ownership. When he spoke, what he said was not at all what she expected.

"I heard a story once, a terrible story. I have never forgotten it. It was the first time, the first night I met Ulf, and . . . Hakon told it, a tale about two men who swore an oath of loyalty, and what it meant for them. One fellow was named Niall, the other Brynjolf, a warrior. They met one night . . ."

It was a long and tragic tale. Now that he had begun, the words flowed fast, and she had to concentrate hard to follow. It was a story to make you curse and weep and rage in frustration at man's folly. He came to the end: Niall the poet, old, alone and filled with a deep sorrow that crept into every verse he made, that shadowed every song he crafted. The girl, Thora, dead in her youth and innocence. The warrior, Brynjolf, living out his span, never knowing the terrible blight he had set on his loyal friend's life.

"That is a truly sad tale," Nessa said. "It is so wrong, so wrong."

"When Hakon told it, I felt the same. Yet every man there applauded Niall's loyalty. Every man believed he had done the right thing. A blood oath is a solemn promise; the man to whom you swear it becomes your brother. More than a brother. How can a man break such a vow?"

She must go delicately here. "A man can make a vow to a god, or a vow to another man. Or to a woman: a marriage is a kind of promise. But it seems to me there is something deeper that must be able to transcend such oaths. Things never stay the same, Eyvi. People change. Paths change. You cannot know, when you are young, what life will hold for you as a grown man or woman. I don't think I would ever swear a vow such as Niall swore, because I would have to break it if it compelled me to act wrongly, to act out of accordance with what my heart told me I should do. It seems to me that there is always a choice, there must be. No blood oath could make me act cruelly, or falsely, or in defiance of natural laws, no matter how solemnly it was sworn. And, Eyvi?"

He looked at her, eyes somber.

"It takes a stronger man, a more courageous man, to walk that path of truth than it does to adhere blindly to a promise. There is more than one kind of courage. This is the harder kind."

"Nessa."

"Yes?"

"I know nothing but war. I was always first: first to attack, first to undertake a dangerous mission, first to attempt a challenge. I could win any fight, take on any enemy. But I have always been quite stupid in other ways, slow to understand, ignorant of matters of law and argument, often lost for words. I cannot read charts, I cannot make verses, I cannot converse with men of learning. Without my strength, without my will for battle, what good am I to anyone? My friend . . . he tried to teach me runes once, he was quite patient about it. But all I could ever learn was my own name."

"Show me," Nessa said. "Here, on the earth."

He let go her hand and began to make markings on the ground with his forefinger. He was concentrating hard, the tip of his tongue between his teeth, eyes narrowed, all his attention on the task. Nessa watched in silence. His hand, moving to fashion neat upright lines, little branches to left and right, was not shaking at all.

"There," he said. "It's not very good, but I think I have it right. Eyvind. That was all I was able to learn."

"Eyvind," she echoed. "A fine name. A name for a leader, a hero. I've been saying it wrong all this time. Why didn't you tell me?" She glanced up from the writing and was surprised to see a strange expression on his face, the ghost of a smile.

"I like the other name," he said. "It is . . . it is between you and me, special, not part of those other things. I like to hear you say it."

Nessa was unable to find words for a reply. She studied the markings again.

"You said mine is a leader's name," he said. "It cannot be so. I am no leader. I have had but one chance, and I took it willingly, confident that I would succeed. In a way, I suppose I did, for we fulfilled our mission exactly as our chieftain ordered. But it was . . . it was a dark thing. Terribly wrong. It was not a battle, but a bloody massacre. I cannot blame the man who sent me there. I was responsible."

"Tell me."

"I don't think I can tell you, not if you want me to stay here. If I tell you this, I must leave. It would be impossible for you to shelter me." Now his hands were shaking again; with a muffled curse, he thrust them under his armpits, frowning ferociously.

"This is what I meant," Nessa said quietly. "Some sorts of courage are far more difficult to find. Putting some things into words can be very hard. You must know, by now, that I have guessed the truth about this. I understand, at least partly, what you have done, and I will not lie to you, the thought of it appalls me. I shrink from it. But I do not shrink from you, Eyvi. I'm here now, aren't I?" If he had not been so tall, she would have put her arm around his shoulders for reassurance. "Give me your hand again, that's it." She moved closer, so he could feel her warmth. "Tell me, Eyvi."

He drew a deep breath and released it, shivering. "I believed your people had killed Hakon, and his small family by him. I saw their charred bones; I set them in the earth. I thought Engus's folk had done that. Then Grim came, and told us the islanders were on the march, coming to attack the settlement. I had waited so long for a battle, all summer, all through the autumn. I did not even want to come here, I had my work back home with Jarl Magnus's Wolfskins. There I excelled; I was a favorite, trusted, there was always a purpose for me, you understand? Scarce seven days would go by without a call to action, and in between, we had sports and good fellowship. And . . . and there was a woman, too. I have missed her. But I came here. Somerled made me come. It was a long wait; my axe lay silent many moons, my sword slept in its sheath. Now, at last, there was a chance to show what I could do. And he put me in charge. He said, look after this for me. It was my first mission as leader. I was determined to do it right, to do it perfectly. I chose my men, a balanced troop, not too many, for it should be a fair fight. Enough, for we needed to be confident of victory. I wore the helm Jarl Magnus had given me, a chieftain's prize, fair and strong. And . . . and . . ."

She stroked his hand gently. "So, you went out, and you found the enemy was not as you expected?"

"Why didn't I see? Why didn't I see before it was too late? Thor's voice, stilled so long, now rang loud and clear; we answered the call. We cut them down, every one. My men did exactly as I had told them to. But . . ."

"Go on, Eyvi. You have come this far."

"Something changed. I was standing there, and the red mist cleared, and I could see them. Not as warriors, not as the enemy, but as real men, men who walked the land and fished the seas, men who had wives and mothers and babes at home who depended on them. And . . . and when I looked further, I saw that most of them were old graybeards or mere boys, not seasoned fighting men like my own. We had slain a troop of grandfathers and children. Still my men were hacking, stabbing, clubbing the living flesh. And . . . and there was a boy, a boy who drew his bow with trembling fingers. My axe left my hand before I saw how young he was, how frightened. I split that child's head in two, Nessa. Then I ran like a coward. I ran and ran, and when I could go no farther, I hid. Thor stepped away from me; his voice was gone. You see what a sad remnant of a man I am? I am become so weak and hopeless that my own mother would disown me."

"His name was Taran," she said, working very hard to keep her voice steady. "Her brother—Ara's little brother. They didn't want him to go, but he wouldn't stay back. He was angry. The Folk are all angry. I heard what was done to him. When I took your axe, when I put it away, I did not know it was fresh from that ill deed. This is . . . it is very hard for me, I find it hard to . . . to look at you and . . ." It became impossible to keep control; tears began to spill helplessly from her eyes, and she let go his hand to brush them aside, fighting the tumult of feelings within her.

"Now I have made you weep. And you do shrink away from me. For all your good intentions, you cannot hide your disgust. I disgust even myself. This is not one error but many; not one ill deed but hundreds. I have a shield, I do not bear it often now. It is marked with little notches, row on row, a count beyond counting, of all the men I have killed. Many were warriors, taken in fair combat. But who is to say whether, among the myriad slain, there were not other ancients, other innocent youths? I will never know. It was not until that day at Ramsbeck that I ever saw them."

"Oh, Eyvi," she whispered. "Oh, Eyvi." Then she got up and stirred the coals to life, and began to heat water again, for the familiar brewing of tea helped her maintain a little longer the pretense that things were all right between them. She sprinkled herbs, fetched the cups. He watched her, unmoving. When she had poured the tea, she put his cup by him and moved away to sit alone, staring into the fire.

"I don't understand it," he said flatly, his eyes empty of expression. "Every waking moment I long for Thor's call; without the god's voice, my life is nothing, and I am nothing. The Warfather has been my vision and my purpose all these long years. Yet now, as well, I . . . I fear his voice, I shrink from what I have done, and what I may do again. There is no path forward,

Nessa. No matter what you say, I think, now, there is no way for me to follow. I see the horror in your eyes; you cannot hide it. As Thor's warrior, I earn only your loathing. And yet, without that calling I am a failure in the eyes of my people, and in my own eyes: a craven coward, crippled by war fetter. I am a lost man: a lost cause."

Nessa said nothing. She felt as if she were being pulled in two directions at once, and it hurt; it hurt as if her heart were breaking.

"You should go," he said, setting down the cup. "It is not right that you should be here alone with me. Take your lantern and go back to the cottage."

"If that's what you want." By all the powers, it was a terrible hurt indeed, and everything he said seemed to make it worse. She should not have come here; she should have listened to Rona, who was a wise woman, after all.

"What I want doesn't matter," he said.

Nessa got up, leaving her tea untouched by the fire. "I'm sorry," she managed. "I need some time."

Eyvind nodded. His face was ashen white, the eyes like dark holes. It seemed a terrible thing to leave him now, but how could she stay? She could not look at him without imagining young Taran facing up to him, and the axe whistling through the air on its mission of death.

"Good night." His voice was the merest thread of sound. "Really, I think it best if you forget me, as Thor has done. I deserve no more than that."

There was no more sleep that night. Nessa lay wide-eyed on her bed, listening to the small creatures rustling in the roof thatch, until she judged it time to rise. It was still dark; the winter days were short indeed on the islands, and one became accustomed to doing what must be done by lamplight. She made up the fire; she brewed tea but could not drink it. She swept the floor, made dough for bannocks, fed Rona's scrawny chickens. Then she packed her little bag with the few possessions she had brought from home, and sat waiting for the old woman to wake.

"I'm leaving this morning," she said as soon as Rona was sitting up on her pallet, steaming cup in hand. "I've made your breakfast. And his. You'll need to take it to him. I have to catch the tide."

"I see." Rona sipped at her tea, pebble-gray eyes sharp on her student. "I thought it was tomorrow Kinart was coming."

"I've changed my mind. Mother needs me."

"And the big fellow doesn't? Your mother doesn't know one day from another, that's what I've heard. Why the rush?"

"I thought you didn't care if he lived or died," Nessa said in exasperation. "This is hard enough, without you arguing the point."

"It's not him I care about, it's you, child. Why lose a day if you don't have to? Why rush off home if you don't want to?"

Nessa pressed her lips together; she would not cry again. She was behaving like a silly girl, and not the priestess she was.

"What do I tell him?" asked Rona quietly.

"Nothing."

Rona looked at her.

"Tell him I've gone home because my mother needs me. It's the truth. I was foolish to spend so long here, I can't imagine why I . . . just say that. I'll come back and see you as soon as I can, Rona. I hope you will be safe."

Nessa took up her small pack and put it over her shoulder; already she wore her light cloak and boots. Her outer cloak, the warm one, was still in the cairn, and she was not going to fetch it.

"What happened, Nessa?"

"Nothing. I have to go now or I'll miss the tide. Farewell; be careful. I'll be back as soon as I can get away." Nessa bent to kiss the old woman's wrinkled cheek. "You might have to . . . you might have to watch him." She could not stop herself from blurting this out, and Rona's eyes narrowed sharply. "I think he might . . . I'm worried that he may try to—" She could not bring herself to put it into words.

"Oh, yes?" Rona pursed her lips. "But you're still off and away without another word?"

"I think I'm only making things worse," Nessa whispered, then turned away and went out into the morning, blinking hard. The sun was struggling up; the wind was fresh from the west, full of the sharp scent of the ocean. One of the dogs stood waiting for her by the cold remnants of the outdoor fire, ears pricked, head up, alert as if on guard. Her heart like a leaden weight in her breast, Nessa turned her back on the tower in the earth and set her steps for home. Her mother needed her. Her uncle needed her. The Folk were in peril. She must be with them, not here; she had been foolish to think this might end in good. She had never misread the signs before, but this time she must have been wrong. She would put this behind her. She would not even think of it. Of him. Of him waking alone and finding she was gone. Of him knowing she had run away. Of him walking into the sea and swimming steadily westward until the waves swallowed him, or wandering off across the winter hills and into cold oblivion. By the ancestors, the pain in her heart was fierce indeed. And yet . . . and yet there was the axe, fresh from the killing of a child, the axe that had slain and slain again, swinging in final, bloody judgment through years of heedless service to the god. That was alien; it was unthinkable. Tears began to fall, and this time she let them flow, hot and painful, for the only one who could see her was the dog, padding steady and silent beside her, all the way home to the Whaleback.

EIGHT

Somerled had a certain style. When at last he came, he strode across the narrow causeway in his billowing cloak and braid-edged tunic, his dark hair held neat by a red silk ribbon, and his men marched behind him with their burnished helms and their fine, sharp weapons. It was noted that this new chieftain bore a round shield, fresh-painted with a black horse on a red ground. It seemed he was not displeased with the name his comrades had bestowed on him. Kinart cursed under his breath, hands white-knuckled on his spear. The men of the Folk discussed the range of their bows, and whether they might pick one fellow off cleanly among so many. But Engus said, let them come. Now was the time for diplomacy, not assassinations. He had invited Somerled to make a treaty, and Somerled had come. It was a little late maybe, since the winter was almost over, but at least the man was here. They must assemble in the hall and hear what he had to say.

Before, the women would have been excluded from such a gathering. In particular, Engus had not wanted his nieces on show. But it was different now. The sickness and a season of fighting had decimated the Folk and weakened their resolve. Now the king wanted Nessa by him, as royal princess and wise woman of his household. Her presence would moderate his own men's behavior, and Kinart's in particular. It would take but one rash outburst to destroy this slender chance of peace.

They waited. Nessa sat on Engus's right, Kinart on his left. Tadhg, newly arrived from Holy Island, stood behind. The men of the household were all gathered there, spears and knives to hand, their faces a study in anger, resentment, frustration, fear. They were weary; they were sick at heart. Yet they were not without hope, for why else would the fellow come here, save with an overture of peace?

Nessa felt Somerled's eyes on her the moment he entered the hall. The nightmare came to her, the cutting, the falling, the hand sweeping with confidence across the board. *Oh, dear.* Now those same dark eyes traveled up and down her body, assessing, admiring, and a little smile played on his lips. He seated himself opposite Engus and folded his hands together on the table. He wore a fine silver ring, wrought with the heads of strange beasts and set with gleaming red stones.

"King Engus," he said pleasantly. "It's been a long time. I trust you've been well?"

Tadhg's voice was steady, translating.

"I am well, thank you, and hope you are likewise, though it seems a strange question to ask in view of what has occurred," the king said gravely. "It cannot be unknown to you what losses we have suffered at the hands of your warriors this winter. You must forgive me if I am blunt. But we had hoped for better, after the promises your brother made. Have you forgotten the words Ulf spoke at the Great Stone of Oaths?"

"Ah," said Somerled. "Straight down to business, then. I like that. No point in beating about the bush, is there? You think me forgetful. You misjudge me. I never forget. I do not forget my brother's murder. I do not forget that your folk burned one of my warriors alive with his woman and children by him. I do not forget their brazen attempt to ambush our settlement, nor the many times they have carried their spears and bows onto my lands with no purpose but to stir up trouble. You speak of promises. Those promises were invalid the moment your folk laid hands on Ulf."

Nessa felt the anger that ran through every one of the king's men as they heard these words translated. Engus's jaw tightened. Kinart's eyes blazed with fury. As for Somerled, he sat calmly, hands relaxed before him, expression bland. He could have been speaking of a fine day's fishing, or discussing what to have for supper.

"I wished to speak of this before, soon after your brother's untimely death," Engus said, keeping his voice steady. "You made that difficult. I understand your grief, your anger at what occurred. It is not easy to lose one so close."

"If you say so."

"But your information is wrong. My men did not kill your brother. We respected him; we admired what he did and were grateful for his help. I had come to regard Ulf as a friend. I must tell you I have made extensive inquiries; I have spoken personally to every one of my men who traveled to High Island that day, and to all who live in the settlement there. Whoever murdered your brother, it was not one of the Folk."

"What are you suggesting? That one of our own would carry out such a barbarous act?"

"I suggest nothing. I simply point out that these accusations are false. So are those concerning the death of the widow, Ara, and her man. It is not the way of the Folk to carry out hallburnings. We do not kill children. For that, too, you must look closer to home for a culprit."

"Where's your evidence?" Somerled raised his brows.

"Where is yours?" Engus's voice had an edge to it now, as if he maintained control with some difficulty. "And what of the slayings at Ramsbeck, a rout so savage there was little left of our men but shattered bone and bloody crow-pickings? What kind of a warrior fights like that, as if death itself cannot satisfy his lust for blood, but he must gouge and pierce and crush until he makes of his opponent no more than a lump of carrion? That was the act of madmen." He glanced at Nessa, as if remembering her presence too late. "I'm sorry, my dear."

"Your men attacked us," Somerled said. "And I too suffered losses that day: two men killed and another missing, my finest fighter, my personal bodyguard. Slain, I presume, or he would have made his way home by now, since no prison is strong enough to hold this particular warrior. Where is Eyvind? Does his corpse lie rotting untended on your land? He was my dearest friend, my companion since childhood. It is as if two brothers have been torn from me. Now I cannot even lay his bones in earth; I cannot bid him farewell. Your men have done this." A flicker of real emotion passed over his pale, impassive features, and was gone. Nessa shivered.

"I know nothing of this," Engus said. "We carried home only the broken remains of our own. We saw no such warrior in that place, dead or alive. I will make inquiries for you. Nobody would deny you the right to lay your friend to rest, no matter what he has done: no matter what he was."

"Thank you. And now to business. I cannot stay long," Somerled said, leaning back and folding his arms. "I'm hoping we can reach some sort of agreement today, so my visit won't have been for nothing. We're busy men."

"Your words hearten me," Engus said cautiously. "I, too, wish for a treaty, perhaps a renewal of that I struck with Lord Ulf. We might discuss initial terms here, and the details in private. I'm grateful for this opportunity. Indeed, I would have welcomed it earlier."

"Really?" Somerled raised his brows again. Nessa watched him and felt the dream, dark as a shadow, lingering somewhere in her mind. He looked so affable, so confident, so relaxed. It was the look of a man who sees no possibility of failure.

"Most certainly," Engus replied. "And we have a gift for you in token of our good will. There have been some difficulties between us since your brother died. We offer this small treasure as a gesture of amity, a symbol of our desire to begin afresh. These are old and quite rare, the only examples of their kind." Engus gestured to one of his men, who brought out a box fashioned cunningly from carven whalebone, a fine piece that had lain long in the king's storehouse awaiting such a moment. Any monarch worth his salt must keep ready a supply of goods suitable to please a dangerous neighbor, a visiting dignitary, a chieftain who might turn from loyal friend to bitter enemy on the merest whim. Such gifts are an essential part of diplomacy.

Engus lifted the hinged lid to display the gleaming set of silver spoons that lay within, gracefully curving implements each fashioned in the shape of a diving dolphin. It was a gift of considerable charm. The workmanship was without equal; Nessa had heard her uncle say so when he took them out of storage on the chance that this difficult chieftain might at last come to the bargaining table.

"Exquisite," Somerled remarked. "Delightful. Quite outside the usual." He was not looking at the spoons. "Introduce me to the young lady, will you?" He snapped his fingers and one of the big, fur-cloaked warriors came forward to clasp the box shut and take it under his arm. Wolfskins: there were two of them here, both formidable men, though neither, she thought, as tall or broad as Eyvind. Nessa stared back at Somerled, willing herself not to blush, not to lower her eyes in embarrassment or shame. She would not give him the satisfaction of that. His own eyes widened a touch as she stared steadily at him; his mouth twitched mischievously, as if he wanted her to share a private joke.

"The lady's name is Nessa," Brother Tadhg told him direct, without translating what Somerled had said. "I caution you against speaking out of turn here. Any sign of disrespect to her, the least ill word, will stir every man present to rage."

Somerled's dark gaze swiveled to the Christian. "Well, well," he drawled in feigned amazement. "So fast to the defense, so vehement. Are you not a priest, and bound to chastity? I would swear you harbored a weakness for the lady yourself, so swiftly you spring to protect her. She is rather delectable, isn't she? I find that "touch me not" air quite irresistible."

"I have warned you," Tadhg said quietly. "Ignore it at your peril."

"Ask the king if his daughter is promised in marriage."

Nessa froze. And now Engus had turned to his translator, demanding an explanation.

"What is he saying? Why do you not translate these words? Did he speak of Nessa?"

Tadhg cleared his throat.

"I am not his daughter." Nessa's words came clear and confident in the tongue of the foreigners. "King Engus is my uncle. I think you know this already. And I am not promised, nor will I ever be. I am a priestess of the Folk, and sworn to a life of solitude in observance of the rituals. My future will be in my own hands, not those of some man hungry for power." That last bit had been rather ill-advised; still, she felt a certain satisfaction for having said it.

"My goodness," said Somerled, his smile widening to something that seemed for a fleeting moment quite genuine, and not at all part of the game he played. "Beautiful, untouchable, and clever as well. A voice like sweet music, and speaking in our own tongue. I'm impressed. I wish I had met you earlier. Sworn to a life of solitude, you say. That's somewhat hard to believe."

"It is true." That would be the difficulty, she could see it: not the times when he twisted and manipulated things, not the times when he was openly unpleasant, but those rare moments when one wondered if there might be a different person here, hidden somewhere deep. For a man like Eyvind, that would be the hard part.

"I don't think so, sweetheart. Someone did tell me a little something about the female line, and the need for an heir, quite a desperate need in view of your people's recent losses. You may find your uncle has something different in mind for you, I think, something a great deal more down to earth. That's a pity. Such a rare creature should not be wasted." He glanced at Brother Tadhg. "Tell the king I, too, have come with a gift: a very special gift. I doubt if he has ever seen its like before."

Tadhg translated, stony-faced. As he spoke, one of Somerled's warriors stepped forward with a roll of parchment, which he passed to his leader. It was fastened with a length of silken cord. Somerled's fingers moved deftly, untying the knot. He unrolled the document on the table before the king. The corners curled up; Somerled reached across to hold them down, and Nessa saw, clear and straight on the flesh of the left forearm, the mark of the knife: the pledge of a lifetime's loyalty. *He was my dearest friend.* A shudder of disgust ran through her body; she caught his eyes sharp on her face, as if he knew what she was thinking. Nessa looked quickly back at the map. For that was what it was: a map of the islands, drawn neat and precise with quill and colored inks, complete to the last line of cliffs, the last tiny rush-fringed lake, the last small clinging grove of prostrate trees. There was High Island, you could see the two great peaks, even the giant-hewn stone lay in its lonely vale. There was the southern coast of the Queen's Isle, and Gartnait's Isle, and Little Spear, and there the small oval of Holy Island, and a house marked with the sign of a cross.

"This is a fine piece of work," Engus said slowly, tracing the coastline with his hand, "very fine. You have a skillful draftsman in your household, that is evident." His fingers stopped; they rested against the northwest margin of the home island, where a little circle showed off shore, with a tiny thread of ink joining it to the coast. The map was meticulous in every detail: cliffs, bays, fissures. Moorings, barns, settlements, storehouses. Stone walls, fortifications, hiding places. "What is written here?" asked the king.

Somerled gave a slow smile. "Have you no men of learning here," he asked softly, "who can read the truth for you?"

"It says *Hrossey,* my lord king," Tadhg said, looking at Somerled. "That could be translated as *Island of the Horse.* This name is written across the whole of the northern part of this island; it encompasses the Whaleback, and your own farms, and also the lands you granted to Ulf's people. It stretches as far south as the safe harbor, and to Silver Bay in the east. The great stone circle lies within this territory."

"I thought the name apt," said Somerled, unsmiling.

Engus rose slowly to his feet. "What is this?" he asked, and something in his voice made Nessa's heart lurch. There was a jingling, scraping sound in the hall as every fighting man put a hand to his weapon.

"My terms for peace," said Somerled smoothly. "You wanted a treaty, and that's exactly what I'm offering you. You need lose no more men. I can be magnanimous. I understand you have barely enough folk left to survive. This chart shows how it will be when we reach agreement. These islands are small. There simply isn't room for two leaders here."

Nessa could no longer hold her silence. "This is—it is outrageous!" Her voice shook with fury. "It is an insult, a mockery which no true leader could suggest without deepest shame. You know what your brother wanted for the islands, for our own people and yours. How dare you bring this travesty of a bargain to the king? You disgust me!"

Somerled put his hands together; she thought he was on the verge of applauding her. "Well done," he said, and he was not smiling now. "Such passion, such fire! We must ensure that is not wasted. And such command of the language, too. I cannot imagine where you have practiced, to become so fluent." There was a question in his tone.

"She learned from me." Brother Tadhg spoke evenly; his eyes carried another message. "And do not forget what I said before. There are those who will not accept lightly your veiled insults to this lady. Now I think you must explain clearly to King Engus what you intend by this. In plain words, and to the point. There are angry folk here, my lord; I hope this does not mean what the lady Nessa thinks."

"Don't try to play games with me, little priest," Somerled said. "Stick to your job, will you, and stop meddling? Now, my lord, it's only fair that I set this out clearly, as I'm bid. I see that. The fact is, I'm afraid your situation is very grave, King Engus. You saw the evidence of that at Ramsbeck. We have superior numbers of fighting men, greater skills on the field, more advanced weaponry. We have mapmakers. We have scholars. We have strategists. What do you have? A handful of would-be warriors with ill-made spears and a whole lot of anger. Perhaps I need to make something else plain to you. Ulf is gone; I am not my brother. As chieftain, I've my own way of conducting my affairs. And in my vision for Hrossey, there is no place for you."

White-faced, Tadhg rendered this speech for the king; he softened it somewhat, to Nessa's great relief, for it seemed to her they were a hair's breadth from a bloody explosion of violence.

"Leave my hall." Engus did not shout, he did not thump the table in his anger. He spoke the words with quiet dignity. "Leave my hall, and leave my lands. I will hear no more."

"I did say," Somerled raised his hands in a gesture of helplessness, "I did say you need lose no men. Or women, or children. If you won't listen, so be it." He turned to go; the two Wolfskins closed in at his sides.

"Uncle," Nessa said urgently, "you should hear him out. Whatever it is, perhaps it is better than a massacre."

There was a silence.

"Very well," Engus said heavily. "Tell us. In this grand plan of yours, where are the Folk? Where are we on these islands that have been our home since the time before memory?"

"Oh, you'd be gone." Somerled's tone was light. "You and your son. I'd be very foolish to let you stay on as a rallying point for the shreds of your tribe, and I don't think I could send you off to these folk you call the Caitt, either. Distant relatives, aren't they? There's always the possibility you might bring back unwelcome visitors. You would, however, make excellent hostages. Rogaland would be a good choice: far enough away, and containing many folk with an interest in the opportunities this place can offer. Your people? You would take any fighting men with you into exile; we couldn't have them here. The boys could make themselves useful on the land. The women would stay; their beds wouldn't be cold long. You see, it's a neat and simple solution, and not a drop of blood shed after today. Ulf would be proud of me."

Engus's face was like a carving in granite. "Your brother would turn in his grave if he could hear you today. He was a peacemaker. You are nothing but an opportunist upstart. Now get off my land and take your thugs with you. The sight of you turns my stomach."

Tadhg rendered these words very precisely.

Somerled laughed. "Family habit, is it, cheap insults? Don't worry, we're going. I have no intention of being trapped here by the tide; I wouldn't answer for what might happen then. Your son is straining on the leash like a hunting dog. Oh, and that reminds me. Whose is that fine hound I saw outside the hall? It looks uncannily like one of my brother's pair, which went missing on the day of his funeral. Sure your people haven't added theft to their catalogue of misdeeds?"

"The dog is mine." Nessa spoke as firmly as she could, though she was shaking with fury.

"Really?" That little smile was flickering again. "I cannot argue with a lady. Keep him, by all means. Consider it a gift from an admirer. And of course, I had forgotten something." He turned back to Engus. "My generosity in sparing your life and those of your followers is dependent on one further condition."

Nessa felt the blood drain from her face.

"I have need of an heir, and I am as yet unwed," Somerled said smoothly. "I've heard this young lady is not yet promised. I want her hand in marriage. That should please you; it befits her status as a royal princess. Indeed, it's very neat. I rule the islands; the lady becomes a queen. In time, my son takes my place as leader here. And, just think, the little fellow is the rightful heir under your own rules of succession as well. A king of the Folk and Norse ruler of Hrossey, all in one. Ingenious, though I say it myself."

Nessa stared, unable to speak her revulsion. Somerled was most certainly a quick thinker: a formidable opponent. Perhaps this had been part of the plan all along, and his words to her mere playacting. Tadhg's hands were balled into angry fists. His translation of Somerled's speech was a masterpiece of tactful rewording. But he could not disguise the message.

"You misjudge me badly," Engus said quietly, casting a stern glance around his restless warriors. "My niece would not give such a proposal even a moment's consideration, and nor would a single one of our folk. This land has been in our custody since the time of the oldest ancestors. We will perish to the last man rather than sacrifice it. If you have chosen not to heed my warnings, let it be on your own head. Make war against us if you will. March through the sacred places, set your boots on the bones of memory. We'll lay down our lives for the islands, every one of us. You are nothing, Somerled. You are a rat with ambitions, a runt who strives and strives to be his brother's equal, knowing he can never come close. You think the lady Nessa would ever stoop to ally herself with such scum? You think I would condone that? I am king here, and these islands are my sacred trust. Now get yourself and your butchers off my lands, and never set foot on the Whaleback again."

"My lord says he scorns your offer. He will fight to the death sooner than accept," said Brother Tadhg. "And he asks that you leave now."

"That much I worked out for myself," said Somerled, "and a little more besides, for I too have a talent for languages. Please say to King Engus that I find his precipitate decision unfortunate, and that, being the thoughtful fellow that I am, I plan to give him time. Limited time. Winter is less than ideal for major battles; the weather's so unreliable. Please tell the king I will hold off until we feel that first hint of spring warmth in the air; he'll know when. I'll send a messenger for an answer then. Goodbye, Nessa. I look forward to meeting you again, and getting to know you much better."

Nessa looked him straight in the eye, keeping her voice level at some cost.

"Most unlikely, I should think," she said. "Of course, you will not accept my uncle's gift now. I'm sure you can see that would be entirely inappropriate."

Somerled gave a wintry smile; the look in his eyes disturbed her deeply. "Put the spoons back, Erlend," he said. "As for our own gift, your uncle may keep that, Nessa. Let it not be said that Somerled of Hrossey was a petty man. This map, I think, will serve as a reminder of the likely future if he remains obstinate on this issue. That would be foolish. Very foolish."

"We have no more to say to you." Engus's voice was that of a king. "Leave this hall, and leave this island. We shall not meet again, save on the field of war."

"I wish you could understand me, Mother," Nessa whispered, pulling her bone needle through the hem of the skirt she was mending, and fastening off the thread. They were sitting outside, the two of them together on a stone bench, for it was one of those winter days when the sun decides to show himself for all the chill, in order to remind folk that he has not quite forgotten them. Nessa ran the cloth through her fingers, searching for the other place where the garment was worn to holes. There it was; a thorough darning would be needed if she were to get more wear out of this. Once, Mother would have taken the work from her hands with a smile, and done it herself, reminding Nessa that she was a priestess. Not now. Mother sat with hands in lap, eyes watery, mouth slightly open. She did not seem to look or listen anymore, though sometimes she spoke: words not even Nessa could interpret. It was hard to see your own mother as a kind of idiot, a madwoman. It was impossible to believe that not two seasons had passed since the time before the sickness, the time when Nessa's sisters had giggled gossip and plaited her hair, and her mother had been so strong, so loving, the sort of mother you could tell all your secrets to.

"I wish I could ask your advice," Nessa went on. "What if you know someone has done a bad thing, a cruel thing, and yet your heart tells you that he is a fine, good man? Do you think it makes a difference, if someone does ill, believing it is right? Can his misdeeds be forgiven if they are done in ignorance?"

Mother gave a little cough and muttered something. Perhaps she said, *Water.* Nessa put down her sewing and fetched a cup. Mother's features were quite vacant; she made no attempt to take it. Nessa held the cup to her mother's lips and waited for her to sip. It was like tending to a dying child, futile and heartbreaking.

"Mother? I wonder if you can hear me, somewhere deep down. What do you think? Am I being really foolish? How can a good, kind man stay loyal to a heartless tyrant? Why is the signs tell me I am right, when it seems so wrong to care like this? I ran away, I turned my back on a friend. I've never done that before. Mother, please talk to me. Oh, please. All I want is a word, just one little word; just a hint in your eyes that you are there somewhere. I'm so lonely here now." *Stop this, Nessa,* she told herself as tears threatened to spill. *Stop feeling sorry for yourself. What about Mother, how hard is this for her? What about Eyvind, whom you abandoned? What about poor Rona? If you want answers, find them yourself.*

She glanced down the slope of the Whaleback to the eastern sward, where Kinart and the other men were taking advantage of the fine weather to practice swordplay. Thrust, block, duck, turn, thrust again. To her untutored eyes, it looked quite expert. She imagined Eyvind there among them. He would be taller and broader by far than the biggest of Engus's men, and probably a good deal more skilled. Kinart was holding his sword as if he fought demons; he was consumed with anger. They all were. When the time came at last for them to face Somerled's men, they would see nothing but the broken bodies of Ramsbeck, the burned-out remains of Ara's cottage. They would charge into the fray with that before their eyes. Their fury would make them blind, and Somerled's men would cut them down like ripe grain. Her uncle would be banished, her kin enslaved. A tyrant would rule the Light Isles, and she herself would be . . . would be . . . She shuddered, unable to envisage a future in which she lay by that man's side. And yet, there was a choice in it. Agree to marry Somerled and bear his son, and she could save the

Folk from annihilation. Wed Somerled, and she would be dis-
obeying the wisdom of the ancestors, the knowledge that ran
deep in the blood. A dark choice. An impossible choice.

Kinart and Ferach were locked in close combat now; their
fierce dedication to rehearsing the dances of war was driving
them hard. The memory of Ramsbeck tormented them like a
bloody goad. Eyvind, too, had seen his friends slain: Hakon,
who had been a Wolfskin, and those Hakon had cherished. He
had thought her own folk responsible. Was it the same for
Eyvind, as he urged his warriors to the attack at Ramsbeck, as
he sent his axe through the air in a glittering dance of death?
Had he felt the same rage? She watched as Kinart put aside his
sword and began to rehearse spear thrusts, eyes savage, mouth
tight. Perhaps there was not such a difference between them.
Perhaps it only had to do with what you believed in.

She stood by the Kin Stone, watching a bloodred sun sink into
the dark turmoil of the western sea. The air was damp with fine
salt spray. Over the final rise of the Whaleback's tilting surface,
cliffs fell sharply, and unseen waves smashed their base far below. Only a fool or a madman would walk too close. Even the
sheep knew to keep away. Engus stood by her side, eyes fixed
on that far horizon: the end of the world, maybe. The dog
sniffed about, scenting rabbits.

The sun was almost gone, so soon, too soon. At this time of
year, all longed for spring; it was hard to keep the heart light,
the spirit hopeful, when night laid its blanket so heavily over
the land. In the brief time of daylight, all must be done, hunting, fishing, tending stock, mending storm-damaged houses,
the movement of sentries, the strengthening of what small de-
fenses they had.

The last glow of the setting sun fell on the carven stone, illuminating the three warriors who strode with dignity and purpose across its face, guardians, keepers, defenders of the
islands. The Kin Stone had stood here long; it was the marker
and center of the realm of the Folk. Yet, on the islands it was
young. The stone circles, the hidden chambers, the ancient
mounds, the unseen folk who dwelt, mysterious and subtle,
within the folds of earth, beneath the shining water, these were

memory and magic, heartbeat and history. These had been a part of the Light Isles since a time so distant, a man's mind could hardly encompass it. They would endure, whatever came. For the Folk, the future seemed much less certain.

"It is unthinkable," Engus said to his niece, "that a man such as Somerled could rule here. Unendurable. And yet, I can see how it could come to pass. That would be the end of our people, Nessa. This is a cruel race of men, heartless and ignorant. I made a grave error in letting them stay. I judged them all by Ulf's measure. It seems to me now that he was a rare breed among them. If this is the end, it rests on my shoulders. I had not thought to see such a dark day come to us; I had not thought to bear such a burden."

"Uncle?"

"Yes, Nessa?"

"About Ulf: his death, the manner of it, and your investigations. It is clear none of our own men was involved. Have you a theory to explain what happened that day? Who do you think did it? It was that death which turned things around. But for that, perhaps your treaty would have held, and the two peoples lived side by side, as Ulf planned."

"Theory?" Engus said, glancing at her. "Oh yes, I have a theory all right, not that it matters, since this fine new chieftain seems to have his people eating out of his hand. Even if there were evidence to support it, I doubt that it would make a jot of difference. This is a subtle opponent, Nessa, as clever as he is evil."

"I'm right, then," she said quietly. "You think Somerled himself was responsible."

"Perhaps he did not perform the deed. But I believe he arranged it. He was missing that night and half the next day. He turned up unhurt, speaking of voices in the darkness, and mysterious lights. The men who were with him told much the same tale. Brude was led astray by these manifestations all night, until sleep claimed him at last. He awoke far away from our campsite, when the sun was already high in the sky. As for Drest, the voices led him high up the crag, where he was set upon by, he thinks, the Hidden Tribe. It was dark; he could not discern if they were men or something other than men. He was lucky to escape with a broken leg. The question is, where was Somerled during that time? He claims he, too, wandered lost. But he had men there in the valley and back at the anchorage. My guards could not watch them all. Somerled's own henchmen could have come to help him. That cruel murder was not a task for one man alone. His hand was on it, Nessa."

"But why? His own brother, that is against all natural laws. And Ulf was a good man. Surely Somerled would not have done such an ill deed in order to take his brother's place here as chieftain. How could any man live with the guilt of that?"

"This is not a man like other men," Engus said heavily. "This is a man driven by some kind of darkness. And I think it is not as chieftain he sees himself, but as king. That is why a treaty, now, is out of the question. One does not make agreements with such as he is. And yet, to do so may be our only hope of survival. Brother Tadhg knows more of this man. Tadhg spoke long to Ulf, on Holy Island; he was privy to the secrets of Ulf's heart. But he will not tell of these things, a holy brother cannot. That is regrettable; such knowledge could help us."

The sun was quite gone now. They must head back to the settlement before all was ink-dark.

"There are other ways," Nessa said slowly. "Other paths to follow, which may lead to answers. I could do it for you, with Rona to help. I would not relish such a task, but these are desperate times, Uncle."

"I don't want you going back to the women's place." Engus's voice was stern. "You saw the fellow, you heard his outrageous suggestion. You saw those oafs in their barbarous cloaks. The only place we can keep you safe is here on the Whaleback, Nessa, and even that may not be safe enough. If it were not the dark season, I would send you away. There are folk in the northern isles would shelter you until this is over. You are too precious to be put at risk. Could not you perform this ritual here, summon the voice you need? We should fetch Rona at any rate; she is in danger if she remains in the place of ritual alone. The secrets of the spirit will mean nothing to Somerled's thugs."

They began to walk down toward the settlement, where torches flared in the chill wind outside the hall.

"Uncle?"

"What is it, Nessa?"

"This ritual . . . I cannot tell you what it is, but it must be done there, in the women's place. The voice I must summon is a very old one, a dark one; there is only one chamber where I might hear her, and that is not on the Whaleback. I must return there if you want your answers. I am safe. I travel under the protection of the ancestors."

The king walked on in silence for a little.

"Only between tides, then, and you must take Kinart and another man with you, so they can watch both sides of the women's place. I am uneasy, Nessa. I saw the look in that man's eye. If he cannot have you by fair means, he will not hesitate to use foul."

"It can't be done by daylight, Uncle. I must be there overnight. Kinart can take me there and come back for me. I don't want him to keep vigil in the dark."

"I don't like this. I should have seen this coming. I should have sent you away before winter."

"I will go tomorrow and come back the next day. Uncle, I must ask you a question."

Engus sighed and stopped walking. It seemed to Nessa her uncle's broad shoulders were stooped, as if the weight of cares he bore were making him old before his time.

"You need not ask," he said gravely. "I understand what is troubling you. Nessa, how can the Folk survive without a king? How can they cling to hope after so many losses, unless the royal line has an heir?"

Nessa found it difficult to speak. "How can they go on without a priestess of the mysteries?" she said tightly. "Without a wise woman, the Folk cannot hear the voice of the ancestors. Without that guidance, we would indeed lose our way."

"A cruel choice," Engus said. "But Rona still lives. And there are girls here who could learn. You could teach, and still bear a child for us. You are the last one, my dear."

"Then why not marry me off to Somerled and have done with it?" Nessa could not restrain the bitter words. "That way at least a remnant of our people survives. Never mind my ten years of dedication and study, the calling of my heart and spirit.

You heard his plan. My child would still be the next king of the Light Isles. Somerled's child."

Engus put his arm around her shoulders, a rare gesture, for he was not a man given to the open expression of affection.

"Impossible," he said quietly. "Unthinkable. And the decision must be yours in the end. In that, I do recognize what you are and what you have accomplished. I know that whatever hangs in the balance, you will never ally yourself with that man. A princess may wed outside the Folk, it has been done before. Men of Dalriada have fathered our kings, men of Northumbria and chieftains of the Caitt. The father of a future king is chosen not just for the alliances he carries with him, but for his courage, his good judgment, his soundness of spirit. That is how we keep our line strong. I had hoped for time to find a mate for you, one acceptable both to the Folk and to yourself. But I would never wed you to a man such as Somerled. As for the need to tend to the mysteries, I respect that; but I ask you to ponder what I have said. You are a wise woman, and you will choose wisely in this as in all other things, Nessa. I understand how hard it is; duty calls you both ways, and this troubles you deeply. I, too, have had sleepless nights. Let us hope your ritual sheds light on these matters for us, for we have sore need of it. Now come, we must go indoors and see if your mother is improved after her rest. I have hopes the spring may bring my sister back to herself."

"I will find Kinart," Nessa said. "Two days, one night, Uncle. And I'll try to bring Rona back with me, but I don't think she'll come."

"She always was a stubborn old woman," said Engus.

Of course, by now he will be long gone, thought Nessa as she went southward on the path through the dunes under heavy skies. The dog kept steady pace, ears alert, feet padding silently on the sandy track. *The moon has run her course nearly twice since I left him, and winter moves on apace. He will have fled away. Perhaps he has gone back to Somerled. Back to his dearest friend.*

"I hope they come," growled Kinart to his companion, Ferach. "I hope they come when we are on guard. I will split their bodies like pigs on a spit. I will crush their thick skulls like lumps of clay. I will account for every one, if they dare set foot near the sacred place."

Perhaps he is quite well again, and in that man's hall preparing for battle. Maybe even now he sharpens the war axe, makes bright the long sword. Perhaps he lifts that shield he spoke of, and ponders the marks he made there, a long record of heedless killings. I hope that Rona is safe. A warrior whose ears are open to Thor's call does not see an old woman's frailty. I trusted him; perhaps I was foolish. Did he learn where the difference lies: that, in taking a life, one must understand what life is worth? Did he ever understand what a precious gift it is?

"You speak no more than my own thoughts, Kinart. My dagger cries out to taste their flesh. Let them come on, we'll give them a dose of their own treatment, a little surprise."

Perhaps he died alone, out on the hills . . . perhaps the tide carries his body even now, dark weed, bright hair drifting on the swell . . . but this is foolish. It is not for him that I return to the women's place. It is for the Calling. And the Calling will take all my strength. Into the darkness, into the hidden places, that is a journey to test the most dauntless spirit. I must think of that. I will not think of him.

"It is hard to wait until spring," Kinart said as they neared the place where the two men must halt and let Nessa go on alone. "Father holds us back when our bellies hunger for vengeance. If I were in charge, I would make an army of my own. I would take the fight to Somerled's door. While we hold back, while we wait, he strengthens his force, he tightens his grip. We should act now. I tell you, the first sight I catch of one of those butchers, there'll be no stopping me."

"Kinart, you must leave me now," Nessa said. "There's no need to wait; the day moves on swiftly and the time of darkness is long and cold. You should go home while tide and light allow it, and come back for me tomorrow."

Kinart's mouth was grim; he showed no sign of moving. "Not this time. I'll keep watch on the shore; Ferach will stay up here on the eastern side by the dike. And when you come out, bring Rona with you. That's what the king wants."

Nessa sighed. For all he was a year older than herself, some-times this manly young warrior still showed he was a boy. She shivered as a wave of cold, a shadow of something not quite seen, passed over her. "I know what the king wants, Kinart, I don't need you to tell me. If you must stay, stay then, but keep your distance. Do not be alarmed if there are voices and lights from the women's place. I am here to conduct a deep ritual to-night; I may awaken forces thus far unknown to us. Rona will help and guide me. I will not come forth until low tide tomor-row afternoon, and for the whole of that time we must not be disturbed. This is an ancient rite. If it is to be attempted, it's im-portant that you heed my instructions."

Kinart nodded, his features somber. "If it helps us win our war and drive these barbarians from our shores, a night stand-ing out in the cold is a small price to pay," he said.

"What about the Hidden Tribe?" Ferach sounded less confi-dent.

"Tonight you stand guard over the islands' oldest mysteries," Nessa told him with a little smile. "I doubt if the Hidden Tribe will bother you. They are fond of tricks, but they are an ancient people, and their blood flows to the rhythm of the islands, as ours does. That makes them akin to us in such times of trial. Do not fear them. If you see strange lights, or hear songs or cries, look away and think of morning. I hope you are wearing your moon charms."

Both young men nodded, hands moving instinctively to the leather strips that held these amulets around their necks. Every child on the islands was given a tiny bag of soft leather holding round white pebbles, three or five or seven in number. Moon charms provided infallible protection against the more mischie-vous local spirits. Even Nessa, priestess as she was, wore such a talisman.

"Then you will surely be safe. Goodbye, now. I'll see you at low tide tomorrow. Do not call me. I will come out when it's time."

The last thing she expected to see as she came down the bank into the women's place was a girl. The girl was young, perhaps fourteen, with a pleasant, nervous face and wispy fair hair. She wore a long, coarse cape with a little hood, and sturdy boots. She was one of them: one of Somerled's people. The girl stood

helplessly before the cottage as Rona berated her in words she
could not understand.

"There's no point coming in here if you can't make yourself
understood. This is a sacred place, a forbidden place. Your kind
are not welcome here. Now be off with you!"

"I only want—my lady wants—I cannot go back unless—"
The girl's voice shook nervously; she twisted her hands together.

"What is this nonsense, don't you know I can't make sense of
a word you're saying? Get out of here before I put a hex on you
and turn you into a beetle!" Rona's mouth curved in a ferocious
grimace, revealing her gapped and darkened teeth. The girl
flinched, but held her ground.

Nessa gave a small, polite cough. "I'll deal with this, Rona,"
she said quietly, coming across to set her bag by the cottage
doorway and give the old woman a kiss on the cheek. The dog
had slipped away to the tower in the earth, perhaps searching
for his mate. There was no sign of Eyvind. It looked as if she'd
been right.

"She won't go when she's bidden," Rona grumbled. "Wants
something, but can't tell me what. Must want it badly. It's a
long way to come, and she's where she shouldn't be."

"I'll talk to her," Nessa said. "Why don't you go inside and
get warm?"

"You're welcome to her," Rona muttered. "Waifs and strays,
more trouble than they're worth, if you ask me. You'll be wanting a cup of tea, I expect, after that walk. This wind's enough to
freeze the marrow in your bones." She disappeared inside the
cottage.

Nessa turned to the girl, speaking in the tongue of Eyvind's
people. "You have come into a forbidden place," she said. "Perhaps you didn't know that. Your people are not welcome on our
land. Why have you come here? What do you want?"

"I heard—my lady heard—that there was a wise woman
here," the girl managed, her voice breathless with anxiety. "I
only wanted—they say she can cast spells, make potions—I
only wanted—"

"You need some help? A faithless lover, a cruel master? We
do not provide such easy solutions here; we do not deal in quick
remedies and instant cures."

"They said—they said the wise woman . . ." The girl glanced

at the cottage door; clanking noises from within told Nessa that Rona was setting water to heat in the iron pot. The smell of herbs wafted out on the cold air.

"Is she making a spell?" the girl whispered, eyes fearful.

"Quite possibly," Nessa said. "Now listen to me. I too am a wise woman, and I have little time for this. Tell me plainly what you want. This is a women's place, and you are a woman, though you are not of our kind. I will help you if I can."

"She wants—I want—what you said, a faithless lover, something like that. A philter, a remedy, to make him turn back. That is what she asked me to say . . ." If this was supposed to be an attempt to disguise the nature of the request, it had failed miserably. This girl had no more subtlety than a chicken.

"This lover. Your sweetheart? Your husband?"

"Yes—no—I mean—"

Nessa regarded her a moment in silence. Whoever had set this on her had been less than fair to her. "I'm afraid I cannot help," she said. "You see, if it were for yourself, I might be able to give you something to use, though I would warn against such charms. They are effective, certainly, yet in the long run they do more harm than good. But it's clear to me what you want is not for yourself, but for another: your mistress, I assume. And unless I can see her and speak to her direct, I cannot provide what she needs. I'm sorry. You must go home empty-handed."

"Oh, but—" The girl's eyes were alarmed, her cheeks flushed with dismay. "Oh, but—"

"I'm sorry. That's the way it is. And I would not advise the lady to come here herself. Our people are on the brink of war. It is not safe to travel so far away from home: not safe for her, nor for you. I am astonished she sent you out here all alone."

The girl's blue eyes were round and guileless. "Oh, but she didn't—I mean, she came with me, but she wouldn't come in here and ask—now I have to tell her no, and she'll be cross with me."

"I see," Nessa said slowly, while her mind raced to Kinart and Ferach, one on each side of the women's place, and the day already growing late. "Where is the lady now? Where does she wait for you?"

"Just up there." The girl jerked her head to the east, beyond the cottage.

"Go and fetch her," Nessa said. "Bid her be quick; dusk will fall soon, and you must be back across the borders by then. Indeed, there may not be enough time for that; it's a long way."

"We have horses. I'll go and tell her." The girl fled, boots slipping on the wet grass.

Rona put her head around the cottage door. "Got rid of her, did you?"

"Not yet. You'd better stay inside. I won't be long."

"If you say so." The head disappeared.

The woman looked familiar. She was young, close to Nessa's own age. She held her back straight, her head regally high. The auburn hair was woven into a coronet, fastened with black ribbons. For all the pallor of her cheeks, she showed no sign of nervousness.

"Gunhild tells me you cannot grant my request unless I speak to you myself," she said coolly, with no attempt at introduction. "I did not wish to come here."

"Believe me," Nessa said grimly, "I had no wish to receive you in this sacred place. But you are here now. It was foolish to come so far. It will be dark soon, and there are guards. Don't you understand how things are between my people and yours? You have put the girl at risk, and yourself, and all of us."

The young woman's brows rose a little. "You care about our safety? That surprises me. I'm not some foolish goodwife after love potions. I need help: real help. But for that I would never have set foot here, believe me."

She reached up an elegant hand to adjust the silver clasp that held her cloak, and Nessa saw the fine rings she wore, rings with bright jewels and delicate filigree work. This was no farmer's wife, no warrior's consort. Indeed, if her memory served her right, Nessa thought she had seen this young woman before under very different circumstances. She must tread carefully here.

"I've said I will help if I can. But you must tell me the truth; the cure must be made strictly in accordance with the malady, or it will have no effect, or the wrong effect. That is why you cannot use an intermediary." Nessa glanced at the girl. "I imagine you wish to discuss this in private."

The young woman inclined her head.

"Right," Nessa said. "The girl must go into the cottage with the old woman. We'll talk out here in the open. Be quick, child. Go on now, Rona won't eat you."

The girl sidled into the cottage; the door closed firmly behind her.

"Now," said Nessa, sitting down on one of the stone benches by the remnants of the cold fire, and motioning the other woman to be seated. "Tell me your name."

The dark eyes stared back at her unblinking. "I cannot do that."

"You must, if you want me to help."

"Margaret."

Nessa shivered. It was as she had thought. This ashen-faced girl, sitting proud and straight in her thick gray cloak, was Ulf's widow. This was perilous indeed. *I will split their bodies like pigs on a spit* . . .

"Very well, Margaret. I am a priestess of the women's mysteries here in the Light Isles. You must tell me what you need. The girl said it is to do with a man." She would not let slip she knew the name's significance. Perhaps there was more than one Margaret among them. "Your husband? Your lover? Or one you wish might be so?"

"I–I don't think I can do this after all," Margaret said tightly. "I don't think I can say it."

Nessa waited in silence. The clouds built overhead; the air smelled of a storm to come. Kinart would be guarding the western path, Ferach the other. It was just as well these unexpected visitors had arrived before she got here, and brought their horses right in. But how would they get out? Curse the woman, how could she be so foolish? Desperation must have driven her.

"It is . . . it is not a love potion I seek. I thought, once, this man might be capable of love, though he has known little of it himself. He was kind to me. He made time for me. My husband did not have a great deal of time; his vision drove him hard." She bit her lip, and looked down at her hands, twisting in her lap.

"So, this man is not your husband?" Nessa asked cautiously.

"I–I don't think I can tell you. You might be a spy. I was expecting an old woman. I can't tell you."

"Then why have you come here, Margaret? You need have no concern about secrets. This is the women's place, sacred to the deep powers of the earth. Confidences are safe here. Now tell me."

"I am a widow. My husband died. He was a good man, a fine man, who strove to do what he believed was right. A true leader. I tried to be the kind of wife he needed. But . . . but there was so much for him to do, too much . . . He was consumed by the will to achieve his goal, to make his vision reality before . . . If he had lived, there might have been time for the two of us. But his life was cut short. He expected that, I believe."

"He is gone, then. What of this other man?"

Margaret's eyes changed; a shadow entered them. "There were such possibilities for him, when we came here," she said in a voice no more than a whisper. "For him, for all of us. This is a man who has followed a lonely road, a man to whom the gods have not been kind. Because of that, he cannot readily give of himself. He lives behind high walls of his own making; he trusts no one. Perhaps that is not quite true. There was one he trusted, besides myself. But he is—he is very much alone. I thought . . . I thought it would change things for him, coming here. I thought he could forget the wrongs he has suffered."

"But this did not come to be?"

"He has changed," Margaret said wearily. "He has not come to himself, but moved further away. I thought . . . I thought he might put aside the terrible jealousy that consumed him, might find his own right path. But even after his brother died, he flayed himself with his failure to be his brother's equal; to have what my husband had. I have tried to put it right. I have tried to reach him. But . . ."

Somerled. She meant Somerled. By all the powers, how could this be? Ulf's own brother: that man, that hideous man with his cold eyes and his little crooked smile.

"But what, Margaret?" Nessa asked gently as her flesh crawled with horror.

"I think some darkness has fallen on him," she whispered. "He looks at me now and does not see me. His mind is set one way only, on his own path. And it is an ill path. This is a man who will never be content. When he gets what he wants, he soon tires of it, and sets his goal higher."

"Did you lie with him?" Nessa asked her. "With your husband's brother?"

A flush rose to Margaret's pale cheeks. "That's none of your concern!" she snapped.

"Perhaps not; still, you did seek my advice. Has this man tired of you? Do you indeed want only a love philter, to rekindle the dying fires of his passion? That could be had from any old woman of the cottages, lady. There was no need to come to me. I am a priestess of the Folk. My work is in the high mysteries, the dark and secret ways of our people. I do not dabble in such tricks."

"They say the Folk are finished." Margaret's tone was flat. "So much for Ulf's bright vision. It lasted no longer than he did."

Anger flared in Nessa. She rose to her feet. "You dismiss us easily," she said. "Yet you come to me for help. Why should I help you?"

"Because you are a woman, and so am I," said Margaret quietly, standing to look Nessa straight in the eye. "And I told you, I do not want a love potion. If a man cannot love me of himself, then his love is not worth much. You despise me, I can see that. You misjudge me. I was never unfaithful to my husband. I did not lie with this other man, even though he said he loved me and begged me to be with him. I did not lie with him until . . . until after . . ." Margaret drew a deep breath; Nessa could see the way she summoned the will from deep within her, a core of iron strength. "And it was only once. I thought to comfort him; his brother's death was a cruel blow to him. It was then that I knew—that I realized he was not the man I had thought him to be. He was . . . he was less than gentle with me. And afterward, disdainful, as if the gift I had given him was no more than his due. I don't know why I'm telling you all this, I don't even know you."

"I do not judge you, Margaret. How is it I can help?"

"I wish to discover how I can turn him from this path he follows, for I see in it only sorrow and destruction and death. He used to listen to me, but not anymore. The other friend he had is gone; he is surrounded by men who jostle to please him. If you have a charm to make him listen, any talisman by which I might influence him, I would pay well for it. I have silver. I only want him to hear me. No matter if he does not love me."

Nessa was silent a moment, seeing how tightly controlled were the pale features, how full of pain the dark, proud eyes.

"If we had longer," she said slowly, "I could look in the fire, and ask the ancestors; I could seek wisdom for you. But there is no time. You must be away quickly, and I'll have to distract the guards. Perhaps it is too late to halt this man. Most certainly there is no easy solution, for he has brought a darkness on our two peoples, a shadow from which we may not escape. I will give you herbs to sprinkle on your hearth fire. Do it alone, at night. Sit quiet before the coals, make your mind empty, and watch the smoke that rises there. If you are open to it, you will receive guidance."

Margaret stared at her. "Is that the best you can do?" she asked. "What if I take this, and try it, and nothing happens? I could be wasting my silver on a bunch of old weed."

Nessa bit back her first answer, and took a deep breath. "I want no payment," she said. "Your silver is no good to me."

"Really? It seems you live in some poverty here. This could help, surely? Blankets for the old woman, a joint of meat?"

"I do not want your silver. And believe me, what I give you is rare, precious, and sacred, bestowed seldom even on our own kind. I give it to you because I see truth in your eyes, honesty in your face. I give it to you sister to sister. Wait here, please."

She fetched what she needed from the cottage. Rona raised her brows as she watched Nessa unseal the small jar hidden deep on a stone shelf, and fill an even smaller bag from its powdery contents. The girl stood shivering by the hearth, an untouched cup of Rona's herbal brew steaming between her hands. She thought, perhaps, that one sip might transform her into a newt or a toad.

It was necessary to find a pretext for going out, for walking with Ferach down to the shore and keeping both him and Kinart distracted while the women took their horses and made their escape. Just as well it was nearly dark; the traces the animals left would otherwise be clearly visible. They lingered on the shore until after the sun set, looking up and down the water's edge for something Nessa said she had seen, a man's body perhaps, a stricken seal, or a mysterious bundle. When she could be quite sure Margaret and her attendant were safely away, and rain was starting to fall in a fine, drenching mist, Nessa told the two men perhaps she had been mistaken: a trick of the light. They must return to their watch, and she to her place of ritual. The rain grew heavier; by morning, hoof marks and other signs of passage would be all but obliterated.

It was pouring. Clutching her cloak around her, Nessa made a dash for the cottage, thrusting the door open with one hand, stumbling in, reaching to push her dripping hair out of her eyes. The fire glowed warm; there was a savory smell of supper cooking. Rona stirred a pot, humming tunelessly to herself. On the other side of the hearth stood a tall man with butter-yellow hair. He was pouring water from a pot to a cup; this was an exercise in discipline, that was clear from his expression of extreme concentration. His hands shook a little, but not much. As Nessa stood mute, he set the pot down, turning his summer-blue gaze on her.

"You came back," he said softly. "I didn't think you would come back."

Nessa was quite lost for words. She only knew the drumming of her heart, the warmth in her cheeks had nothing to do with fear.

"You've shaved off your beard," she said. "You look younger."

"Get out of that wet cloak!" Rona snapped. "Foolish girl. Sit close to the fire; drink that tea. Give her the tea," she ordered, and made a series of signs with her hands, *pass, drink, shiver, cold*. Eyvind put the cup between Nessa's frozen fingers; the warmth of his hand, brushing against hers for the merest instant, seemed to go deep inside her.

"Thank you," she said. "I thought you would be gone. I was sure you would be gone. Back to the others, or . . ."

"I could not leave the old woman on her own, unprotected," he said.

"You see?" Rona put in. "The fellow's still here. Loves my cooking. Can't get enough of it. In fact, he's not without his uses. Knows how to fish, even in this weather. Quite canny with a hand line."

"Fish?" Nessa swung from relief to terror. "You let him go out, down to the rocks? He cannot do that, my uncle's men could see him, they would finish him—"

"What's wrong?" Eyvind asked. "What are you saying?"

"You mustn't go out. Rona told me you've been fishing. I'm glad you can walk so far; glad you have recovered enough to attempt such tasks. But it's not safe for you. Things have changed. They've changed terribly since I left here."

His face was grave. "You'd better tell me," he said. "You look pale, and you're thinner. What's wrong, Nessa?"

Rona's spoon clanked against the bowl, ladling dumplings in onion broth.

"I don't know what you're saying to her, lad, nor she to you, but it can wait until the girl's had her supper. She's worn out as it is. And you're still skinny as a wraith, great thing that you are. Here, eat this and sit quiet a while."

"She says, supper first, talk later," Nessa said, managing a little smile. His eyes were so bright in the firelight, she could hardly look at him; and yet she wanted to look, to go on looking, so she could be quite sure he was really here. She felt strangely as if she might start to cry. This was no good at all. Kinart and Ferach were on guard, and she had a ritual to perform. It would have been better if Eyvind had gone away, as she had expected. Much better for everyone. And yet, there was no denying that sweet warmth, that flood of delight that had swept through her the moment she saw him standing there, so tall, so quiet, so solemn. As if he belonged here. As if he were a part of her. She was so glad, so glad that he had waited.

"Stop dreaming, child, and get that food into you," Rona commanded, gaze shrewdly assessing. "Then tell me why you're back. Not just to pass the time of day; I see that in your face."

"Who was here?" Eyvind asked as soon as they had finished eating. "I heard voices. I thought it best to stay in the old place until they were gone."

"Just a couple of women after remedies," Nessa said lightly. "Folk come here for such trifles sometimes. They're gone now. But you must be careful, Eyvind. I'm not allowed to be here without guards now. My cousin watches the seaward track, and his friend the eastern way. They're well armed, and will not hesitate to attack. Promise me you won't go out again. It was foolish to do so. I can't understand how Rona could make such an error of judgment."

"I may be weakened and unable to wield a weapon, but I have not lost all my skills, Nessa. I was a hunter by the time I was five years old. I can walk silently, and pass a wild creature, or a man, not seven paces away unseen and unheard. There was no risk. Trust me."

Nessa shivered, saying nothing.

"What is it? What has happened?"

"I must speak to Rona first. I am not here for you, but to enact a ritual, a dark and secret observance. It must be done tonight, in the tower: in the chamber below, the hidden place deep under the earth. And tomorrow I must go home again."

His face altered as if she had hit him. He said nothing.

"What did you say to him?" asked Rona sharply. "No need to be cruel. The big fellow's been trying hard while you were gone. Cleaned himself up, made himself useful, and putting himself together again as best he can. He's been waiting for you a long time, lass. You could manage a kind word."

"I thought he was just a nuisance to you," Nessa retorted, amazed. "A big man with a big axe, who can't even talk properly. Isn't that what you said?"

"Times change," Rona muttered, suddenly busy picking up platters and spoons and stacking them to be cleaned. "You forget how long you've been away. There's a hint of spring in the air, and spring may not be good this year. No doubt you can tell us more. The big fellow still can't speak our tongue, but we've managed well enough between us. Yes, he's a warrior; that may never change. But there's a great kindness in him, Nessa. It's easier to see with each day that passes. Kindness and strength, for all the trembling and the dark visions that haunt him. I never thought I'd say this, but perhaps a warrior's what we need, you and I."

"He is Somerled's friend. And Somerled has declared ownership of the islands. He wants to take my uncle's place."

"What are you saying?" Eyvind put in, frowning. "What about . . . what about Somerled?" He seemed to speak this name with some reluctance.

"Why are you here now, lass?" Rona's eyes were searching, her mouth grim.

"For a Calling."

"I thought as much. Sure you can do it? It's Engus wants guidance, I suppose."

"Somerled has given him only until the first day of spring to decide. The choice is, surrender everything or be wiped out. My uncle says he will never give up. I'm scared, Rona. This could be the end of the Folk. And . . ."

"And what?" asked Rona sharply.

"Nessa?" Eyvind, too, was watching closely from where he sat by the hearth, hands clasped together to keep them still. "Please tell me what you are saying. You look frightened. What is it?"

"Later," she told him, and saw that look on his face again, like the sad expression of a faithful dog chastised for no good reason. Curse the man, why did he have to make her feel so guilty? "Rona," she went on, "I can hardly bear to tell you, but I must. It seems to me that I can influence the course of events here, though my uncle does not wish it so. It weighs on me. Somerled asked . . . he said a part of the agreement would be that I marry him, and our son would be ruler of the islands after him. If we agreed to that, he would spare our people's lives, though my uncle and Kinart would be exiled. Rona . . ." Nessa felt tears close and willed them back, "if I persuaded my uncle to agree to that, there would be no more killing. I could save the Folk, men, women and children. We have lost so many. The prospect chills me, for that man is not fit to lead anyone, he is not of the Folk, he can never understand what the islands are and what it means to be their guardian. But the other way is the end for our people. That's why I must perform a Calling. Always, before, I've been able to tell which way is right: which path to follow. But this time, both choices feel terribly wrong."

Rona shook her head and put her arm around Nessa's shoulders, muttering something about bones and ash, and suddenly Nessa was crying. In her mind, she saw her mother's empty eyes, and the broken bodies of Ramsbeck, and she heard Kinart's furious vow of vengeance. Over it all, Somerled's voice came with studied calm. *In my vision for Hrossey, there is no place for you.*

"Right, lass," Rona said when Nessa's sobs had subsided. "This is what we're going to do. First, you sit down here and drink some more tea." Eyvind was standing by the hearth, his blue eyes fixed on the distressed Nessa. Rona's hands showed him what was required; he moved obediently to set the pot back on the fire, to find a bunch of dried mint, a crock of honey. It was clear to Nessa, watching his careful, methodical movements, that he and Rona had established an efficient way of talking with no words at all. Eyvind made no attempt to ask her what was wrong.

"Now do as I say, Nessa, and no arguments," Rona instructed. "Tonight's ritual will take every bit of strength you can summon. Drink the tea. Get warm, sit quiet for a while. Let me prepare the chamber for you—no, don't interrupt—I'm not yet so ancient that I can't go down there and set things out the way they should be. You've done it for me often enough over the years. While I'm gone, you must talk to the big fellow. I can see from that stubborn look on your face that you shy away from it, but you owe him that much for waiting around until you came back. He needs you to listen to what he has to say."

"What if I talk to him, and he goes straight back to Somerled? The whole thing might be set up for that. It might all be some terrible game designed to trap us. I can't trust this man. He killed Ara's brother. He split Taran's head in half with his axe."

"I know that, child."

Nessa stared at her. "How can you know?"

"We've had our ways of talking, and I can put two and two together as well as anyone. What he can't tell me, I see in the fire. And it seems to me that I've seen what you refuse to recognize."

"What's that supposed to mean?" Nessa retorted, watching as Eyvind poured water from the pot again, mouth set tight in concentration, willing his hands to stay under control. This time he was less successful; there was a small hiss as drops spilled on the hot coals, and she could see the trembling. Perhaps that was her fault.

"I've seen what you saw that first night, when you told me we needed to keep the big fellow safe," Rona said. "You've forgotten that, in your anger at the blood spilled. But you were right. He's part of this, Nessa. We need him. Now sit awhile and let him talk. Ask him about Somerled. That's what's going through his head."

Nessa sat. When Eyvind put the cup in her hands, it seemed to her that he took particular care not to touch her. The tea was good. Rona was filling a bag with small items from the shelves and the storage baskets: bone and ash as she had said, herbs too, and other objects—secret things that Eyvind should not see.

Rona was not going to go until Nessa started talking, that much was plain.

"Rona's preparing what I need for tonight," she began awkwardly. "She says I must talk to you. But I don't know where to start."

"How is your mother?" he asked. "Is her health improved?"

Nessa had not expected that, and did not guard her answer. "Still living, but . . . but she's like an empty vessel, with nothing but sorrow left in it. She's already gone away. I don't think she will see the spring. She forgets to eat and drink; she forgets everything but the children she lost."

"Children?"

"My two sisters; I was the youngest. They died when the sickness came, last summer." She had not meant to tell him this.

"No wonder you weep," he said quietly. "What of your father?"

"Killed in a war against the Caitt. I was very young. I don't remember him."

"Your father was a warrior, then?"

Too many questions. "Only to defend the islands. Not for the love of killing."

Eyvind made no response. She had hurt him again, and instead of satisfaction, she felt only confusion. She must take control of this conversation, ask what she needed to ask, and let that be an end of it. She looked straight at him, summoning her will. His hair gleamed honey-dark in the firelight; his eyes were solemn. She could not tell what he was thinking. Nessa drew a deep breath, but Eyvind spoke first.

"It was a grievous blow for me, Thor's silence," he said. "Without you, I could not have survived it. Now, it seems to be your forgiveness I need, before I can begin to seek a new path. It's all right. I do not expect you to give it, not after what I have done."

Everything she would have said, everything she needed to ask fled from her mind. All she felt was the urge to put her arms around him, and weep again, and say that of course he was forgiven, and that she was sorry she had wounded him when he was already stricken. It was not like her to lose control so easily. She must not let this rule her.

"Tell me about Somerled," she said severely.

Eyvind's mouth tightened. "What about him? You spoke of . . . Somerled . . . before, to the old woman. Do you have news?"

"Some," she replied cautiously. "He thinks you dead; he accused King Engus of hiding your body. He called you his dearest friend. How can such a man be your dearest friend, Eyvind?"

He hesitated. "Somerled is . . . he is a complicated man," he said. "Determined. He takes what he wants, that's the way he plays his games. We have been friends since childhood; I owe him loyalty, in accordance with that. I know he can be ruthless."

"I met him," Nessa said. "He came to my—to King Engus' court. With a plan for peace."

"He did?" Eyvind's eyes lit up, and he leaned forward eagerly, elbows on knees. "He told me he would do so, as Ulf wanted, but I confess I doubted his will to go through with it. Has an agreement been reached? Perhaps I can go back; relieve you of my presence. It's plain I am no longer welcome here."

"I'll tell you," Nessa said. "I'll tell you what this man proposed, this great friend of yours. The bargain is simple. Engus forfeits the islands and the kingship, Somerled takes all. He'll be chieftain of Hrossey. Yes, he even has a new name for this ancient land. He said, "There simply isn't room for two leaders here." Engus and his son go into exile with their warriors; the rest of us stay. And . . ."

"And what?" His face had gone white.

"And . . . no, nothing." She would not burden him with this, too. For one of his kind to befriend the king's niece was perilous for both of them; tell him who she was and he would be gone by morning, she was sure of it. She could not tell him his dearest friend had marked her as the price of her people's survival. In time he would have to learn this, but only when he was strong again. "He has given the king until spring to make up his mind," she said. "If Engus says no, and he will, then it is outright war. If that happens, the Folk don't stand a chance. This Somerled, he wants to be a great leader here, founder of a new age, I think."

"He wants to be a king," said Eyvind. There was a grim ring of old knowledge in his voice.

Rona had gone out; it would take her some time to prepare

the secret chamber. It seemed to Nessa that in the soft crackle and hiss of the fire and the sigh of the wind around the cottage, there were whispering voices, an ancient story.

"Talk to me, Eyvind," she said. "Tell me about Somerled."

"It is . . . it is hard for me to speak of this. There is the promise we made to one another as children. It binds me to loyalty; it locks me into a silence that has become a denial of truth. Through every long day, through every dark night I see the same pictures, like the dream you spoke of, falling from a tree: so many pictures. I shrink from them, yet they pursue me. I think I can no longer pretend; I can no longer be blind to this. But I don't know what to do. The truth is . . . it is unthinkable, Nessa. He is my brother. Closer than a brother."

"Tell me, Eyvind. Tell me about the time when the two of you cut yourselves, and swore an oath of loyalty."

"He was a strange child: wary, proud, very much alone. Ulf brought him to Hammarsby, and I was given the job of . . . of teaching him to be a boy, I suppose. I didn't know what to make of him. He had been badly treated. His mother had died, his father had neglected him, and Ulf simply did not know what to do with him. So I—well, I did what I thought was right. Taught him to defend himself. Taught him to hunt, to skate, to swim. I never managed to teach him to enjoy those things, but he learned the skills; if he thinks he needs to master something, he applies himself with fierce dedication. Nobody liked him. He had no friends other than me. I was . . . sorry for him, I suppose. And I admired him; he was clever. He could do so many things I couldn't."

Nessa nodded. There was plenty she wanted to say, but she stayed quiet.

"That was the reason I did it. Swore the oath. He had heard he was going away. Despite himself, he had been happy at Hammarsby. I think it was the first time he had had a friend. How could I say no? So we did it. At first, it did not seem so very important; we were children. But I knew soon enough that the oath was binding. He saved my life; I saw in his eyes, then, that this pledge of loyalty was forever. It has bound me close to Somerled. It has bound me to . . ."

"To let things pass, when you should have acted on them?"

"I don't think I can tell you. I don't know much about the

.law, but I do know one should not accuse a man without evidence. I have had doubts, increasing doubts as time passed. There is nothing that can be proven. I am his one true friend. If I were to turn against him, he would again be quite alone. That is a terrible thing, Nessa, to be alone. I know that now. After the . . . after what happened at Ramsbeck, I wandered a long time in a place where nobody else could reach me. Until you came."

"I have felt the same," she whispered. "I miss my sisters so much, though when they were here I often thought they did not understand me. I miss my mother. I talk to her and she does not hear me. Eyvi, you must not rely on me. My people need me, they are in terrible danger. I cannot—I should not—"

"I understand. You still can't trust me. That is no more than I deserve. I hoped . . . no, that is foolish. Do you have a comb?"

"What?"

"Your hair's still wet. You'll catch a chill if you spend the night down in that chamber with wet hair."

He was telling her she looked a mess, just as Kinart might do. Nessa was annoyed to feel a blush rising to her cheeks. She fished in her bag, found the little bone comb with seals on it, and unfastened the damp ribbon on the end of her long plait. A pox on the man. How did he manage to make her feel like this, confused and upset and happy all at the same time? Was she not a wise woman?

"No," he said, taking the comb from her hand. "I'll do it. Practice for me. I've been trying to use my hands for different tasks. I even brought some driftwood up from the beach for the old woman. I cleaned the fish I caught. When I concentrate I can keep them almost steady. Sit still, now. That's it."

This was something mothers and sisters did, not some young warrior one hardly knew. Ridiculous man. He'd simply knelt down behind her and started drawing the comb through her wet hair without so much as a by-your-leave.

"Ouch!"

"I did say, sit still. Is that better?"

"Yes, but—"

"You can trust me to perform this small service, at least. I missed you, Nessa."

"Soon enough I will be gone again. Eventually you will go

back to him, to Somerled. It is not possible that we—that we . . ." The steady movement of the comb was soothing; it made her feel warm and content. She could not bring herself to tell him to stop, though this was entirely inappropriate. "You could be a spy," she went on. "You are Somerled's friend, after all. He could have sent you here, set the whole thing up to trap me. He could have been pretending when he said . . . when he said he thought you were dead."

"Why would he want to trap you?" Eyvind asked as he kept up his steady work, teasing out the knots. "I understand that as a keeper of the mysteries you would have some influence over the king. But—"

"It's a long story," Nessa said. "Now answer me a question. Ulf came to the islands wanting peace; his men supported that. Some of them took up with our women. One even got married. And yet, as soon as Ulf died, everyone was following Somerled, who didn't want a treaty at all. He's made it clear enough he has no respect for the Folk; he doesn't even want the islands, not really, all he wants is power and influence. And what Somerled wants, he takes. A man who, as a child, had no friends. Why didn't you stand up to him? Why didn't anyone? Couldn't you see what he was doing was wrong?"

"I . . ." The movement of the comb stopped.

"Tell me, Eyvi."

"Whether it was true or not, folk believed Ulf sought baptism as a Christian. If a chieftain takes such a step, it is not long before he expects his people to follow him. That disturbed folk; it made them afraid. When Somerled became chieftain, he confirmed his strong allegiance to the old gods, and it won him loyalty. And there were men who had become his inner circle, men whom he charmed by . . . by making himself into the sort of fellow they admired. Some folk might have spoken out against him, had not fear stopped their tongues. Many found no fault in his warlike aspirations here. In my home country, a leader who is strong and decisive, who cuts down enemies and seeks to expand his own influence is a man to be respected. But . . . there was one who did speak out. Hakon came to court, after the killings began. He refused to swear an oath of loyalty. He gave up his wolfskin."

"And Hakon died."

"Yes, but—"

"I told you, Eyvi. Our people do not burn men and women alive in their homes. We do not kill children."

He was silent. She felt his hands against her neck for a moment, and then he put the comb down.

"What better way to command loyalty," she said quietly, "than a graphic demonstration of what happens to those who disobey?"

"I think you know my puzzles as well as my dreams," he said. "That is one. After we buried them, Hakon and his family, my brother Eirik went away. He told me he would stay at Hafnarvagr, something about nobody hearing much from him before the spring, because he wanted to get back safely to his woman and children in Rogaland. He told me there was danger all around me. I–I hid from the truth, Nessa. I convinced myself I did not understand those words. But . . ."

"But?"

"Somerled was always fascinated by death and dying. When we caught creatures in snares he would not administer a merciful end; he liked to watch them go, slowly. When he heard that story, about Niall and Thora, all he wanted to know was . . . and yet, he has such ability. I know he is capable of great things, if only . . . if only he understood what it means to hurt. He plays his games with real men and women, and treats them the same as the little pieces carven in stone."

Nessa nodded grimly. "Come, sit back here where I can see you," she said. Now that her hair was unbraided, it would dry quickly before the fire. "That's better. And thank you. I see there are at least three things you can do, besides fighting and killing. You can provide for a family, since you have not lost your hunting skills. Perhaps, as you said, you are not a clever man, not in the way Somerled is clever. But it is clear to me you are wise. That's why it takes you so long to solve your puzzles, Eyvi. You must examine every possibility, weigh them up, before you reach a conclusion. Only a wise man does that. Only a wise man keeps silent lest he speak before he has fully considered a matter. No wonder the ancestors did not bar you from entering this domain."

He was watching her intently. "And the third thing?" he asked softly.

"You know how to comb a woman's hair," she said dryly. "As

you have no little sisters, I expect it was a woman who taught you that."

Eyvind grinned, and was instantly solemn again. "Signe. It seems so long ago now. Her hair was fair as wheat, not dark like yours. Though yours glows red in the firelight, there's a sheen on it like ripe chestnuts."

"This Signe, she is your wife? Your sweetheart?" Curse her stupid tongue, why had she asked him that, as if it mattered the smallest bit to her?

"No," he said gravely, "though it was not for want of asking, on my part. She is—was—friend and lover, a person of great kindness."

"I see." For some reason that made her feel no better. "So, she will be waiting for your return?"

"We said our good-byes. There are no expectations between us."

"Rona will be back soon, and I must go down for the ritual. Eyvi, there is another puzzle. It is a strange and difficult one. It concerns a man hung up in a fishing net and left to die between land and water, a good man whom we welcomed to these islands. Have you a solution to that puzzle, too? I think I have, and mine is the same as King Engus's."

He nodded slowly. There was a look of misery in his eyes. "The manner of it suggests only one answer. Yet, at the time, Somerled was distraught. His shock and grief seemed entirely real."

"Still, you said yourself, he made himself into the kind of man some folk admired. Perhaps, on that day, he made himself into the sort of man who mourns his brother's death. Another game."

"But there's no proof," Eyvind said. "Only that, because I know him well, I see something in the execution of it that points to one man only. A clever killing, all tracks covered, and the prophecy accounted for down to the last detail. I don't want to believe I'm right, for this is a crime against blood, against kinship, against natural law." His tone was hushed.

Nessa inclined her head. "But you do believe it," she said. "This is what keeps you from going back, even now that you are regaining your strength. You fear to confront him with the truth."

"How could any man perform such an act? It was surely a vengeance far too great, even if Ulf did use Somerled's birthright to help pay for the journey here. After all, Somerled is well equipped to make his own way; indeed, that is what he prefers. I asked myself, would he do such a deed, take such a risk, simply to punish his brother for not loving him? And I remembered . . ."

"What, Eyvi?" She saw his hands shaking again and, without thinking, put her own out to take and steady them.

"I remembered another time when his vengeance was terrible indeed, another time with no evidence, no proof. When we were young, back in Hammarsby, there was a girl hurt—taken by force, and got with child before she was ready for it. She killed herself. They never knew who was responsible. I knew, but I denied it to myself, I refused to believe he was capable of it. There was a lad, Sigurd, who was fond of the girl; he left Hammarsby soon after she died. Later, on the voyage here, we met Sigurd again, a man still consumed by rage after all those years. He tried to kill Somerled; I stopped him. And then . . . then there was a terrible accident. Or it seemed like an accident. Sigurd was killed. He was gored by a bull. It was Somerled's little knife that goaded the creature to charge. But . . . but I stood there too, on the other side. Somerled had no way of knowing if the bull's horn would pierce Sigurd's breast or mine. That made me think. It made me think more than I wanted to."

"He, too, swore a blood oath," Nessa said. "But you cannot expect loyalty from such a man. Your brother was right to warn you. Somerled is only interested in winning. He doesn't care who falls by the wayside."

"He has been kind to me."

"Can such a man understand kindness?"

"I told you he saved my life once, when we were boys. That day, he was heroic, strong, altogether admirable. I owe him a great debt for what he did. And he helped me, at the Jarl's court. I hated the clever talk, the game-playing, the need to summon ready words in order to avoid ridicule. I was respected as a warrior, but I never learned to be a courtier. Over and over again, he got me out of trouble, stood up for me. He could always find the words I needed. And he was kind to Margaret, Ulf's wife. When she was lonely, he made time for her. She is, I think, the only other to whom he reveals himself, and then but rarely. I cannot believe he is all bad, Nessa. If only he could stand in the other man's shoes, if only he could understand that it is not a game he plays, but his own life, a precious thing to be lived well and fully: his chance to get things right, to prove his worth. If he knew that, he would have much to give."

Nessa's hands tightened around his. She felt curiously close to tears again. "It seems to me you judge him by your own measure," she said a little shakily. "It's clear you have not wasted your time here."

"Really?" he asked softly. "But I still don't know where to go or what I should do. How can I turn against him? How can I walk away from a vow of lifelong loyalty?"

"I cannot tell you that," said Nessa. She was aware of the door opening behind her, and Rona coming in. No doubt the old woman was looking at her unbound hair, and her hands clasped around Eyvind's; the two of them sat quite close. Nessa did not snatch her hands away. "But tonight I will seek answers," she told him. "So much hangs in the balance here, it seems impossible that we may influence it, Eyvi. A terrible task, a task demanding so much courage, so much strength. I don't rightly know how it can be done. But we must do it."

"We?"

She looked into his eyes and nodded. Then she withdrew her hands and got up.

"Is everything ready?" she asked the old woman.

"You did the right thing," commented Rona. "Gave him your forgiveness. You can move on now, and so can the big fellow. Yes, I've set it out. Pity I can't do the whole of it for you, but the old bones are too stiff for a Calling now; it takes a lot out of you. Ready?"

"Yes," said Nessa. "I'm ready."

It was cold and dry. It was dark, a place enclosed in stillness. The lamps Rona had lit conjured looming shadows on the walls. By the steps leading up, the seven small skulls regarded Nessa unwinking from their stone shelf. By them was set a helm, a fine, glittering object with a spike on top, a curtain of delicate metal rings, and a masklike eyepiece. The Hidden Tribe have a fondness for shiny things. That made eight faces looking on as Nessa settled cross-legged on the earthen floor.

The nightlong vigil of a Calling was too much for an old

woman, so Rona had stayed in relative comfort in the topmost chamber, with the dogs. She would remain awake; a watch was essential for the seer's safety. Eyvind had been instructed to stay in the cottage, as far away as possible. Many rules had been broken by his presence in the women's place. He must not come near this most secret of observances. Nessa had never done it before, not on her own, and it was vital that everything be right, or she might wait the whole night and still find no answers.

Layer by layer she sank deeper into trance. First was the calm, the quiet, the slowing of the breath, listening for the ancient heartbeat, the deep pulse of the earth. Then the gradual withdrawal from the clay self, finger by finger, toe by toe, from soles of feet to crown of head, leaving the body behind: a shell seated there in the dim light, with her back straight and her dark hair flowing over her slender shoulders. That took time; the wisdom of the earth has not been gathered in a year, or a hundred years, or a thousand, but over an age man's mind cannot encompass, a span greater than the arch of the heavens, deeper than the ocean at world's end. Long and longer she sat there into the night, until her mind began to merge with an ancient mind that was rock and earth, seeping water and probing tree root, chill air breathing in the underground chamber, a voice that was both within and without. The empty vessel that was Nessa leaned forward, obedient to her will; her hands moved the ritual objects, sprinkling water, letting ash trickle between her fingers to make a pattern, casting the fragments of bone. When the voice spoke, it was her own and not her own. The seer and the vision were the same.

Where is the Wolf?

"The . . . the wolf . . . the dog? Upstairs, in the outer chamber."

Where is the Wolf who shadows the steps of the priestess? Where is the chieftain?

"Not far away. He is a man. He cannot enter this place."

His helm gleams there in the shadows, another mask of death. He will wear it once more in battle; I hear his axe blade ringing in the chill wind from the sea. He will go down fighting, as befits his kind. He does not know surrender.

"Are you telling me he will die?"

He is a warrior. You need a warrior.

Silence. The husk that was Nessa inclined her head to look

at the pattern on the ground before her, the alignment of the bones, the subtle markings of ash and water. Shadows flickered past; whispers haunted the air. The eye of the spirit watched unblinking.

What is to be seen?

"I see death, Mother."

You see true. But you do not see all. Drink of the cup the wise one set for you, and look again. Your voice trembles. Do not let fear blind you to what is there. That is not the way of the seer. Make yourself empty.

Nessa sipped from the cup; the brew was strong and bitter, herbs used to deepen the trance and open the pathways of the mind. She forced herself to finish it. Now there was no sense of time passing. There was only the earth above her, and the voice inside. The bones, the ash shifted and stirred of themselves; now she could see an image there, fire, men running, and somewhere in the shadowy corners of the underground chamber there was a terrible screaming that went on and on, and behind it the sound of the sea. There was a vision of the islands, but the islands were changed. The Kin Stone was cast down, the great circle was laid waste, there was burning and destruction and hatred. She could not see herself or Rona. She could not see Engus or Kinart or any man of the Folk. She could not see Eyvind. It was a place empty of spirit.

What do you see?

"I–I cannot say . . ."

You called me forth from my sleep, daughter. This is no time for cowardice. A wise woman does not shrink from the truth.

"This cannot be the future! It cannot be! We must be able to stop this!"

Is the Wolf faithful?

"Yes." Her voice was a whisper.

Is the old woman strong?

"Yes."

And what of you, priestess? You flinch away from these images. But there are no easy answers for you. You think you have seen sorrow, but you face a sorrow far greater than any your mind can imagine. You will see all that is dear to you hanging by a thread fine as a single filament of cobweb. Are you strong enough to lose all you have, and still go on?

"This is . . . it is a true vision, then? This is what awaits the Folk, as Somerled threatened?"

The answer is within you, daughter. In ash and bone you seek the truth, in the shards and dust that are man's destiny. In ash and bone shall you find the truth, hidden deep. Summon your courage, for tonight's dark vision shows you the path to come. Follow it steadfastly, or all fails.

"*Or* all fails? Then . . . there is some hope to be found in this, a chance? The single strand? Tell me. Tell me, can the Folk be saved? Or are we—are he and I destined to fight and fail, each of us alone in this dark time to come?"

The Wolf does not know surrender. A cruel god binds him.

"He's changed. He has learned what it means to take a life, and what it means to live one."

He will go unarmed into this battle. His adversary has all the weapons.

"I should send him away, then." The chill deepened. The lamps flickered, the shadows moved. "I would not bind him to me, and have him go before me to be vanquished, to die for me, for us. I would not throw him at Somerled's feet. Better that he go home: that he sail away and never return."

Too late for that. The Wolf follows in your steps. He will be loyal to the end.

"My uncle . . . my cousin . . . what about Rona? None of them were there, none . . ."

How strong are you, daughter? Are you as strong as the standing stones? Can you endure as the deep caves endure, does your heart keep time with the heartsong of the islands? How strong are you, Nessa?

"Strong enough. I must be."

Ahhh . . . The sound rang through the cavern, a sigh, a sob, a whisper, a great call, a deep prayer. Nessa covered her face with her hands, and felt the darkness close in around her.

She stirred, half-waking. Her head swam; her limbs were heavy, her mouth dry. To go from trance to sleep is not kind to body or mind. It is best to come out step by step, through the misty layers of thought, until the mind attains full consciousness again. Only then can one surrender to sleep in safety. She had not done that; exhaustion, despair, and denial had claimed her, and now she felt drained, deadened, unable even to run her tongue over her parched lips. Slowly her awareness grew. She was warm; she was lying somewhere soft, in bed, with a pillow under her head. It was no longer dark; though her eyelids were heavy with slumber, she could feel the light streaming in . . . If she was in the cottage, and it was as bright as this, it was not only day, it was already afternoon . . . It was nearly low tide . . .

Nessa's eyes snapped open. The warm fingers that had encircled her own were abruptly withdrawn. She tried to sit up and collapsed back with a groan as her head began to throb, an insistent drumbeat starting up somewhere just behind her eyes.

"It's so late . . . why didn't you wake me?" she whispered. "Kinart will be waiting . . . I have to go."

"Water." That was a command, in Rona's voice. Nessa turned her head very cautiously to the side. There was Eyvind sitting by the pallet with jug in one hand, cup in the other; he was getting plenty of practice at this. He held the cup for her; she propped herself up on one elbow and drank. Why was he so pale? Why did he look so anxious? She had not even told them yet. They did not know what she had seen.

"Good," said Eyvind, "good. Not too fast. That's it. Now lie down again."

"No!" She struggled to sit; gave up and lay back on the pillows. "It must be time for me to go. The sun is already low in the west." There were knives prodding into her head.

"Kinart can wait a bit longer," said Rona, coming into view behind Eyvind's shoulder. She, too, was looking pale and tired; a night without sleep takes its toll on an old woman. "You're worn out, you look like a wee shadow. Take your time. If needs be, I'll go out and have a word with your cousin. You've time to rest a bit, and tell us what you've seen. Then you can go, if you must."

"My uncle made me promise. Rona, he wants you to come with me. And I think he's right. It's not safe for you here, not anymore. There is . . ." A shiver coursed through her body, for all the warm blanket. "There is a bad time ahead, the darkest of times. Will you come?"

Rona shook her head. "Me, settle on the Whaleback? Hardly. I'm not afraid of dying, Nessa. I'm an old woman, I've done what I have to do here, and I'll go when I'm called. You're the priestess now, lass. The ancestors will watch over me, and I over them, as long as it's meant to be."

"That's just it," Nessa whispered. "I don't think you've done it yet, not all of it. I was asked if you are strong. I think there is another task for you, Rona, but I fear for you if you stay here unguarded. There is . . . there is an empty future for us, for the Folk and the islands, if we cannot be strong enough."

"We?" queried Rona, eyes shrewd.

"You, and me, and . . . Eyvind."

"Ah," said the old woman. "We were right about him, then. Will you tell him?"

"I don't know how. It sounded as if . . . it sounded as if by helping us, he would sacrifice himself. I don't want to send him to a certain death, Rona. How can I do that? He's not even one of us. It's like using a warrior whose only part in a battle is to rush in first, and die."

"Tell him. I'll go out and have a word with Kinart. I'll let him know you'll come as soon as you're strong enough."

The door creaked open and shut. She must sit up, must summon her strength, for all the piercing pain in her head and the leaden weight in her heart. Now she felt bile rising, she was going to be sick. Curse it, this wasn't fair at all . . .

"Here," said Eyvind. He held a bowl for her, one hand on her brow as she retched helplessly. "It's all right," he murmured. "It's all right. You'll be better soon."

And, remarkably, she was. With her stomach empty, the headache receded to a dull throb. Eyvind wedged the pillow behind her back so she could sit upright. He cleaned up; he returned with a wet cloth, and held it to her brow.

"I was worried," he said. "You seemed so far away."

"It's the trance. And—and what I saw was bad. It was so bad I couldn't come out of it properly; I went to sleep instead. Running away again. That's why I'm sick now. It will pass. I must go soon, the tide will be at its lowest. How did I get here? How did I get out of the chamber?"

Eyvind smiled. "Well, the old woman didn't carry you, that much is certain."

"But . . . you mean she let you go down there and fetch me? You brought me back?"

"She gave me permission, with instructions to keep my eyes down. You were freezing cold; breathing as slowly as a man left out in the snow at night. We might have lost you."

"Thank you for bringing me back."

"It was quite awkward. That passageway is narrow, and you're tall for one of your kind. Almost up to my shoulder."

"When we were little, my cousin used to call me Beanpole," Nessa said dryly.

Eyvind said nothing for a while; she began to wonder if she had got the word wrong in his language. Then he said, "I would not give you such a name."

She glanced at him. There was a look in his eyes that seemed new. It troubled her, for she felt its reflection in herself, something fragile and lovely, so painful she could hardly bear it. "What name would you use, then?" she asked him, not sure what he meant.

"I would call you Pearl, for your beauty. I would call you Dove, for your sweetness," said Eyvind softly. "I would call you Bright Star." He would not look at her now, but stared with apparent fascination at the ground by his feet.

Nessa's heart seemed to turn over, and steady, and beat again. Men did say such things, of course, she knew that. But they never meant them; her sisters had told her it was only a trick to make women give them what they wanted. She drew a breath to rebuke him, but could not find any words. It was quite plain to her that Eyvind was not that kind of man. Indeed, she doubted very much if he had ever spoken thus before. He seemed to be blushing.

"Men do not say such things to me," she told him, not managing to keep her voice steady.

"No?" Now he did look at her, gaze deep as the summer sea.

"I am a priestess. Men do not address me thus. It's not . . . appropriate."

"Have I offended you?" he asked quietly. "Are you telling me that you are sworn to your gods for life? That you will never lie with a man?"

Suddenly this was becoming much too difficult. Nessa shivered and wrapped her arms around herself. She chose the easiest question to answer.

"You haven't offended me, Eyvi. We are friends. Now listen

to me, please. I must go soon, my cousin is waiting. Last night—last night I saw some terrible things. It seems to me we will walk close to a cliff edge, all of us, and that if we slip, the Folk are lost and the islands are lost and we are lost too, Eyvi: you and me and Rona. I want to ask you, will you help me? Will you help me to save the Folk?"

He nodded without hesitation.

"You must fight a battle. The Wolf, that was what I was told, the Wolf must go into battle against an opponent who has all the weapons. But I don't think it is the sort of fight in which you have excelled in the past. And I must tell you, to do so is to act in peril for your life. I do not . . . I don't want to bind you to a promise, Eyvi, only to see you die."

He gave a mirthless smile. "That's all I'm good for, I think."

"Don't say that!" She swept aside the blanket and rose to stand by the bed, swaying as the cottage walls and floor and roof beams whirled in a circle before her eyes. Eyvind sprang up to support her by the arms; his hands were warm and sure, the same hands that had held hers safe through the dark time of oblivion. "Don't say it, Eyvi! There is a future here, I will believe it, I will believe we can make things good and bright again, I will not give in to despair! And there are so many things you can do, so much you can give, stop trying to hide behind your helm and your axe and your battle cry! The man inside is kind and sweet and strong. He is the one who will win this fight!" With a considerable effort of will, she stepped away from his touch, though everything in her urged her to move forward, to fling her arms around him and put her head against his breast, and . . . and there were so many reasons why she could not do that, reasons within reasons. She must indeed be sick and exhausted, to allow such a thought to enter her mind. She found her cloak, her bag. She thrust her feet into the pair of boots someone had set neatly by the bed.

"You didn't answer me, before." His voice was so quiet she could hardly hear him: a thread, but strong. She could not bring herself to meet his eyes. "Are you sworn to a life of celibacy in the practice of your rituals? Is that what you were saying?"

"I don't know," she whispered. "I don't know the answer." She fumbled with the boot straps.

"Let me," he said, and knelt down by her to tie them carefully. For a man with such big hands, he had a neat touch with knots.

"Your hands aren't shaking at all," Nessa said.

"No," replied Eyvind, "but I am frightened. Frightened for you, frightened for the old woman, terrified of the task ahead of me. He could always cut me down with words. They are his weapon of choice, and he uses them like a master."

Outside there were footsteps on the path; Rona was returning. The old woman coughed loudly, a warning perhaps.

"Can't you tell me more of what you saw?" asked Eyvind urgently, rising to his feet. "What about you? I don't want you in the path of an attack, you should go away to safety—"

"Shh," Nessa said. "There's no time left. There's no time left for anything but good-bye." She stood on tiptoes and gave him a little kiss on the cheek. It was a touch as quick and light as the brush of a feather, the brief dance of a butterfly on an open flower. She heard his indrawn breath, and knew that if she lingered an instant longer his arms would come up and wrap themselves around her, a cloak of love and warmth and protection. That could not be allowed to happen. She stepped away and fled out into the fading light of late afternoon, down to the shore where her two guards waited, and they raced the tide back home.

NINE

Once he would have acted without hesitation. He would have strapped on his sword belt and put Biter on his back and marched away from the secret place, straight to Somerled's court. Once he had been a Wolfskin.

It was not only his own doubts that made him wait. Rona, too, urged caution. He understood her gestures well enough; he could even make out a word or two now. *Not yet,* she was telling him, *not just yet.* And because he had not forgotten, and never would forget what he had been, Eyvind spent the time preparing himself as best he could. He would not be fighting

Somerled with sword or axe or fists. But neither did he wish to be murdered by the wayside before he even got there. He could imagine what Grim and Erlend and Holgar would say if he went back, and could not even lift a drinking cup without spilling half the contents. He could imagine what Somerled would think if his chief guard could scarcely walk from sleeping quarters to hall without stopping to rest his trembling legs. So he readied his body, and in the harsh tests he set himself, he tried to clear his mind of Nessa. He would do what she wanted, he was bound to that. Probably he would die. He had seen that in her eyes, though she had not put it into words. Perhaps it was better if he did die, for try as he might he could not banish her from his thoughts.

That moment came to him over and over again, at dawn's first waking, at night falling asleep, by day as he lifted Biter over his head and put himself through his paces. He could not forget the touch of her lips against his cheek, the sweet smell of her, like new violets, the brush of her slender body against his own, stirring him to an instant desire that shamed him deeply. Nessa was a priestess, forbidden, untouchable. Even had it not been so, she was so far beyond him, with her composure and wisdom, that it was ridiculous that such an idea should ever occur to him; outrageous that his body burned for her, even now when she was long gone. He had only to imagine . . . he had only to remember . . . he would not remember, Eyvind told himself savagely, hurling Biter at a lump of driftwood he had set against the bank as a target. The axe struck true; the massive log split neatly in half. He must not imagine her. He would think only of today, of this moment: the axe, his arms, the target. He was once more a weapon, not Thor's now, but hers. His mission was to go to Somerled and tell the truth; to use what he knew, somehow, to influence his friend's actions. He could not accuse Somerled in front of others, not without proof. To do that would be to seem a madman or a fool; it would change nothing. All he could do, he thought, was speak to his friend in private, and try to shame Somerled into making peace with Engus. He must trust in the strength of that childhood bond, and hope he could set Somerled on a new path. *I know you killed your brother. From now on, I will be watching you, to ensure you walk straight. Every day, every step.* Odin's bones, the oath had indeed fettered him. The task would be hard; harder than anything he had done before. He must work to grow strong, so he would be ready.

Eyvind gave the dog a name: Shadow. Perhaps she had once had another name, one Ulf had bestowed on her, but that was forgotten. Shadow stayed close; if she missed her mate, who had gone away with Nessa, she gave no sign of it. She lay by the entrance to the howe, nose on paws, watching gravely as Eyvind practiced with the sword, lifting it high, sweeping it low, turning, blocking, slashing, holding it steady. His weapons had been laid away carefully, but not hidden from him. That meant Nessa had trusted him from the first, when she had every reason not to. There were reminders of her everywhere: the cloak that she had left behind, in whose folds lingered a trace of the sweet scent that so beguiled him; the small pattern of stones she had made beside the place where Biter was stored. He took the axe out every morning and laid it back every night, without touching those secret symbols. He could imagine the solemn expression in her strange, light eyes, he could see how her silky brown hair might flow over her shoulders as she bent to move the little stones delicately into place. He could envisage the play of lamplight on the pale skin of her cheek, and the soft rosy curve of her mouth. He could see her as if she were right there before him . . . Curse it, this was a slow torture, and he was a complete fool. There was a job to do, and he must do it, and that was where it ended. That Nessa had enough faith in him to seek his help must be enough for him. It was not her fault that his eyes saw only her image, that his body ached for her touch, that his mind was full of terror that she might be in danger, and himself not by her side to protect her. She did not know that she had stolen his heart the moment she folded her hands around his, and called him Eyvi. She had not asked him to love her. That part had been his own stupid fault, the weakness of a man who, in Somerled's words, had never been very good at thinking. Now he would have to think, and think fast, because spring was nearly here, and he still didn't know how he would say what must be said. *What you're doing is wrong. Your whole strategy for the islands is wrong. These are real men and women here, not toys.* He could already hear Somerled's reply. *Oh dear, Eyvind. You've got it all muddled. Leave this to me, will you, and stick to what you're good at?*

Every evening he asked the old woman, in signs and gestures, in words half understood, *Is it time yet?* And every evening she answered him in the same way, *Not yet. Wait a little longer.* But there came a time when there could be no more waiting.

Maybe there was a trace of spring in the air that day. Rona spent a lot of time watching the sky, and even more time staring into her small fire and muttering to herself. As Eyvind sat polishing his helm and sword, he caught her gaze on him, sharp, shrewd, as if somehow measuring him.

"I will do what I can," he said, though she could not understand his words. "Everything that is in my power. I'll try to protect her, to help her. It's just that—"

He fell suddenly silent. Rona froze; her old ears had heard it too, a footstep not far away, a man's boot set down where it should not be, inside the border of the women's place, on the western margin. Shadow began a low growling, deep in her throat; Eyvind silenced her with a quick gesture. He rose to his feet, listening as a hunter does. Rona sat motionless.

Another tiny sound, to the east this time. He thought there were four of them. Either they were quite skilled, or he was losing his touch, to let them come in so close. Four. Very well, he had no choice but to confront them before the old woman was harmed. He rolled his eyes at her, then jerked his head toward the howe: *Go in there, quick, hide.* No need to worry about her making a noise, she moved as if she were a ghost, in complete silence and with remarkable swiftness. He tried to convey the same message to Shadow, *Go, guard her,* but Shadow would not obey. She stood by him, teeth bared, moving her whiskery muzzle from side to side as if to guess which enemy would dare strike first.

The footsteps came closer, stealthy but unmistakable. At least four, maybe five. Eyvind put on his helm. He took Biter in his right hand and his sword in his left, and moved into a dark corner behind the water barrel. Something inside him was saying, *Let it not be Holgar. Let it not be Grim. Let it not be Erlend or Thord. Let it not be my brother.* His fingers tightened around the axe, and then something flew in a great arc through the air, a ball of fire, a torch, and flames were suddenly crackling from the heather thatch of Rona's cottage, and armed figures ran into the women's place from both sides at once.

"Find the girl!" someone yelled. "Check the place before it burns down. Kick the door open!"

"I'm not going in there!" another man shouted. "What about the witch? Smoke them out, that's safer!"

"You heard what Somerled said. Get the girl out alive. That's who he wants. Go on, he won't thank you if you bring him back a pretty little charred corpse."

"All right, all right." One of the fellows was setting his boot to the cottage door; it gave little resistance, being almost as old as Rona herself. Clouds of dark smoke billowed out; the man blundered inside, coughing.

"What about over there?" It was one of the knarr's crew, Eyvind knew him. "A cave or something; she could be inside. Come on!" He knew them all; men who had been Ulf's loyal companions and men who had simply been hired sailors. Now all bore cold iron; now they were Somerled's men.

"Nobody in there!" wheezed the fellow from the cottage doorway. Behind him the rafters were beginning to give; strange sparks fizzed and popped through the smoke, purple and green and scarlet. There would be little left of the wise woman's possessions, meager as they were.

Now all five men were making for the howe, and suddenly there was Shadow, her growl menacing, her mouth a drooling trap of long teeth fit for rending bear or deer or wild boar. Her eyes, so mild when she walked by Eyvind's side or played with her mate, now seemed the reddened orbs of some crazed, feral creature. The men hesitated.

"Odin's bones!" their leader muttered. "What in the name of all the gods is *that?*"

"It's a witch-wolf!" someone whispered. "One bite and you drop dead in agony."

"Poison in the fangs," agreed someone else in shaking tones. "Where I come from, they call them demon dogs. Better back off."

But one fellow had a spear ready, and it was aimed squarely at Shadow's heart. His arm went back, the shaft flew through the air, and Eyvind stepped out neatly from his hiding place to deflect it with his sword. Shadow began a ferocious barking.

Until that moment, Eyvind had not known what he would do: what he might say. Now he raised Biter high, and the flames of the burning cottage shimmered gold and orange across its blade. A voice came to his lips unbidden, a voice of wrath, powerful as the darkness in the moment before death. It rang across the hollow like a summons from another world. "Who dares challenge me?"

"Eyvind!" someone gasped in tones of abject terror. The men's faces grew pale as cheese, their eyes filled with panic, and they began to back away, stumbling in their haste. "It's Eyvind! But–but he's dead!"

There was a stampede for safety, men scrambling past one another in their frenzy, with Shadow snapping and snarling at their heels. Within moments, the women's place was empty again, save for Eyvind and the dog. He noticed a strange kind of green mist on the ground and around his knees, a sort of vapor that clung and coiled eerily up his body. And when Rona came slowly out from the tower in the earth, the same green veil seemed to linger around her hands and her skirts before dissipating in the cool air. It appeared she had added a few touches of her own.

They stood side by side, watching the last remnants of the cottage burn. It was a hot fire; there was nothing to be saved. Eyvind put his arm around Rona's shoulders; she was as fragile and bony as an ancient owl. It came to him that she was a being both wise and precious.

"I'm sorry," he said. "I'm sorry I couldn't save it."

Rona muttered something and gestured with her hands. The house; her possessions. A sweep of the arms: all gone. She cupped her hands to her heart, tapped her fingers to her head, and gave her gapped and crooked smile. He thought he understood her. *It's all in the heart and the head, lad. That's what matters.*

After the burning, it was clear neither of them could stay there. They sheltered in the howe as night fell. Shadow stayed outside, perhaps knowing that now a constant watch must be maintained. Eyvind tried to explain to Rona what he had heard. It seemed vitally important.

"Nessa," he said, knowing this name, at least, they had in common. He used his hands. "Men come—not for me, not for you—men come for Nessa. Somerled—find Nessa. Why? Why does he want her, Rona? Tell me."

But like many old folk, the wise woman chose her own times to be helpful and her times to stay silent. She shrugged and said nothing.

"Please," begged Eyvind, knowing he was talking to himself. Rona lay down on the ground with Nessa's cloak over her for warmth. It was not a kind bed for an old woman. "Please tell me. I love her, I can't let him hurt her. I understand what she is, and what I am. I know the best I can do is try to stand between her and danger, to help her as I promised. All I'm trying to do is put it together so I can understand: so I can know what to do next."

It was pointless. Rona's eyes were closed; she snored peacefully. As soon as the sky began to brighten, he'd have to wake her, and they'd have to go . . . where? A fugitive, whose own folk thought him a ghost, an ancient crone and a very large hunting dog: the three of them could surely not travel far, unobserved. He did not like to think of Rona in Somerled's hands. Somerled's treatment of the cat woman all those years ago had shown what he thought of priestesses. Where could they go? Where could he take her? To the Folk, he was the enemy, a butcher who had slaughtered their sons. And what about Somerled? Every moment that passed seemed likely to put Nessa and her people in greater danger. If only she were here by his side; if only it were that first night again, when he had woken from his long nightmare to see her there in the shadows, with all the mystery and gravity and wonder of the islands written on her delicate features. No wonder he had thought her a goddess, a spirit. No wonder he had sat close by her, with her body warm against his own, as if there were nothing untoward about it. That night had not been part of ordinary time; it was its own time. Where was Nessa now? Did she think of him at all? Did she wonder if he had begun to fulfill the quest she had given him, or had she forgotten him the moment she'd turned and run from him, back to her own people? Eyvind put his fingers up to touch the place where she had kissed him, and, knowing himself foolish beyond belief, he whispered his goodnight words to her. "Rest sweetly, my Bright Star. Walk safely. My hand in yours." He closed his eyes and slept.

* * *

It was quiet. It was so quiet he knew the moment he woke that the old woman was gone. A glance around the howe found no sign of her. Eyvind made his way outside, hoping Rona was merely dipping water from the spring, or perhaps rummaging through the pitiful remains of her home, hoping to salvage some small treasure. But the place was deserted. A gray film of fine ash coated the small bushes and dusted the banks of the stream. Rona was gone, and so was Shadow. A raid, an abduction, even murder—had he slept through that? *Think, Eyvind.* No sign of a struggle, no blood, nothing touched as far as he could see, though the boot prints Somerled's men had left behind them still marked the soft soil. Where did Rona's footsteps lead? Did she walk as subtly as she wove charms of green mist and ghostly voice, so cleverly she passed with never a trace?

"Rona!" he called, knowing in his heart she would not reply. "Where are you, foolish old woman? Who will guard you, wandering alone?" Here were Shadow's paw prints overlaying the others, a steady trail across the sacred space and off up the eastward track toward the hills. They were gone, the two of them. Rona had solved his first problem for him; the wise woman had freed him from the need to protect her, so he could pursue his quest. Eyvind wondered in what chill corner of the land she would lay her aged bones tonight.

"I'm sorry," he whispered, and went back into the howe, for he must move now, before Somerled sent his men back with instructions to conquer their fear of ghosts and complete the task he had set them. *Find the girl.* Why? Why was Nessa so important to Somerled, who respected matters of the spirit only when it suited him?

It had been easy yesterday. His burnished helm and weapons, the terrible voice that had not been his own, the dog's courage—these things had set the attackers sprinting in retreat before he needed to wield sword or axe in earnest, before he had to test himself. He still didn't know if he could have done it. There was no saying if he could even begin to fight a man without the voice of Thor to spur him on. The time would come, soon enough, when he must find out. Could he kill, now he had begun to understand how precious life was?

He must erase all sign of his presence from the women's place. There was no doubt in his mind that Somerled's men would return. He must take all his things, his weapons, his boots, his cloak. He must wear his wolfskin. Setting it on his shoulders felt very strange indeed, as if he dressed in another man's clothing. He should take the helm as well. Where was it? He was sure he had left it there in the alcove beside Biter, but now it was gone. Eyvind had no desire to go back into that shadowy chamber far underground, the place where he had found Nessa lying limp and white after her long, lonely ritual. For an instant, that night, he'd thought he had lost her, and a wave of anguish had swept through him that was like death itself. In the moment of realizing that she still breathed, Eyvind had begun to understand why Thor had released him from his vow, and he had thanked the god from the depths of his heart.

Now there was no choice but to descend into the darkness and seek what was his. The helm was back on the shelf beside the little skulls with their blank, staring eye holes. Eyvind tried not to look at them as he reached up. He needed no reminding that this chamber was a forbidden place. The talk of a Hidden Tribe was more than enough to curb a man's curiosity. His fingers encountered something hidden underneath the helm, a small soft object. He shuddered, and tried not to imagine what it might be. As his hand felt it, he seemed to hear a voice, a fierce, dark whisper: *Take it. Take it, warrior.* He did not look around, but seized the small bundle in one hand and the helm in the other, and fled up the crumbling stone steps to the top chamber and out into the light of day. Only then did he squat down to lay what he held on the ground before him and examine it.

There were two items there, and one of them was his own: the pouch he'd worn on his belt when first he blundered into this forbidden place. Until now, he had not even thought about it. The other was a folded scrap of cloth, tied with blue ribbon into a neat, tiny bundle. The ribbon was Nessa's, the same that had fastened her long braid the day she had dried her hair before the fire. Carefully he untied the knot and spread the small cloth flat. Looking at what it held, he could hear her voice, calm, serious, and see the graceful movements of her hands as she gestured, explaining. *Here is all that the islands are, Eyvi, all that the Folk are, and all that I am. Earth, fire, water, air: the enchantment of light, the patterns of being. Hold these things close, for they are life itself.* On the unfolded cloth there lay a small gray feather, whisper-soft; a smooth brown stone from the shore, which bore a delicate network of lines in silver-white, like some strange earth runes; a frond of dried seaweed with fine grains of sand still clinging to its crevices; and a twig from the hearth fire, white at one end, charred black at the other. As well, the little bundle held three tiny round pebbles, pale as winter moonlight. Holding them in his hands, Eyvind felt his breathing grow slower, his mind become calmer. The beating of his heart seemed strong and steady. It was as if he sat in an island of quiet, outside ordinary things; as if he were back in that place the two of them had shared the night he first met her. He thought how exhausted she had been in those last days; how fear had shadowed her sea-gray eyes and turned her cheeks wax-pale. Yet she had made time to gather these things for him; had probably asked Rona to keep them safe until he should be ready to receive them. Carefully, he wrapped and fastened the tiny bundle again and opened the pouch to stow it away inside.

His hand encountered a tangle of cord or string twisted about something metallic and sharp. He drew the object out. A buckle: Ulf's belt buckle, he had thrust it in here that day on High Island, thinking to return it to Somerled, and he had completely forgotten about it. It was a fine silver piece of considerable value; it should have been buried with its owner, or gone back to his brother. He must take it now . . . Eyvind's heart lurched; a chill seemed to creep over him. His eyes understood, but for a moment his mind refused to accept. By all the gods, how blind had he been to miss this? Why hadn't he taken the time to look at it properly, the day of Ulf's killing? The belt clasp was twined about with scraps of fine, strong cord, the same cord that had pinioned Ulf there on the cliff face so tightly that his struggles had only served to sever his wrist nearly in two. Eyvind's knife had slashed him free. The stained cord was frayed where the buckle's edges had chafed it, and it was unravelling where the knife had slit it, but, above and below those points, he could still see the knots tied in the cord. No wonder Ulf had been unable to free himself. Eyvind knew this knot. It was neat, small, and decorative; it looked a little like a flower. It was a knot that tightened quickly at first and then more slowly, an infallible knot for a snare. There were only two people he knew who could make this knot: himself, and Somerled.

He thrust the buckle back in the pouch and fastened it to his belt. His gut churned; his mind was in turmoil. *Think, Eyvind.* Very well, he had evidence, though he almost wished there were none. For now he must confront the truth: Somerled really had done the unspeakable. The friend to whom he had sworn lifelong loyalty had killed his own brother, killed him with cold premeditation and devious, imaginative cruelty. And he had lied; he had convinced them all of his grief, of the guilt of the islanders, of his genuine wish to discover the truth about his brother's murder.

Images ran through Eyvind's mind with terrible clarity: Hakon laying his wolfskin down before his brother warriors for the last time; a bull's horn piercing a man's chest; a girl lying open-eyed under a stream of clear water. So many lies: so many betrayals. If Somerled was guilty, was not Eyvind equally guilty in his blind adherence to the oath that bound him to silence? And yet, a promise made in blood was a promise never to be broken. What was to be done? There was no Jarl Magnus here, no priest of their own kind, no impartial men of law to whom he could go for help. He could try to find Eirik or Thord, he could ask them to support him. But there was no place where charges might be brought formally, since Somerled had dispensed with the Thing. Besides, even if a charge of murder were proven, what penalty could be imposed here in this isolated realm? Somerled could not be banished; he could hardly pay reparations, since he himself was the dead man's closest kin. This could not be done openly, as if they were still in Rogaland. Besides, he did not want to destroy Somerled. He did not wish to wrench from him all that he had desired in life: recognition, authority, a place of his own. As a true brother, he must persuade Somerled to change, to become the kind of chieftain they needed here, a man of vision and balance. That pale, fierce-eyed child had had the seed of greatness in him; Eyvind had seen it. Somehow, he must turn Somerled from the dark path he followed, and into ways of true leadership. That was the answer. If he could convince Somerled to remake the treaty, Nessa's people would be saved. After that, Eyvind must ensure this chieftain led his people justly and fairly. He would use what he knew to force a change. *Stand back from this battle, leave the Folk in peace, or I will tell the world you killed your brother. Renew the pledge of amity Ulf made, or I will expose your crime before all.* Rona had known. Somehow she had known what this buckle meant, and saved it until Eyvind was ready to use it. A wise woman indeed.

He slipped Nessa's small talisman inside his tunic, close to his heart. He would not lay this precious thing away beside the dark remembrance of a brother's treachery. He took a last look around him. The cottage was no more than a shell, the earth still bore the marks of raiders' boots, the little fire where the three of them had sat together was cold. Eyvind looked up at the sky as he had seen Rona do, and as he gazed, a flock of birds passed over, a scattering of silver flashes against the palest gray of morning. *The enchantment of light . . . the patterns of being . . . they are life itself.* Perhaps he would never come back here. Perhaps he would never see his two wise women again. With axe, sword, and knives, with wolfskin on shoulders and bright helm held ready, Eyvind felt as naked as a new babe, a warrior going forth quite unarmed to face the enemy. He set his face to the southeast and walked away from the women's place. All that he had was the truth; it must be enough.

It seemed much farther than he had remembered. He skirted the shores of the large loch that lay inland from the women's place, stopping to hide several times as parties of armed men passed by. He was not covering the distance as quickly as he had expected, and yet he was already tired, his legs aching, his head throbbing. By the time he reached a crossroads that he judged to be the halfway point of his journey, the sun was moving down toward the west, and the wind was brisk and chill. He noted that there were far more of his own folk about than islanders. Now he was in a part of the island where King Engus had said Ulf's people might travel freely. Not that that seemed to matter anymore. Had not Somerled's men marched boldly into the most forbidden of places with weapons drawn? Perhaps it was already war.

Odin's bones, he was weary. Sitting down to rest under this rocky outcrop had been a mistake, for while he forced himself on he could ignore the pain in his legs, the dizziness in his head, the powerful urge to find a place of refuge and seek respite in sleep. He could not allow himself to give in to that. There must be no more running away. Before dusk today he must walk into Somerled's hall and ask to speak to him in private. He must find the right words and make Somerled believe them. He would sit just a moment longer, and then he would go on.

He slept, or half-slept. Nessa's image was in his mind. He saw her slight, ethereal figure walking on a lonely shore, turning to gaze at him with those strange light eyes, shell-gray rimmed with darker blue. They were like the eyes of some wondrous wild creature . . . A tiny sound roused Eyvind abruptly from his reverie. He was on his feet in an instant. There was someone on the other side of this rock, someone treading very softly as if to creep up and attack him unawares. Very well, two could play that game. Eyvind moved swift as a hunting dog, stepping around to pinion both the fellow's arms with one of his own, while he clapped his other hand across the man's mouth to stifle any screams for help. Good: this, at least, he could still do well enough. He glanced quickly across the hillside and over to the grazing lands fringing the lake. No sign of anyone; with luck this fool was a lone assailant. He relaxed his grip a little. The man was putting up no fight at all. As Eyvind removed his hand from the fellow's lips, his captive began to speak quietly, in measured tones. The language was vaguely familiar, the voice instantly recognizable.

"Pater noster qui es in coelis, sanctificetur nomen tuum . . ."

Eyvind released his grip altogether. "You'll get yourself killed one day, creeping about like that," he said sternly.

Brother Tadhg fell silent, turning mild eyes on his captor. He did not appear much shaken; perhaps a man with such faith in his god is difficult to frighten. "Ah," he said. "It's true, then, what they say. Your ghost walks, a warrior still wielding his axe from beyond the grave."

"You speak in jest, I take it."

"Not entirely," said the priest. "For myself, my ribs tell me all too plainly that you are flesh and blood, and that you have somehow survived a battle and a long disappearance. Others tell the tale of your manifestation in a most unlikely place, your axe and helm glittering with eldritch light, and a great ruby-eyed wolf-dog by your side. I see you are heading southward."

Eyvind nodded. He had plenty of questions, but he could not ask them. It was not safe to tell where he had been, not even to this mild-mannered Christian; he could not say what he had learned.

"I did not intend to do you any harm," Tadhg said.

Eyvind smiled. "No, I don't imagine so. I'm sorry I was rough. It could have been anyone. Can you tell me—" No, he could not ask.

"What is it you wish to know? I spend little time with your people now. Somerled finds my style of translation ill suited to his purpose. King Engus was less than pleased with the offer of peace your friend made to him."

There was an assumption there, Eyvind thought, that he would be aware of this; surely Tadhg could not know where he had been?

"Has Somerled sent a messenger yet asking for the king's decision?" he asked cautiously. "Has Engus given an answer?"

"Not yet," Tadhg answered, showing no surprise whatever at these questions. "The first day of spring, that was the deadline. We are coming close. But matters have overtaken Engus somewhat. His sister died this morning. It is a time of great sorrow for the Folk, made more painful yet by so many other losses since the summer. For these people the royal line is always the women's line, and this lady was a princess in her own right."

Eyvind bowed his head and said nothing.

"Tonight is a time of solemn ritual on the Whaleback," Tadhg went on. "I saw them this morning, but I will not stay for that; it is an observance of deep mourning. All will gather there to bid the lady a last farewell, and the ceremony will last deep into the night. Once she is laid to rest perhaps Engus will be ready to make his decision."

"I heard—it seemed to me—the king did not see this as a choice," Eyvind ventured. "It seemed that he would sacrifice his people rather than agree to Somerled's terms."

Brother Tadhg was watching him intently. "It seemed to me thus, as well," he said. "I believe we are poised on the edge of disaster, Eyvind. There are others on the Whaleback who agree with me." There was a question in his tone.

Eyvind looked down toward the ruffled waters of the lake and the sweet soft curves of the hills beyond. He felt the strength of the great stone at his back, he saw how the sky here seemed so wide, so open that it bathed the land in light. "You remember," he asked, "how you once spoke to me about truth? About being my own man?"

Tadhg nodded.

"How much time do you think we have left?" Eyvind asked quietly. "I am hoping he will listen to me, if I go there now and try to tell him—he is my friend, after all, almost a brother. How long before the first day of spring?"

"Long enough, warrior." Tadhg's eyes were bright. "But you should make haste. Your friend has gathered quite a force of armed men. My knowledge of warfare is somewhat limited, but it is plain even to me that Somerled will be ready to move the instant he hears from Engus. His men are hungry for battle."

"It would not be battle," Eyvind said, "but a bloody massacre. He must not do it. The treaty was ring-sworn; a man who breaks such an oath must bring down the gods' fury not just on himself, but on all his people. He must listen to me. I should go now. It's still a long way, and I'm not as strong as I was."

"As to that," observed Tadhg, "it seems to me you are a great deal stronger: a different man, almost. I think you have made a new friend since I saw you last."

"Two," Eyvind said.

"What will you say to Somerled when he asks you where you have been all this time?"

Eyvind had been pondering this earlier as he walked. "I can't remember anything at all since the day I left there—since Ramsbeck. It is all gone from my mind."

Tadhg gave a nod of approval. "I've heard a blow on the head can do that. Now let me give you some advice, and then I too must be gone. I'm to meet Brother Lorcan not far from here and go on to the safe harbor. We've a chapel there and a small house where three of my brothers dwell. It looks across the water to High Island. Eyvind, if you have friends you can trust among your own people, make use of them now. If there is any way I can aid you, tell me. We both seek truth. We both seek to avoid the dark path that lies before all of us if Somerled proceeds unchecked."

Eyvind looked at him. There had been a great deal unspoken. Still, the priest knew, as Somerled would know by now, that it was in a sacred place of the Folk that the ghost of Eyvind and his spectral hound had manifested themselves. And Tadhg, it seemed to him, was the sort of man who worked things out rather quickly.

"I . . . there is one thing," he said with some hesitation. "My brother Eirik—you said you were going south? Will you be close to Hafnarvagr?"

"Indeed I will. Our little church and cottage are a short walk along the shore from that settlement. You want me to find Eirik? Will he listen to me?"

"I must speak openly, I think, and hope I can trust you."

Tadhg waited.

"My brother should be told that I am safe and well; my disappearance will have caused him some grief. But any messenger could bear him that news. It is for another reason that I ask you to seek him out. I intend to lay the truth about . . . certain matters . . . before Somerled today, as soon as I reach his hall and can speak to him in private. I have a piece of evidence that may surprise him. But I know he is clever, and highly skilled in matters of law; I know he has many supporters. It would be useful if . . . it would strengthen my case if—"

"I understand. It's highly unusual for a crime of this kind to have no witnesses at all, Eyvind. Your brother, placed as he is among the remnants of those men who sailed to High Island, might be in a position to gather information for you."

"It must be quick, I think. Who knows how soon spring will be here? But I don't want to put Eirik at any risk. Getting home safe to his woman and children in Rogaland is his first wish."

"Then I will simply lay things before him as best I can and leave the choice in his own hands," Tadhg said quietly.

"I am grateful. You're a man of great courage. But you should take care. There are some on this island who have little respect for what you represent. I think even a priest must guard his speech and watch his step now."

"We are all God's children, whatever our beliefs," said the brother. "He holds us in his hand. If we can protect these innocent people from further losses, we are bound to do so. I frowned once to see those matching scars, yours and his; it disquieted me to learn of the bond between you. But that very link may be our most potent weapon. If it gives you the power to alter Somerled's course, to turn him from his dark pathway, then you may yet make all good. Be brave, warrior. Hold fast to the truth."

"That was what she said," Eyvind whispered. "*We can make things bright and good again.*"

"If she can hold on to that hope," said Tadhg, "after such terrible losses, then it should not be so difficult for us. Now I must be off; Brother Lorcan does tend to fret when people are late. Farewell, Eyvind. I hope we may meet again in better times."

"Farewell, and thank you. You should find Eirik staying with a man called Thord, a big fellow with a scar on his face. The cottage is at the eastern end of the settlement, by the water. Tell him to be careful."

"I will. Go with God, Eyvind."

Eyvind walked on as fast as he could, cursing his weakness. Once, before Ramsbeck, he could have covered this whole distance easily between sunup and midday. Now he would be lucky if he reached Somerled's hall before darkness fell. His mind was on Eirik, and the good times back home in Hammarsby: the snow fights, the long solitary walks under the dark pines, the exhilaration of speeding across the wide expanse of the ice-hardened river. Then there were those long evenings by the fire, warm together in the light of seal-oil lamps while the snow fell outside, blanketing the longhouse in quiet: the women's fingers fashioning things of beauty with needle and fine wool, Karl carving a tiny walrus from soapstone, and Bjarni frowning over his pattern board. He could imagine Eirik telling some tale of battles won, watched by dark-haired Oksana and her small, blue-eyed sons. Eyvind felt a wave of cold pass over him. Eirik must go home, he had folk waiting for him there. He should not have asked Tadhg to find Eirik. When the *Golden Dragon* sailed again for Rogaland, his brother must be on board, fit and well. They owed that to Ingi, and to all who waited, counting the days until their men came home again. It was strange, Eyvind thought, feeling the deep aching of his legs as he climbed a rise between dark, looming rocks—it was quite strange that he could no longer see himself anywhere in this vision. For one reason or another, it seemed to him that he would not be going back.

* * *

By the time he reached the outer perimeter of the settlement, his legs felt as if they scarcely belonged to him, and his sight was blurred by the throbbing in his head. The place was surprisingly quiet; only a few torches burned in the creeping dusk, and there was no movement of folk. The sentries challenged him; he stepped forward into the light, helm safely under his arm this time, and saw terror blanch their faces and cause their swords to shake in their hands before he summoned words of reassurance.

"Easy, lads," he said. "I'm no ghost, but flesh and blood: the same man who shared your voyage from Rogaland last spring and sat with you at table many a night. I've been away. Sick. Now I am returned and I must see Somerled without delay. Will you let me pass?"

"Eyvind!" The man's tone suggested there might still be some doubt. "You're alive!"

"Most certainly." Eyvind slapped the fellow on the shoulder, and felt the ache in every muscle of his arm. It was just as well he had not been called upon to draw sword or brandish axe, for he doubted he'd the strength to lift either right now. "Feel this? I am no specter, but a living man."

"Maybe so, but you seem far from yourself, Wolfskin," observed the other fellow, an older man who had been one of Ulf's household guards. "You're nothing but skin and bone. Best be off indoors and stir the women to find you a bit of roast meat and a pot or two of ale. Then you'll want to be away again, no doubt."

The first man nodded. "You got here just in time. That'll please the king well."

Eyvind's head was fuzzy; he didn't seem to be understanding. "King?" he echoed.

"Not yet, maybe, but he will be by morning."

Through the pounding of his head, Eyvind struggled to comprehend. "What do you mean?" he asked. "Who?"

The younger guard raised his brows. "Where've you been?" he queried in amazement. "Somerled Horse-Master, of course, King of Hrossey. I'll tell you something, that fellow may seem hard at times, but there's a man who knows how to make up his mind quickly and step forward without hesitation. A true leader, he is."

There was a shadow in Eyvind's thoughts, though he still struggled to piece together the full meaning of the man's words. "I must see Somerled," he said, "now, straightaway. I must talk to him, and persuade him—"

"He's not here," said the older guard. "They left a while back. Best go in, have a bite to eat before you head off again. Long walk. Not so hard for your kind, I suppose." And when Eyvind only gaped at him, he added, "Dawn attack, that's the plan. He'll welcome you with open arms, lad. How can they fail, with the hero of Ramsbeck leading them forward?"

Somewhere within Eyvind's mind the pieces of the puzzle locked together, and gave him an answer that turned him cold with horror. "You're saying he plans to attack Engus tonight? That he has already gone to the Whaleback?"

The two guards nodded. "Just our luck," observed one, "to score sentry duty. Still, someone has to keep an eye on the womenfolk. There might be a few more of them by tomorrow; some of those island girls aren't half bad, though they're on the scrawny side. I wouldn't say no, given the chance."

"You've time to get there, Wolfskin," said the other. "Low tide's just before dawn; that's when he'll move in."

Now Eyvind's heart was thumping like a deep warning drum. Miraculously his head cleared and his mind began to work fast, faster than it had ever done before. "Who is here?" he demanded. "Thord? My brother?"

The sentries shook their heads. "Still in Hafnarvagr, the two of them. Somerled never called them in."

No help to be had there. Very well, he must cast wider. "What about Lady Margaret?"

"Gone away. Somerled sent her off to stay on one of the farms, with her woman and a couple of guards. Safer, he reckoned."

There was no time to ponder the oddity of that. It seemed to Eyvind quite obvious that the safest place was the settlement itself; besides, did not Margaret have a role to play as a leader of this community? Never mind that. She wasn't here; there was nobody else he might approach for help.

"I must go," he muttered more to himself than to the guards. "I must be there before he advances on the Whaleback. It seems Somerled does not know these folk are in mourning. King Engus's sister died today: a royal princess. Tonight the king's people will be gathered for the solemn ritual of farewell. To attack at such a time is against all the rules of right engagement; truce in time of funeral rites is understood and respected even between the bitterest of enemies. Besides, didn't Somerled say he would await King Engus's reply before he attacked? Wasn't that supposed to be the first day of spring?"

The older guard's eyes narrowed. "Where have you been?" he asked sharply. "Who have you been speaking to?"

"Maybe we should take you in to answer some questions," said the other. "Somerled doesn't like that kind of talk."

Eyvind's hand moved to where Biter was slung on his back; his fingers curled around the handle. "Have you forgotten everything you learned among Ulf's fighting men?" he asked quietly. "Have you forgotten the very principles of combat? These folk will be weary, distressed, ill equipped to put up even a rudimentary defense. To mount an attack at such a time is an act of barbarism; it would be like mowing down a group of children."

"New place, new rules," grunted the older guard.

"You're not in Rogaland now, Wolfskin," growled the other. "Best be off with you before we decide to lock you up for the night. Go find food and shelter. Living wild so long has addled your wits, I think. Go on." His eyes flicked nervously to the axe, and back to Eyvind's face.

Food and shelter; somewhere in the back of his mind Eyvind knew he was hungry. He could not remember when he had eaten last. Somewhere inside him was a profound longing to lay his aching body down on a comfortable pallet and surrender to dreamless sleep until morning.

"I won't stop," he told them. "As you said, Somerled needs me. Best head off now." Quickly, before they could change their minds about letting him go, before they could discover how little strength he really had, he strode away into the darkness. He managed to walk like a Wolfskin, straight, fast, confident, until the guards were well behind him and out of sight. After that, the pretense that he was himself again became too hard. Perhaps he should have stopped and rested first. But there was no time.

* * *

Eyvind staggered onward. After a while, the cool light of a half moon aided him, and he followed sheep tracks and stone dykes, trying to keep his course northwestward, back the way he had come. He tried to rehearse what he would say, but his mind was in a small circle of its own now, a pattern that said over and over, *Let Nessa be safe. Let me be there in time.*

He stumbled on, falling, picking himself up, falling again. Once, when he caught his foot on a rock and sprawled head-long, he simply lay there in the dark, face down on the hard earth, wondering how he could ever be strong enough to do what must be done. Nessa was strong, and she was only a slip of a thing, insubstantial as a lovely shadow. Brother Tadhg was strong, yet he was a small, weedy fellow plainly ill suited to tests and trials. That should mean something. Rona was strong, too; she was old and frail, yet she had made that decision to go away into danger and free him for this mission. She had sheltered him at great risk. He thought of them and felt the earth beneath him, holding him safe. There was something small and hard under his chest, pressing against him: Nessa's gift, the mystery of being encompassed in the space of a cupped hand. Eyvind rose shakily to his feet. He looked across the moonlit folds of land and up into the great starry expanse of sky, and then he began to walk again.

The distance seemed endless. At some point there was a small streamlet fringed by grasses and ferns; he stopped to drink, and tried to judge how far he had come, and how much time had passed, but he was too weary to calculate either. The best he could do was keep moving forward, and hope.

It was still dark when he stumbled over the bodies of Engus's sentries, each slain quickly and, he suspected, silently, so they could not alert others. The moonlight shone on their tunics of bold red and blue and green, on their dark eyes open in surprise and the blood staining the earth beneath them. The killing had a Wolfskin's mark on it, efficient, professional. There would have been no running to raise the alarm, no signaling the isolated settlement on the Whaleback with smoke or flame, with flag or banner or shouts of warning. By now, perhaps, Engus's folk were sleeping, worn out by prayers and tears, little dreaming what horror the dawn might bring. Eyvind had passed the western margin of the big loch, and now, not so far off, he could hear the great, deep roar of the sea. He forced his feet to move more quickly, knowing he must be close to the headland that jutted out toward the Whaleback, knowing somewhere near at hand Somerled and his forces must be waiting for first light. He was no longer tired, though every corner of his body seemed to have its own particular kind of pain. Something was keeping him awake, something was keeping him moving, the same thing that made his thoughts swarm and seethe in his head. *Let him listen to me,* he told himself. *Just let him listen.*

He heard them just before they moved in, one on each side and one looming up before him, quick as some wild predators. There was just time to say, "Friend—" before a hand was clapped over his mouth, and his arms were improbably twisted behind his back. Pain scythed through his shoulders; he could guess who had grabbed him. Once, he would have heard them earlier; once, he would have put up a good fight against any man foolish enough to try to attack him thus. Now he could barely stay on his feet. The moon had hidden behind a cloud; he hoped they would not kill him as they had those others, before they saw who he was.

"What's this?" hissed Grim's voice in his ear, and the vice-like hold was abruptly released. It was, perhaps, the sheer size of the captive that had revealed his identity. "Eyvind?" The tone was of incredulous joy.

"Great Thor!" Erlend removed his large hand from Eyvind's mouth and gripped him by the shoulders instead, his touch now speaking welcome, not capture. "It is you!" He was holding his voice low; the darkness and the hush told of a covert camp, the preparation for dawn's surprise attack. "By all the gods, they told us you were a walking corpse, a thing of light and shadow to be seen only in visions! This is wondrous!"

"Where have you been?" Holgar asked sharply. "Where have you come from?"

"I have to speak to Somerled. Now, straightaway. It's urgent."

"Shh, keep your voice down," Grim whispered. "Come on then, he's not far off. Now that's a man will be even gladder to see you than we are. He thought the islanders had accounted for you that day at Ramsbeck, and dragged your body away like a lump of carrion."

"We're sure of victory now," Erlend said, grinning fiercely. "Thor's hammer, I can hardly wait. My blood boils in anticipation, my heart beats as it did on the longship's prow, with Danes in sight across the whale's way. Four of us together in the vanguard; four of us screaming Thor's name and wielding bright weapons together! I've a great thirst on me for blood, lads."

"It's been a long time coming," grunted Grim. "That was an endless winter. Spring will be glorious; we'll wipe out this scum and set our own names on the land as we should have long since. Our own names: our own king."

"Somerled," Eyvind said. "Take me to Somerled. Now." He saw the three of them exchange glances; it seemed to him he could see more with each moment that passed, as if dawn were not so far off. Gods, had it taken him all night to walk here? An infant could have done it quicker. Why were they frowning? Had he said something wrong, had he shown some sign of weakness? He held his head high, his back as straight as he could; he willed his legs to carry him on.

Somerled had made his headquarters in one of the fishermen's cottages near the point. There were no lamps lit, but the sky was perceptibly lighter now. Armed men waited in total silence all around the cottage, and Eyvind could see them deployed along the shore, keeping down behind crumbling stone wall or low scrubby bush, invisible to any sentry who might be patrolling the shores of the Whaleback. A forest of spears, a wall of swords, a deadly rain of arrows. Odin's bones, nearly every Norseman able to draw arms must be here save Thord and Eirik, who had strangely not been called. This force would surely outnumber anything Engus could maintain in the small settlement on the Whaleback by three to one. *Let her be safe.*

He went in silently, unannounced. "Somerled?"

In the shadows within the hut Somerled's white face jerked around toward him, Somerled's dark eyes widened, and then, something Eyvind had never seen before, Somerled's features were transformed by a dazzling, joyful smile.

"Eyvind! Thor be praised!" Somerled took two steps forward and threw his arms around his friend in a strong, brief embrace. "They told me you were slain; then they said you were a ghost. I cannot believe this! It is surely a miracle that you are here now, at precisely the time when we most have need of you. Where have you been? You're a mere shadow of yourself, old friend. What have they done to you? Come, sit here awhile. We still have a little time left."

"Somerled—" Eyvind's voice shook. He took another breath. "Somerled, I have some information for you, it's important. I will answer your questions later. I must give you some news. This invasion cannot go ahead; you must call your men back."

There was a little silence.

"What?" asked Somerled quietly.

"There's been a death on the Whaleback: the king's sister. These people are in mourning, conducting her funeral rites this very night. You can't attack now, Somerled. Everyone knows there must be truce at such times. You must withdraw and leave these folk in peace to bid their kinswoman her farewells."

There was a longer silence.

"Where have you been, Eyvind?" There was an edge to Somerled's tone now; his eyes had narrowed.

"I–I can't remember. I can't remember anything since Ramsbeck."

"Then how did you come by this information?"

"I heard it as I journeyed here: a couple of fellows traveling by the wayside."

"Really. You never were very good at subterfuge, were you? Much more the smiting axe and piercing sword type of man. Never mind. I am so pleased to see you alive and by my side, I'm prepared to forgive much, even an ill-considered attempt to protect those who are our sworn enemies. Your news is no news to me, Eyvind. I'm already aware of this death. Indeed, I have chosen my time quite deliberately, knowing it gives me great strategic advantage."

"How can you say that?" Eyvind stared at him aghast. "Jarl Magnus would never have disregarded the rules of fair engagement thus. Ulf would never have sanctioned such a shameful attack. Are you a coward, that you must move against these folk when they are at their most vulnerable?"

"What did you say?"

Eyvind had heard that tone before, but never used against himself. It set a chill on him. "You heard what I said, Somerled.

Besides, you made King Engus an offer. He was to answer on the first day of spring, and that day has not yet come. Have you forgotten every rule a leader of Rogaland lives by? Have you put aside every law?"

"If you've lost your recall of everything since Ramsbeck, how can you possibly know of any offer I may have made to this barbarian leader?" Somerled's tone was smooth as silk. "This game is far beyond your limited understanding, Wolfskin. And it hurts me deeply to hear you speak thus, as if you scorn my efforts to achieve my life's goal. Did not you yourself encourage me to keep my dream in sight? Did you not counsel me to hold on to my vision, when I was in despair? I thought you shared my aspirations, Eyvind. I thought we would move on together, the king and his valiant war leader. Then you were lost to me, or so I believed; from that day on I vowed to keep striving for the prize, in memory of your courage and loyalty. Now you are restored to me, wonderfully, miraculously, beyond all hope. I am alone no longer. Yet you speak strangely, and you wound me. It is as if . . . it is as if you despise me."

Somerled's voice was unsteady; he seemed almost on the verge of weeping. Eyvind could see that lost child again, the friendless boy who had slashed his arm in the forest and challenged him to be a brother.

"The attack must go on," Somerled said. "The men are balanced on a knife edge; they're hungry for battle. It's too late to back out now. I'd have a riot on my hands. They respect me, Eyvind. They like my way of doing things. And it seems to me this kingship can only be won by finishing Engus and his pathetic warriors once and for all. He simply can't be allowed to live, nor can his son or any of his kinsmen. I will spare the women, to the extent possible. Eyvind, I'm detecting a definite change in the light. We're running short of time, old friend. Will you stand beside me in battle? Will you be my chief Wolfskin as we planned so long ago?"

Eyvind closed his eyes a moment, summoning what strength he could find. He was going to have to say it, and rob his friend of this victory. He would have to threaten Somerled with the loss of everything that fierce, lonely child had ever striven for. His hand moved to his breast, where Nessa's gift lay under his tunic, next to his heart. "These men will not follow you when they learn you killed your brother so you could take what was his for yourself," he said quietly. He waited, a cold sweat breaking out all over him, while Somerled stood staring back at him. Now it was Somerled who looked away first, folding his arms and frowning.

"This is very foolish, Eyvind," he observed levelly. "I don't think you realize just how foolish."

"I have evidence, and I will not hesitate to use it. Call off this attack or I will tell the world what you have done. I don't care what happens to me, Somerled. You can do what you like. Just call off the advance. It's not dawn yet, you still have time."

"What evidence?" Somerled snapped. "Show me! This is nonsense, Eyvind. I'm sure you have simply got things mixed up again, you do tend to do that—"

"Here." Eyvind stretched out his open hand; on it he showed Ulf's belt buckle, entangled in its bloodstained network of knotted cords. An instant too late, his fingers closed to keep it secure, but Somerled already held it in his hand.

"Where did you find this?" he hissed.

"Perhaps you have forgotten that it was I who descended the cliff to retrieve your brother's body," Eyvind said. "I would have returned this, but I forgot. Then I was . . . away. You recognize these knots, don't you? They are not my work, and so they must be your own. Perhaps, that long morning, you watched your brother die as once you relished the slow torture of the rabbit in the snare. What will your men think of their fine leader when they know that? What will they think when they learn it was you who ordered the burning that killed Hakon and his family? There's a certain cleverness about that, the setting up of crimes so you can blame your enemy for them. That makes it much easier to turn the tide of opinion against him. No wonder these men hate, no wonder they long to sink sword in flesh, hew head from shoulders. Those killings have your mark on them. I have known you a long time, and I recognize it plainly. Call off the attack, Somerled. Call it off now, and I will keep silence. It is another chance for you, a chance to set your feet on the right way." He looked into his friend's dark eyes, and saw the same eyes staring back: intense, single-minded, as a thin, pale boy dragged his injured companion to safety down the impossible slopes of the hillside at Hammarsby. Surely that spark of goodness, of greatness, was still there, deep down. Surely such promise did not wither and die. Somerled had shown him kindness as a child and friendship as a man, for all his odd ways. Surely he must listen now.

Somerled's fingers closed around the buckle. He slipped it in his pocket. "Not very good at this, are you, Eyvind?" he said. "I keep waiting for you to surprise me with some piece of cleverness and it never happens. I have to say your disloyalty makes me very uneasy. It wouldn't have something to do with the company you've been keeping, would it? I did hear your ghost was spotted at the site of a certain hovel on the barbarians' land. They say some sort of old crone used to live there before my men put the torch to her sorcery. And there's another little witch too, a comely young one with quite a head on her, and a fiery temper. I met her recently. She was remarkably fluent in our language, and I did wonder just how she had managed that, her uncle being generally so reluctant to have her on show. An impressively forthright young woman. I liked her."

"Uncle?" Eyvind echoed as the light brightened in the hut around them, and sounds of scraping metal and booted feet on the move increased outside.

"Oh, yes." Somerled raised his brows. "I refer to Engus's niece, the lovely Nessa. Last princess of the Folk: last hope of an heir for the old man. The girl won't be a priestess long; she has to bear a son. Oh dear, Eyvind, you've gone quite pale. Had she become a special friend? I will ask the lads to watch out for her while they're over there, it's in my own interests to get her out alive, after all. It seems to me a king needs a wife, and there's a distinct shortage of princesses in these parts, so I can't be too fussy. But the sad fact is, my warriors have been spoiling for a bit of action. I can't be certain they'll look too carefully before they start laying about them. Maybe we'll retrieve her safely, maybe not. Now, I think we're out of time. Interesting talk. Shall we resume later? I don't like that look on your face, Eyvind. There'd be no point in putting those big hands around my neck and squeezing the life out of me, Wolfskin. That would only spur the men to greater effort. I think you have forgotten that I am your chieftain now. I suggest you put that fine helm on your head and go out to join the others— back where you belong, in my front line. I don't need to remind you of your own lifelong ambition, do I?"

"You can't do this," Eyvind whispered with terror clutching at his vitals. "You can't do it. Such an act of evil denies the man you are, the boy you were. It will set a dark curse on your future. These people are blameless, your brother befriended them. The treaty was ring-sworn. Don't do it, Somerled." And he backed to the open doorway of the hut, as if to prevent the other man from stepping outside. Somewhere across the fields small birds were uttering their first cautious greetings to the day; the dark sky was washed now with palest gray, shading to a rim of darker blue. "You must not," he said aloud, putting his arms out to block the way. "I beg you, on our oath of brother-hood."

Somerled looked past him as if he were not there, speaking to someone who stood outside the hut. "Move up," he said. "Wait for Holgar's sign, then advance. Keep to the center as I told you, those rocks are treacherous. There's to be no sound until you reach the far shore. We want to surprise these people."

Behind Eyvind there was a surge of movement, men grabbing spears, men drawing swords, men striding fast, too many men to be counted, their booted feet carrying them in a relentless tide to the west, toward the Whaleback.

"Don't run away again, Eyvind," said Somerled with a crooked smile. "The next move's yours, and you must play properly now you've started."

Too late, too late, what point in shouting out accusations now, what point in branding their leader as brother-killer? Eyvind knew all too well how it felt, that moment before the call to advance, every sinew tensed, every muscle bunched, the mind tightly focused on the challenge to come. It would not matter what words of truth he uttered, for they would not even hear him. Quick, then, there must be another way. Holgar was to signal the advance. Holgar and Grim and Erlend would be first, leading the troop across the causeway, spearheading the attack on the unsuspecting islanders. He must be on the causeway before Holgar, and somehow he must stop them.

Eyvind ran, jamming his helm on his head, seizing Biter in his hand, willing strength into his exhausted limbs and courage into his anguished heart. He ran as he had never run before, out along the track that skirted the promontory above the wide rock shelves where gray seals had sunned themselves in warmer

times. The tide was well out already, the rocks stretched slick
and dark toward the sea. The Whaleback reared up from the
waves, its great sloping surface tilting high toward the western
end where cliffs fell away to the ocean. Gulls cried; it was
morning. He passed men with bows and men with hammers,
men leather-capped and iron-helmed, men with spears and
staves and swords, silent, all of them, obedient to Somerled's
command. Now he could see the causeway that stretched across
to the tidal island, a narrow safe path of meticulously laid
stones, a great work of construction that had held firm against
the pull of the tide through many seasons. At low water it was
exposed, its flat surface draped with shawls of dark weed and
scattered with pale shells. Two men could walk there side by
side, or pass one another. At high tide, the sea would submerge
it, making the Whaleback both fortress and trap. To either side
of the path great tumbled stones glistened, wrack was strewn
thickly in slippery heaps, sudden pools lay dark and treacherous between rock slabs. It would be possible to pick a way
across there, if one were prepared to risk the hazard of broken
limbs or sudden drowning. The causeway was the only choice
for armed men looking to cross in a hurry and silently.

There, where the safe path began, stood three familiar figures,
wolfskins on shoulders, weapons held ready, close together with
eyes shut and hands clasped in a brief ritual of silent preparation.
Eyvind could hear it in his own head, though it was not to him that
Thor spoke. *Burn bright for me, warrior; strike true.* This was the
moment he needed, and he moved with the breath of terror at his
heels, running past the three of them, leaping to stand, legs
astride, on the narrow path. He looked ahead to the Whaleback as
the first rays of sunlight pierced the sky, touching the sloping
fields of the great brough with warm gold. *Let her be safe.*

"Wait for the sign, Eyvind," Grim whispered behind him.
"We advance together, running single file, or this will be chaos.
Half of these fellows have never fought a proper battle before.
Quick tussle behind the drinking hall, that's about it. Wait for
the sign, man."

Out of the corner of his eye, Eyvind saw Holgar's arm go up,
a red cloth held in his fist. The men began to surge down from
the low headland to the shore, lining up haphazardly in preparation to make the run across the narrow path.

"Now!" called Holgar, and both he and Erlend sprang onto the causeway behind Grim, with others following close. Eyvind gathered breath and will. He turned to face them, lifting Biter high. His voice was a mighty shout. "You cannot pass! These folk are defenseless; they are in mourning! Back off! You cannot pass!" Biter swung through the air, this way, that way; Grim took a step backward, his face a picture of shock and dismay.

"What are you doing, man?" hissed Erlend. "Let us by, you fool! And keep quiet, will you, you'll wake the lot of them! What's got into you?"

Grim had raised his hammer, but he did not step forward. "Eyvind?" he ventured. "Move aside, lad, let us through."

"You cannot pass! I will cut down any man who tries to go this way! Back off now and leave this place. Would you follow a chieftain who killed his own brother?"

He saw Erlend look at Holgar, and Holgar give a tiny nod, and the two of them moved together, pushing Grim out of the way. Holgar came in with the sword, Erlend with the thrusting spear; Eyvind twisted and hacked and turned. Behind Grim, other men were muttering, whispering, "Shadow warrior . . . walking dead . . . witch's curse . . ."

"Back off, Holgar," Eyvind gasped, wondering how long he could keep up the pretense of strength. "Order these men to retreat. Somerled is a murderer; he ordered Ulf's killing and Hakon's. I've got proof. Back off before I have to do you some damage."

The Wolfskins paused; they exchanged glances. It was clear to Eyvind what they were thinking. Two might not be a match for him; three could bring him down. They did not seem to be hearing what he told them. Now Grim had stepped down from the causeway as if to retreat, but instead of going back he moved to the left, nimble on the uneven rocks, his hammer ready to deliver a crippling blow at knee level. Eyvind swung Biter out low; iron glanced off iron, Grim reeled and fought for secure footing. Eyvind completed the axe's circle, thinking to take Holgar with the returning arc, but Holgar had moved too, down to the right, and Erlend stood ready on the path with spear in hand.

"Stop this, you fools," Eyvind panted, "I don't want to have to kill you! Just give up, will you?" Odin's bones, Biter was heavy; he had forgotten how heavy. And his head was starting to ache again, a fierce pain that came close to blinding him. The rising sun was dazzling now; perhaps it was the first day of spring. Small birds passed high above, fluting their songs to the morning. "Back off, will you?" Holgar's sword slashed at his legs; Eyvind jumped sideways, willing strength to his limbs, willing his mind to stay clear enough. He shifted his grip on the axe. Now Grim had come up behind him, and in front, Erlend's spear-tip was pointed neatly at his heart. Holgar slashed again; Eyvind staggered. The men on the shore were starting to call out helpful advice, voices still low. "Kill the treacherous scum!" "Go in on his left flank, man, take him down!" "Get off the path, we're wasting time!" It would not be long before they began shouting. Eyvind ducked suddenly, and as the thrusting spear came toward him, he rose to grip its shaft in his left hand while Biter struck a glancing blow to Erlend's shield. Erlend dropped the shield and laid both hands to the spear, seeking to use it to push Eyvind off balance and down to the rocks. What was Grim doing? He was somewhere behind, but not moving. Holgar was the danger, coming in again now with the sword; he must kick out, he could not twist to dodge the blow with the spear shaft in his grip. He let go abruptly; Erlend was caught off guard and fell toward him, too close for the axe. Holgar paused; the target was no longer clear, his sword could not strike without risking Erlend. Eyvind let Biter fall; with the last of his strength, he lunged at Erlend, bringing him down, nearly falling himself to sit astride the other man with his hands around Erlend's neck. "Back off or he dies," Eyvind hissed, not at all sure he had either strength or will to carry out such a threat. He was dizzy now; his limbs were full of a fiery aching, his breath came in labored gasps. It must be all too clear to the others how weakened he was, for did they not know him like a brother? "Back off! I will kill him! Fetch Somerled, tell him the advance cannot go ahead!"

"What is this?" It seemed Somerled was already here; his clear, crisp voice came from the shore, beyond the crush of waiting men. "Are you not under orders to keep silent? What's going on here?"

Nobody ventured an answer.

"For Thor's sake, man!" It was Grim's voice behind Eyvind, a hoarse whisper. "Let him go; it's Erlend, you fool, a friend and comrade! We've work to do here. Step down. Don't make me—"

"Halt the advance," Eyvind said, gritting his teeth. "Somerled killed his brother. He burned Hakon. He lied to me; he lied to all of you. I swear on Thor's name that this is true. You cannot go forward." His grip on Erlend's throat seemed to be slackening, try as he might to maintain it. He could feel Erlend's shoulders tensing, his legs seeking leverage to dislodge Eyvind from his back. Everything was starting to blur; through the eye-guard of his helm he could see Somerled not far away, but his features were swimming, the men around him fading to shadow.

"Now then," said Somerled firmly. "You can see what's happened here. This fellow is sick; it's plain enough what his malady is, they call it war fetter, though no warrior wants to put a name to such an illness, one which slows the feet and weakens the will for battle. Eyvind is suffering from delusions; it comes of spending too long as a captive of these primitive tribesmen and listening to their poisonous tales. It's them we must blame for this sad change in what was once a fine man, the hero of Ramsbeck. A sorry sight indeed. A sorceress of the Folk has put a spell on our dear Eyvind. As to what he says, it is no more than nonsense. I, kill my brother? Have I not sought vengeance for his murder with all my strength and all my will since the very day those barbarians hung him up to die? Let your fellow warrior go, Eyvind, old friend. It's rest and help you need, not combat. Let others do battle today in your place. Your arm can barely support the axe's weight; your legs can scarcely carry you. See, men, even now his hands slacken their grip, even now his head bows with the weight of the fine helm he once wore gloriously into battle. This is no Wolfskin, but the merest shadow of what once was."

"Don't listen to him!" Eyvind snarled, fighting to keep his grip as Erlend began to thrash and twist, sensing his captor's flagging strength. "I am in my right mind, and I tell you this attack must not go forward. I will kill this man if even one of you seeks to pass me." *Run, Nessa. Hide.* Thor's hammer, it seemed to be growing dark; if he lost consciousness now it was all over. He could not fail her, he must not . . . The world was going hazy; the rising sun dazzled his eyes. "Run!" he shouted. "Hide! Beware attackers!" but his shout seemed to be no more than a whisper inside his stricken heart.

"Oh dear, Eyvind," someone said. A moment later there was a ringing blow on his helm, Grim's hammer used with just enough force to disable him without cracking his skull open. A darkness fell on him, a darkness that was not oblivion, for he could still hear the tramping of boots all around him as men surged across the causeway and picked a path on the slippery rocks beside it. Feet passed before him, behind him, on top of him, ever forward to the attack. There were no cries save the harsh warnings of gulls, and the Folk would scarcely heed those. Other sensations returned; there were rocks under his head, his legs were in water, his axe and helm were gone. He was still blind; Grim's hammer had taken away the daylight. After a while, the footsteps ceased. He crawled forward, not knowing who was near, not knowing if he were alone or no. Perhaps they were all gone across, with their spears and swords and axes . . . *run, hide, quick, quick* . . . He couldn't see and he didn't seem to be able to speak either. Perhaps it was grief that set this choking lump in his throat. He must go on, he must get across and help her, perhaps even now it was not too late . . . In the distance, men were shouting, and there was an ominous crackling, and suddenly above the war cries came the sharp, terrified scream of a woman. *I wonder if she screamed*, Somerled had asked him once, long ago. He must move, he must go on, perhaps he could still find her in time, perhaps . . . He seemed to be back up on the causeway, he could feel the close-laid stones, but he could not get up, his legs didn't seem able to carry him . . . right, he would crawl if he must, he would find her, blind as he was . . . he had given his word . . . he must make it good . . .

"I don't think so, Eyvind." Somerled must be right beside him; must have watched each pathetic move. "What can be so important over there that you still strive for it, wreck of a man that you have become? It saddens me to see this. You simply cannot be allowed to torture yourself thus. Grim's blow was meant to render you unconscious, not turn you into some pitiable excuse for a hero. Now give up, will you? Tie him!" he ordered. "Bind his wrists and ankles tightly. Then put him up there on the point. Let him watch, since he seems eager to be a part of this. And keep guard, vigilant guard, you understand? If he tries to get away, hit him hard."

Hands seized Eyvind and hauled him unceremoniously back across the rocks. Dimly, he was aware of pain. The screams grew louder and shriller, then abruptly stopped. Men were still yelling, metal rang on metal, and now there was a roaring sound as of a great consuming fire. They were dragging him across the shore, up the path; his head hit a stone, and he could see again.

"Somerled!" he tried to shout, but the sound was hoarse and breathless, drowned by the voices of the gulls. "Somerled, please! You don't know what you're doing! Somerled!"

But Somerled could not hear. Already he was striding across the causeway, slender and straight-backed, this time with no guards at all. There was no need of them, for it seemed the battle would be all but over by the time he set foot in his new domain.

Eyvind's captors did as Somerled bade them, adding a gag for good measure. They lashed their prisoner to a stone on the point, facing the causeway and Engus's settlement. The bonds were indeed tight; at first, Eyvind fought against them with all his remaining strength, kicking, twisting, straining, but his efforts were futile. He tried to shout, but the wad of coarse cloth in his mouth made his words into harsh animal noises, which echoed the turmoil in his head. Smoke arose thick and dark from Engus's hall; beneath it flames flared bright gold. Most of the fighting seemed to be over; bodies were strewn about the sward, all around the small cluster of dwellings, bodies with tunics of brave red and green and blue. He could see Somerled's men strolling between them, and the sharp downward movement of axe and sword. Other men stood around the burning hall at a safe distance, ready to seize any who might seek to escape from door or window. There didn't seem to be anyone coming out. There was a movement of folk toward the far end of the causeway, women among them; perhaps prisoners were being taken. *Nessa.* How long would it be before they came back? It could not be long, the tide would turn and trap them if they delayed. Maybe she was still alive, maybe he would see her there in bonds of captivity, her head held proudly high, her lovely eyes turned on him in sorrow and reproach. He had failed her; he had not kept his promise. He had sworn to aid her, to be her champion. He had thought he could do it. But in the end, he had not been strong enough.

Eyvind wrenched at his bonds anew; Odin's bones, he was as weak as a newborn infant. Perhaps it was indeed as Somerled said. War fetter. Everyone knew what that was, though fighting men never spoke of it openly. It was the ailment a warrior feared above all, for it rendered a man useless, stealing his will to go forward, turning him into a trembling, pathetic husk. He had seen such a one at home in Rogaland, a quivering, weeping wreck who sat in a corner of the drinking hall nursing his ale, shunned even by his own wife. War fetter robbed a man of his very purpose for living. That Somerled had named it was like a curse; it was like setting a darkness on him. He had seen the look of pity and horror on Grim's amiable features. He had seen revulsion in Erlend's eyes, confusion and shame in Holgar's. It seemed as if Somerled was right.

For now, Eyvind could do nothing but sit here and witness the destruction of what he had vowed to preserve. He watched as the hall burned down to stones and ash. He watched as Somerled's men began to march back across the causeway with the heads of their enemies held up on spears, fresh blood painting the shafts a glowing crimson in the light of morning. Gulls circled, screaming a song of death. After the heads came captives, one or two old graybeards, a few women, no more than six or seven. A single glance told him Nessa was not among them; none had her height, her proud carriage, her glossy brown hair. A warrior with a sword herded a gaggle of terrified children. One girl clutched a tiny infant, another shepherded an ancient grandmother hobbling on a stick. Not Rona: this one had sparse white hair in wisps, and stooped shoulders. *Nessa* . . . He watched them come, so few, a pathetic few. There were no boys, no young men, no warriors of middle years. Those had come already, their furious dark eyes and blood-drained faces paraded high on their conquerors' spears.

Now there was nothing moving on the Whaleback, save the drifting smoke from smoldering buildings, and the white dots of sheep on the sloping pasture beyond the ruined settlement. The men of the Folk lay where they had died; there was nobody left to gather their headless bodies up. Somerled's warriors streamed back across the causeway, not silent now but jubilant: it was a great victory. On the shore below Eyvind, the captives now stood in a tight group, ashen-faced; the infant squalled shrilly, the children sobbed in terror. The women were quite silent. He saw Somerled down on the beach, lifted high on the shoulders of his men, arm raised in gesture of triumph. They were setting the heads in line along the pathway, driving the spears hard into the unyielding earth. The curve of the shore was fringed with them, the eyes of these dead warriors fixed westward toward the place where the last king of the Folk had fought his last, brief battle. Someone thrust a spear into the earth by Eyvind's side. Despite himself, he looked up. Atop the shaft, the severed head of Engus's son, Kinart, was set, fierce-eyed, grim-jawed, so young, too young . . .

"Well, Eyvind." Somerled was standing on his other side, expression mildly amused. "A pity you missed that: a fine battle, if all too easily won. But I'm afraid I have some sad news for you."

The gag smothered the words of fury that Eyvind would have shouted; the sound he made was the bellow of a beast in pain.

"Now, my old friend, hold still and keep quiet, will you? You're making my guards quite nervous, thrashing about and roaring like that. I think they're still mindful of ghost warriors and witch-hounds, even though you've manifested in flesh and blood. Easy now; you're not well, anyone can see that."

Tell me! Tell me! He tried to convey with his eyes what he could not say; not that there was any doubt Somerled understood. Somerled was simply playing again; there was a little smile on his lips.

"Very unfortunate. We accounted for the son." He glanced upward. "The young fool thought himself a warrior, but these folk have limited skills in the field; he didn't last long. I'd hoped Engus would come out and face me, but he chose to stay in the hall, and I'm afraid the young woman I mentioned before was by his side, loyal to the end. It was impressive, the stuff of a fine tale. I'm told there wasn't a sound from in there, not a scream, not a cry. They perished in silence. Quite dignified, I thought; the pain must have been considerable. It was the ones outside that made all the noise. So, she's gone, Eyvind. I'll be looking elsewhere for a bride. Perhaps it's for the best. Cleaner this way, complete break, no question whatever of my authority here. Somerled, king of Hrossey. It has quite a ring to it, don't you think? Oh, Eyvind. Are those tears I see in your eyes? They are! My dear fellow, I did not expect such a display of feeling. It is a great victory, I must acknowledge that."

Eyvind let his lids close over his eyes. This grief was bone-deep, earth-deep, beyond words, beyond thought. This rage could not be spoken; it smoldered in the head, making the thoughts a white-hot furnace of hate. This loss flowed in the very veins, scourging the wounded heart until it cried for mercy. But there was no mercy. She was gone. Nessa was gone, and Eyvind had failed.

"Best if we take you somewhere safe, my friend," Somerled said. "Somewhere really safe and really quiet. You need time to recover, time to ponder what's happened and think about your future. Later, we'll talk. Not now. I think this gag had better stay on until we have you securely locked up, just for your own protection. Wild accusations do make folk angry, and you don't seem to be able to defend yourself anymore, poor Eyvind. A nice long rest in a nice secure room, that will be best. Now, if you'll forgive me, I have things to do. It's not every day one becomes a king."

Not so long ago, when Thor had deserted him and he'd lost his will to go on, Eyvind thought he had plumbed the depths of despair. He had come close to giving up altogether in that dark time. Perhaps that had been the illness Somerled had named, yet Eyvind did not see it thus, not now. He thought it had been a kind of test, a trial set on him, and because of it he had begun to think clearly, and see truly. He had not known the real trial still lay ahead of him. Now hatred gnawed at his belly, grief played tricks in his head, something else which he could not name made it impossible to do as he had done before, simply curl up in the darkness and flee inside himself. Something kept his mind awake, telling him this was not over yet, even though he had failed, even though Nessa was gone, even though Somerled had got exactly what he wanted. This time there would be no running away.

They had locked him in a cell-like room, whose only light came from chinks in the rock walls and up under the musty thatch; a storehouse, probably, for there was a sprinkling of grain on the earthen floor and shelves where sacks might be laid to keep dry. He had heard a heavy bolt being slid across the door. Now and then came men's voices beyond; no more than two, he judged. Somerled must believe him much weakened to set so meager a watch on him. Everyone knew you could not hold a Wolfskin prisoner long. Eyvind shivered. He had not been much of a Wolfskin this morning. He hadn't even wanted to fight, but in the end, his flagging strength had been all he had, for the truth had been a poor weapon; not one of them had believed him. How could men like Erlend and Holgar follow Somerled so blindly? Was the thirst for battle so fierce in them that it overwhelmed all sense of what was right and fair? But then, had not he himself charged forward in the forefront of Jarl Magnus's fighting men, and never questioned his enemy's claim to land or goods or whatever it was the Jarl sought to take from him?

Eyvind sat on the earthen floor, arms around his knees, staring at the wall not two paces before him. It *was* different. The difference was Magnus himself, a man of good judgment, a man whom they had seen arbitrating at the Thing and balancing each matter with gravity and rightness, a man who would make his decision only after due and full consideration of all the relevant matters. Magnus could be hard; he had quashed that rebellion in the east with speed and blood. But he was always fair, and what he did was for the benefit of all his folk in the long term. Magnus was a true leader. Somerled was . . . he was dangerous, not just to his enemies but to friends and family and to all he touched. He was even a danger to himself.

Eyvind had never forgotten the words of the seer's foretelling. For him, it had been true: in this far place he had indeed found a treasure beyond price, found her and lost her in one season's span. As for Somerled, the cat woman had seen two paths for him, one leading to kingship and glory, the other shadowed and lonely. It seemed to Eyvind it was by no means sure which one of them Somerled followed. But one thing was plain. Somerled must be stopped. He could not be allowed to go on as he had begun here, setting his stamp on land and people until Nessa's folk were entirely destroyed and her fair islands shorn of their ancient mysteries and peaceful beauty. Better no chief-

tain at all than one who plunges his followers into blind wrongdoing and sets the sword to those who extend the hand of
friendship.

It grew dark outside. At one point the iron bolt was slid open,
and the door widened a crack, and a cautious hand came around
with a hunk of bread and a cup of water. Eyvind made no move,
no sound. The door closed; the bolt slid home. He could endure
a night or two in this stinking hole; he still had his wolfskin to
shelter him, he still had Nessa's gift lying small and warm
against his heart. Rushing out blindly with nothing in his head
but the desire to strangle Somerled was the sort of thing the old
Eyvind would have done: the sort of thing a Wolfskin would do.
He was not a Wolfskin now. He had a mission; he had given
Nessa his word, and he would keep it as best he could. It was
too late for her, but somewhere in the islands were the remnants
of Engus's people, in hiding here on the mainland, or captive in
Somerled's settlement, or eking out their living by land and sea
on the remoter islands, not knowing yet that their good king
was gone forever. Those folk he could warn; them he could protect, somehow. He could tell them what Nessa had wished and
hoped for them, he could give them heart. And he could stop
Somerled. That part was first.

In the dark, Eyvind unwrapped the little bundle of cloth, fingers gentle on the narrow ribbon. This she had worn in her hair,
her lovely long fall of hair like dark shining silk. He had been
bold that day, he could not believe how bold, taking the comb
from her hand, drawing it gently through, stroking her hair with
his fingers, softly so she would not know what he did. So close,
so close she had been to him, yet quite unaware of the longing
in him to wrap his arms around her, to kiss the hollow of her
neck, her pale cheek, the sweet curve of her lips . . . He would
not think of how it had been for her at the end; of how she and
her uncle had sat quietly in their hall as the fire came all around
them, as the smoke filled their lungs and the heat seared their
flesh. He would not think of it, and yet as his jaw tightened and
the lump came to his throat and his tears began to flow again, he
could not stop thinking of it, her pain and terror tore at him. Engus's niece: no wonder Somerled had pursued her. Now she
was gone, and if Somerled had spoken the truth, the royal line
of the Folk was ended. He touched the small feather, the moon-

white stones. The heartbeat of the islands was not so easily stilled. The ancient beings Nessa had spoken of dwelt yet in the deep places, though their clear-eyed priestess could no longer summon them forth. Beneath his grief, a chill purpose had begun to possess him. This was not finished yet.

Sleep was not possible. He made himself lie down on the cold ground, made his body still and quiet, a discipline well-practiced in long years of sea voyaging and hastily improvised shelter. His mind he could not set at peace; it showed the images of fire and terror over and over, until he could have howled his anguish aloud as a wild creature does. He recalled the tale of Niall and Brynjolf, and a blood oath that bound a man to a lifetime of guilt and sorrow. It seemed to Eyvind that Niall should never have made the vow at all, knowing Brynjolf far less well than he thought. But having pledged himself, and having done the deed, he should not then have let it go as he had, simply pouring his grief into his songs. He should have challenged Brynjolf, made plain the truth of what he had done. He should have made sure such an ill course of events could never happen again. That was what Eyvind would do. It would not make good his own loss, nothing could ever do that, but it was at least a path of purpose, a course of action that set folk's feet in right ways.

Somerled had robbed him of Ulf's buckle. Very well, without material evidence one must produce some other kind of proof. What had Brother Tadhg said? That it was unusual for such a crime to have no witnesses at all? Somerled could not have killed his brother thus, with such elaborate attention to detail, without at least one accomplice. Find that man, persuade him to talk, and there would be a case. Present that before the men of the court, Olaf Sveinsson, Harald Silvertongue, the more reasonable of Ulf's advisers, and he could sway the balance here. The men of Rogaland were not blind to what was right. A warrior might charge in to the attack without weighing the character of his enemy, but he would never pledge allegiance to a brother-killer. Prove his guilt, and Somerled would be finished.

He'd need help. It would have to be Eirik: Eirik who now dwelt in the south, where it was just possible witnesses might be found and coerced to speak out against their chieftain. Big, wild-bearded Eirik was quite good at getting people to talk, with limited damage. A course of action began to emerge: get out of this hole, find his brother, hide while a witness was sought, return to Somerled's court and present the case. If only Somerled conducted matters as Magnus did back at Freyrsfjord. The formal proceedings of a Thing would provide the measure of protection needed to put a case together, as well as a forum where all arguments must get a fair hearing. That was all he asked. But it seemed Somerled had dispensed with the Thing, making himself sole arbiter and judge. He alone would determine punishment. That, surely, was too much power even for the wisest of men. Odin's bones, he hoped Eirik would not look on him with the shock and scorn he had seen in the eyes of Erlend and Holgar.

Escape: he knew how he would do that. It was just a matter of resting, of eating this foul lump of moldered bread and drinking this brackish water, and being ready at dawn when they opened the door, tomorrow, or the next day, as soon as he was strong enough. Rest, now. Slow the wild thoughts, calm the thundering heart, make the limbs easy. *Sleep safe, my Bright Star. Dream of fair things. My hand in yours.*

Two days later when Somerled's men came up to the isolated building to relieve the guards on duty, they found one fellow sprawled in the entry to the bolted cell, quite unconscious, with a red lump the size of a goose egg on his head, and a bowl of cold porridge splattered all about on the ground. If the man had borne any weapons, they were gone now. The other guard was face down over the stone dyke that ran from hut to farmhouse; his skull bore a nasty gash, as if struck with some force by an iron rod or bar. Now that they looked closer, it seemed the very bolt that served to keep the prisoner in had been wrenched from its pins and used to render this fellow insensible, for the great length of rusted metal lay there in the field beyond; a flock of ewes with early lambs at foot grazed peacefully around it. When they saw that, the men muttered and threw glances at one another. Perhaps it was true what folk said, that this was no ordinary warrior but a vengeful ghost come back from beyond the grave. Did not such a feat demonstrate a strength beyond the purely mortal? As for war fetter, Somerled must have been wrong. This was no shrinking invalid, but a warrior best avoided unless you had a troop of heavily armed men at your back, and even then you couldn't be sure he wouldn't fell you with a neat little tap of the fist. And what about the dog? The dog might be back at any time, creeping up with its bloody fangs ready to rip you to shreds. The man was best left alone, if you asked them; trying to get hold of a fellow like that was a bit like trying to bring a dragon or hill troll to heel, both exceedingly daring and very, very stupid.

But when they took the news to Somerled, he sent them straight back out again, and two of his Wolfskins with them. They must spare no effort, leave no possibility unexplored. Eyvind had been his friend; Eyvind was to be found and brought back alive. What the man had done could in no way be disregarded. He had stood against his chieftain's forces at the very moment of their great endeavor and shouted words of basest treachery; lies, poisonous lies. He must be brought to justice and made to see the error of his ways. Eyvind was an oath breaker, and he must pay the price.

And because no man in his right mind questioned Somerled when he had that particular expression on his face, and used that particular tone of voice, they took their weapons and went out again, one party to Engus's lands in the west, one north toward Holy Island, and the last southward in the direction of Hafnarvagr. Somerled watched them go, and then he went back into the hall and took out the kidskin bag that held Margaret's fine set of game pieces, her farewell gift from the Jarl. He hummed to himself a little as he set them up, pale ivory, banded silver, polished board adorned with fair inlay of beasts and twining leaves. A pity there was no worthy opponent here; he must fetch Margaret back. It was time; she'd have learned her lesson by now. She must see that it was unacceptable for Ulf's widow to speak out openly against the new king's policies. Margaret had surprised him with that. After all, she had given herself to him, and that, surely, implied a certain level of loyalty. The experience itself had been less than a stunning success; where was the enjoyment when a woman had no fight in her? Unfortunately, her outspoken comments had continued, beginning to awaken doubts in his household. It had become necessary to remove Margaret from court. Still, in due course she would make a satisfactory wife. One could seek one's physical release outside the marital bed, after all. And Margaret was still the only one who could match him at games. Yes, he would recall her soon. He recognized with surprise that he missed her; her cleverness, her ready wit, her elegance still pleased him as they had from the first. He'd just have to make it completely clear what might happen if she didn't keep her mouth shut.

Meanwhile, lacking a suitable adversary, he must pit his skills against himself. His fingers reached with confidence to grasp the carven head of the small white king; smoothly, he made his move.

TEN

The little boat had carried her safely to the shingly beach near Rona's cottage. But she could not leave it on the shore; that would be as good as leaving directions for finding her. Nessa scrambled over the side into hip-deep water. She scarcely felt the cold; there seemed nothing left but the weight of her grief, like a hard stone lodged where once her heart had been. She holed the boat's hull, ripping her knife through the tarred skins that stretched across its light frame of wattles. Kinart would have been outraged. From this small craft, he had drawn in many a harvest of fine cod and sweet mackerel; he had made the curragh himself over the nights of a long, dark winter, and its neat form, already slipping down beneath the sea as Nessa waded ashore, bore his love for the ocean and its bounty in every tightly fashioned seam, in every finely curved rib. Kinart could not see his boat destroyed. Kinart was dead. They were all dead: all but Nessa. Her uncle had held her to a promise, and she had lived.

She wished she had not promised. She wished they had planned better, or not so well. They had not been unprepared for attack. If it came, Nessa was to take a small bundle and run straight to the hidden cove, below the Whaleback's southern flank. If things went badly for them, she would take the boat and make her escape. Engus had refused to listen to her protests. He had put it quite bluntly. If anyone were to survive, it must be Nessa. She knew why. So he made her swear, and when the worst came to pass, she had kept her promise. There had been other parts to the plan: men designated to defend the causeway, to guard the hall, to protect the women. Women to watch over children, hide treasures, herd away stock. None of them had trusted Somerled's talk of sending messengers and waiting for answers. But to choose today, the very dawn after her mother's passing, to attack in time of deepest mourning, this betrayal had caught them quite unaware. Nessa had woken abruptly, heart pounding, not knowing what had startled her; all seemed quiet outside, yet it was as if someone had screamed her name, as if some power outside her body compelled her to run to a place of hiding now, quick, before it was too late. Yet nothing stirred. She could hear gulls passing, crying, and the soft song of the sea. She rose, thrust feet in boots, grabbed a cloak, woke the other women in the hut. She ran toward the hall, where the men still lay sleeping on the benches, worn out by the long night's solemn ceremony, senses dulled by exhaustion and strong ale.

"Uncle!" she cried. "Kinart! Wake up!" For now, as she ran, she looked toward the mainland in the wakening light, and what she saw turned her chill with terror. Armed men were swarming on the point, more men than she had ever seen gathering in one place before. And now there were cries, she heard them, and one warrior was standing there on the causeway, a tall, broad man with a beautiful helm fringed by a curtain of fine metal rings, and a big axe in his hand, and he was facing his own comrades, yelling, brandishing the weapon before him . . . *He was trying to stop them* . . . Around her, Engus's men began to emerge bleary-eyed from their beds, slow to wake fully, slow to grasp what lay before them. She watched a moment longer, saw Eyvind kick and duck and turn amidst his attackers, saw him felled with a single massive blow. No man could survive such a blow . . . she felt it like a great wound to her heart. Now Somerled's warriors began to stream across the causeway, swift-paced for all the forest of spears they bore, the axes, the hammers, the flashing swords. Somewhere beneath that pounding stampede of booted feet lay Eyvind's body. She heard herself make a strangled sound, half sob, half scream, and then her uncle was there before her, buckling his sword belt, gray-faced, with a look in his eyes she had never seen before.

"Farewell, Nessa," Engus said. "Go now, quickly. You must not be seen. Our hope rests in you. The future is in your keeping. Go now." From his finger, he drew the heavy silver ring ornamented with the symbol of twin shields, and placed it in her hand. This was no royal token, but his own personal ring of lineage. It should have gone to his son.

Nessa was wordless, knowing it was the last time she would ever see him: the last time for them all. So quick, so sudden, it snatched the breath from the lips and clutched at the very core of the heart. Down beyond the hall, Kinart was running, spear in hand, desperate to be there when the first of the invaders tried to step onto the Whaleback. His young face was radiant with courage. Nessa stood motionless, her whole body aching with grief.

"Go now," Engus said again, and bent to kiss her on the brow. She reached up and gave her uncle a fierce hug, and then, blinking back blinding tears, she ran. This was a promise that must be kept. The dog followed her; she hoped he would remain silent, for she could not row away until the tide came up again.

Nessa had no need to see, to know her people's terror in those last moments, and their courage. She sat with eyes tight shut, and somewhere deep inside her, as she heard the screams, the clash of weapons, the roar of fire, was the small image of a lone warrior making a terrible, heroic stand, one man against fifty: a vision of Eyvind fighting and falling, just as an ancient voice had told her he would. As the sounds of slaughter came to her ears, as her home was laid waste not a hundred paces from where she hid, shivering, in this stark crevice above the tide-bared rock shelves, she bore within her the knowledge that she had sent her warrior before her to die in vain. *How brave are you, Nessa? Do you have the courage to lose all that you have, and still go on?*

After a while, not so very long, it grew quiet again. For a little, there still came sounds of men's voices, not shouting now but speaking more levelly as if establishing order and issuing commands. She was glad she could not hear what they said. The dog, Guard was his name now, sat close by her, his dark eyes anxious. From time to time he licked her hand, and she laid her fingers on his head, drawing some slight comfort from his warmth. She had bid Guard be silent, and he was obedient, though the sounds from above made him lower his head and flatten his ears, trembling.

Nessa had learned long ago to read the subtleties of the tide. It was turning now. The voices were gone, the crackling had died down; a pall of smoke turned the morning light to sickly yellow. The water washed in gently over the rocks below her. It would not be easy to launch the curragh on her own, light as it was. In a little while, she would leave here. Her uncle had said she must go as soon as she might. "Don't look back, Nessa," Engus had said. "If we are attacked, we will fight to the end, as befits true warriors of the Folk. But the odds are not in our favor here. If we fight and fail, turn away and leave this place. Find Brother Tadhg; seek safe refuge on the outer islands, then passage to the land of the Caitt. Our kinsmen there will shelter you. You must not look back."

He had forgotten, maybe, that she was a priestess. Whatever lay unseen above her on the fair sloping grassland of the Whaleback, she could not leave without ensuring certain things were done, certain words spoken. So, when it seemed to her all was quiet above, and the tide was rising apace, so that Somerled's men had surely passed back across to the mainland to celebrate their great victory, Nessa crept out of her hiding place. She approached the settlement cautiously; there might be guards, set here by Somerled to watch over the field of his triumph, lest there be one enemy they had missed, one youth unslaughtered, one old wife cowering in the blackened ruins. But there was nobody there: nobody but the dead. She walked down across the trampled sward.

This was the stuff of dark dreams. It was a sight to wring the stoutest heart, to pale the rosiest cheek. She was prepared to see death; she had stiffened her will for that. But these pitiful corpses, not even afforded the dignity of resting whole on their home soil, these bodies cruelly mutilated, so that not one of the men lay as he had died—this was a scene of deep unrest, a heart wound never to be healed. This place would never be a safe haven again. A blight of wrongness lay over it; the drifting smoke from the ruined hall was heavy with the memory of shame. Nessa did not weep. Her eyes were dry, her breathing calm. She felt only the cold, hard thing in her chest, a shriveled kernel of grief, a tight knot of suffering and loss. There was no sign of activity over on the point now. No sentries watched her; only the dead eyes of her kinsmen looked on across the swirl of the incoming tide, each blanched face gazing westward atop its savage spike as their priestess knelt by each headless corpse, crossed each warrior's limp hands on his chest, and spoke the ritual words of farewell. *Rest, brave spirit; may the earth hold you gently in her hand. Great Mother, receive your warrior, Ferach . . . your warrior, Brude . . . your dear warrior, Kinart . . .* She knew them like brothers, one by his long, ringed fingers, one by the way he bit his nails down to the quick, one by the many freckles the sun drew on his fair skin.

Down by the hall, there were three women dead. They lay huddled in a pitiful heap, speared through chest and stomach and throat, still clutching one another close in their terror. All were older women, who had served faithfully in Engus's household. One had nursed Nessa's mother. There were no young wives among the dead, no girls, no children. The plan had been for these to shelter in the outer hut, where stock were housed in rough weather; two of the bigger boys, who were to guard them, lay in their blood there by the wall. *Mother, receive your fine sons, Gartnait and Drust, who never came to manhood, yet who died as men . . . Mother, receive your daughters, who have served you loyally. They cannot be laid in earth, but see, I prepare them as well as I can, and tonight I will keep vigil and say full prayers for their passing. Take them to their rest, and forgive the stain of heedless killing that has darkened this fair place . . . Receive your son, Erip . . . receive your son, Conal . . . receive your son . . .*

She could not enter the hall, for the smoldering rubble was still full of heat, but she could see at a glance that if anything remained, it was no more than bones and ash. Nessa bowed her head. *Mother of us all, here perished the last good king of the Folk in the Light Isles. Receive your son, Engus.*

Guard was keeping very close by her side; tail between his legs, body shivering with unease. From time to time he gave a little whine, and she bade him be silent, but kindly, for his deep unquiet mirrored what was in her own heart. Here was the cairn where her two sisters slept their long sleep. Her mother would never rest now beside these two lost daughters, for her shrouded body had not yet been laid in earth before the fire had ripped through the hall, taking dead sister and living brother together in its frenzy. When all was lost, a king must die honorably in his hall; that was a true sign of strength, and Engus was one of the strongest men she had ever known.

There was yet one thing to be done before she might leave this place of shadow. Nessa walked up the slow rise of the Whaleback, and Guard followed her. The sheep ambled away and dropped their heads to graze again. Guard kept perfect pace as she came up the hill to a place from which the Kin Stone might be seen on the western clifftop, standing proud and strong between land and sea. There she would promise her uncle loyalty and truth; there she would swear by the stone to be worthy of the trust he had placed in her. She climbed higher, gazing westward. She blinked and looked again.

The Kin Stone was gone. How could that be? Her eyes must be deceiving her; it had marked this ancient domain since a time of story, since the first man and woman of the Folk settled on the Whaleback. It could not be gone; the ancestors would not allow such sacrilege.

"Guard," Nessa whispered as a terrible cold began to creep through her, "I don't think I can go on. Guard?"

But Guard went forward, and she followed. There was no choice. What carried her was fiercer than pride, darker than fury, more powerful than love. It was something old and deep, something that had no name.

The Kin Stone was broken: shattered. It lay in pieces on the sward, the crescent split apart, the carven king sundered from his sons, who gazed blindly up into the empty sky. Here was the eagle, its flight cut short, here the sea-beast, fractured and crumbling. Somerled had not been content with his slaughter of the Folk, it seemed, but must obliterate the very core of their identity. Nessa knelt by the broken pieces, reaching to touch the ancient king's curling hair with her finger. Such blind hatred was surely born of fear; there could be no other reason for it. And Somerled was right to fear. What spoke in her blood now was powerful and dangerous. It was the same pulse that beat in every fold of this land, that sounded in every surge of waves on the shore, that rang in the heart of the standing stones and cried in the wind from the west. *The islands live. The islands endure. The islands do not forget.*

Nessa could not gather up the broken pieces of the Kin Stone; they were too heavy. This work of healing must come later. She took up a tiny fragment, perhaps part of the sea-beast's strange tangle of limbs and tail, perhaps not, and put it in the little pouch that held her moon charms. She found she could not chant the solemn vow she had intended. Somewhere inside her there was an anguished wailing, a wild lament that refused to be set free. The cold calm that had come over her as she settled the lost men of the Folk for their long sleep had banished tears and muted her voice. That mattered little. The ancestors hear even a whisper, and an oath can be stone-sworn even when the sacred stone itself is shattered, for the truth can never be destroyed. Nessa looked to the east, down over the ruins of the settlement, and knelt to lay her hand on the head of the brave carven king. *Receive our poor broken ones, gentle earth; cradle their spirits sweetly; give them rest.* She stood, turning to face the west, and the sun laid her shadow long and straight across the earth to touch the farthest margin of the isles. *Great ocean, bear their song of courage west and east and north and south, to all the corners of the world. Let it not be forgotten, what the Folk were.*

Then she took the boat and rowed away southward to the shore near the women's place. The sun was high, but veiled by heavy cloud now; she had tarried long in that place of death, too long maybe. Nowhere was safe; it was a time for flight and concealment. Somerled understood what Nessa was; he knew what she stood for. She must move quickly, and stay ahead of him. There was a task to be completed, and she must find the strength to do it, and do it alone. Once it was accomplished, it would be the time to step forward and confront him, though the thought of that filled her with dread. She had clung to hopes of Rona, but when she stumbled into the grassy hollow of the women's place, she found the cottage burned to the ground, and her old friend gone. It was clear men had been here; the earth still bore the traces of their boots. She did not see how the wise woman could have survived such an attack. Even then Nessa could not weep; this sorrow was beyond that. It was a thing of bone and shadow, dark and deep; it had laid its hand heavily over these fair isles, so heavily it seemed beyond the strength of any priestess to lift it, be she skilled in lore and steeped in wisdom, be she brave as a hero of the old tales. She would not give in to weakness; she would not lie here in the dim quiet of the tower in the earth, huddled under an old cloak that once had sheltered a damaged warrior, she would not release the tears that built and built inside her.

Her little bag had been carefully packed, ready for just such a flight as this. Engus had known, as she had, how slender their hope of survival would be once Somerled had his grip on the land. She could make fire; she could feed herself for a day or two. She had a tiny lamp, and oil in a corked jar. She could cast the bones in augury; she could burn herbs and sing prayers for the dead. She could perform the duties that had been set out for her since the day long ago when she ventured a little too far into the dunes and first met the wise woman.

Nessa did not sleep that night. Guard curled up on the cloak, alert enough to warn of intruders, yet not his old self; perhaps he had hoped to find his mate here, or the man he had helped watch over, for there was something in the droop of his tail and the sadness of his eyes that touched her deeply. He did not go to hunt; he ate a scrap of hard bread from Nessa's small store, and settled by the entry to watch.

She sat between lamps in the bottom chamber, and told the tale of the dead: so many names, so many farewells. She sang the story of the Folk in the islands, generation by generation: how they had worked the land and fished the seas, how they had borne bold sons and brave daughters, how their kings had ruled justly, how their wise women had brought them the lore of earth and sky, had woven the rituals of fire and water, bone and moonlight. She told of her mother, her sisters, King Engus and his son Kinart, a fine fisherman, a valiant fighter. The darkness gathered around her in the small, round space; shadows were close. Above her on their shelf, seven small skulls watched with somber attention.

"I have lost two more this day," whispered Nessa into the silence of the underground chamber. "My friend and mentor all these years, Rona, priestess of the mysteries. Mother and teacher she was to me, a wise woman indeed. It seems to me she met an unkind end, yet I know she faced it tranquilly, with courage, for if ever one were ready to move on, it was she. And I have lost another: my faithful warrior, slain in a valiant fight for truth. But for me, Eyvind would still live, and could still return across the sea to his own people. I sent him forth to do my work; I sent him to his death." Her voice wobbled; this was no good, she would be strong, she must be strong. "I don't understand why I had to do that, why your words told me he must fall in one last battle. That seems nothing but waste, since all his efforts could not stop the slaughter of our people. And to die just when he was starting to see his way forward—did you seek to teach me that a priestess cannot entertain such feelings as I did for him? It was a harsh lesson, and I bear it in my heart along with all the others I have learned today. I did not know how dear this man was to me until I saw him fall." She would not weep, not over this, not when so many losses must be endured. And yet, this seemed the cruellest, as she sat here alone. The knowledge that she would never again sit by him as she had that night, sharing the warmth of a single blanket, speaking as if to another part of herself, so close-attuned were they each to the other—to know that would never come again seemed unendurable. "It is hard to be faithful at such a time," she whispered fiercely. "Very hard. Have you taken him from me for this reason alone, that if he had lived, perhaps I could not have remained your priestess? Have you robbed him of his future solely so that I can remain your conduit? It is very hard; so hard I don't know if I have the strength to go on."

There was no reply; the ancestors had no answers to her questions. So, when the long farewells were ended, Nessa sat in silent meditation, for one could not command this voice if it would not come. Upright she sat, cross-legged, straight-backed, eyes open but unseeing, and made her mind still, empty, ready for what might come to her before another dawn sent its first fingers of light into the upper chamber. For a long time there was nothing. Perhaps even the ancient powers were silenced on a night of such loss; perhaps it was beyond even them to find a meaning in such sorrow and waste. On some level, Nessa understood that the night was well past, that light would come soon. Her ears registered the little sounds of the dog shifting about in the upper chamber, snuffling, sighing, settling again to rest and watch. And at last came a fragment of thought.

*Bone and ash . . . bone and ash . . . in bone and ash shall you
find truth . . . how strong are you, Nessa?*

Strong enough, came her answer. *I must be.*

Are you sure of that?

*How can I not be sure? There is nobody else to do what must
be done.*

*You are not quite alone, Daughter. Summon your strength.
Find your path now. Time runs short for the Folk. In bone and
ash, find the true way . . .*

Morning came. As the light filtered into the chamber above
her, Nessa withdrew from her trance, slowly this time, careful of her weary body and shattered spirit, until she could
move fingers and toes, stretch her back, rise at last to make her
way up the crumbling steps to be greeted ecstatically by a licking, whining Guard. She went out into the day. The air was
warmer; the sky was a sweet, mild blue, the color of her warrior's eyes, but she would not think of that, she would not think
of him. She must make a plan and go from here. If Somerled
suspected she still lived, surely this was the first place he would
look for her.

She shared a crust with the dog. "Let me tell you a story,
Guard. It's an old one, about two sisters; a king's daughters,
they were. They both loved the same man, but they couldn't
both have him. He wanted the younger one, her name was
Dervla. One day, the elder sister pushed the younger into the
river, and Dervla drowned. She floated a long way downstream
in her white gown, until she came to a place where a mill wheel
turned in the water. The miller thought it was a beautiful bird he
saw swimming there, and then he looked closer at the lovely
dead maiden, and drew her in to the bank. Poor girl, he thought,
so sweet and so sad: I wonder what her tale was? And because
he had a fancy to do it, he turned her body into a little harp,
white bones for the frame of it, golden hair the shimmering
strings. There was no need to touch fingers to this delicate instrument, for the instant he set the last peg in place the harp began to sing all by itself, and such was its song, the miller knew
it for a thing of wonder and enchantment, and he bore it forth to
the king's hall. A little abashed, for many grand folk sat there,
the king's elder daughter and her new husband among them, the

miller set his harp on the board before the king and took a step back. Then the harp began to play, Guard; oh, such a tune it played:

"Oh my father, hearken here
Hearken to me, mother dear
By you my false sister stands
Who drowned me with her own two hands
For the love of Conall sweet
Dervla swam in river deep
I, your daughter, now come home
Voice of truth in harp of bone."

Guard looked up at Nessa. He licked her hand.

"Everyone knows that story," Nessa said, "or another like it. A bone harp always speaks truth; it draws its voice from the deep well of earth, from the very core of being. I think that's what it means, ash and bone. Somerled did not listen to Eyvi, nobody did, that much was plain. With no evidence, no witnesses, he had nothing but his axe and his courage. That wasn't enough, and so he died."

Guard whined and laid his muzzle on her knee; Nessa stroked his head. "And so, you see," she whispered, "you see what we must do. You understand where we must go." A deep shudder ran through her. "I cannot do as my uncle bade me. I cannot run away, seek shelter, go into hiding. There is no point in that. I will not rally the last of my people only to see Somerled cut them down once more, to see him make a show of their remains in some perverted parade of conquest. That must not be allowed to happen. Somerled must be stopped. Now that Eyvind is gone, the one man who might have made him listen, this quest has fallen to me: to summon the voice that cannot be denied, the only true witness to that man's evil deeds. I must make it known to his own folk just what Somerled is, and where he will lead them if he is not curbed. Will you go with me, Guard? We must cross Somerled's land: go right to the heart of his realm unseen, and quickly, for there are women and children of the Folk held prisoner in his settlement, I think, and we must do this in time to save them. Will you go?"

Guard's eyes were steadfast as only a good dog's can be; he wagged his long tail.

"Right, then," said Nessa, trying not to think too hard of the details, now that she knew what must be done. "I suppose we'll need a shovel, and . . . and a sack or bag, and a sharp knife—I have that already. We'd best look over in the rubble there and see if anything escaped the fire."

She moved across the empty land like a shadow, and Guard moved by her, her last loyal companion. Slipping silently from rock to bank, from standing stone to desolate barn, she made her way southeastward as the sun edged across a pale spring sky. There were early lambs in the fields, frisking and playing in their pristine white, as if there were no such thing as sorrow.

She rested in the shade of a tall stone close by the lake, recognizing that its huge form had wandered somewhat since last she came this way, in a long-ago summer in a faraway world. It was well known that the stones moved, though nobody ever saw them do it. Seeking water, seeking warmth, seeking wisdom: who could say what was in their ancient hearts, save the earth herself? This one had shifted closer to the lake, and now it sheltered Nessa's rest. She felt its warmth at her back, saw without needing to look the complex pattern of lichen that crusted its rough surface, gold, red, gray, yellow-green, a whole small world of subtle, mysterious growth.

She leaned back against the monolith, eyes closed, and knew in an instant that there was one image she could not put aside, one loss that stayed starkly foremost in her thoughts. Gold, red, the sun glinted on the waterfall fringe of his helm; silver, gold, the light caught the fire in his axe and flashed it like a beacon. He fell. Boots trampled his limp body. Gold, red, his blood-soaked hair curled gently around his solemn, pale features; blue met blue, his empty eyes gazing up on empty sky, seeking answers where there were none. She had sent him before her to die. She had sacrificed him for nothing. She had squandered what she had not known was precious. This was a small loss beside the slaughter of the Folk, a little thing beside the death of their king. The priestess understood that. But the woman felt it like a heart wound, she knew in this hurt her own frailty, her own longing, her own mortality. He was hers, and she had killed him.

"Come," Nessa said to Guard, and he rose obediently from where he lay panting on the grass by the ancient stone. "Time's passing. We must find our way there before dusk." She shouldered the bag, picked up the shovel, moved forward. The dog stepped by her lightly; he disregarded grazing sheep and hovering meadow birds and tantalizing rustlings in the bushes. The two of them went together with a single path and a single purpose.

They had come a long way, and now there were people about, Somerled's people, soldiers, sentries, and Nessa knew she could not go where she must without passing them. Down the hill, below her, she could see the settlement Ulf had built in those first days of bright hope and purpose. There were several buildings, long and low, made of neat-laid stones and heather thatch over a frame of pale timbers, gifts from the sea. Men and women were walking about there, and a child ran, chasing a ball. A dog barked and Guard tensed, hair rising, teeth bared. Nessa quieted him with a look, a gesture. Standing still by an outhouse wall, she gazed down the hill, seeking clues. Were any of her people captive there? The child she had seen was stocky, fair-haired, pink-cheeked: one of theirs. Where were the young women of the Folk, the infants, the grandmothers? Perhaps it was already too late for them.

Now there were guards coming through the gateway from the settlement, a group of them clad in leather-belted tunics and short woolen cloaks, with caplike iron helms on their heads and short swords by their sides. They were walking straight up the track toward her. Nessa shrank back into the shadow by the old building, her heart sounding a fast music of alarm. Guard growled; she moved her hand, hushing him. The men came closer; she could hear them talking, she could hear them laughing about what they had done at the Whaleback, about how easy it had been. Panic gave way to fury; something in her was desperate to step out in the open and confront them, to scream her outrage, to awaken some semblance of shame in their complacent eyes. She stood still as if she were herself part of this stone wall, as if she could melt invisibly into its cracked surface, become one with the mosses and fine-leaved creepers that had made their home here. Guard was struggling to hold back his instinctive fanfare of challenge. Nessa kept her hand on the

dog's neck, made her touch gentle and reassuring for all her
own tumult of feelings. The men passed by not five paces from
them, seeing nothing. Their voices rose and fell, joking, jubilant, unthinking. They walked on up the hill and were lost from
sight.

"Come," Nessa whispered, and the two of them moved on
again. Lone tree to solitary stone, small hollow to crumbling
sheep pen, broken wall to clump of tattered grasses, they passed
to the south of the settlement, and before the sun went down
they reached a gentle hill amidst meadowland, a place of immense quiet, whose stillness was broken only by the peep and
trill of inland birds, the mellow call of ewe to lamb, the soft rustle of a spring wind. Atop the hillock, a cairn had been raised;
grasses were already creeping over its surface, where earth had
been laid on the stones that formed its structure. Small flowers
showed here and there, yellow, purple, white, a delicate quilt to
shelter a good man's slumber. There was a long view to the
west. From this resting place, the dreamer of dreams could see
as far as the world's end. Nessa had heard it said Ulf's wife had
chosen this spot. If that were so, it seemed Margaret had understood her husband well.

Nessa waited until it was quite dark, forcing down a cup of
water, a crust of dry bread. When rabbits came out to forage in
the dusk, Guard disappeared for a little and came back licking
his lips. Both of them would need their strength, Guard to stay
alert and keep watch for her, Nessa to dig.

Over the years of Rona's tutelage, growing from child to
young woman, she had learned many rituals. There were high
ceremonies for the year's great turning times, the stepping forward into light or darkness. There were those that acknowledged a man's or woman's journey in the world, birth,
handfasting, death. There were observances to honor the powers that sustained life, the elements, the ancestors, the deep
eternal beings. There were prayers for the hunt, prayers for the
fishing boats, prayers for harvest. And there were the most secret, the most enclosed and guarded rites, such as the Calling of
an ancient voice, the summoning of one who might be woken
only in times of direst need. Bone Mother, deep as the core of
hard stone that held the earth's heart, old as the world itself and
older, dark as the shadows of a prophetic dream, she was the

one who had spoken. It was she who had sent Nessa here to this place of death alone. But Rona had taught no ritual for what must be done now. Nessa must pluck the words from moon and darkness, from mounded earth and the ash of memory, from her torn heart and the knowledge that truth is the sharpest knife of all. With her small voice in the darkness, with her faltering steps on the sward, she must speak the words and pace the circle to make this an act of power. With the strength of her own hands she must wrench bone from earth and make a new voice, sound a new song that could not be disregarded. It was dark and cold, and she was weary and heartsick beyond belief. She was the priestess of the Folk, the last of the royal line in the Light Isles. She would be strong.

Nessa loosed her hair from its binding to flow across her shoulders and down her back. From her little bag she took the tiny pot that held her ceremonial clay, blue as sea shadows. She sprinkled the powdery stuff into her cupped hand, damping it with moisture from the grass, and made the spiral on her brow, the spirit tracks of owl and otter on her cheeks. She made the bone-lines on her hands. No need for clear water or shining metal; this was a practice perfected through long seasons of discipline. The eye of the spirit needs no reflection; the hand of the priestess writes truth, even in darkness. Her ritual knife was of bronze, its handle finely carved bone patterned with animals of many kinds, her own signs of otter and owl, with dog, hare, and sea serpent. This had been Rona's gift at the time of her student's first bleeding, when she had become a woman: a reminder, perhaps, of where her true path must lie. Now the knife's point traced the circle widdershins, for this was a ritual of darkness. Under a waxing moon, Nessa acknowledged the spirits of the quarters and stood awhile in silent meditation, knowing this night to be a turning point, not just for herself, but for the islands and all who dwelt there. One way hatred, blood, and sacrifice: the other struggle, healing, hope.

"The circle holds," Nessa whispered, "until my work is done here. Mother, watch over this task of darkness; know that I do not come to desecrate, to lay waste what should be left sleeping, but to seek the aid of this man named Ulf, untimely slain, a man who sought peace and light for these islands, but who brought only sickness, slaughter, and chaos. He must lend his

voice now in the only way he can, and so set all here on right
paths. What I take this night, I take with reverent hands, knowing and accepting the power of the dark one who gathers us all
to her in the end. That which I bear forth, I will return with
solemn ceremony when my purpose is achieved. This I swear
as your priestess. There has been enough loss in this place,
enough sorrow. Let there be no more."

The moon shone silver-white, cool, impartial. Stars grew
brighter, a high arch of jewels on a blanket dark as a seal's eye,
dark as winter sea-wrack, dark as deep cave shadows. Nessa
fetched the shovel.

The burial mound was sealed tight; there was no easy entrance way. It came to her—as the night wore on and she felt the
sweat drenching her body, and the pain creeping to lodge itself
up and down her back and along her laboring arms—that an old
tale was one thing, reality quite another. Old tales did not dwell
on the practicalities of a task such as this, the backbreaking toil,
the unbelievably slow progress, the growing fear as time passed
and she had moved so little soil, shifted so few great slabs of
flagstone. She started at the top, hoping this cairn was constructed in the old manner, its stones layered to form a gradual
inward curve all the way up. She hoped they had not filled it in,
blanketing the dead man in earth. If they had left space, she
would reach him more easily. There must be enough time before morning; there had to be.

It was very quiet. Once or twice, Guard growled softly as
some small creature rustled by in the grass on a nocturnal errand. Once or twice, an owl hooted overhead, passing by on the
hunt. Nessa could hear the gasp of her own breathing, she could
smell her own fear. One stone; another. She would not throw
them down, that was to offend the earth, to disturb the sanctity
of the place still further. They must be set aside each in its turn,
ready to be laid back in place when the task was over. But they
were heavy, each heavier than the last, monumental slabs that
seemed weighed down by an ancient grief. Tears spilled down
her cheeks now; she labored on, letting them flow. By all the
powers, she was weary. How sweet it would be to lie down and
feel her warrior's arm around her warm and strong, and his
breath against her hair. Right now, she did not want to be a
priestess.

She rested a moment, crouching as still as if she were herself another stone, an insignificant mark in this vast, quiet place under the star-pierced sky. It was so late; what if she could not achieve the task by dawn? What if she were still here, the cairn uncovered, her hands dark with soil, her tools by her in plain view? What then? She could not leave this half-completed and seek a place of safety, for Somerled's men would pass by and see what she had done; such an act of sacrilege would ensure she was hunted down. Besides, tonight's work was only the first part of the task. She stirred; she set hands to stone again, tugging to free another slab, scraping at the soil, which had settled over and between the layers to anchor them ever more steadfastly to the earth. She strained, screwing up her eyes. *Please, please.* This one did not want to move; it fought against the weakening grip of her hands. *Please. Help me.*

Guard growled again, an eldritch sound that spoke both challenge and terror. Nessa opened her eyes. There were lights, many lights across the fields around them, coming closer, moving in. Her heart lurched. Somerled's men. It was finished, then. But there was no sound save a kind of whispering, like a language almost past the edges of human hearing, and the lights were surely not those of torches, for they shone eerie blue, beacons of a kind found in the tales of wrinkled grandmothers, in the songs of ancient shepherds. Bobbing, weaving, they made their progress toward the cairn where Nessa sat staring, knowing the circle kept her safe, knowing the signs marked on her face protected her, but trembling all the same. Guard had moved in close to the mound's base; he was silent now, standing over the bag that held Nessa's small store of belongings. The moon caught the wild look in his eyes, the half-bared teeth, but he stood steady, true to the name she had given him.

They came through the circle she had cast, making a ring of their own around the burial mound. Still she could see little of them beyond those wavering blue lights, yet here and there she half-guessed shadow forms, dark opaque eyes, squat bodies marked with ritual scars, faces that might or might not be masked, for there was no telling if they were man or creature. There was no doubt in Nessa's mind that this was the Hidden Tribe of the tales. Most folk had seen the lights at night in the distance, gathered by some ancient cairn or weaving a pattern through the great stone circle in the south. One or two people claimed to have met them, and were half-believed. Every farmer had lost stored grain, or a bright cloth from a washing line; once, folk said, it had been a babe from the cradle, and nothing but a turnip in its place, with stones for eyes. Every farmer left out bowls of milk at full moon, and small sweet cakes at harvest time.

They climbed toward her from every side. Nessa shivered. What did they want? Who had sent them? She could not hide, she would not run. Instead, she set her hands to the stone again, grimacing with effort. Sweat made her fingers slip, pain shot like fire across her shoulders. She gripped the rock anew, and now other hands set themselves by hers, hands as gnarled and knotted as dead roots, one pair, two pairs, three, and all heaved together, and the great stone freed itself from earth with a wrenching, rasping sound like a death rattle. Foul air arose from below; Nessa recoiled, her hands over her mouth and nose. There was movement around her now, stones shifting, rising, being passed down to the ground below, long hands scrabbling in the dirt, lights moving in total silence save for the constant, rustling whispering. The hole widened, the stench dispersed in the night air. Guard whined, looking up at her anxiously.

The cairn was open. Dark forms dropped down within, blue light shone up from the interior. Hands like bleached bone reached up toward her. It was at that moment that Nessa remembered how she had called for help; it was she who had summoned them. She moved, lowering herself, until the stretching hands caught her and their owners lifted her down inside as if she were no heavier than a single owl feather. She stood by the slab where Ulf the far-seeker lay on his bed of heather, covered by his brave red cloak, and the Hidden Tribe stood about her in a circle, waiting.

Lifting the stones, making the way in, had required strength, and she had found it, with a little help. What she must do now required an entirely different kind of strength. Every instinct shrank from the task; her thudding heart told her the fear she had felt before was nothing to this. She took a corner of the cloak between her fingers and peeled it back.

Time and the small creatures that dwelt within the earth had wrought their changes here. Decay had touched this chieftain's noble form, had shrunk and crumbled his fabric and painted him livid and gray and night-dark. The skull showed stark beneath the matter that still covered it, the body was collapsing within its shroud of fine clothing, braid-edged tunic, cape of close-woven wool, broad studded belt, fine soft boots. Ulf's weapons lay by him; a helm with gilded eyepiece, a long sword, a dagger whose hilt bore a pattern of waves and suns, as if to show the will to voyage, which had been so strong in this chieftain from the snow lands. His hair lay long and dark about head and shoulders; the band of braided cloth, which had kept it neat, still circled his skull above the empty sockets of once far-seeing eyes.

The hair: that was the easy part. She would start with that. Nessa's knife moved, sliced; the soft strands fell into her hand, a whisper against her blistered palm. Other hands reached out, ash-pale, and took the strange harvest from her. She stepped across to stand by the dead man's right arm. In her mind, she pictured the thing that must be made. She lifted the knife, poised it in place, began to cut.

The sky was beginning to lighten by the time they were finished. The folk of the Hidden Tribe bore the hard-won burden forth from the chamber; they lifted Nessa out and set her back on the earth by Guard, and they passed the bones between them until she had packed them all safely away in the bag she had brought. She was feeling very odd indeed, as if she were not really here, as if it were some other girl who did these fearsome things and walked by these beings of story, and the real Nessa were still at home on the Whaleback, tucked up asleep by her sisters in a time when the world was to rights, and no blond giants had come across the sea to set their booted feet on this quiet shore. But she was here; she could feel the burning ache in her back, she could see the circle of shadowy figures in the darkness and hear their whispering. Oh, she was tired; she was so tired, and this was not yet finished.

"Cover up," she managed. "We cannot leave him thus. The stones, the opening . . ."

Already, behind her on the mound, there were faint sounds of activity, and yet the strange companions of her moonlit endeavor stood here close by her, the blue light which shone about them fading slowly as dawn came closer. She ventured a glance over her shoulder and blinked in amazement. The Hidden Tribe, it seemed, was not the only force the islands had summoned to aid their priestess this night. Now small creatures of the dark crept forth—some on two legs, some on four; some furred, some feathered; some many-limbed in jewel-bright carapace—and as Nessa stared, the cairn was mended, grain by grain, pebble by pebble, the surface growing smooth and unbroken in the gray of early light. She had not seen the big stones move, but this was a place where the impossible happened every day, folk knew that; what about the woman who had once been a seal, what about the turnip baby, what about the monolith with a powerful thirst for lake water? Nessa looked away. Whatever had moved that weight so quickly, she thought, she would rather not look in its eyes. Still, she could see ferns rustling upward, creepers twining and binding to cover the earth she had bared, she could see spring's soft blanket moving up again to shelter Ulf's rest, until she might return to make him whole again.

Now she must go; she must find a place of hiding as far from here as she might travel before the sun rose bright in the spring sky. Her helpers seemed to be waiting; perhaps they expected some reward. Nessa took her knife again and moved sunwise around the circle, undoing what she had made here. She spoke a few words to the guardian of each quarter, spending a little longer in the north, home of Bone Mother, for she knew the ancient one had sent courage to her heart and steadied her hand in this night's work. There: the circle was unmade, the morning brightened, the wide sky showed a faint rim of rose pink to the east. Still they waited there, eyes dark and solemn, bodies clad in tattered rags, whose openings showed old, deep slashes to the skin, neat patterns of lines on chest, belly, back, or thigh. Some wore talismans of whalebone driven through ear or nose, and one had a necklace of tiny skulls.

"Th—thank you," Nessa stammered, not at all sure they would understand. "I honor you for coming to aid me. Without you, I could not have completed this task."

They stood unblinking.

"I would like to give you something, some token of my gratitude," she said, "but I came away in haste; I have very little."

Now they were staring at Guard; one licked his lips. The hound growled a warning.

"I have a little food. Bread, some hard cheese, some dried fruit. You are welcome to that." She bent toward the bag, wondering how she would manage if even this meager supply were gone.

A bony finger tapped her shoulder. Nessa looked up. Its owner motioned toward her face, then to his own, touching the lips. A rustling went around the circle; they edged in closer.

"A kiss?" Nessa rose to her feet, blinking in amazement. "That is all you want? This I will give gladly, and then I must be on my way. I will remember each of you, and do my best to keep your secret places safe. Our kind and your kind, we are both of the fabric of these islands, though our feet seldom walk the same path."

Right around the circle of them she went, stooping here, rising on tiptoe there. Each got his kiss; each felt the touch of her lips on cheek or mouth, each felt the warmth of her hands, and one or two were bold enough to put an arm around her, to touch roughened fingers to soft hair or narrow waist. When she was done, she opened her mouth to thank them again, and saw the grins that creased their fierce faces, but before she could speak, the lights faded away and, with a whisper of shadow on dew-touched grass, they were gone. Behind her, the mound still rustled with life as myriad small creatures worked their magic of remaking.

"Come, Guard," said Nessa, shouldering the little bag and picking up the other with its strange cargo. The shovel she must leave somewhere in the fields; it would slow her progress, but could not be abandoned in this place. "We must seek shelter until it is dark again. Come, good friend."

When it came to it, they did not go far, for there were soon men about, Somerled's men, and it was quickly clear to Nessa, peering out from what refuge she could find, that they were looking for someone. Perhaps they had learned of her escape, finding the ruins of Kinart's boat, her footsteps on the shore, some other trace. Perhaps Somerled sensed her purpose and sought to silence the voice she would summon. She could see small groups of warriors scouring the countryside, going into every cottage, every barn, searching each fold and cranny of the land, perhaps on orders not to return until they had found their prize. Of her own folk, she saw none as she fled, nor would she have sought them, for to ask for shelter among what survivors still lived in isolated farmhouse or far-flung settlement was to bring down Somerled's wrath on them. What must be done, she would do alone.

She was tired; she was so weary her legs would hardly go forward, her eyes barely remain open to see her way. She would have to stop. She would have to rest and go on at dusk when she might move more freely undetected. She watched while a group of five warriors searched a hay barn, now all but empty of its summer harvest. The best stock had not long been let out of winter confinement to feed on the first new growth in the fields; it was strange to remember that, but for Margaret and Ulf, the crop that had been stored here might never have been gathered in to nourish the herd through the dark season. When the search was over and the men moved on, Nessa stole into the barn with Guard by her side, and crept into a dark corner among the remnant hay. She lay down with her pack under her head and her arm curled protectively around the other bag. She was too weary to eat, to drink, to do anything at all. In the far corner, Guard caught some small, squealing thing and ate it hungrily. Nessa thought about Margaret. A fine, strong girl: a pity she had not been able to sway Somerled. He had not listened to her, and he had not listened to Eyvind. He had scorned the good counsel even of those who loved him. He had gone his own way, and now it seemed he would make the choices and determine the path for all of them. That could not be allowed to happen. She would stop him. When it was dark, she must head southward to the great circle, and then to the coast again. The Hidden Tribe had come to her aid. Now she must seek help from another quarter, though she trembled to think of it. She would go on . . . she would . . .

Nessa slept. In the doorway lay Guard, one eye half-open, ready for trouble. The sun passed over, the breeze brought a shower of rain, and another. Down the hill, armed men passed and passed again, searching. The sunlight glinted on their spears, on their helms, on the burnished bosses of their round shields.

"Not a whisker," said one warrior to another, easing his back. "Whatever way he went, it wasn't this one."

"So what do we do?" asked a second. "Report back empty-handed? Who wants to tell Somerled we searched from dawn till midday and found nothing? Not me."

"We could try northward," suggested another.

"Fool's errand," grunted the first. "The man's a Wolfskin. Wild creatures, they are. Slip across the land like the hunters they're named for. Like shadows. Like ghosts."

"Bollocks," said the second. "Any man can be caught, so long as he's flesh and blood. Somerled's right. Eyvind turned into a traitor. Traitors have to be taken and punished. No chieftain worth his salt lets a man turn against his own and get away with it, Wolfskin or no Wolfskin."

"Never catch him, not unless he wants to be caught," muttered the first man. "If you ask me, Somerled's a fool."

"What?" Four voices spoke as one. His companions turned toward him, eyes narrowed, mouths grim. Each fingered his weapon.

"Nothing. Come on, then. North it is."

They moved across the land in silence, leaving no tumble-down hut untouched, no cave, no sheepfold, no heap of weathered rock unsearched. In the hay barn, small creatures stirred in the walls, and Guard's ears twitched. Nessa slept a sleep of dark dreams.

ELEVEN

As night fell a chill wind came up, numbing his ears, hurting his head, setting a shiver in his bones. He had stolen sword and knife, a pair of boots, a haunch of meat which he'd already eaten, crouched motionless in the lee of a stone wall between fields, some time during the day's gradual journey southward. Without fire it would be a cold, dark night. But fire could only attract pursuers; in darkness, he was safe from Somerled. A wolf finds his way by moon and stars, by the faint scent of the enemy, by the subtle movement of leaf and twig. Thus Eyvind must go; but for now his aching body demanded rest, his throbbing head and hazy eyes cried out for sleep. Ah, sleep: he longed for it and dreaded it. Sleep brought a bright tangle of dreams, and all the dreams were of her. The bad ones: Nessa frightened, Nessa captive, Nessa burning; from those he would wake with flesh bathed in cold sweat, heart racing, eyes full of tears. The good ones: her soft voice, her elusive smile, the scent of spring flowers; words of love she had never spoken, sweet touches she had never given. He walked with her on the shore in summer; he sat silent by her on the clifftop in springtime. Waking from those dreams was bitterest of all, and he did not know which was strongest in him, the craving to see her or the horror of confronting, each time anew, the knowledge that she had been taken from him. He cursed the gods for sending him such dreams, and yet he would not have been without them.

He could not go much farther; he must find the nearest hiding place and seek rest, at least for a little. Before dawn he would move on, and with luck be close to Hafnarvagr tomorrow, close enough to get a message to Eirik somehow, and find help. All day he had observed armed men swarming across the fields in search of him; to go to his brother's dwelling was impossible. He would need all the stealth he could summon, and all the subtlety that Somerled had always told him a Wolfskin did not have. Perhaps that was what he should be trying to do: to think as Somerled would think, cleverly, cunningly. Somerled had always known how to put a legal argument, setting it out in logical sequence, clearly and wittily; when challenged by the opposition, Somerled could always summon some trick of words, or aim some barb at his adversary in order to extricate himself. Eyvind had never seen him lose. Very well then, he'd need to do something like that. A shiver went through him, for he knew this challenge was near impossible. Without help, it seemed quite beyond him. And to seek help, from his brother or Thord or others such as Brother Tadhg or even Margaret, that was to set those others at grave risk. What if something happened to Eirik, and his brother never returned home to his family in Rogaland? What kind of burden was that to have on your conscience?

Pondering this and trying to ignore the creeping cold, Eyvind marched grimly on in the darkness until he came to a place he

recognized. He had come too far to the east, and was close to
the great ring of standing stones, set by a narrow neck of land
on rising ground. He had walked this way before, in the days
when any man might pass freely across this land without fear of
sudden ambush. But no man came here by night unless he must.
The stones were full of ancient power; all felt the slow dance of
spirits weaving around and between these grave giants. Dotting
the landscape close by the great circle were earthen mounds,
some sealed, some with low entrances leading to darkness.
Only a fool would seek shelter in such a howe after sunset;
they'd all heard the tales the locals put about, of how a night in
there would turn your hair white as snow, and leave you screaming crazy things the rest of your life. Without saying it in as
many words, it was made clear these old places were forbidden.

Eyvind walked on until he saw the form of one such barrow
looming up ahead. He thought he could discern an opening,
though all was shades of gray on gray. The moon was low in the
sky, casting the stones' long shadows across the heather-clad
hillside and touching the lake water with a faint glimmer of silver. It was apparent to him that he could go no farther; he recognized the gradual numbing in his legs and knew they would
buckle and disobey him if he asked them to carry him on.
Crouched double, he crept into the secret depths of the howe.
He walked the edge of the chamber once, touching the neat-laid
stones with outstretched fingers, judging the size, the positions
of three small alcoves. He did not reach within them. If precious things were hidden here, it was not for him to disturb
them. Eyvind unbuckled his stolen sword; he spread his wolfskin on the earthen floor and sat, leaning his back awkwardly
against the sloping wall, staring into the blackness. The wolfskin was all he had left, the last thing that was his own: that, and
the small tokens Nessa had given him. His captors had tried to
seize even those, with muttered words about spells and witchcraft. He had not fought them for his bright sword or his dagger,
he had not even fought them for Biter, so great had been his anguish on that day of death and betrayal. But he had fought them
for this scrap of cloth, this ribbon, these little things that
seemed of no consequence, yet encompassed the world in the
space of a girl's cupped hand.

He did not want to dream. He sat thinking, delaying the moment when his weary lids must drop over his eyes and the longed-for, the dreaded visions again assail him. The wolfskin was warm beneath him; he welcomed that. Not one of them had dared lay hands on that badge of honor, that garment of power. It was strange. In one way, he did not deserve the skin anymore; in another, it had never been more truly part of him. Thor had let him go. He would never again hear that golden trumpet voice calling him on, would never again know the thrilling flood of rage that threw the warrior forward in blind courage to do the god's will, the call that made of a man an unthinking weapon of sheer unassailable power. Invulnerable, that was what they said: a Wolfskin could be stopped neither by spear nor axe nor broadsword. The Warfather's silence had seemed a death blow; without that voice, he had indeed been lost, cast adrift, bereft of strength and robbed of purpose. A Wolfskin vowed lifelong loyalty; to break that vow was a kind of death. But he had been human then, as full of doubts and aspirations, of love and sadness as he was at this moment. Thor's cry had made him deaf to that, the red haze of battle frenzy had made him blind to it. Now he understood what it was to be a man: that it was to be weak as well as strong, to be foolish sometimes and wise sometimes, to know how to love as well as to kill. And he had learned that there were other paths for him, other gods who called in the deep places of the earth, in the lap of wavelets on the shore, in the breath of the west wind. He had learned that there were other kinds of courage. He knew, with deep certainty, that the islands held a new path for him. He need only move forward to find it.

His fingers moved across the fur of the wolfskin, feeling its softness, its strength, its beauty and power. He thought he saw the wolf's eyes glowing in the darkness, but now they were not yellow and feral, they were the blue of a spring sky, full of courage and sorrow. They were his own eyes. It was his own skin. So long, so many seasons it had taken him to learn this lesson. He had believed it bravery, to feel no fear. It was only now, when there seemed nothing left but the darkness, that he understood what it was to be the wolf.

His eyes closed despite himself; dark turned darker. This time the dream came at once, a soft rustling from the entry as of gentle footsteps, a flickering gold light across the small chamber. She was there, standing hesitant by the opening, clad in blue tunic, dark skirt, her soft hair loose over her shoulders, a little bag on her back, a bundle under her arm. In her free hand she carried a tiny lamp; its glow illuminated her pale skin, her deeply shadowed eyes, her lips parted in the sudden shock of recognition. Her hand began to shake; the lamp wobbled perilously, spilling oil, threatening to fall. He heard her voice, a whisper of astonished disbelief.

"Eyvi?"

Gods, this was cruel indeed, for the nightmare to copy so closely what might have been real. How could he bear this? The urge in him was fierce to leap to his feet, to take two strides across and fold in his arms this lovely phantom, this beguiling trick of light and memory, yet he knew the moment he reached her she would fade, and he would be left with the night and the loneliness. He sat quite still. He scarcely dared to draw breath lest she vanish.

"Eyvi?" the vision said again, and now a hairy gray form pushed past her skirts and hurtled toward him, tail thrashing in delight, tongue licking his face in an exuberant display of recognition. Eyvind rose slowly to his feet, eyes fixed on the slender figure opposite. The lamp shook; she was going to drop it, and it would go out, and she would disappear forever.

"Careful," he said, stepping forward. "Here, let me take it." He reached out; he took the little light carefully from her and turned to place it safely in one of the alcoves. A warm glow spread through the round chamber, echoing the warmth that seemed to be flowing now, miraculous, incredible, into every corner of his wounded heart. The moment his fingers had touched hers, he had known that she was real.

Eyvind turned back. There was no need at all for words. His arms went around her, and hers around him; they stood thus enfolded a long time unmoving, for the message that flowed between them was deep and solemn, and needed no more for understanding than the beating of heart on heart.

The hound, however, had a wish to be a part of things, and at length made his presence known again by jumping to plant his great forepaws on Nessa's shoulder and giving little whines of excitement. Reluctantly, Eyvind released his hold and moved back a step, staring at her in wonderment.

"I thought you were dead," he said, finding his voice did not come as readily as usual. "I thought you had perished there in your uncle's hall. I'm sorry, I'm so sorry I failed you, I tried, but—"

"Shh," Nessa said, putting her fingers up to touch his lips to silence. "You are here, that's all that matters now. How is it you are here, Eyvi? I saw you fall, I saw you clubbed down and trampled . . . I thought I had lost you, too, that day . . ." Her voice was shaking; in the lamplight, he could see the tracks of tears on her cheeks, he could see the deep weariness in her eyes, the pallor of her skin.

"You must sit down. Here," Eyvind said, drawing her over to the place where the wolfskin was laid on the ground. "You look exhausted. You should eat and drink, you must rest. I have some water here, but no food; I made a rapid departure and brought only what I could snatch before I ran. Nessa—"

She sat; she looked up at him and he was instantly lost for words. In silence, he fetched his stolen water skin, and offered it for her to drink.

"I have some food," she told him. "Bread, cheese, it's in my pack. We may as well share it now; who knows what tomorrow may bring? No, not that bag," she said sharply as he moved to open the larger bundle she had carried. "The other, the small one; that's it."

It was another night like that first one, when they had sat together by soft light under the earth, and spoken as if there were no barriers between them. Eyvind saw the recognition of that in Nessa's eyes. Yet, it was different as well. That first time, they had sat side by side, hand in hand, as if that were quite natural. Tonight, after that first fierce embrace of recognition, a sudden constraint had fallen between them; they sat close, but each was careful, now, not to touch. Their eyes met, and looked away, and met again, as if unable to deny what was as yet unspoken. Eyvind fetched the small store of food, Nessa divided it, giving the dog an equal share, and they made pretense of eating.

"How did you escape?" she ventured. "I cannot understand how you survived so harsh a blow."

"Grim's an expert; he did not intend to kill me. And I've a

hard head, and a will to go on. That much has brought me here. And you—Somerled told me you had perished. He told me you were in the hall with King Engus. With your uncle."

It seemed she grew still paler, her eyes full of dark memories. "My uncle expected an attack sometime, though not so soon. He made me promise to run and hide if it happened, and I kept my promise. I came away in the little boat, when all were gone. Somerled killed them, Eyvi. All my people, all the fine young men, every one. He hacked off their heads and left their bodies strewn on open ground, gull pickings, worm fodder; he defiled the Whaleback forever with that unthinking act of desecration. I walked among the fallen; I saw this work of madness. He struck down the Kin Stone. It seems to me an ocean of tears cannot speak such sorrow as this."

Eyvind nodded. No words seemed adequate. He longed to take her in his arms again, to offer simple comfort, but he did not think he could.

"Why are you here? Where are you going?" she asked him suddenly.

"To Hafnarvagr, to seek my brother. I had evidence, clear proof of Somerled's responsibility for Ulf's death. I was foolish, I showed it to him, thinking to prevent the attack on the Whaleback, and he took it from me. He would not hear me, Nessa. And the others, I tried to tell them, I tried to stop them, but it was too late. The light of battle blinded them to the truth. But I will prove my case, despite all. I will find witnesses to what happened that day on High Island, and witnesses to the burning that killed Hakon and his wife. My brother can help me. I should move on at daybreak. Somerled's men are everywhere, searching for me. But I cannot leave you alone with nobody to guard you. Where can you go? Where can you be safe? I should be by your side to shield you."

She was silent a little, toying with the crust of bread she held. Guard's eyes followed every movement. "I—I have something to do, a task that must be completed. It's a little like a ritual, that's the only way I can describe it. To do this, I must have some time alone, in a particular place. I'm traveling there now. It lies to the west; I came this way only to speak to the stones, to tell them my uncle's story. Eyvi—I cannot describe for you what comes next, it is dark and secret. But if I achieve this task, it will help. Its purpose is to confront Somerled with the truth of what he has done. So, my quest is the same as yours."

Her words troubled him deeply. "You can't go on alone, it's not safe for you," he said. "His men are everywhere, you must have seen them. He heard me accuse him openly and he will not stop until he silences me. As for you, you wouldn't get across the fields, you'd be taken prisoner the first day. I don't think you fully understand Somerled's purpose: what he may intend for you. He spoke to me of making you his wife, of claiming the royal bloodline for his own sons. It is this he will pursue once he learns you live. I know him."

Nessa nodded gravely. "I am aware of this. He visited my uncle's hall. He spoke of it quite openly."

"When?"

"Long ago, when he threatened us with annihilation. My hand was to be part of the price for sparing our people's lives. That gave me many sleepless nights, Eyvi, sleepless nights and troubled days."

"Why didn't you tell me?" he whispered.

"I wanted to, but I couldn't. It was . . . it was too hard, I couldn't find the words. It would have been a high price to pay; but I did wonder if I should agree, to save the Folk. Now that I have seen Somerled at work, I know that I was right to refuse. Such a bargain would have won my people only a life of bitter servitude. Besides, I–I knew I could not wed Somerled. I knew it."

"Because you are a priestess," Eyvind said, finding again that his voice was not quite obedient to his will. "I understand that."

Nessa was regarding him very intently. "I could not wed Somerled," she said again. "I realized it was not possible."

"Let me come with you," he blurted out, "let me guard you and help you with this task, whatever it is. I–I thought I'd lost you forever. I can't lose you again."

"I don't know," she said slowly. "The task is . . . it is something I have to do alone, it is a work of magic in which you cannot play a part. But . . . but if I could have a companion on this journey, save my faithful Guard here, it would be you I would wish for above all others, Eyvi."

"Can I not at least watch over you, so you can complete the task undisturbed? I would keep you safe. I ask for nothing more than that. Please don't turn your back on me and walk away, not when I can place myself between you and the peril that shadows your steps."

"What about your own quest, your own task?"

"It can wait." He knew even as he said it that this was not so.

"I don't know. I, too, dread saying farewell again, lest it truly be the last time. I'm not sure I can bear another loss. We need some guidance in this, a sign. If only Rona were still alive. I miss her wisdom so much."

"She may be still alive," Eyvind told her cautiously, "though she did place herself at great risk. She's an old woman, certainly, but there's a core of iron there every bit as strong as your own."

Nessa's eyes widened. "What do you mean? Don't you know her cottage was burned with everything in it? Somerled's thugs devastated our holy place, laid waste its secrets. An old woman does not survive such an attack."

Eyvind smiled. "Ah. That was not quite the way of it. She and I, we watched the burning, and it was sad to see her things go up in smoke; that was indeed an act of barbarism. When Somerled's men sought to find us in the howe, I stepped out to confront them, I and the dog, Shadow. My body was still weak, I doubt if I could have fought them off if it had come to that. But they fled in fear, thinking me some ghostly warrior. That night we slept in the howe, and in the morning Shadow was gone, and so was Rona. I don't know where they went, Nessa, but there is at least some cause for hope."

"Thank you," she said softly. "And I know what she would advise. In the morning, I will cast the bones and see what the signs tell us. Maybe we will go on together; maybe each of us must take a different path. I cannot think of this now; my mind is crowded with other things, my heart is too full to let me see my way clearly."

Eyvind nodded, thinking her heart and her body could not possibly be full of as many conflicting feelings as his own. He could hardly think straight, so powerful was the longing in him.

"You're exhausted," he said. "You must sleep. I have no blanket, not even a cloak; still, the wolfskin is warm. Lie down there; I will sleep over at the other side. A warrior is accustomed to a bed on hard earth. Your dog—have you given him a name?"

"Guard, I called him."

"Guard will listen for intruders, though I think there will be none here; all fear to approach this place."

"You did not fear it."

"I was beyond fear, I think, once I thought you were lost. Now I know it again; I can scarcely bear to think of you going on alone."

"Hush," Nessa said. "Tonight is time out of time; there is no place for fear tonight."

"You must rest." He made himself move away, settle on the earth as far from her as he could go. Not far enough. For him, there would be no sleep; the aching of his body would torment him, her presence would ensure he fought back his desire, moment by moment, until dawn. "I don't like to see you so pale, so troubled. Have you held back your tears all this while, for those you have lost? You should not fear to weep; it does not make you any less strong, to let your tears flow. Shall I blow out the lamp?"

"Not yet." Her voice was very small, and wobbled. "Eyvi?"

He waited in silence.

"I feel so lonely," she said in a whisper. "They are all gone: my family, my people, all of them taken. And I'm tired, but I don't want to sleep, not here in the dark; I don't want to see their dead faces in my dreams."

He clenched his teeth together, willing himself not to move.

"You remember that night, the first night you woke up, in the tower in the earth? We sat by lamplight then and talked about dreams, and you put your arm around me and held my hand. It was a different sort of time, a time when hurts could be salved and secrets spoken and understood as if . . . as if . . ."

"As if the two of us were one." He said it, despite himself.

"Could we do that again?" she asked him. "Will you stay by me and keep away the visions, just for a little? If you would do that, this might be easier."

Not for me, he thought grimly, cursing his own selfishness. What kind of man was he, that he could not suppress his body's urges in order to help a friend? How weak was his self-control, that he could not trust himself to touch without taking?

"Would you, Eyvi?" He could hardly hear her soft voice, and yet he felt it in every corner of his body.

He did not speak, but moved to sit as he had that first night, close by her with his arm around her shoulders and his other hand clasped in hers; her sweet scent filled his nostrils, her warmth flooded into him, and his breathing quickened, despite his best efforts to keep it steady.

"Mmm," Nessa said, and laid her head on his shoulder. "That's good, Eyvi; that's so good. I did not know how much I had longed for this." Then she fell silent, and he could tell she was weeping, but he dared not hold her closer, he dared not reach to brush away those tears with his finger, to stop them with his lips, to . . . no, he would not think of that. His hand clasped hers tightly; he felt his breath escape in a great sigh. The gods were kind, and cruel. They had delivered her to him, safe and well, when he had thought her lost; it was his own fault that he was no longer contented with what he had.

"I'm sorry," Nessa said after a while. "I didn't know I was going to cry. I'm all right now. Perhaps we should try to sleep." Still she held his hand; even when he made to get up, she clung to it.

"Perhaps we should," he said. "You stay here; the wolfskin is the warmest place. I'll go back to the other side." He got to one knee, seeking to rise, but her hand held him fast.

"No, Eyvi," she said quietly. "Here, by me."

His heart lurched. "You don't understand," he said. "It shames me to say it, but I see I must. I cannot lie here by you, so close, and not—and not—I'm sorry, I wish I could hold you and comfort you and not want you so much, but I have dreamed of you every night since we parted; I have thought of you every waking moment. So now, you see, I must sleep elsewhere . . ."

She released his hand. He didn't seem to be able to move. He knelt where he was, staring at the ground, full of shame at his own weakness, full of sorrow at what could never be. Nessa was silent a little. When she spoke, her voice was both gentle and sure.

"Eyvi," she said, "listen to me. There's no saying what tomorrow may bring for us. Maybe flight, maybe captivity, maybe death. I can't tell you about that. All I can tell you is what I'm feeling now. I have never lain with a man; I thought I never would. But my body's aching for you, it has been this long time. I don't want to die without holding you in my arms, flesh to flesh; I don't want to leave this world without doing what a man and a woman do when they love each other. That's all I can say, dear one. Of course, if you think it's better that we don't—"

A sound came out of him, somewhere between an agonized groan of pent-up desire and a snort of astonished laughter. An instant later, she was in his arms, her lips soft on his, parting for him, hungry for him, her hands were making patterns of sweet fire against his skin, and they lay down together on the wolfskin and forgot the world for a while in the fierce joy of coming together. She was new to this, and Eyvind's desire so strong it threatened to rob him of all control. He had thought Signe beautiful, with her lush figure and her fair wholesomeness, and so she had been. But this girl, birch-pale, willow-supple, her long brown hair a tantalizing, silken shawl half-revealing the sweet small curves of her, this lissome woman was his heart's delight. She was his Bright Star, his joy and fulfillment. And he blessed Signe now for the skills she had taught him over those long nights in Freyrsfjord: how to be slow and careful, how to wait, how to make sure he did not hurt her. Such restraint took strength; he found that strength within himself, and it was only when Nessa cried out beneath him, her body trembling in the moment of fulfillment, that Eyvind let himself plunge over the brink into the darkness of his own pulsing release. They slept close-folded, arms wrapped around each other, legs entwined, breathing as one. Once or twice in the night they stirred, each moving a hand across the other's skin, stroking, touching softly, making quite sure this was not just another cruel dream. And once Nessa whispered,

"Eyvi?"

He stirred, not fully awake. "Mmm?"

"I think this is the first day of spring," she said, and slept again.

His eyes snapped open. In an instant body and mind were aware of danger. Here, inside, was the warmth of Nessa still sleeping, folded in his arms. There, outside, Guard was barking a frenzied warning, and men were raising their voices to be heard over it.

"He's got to be in there! We've tracked him down at last!"

"Good work, lads! Who's going in to fetch him out?"

"Going in? You must be joking."

No time; he woke Nessa quickly, silently, his hand over her mouth to warn her. She, too, was instantly alert, moving to dress herself, to hunt for her few possessions in the half-dark, to slip her feet into her boots. Morning light came dimly through the tunnelled entry. Nessa's eyes met his, wide with shock, recognizing that this time there was nowhere to run to. Eyvind struggled to keep his expression reassuring. The voices came again.

"What do you suggest, then? We've got to get him out somehow. There'll be a handsome reward in this, boys. Go on, Thorvald. You're a big, strong fellow. It's only a dog."

"Anyone got a thrusting spear? That thing's no dog, it's a fiend from the Underworld. Take it from a distance, you might have half a chance."

Nessa's fingers moved to touch Eyvind's in the shadowed silence of the howe. Their hands clasped tightly together. Even if it had been possible to speak, there were no words for this.

"Hang on," said another voice. "Don't be so ready with your talk of spears. That's Ulf's dog, don't you recognize it? Shouldn't think Somerled would be too pleased if you ran it through like a pig on a spit."

"Here, give me that hammer of yours," said another man. "Let me take a shot at the creature." There was a shuffling followed by a dull thud. The barking ceased abruptly, and Nessa drew in her breath in a little gasp.

"Right. Now let's see you go in, Thorvald. You're the biggest. Fellow's quiet enough; maybe he's still sleeping."

"Very funny." Thorvald sounded anything but amused. "Great way to get us all killed. We creep in one by one and he finishes us off one by one with his little knife the moment we come out the other end of that tunnel. This is a Wolfskin, lads, not just another miscreant on the run. You won't see me crawling in there, reward or no reward."

"Why don't we just wait?" offered somebody. "He's got to run out of food sometime."

"Stay out here in this place overnight?" This voice was incredulous.

"Smoke," someone said suddenly. "Make a fire at the entry; there's no hole on top, place'll fill up quick as a flash. He'll have to come out then; if he doesn't, he'll soon fall unconscious and we can go in and get him trussed up before he knows what's what."

Eyvind bent to touch his lips to Nessa's brow, to stroke her soft hair with his fingers. *Farewell, Bright Star. My hand in yours.* His heart was thundering in his breast. It was apparent to him that there was only one thing he could do.

"Good idea. You've more wit than I gave you credit for, man. Right, let's do it quick. Look around for what'll burn. I see that reward coming closer and closer. Might even be one of those handsome little islander girls in it, who knows?"

Eyvind relinquished Nessa's hand and took up his stolen sword, his small dagger. He motioned again that she must keep silent, pointed to the back of the howe, where she would be least visible to anyone looking in from the entry. *Go there. Hide. Wait.*

Her eyes were frantic, though she kept her silence. "No!" she mouthed. "Eyvi, no!"

"I love you." His lips made the words without a sound, and then he turned his back on her. "Thorvald!" he shouted. "Gudbrand, is that your voice, old scoundrel? I'm coming out; I'm weary and hungry, and I've no desire at all for a lingering death by choking. I'll hand my weapons out before me, no tricks." He crawled into the narrow passage as the men's voices rose in startled reaction. Behind him all was silence. He came out into the light of morning, on his knees, half-blinded by the brightness, proffering sword and dagger hilt first.

"Thor's hammer, Eyvind," someone remarked in tones of disgust, "you're not the man you once were, that's for certain."

"Tie his hands quick," another man advised. "Can't trust his kind."

Eyvind put up a slight struggle; it was best that this be done quickly, yet to give in too meekly was to invite suspicion. The dog lay prone near the entry, perhaps dead, perhaps merely stunned. Eyvind did not look back at the howe itself.

"This all you've got?" Gudbrand, who seemed to be leading the expedition, stared hard into Eyvind's face as the others bound his hands tightly behind his back. "No axe, no spear? No supplies?"

Eyvind shook his head. "I came away in haste, as you know," he said. "My own things are gone."

"Still," Gudbrand mused, scratching his chin, "maybe we should have a look inside. Could be a trick. Not like your kind to give up so easily. Thorvald? Why don't you go in and take a look?"

"Me?"

"Why not?"

"Ever heard what happened to that fellow from Hafnarvagr that went in one of those and scratched his name-rune on the stone? Spent the next three days babbling about ghosts and then jumped off a cliff into the sea. Come on, let's go back. There's a good pot of ale in this at least."

"What about the dog? Didn't you say the thing was Ulf's?"

"Anyone volunteering to carry it? I say leave it where it lies. Offering for the spirits, keep them off our backs. Come on, then. Move, you!"

These men may have been his comrades once, but it was clear he was now no more to them than another captive to be harried forward at spearpoint. Eyvind did not look back. He set his eyes ahead, northward to Somerled's hall, blessing each step that took them farther from the place where Nessa still hid in shadows. They had not found her; she was safe for now. He must hope that she could go on alone and complete the mysterious task she had spoken of. At least, now that he was recaptured, there would be no need for Somerled to send warriors out in great numbers scouring the countryside. Nessa had at least some chance of evading the few who would still patrol what had once been the borders of Engus's kingdom. As for himself, despite the terror of seeing her so close to capture, his heart was whole again: he bore the sweet memory of last night within him, and it seemed to him that talisman had the power to arm him against much. It would be back to the little cell, he supposed, back to the darkness and the company of his own thoughts. So be it; if he must break out again, he would, no matter what guard they set on him. He'd have to let them hold him a few days at least, so Nessa had time to get away, time to do the thing she had to do before his own escape drew forth pursuit once more. Then he would go back to the old plan, to seek out Eirik. Perhaps he would find Nessa again, drawn to her side by whatever ancient power had sent the two of them to find refuge in the selfsame hidden place, on the selfsame night. That could hardly have been chance. If those forces were kind enough to lead him to her again, he would not leave her. He would do all that was in his power to keep her safe from Somerled. Time, that was all he'd need, enough time. As they marched northward, his guards now grimly silent, Eyvind planned it out in his head, imagining the musty outhouse where he'd been locked up before, picturing where they might deploy an increased guard, working out how long he would wait, this time, before making his move, and what path he would follow to come back to the south undetected.

But it seemed they were not taking him to the isolated farm hut that had held him before. The group was passing to the west of that place, skirting wide around the fields that fringed Ulf's burial mound, then curving northeastward again to make their way straight toward the settlement and Somerled's hall. Eyvind held his silence. It was clear to him from the disapproving scowls of his escort that useful information was unlikely to be forthcoming. He knew what was in their minds. To defy your chieftain's orders and turn against your own forces was bad enough. But what sort of warrior surrenders with no resistance at all, merely for the sake of a warm bed and a joint of mutton? Their eyes told him their opinion. He whom they had once admired, envied, even idolized, was now sunk as low in their estimation as a worm beneath the boot heel: lower, even, because of what he had once been. His shame had robbed them of words.

The sight of the settlement wall, the calls of sentries, brought light back to their eyes and grins to their faces soon enough. Gritting his teeth, Eyvind let them drag him into the enclosure with more than a few glancing blows to ear and jaw inflicted on the way. They tied him to a post while Thorvald went ahead into the hall; it was not long before this new captive attracted a crowd, folk muttering and whispering at first, then jeering and shouting insults as confidence grew. Someone spat in his face. Eyvind held himself still and quiet. His mind showed him small images: Nessa sleeping, a standing stone, dark under the moon with the glittering lake water beyond, a lone, pale beach where slow waves washed the sand. He breathed carefully; there were parts of him that hurt from blows received during that long walk north, blows he had chosen not to return. It was important to stay alert and save what strength he had. These men did not matter. Only Somerled mattered. At the back of the group that now surrounded him, their taunts increasing in the face of his own silence, he saw Grim, a tall, broad figure clad in wolfskin and woolen tunic, the hammer slung on his back. A clever blow, that had been; Grim had known just how hard to strike, to stop but not kill him. He thought neither Holgar nor Erlend had shown such judgment. Still, one could not know who was a friend and who an enemy. Good and bad had become blurred on this island since Ulf's death. And Grim, too, had charged across the causeway that morning to hew men limb from limb, to part head from shoulders.

Someone threw an egg; it cracked on Eyvind's cheek and splattered across face and neck.

"Enough!" Grim's voice was deep and rough like the growl of a bear; folk fell silent. "What are you, some rabble starved of cheap entertainment? Take this man inside; get him cleaned up before Somerled sees him. A fellow's got the right to be heard before you set him up as a figure of fun, hasn't he? Now get out of here; I feel the itch in my fingers for a little hammer play, and right now I'm not particular who's in my way."

The enclosure cleared as if by magic, leaving Eyvind and his captors. Grim looked on with a heavy frown. He wasn't talking now. He stared at Eyvind, and Eyvind glanced back at him, and thought he saw the smallest of nods from the bearded warrior before Grim turned on his heel and tramped off indoors. Then Gudbrand was tugging on the ropes that bound his prisoner, and he was hauled away.

Inside, he was conveyed none too gently to the quarters where he had once slept with his fellow Wolfskins, but nobody seemed to be prepared to unfasten the tight bonds that tied his hands behind his back, nor to tend to the cuts and bruises on his face, nor to offer a clean tunic or a bowl of fresh water. He waited, standing very still in the center of the room while his captors conferred in low voices. A hearing, he thought, that would be the next thing. They'd lock him up for a while, and then he'd have to walk out in front of everyone and say what he had to say with neither evidence nor witnesses. This wasn't how it was meant to be; he'd just have to do his best. At least he was buying time for Nessa. He wondered where she was now. He wished she would slip onboard a fishing boat and go off to the outer islands, where Somerled's hand had not yet tightened its grip on her people. This new king would be busy enough establishing his realm of Hrossey without turning his attention to the far-flung remnants of the Folk on Sandy Island or West Island or the smaller, remoter places. But Nessa wouldn't go; he knew her. She was a leader. She would not rest until she had completed the task she had spoken of. He hoped it would not bring her here to the settlement. He did not want her to be here, so close to Somerled.

"Right," said a voice from the entry. "The king wants to see him straightaway. In his own quarters. Alone."

"Alone?" Gudbrand scowled. "That's hardly wise. A guard or two inside the chamber, surely?"

"Alone, and now," said Thorvald, who had brought the message. "That's what he said."

At the entry to Somerled's private quarters, which had once been his brother's, stood Holgar and Erlend, one on either side of the doorway. Erlend stepped forward, seizing Eyvind by the arm, and jerked his head at Gudbrand in dismissal.

"That'll be all," he snarled.

Gudbrand hesitated; perhaps his mind was on the reward.

"What's the matter? Lost your hearing suddenly?" Holgar loomed up behind Erlend, frowning ominously, and all at once there was nobody left but the three Wolfskins.

"Says he'll see you on your own," Erlend muttered, avoiding Eyvind's eye. "Not very sensible, if you ask me."

"Just don't try anything." Holgar's voice had an edge to it; he seemed ill at ease, jumpy. "We'll be right outside the door. No tricks. We know them all."

The length of thick woollen cloth that hung across the entry was drawn aside.

"Eyvind is no threat to me." Somerled stood there, his expression calm, his voice tranquil. He was plainly dressed in dark tunic and trousers, his hair gathered neatly back by a scarlet cord. "We're like brothers. You know him less well than you think, if you imagine he'd ever raise a hand to me. But, by all means, stay out there if it makes you feel better. Down the hallway a little, if

you please; this conversation is private. Come in, Eyvind." He
stepped back, and Eyvind walked into the chamber. "Oh, and by
the way," Somerled had put his head outside again, "tell someone we need a bowl of warm water and a cloth. And I think a jug
of ale and a bite to eat wouldn't go amiss either. Those who
treated this prisoner so ill have erred; tell them that hasn't gone
unnoticed." He pulled the curtain firmly closed.

Eyvind waited. This was not at all what he had expected, not
after that bloody dawn at the Whaleback, and Somerled's challenge to him. This game seemed to have no rules at all.

Somerled regarded him gravely. "You don't look well,
Eyvind," he observed. "Let's get these cuts cleaned up, at least.
Turn around."

Mutely Eyvind obeyed. He felt the light, deft touch of
Somerled's fingers as the rope which bound his hands was untied.

"There," said Somerled, rolling the cord into a neat coil.
"Now, sit down, and we'll talk a little. It's good to see you, old
friend, no matter what has passed between us. I've missed you;
so much is new here, and strangely enough I find I don't particularly enjoy doing it all by myself."

Eyvind sat. His arms ached; red welts made broad bracelets
nearly a handspan wide around his wrists. His hands were shaking; he clasped them tightly together and made himself breathe
slowly. A man sidled in with water and a small towel; another
brought a tray with roast meat and a jug of ale. Somerled filled
two goblets.

"You're very quiet," he observed.

"I don't know what to say to you." Eyvind looked into his old
friend's eyes. He could read nothing there but anxious concern.
"I don't know where to start."

"Here, eat and drink a little. Let me tend to those cuts first;
there's crusted blood all down your cheek and across the brow,
not to speak of what looks like egg yolk. You've managed to
surprise me, Eyvind. The man who brought the news said you
gave up without a fight."

"I'm tired," Eyvind said. "It seemed to me there was nowhere
else to run to."

"But you escaped my custody. Where did you imagine you
were going?"

Eyvind did not reply. He would not mention Eirik or Thord; he would not speak of Brother Tadhg. No need to draw others into this. What he must do, he must do alone.

Somerled damped the cloth, dabbed at the wounds on Eyvind's face. After a while he said quietly, "You can talk to me, Eyvind. I'm not some monster, you know. I am your friend as I always was; like you, I swore to be loyal above all else. That's why you are here alone with me, not dragged forth to account for your actions before the whole court. I want this settled properly, and I want to protect you if I can. Here, drink this ale, you look like a walking ghost. That's it. And eat. I suspect you've had nothing at all today. The men are angry; you cannot expect them to treat you kindly. They saw the way you defied my orders. They saw the way you stood against your own comrades."

Eyvind felt confusion and doubt creeping back into his mind; his hand shook, and he set the ale cup down. "What do you mean, protect me?" he asked. "I've come here to tell the truth, that's all."

Somerled was watching him closely. "Truth?" he queried, brows raised. "Which truth is that? The same you were shouting that morning when you came back from the dead? Unfounded accusations wholly without proof, the rantings of a man driven out of his wits by long captivity and torture? You may choose to call those ravings truth, but I am king here, and these men follow me. On these islands, mine is the only truth that counts."

Eyvind drew a deep breath. Thor's hammer, his wrists felt as if naked flames licked at them. "So, you expect our people to follow a man who murdered his own brother?" he asked. "It seems to me you have let nothing and no one stand in the path that leads to your desires. I'm not sure you understand what you have done."

"If you want to explain it to me, please go ahead, Eyvind. I'm here to listen."

"On one count you are right." Eyvind's fists clenched tight; the shaking was getting worse. "I did swear loyalty to you once, and I meant it. I have never forgotten that you saved my life. From the first, I recognized in you what others could not see: courage, determination, fierce strength of will. A cleverness I could never come close to. A desire to be your own master and set your own course. I admired that in you; I saw a future in which those qualities would flower, a time in which you would set them to some great and noble purpose."

A light had awoken in Somerled's dark eyes. "Now is that time!" he exclaimed, springing to his feet and setting a hand on Eyvind's shoulder. "Can't you see that? We are here together, and I am king, and we have a whole new world to make as we will. These people look up to me, Eyvind, they like a leader who's prepared to make hard decisions and to abide by them. They want someone who will adhere to the old gods. They don't want some vacillating peacemonger with his head in the clouds, they want direction. I've given them that. They're grateful. They'll do anything for me. Look at your fellow Wolfskins, lurking out there in the hallway. They're more loyal to me than they ever were to Ulf. I've given them real work to do, the only kind they understand."

"A kingdom founded on a brother's blood is not much of a kingdom," Eyvind said quietly. "A battle fought on such uneven terms as yours against King Engus can bring no glory, only shame."

Somerled's eyes narrowed. "Are you telling me you would break your blood oath? That now, in the light of day, after time for reflection, after weighing the consequences, you would still stand against me, Eyvind?"

"I don't think that's what I'm saying at all. It seems to me my blood oath ties me to guide your steps in right paths. It forces me to tell you when you are wrong; to make sure you don't do anymore damage to yourself or to others. What crime did Ulf ever commit, to bring down such doom on himself?"

Somerled's lips tightened. "You are more brother to me than he ever was," he said. "And yet you turn against me. In your efforts to destroy me, you will only destroy yourself. You said I didn't understand what this meant. But you're the one who doesn't understand."

"Maybe not. You always called me stupid, muddled. Perhaps it's true. All I can tell you is that if you continue to follow this path of slaughter, destruction, and fear, I will fight you to the end, blood oath or no. Good folk have perished here, folk who were slain for no reason, save that you wanted what was theirs. A treaty was broken, the rules of right engagement callously disregarded."

There was a pause. Somerled's fingers toyed with an ale cup, rolling it against the tabletop. "And the girl died," he said eventually. "That's what this is all about, isn't it?"

"What girl?" Even to himself, Eyvind's voice sounded strained.

"The princess. The little priestess, Engus's niece. That was a pity. I liked her. And I suspect you did, too; weren't you hiding in that place where the island witches brewed their potions? I suppose you fell for her, though I did think your tastes ran more to the buxom, fair type. But there can be no other explanation for your sudden insanity. She could never have been for you, old friend. She was far above you, a bride for royalty. Well, that's of no account now; she's gone. Never mind, there are several others to choose from, though the best we captured are already taken. I'll give you first pick of what's left."

Fury quickened Eyvind's breathing; with difficulty he held his features calm. "I don't want a woman," he said.

"What do you want, Eyvind? Why have you allowed yourself to be brought back here? Tell me."

Eyvind swallowed. "A fair hearing, that's all. Let me put forward the truth as I know it, call witnesses, present evidence before a Thing, or whatever assembly you wish to convene. Give me the usual time to prepare my case. I will accept the judgment of worthy men."

"You? Prepare a case? Oh, dear, Eyvind. This time on the run really has addled your wits."

"It is possible," Eyvind said, "that truth may outweigh the cleverest arguments. I may be muddled and stupid, but I understand that. Are you afraid of the truth?"

"Of course not!" Somerled snapped. "I'm afraid of having to pass judgment on you, my oldest of friends. You're such a fool you haven't worked that out even now. Eyvind, I know you as well as anyone does. You just don't have the capacity to win this. I have my own rules here, new ones. I don't convene assemblies, I hear all cases myself. Judgments are summary and swift. That's essential to maintain discipline. I've called you in here because it's the only way I can save you. You disobeyed a direct order, you made wild accusations, you fought against your fellow warriors. If those charges are brought against you formally, and proven, I can only pronounce a sentence of death. It would be carried out within a day."

"Death?" This was new indeed. In the formal hearings of Rogaland, a lifetime's banishment was the harshest penalty a man might receive. Of course, unofficial executions by fire or ambush were possible, but these attracted their own penalty; such feuds could last for generations.

"It's indeed so; I have decreed it. Necessary in these times of instability. I can't afford any insubordination, any half-baked rebellions. Now, Eyvind, what's it to be?"

"I'm not sure what you mean." Eyvind rose to his feet, and instantly regretted it; after the day's forced march, the old weakness had returned to his legs, and he had to set a hand on the table for support.

"I'm offering you a chance to redeem yourself. More than offering—I'm begging you to take it." Somerled was pale; his eyes were deadly serious. "Let there be no more talk of Ulf and of murders. Let there be no more talk of Engus, of the battles we have won here, of treaties and the like. You cannot make the dead live again, Eyvind. Come back to my side; let us go forward as we planned once, long ago, a great king and his peerless Wolfskin. Your behavior can be easily explained, readily forgiven once the full tale is told, of how these islanders took you prisoner after Ramsbeck and played tricks with your head so that you could no longer tell friend from foe, right from wrong. You're clearly still very weak in body as well as mind. Why else would the foremost of my warriors give himself up so easily? You can have rest, good care, as many little islander girls as you want to warm your bed. No need for any sort of hearing; I'll announce that I've pardoned your indiscretion, and we'll move on from there. What do you say?"

Eyvind was silent. In his mind he saw Nessa, a slight, graceful figure walking on the shore, turning her head to look at him, her long brown hair tossed like a banner in the west wind. He saw a young warrior's severed head, fierce-eyed. He saw Ulf's tortured body hanging in air. He wondered how Somerled would kill him, when the time came.

"Eyvind? Don't make me do this, I beg you." Somerled's voice was shaking. It was the voice of a child who had once said nobody cared.

"I want a fair hearing," said Eyvind quietly. "If you will not call an assembly, then let me tell the truth as I know it before all the folk of this settlement. Then, since you have appointed yourself sole arbiter, I suppose you will pronounce sentence on me. But I will be heard. I would like my brother to be present, if he can be called back from Hafnarvagr. I would like Lady Margaret to hear what I have to say."

"It's not up to you to determine who should be there," Somerled snapped. "Odin's bones, Eyvind, you're such a fool! Why sacrifice yourself for nothing? Curse it, man, I can't do without you!"

Eyvind managed a smile. "I think, for both of us, there is now no way forward but this," he said. "You cannot undo what you have wrought here. Even if you stepped on your ship tomorrow, and set sail home to Freyrsfjord, the legacy of your deeds would shadow this place for long years to come, for you have robbed these folk of a whole generation of men. As for me, I can see no other way than to set things out as I understand them, and call on the gods and on the wisdom of ordinary folk to make wrongs right again. That is all I can say, Somerled, except that I am sorry: sorry that it has come to this between us."

"Please," said Somerled in a whisper. "Please don't do this. You don't know what you're throwing away."

The little image of Nessa came again, tiny and perfect, her grave features, her graceful hands putting a pattern of white stones in place, her dark hair shining in lamplight.

"I do know," Eyvind said quietly. "I know how high the stakes are. And I know I must play to the end."

TWELVE

Guard was slow, so slow. A brave dog and loyal, he did his best to keep up with her, staggering along behind, his long legs shaky at best. Nessa stopped three times on her journey so that he could rest, once by a stream where the hound lapped thirstily, once by the burned-out ruin of a cottage—she shrank to think what had become of the fisherman and his family who had lived there as long as she could remember—and later, in the shade of bushes as they neared the cliffs above the place she sought. She gritted her teeth in frustration each time. Poor Guard. Somerled's henchmen had struck him insensible; it was not fair to expect so much of him. He struggled to maintain even a walking pace, and there was no time at all to spare. The women of the Folk had been taken, and now Eyvind was captive, at Somerled's mercy. She had seen what this new king could do.

The sun passed across the sky. It seemed to Nessa the day moved on with cruel and unreasonable speed. Her burdens were heavy: the bag with its strange cargo gleaned from a chieftain's barrow, and under her other arm the wolfskin, rolled tightly and bound with a strip of linen torn from her shift. She would not leave this great shimmering pelt behind, impractical though carrying it had proved. She had already allowed Eyvind to sacrifice himself for her, not once but twice. It was clear to Nessa that the skin was part of him, as integral to his self as steadfast heart or loyal spirit. The wolfskin must be kept safe. Thus, she reasoned, she might in some way protect him until the truth was at last laid out for all to see and understand. All the same, she chafed at every small delay, and as she passed through hidden vales and over gentle hills toward the sea, her mind was beset by images of what might be: Eyvind imprisoned, Eyvind beaten, Eyvind desperately playing for time so that she might be safe. He was in terrible danger. A man who would slaughter and burn as Somerled had would not hesitate to wipe another from the face of the earth if he believed him a threat. Friendship meant nothing to such a man. Nessa shivered as she stood on the edge of the cliffs above the hidden cove. *Let him live.* She sent a prayer to whatever god might be listening: Thor, perhaps, for surely this warfather would not abandon so patently heroic a warrior, whatever Eyvind himself believed. If the god had fallen silent it was for a reason, perhaps so that his son might listen to his own heart awhile, and make his choices in another way. *Keep him safe until I have made what must be made, and journeyed back to find him.*

She expected no answer, and there was none. She must simply get on with this. The way down to the cove was steep and narrow; she bore her burdens carefully, picking cautious steps on the slippery cliff path. Far below her the ocean rolled dark and chill to the shore, and all the way down birds screamed, gliding and diving in endless dance about the ledges and crevices of the rock face. Nessa had no free hand to protect her eyes, nor could she shut them as beak or claws flashed past a handspan from her face. It would be thus all through the nesting season. Guard faltered after her, edging his way down the precarious track. At last they reached the foot of the cliff, where a small stretch of sand lay before shallow caves, and shelves of flagstone spread out on either side, offering a safe haul up for seals and a fine spot for line fishing when wind and tide allowed. There were no fishermen here today. Perhaps there were none left at all; she had passed several cottages whose roofs were burned, and whose stock wandered untended. Once, she had thought she saw the body of a man sprawled in a yard; once, she had heard a dog howling. She had not ventured closer. How many of Engus's people survived here on the home island? Did Somerled seek to crush every last one of them, to wipe out all trace of the Folk, so that even in the tales of future generations the knowledge of them would be lost?

She was here at last. Now she must work quickly to finish the making. Afterward there was another hurdle to cross, but she would not consider that yet. Nessa glanced at the sun. It was already sinking toward the west. If she made this tonight and traveled tomorrow, would she be there in time? How long could Eyvind hold out? He had been a prisoner since dawn: nearly a whole day. He might already be dead. Her fingers reached to untie the wolfskin and spread it out on the floor of the small cave. It was indeed a wondrous and powerful thing, whose magic could be sensed in every strand of its glossy surface. *Wait for me*, Nessa whispered. *Don't go on without me.*

The task could not be completed without help. She knew that; it was the purpose of her journey here. Nessa unfastened the bag and emptied its burden out. With a faint, clinking music, the bones tumbled moon-white onto the silver-gray wolf pelt. A tangle of dark hair wrapped itself around them. She stared down at the jumble of shapes, biting her lip. It was only an old tale, after all: *voice of truth in harp of bone*. She be-

lieved it, of course she did; the only thing was, the stories never
gave step-by-step advice as to how one might go about constructing the mysterious objects of which they told. Practically
speaking, it was impossible. The frame could not be locked together; what might one use in place of pegs of wood or whalebone? How might one shape the curves with only a small knife
and so little time? And what about the strings? A man's hair
could not provide the tension required to sound notes in a
melody. It would snap the moment the pegs were tightened.
Still, she had no choice. Such doubts must be set aside. Truth
was the most powerful voice of all; truth would make itself
heard against impossible odds. And for such a work of magic,
Nessa must seek help from those who understood the deepest
secrets of the heart and of the blood: those whose existence was
part of the ebb and flow of the tide itself.

She settled herself on the flat stones above the dark water.
She cast her mind back a long time, to a day when small Nessa
had been watching the seals on the shore and thinking about the
lonely fisherman who had built the tower in the earth.

"Rona," she'd asked, "how could you call the Seal Tribe? If
you wanted to talk to them, how could you make them hear you?"

"That depends," Rona had replied guardedly. "Such folk
don't just come when you want them. They're not at the beck
and call of the human kind, and they never will be."

"So you've never—?"

"Ah," Rona had answered, "I didn't say that. For you and me,
it's a bit different. You'll find out, as you study the mysteries.
They start to hear you, and recognize what you are, and then you
begin to hear them. These old ones, the sea people, the earth
folk, they understand our part is to preserve the heart of the islands, Nessa. We all want that. One day you'll be casting your
circle, and you'll look westward to invoke the powers of the
ocean, and the people of the Seal Tribe will be there watching
you. And there is a way to call them, if you've a desperate need."

"What way?" At nine years old, Nessa had not been sure of
what a desperate need might be, but she was always eager to
learn whatever the wise woman had to tell.

"You must sit by the water in a place you know they love,
and you must shed seven tears into the sea. Then ask them to
help you."

"Does it work?"

"I don't know," Rona had said dryly. "Let's hope we never have to put it to the test."

The time had come now. Seven tears, no more, no less. It was not hard to weep. Think not of the deaths of her uncle and Kinart and all the fine men of the Folk, not of the Kin Stone laid low, nor of her mother's slow fading and the fever that had snatched her sisters away before she could say good-bye. Think not of the women of the Whaleback, captive and frightened. Think not of Rona wandering off into the wilderness alone so that Eyvind might go on to confront the friend who was his enemy. Think not of Eyvind giving himself up so Nessa would be safe, nor of what he might be enduring now. Oh, no: think only of last night, think of the look on his face, his smile like a flash of sunshine, the touch of his hands on her body, so gentle, so careful for all the passion that made his breathing falter and his blue eyes darken. Think of the way their bodies moved together, as if they were two halves of one wondrous whole; remember the secret darkness of their longing and the shattering brightness of their fulfillment. Even now her body ached with it. Think only of the unthinkable sweetness of that, and of how much she had to lose if she failed. Think of that and weep. One, two, three . . . seven . . . now cover the eyes with sudden hands, lest a whole flood of tears drop to the cold sea, and this charm be undone before ever it was made.

She sat silent thus, palms over her face, head bowed, with no room in her thoughts for anything but him. Yet all around her the magic flowed, ancient and true, for this was not just for woman and man, for the bond between them; it was for the Folk, for the islands, for life itself. Seated there, blind and weeping, Nessa felt the power of it deep in the bone, flooding the heart, filling the spirit with brightness, and knew she had never been more priestess than she was in this moment.

She opened her eyes to Guard's barking. There were five of them seated on the rocks around her, women and yet notwomen, fragile, wild sea creatures with eyes all liquid darkness and hair draping their white shoulders like fronded leaves, gray, blue, green as the deep below the swell. Their bodies were naked and wet, pale skin pearled with droplets as if they had but a moment ago emerged from the ocean's chill embrace. Perhaps what lay on the sandy beach beyond them was merely a drift of dark weed; perhaps it was sealskins set neatly down until their owners should need them again. Guard was hysterical, running up and down the shore, squandering the last of his flagging strength in a frantic warning.

"Hush now, Guard, good boy." Nessa rose and walked back to the little cave, and they followed on their narrow white feet. They settled in a circle around the wolfskin, and long-fingered hands reached out immediately to touch the bones, to stroke and examine. They seemed to speak one to another, but their voices made notes, not words: a deep, antiphonal humming that told their understanding of what Nessa had prepared here. With pointed finger, with nod or shrug, with little notes of song, they proceeded to show her how the task must be done. Shreds of dark matter adhered to the bones, near the joints; these must be cleaned away, and the long, pale shafts polished. A handful of sand, shreds of dry seaweed, she must rub harder, harder, this was to be a thing of beauty, pure and bright as the moon itself. This took time. As each bone was judged ready, it was laid out in place, flat on the wolf pelt, so the shape of what must be made could be seen. Shin bones, thigh bones for the frame: these must be trimmed, pared, shaped with Nessa's little knife. Once or twice, the sea women were not satisfied with her efforts. They would not use the knife, but took up the bones and set their teeth to them with precision, gnawing a hollow, grinding a curve more precisely. The joints must be a perfect fit, matching as sweetly as the timbers of that great vessel that had borne Ulf, the far-seeker, safe across the ocean to the islands of his destiny. They watched her intently, shining eyes fixed on every fumbling attempt to hold the sliding pieces in place, attention sharp on every cautious shaving away of a tiny shard so that the instrument would be perfect in form and function. Later, they chewed weed into long strips for bindings, passing her the dark, wet strands, showing her cunning knots, clever twists. These wrappings would tighten as they dried, giving strength to the frame.

The day passed swiftly; the sun bathed this small patch of western shore in deep gold, lighting the faces of Nessa's companions to a translucent glow. A note of urgency had crept into their voices now, the pattern of their speech-song conveying a clear message: *Hurry! The sun moves lower. Make haste, or it will be too late!*

Pegs, little pegs of finger bone. Notches almost too small to see. So small, her hands were shaking, she must concentrate, she must slow down. She must keep her mind only on the task of making, and put those other images out of her mind: Eyvind hurt, Eyvind fighting and falling again.

"There must be time," she murmured to herself. "I'll light a fire, I'll work all night. In the morning, I'll find a horse at one of the farms, I'll ride there as swiftly as I can. He's only been captive one day. They must have some sort of hearing, these things take time . . . Tomorrow, tomorrow must be soon enough."

Even as she spoke she saw the look in the sea women's wide eyes, and heard the tone of their wordless voices, and recognized what they were trying to tell her. One raised a delicate hand, gesturing toward the sun, and ululated a warning. Another pointed to the cliff path, to Nessa herself, and to Guard, who now slept with eyes half-open at the rear of the shallow cave, twitching and trembling. The sea woman used her hands to show running, running. She pointed eastward, her hum rising to a kind of scream, which rang from her mouth and nose, a braying danger call like the voice of a war trumpet. There was no mistaking the message. *Finish it and go now. Now. Tomorrow is too late.*

They began to work alongside her; it seemed they had decided she could not finish in time, not on her own. Their thin, pale fingers plucked the hair from the tumble of discarded bone and began to twist and weave it together with a speed and dexterity that made Nessa stare in wonderment, until one hissed at her, motioning to the harp frame where the small holes still lacked their pegs. These finger bones were so little, and it was getting dark. She had made the holes as neatly as she could, not easy with a knife better suited to the casting of ritual circles than such a delicate and precise task. She fitted one peg, working hard to keep her hands steady as the sky darkened and the sun turned red, sinking until it was a finger breadth above the slate gray of the western sea. She eased another into place.

"I must make fire," she said, hoping they might understand. "I can't see to do such fine work. It's almost dark, and there are four more of these to fit, and then the strings. Must I go there by night? Is that what you mean?"

The only answer was wordless, incomprehensible. One of the sea women held the frame upright, two others were still fashioning strings, and there were two down on the sand now, crouching over something they were making. Nessa fitted the next peg.

"You should tell me the truth," she said, fumbling to find another of the tiny bones, to trim the end narrower while she could still see. "If I don't get there before morning, will Eyvind die? How can I get there? How can I go up this path in the dark, with—" She looked at the thing she had made, so delicate, so fragile. She looked at the wolfskin, bulky, heavy, but not to be left behind. Guard whimpered in his sleep; he was exhausted and hurt. "I don't think I can do it," Nessa whispered. *Oh, Eyvi, how can I do it?* She reached to slip the peg into place, but it was too wide and would not fit, and now the sun sank abruptly, and all at once it was too dark to see, too dark to calculate the fine adjustment necessary, to shave off the smallest fragment of bone so this could fit snugly but still be turned. *I can't do it.*

The sea woman suddenly let go of the harp, and Nessa's hands shot out to keep it from falling. A thrill ran through her, a ripple of power that made every corner of her body tingle with a terrible awareness. In that moment, she felt what this was. As yet it had no strings, no voice, yet she sensed the magic hidden in the graceful frame, the energy concealed in the elegant small shape. *I am . . . I am . . .* Its voice hovered on the edge of hearing, urgent to come forth. Oh, it would speak all right; it would tell a tale to freeze men's hearts and set tears of shame in their eyes, it would make them shiver and quail with its song. This harp would bring truth to the tyrant's hall. It would save the Folk. It would save Eyvind, if only she could bear it forth in time.

There was a certain amount of dispute as to where Eyvind might be held securely until all was prepared for a formal hear-

ing. Erlend and Holgar recommended some form of shackles,
and a bolted door. Somerled thought such precautions unnecessary. After all, Eyvind had demanded a fair hearing. Now that
he was getting one, why would he take the trouble to escape?
Hadn't he given himself up with no more than a token struggle?

A compromise was reached: hobbles for the ankles, locked
securely, but the hands left free, since the prisoner's wrists were
red raw from the tight bonds he had worn during his march
north. The chamber where they placed him seemed new.
Eyvind thought it purpose-built for captives such as himself, for
the door was an iron grille, heavily bolted. There was a high,
small window in the stone wall; none but vole or finch might
escape this cell. A straw-filled sack and a bucket provided the
sole furnishings. Guards paced the hallway beyond the door,
not Grim, not Holgar, not Erlend, but others, men who did not
know their prisoner well. Perhaps Somerled thought that safer.
Or maybe the Wolfskins did not like to see their old comrade
sunk so low. He had seen the unease on their faces, the confusion in their eyes. Now, he was not only a traitor, he was something worse: a coward.

For Somerled was right, as usual. Eyvind would not attempt
an escape, though as soon they'd brought him in here, he had
instinctively sized up door and bolts and guards to weigh the
chances. For a Wolfskin, this was a natural reaction. But he
would not try, even though he suspected Somerled's idea of
what constituted a fair hearing would differ markedly from his
own. If he broke out and fled, he would be pursued. Somerled
could not afford to have him abroad spreading dangerous
truths. And if they hunted for him, they would find Nessa. That
could not be allowed to happen. He was not so much of a fool as
to believe there could be a future in these isles for him, even
though she had lain in his arms one whole, sweet night. She had
a place here as priestess, as leader. As for himself, it seemed he
had earned the scorn of all who had once admired and loved
him. There was nothing to do but go on in the manner of a warrior, with what strength and dignity he could muster. He would
face death as the wolf did, steadfast to the very moment of
darkness.

Time passed. The guard changed and changed again. Someone brought food and drink. Eyvind wasn't hungry, but he ate it anyway, simply for something to do. The silence, the shadows sharpened his awareness of the pain in his wrists, the trembling in his hands, the weak, numb feeling in his legs. He made himself move about within the tight confines of the cell, bending, stretching, always hampered by the shackles. He tried to imagine what the hearing would be like, what Somerled would say, and how a man such as himself might counter the arguments of such an expert law speaker.

The light from outside suggested late afternoon or early evening. Eyvind sat on his straw pallet, concentrating hard, making sure he could remember all the details of Ulf's death, and what had been said during that day on High Island. The blood . . . the dead eye . . . the knots . . . Somerled's voice, shrill with shock . . . He was jolted back to the present by a hoarse whisper from the door. Grim stood beyond the grille, flaxen hair, bristling beard, anxious eyes.

"Eyvind!" he hissed. "Wake up, man!"

Eyvind rose and moved forward. He said nothing.

"Listen," whispered Grim, mouth close to the narrow bars of the door. "Shouldn't be here, haven't got long. Might be able to get you out. You game for it?"

Eyvind could not help himself, his heart thumped, his blood surged with hope. A friend, freedom, a chance to live—gods, how he wanted that!

"How?" he murmured.

"Suppertime, little diversion, one of us slips the bolt. End of the hallway, there's a yard, and a couple of old nags. Up to you then. We'd keep them busy, give you a fighting chance. Better than nothing. What do you say?"

"I can't." There was no choice; he had known that all along.

"What!"

"I can't. I have to face him; have to tell my side of the story. But thanks. I thought I had no friends left here."

"Huh." Grim's eyes flicked one way and the other, watching for the returning guards. "We don't think much of what you've done. That doesn't mean we want you dead. Why not? Why not get away? You've about as much chance against *him*," he jerked his head in the general direction of the hall, "as a naked babe against an armed warrior. None, that is. Better to die a free man, surely."

"I can't. Someone has to tell the truth, and it looks as if I'm the only possibility. Grim?"

"What?"

"Where's Eirik? I sent him a message, a while ago. Why isn't he here?"

Grim scowled. "Don't know. Seen nothing of the pair of them, him and Thord, since long before we took the Whale-back. Busy with the ship, I should think. Nearly time to sail. Still, this isn't like him. Eyvind—"

Grim broke off as footsteps sounded along the hallway: the guards returning. "You sure?" he hissed.

Eyvind nodded. Inexplicably, there seemed to be tears in his eyes, and he turned away so his old comrade could not see this sign of weakness. He had to be strong: strong, clever, and calm, like Somerled. The arguments, the facts; he would go over them once more, make sure he would be able to relate them clearly, even with Somerled looking right at him, ready to pounce on any flaws. He sat down again on the straw pallet and tried to concentrate, but his mind seemed to have stopped cooperating. The images he saw in the shadowy cell were not of the voyage to High Island, the climb, the mist, the desperate search and sickening discovery. Instead, he saw the forest above Ham-marsby and two boys walking along a narrow path under tall firs. They went soft-footed, knives and spears ready for the hunt, moving together in a silence of complete understanding. One felt pride: *He's good at this now, and I taught him.* What the other felt, there was no telling. He saw them younger, in the red light of a winter dawn on the frozen lake, one unsteady on his new skates, the other supporting with kind words and strong arms. He saw himself with crudely splinted leg, face white as chalk, staggering down the rocky hillside, and a small, fierce-eyed Somerled struggling to keep him upright. The grim jaw, the scowling determination of that exhausted child set him apart; surely, Eyvind thought, such single-minded courage had destined Somerled for greatness. And he had indeed become a king, just as the seer had foretold.

But . . . this travesty based on murder, cruelty and lies, this mockery of a true monarch's rule, surely it was not this the cat woman had spoken of? Even he, stupid, muddled Eyvind, whose only skill was with sword and axe, could have done a better job as leader here. For all his cleverness, Somerled had got everything wrong. They must be made to see that. He would make them see it. Eyvind lay down and closed his eyes. Without rest, he had no hope of keeping his wits about him when the time came. *Sleep safely, Bright Star. My hand in yours.*

Sometime in the darkness Eyvind was woken by voices and the flare of torches, and the sound of bolts being scraped open. It seemed to be time to move. Erlend and Holgar conveyed him out to the hall, his feet still hobbled. Neither said a word, nor did they lay hands on him this time, but walked on either side as if uncertain which they were, warders or bodyguards.

The hall was alive with lamplight and movement and the buzz of anticipatory voices. They ushered Eyvind to the center, facing the table at which Somerled sat, flanked by the men who had been his brother's advisers, and by some who had been elevated by the new chieftain's favor. The captain of the knarr was there: the knarr on which a man called Firehead had died. On every side of the long chamber, men sat on benches or stood in small groups, talking among themselves; the place was packed as full as a temple at the time of sacrifice. *No white goat this time, only a man.* Eyvind's thoughts spun in a way he much disliked, but could not halt. *And Somerled has learned to use the knife; I taught him myself.* He blinked and straightened his shoulders. There must be no sign of weakness. Keep still, stand upright, set a guard on eyes and tongue that they betray no secrets, tell no more than was strictly necessary.

The hum of voices ceased. Somerled had risen to his feet. He wore a little circlet of finely wrought silver in place of his customary neat hairband; he appeared quite pale, very serious, and every bit a king.

"I call this assembly to order," he said gravely, not raising his voice. "The matters we must deal with tonight are dark and troubling. They touch on the very safety and security of our settlements on this shore. Our enemy works subtly. He seeks to undermine us by turning our most loyal servants and comrades to traitors, our dearest friends to enemies. Do not think that the great victory we achieved at the Whaleback was the end of this struggle. Oh, no. The fight goes on in the hidden crevices and corners of this land, in the dark caves and sinister places of the earth, on the far-flung islands. The evil works subtly; it is under our very noses, in front of our very eyes before we see it in its true colors." Somerled sighed, his dark gaze intent on Eyvind. "That is why this hearing has been called without delay. I will not lie to you. You know this man has been my closest friend since childhood, dearer than a brother, sworn to me by blood. You know the pain I feel in pursuing this. I did indeed speak with him, offer help, seeing, as he could not see, the poison our enemy had slipped into his mind. But Eyvind would have none of it. It was he who demanded the formal hearing I conduct tonight. Perhaps he was right to do so. These charges are of the gravest kind, and if we find him guilty, the penalty will match them in severity. You all know what that means." There was a slight shuffling of feet, a fidgeting around the hall. Grim stood by the western door; Eyvind saw his ferocious scowl. Where was Eirik? Where was Margaret?

"So, we shall commence. I will set forth the charges; Eyvind will have his turn to speak. Decision and penalty will be pronounced tonight, and the sentence carried out at dawn tomorrow. Such affairs unsettle us all; they stand in the way of our plans and endeavors and cast a shadow on the fair fields of our conquest. I cannot have this. I want this over quickly, over and done with."

Men muttered among themselves again; it seemed to Eyvind to have the sound of agreement. Were there no friends here, nobody who would listen? Had Somerled convinced them all before this had even begun?

"Very well, Eyvind." The tone had changed now; it was a silky, deceptively soft voice, one Eyvind had heard before in a court of law, deliciously anticipatory, like the sound in the throat of a cat before it moves to take the prey. "The facts are thus. You led your men forward at Ramsbeck with a courage nobody disputes . . ."

It was an expert account. Somerled held the audience in the palm of his hand as he set out the tale of his Wolfskin's disappearance, his own grief and fury at Eyvind's apparent demise at the hands of King Engus and his warriors. Then there was the ghostly sighting at the lair of the island witches, when he sent his men out to capture Engus's niece. The girl was a sorceress, and had needed to be stopped before she employed her dark arts against his own forces.

As he spoke, Somerled moved out from behind the table and paced to and fro, sometimes behind Eyvind, sometimes before him. Eyvind noticed how this king looked each man in the eye as he passed, as if speaking directly to him. It was unnerving. He set his own gaze forward, fixing on a particular point in the stone wall above the heads of the intently listening arbiters. Soon he himself must speak; he must try to set his case out clearly, weary as he was. He must keep this going, he must not give in. The longer the hearing lasted, the more time he bought for Nessa.

"Then he came back," Somerled was saying, "in the flesh this time. Odin's bones, I've never felt such joy as I did at that moment, seeing my old friend alive, though a mere shadow of himself. We were poised on the brink of our great victory; I needed no more than my Wolfskin's presence to make that day perfect. I sent him forward to take his place among the others in the vanguard, for despite his obvious weakness he seemed hungry for it. And then . . ." Somerled's voice faltered. He looked down at his hands, folded before him. "And then . . . it pains me to put into words what all of you know already. Erlend, lad, stand forward and tell this assembly what happened that dawn at the Whaleback."

Erlend cleared his throat. He was a man of few words; a Wolfskin's realm was the field of battle, the prow of the longship, not an assembly of law, if such a title could be given to this makeshift proceeding.

"My lord, and all gathered here—I can only say what we all saw that morning. Eyvind's return gladdened our hearts. It seemed a bright omen that he had come back to us on that particular day, at that particular time. It had Thor's mark on it. I did think Eyvind somewhat . . . somewhat changed, ill perhaps, and weakened from so long living wild. We did not know where he had been, and he told us he had forgotten. Then, at the moment of advance, he . . ."

"Take your time," said Somerled kindly.

"He did the unthinkable," Erlend muttered. "Disobeyed Thor's call and your orders, my lord. Tried to stand against us. He was shouting nonsense, wild accusations, a madman's babble. We had no choice but to take him down, the three of us. He endangered the mission."

Eyvind kept his gaze on the wall. He counted the stones up to twenty and started again, trying not to hear the anguish in Erlend's voice. To jeopardize the mission was the worst offense a warrior could commit—almost the worst.

"Thank you," Somerled said. "You can sit down now." He lifted his hands wide, turning to encompass the entire crowd assembled there with his gesture. "What could one do?. What could one think? There was a woman in it, of course: who but Engus's own niece, the witch whom we burned with her uncle that morning? I saw the fury in the Wolfskin's eyes when he heard of her demise. It was clear to me he had been seduced by this girl's sorcery. Eyvind's always been a little naïve where the ladies are concerned. There was a whore back home in Freyrsfjord; half the men of the settlement had been through her, but our friend here still bristled with righteous anger if one made the slightest reference to the lady's . . . generosity."

Laughter rippled around the room. Eyvind clenched his teeth. *He's trying to rattle you,* he told himself. *Stay calm.*

"Eyvind gave the slattern flowers and words of love. The rest of us gave her no more and no less than she expected," Somerled said dryly.

Eyvind closed his eyes a moment. *Signe never lay with you. She would have told me.*

"This is a simple sort of fellow, one you want beside you in the field, for he is—was—renowned for his courage and his skill in arms. He's not a man you'd send on an errand requiring wit or diplomacy. In many ways, this great warrior is like a child: easily pleased, easily led. He was like unformed clay in the hands of these people. It took but the space of a season for them to confuse and corrupt him. He returned to us damaged beyond repair. My friends, this man you see before you can no longer tell right from wrong, friend from foe. I tried to reason with him, I tried to help him. Eyvind would have none of it. He seems fixed in this skewed vision. And alas, in such a state he is

a danger to us and to all our endeavors. A man strong as an ox
and addled in his wits cannot be let loose in a small, contained
realm such as this. And who would bear him across the sea as
an exile? One does not undertake a long ocean voyage with a
dangerous madman on board. I weep to say it, but I see only
one answer here."

There was silence, a silence that drew out as Somerled folded
his arms, and gazed at Eyvind a while, then slowly, as if himself stepping toward an executioner's axe, walked to resume his
seat among the arbiters. Not one man present uttered so much
as a whisper.

Eyvind drew a deep breath. He gripped his hands together
before him, lest they begin to shake. "May I speak now?" he
asked as steadily as he could.

There was a stir at the side of the hall, near the doorway.

"I've a question first!" It was a rough voice, Grim's, loud
with nervousness.

"You speak out of turn." Somerled's tone was chill. "The accused man is next. Questions later."

"In the Thing, at home, a man has his kin to support him.
This isn't right. Where's his brother? Eirik should—"

"Enough!" This time the voice was a lash. "Do you accuse
me of being inequitable in my treatment? You, a Wolfskin?
What do you know of the law?" Somerled turned to the man by
his side, Harald Silvertongue, who had been Ulf's law speaker.
"You explain," he said sharply.

Harald rose slowly to his feet. His hands were restless, nervously plucking at the fabric of his long robe, twisting and
twining together. "Eirik Hallvardsson was sent for some time
ago," he said. "As you see, he hasn't made an appearance. If an
accused man's brother does not come to his aid, that says something about the nature of the offense, does it not?"

"Where is Lady Margaret?" Eyvind asked suddenly. "Should
she not be present here, as the widow of our former chieftain?"

Somerled raised his brows. "We're dealing with a matter between king and subject here," he said coolly. "This has nothing
to do with Margaret. Besides, she's away from the settlement."

"What I have to say has everything to do with her," Eyvind
said. "We should wait for her, and for my brother. Back home in
Rogaland, a man has time to prepare his case, to gather his sup-

port—" He faltered to a stop, seeing the hard finality in Somerled's eyes.

"We're no longer in Rogaland," the king said. "And you're wasting time: your own time. Speak up. What explanation can you offer for your bizarre acts of treachery? Or do you tell us it was some other man who stood up there on the causeway and swung his axe against his own comrades?"

The moment had come, and there was no help at all. Even Grim had been cowed to silence. "No, my lord." Good, his voice was steady: a pity about the hands and the thumping heart. "The charges as you lay them are true, in terms of fact. I did stand against your forces, and I do not regret it. Your actions at the Whaleback were wrong, deeply wrong." He felt the shudder that ran through the hall; he had just signed his own death warrant. "I trust only that tonight I may give you an account of my reasons, an insight into what you call a great victory." He tried the trick Somerled had used, turning so that every man present might meet his eyes for a moment, read his expression. It was awkward; the iron shackles that hobbled his ankles were but a handspan apart, joined by a heavy chain that clanked as he moved. "Do I seem crazed or wild? I am as sane as I ever was; saner, maybe, for now I see truth where once I hid from it. That was no victory, but a cruel and barbarous massacre, and the man who led it holds kingship here on the flimsiest of grounds. He sent you into attack on a day when your adversary held mourning rites for close kin. That breached the rules of right engagement; any leader worth his salt knows that. Yet not one of you dared challenge his decision."

"It's not I who am on trial here," Somerled said quietly. The men beside him murmured agreement.

"Get on with it," said Harald Silvertongue testily. "We're not interested in the pros and cons of the battle, only your part in it. Right engagement, and so on, is all very well when you're facing an enemy of your own kind; the Danes, for instance. With primitive tribes, like this one here, such niceties are inappropriate."

"Have you forgotten the treaty sworn on both ring and stone?" Eyvind asked. "Ulf made peace with these folk, a pact solemn and binding. Do you clasp hands one day in promise of amity, and the next day stick a knife in your ally's back?"

"You're a fine one to speak of promises," Somerled said

evenly. "Did you and I not swear an oath of loyalty in blood? Yet you sought to undermine my great endeavor. Even now, you stand in my hall and accuse me of some kind of double dealing. And you have broken another, deeper oath: your oath to Thor. That show of defiance at the Whaleback, that brief display of dazzling strength, it was all an illusion, wasn't it? Thor has lost patience with you; he has abandoned his favorite son. You just can't fight anymore." He gazed about the room, eyes bright. "War fetter, my friends, the malady men dare not name. It has clutched even at our brightest and most dauntless warrior. What other reason could there be for his flight after the battle of Ramsbeck?"

A great weariness descended on Eyvind. He was aware of the trembling in his hands, the ache in his knees, the haziness in his head. Sounds seemed to come and go in waves. This would not do at all. He had barely begun to tell them. His hand came up to touch the place where Nessa's small token still lay beneath his tunic, next to his skin.

"I acted as I did to preserve the treaty," he said, finding the strength somewhere to make his voice steady. "The Folk of the islands treated us with generosity. We repaid them with death. If that is what it means to be a warrior, then perhaps it is a blessing I can no longer wield the axe as once I did. I know one thing. I cannot follow a chieftain who has his own brother's blood on his hands."

"What!" Harald Silvertongue had risen to his feet again, and so had Olaf Sveinsson on the king's other side. The hall buzzed with shocked voices. Somerled himself sat tranquil as ever.

"The fellow's crazy!" Olaf exploded. "This is dangerous nonsense."

"Indeed," put in Harald. "Let us hear no more of this rubbish. If Eyvind Hallvardsson can't keep to the point, his account of himself is not worth listening to."

"Not at all," said Somerled gently. "When a man faces a sentence of death, we must at least give him a hearing, however distasteful his manner of expression. Far be it from me to gag his arguments as soon as they seem to touch too closely on my own actions. Do go on, Eyvind. I never thought to hear you putting forth a legal case, old friend; this is truly a novel experience."

There were a few chuckles, but the prevailing mood was as somber as the look in Somerled's eyes; for all the king's banter, it was clear to Eyvind that he understood this was a fight to the death.

"I make no apology for my manner of speaking," Eyvind said. "Like Erlend, I'm a fighter, not a courtier. I'm here to tell the truth, that's all, to be heard before you decide my fate. I stand by what I've said. As Somerled told you, I'm a simple man. I cannot spin magic with my words to change men's minds for them and make them see black as white, or white black. I wish to speak of a day on High Island, a day when our good chieftain, Ulf, was slain in accordance with a foretelling, and his brother took his place as leader. Will you hear me?"

There was a frozen silence. Then Olaf Sveinsson said thinly, "This matter has no relevance to the charges. My lord king, it grows late. Must we listen to this?"

"Why not?" asked Somerled lightly, and leaned back in his chair, narrowing his eyes to slits and folding his arms. "It's free entertainment, after all; we get little enough of that in this god-forsaken corner of the world. Please continue, Eyvind."

Borrowing a trick from Somerled, Eyvind turned around, spreading his hands in a gesture that encompassed those at the rear of the hall, the Wolfskins, the guards, the men of lesser rank. "You know me," he said simply. "You know I don't have it in me to tell falsehoods. Somerled was my friend. As boys, we spent many a season in close companionship, on the hunt, in the fields of my mother's holding at Hammarsby, skating on the lake there, telling tales by the fire. Know then that it pains me deeply to speak thus against him, for he is a man of many admirable qualities, whom once I deemed well fit to lead. When we were children, he told how he would one day be a king, and the others laughed. I believed him. I think I sensed then what I understand now—that he would let no one stand in the way of his ambition, not even his own brother."

There was a rumble of voices around the hall, then silence as Eyvind spoke again. "I have strong cause to believe that Somerled intended all along to take Ulf's place," he said quietly, fixing his gaze again on the stones of the wall above the king's head, for he could not look into those implacable dark eyes and say what he must say now. "There was no love lost between them; there never had been. Ulf did not want Somerled at court. He seized at every chance to leave his brother with us on the farm. Ulf dreaded bringing him on this voyage."

"Dreaded," Somerled drawled, "that's a little strong. But it's true Ulf didn't want me here. It was Eyvind himself who won me a place on the knarr: a fine act of friendship for which I remain immensely grateful."

"I did so, it is true. It is to my continuing guilt and shame that I ensured he could travel to this shore. For when Ulf brought his brother to the Light Isles, he brought unquiet. He brought blood and cruelty. He brought his own death."

Now there was complete silence. Harald Silvertongue's fingers seemed the only thing moving in the chamber as they played restlessly with a spoon someone had left on the board from supper. Eventually Harald cleared his throat and spoke.

"These are grave matters, Wolfskin. Since my lord king wishes to hear your tale, it seems we must let you speak. I see no way in which these accusations can aid your own cause. Spare us the details, at least, and keep your account brief."

Olaf muttered agreement; Somerled was silent. He was gazing with interest down the hall past Eyvind, and despite himself, Eyvind turned his head to look. There were women passing along the chamber now with jugs of ale, filling the cups as they went, young dark-haired women clad in plain skirts and overtunics, green, red, blue; girls with ghost-pale skin and shadowed eyes. One bore a livid bruise to the cheek; the other walked carefully, as if bearing an unseen hurt. They were daughters of the islands: Nessa's people. The sight of them captive in this place stirred Eyvind to fury and terror. He saw, in the moment before he looked away, how the hands of men moved to grope, to fondle, to pinch as they passed, and how fierce resentment warred with fear on the drained young faces. One of the girls spat at a man's feet, and the fellow cuffed her on the ear, and there was a roar of laughter from the knot of warriors who stood nearby. Eyvind turned back to face Somerled, and Somerled's lips twisted in a smile.

Time, Eyvind reminded himself. *Play for time; keep Nessa safe.* "Very well," he said. "If you want a brief tale, you shall have one, brief and bloody, a tale to sicken men's hearts . . ."

He set it out as well as he could. It was a plain account; he had not Somerled's flair with words, his dazzling wit. There was the journey to High Island, the climb, the mist, the terrible search and grisly discovery. He did not think he had left anything out, though it was getting harder and harder to think straight. The faces of the arbiters were blurring now, and the lamps seemed to be dancing before his eyes. He tried to explain how fear and prejudice had blinded them all. Why would King Engus want Ulf dead? The respect between the two of them was plain to see, and never more than on that visit to the ancient tomb. Then he spoke of Hakon's death. They must understand that the islanders could not have committed that crime, it went against all they believed in. Didn't anyone remember how Somerled had threatened this most loyal of Wolfskins? The fire that killed Hakon was lit on Somerled's orders, as a demonstration of control. They must see that. They must see how this new leader had turned Ulf's vision of peace into a nightmare of blood and conquest.

Eyvind's voice was shaking; he needed to sit down. He tried to brace his legs, to square his shoulders. The young islander women were leaving the hall now, ale jugs empty. The fine small features, the proud carriage, the moon-pale skin brought Nessa sharply back to his mind. Thor's hammer, was it only this morning that he had held her in his arms, felt the whisper of her long hair across his skin, the warmth of her body close-folded with his own, his other half, his completion? The women were gone. He turned back; watching him, Somerled gave a slow smile.

"What are you trying to do here, Wolfskin?" Harald Silver-tongue took a draft of ale and set the cup heavily back on the table. "Your account is rambling and incoherent. Are you laying charges against the king, that the penalty for your own misdeeds may be set against the price of his? Justice is not dispensed in the old way here in Hrossey. Did you not understand when the king explained that?" His tone was not without kindness.

"Eyvind's never been quick to grasp such matters," Somerled said gently. "I well remember the time I tried to teach him how to make his name in runes; that task tested my patience hard, I can tell you. I might make this a little easier for him, or we'll be

here all night. Eyvind, you can't press charges purely on
hearsay. You must have proof. If I tell you I had no part in what
happened to Hakon, that must be good enough for you, unless
you can find witnesses who will tell otherwise. A legal assembly can take no account of unsupported claims such as these.
Do you understand?"

Eyvind's vision blurred again, and cleared. He didn't seem to
have any feeling in his legs. He set his jaw and made himself
look directly into Somerled's dark, unreadable eyes. "I understand," he said, drawing a deep breath. "I will speak no more of
Hakon, whose killing was designed to inflame us against Engus's people. I will not speak of other actions that must lie
heavily on Somerled's conscience: the rape of a girl who was
little more than a child, the cold-blooded killing of a man who
sought to avenge that ill deed. I asked for an open hearing for
one purpose only: so I could tell all assembled here that this
man murdered his brother. He did it to achieve the kingship he
has craved since boyhood. His rise to power has been based on
a heinous crime against nature and kinship. That morning at the
Whaleback, I knew I could no longer follow him, and I believed
all had a right to know the truth about this fine new leader before they made their own choices of allegiance. Either Somerled
did the deed himself, or he hired others to do it for him. I know
how ruthless he is. I have seen it over and over, since he was a
mere child. I know him better than anyone. The mark of his
hand is clear in the manner of Ulf's death, so carefully planned,
so faithful to every detail of the foretelling whose shadow our
good chieftain bore with him even to this fair place. Believe
that I speak the truth. That is the only way I know." His breath
was coming shorter, as if he had run a race; he ended on a whisper, and the lights seemed to brighten and fade in a sort of pattern. He wondered if he were about to faint.

There was a scraping sound; Grim had come up behind him,
kicking a three-legged stool in place next to Eyvind's hobbled
ankles.

"What's this, Wolfskin?" Somerled's voice, for the first time,
betrayed a hint of annoyance. "Did I give you permission to approach the prisoner?"

"Sit down, you fool," growled Grim under his breath, and

Eyvind sat. He would be precious little use to Nessa's cause, or to himself, if he collapsed unconscious on the ground. Somerled would not hesitate to conclude the proceedings without him, pronouncing both verdict and penalty in his absence. He must keep going: every moment was time gained for Nessa.

Somerled's eyes bored down the long chamber in Grim's general direction. "I'll speak to you later," he said crisply. "A man who does not heed orders has but a short stay in my household, and there's precious little else offering in these parts. Now, where were we? Ah, yes: my brother. I'm impressed by the boldness of your statement, Eyvind. I can't conceive of how I could have carried out the murder. Indeed, it's difficult to imagine anyone committing a crime in such bizarre circumstances. To do such a deed would have required a man of exceptional strength. My brother was no weakling, and his will to survive would have been formidable. He had a quest here, a vision that had driven him a long time. It was Ulf who was the ruthless one, Eyvind, not I. He could barely wait for our father's death to sell up and start making his great ship. The old man was scarcely cold in his grave when the agreements were drawn up."

"And you lost your birthright," Eyvind said softly, feeling the strange dizziness come and go in his head.

Somerled shrugged. "That meant little. I have always gone my own way."

"Wolfskin?" Olaf's voice was sharp. "You accuse the king of no less than fratricide, a crime abhorrent to any right-thinking man or woman. Your allegation appears to be entirely unsubstantiated. We can go no farther down this path unless you have proof. Are there witnesses whom you can call? Is there material evidence? If you have neither, then we will hear no more of your arguments. I remind you, Somerled is not on trial here, but you are, and it is your life that rests in the balance. You'd be wise not to forget that."

"I understand," Eyvind said, wondering vaguely whether the odd way his sight and hearing were behaving had anything to do with the injuries he had sustained during the day, or perhaps with Grim's well-aimed hammer blow. "If I had been afforded time, as I would have been had Jarl Magnus presided over this hearing, I would most certainly have found witnesses. A crime such as Ulf's murder, carried out with such delicate attention to detail, is not achieved without the knowledge of several men, at least."

"Not unless the fellow that does it is of superhuman strength," observed Olaf. "So, you're telling us there are no witnesses?"

"I cannot produce them tonight. Will you not at least consider the manner of the killing? Ulf and his brother were together on the cliffs. They disappeared together when the mist came down. We did not see Somerled again until the sun had risen high on another day, and when he did reappear, his account of himself was sketchy and implausible. My lords, I myself trained Somerled in hunting and tracking, in the pathless forests of Rogaland. High Island is a bare, open place, where crags and hillsides offer wide vistas of land and sea. Somerled could never have been lost that day. He knows his way by sun and shadow. He knew the foretelling in every aspect. He had influence, men who would spring to do his bidding, men whom he had charmed into becoming willing lackeys, men who would murder without scruples to win a place among his inner circle." Eyvind glanced at the knarr's captain, and the man stared back, red-faced, his small, angry eyes full of dislike. "There was nobody else there that day who could have done this."

"Nonsense." Somerled's tone was smooth. "There were four men scattered on the hillside that night, and none returned at dawn. There were nine men waiting at the starting point, sleeping rough, unable to see their own hands before their eyes in the mist. I put it to you that any one, or two, of those men had as much opportunity as another to carry out the killing. All was confusion in the morning, so I'm told. I wandered dazed for the better part of the day, as did others. Who can say what took place there on the cliffs, and in what sequence? I only know my brother was cruelly slain, and that the nature of it pointed to King Engus. These island folk don't think the way we do. The place is rife with superstition and sorcerous practices. Does not the manner of this killing suggest a sacrifice, perhaps to propitiate the anger of the ocean? One cannot make allies of a people so different in beliefs and in blood.' "

"Eyvind." It was Olaf Sveinsson who spoke, his gaze intent on the accused man. "Without evidence, there is no validity in your accusations. It is time for these proceedings to be drawn to a close. We're all weary. If the king agrees, I think we should take time now to discuss this in private, and you should be returned to your cell. You seem unwell; rest will prepare you better to face what is to come. Are we agreed?" He turned to Somerled, and Somerled nodded.

"There is evidence!" Eyvind sprang to his feet, his voice cracking with desperation. This could not end now, so soon: what about Nessa? "I had it in my possession that morning at the Whaleback, and Somerled stole it from me. Ask him, if you dare."

Harald and Olaf both looked at Somerled. Somerled was watching Eyvind, and he wore once again that smugly anticipatory look. Now, thought Eyvind, now Somerled will say something like, *I can't imagine what you mean, Eyvind,* and remind them all how dangerous a strong man can become when he loses his mind.

"Do you know what he means, my lord?" asked Harald. There was a little pause. The hall had fallen very quiet, save for a slight disturbance at the far door, where it seemed somebody had just come in.

"I believe I do," said Somerled smoothly, reaching into a pocket of his tunic. "You mean this, do you, Eyvind?" He drew out a small object and placed it on the table before him. Eyvind shuffled closer. Thor's hammer, Somerled was indeed a bold player; there was surely no way he could twist this to his own advantage. Eyvind's heart was drumming violently; he felt the rush of blood in his ears, the sweat breaking out all over his body. For there on the table, clear and plain for all to see, still twisted in a tangle of knotted, bloody cords, lay Ulf's silver belt buckle.

There was one peg left. The sea woman held it between her sharp white teeth. She gnawed gently, taking it out from time to time to squint at the shape, slipping it back to grind away again. At length, apparently satisfied, she fitted it into the last little hole and sat back on her heels with a contented burble of melody. The others reached out their hands, gravely offering Nessa the six strings they had crafted from close-plaited hair.

Though the strands were silk-fine, she had seen the making and knew each had its particular thickness, its note, and its place. Now she must string them on the frame and awaken the voice of the dead. But it was dark; none but an owl or night mouse might see to perform such a task. Without these wondrous daughters of the ocean, she could not have come even this far. Still, she almost wished for the Hidden Tribe again; at least they brought their own light with them.

"I can't see," she said, her voice trembling. "How can I do this?"

Around her, the women of the Seal Tribe sat in silence now, as if waiting. *Think, Nessa.* It was hard to obey her own command, for she was weary, and her back hurt, and it seemed like a very long time since she had last eaten. And there was the nagging fear: her own folk enslaved, abused, Eyvind at terrible risk, because of her. *Think.* The beach, the stillness, the knife in her hand: the knife, that was the key to this. Nessa rose to her feet; she faced the west and moved in place to cast her circle, quite a small one in the darkness. She breathed the words of salutation and acknowledgment to each quarter, and turned back toward the ocean. Now her voice was not a whisper, now her chant did not waver but came pure and true. Around the circle, the five sea women stood silent as the last priestess of the Folk uttered her invocation.

"Powers of the earth, spirits of the ocean, deities of air and fire, I salute you! I acknowledge your power; I thank you for your guidance. My call is a grave one and desperate. You who watch over our steps day by day, season by season, you have seen what has befallen these peaceful isles. Our king is slain, our men cut down like stalks of barley harvested too soon, lost and wasted. Our women are captive, our little ones walk with fear-filled eyes, the wisdom of our old folk is cast aside. The Kin Stone is thrown down, the Folk are shrunk to a shadow of what they were. We cling on by the merest finger; we are a hair's breadth from destruction. So soon have the islands been shorn of their human guardians, in the space from one springtime to the next. An evil has come to this shore, a darkness, which has stolen our lands, our homes, our lives. Somerled Horse-Master would rob us of our future; he would erase even the memory of what we were."

The sea women had begun to sing again, low and pure, a flowing chant that wreathed itself around Nessa's words. Their voices hummed in her blood, chorused in her breath, lending her strength.

"These men from the snow lands were not all bad. He who led them here sought peace; he came in friendship. For that, he was himself struck down. I seek to awaken his voice. I would bear him home to his own hall, and let him speak truth for all to hear. And there is another, who even now risks death to bear witness on our behalf. If I am not by his side in time, he will be slaughtered as our own men were. This must not be. I have heard the voice of deep earth, the voice of Bone Mother. Eyvind is our warrior. He fought and fell for us on our day of blood and terror, because I sent him forth to speak for the Folk. A lesser man could not have survived what was done to him, but he freed himself and came to aid me. This champion has yet a part to play here, a part far greater than simply to suffer a senseless death. We have lost too many good men in this season of carnage. Help me to save him. Help me to save the daughters of the Folk, held captive in Somerled's settlement. Help me awaken the voice of Ulf, dreamer of dreams, the only true witness to what this cruel chieftain really is. Give me light! Guide me forth on this journey!"

The song of the Seal Tribe rose into the night, complex and lovely, strand on strand of graceful melody, weaving and tangling around Nessa's still form as stars appeared one by one, glittering points of brightness in the shadowy blue of the sky. Her heart keeping time with the wild music, Nessa raised her hands in a gesture that was more fierce demand than respectful supplication. Guard now added an eldritch howling to the night sounds, and overhead an owl hooted, passing by on the hunt. The sea washed in and out, in and out; a whisper of breeze shivered through Nessa's hair and stirred the fronded tresses of her strange companions.

She closed her eyes in silent meditation, stilling her racing heart, slowing her breathing, calming her mind until the deepest of voices spoke inside her. *What of you? There is a part of this tale not told. What does your heart tell you, priestess? Will you keep faith with me?*

"I will," she breathed. Tears pricked her eyes; she did not allow them to fall. "All that I must do to keep the islands safe and to preserve their secrets, I will do. All that I must do to ensure the Folk survive and endure as custodians of this fair land, I will do. I swear this as your priestess. And I swear it as the last of the royal line here in the Light Isles."

She stood unmoving, feeling the weight of exhaustion through every part of her body. It was necessary to go on. She would find the strength somewhere. Nessa opened her eyes and saw pale light beginning to creep over the landscape, touching the sand to faintest silver, illuminating the delicate, naked forms of her companions, pearly breast, snowy arm, long flank, the sweet curves of bodies that were not quite those of women. She turned; the little harp stood gleaming white under the rising moon, awaiting the strings that would release its voice.

"It is good," Nessa said gravely. "Very good. I thank you from the bottom of my heart. And I will be true to my word." Then she stepped around again, unmaking the circle, as the sea women's chant ebbed and flowed like a powerful tide. They crouched again by the harp, and one by one the dark strands of woven hair were looped and hooked at the base, where Nessa had made notches in the bone, and wound with cautious fingers around the cunning small pegs set in the upper part of the frame. One, two . . . four, five . . . As each was strung in place and the peg turned to tighten it, Nessa could feel the growing power of the thing she had made; it did indeed bear the life of the chieftain whose body had furnished its materials, and it seemed eager, straining to sound forth the words that had been snatched away from him by death.

I am . . . Ulf . . . She felt the hairs on the back of her neck prickle, and a cold thrill go down her spine. *Twisted . . . bound . . .* the harp whispered. *Som . . . Somer . . .* Nessa was almost afraid to set the last string in place. But the sea women were hastening her along again: *The path, up there, to the east, run, run, hurry, hurry!* She slipped the slender fiber into the notch, twined it around the little finger bone, turn on turn so it held itself in place; she began to tighten the peg. There was a sudden hissing, and when she looked up, they were shaking their heads in warning, their liquid eyes anxious.

"Not yet?" Nessa queried, heart thumping. "Ah, I understand. Not until we reach Somerled's hall. Only then do we re-

lease this voice." She wrapped the little harp carefully in the
bag, which not long ago had held only jumbled bones. "Now I
must leave you. I thank you for your aid. Without you, this
would not have been made."

They acknowledged her with a flurry of notes like the fluting
of meadow birds, a dazzling, bright music of recognition. *We
are sisters. Go safely.*

There were scraps of bone left over, slivers and shards.
Nessa gathered them with respect and laid them gently in a
sheltered corner of the cave. She rolled the wolfskin up once
more and fastened it tightly. Guard was waiting, his ears laid
back, his tail between his legs. He seemed less than steady on
his feet. It was a long way up the cliff path, and a longer one
across the moonlit fields to Somerled's hall.

Now two of the sea women came forward, a small bundle or
package held before them on outstretched hands. The tone of
their song, the courteous bowing of their heads indicated this
was a gift, and Nessa must take it with her. It was wrapped in
what might have been cloth, or dried weed, or the hide of some
creature only seen in deepest waters.

"Th–thank you," Nessa faltered. "I don't know how I can
carry—"

Long hands reached to fasten the package on her back, a
cord of twisted seaweed tying it in place. Nessa drew a deep
breath. She bore the wolfskin under one arm, the harp cradled
by the other. It was a steep path, and narrow. There was simply
no room for any error. She had sworn she would do this, and
she must.

"Farewell," she told them. "I won't forget what you have
done. I understand its importance. We are of one kind, my sisters, for all our differences."

They reached to touch her then, a whisper of fingertips
against her cheek, brushing her hair, stroking her arm, clinging
to her hand. Their skin was so cold, as cold as hoarfrost, and
there was a faint, constant trembling in them, as if the ebb and
flow of the sea were present in their flesh, even while they so-
journed on land. Their voices sang greeting and farewell: *Sister,
our sister. So brave, so true. Go forth, go safe.*

Guard hung back, reluctant even to begin the journey. He
stood at the foot of the path whining, a sound that increased in

anxiety as Nessa, heart sinking, made her cautious way upward in the faint light from the moon, which hung low in the sky somewhere beyond the clifftop. There could be no delays. There was no mistaking the message: if this was not done to-night, it would be too late. Behind her, Guard whimpered again. It sounded as if he was a long way back. She waited, trying not to look down, making her voice reassuring.

"Good boy, Guard. Come on, now. It's not far."

There was a hissing from below, as if the sea women sought to harry the hound on his way; a sudden scrabbling followed, and then silence. She could not tell where he was. She turned her head, peering back in the dim light. Below her, far below, the moonlight gleamed on white water. Her stomach churned; a wave of dizziness swept over her. On, she must go on, that was the only thing that mattered.

"Guard?" She had spotted him, crouched frozen on the path a short way up from the shore. She could not help him, burdened as she was. Perhaps she could reach the top, put down what she carried and then go back for him. He had been so faithful, so strong; she could not leave him behind. But suppose she fetched him safely up, what then? To reach the settlement in time she must ride, she must steal a horse from somewhere, and if she did that, Guard would not be able to keep up.

Nessa crept on up the path. Behind her, there was now no sound but the sigh of the sea far below, the sleepy calls of gulls on the ledges. She was breathless and her body ached. It had been foolish to forget the importance of eating, for now she was faint and her strength was flagging fast. She could imagine what Rona would have said. *Foolish girl! Even a priestess must eat and drink. The mind can't help you if you don't help the body. Here, get this broth into you.*

A cloud came over the moon, and the path in front of her vanished. She froze in place. Her burdened hands could not be used to feel the way; all she could do was stand completely still on the ledge, her back pressed against the rock wall. By day, the wide vista of western ocean would make a fine sight before her, criss-crossed by the flights of foraging birds, gull and puffin, tern and guillemot, circling and passing in their dance of survival. Now, in the darkness, she knew only the immensity of the drop before her, the narrow margin of safety, as small as the length of her foot, the yawning black emptiness ready for her fall, her own last flight. Nausea gripped her belly; she fought for control, her fingers curling into the long, soft pelt of the wolfskin. *I want so much to live. More than I've ever wanted anything before.* The moon emerged once more; cool, pale light frosted the cliffs with silver, and made a shining pathway on the dark water. Nessa walked forward, not knowing if the voice she had heard was her own or another's, borne on some strange wind from the east. "I'm coming," she whispered. "I'll be there soon. Wait for me."

Guard's whine came faintly from somewhere far below. He was surely no farther up the path than he had been that first time, and now she was near the top, and must go on. How could she fetch him? He was a big dog, and her own strength was ebbing even as his had. He whined again, and now there was an answer from above her, a strong, spirited barking ringing out from the clifftop. Nessa's heart clenched tight with alarm. Somerled's men, with dogs: they had somehow followed her, and now waited up there to seize her as they had Eyvind. The harp would be lost, the one chance gone, for the fragile instrument would fall in pieces if it were dropped or manhandled. Somerled's people thought her a witch, working her spells to harm them. They would surely destroy what she bore before ever its voice might be heard.

The barking continued, deep and vibrant, and now there was a scrabbling, sliding sound of claws on the slippery rocks of the path, and all of a sudden Guard was right behind her, the noise he made surely not a warning but a call of recognition, a joyous greeting. Against the odds, he had made the climb in a fraction of the time it had taken Nessa.

"Good boy," she breathed, and since there was no other choice possible, she took the last few steps up to the clifftop. The moment she set foot on level ground she was all but bowled over, for the hound that bounded up to greet her was healthy and strong, and it came close to sending her straight down to the ocean far below in its frenzied excitement. Now Guard reached the top, and the two of them, like as peas in a pod, ran and chased and sniffed in ecstasy, tails thrashing furiously in the delight of reunion. Shadow. Shadow had disappeared with Rona, that was what Eyvind had said. But it seemed Shadow had come here alone. There were no warriors, there was nobody at all, only the moonlight and the stones.

"Good girl," she murmured, setting the wolfskin down a moment to rest her arm. She stroked the bitch's head, feeling the wet warmth of its tongue against her fingers. "Well done. Now we must move on. I need a horse, and I'll have to catch it in the dark. And then . . ." She could not dwell on the difficulty of doing this, on the impossibility of riding thus burdened. What would Rona say? She imagined her old friend by the fire, stirring a pot of something fragrant—gods, she was hungry—and gazing at her wryly. *You're a priestess. Make things happen.* Some help that was.

Shadow had ceased to leap about and now headed off along a near-invisible path, turning her head as if to check whether Nessa followed. Guard stayed close by his mate's side. It seemed he, at least, had found some untapped well of inner strength, and would keep going beyond the point of utter exhaustion. Perhaps what he had found was hope. Picking up the wolfskin, easing cramped fingers around the other precious item she bore, Nessa followed the two hounds across the dark fields to the east. There were farms not far away. At least, there had been farms not long ago, three snug cottages separated by walled fields, with well-tended beasts, including a horse or two. The men who looked after the stock there had perished at the Whaleback. There was no telling where the women might be. It was toward those dwellings that Shadow was leading them. They walked onward under the moon.

Shadow kept a wide berth around the first house, where the shutters hung splintered and broken, and something made a rhythmic banging in the freshening breeze. There was no sign of life. The second house was burned to stones and rubble, and across its outer yard objects lay scattered: a woollen shawl rent almost in two, a child's shoe, a basket whose cargo of shriveled turnips lay scattered on the ground. Was that blood, or merely some natural darkening of the soil here in the corner where a stile straddled the stone dyke? Shadow jumped up; Guard followed, clumsy in his weakness. Nessa scrambled after them and did not look back. Later, when this was finished, there would be time for sorrow, for grieving, for the rituals of farewell.

They neared the third house. Nessa's heart sank. Lights shone from inside, and the figures of armed men could be seen on watch in the yard. Their garb was that of the Norsemen: iron helms, short cloaks, dark, belted tunics. A great deal of weaponry hung about their bodies.

"Shadow!" she hissed. "Shadow, come back!" For the bitch was sprinting forward now, her barking drawing instant attention to their presence. Guard loped trustingly after her. Nessa crouched by an outhouse, her heart pounding. It could be only moments before the men found her.

One guard was reaching down to pat the bitch; he seemed quite unperturbed by her dramatic arrival. The other came over to stand by his side, hands on hips. They were staring at Guard now; Nessa could hear their tones of astonishment.

"Well, well. What have we here?"

"Thor's hammer! Two of 'em! Didn't they say one went off with . . . ?"

"With the Wolfskin. That's what they said. Vicious brute with teeth like knives, nearly took one fellow's hand off."

"Can't be the same dog," said the second man, reaching to scratch Guard behind the ears. "Skinny thing, but friendly enough. Looks like he's been on the run a while."

The two of them exchanged a glance. Then, without a word, they drew their knives and moved forward, straight toward the most obvious hiding place, the solitary outhouse where Nessa huddled, trembling, by the wall. Shadow bounded ahead, showing the way. In despair, Nessa rose to her feet and moved into the open, speaking in the tongue of the Norsemen.

"I am alone and unarmed. All I want is to travel north unhindered. Please, let me pass."

The two men halted in surprise; whatever they had expected to find, it was not a young woman out in the night alone. They looked at each other again.

"Please," Nessa repeated, keeping her tone soft and sweet though anger burned inside her for the wrongs these folk had done to her people, and fear still clutched at her vitals. "Please, just let me pass. I mean no harm."

The first man's eyes narrowed; he was looking at the rolled-up skin under her arm. "What's that you bear, girl?"

Nessa held her head high. She would tell no lies. "You can

see what it is: a badge of honor, the recognition of your Warfather, Thor. I am a friend of the warrior Eyvind; I journey to Somerled's hall with a message of truth. I must be allowed to proceed unhindered. I must reach that place tonight."

They gazed at her. "Hmm," said one. "Just let you go, is it? I don't think so."

"What's your name?" snapped the other. "Where do you come from? Answer quickly, now." And he reached out to seize her arm in an iron-hard hand. In its wrapping, the harp trembled; Nessa struggled to keep hold of it.

"My name is Nessa. Let me go. I won't try to escape. I'm not so foolish as to believe I can outrun you. Only a weak man, or a very stupid one, uses force against a woman. These dogs will protect me. Look at them."

And indeed, the moment the fellow had laid his hand on Nessa, Shadow's affectionate demeanor had changed. Now her ears were laid back, her head lowered, and a deep growling sounded in her throat. Guard had stationed himself close to the second man, forelegs planted wide, eyes intent as if he were ready to leap into attack the moment the fellow made a move.

The first man cleared his throat. "You can't pass," he said bluntly, but he had relaxed his vise-like grip. "You must come with us."

The door of the cottage opened; a warm light streamed out as the two men made their way back with Nessa walking between them, still holding fast to her precious burdens. The dogs followed, watchful.

"What's going on? Why was the dog barking?"

It was a woman's voice that spoke, and a woman's form silhouetted in the doorway, a slender woman clad in dark gown and pale overdress pinned near the shoulders with twin brooches of silver that glinted in the light.

"What is it, Ash?" she asked.

"An intruder, my lady. Found her out yonder by the grain store. Says she's a friend of the Wolfskin, Eyvind that is, heading for court to see him. Sounds like nonsense, but she's got the skin, and she's got his dog, too."

"Up to no good if you ask me." The other man's voice was gruff. "Girl on her own, wandering around out here at night,

Must be a trick. An ambush; pack of her kinsmen out there waiting to move in. We'd better rouse the other men quick."

"I told you," Nessa said wearily, "I've come here alone, but for the dog. Please let me pass; there's no time to waste. I must reach Somerled's hall before dawn. Please," she said again, looking up at the figure in the doorway.

There was a moment's silence, and then the woman turned slightly so the light from inside caught her features, and Nessa saw that it was Margaret.

THIRTEEN

Olaf stared at the buckle and its tangle of knotted cord, frowning deeply. "Wolfskin," he said, "tell us how you believe this object implicates the king in his brother's killing. There's a mystery here; indeed, I confess myself taken aback that the king did not produce this item far earlier in the proceedings if it has such import." He glanced nervously at Somerled, and quickly away.

"Why bring it out at all if it's got no bearing on the case?" growled the knarr's captain. It was his first contribution to the hearing.

"I will tell you what it means," said Eyvind quietly. "When I was forced to cut this buckle away in order to free Ulf, I thought only to preserve it for my friend, for I knew it to be a family heirloom of some value. I thought it would please Somerled to keep this remembrance of his brother. I did forget it for a long time; my mind was taken up by other matters. Then I had cause to examine the buckle anew, to look at the cords, which you can still see tangled and twisted about it, cords knotted so tightly I could not free the dead man's body without cutting the buckle itself away from his clothing. Look closely, my lord. Have you seen such a knot before, a decorative, neat construction resembling a close-furled flower? It is a difficult knot to make, one

WOLFSKIN 417

that tightens quickly at first, and then more slowly: a knot no
living creature can escape. Ulf fought against it so fiercely that
he came close to severing his own wrist; your chieftain bled to
death from that self-inflicted wound. Whether the gulls came at
him while he still clung to life, or later, there is no telling, but
his body was still warm when I cut him free. No man deserves
such a death, whether it is foretold or no. No man inflicts such
torture on another, save one driven by the deepest of hatreds,
the most carefully nurtured of resentments. My lords, this knot
is a thing of beauty and horror, to be employed only in the cruellest trap, for a creature caught thus dies painfully, by slow de-
grees. I have never used it in a snare myself, for I have always
believed in a clean kill, a sharp, merciful ending. But I do know
how to make this knot; Somerled taught me long ago when we
were children. It was his invention, his secret. There are only
two I know of who can do it: your new king there, and myself."

Now the silence was profound. Harald Silvertongue had
picked up the buckle; his fingers touched the little knots gingerly, his mouth was tight with distaste. Olaf had his chin in his
hand, as if thinking deeply. *Now,* Eyvind thought; *now they
must believe me. Somerled was a fool to keep this, and think not
to be damaged by it. Now they must at least feel some doubt
about his motives.* But Somerled was smiling.

"You heard the man," the king said mildly. "Only two can
make this knot. That may or may not be true, of course; who's
to say I did not teach others my invention? Eyvind has no mo-
nopoly on my friendship, for all we are blood brothers. Let us
say I did not do so. Let us say this secret skill is shared only by
the two of us. Now think of the manner of Ulf's killing. A fit,
able man, desperate to survive—did not Eyvind say Ulf fought
against his bonds so hard that he caused his own mortal injury?
What kind of killer could have brought about Ulf's murder in
such a manner, tying him, moving him some distance probably,
stuffing his mouth with weed to silence him, suspending him
from the clifftop in the most perilous of places? Didn't someone mention that would take a man of exceptional strength? So,
we narrow our field of suspects down to one who can make the
knot, and who also possesses physical prowess somewhat beyond that of an ordinary warrior. While I wouldn't mind claim-

ing the latter for myself, my friends, all of you know my own skills in feats of strength are adequate rather than outstanding. Eyvind's a different matter. If you had asked our people on the island, last summer, who among us was foremost in bodily strength and skill, every single one of them would have named this man you see before you. Eyvind, old friend, I'm afraid your stunning piece of evidence has done nothing but point the finger straight at yourself."

"But—" Eyvind began, appalled that such a cruelly twisted version of events could come from the lips of a man who, not long ago, had professed the deepest friendship for him. *Curse it, man, I can't do without you.* All the arbiters were staring at him now; he saw in their eyes shock, disgust, stunned realization. Only on Olaf Sveinsson's shrewd features did he recognize a shadow of doubt. It was to Olaf he spoke now in shaking tones.

"My lord, this is nonsense. What reason could I possibly have had to kill Ulf? I respected the man, I thought him a fine leader."

"Heard you grumbling often enough about how you couldn't wait to get home," put in the knarr's captain. "Cursing the idle days—a waste of time, I think you said once."

"Maybe I was bored. That doesn't make me a murderer," Eyvind said. "Besides, I slept by my brother and the others that night. I could not have carried out the deed."

"He's right." Heads turned; Erlend had stepped forward at the bottom of the hall. His blunt features were tight with unease. "Holgar and I lay close to Eyvind that night in the mist. It was cold enough to freeze your bollocks off. None of us slept longer than a snatch at a time. Eyvind couldn't have gone away without our knowing it. It wasn't possible."

"That's true." Holgar came out to stand beside his fellow Wolfskin; the two of them together made an impressive sight with their great height, their broad, fur-cloaked shoulders, and their fierce eyes. "And he couldn't have done it next day either, nobody went out searching alone. Eyvind had one of Engus's men with him all morning, until he went off with Somerled. They called me when they found the body. Eyvind didn't have the demeanor of a man who'd just murdered his chieftain."

"And I did?" queried Somerled very quietly. A little muscle in his cheek had begun to twitch, something Eyvind had witnessed before from time to time. At long last, perhaps Somerled was worried.

"No, my lord," Holgar said. "If I'd been asked, I'd have said neither of you could have done it. Eyvind was distressed, and you were . . . beside yourself with grief, it seemed to me, almost as if you'd have leaped off the cliff yourself. That was a terrible day."

"A black day," put in Erlend. "My lords, I cannot condone what Eyvind did at the Whaleback, for it runs contrary to a warrior's code to turn against his own comrades, to defy his own leader. In mitigation, I'm obliged to say it was quite clear to the three of us that Eyvind didn't intend to kill us, nor to inflict any serious injury. If he'd wanted to do that, he would have done it, war fetter or no. The man's unparalleled in close combat. We knew he sought only to delay the attack. We didn't understand why. Perhaps the revelations of tonight are the key to that. I can only tell you, Eyvind is well known to all of us, and all of us will say, Eyvind would never have slain Ulf. Not only had he no reason to do so, the manner of Ulf's death rules him out as a suspect. Eyvind's been an expert hunter since he was a boy, we all know that. A hunter kills efficiently, with compassion. With respect for the life he takes."

"Theories, theories," grumbled Harald Silvertongue, "no case was ever proven on speculations such as these. What about some hard facts? Say we accept the premise that Eyvind could not have done the deed that night. We must, of course, bear in mind that you are the accused man's close comrades, bound by your oath to Thor, and that loyalty may play a greater part in your testimony than truth. However, say we accept what you tell us about that night. There is still the next day. You mentioned that no man went off alone in the morning. You say Eyvind had one of the islanders with him. In view of the king's talk of treachery, of the poison these folk put in the Wolfskin's mind, the presence of one of Engus's men by his side scarcely constitutes an alibi."

"It's the opposite," put in the knarr's captain suddenly. "That just made it easier to do the deed. Ulf was wandering as his brother was; they ambushed him, they set it up. Easy. There had to have been accomplices on the island to bring the net and the ropes. It could only have been done thus."

Somerled nodded gravely. "Indeed. A shocking affair. Of course, nothing's proven. It's my word against Eyvind's. I would only ask you to bear in mind that I have been as open as I could, allowing Eyvind full rein to speak his mind although his account of himself was rambling and irrelevant. I produced the evidence he wanted, evidence he thought to use to incriminate me. I had no reason to do so, I could have concealed the fact that this buckle was in my possession. I've told you honestly that I would have pardoned the man's transgression had he been prepared to admit the islanders corrupted and used him. Why would I lay myself open thus if I were guilty of the heinous crime Eyvind seeks to pin on me? Still, it's not that particular offense we're examining here tonight. We risk forgetting the nature of the original charges if we allow this thread of argument to continue."

Nobody commented. Harald was nodding sagely, even as his fingers played restlessly with the buckle. Olaf was staring down at his linked hands as if they were of deep interest to him. Others shuffled restlessly.

"You heard what Eyvind said." The voice was Grim's, though Eyvind could not see him, for he was lost in the press of men by the west door. "Did it sound as if he was lying? The fellow's never told a lie in his life, he wouldn't know how. He's confessed to the charges against him, and he's given his reasons for doing what he did. Why would he let himself be brought back here, except to tell the truth?"

"We're all tired," said Somerled, rising to his feet. "Tired and distressed. You men can sit down." His eyes passed over the tall figures of Erlend and Holgar; there was a chill in his gaze that made Eyvind shudder. To speak out as his fellow Wolfskins had done was to place one's whole future at risk. He did, indeed, have friends here, brave friends.

"This part of the proceedings is closed," Somerled continued. "We'll discuss the evidence in private, and return with a verdict. Meanwhile, I want you all to enjoy some ale and a bite to eat; you've been patient. Let's finish this and allow Eyvind here to return to his cell and rest those shaky legs. Unless anyone else has a mind to jump up and say their little piece in his defense."

Surely, Eyvind thought, the edge in the king's voice and the glint in his eye must be enough to deter the most determined of advocates. This was over. Harald Silvertongue began to rise, somewhat creakily, for he was getting on in years and the cold weather hurt his joints. The knarr's captain was already up and talking with some animation to those of his crew who stood nearby.

"I'd like to speak in Eyvind's defense, if I may." It was a mild, inoffensive voice, which nonetheless carried right down the length of the hall, over the hubbub of chatter.

"Quiet!" barked Olaf Sveinsson, and silence fell. In the hush, the man who had spoken moved on his sandalled feet to the center of the hall, facing the table. He gave Eyvind a courteous nod. The curiously tonsured head was held high, the shoulders square; the little man in the threadbare brown robe made a strangely dignified figure amidst this company of tall warriors and richly dressed courtiers. There was a livid bruise on his left cheek and a deep, oozing cut over his eye.

"I have some words to add to the case, before you conclude," Brother Tadhg said. "I came in late, of course. It's quite a way from Hafnarvagr, and my journey was interrupted. But I think I follow the thrust of your arguments. May I speak?"

Margaret dismissed the two guards with a few crisp words, then reached out a hand to guide Nessa up the steps and into the cottage. A savory smell wafted out the door; supper was cooking. Nessa's mouth watered.

"Here," Margaret was saying, "let me take that," and her hand came out toward the bag Nessa held.

"No!" Nessa started in alarm, her grip tightening instinctively. Within its covering, the bone harp shivered and spoke. *I am . . . I am . . .*

Margaret froze in the doorway, her hands at her throat, her face blanching to a sickly white. *"What is that?"* she breathed.

Nessa swallowed. "I'll explain," she managed. The ancestors aid her, what she bore was made with the very bone and sinew of this girl's husband; it was his body she had opened to find the makings of her charm. Explain? How could she even begin?

"Let me come in first; this is not a matter we can speak of out here. I'm cold and hungry, and I badly need your help."

Perhaps something in her eyes spoke to the young widow; perhaps Margaret remembered a time not so long ago when she herself had asked for aid.

"Come, then. Warm yourself by the fire and share our supper. I am not so neglectful of my duty that I would leave you out in the dark. Come in."

The cottage was cozy; a fire burned on the central hearth, and lamps stood at either end of the room. Shelf beds were well furnished with rugs and linen, and cups and bowls stood on a stone slab. The two dogs were already making themselves at home, Guard lapping thirstily from a bowl of water, Shadow sitting quietly next to a woman who was crouched by the fire, stirring the soup pot. Nessa blinked. Surely she was seeing things; hunger and exhaustion must have addled her wits. Yet the smell was unique; there was nothing in the world as good as Rona's onion broth.

"As you see," Margaret said awkwardly, her eyes sharp on the dark, swathed form of the harp, "you are among friends here."

Nessa came close to dropping the instrument then, overcome by a sudden flood of feelings, hope and sorrow and fear, grief and joy and terrible anxiety. Half-blinded by hot tears, she set harp and wolfskin carefully on the floor and ran to throw her arms around her old friend and mentor.

"Rona! By all the powers! I thought you were dead, Eyvind said you went off all by yourself—how is it you are here, with her? Don't you know what happened? They're all dead, all of them, Engus and Kinart and all the men who stood up with them, they cut off their heads and left them lying, and they took the women from the Whaleback, and now Eyvind is a prisoner, and Somerled—"

"Hush," Rona said, patting Nessa's shoulder, "hush now, little one. I'm very well, as you see. This girl's been nothing but kind to me, though she's weary and sick and full of sadness, and I can't understand a word she says. Hush your weeping, now. I know what happened at the Whaleback. That's a morning will never be forgotten. A terrible sorrow; a great wrong.

Knowing such evils are to come makes bearing them no easier. You must sit down, Nessa. Here. And get this soup into you, girl. There's a task to be done, and your mind won't be fit for it if you neglect to nourish your body. There, now. Dry your tears."

"I have—I made—"

"Shh. Drink the soup first. Then tell us." Rona's deep eyes were calm, watching as Nessa ate broth and bread, as Guard feasted on crusts and scraps of mutton bone. Margaret did not eat. She stood silent by the fire, waiting.

"How can I tell her?" Nessa whispered when the meal was over. "What I carry here is . . . it is the final witness to her husband's murder, the only voice that cannot be denied. You remember what I was told. *Find the truth in ash and bone.* Already this harp speaks, though the last string is not yet wound tight. How can I say it? She'll think me no better than a graverobber."

Rona nodded. "Tell her the truth. What else can you do?"

"You must explain yourself now," Margaret said. "Speak in this language so that I can understand. There's to be no more talk in the island tongue. I must be careful here; how do I know I can trust you? Tell me why you are on this land, and where you are going. Tell me how you escaped the . . . tell me how you got away from the Whaleback, that morning. Show me what you carry in this bag. And be quick about it. I have many armed men here, and I am under no obligation to help you."

"I understand. Still, we share a bond as women, the three of us, and I see honesty in your face, as I did the last time we met," Nessa said. What was this girl doing here, all by herself among guards in an isolated cottage? Wasn't she Somerled's sister-in-law? Why wasn't she at his court? "I helped you then, or tried to. Did you make use of the charm I gave you?"

Margaret's lips tightened. Nessa noticed how thin she had grown, thin and worn, the skin of the cheeks pale and dry, the eyes shadowed. Her hands were clenched together, her shoulders tense.

"It doesn't matter," Margaret snapped. "That's past now. Tell me. Give me answers, and quickly."

Nessa's heart was pounding. There was no right way to say

this. "Before I do that, I would thank you for giving Rona refuge here. I don't know how that came about, but it is no longer safe for my folk to wander abroad, and I recognize that your kindness has probably saved her life." She turned to Rona. "I said thank you," she told the wise woman in her own tongue. "For putting up with you, that is. You're a stubborn old woman, and too brave for your own good."

"It was no trouble," Margaret said gravely. "Your friend makes undemanding company, and she's earned her keep cooking for the men, though I could do without her herbal teas. Now go on. I need your account of yourself. They say you are King Engus's close kin. I did not know that the day I came to your dwelling. You must have thought me somewhat ill-mannered."

Nessa managed a smile. "No, my lady. I thought you a little misguided, but courageous and open. You've given me no cause to change my mind, even though your people have cut down my own with heedless savagery. I need your help tonight. I must make my way to Somerled's hall. I must be there by dawn. I need a horse, and I need you to let me pass unhindered."

Margaret's eyes widened. "That, surely, would be the height of folly," she said. "If you are indeed Engus's kin, you should go anywhere but there. If Somerled knew you lived, he would see you only as an enemy and a threat to his authority. You should leave the islands forever. To travel to the settlement spells only death or captivity for you. Why would you do it? You do not seem a foolish girl."

"I can explain. But . . . this will be very shocking to you; it will distress you greatly."

"I can't consider letting you go unless you tell me what you're doing," Margaret said gravely. "My husband was chieftain here. I have a certain responsibility."

Nessa could not hold back a flare of sudden anger. "Forgive me," she said, "but is not that responsibility somewhat shadowed now that your husband's men have hacked down my kinsmen and taken my kinswomen captive? You should hang your head in shame that our good king was burned in his hall, and the ancient seat of the Folk made into a bloody killing field, only because your husband's people chose to set foot on these islands. This place has been our home since the time before memory. You tell me to leave forever. It is I who should bid you leave, I think. Your responsibility should have been to stop those acts of slaughter. It is too late now."

Margaret stood very still. Her lips were a thin line. The restless hands clutched and twisted together.

"If it is too late," she said in a whisper, "then why are you here?"

"Ah," said Nessa. "Will you listen? Will you listen until I am finished?"

Margaret gave a tight nod.

So Nessa told the tale: how they had found Eyvind and sheltered him, how she had spoken to him about Ulf's murder, and how the Wolfskin had confirmed what the Folk already knew in their hearts for truth. Somerled had killed his own brother because he wanted what Ulf had: land, power, chieftainship. She did not say what trembled on the tip of her tongue: that perhaps Somerled wanted Ulf's wife as well. That part of it was Margaret's; the truth of what was between those two would probably never be told. Nessa described Eyvind's stand against the men who would have captured Rona; she told how he had gone to confront Somerled, and escaped, and how he had given himself up so that Nessa might go free. There was a part of the tale she left out; it was just as well, she thought, that Rona could not follow the details of this narrative, for the wise woman was an acute interpreter of the unspoken. And Nessa could barely utter her warrior's name without trembling, without feeling such conflict inside her that she was hard-pressed to keep her mind on what must be done. She had made a promise, a deep and solemn one. Just how she would keep it was a matter for later, once the task was complete.

Margaret listened in silence. At one point she bowed her head; later she sat down and put her hands over her face. It was not so much a reaction of shock, more the response of one who sees that her worst imaginings are indeed true.

The hardest part was still to come. "I need to ask you," Nessa said carefully, "if, in the old tales of your people, the stories of Thor and—and Odin, and your ancestors, there are any that touch on—" She glanced helplessly at Rona, but Rona only shrugged, unable to comprehend the foreign words, though her eyes showed she had an idea of what it was that Nessa wrestled with. "Among our tales, there is one about a princess drowned by her sister," Nessa went on, her voice shaking. "Her body floats downstream and a miller finds it. He makes a—he makes a harp from her bones and hair and carries it to the king's court, and there it plays a terrible tune, a song that relates the tale of the wrong that was done." She was unable to look Margaret in the eyes. "Have you any such stories? Do the people from the snow lands know of the instrument of bone, which speaks only truth? The undeniable witness?"

Margaret said not a word. She rose and took two steps forward, and with trembling fingers she reached to draw back the wrapping, revealing the graceful, small harp gleaming in the firelight, the neat pegs of finger bone, the twists of sea wrack that bound the joints, the dark, silent strings. The harp quivered of itself. *Ulf . . .* it hummed low. *Ulf . . . chieftain . . .*

Margaret's face was gray, her eyes dark pools of horror. She stepped back, made a choking noise, and fled out the back door of the cottage. Sounds of painful retching could be heard, punctuated by strangled gasps for air. Nessa's heart was pounding; she made to go after the other girl.

"No," said Rona. "Leave her be. There's nothing ails her that time and a bit of hard thinking won't cure, poor lass. Now tell me. I see what you've made, and I know what it's for. I'm impressed. You summoned the Seal Tribe? That was risky. What did they want in return?"

"They didn't ask me for anything," Nessa said, shivering. "Not yet, anyway. The Hidden Tribe helped me, too. All played a part."

"It's as well the old ones are stirring." The old woman's voice was grave. "There aren't many of us left. That day on the Whaleback, the flower of our people was plucked before its time. Say you get to court with this harp, and it tells its tale, and people believe it. What then? The Folk are weakened almost beyond saving, and these Norsemen have weaponry and numbers. Maybe you persuade them this cruel chieftain is not the best leader they have, but what do you see them doing about it? They'll set up another in his place and start the whole thing again."

"This is not like you," frowned Nessa. "Where is your faith? Where's your belief? We cannot fail. Truth must win here, truth and goodness. Eyvind will help me . . ." Her voice trailed off.

"Oh, yes?" Rona asked, brows raised.

"If I can reach him in time," Nessa whispered. "If I can get there before Somerled kills him. Trust me, Rona. I haven't forgotten that I am a priestess."

Margaret was coming back; she held herself very straight, shoulders square, head high, as if determined to show she was a noblewoman, and in control. She walked past the harp, not looking now, and sat rigidly upright on the bench by the hearth.

"Cover it up," she said. "I don't want to see it. Did you—no, I can't say it—was it you—?"

"I made this," Nessa told her gently. "I am a priestess of the mysteries. Our faith has sustained us since the days of the oldest ancestors; it has guided us since time before time. Its pathways are found in the depths of earth and ocean, the eternal patterns of sun and moon. I have studied the ways of it since I was a small child, and Rona has been my wise teacher. There is a solemn ritual for the making of such charms. Both the taking and the returning are carried out with deepest respect. If you visited your husband's grave mound tomorrow, you would see it quite untouched. Would not Ulf want justice? This is the only way he can have a voice here, my lady. Let us grant him the right to speak. Once that is done, he can rest peacefully in this place that he loved and honored. Ulf was a good man; what happened here was not his doing, though it was his desire for voyaging that began it. We owe it to him, and to King Engus, and to all the fine men whose blood has been shed in this dark time, to carry this witness to Somerled's hall and ensure the future of the islands does not descend into chaos and darkness. I need your help, Margaret. Without you, I cannot be there in time."

"You can see I'm sick," Margaret said flatly. "Sick and weary. What help could I be? You told me yourself, it's too late now. I should have stopped him, I should have been strong enough. I did try. I thought I could sway him, I thought he would listen to me as he did in those early days. But he wouldn't listen. Nobody would listen, they're afraid to speak out, since they know what he can do to them. In such a place as this, there's great power for the taking, if a man is bold enough. I spoke, and he sent me away so he didn't have to hear me. Nothing has gone right here, nothing. I was angry at first to be banished from his court, but now I'm glad. Out here, I don't have to think about those things. I don't have to think about anything."

The voice was expressionless, but Nessa saw the trembling of the young widow's hands, the clenched jaw; she saw what it was costing Margaret to maintain that tightly held control. There were tears very close, but on no account would Margaret allow them to fall.

"Is it love that weakens your will for justice?" Nessa asked softly. "Love for a man in whom, against all the evidence of your eyes, you still see some spark of goodness? Or do you not believe what I have told you of the manner of your husband's death? There is a voice here, which can give you indisputable proof of the truth, if you will let it speak."

"Love?" Margaret whispered. "Love weighs nothing in this balance. I have come beyond caring. There is no point in it."

"Would you give up so easily?" Nessa asked her. "How old are you, my lady?"

Taken by surprise, Margaret answered automatically. "Seventeen. Old enough to learn a woman's opinion means nothing in a world where men play all the games that matter. Old enough to know how it feels to be discarded once I am no longer deemed to be of value." She bit back more words; her eyes glinted with tears.

"You and I are of an age," Nessa told her. "You have decided not to act. That is your choice. I will tell you what I will do tonight. I will get on a horse and ride to Somerled's hall. I will walk into that place and demand to be seen. I am Engus's only surviving kin, and the last of the royal line in the Light Isles. In that court, I will be surrounded by enemies. And I am afraid, believe me. There I will speak of the way Somerled murdered his brother, and brought darkness to this fair place. And I will release the voice of the only true witness to that crime. Your people are not all bad; they are merely slaves of fear and of custom. I hope this voice will awaken them, and open their eyes to

what is true and just. There are women and children of my own
folk captive in that settlement, Margaret. The Wolfskin is a
prisoner there, and Somerled will silence him forever if I do not
reach him by dawn."

"The Wolfskin? You mean Eyvind?" Once more Margaret
was startled into speech. "Somerled would never kill Eyvind.
He loves him. Eyvind is the only person he has ever really
cared about."

Nessa nodded. "Perhaps that is why he will do it, because he
cannot bear to see his own reflection in his friend's eyes: the
image of a man who has failed utterly in his life's great ambition. This is no king, it is no more than a warped and crazy
shadow of a leader, deformed by the cruelty he carries within
him and can never be rid of. The sound of truth on his dearest
friend's lips must cut him like a knife. I cannot say what is in
Somerled's mind. But I am a priestess, and I hear the voices of
the spirit. I know that if I do not leave soon, it will be too late.
Stay here if you will. It is your choice to shut your eyes to the
truth as soon as it becomes too hard to bear. It is your choice to
block out what is too difficult for you. Never mind what your
husband wanted. Never mind the courage I once saw in your
eyes, when you sought me out at great danger to yourself. That
strong girl has disappeared. At seventeen, you have become a
frightened old woman. I see that you are sick; I suppose that is
an excuse of sorts. Give me a horse, Margaret, and let me go
unpursued. Let me go now. That's all I'm asking."

Margaret had moved away; she had her back to them, her
arms tightly folded. There was tension in every corner of her
slender frame.

"I hope you weren't too cruel," Rona muttered. "The girl's a
good girl, and she's been kind to me. She's had a hard time of it."

Images of that bloody morning on the Whaleback flashed
through Nessa's mind in stark and uncompromising detail. She
said nothing. Time was passing; how long would it take to ride
there in the dark? Margaret was silent. Oh, quickly, answer
quickly. She heard that voice again, *I want so much to live.*

"Right," said Margaret curtly, not turning. "Right. I still understand duty, no matter how low your opinion of me. You realize
you can't ride with the—with the instrument, and the wolfskin.

You've no hope at all of getting past the sentry posts, or of reaching the hall itself without their taking everything away from you. Perhaps you're not so clever after all."

"Perhaps not," whispered Nessa, torn between hope and despair. "And nor is Eyvind. Just stubborn, the two of us, and set on truth. It is Ulf who must be clever for us: Ulf, and yourself."

"Stop it!" snapped Margaret furiously. "Don't make me weep, then I won't be able to do anything!" She walked briskly to the door, flung it open and called out into the night. "Bjorn! Ash! Come here!"

There was a sound of running feet, and a rapid exchange of words outside. Nessa bent to gather up the harp.

Rona's eyes narrowed. "What's this wee pack you bear on your back?" she asked.

Nessa had completely forgotten the sea women's gift. "That? I don't know. I was given it. Perhaps it can be left behind; it will be hard enough to ride and carry the harp safely without this as well."

"Left behind? I shouldn't think so," Rona said. "A gift from those who helped you in the making, was it? Best open it up now. Such bounty is rarely bestowed, and never without a purpose."

"There's no time—"

"Open it up, Nessa."

She slipped the small packet from her back and unrolled the strange, weedlike wrapping. The contents flowed out, iridescent, pearly, a lovely green-blue length of finely woven fabric. It was whisper-soft to the touch, and smelled faintly of salt.

"Oh!" Margaret's voice came from behind them; she stood on the threshold staring. "Oh, how beautiful!"

"A fine gift," Rona said, lifting the gossamer stuff with careful fingers. "Beautiful, magical, and, as I said, for a purpose. You don't go out to confront a king dressed in your old working clothes. Nessa, you must wear this tonight."

"Highly impractical," Margaret observed, guessing at Rona's meaning. "I'd better find you a warm cloak."

"Rona, there's no time for this!" Nessa hissed. Why didn't they understand it must be now, straightaway, for every moment that passed took Eyvind one step closer to death? She knew him; he would not wait for her. Was it not in the very nature of a Wolfskin to charge forward, heedless of danger, to risk all in each glorious act of challenge? Perhaps Eyvind had changed, but that crazy courage was still in him, and he could not deny it. She had seen it at the Whaleback; she had seen it again on the morning they woke in each other's arms, when he sacrificed his own freedom for hers. Eyvind would want her out of danger, away from Somerled. He would not wait for her. "Let me be, Rona! I must go now!"

"Hush, lass. This will only take a moment. Let me help you."

The gown was of simple cut, high-waisted, narrow-sleeved, with a skirt that fell straight to the floor in graceful folds. The shimmering, shifting fabric, holding all the hues of the ocean in its fluid surface, made this a garment fit for some mysterious queen of ancient story. There was a circlet for the head, and Rona insisted this, too, be worn. Chafing to be gone, Nessa submitted to the wise woman's attentions, since to argue was to delay her departure still farther. Margaret waited, pale and silent, a warm cloak in her hands, another around her shoulders. At last, Rona turned her student around one, two, three times and announced herself satisfied.

"I can't come with you, lass," she said, eyes shrewd but gentle as she scrutinized Nessa's face. "I believe in you; I believe you can do it. You wouldn't have come this far if all the powers of the islands hadn't been there behind you. Win the day for us, Nessa; let the truth be heard."

Nessa bowed her head, saying nothing. If she allowed herself to think too much about what this meant, the magnitude and importance of it, it might become just too difficult to go on. But she must go on; there was nobody else to do it.

"I'll come after you," Rona was saying. "I'll come when it's light, at a pace befitting an old woman. I hope you'll save the big fellow. There's goodness in him; it took me a while to see it, but he's got a spirit to match his stature, and a great will for survival, our warrior. I just hope the two of you don't break each other's hearts. Don't cry, Nessa. This task will need all your strength. Time enough for weeping later, when it's done."

"The men are ready," Margaret said. "I'll bear the wolfskin for you, if you're prepared to let it out of your hands. It's a long way, and we'll need to be quick if what you say is true."

"Do you mean—?"

Margaret had already gone outside. Through the doorway,

Nessa could see several men on horseback, waiting; some of them bore torches.

"You can't possibly go on your own," Margaret said over her shoulder as she made her way down the steps. "In my company, you can be admitted to the hall without question. After that it will be up to you. These men will guard us on the journey. All are loyal to me." There was a subtle emphasis on the final word. "Give me the wolfskin, I'll carry it behind me. The old woman must pass the—the other thing up to you; I cannot lay hands on it." A visible shudder ran through her.

"Thank you," Nessa breathed, not sure exactly why Margaret had made this decision, but recognizing the courage in it

"What does she think she's doing?" Rona's voice was sharp; she stood in the doorway behind them, eyes fixed upon Margaret, who had mounted her own horse and was directing a man to tie the wolfskin behind her saddle. Another fellow waited to help Nessa up on a steady-looking gray mare. "She's not planning to go with you? She shouldn't be riding. Tell her, Nessa."

"What?"

"Tell her what I said."

The message was passed on. Margaret's lips tightened, her face turning still paler in the torchlight.

"You think I care about that?" she snapped, looking straight at Rona. "It's nothing. It's less than nothing. Now come on, we're wasting time."

"Foolish girl," Rona muttered. But she said no more, merely cradled the little harp in her arms while Nessa mounted the horse, then passed the instrument up to her pupil. Shadow danced around the horses' feet, setting them astir with her excited barking. Guard stood on the steps beside the old woman, and her gnarled fingers stroked his head abstractedly as she muttered ancient words of blessing under her breath. The horses moved out of the yard and away across the moonlit fields to the east. Rona watched until they were hidden in darkness, and then she returned slowly to the fire, Guard padding after her. She delved deep in a little crock set on the hearth, and scattered a handful of dried weed into the flames. As the pungent smell of the herbs of divination rose into the warm air within the cottage, Rona closed her eyes and summoned the trance. There would be no sleep tonight.

* * *

Somerled gazed at Brother Tadhg with chill eyes. "Why should we hear you?" he inquired. "You've been in these people's pockets all along, Engus's right-hand man, with your skewed translations and your pathetic attempts to conceal your spying under the cloak of spreading your ridiculous faith. The whole case against Eyvind is based on the way the islanders ensnared and corrupted him. Any evidence from you in his support can only strengthen that case, surely."

Olaf turned his searching gaze on the brother. "How did you come by that injury to your face?" he asked bluntly. "A priest, of whatever persuasion, should never be the target of acts of violence. Are we to take this as evidence that Somerled is right, that you are not in fact a holy brother but some kind of spy?"

Brother Tadhg smiled. "No, my lord. My only allegiance is to God, and to truth, for the ultimate truth rests in God. I see here tonight a man on trial, a man I know lives by truth because he can conceive of no other way to act. I see him trapped by falsehood and deception into a position where he cannot prevail. Perhaps I cannot change that. But my faith compels me to speak on his behalf, since his brother has been prevented from doing so. As for the injury, I came by it on my way here. You all know the dangers that lurk by the wayside for lone travelers in these parts, dangers the islanders knew nothing of until your kind made this place your home. It seems even priests are not immune from such attacks."

"This is . . . unfortunate," Olaf Sveinsson muttered, narrowing his eyes as he scrutinized the priest. He turned to Somerled. "What do you think? Shall we hear the fellow?"

"What do you mean, 'prevented?' " Suddenly Harald Silvertongue's voice had changed. He sat down heavily. "The word was that Eirik Hallvardsson was asked to come here in support of his brother, and refused to do so. That's what I was told."

Somerled opened his mouth to reply, but Tadhg was quicker. His voice was quite soft, but resonant with long practice at psalms and prayers.

"Eirik was on his way," Tadhg said. "Both he and his companion, Thord, were much concerned when I brought them the news that Eyvind was in a position of such danger. They intended to depart that same evening. If they have not yet arrived, it can only be that someone stopped them, perhaps the same someone who attempted to assault me on my way here. Not being a Wolfskin myself, I'm afraid I fled; very fortunately, I was close to the lakeshore, and while I can swim a little, my assailant lacked that skill. So here I am, somewhat damp and bruised, but otherwise none the worse for wear. God watches over his children. I imagine Eirik and Thord put up a great deal more of a fight; it would have taken many men to subdue them."

"Wait a moment," Somerled said sharply. "What do you mean, *you* took them the news? News of what, exactly? When was this?"

"I came to the safe harbor in the evening, the day before King Engus and his household were slain. I went straight to find Eirik, and gave him the message before Brother Lorcan and I continued on to our lodgings. Eirik and Thord were readying themselves as we left."

"Message?" snapped Somerled. "What message?"

Tadhg glanced at Eyvind. "I had encountered your Wolfskin earlier that day, making his way here to the settlement. The poor fellow had completely lost his memory of the winter months. But he was determined to find you and do his best to deter you from any attack on the Folk."

"I see." There was a dangerous note in Somerled's voice. "Do you know who sheltered Eyvind during this mysterious absence from our settlement? Was he indeed harbored by these two witches we hear of, the old and the young?"

Eyvind found he was holding his breath; he took care not to look at the priest.

"I know nothing of that," Tadhg said. "I spent the best part of the winter on Holy Island; I saw no trace of your Wolfskin, nor did I hear mention of him all that time. I was most surprised to encounter him on Engus's land. More than surprised: he nearly broke my arm before he realized I was no warrior."

"Indeed." In a single word, Somerled managed to convey both disbelief and scorn. "Did Eyvind speak to you of Ulf's death? What did he say of that?"

"My lord," Tadhg replied calmly, "it was common knowledge among the Folk that you yourself were responsible for that deed." A gasp went around the hall; hands moved to sword hilts, as if this small, mild man were more threatening than any monster in their midst. "It made sense. They knew their own kind had no part in it. King Engus conducted a most thorough investigation; even his closest comrades and kin were interrogated at length. Engus knew you to be both ambitious and ruthless. It was clear to him that you had set up the murder to win your brother's position as leader here, and at the same time to incite your people to acts of violence against the Folk. I congratulate you. You succeeded on both counts."

"Young man," Olaf Sveinsson's tone was incredulous, "have you no fear at all for your own safety? A fellow can't simply walk into a king's hall and call him some sort of—some sort of—"

"Butcher?" Somerled supplied the word coolly. "Priest, we have heard your ramblings and, frankly, they make even less sense than Eyvind's. I remind myself that you are not of our people and have little understanding of our ways. Yours is a soft faith, a comfortable faith, based on love and forgiveness, gentleness and inaction. We endured a perilous voyage to make our way to these shores. We are a proud and warlike people, whose deeds of courage in battle, whose raids and conquests are known and feared from Halogaland to Saxony, from Birka to Novgorod. We stride forward boldly, we vanquish the most tenacious of foes, we seize rich plunder, and set our stamp on new lands where we will. Look at our Wolfskins. They are warriors of godlike strength; indeed, they are inspired by Thor himself in their valiant deeds of combat. Odin, the trickster, gives us our cunning, our cleverness, and our determination. If we have triumphed here in the Light Isles, if we have deposed King Engus and his hapless underlings, that is no more than the natural defeat of a weaker breed by a stronger. I will speak no more of my brother's death; I relive the pain of that day every time the tale is told. But I will say one thing. In a place like this, remote, harsh, virtually untenanted, there is only one kind of leader who will succeed. It is not a leader who dreams and philosophizes and keeps company with Christian priests. It is a man who is unafraid to take his people forward into their new world, a chieftain who keeps control, and knows enemy from friend. All that I am doing tonight, little priest, is being that leader. Without firm authority, there can be only chaos. That is why this case must be decided quickly, the penalty determined, the sentence carried out at dawn, in accordance with the new

laws I have decreed. Men who oppose my rule have no place on
the island. Men who act against me can expect to pay the price
of their treachery with their lives. This is a frontier realm, the
farthest point of man's voyaging, a place from which there is no
going on and no going back. And I am king here. Would any
man among you dispute that?"

Nobody said a word. It seemed to Eyvind that Somerled had
spoken a terrible kind of sense. After Ulf's death, he himself
had believed for a little that his friend was the only possible
leader here. There were other chieftains like him back home.
Such men ruled by fear. The look in their eyes, the edge in their
voices were enough to command instant obedience. Yet, tonight, four other men besides himself had summoned up the
courage to speak against the king. It was not enough. He pondered, dimly, what sort of chance the Wolfskins might have
against the fifty-odd other men who were gathered in the hall
tonight. They could create havoc, certainly, crack more than a
few skulls before they were brought down. He thought about the
shackles, and how he would go about felling a man when he
could scarcely walk. Foolish, even to consider such a possibility. If this could not be won by truth and courage, it most certainly would not be won by another descent into violence and
blood. His fellow Wolfskins had already put themselves at
grave risk on his behalf; they had done so even though they
thought him a traitor. He must not set them in still greater peril.
Perhaps it was just as well Eirik had not come.

"Eyvind?"

Someone was speaking to him. His mind had wandered;
while he thought of escape, the arbiters had risen and retired to
a smaller chamber, and now only Olaf Sveinsson was left.
Around the hall, ale was being poured, and the place buzzed
with speculative chatter. Tadhg still stood there, his arm now in
the grip of the heavily armed Thorvald; Gudbrand stood ready
to convey Eyvind himself back to the cell.

"Eyvind?" Olaf spoke again. "It's time to go now. I don't
think you heard the king. The two of you must return to your
place of confinement until we reach our decision." Olaf turned
to Gudbrand. "Treat them well. Give them food and drink. No
rough stuff, understand? This man is sick, he's close to passing
out. Don't forget he took a knock to the head that morning at the

Whaleback, and that was after a long winter of imprisonment in Odin only knows what conditions. Go on, take them down now."

"Wait—you can't lock up the priest—" Eyvind blurted out, alarmed to see the way Thorvald hustled his captive out into the hallway. "I'm the prisoner here, not him—he hasn't done anything—"

"The king's orders," Olaf said. "Believe me, I don't like this at all. If there were but one credible voice to speak on your behalf, Eyvind, one unbiased witness whose account could not be challenged, I would demand an extension to the hearing, with time for further evidence to be gathered. As it stands, your case is very weak, son. We can take little account of the testimony of your fellow Wolfskins, bound through old loyalties to speak up in your support. This priest, who was so close to the ear of King Engus, is not an impartial witness. As for your own account, you are a guileless fellow, at times almost too truthful. I think you must prepare yourself for the worst."

Eyvind bowed his head. "Thank you for your honesty," he managed through an increasing fog of dizziness. "The priest . . . can you try to ensure he is released? He is a good man, he has taken a risk to help me, and—"

"Believe me," Olaf said quietly, "there are times when I would give much to be back in Rogaland. My influence here is far less than you imagine. Go on, now. Take what rest you can."

Tadhg was saying a prayer. Eyvind heard it in snatches, through the buzzing in his ears and the throbbing in his head. The sound of it was pleasing, something about a shepherd who kept his flock in right ways, leading them to sweet water and green pastures. The words reminded him of Hammarsby, the fair meadows rich with the myriad hues of spring flowers, the sound of Karl whistling as he checked the progress of his thriving new lambs, the clank of a bucket as Thorgerd drew water from the well. He saw his mother sitting on a bench in the sun, her hair pale wheaten-gold under the neat lace-edged cap, and dark Oksana by her side, brow creased as she concentrated on some fine detail of embroidery. Eirik's small sons played about the women's feet. It was another life, another world. Tadhg was talking about death now, how the shepherd would lead his lambs safely through its shadow into a place where God himself dwelt, a place where there was no more darkness. Odin's bones, this headache was fierce indeed. It drove out all hope of reasonable thought.

"Eyvind?" The brother had finished his prayer. His voice came clearly from the cell next-door, which had the same barred door as his own. "Eyvind, is all well with you?"

"Sorry," Eyvind mumbled, moving closer to the door grille. "My head hurts; my ears are full of noise. Can't seem to . . ."

"Have they given you water?" Tadhg was keeping his voice low; they had been instructed not to speak to one another, but so far the guards had taken no notice. "Drink that, it may help you. Then lie down; bring your pallet up to the door. I want to talk to you. Have you done that? Good. Lie quietly, breathe slowly. I want you to tell me something, Eyvind. We have a friend in common; you know the one I refer to, I think."

"Mmm," grunted Eyvind, who had done as he was told and now lay on his back with his head on the straw pallet, his knees bent up awkwardly, for the cell was far too small to allow such a tall man to stretch out his full length. Tomorrow, perhaps they would lay him in the earth. Then, he would get as much room as he wanted.

"This friend, I sense, still pursues the truth, though you and I appear to have reached the end of our road," Tadhg said in a voice that was little more than a whisper.

"Mm." Nessa. Where was she now? He prayed that she would not come here, he implored Thor and Odin and Freyr and any other god there was to take her away safely somewhere, so she might never again come within Somerled's grasp.

"So, all is not lost," Tadhg breathed. "She is alive?"

"Not here," Eyvind murmured. "Best . . . not here."

"You think our friend would agree with you? We are all fighters for truth, Eyvind, the three of us."

"Best . . . finish. In the morning. Not you. Not her. Just me . . ." Thor's hammer, now he was going to be sick; foul-tasting matter welled in his throat. He crawled to the corner where the bucket still stood and retched as if he would disgorge his very entrails. If he had to face death, if this were indeed his last night on earth, this was surely a most pitiful way to pass the time left to him.

"Eyvind? Are you all right? Eyvind!"

For a long time he could not answer. At length the spasm died down; he crept back to the pallet and curled himself up on it. The headache had retreated; he could hear more clearly now, though he kept his eyes firmly shut, for even the dim light from a lantern down the hallway was like knives in the skull.

"Eyvind?" Tadhg's voice was anxious.

"I'm all right. I just want . . . sleep . . ."

"This is a sorry business. Still, you must not lose hope. We are all God's children, and his hand stretches out over every one of us. For myself, I do not fear death. The manner of it, that gives me pause; I may be a priest, but I am still a man, and I had not thought to meet such a violent end. But I will go to it open-eyed, if our Father determines this is my time. I will walk forward unafraid to meet my Maker. For you, this is another matter, I know. You do not share my own faith, and I have no intention of spending my last night on earth persuading you to it, although you are in all my prayers, Eyvind. Our heavenly Father watches over you, as he does over each of us, priest, warrior, fisherman, and king alike. Perhaps both of us will die tomorrow. You spoke to me once of your god, Thor. What does the afterlife hold for you, Wolfskin?"

Eyvind smiled grimly in the half dark. "If we die on the field of battle, we are assured of an eternity spent at the god's right hand. Thor's warrior women descend to bear such loyal fighters home to Valhöll, to feast there among the great ones for all time. It will be another matter for me, I think." His voice shook. "Thor abandoned me. He ceased to call me. In time, I accepted that; I learned there was another path for me to tread, the one I followed in returning here to confront Somerled with the truth. Now it seems that path was short indeed, and I have failed utterly in my efforts to stand up for what is right. I find I cannot, after all, face death bravely as a Wolfskin should." Nessa was in his mind, her wide gray eyes, her sweet lips parting to his own, the soft, tender warmth of her body. "I want so much to live," he whispered fiercely, sudden tears flooding his eyes. "More than I've ever wanted anything before. I cannot die now, not when this task is yet unachieved, not when there are so many paths still to explore . . . I'm not ready to die, Tadhg. How can I leave her on her own? And yet . . . and yet, if it made the difference between keeping her safe or putting her at risk, I would give up my life gladly. That probably seems foolish to you."

There was a little silence.

"The greatest love is the love of God, Eyvind," Tadhg said at length. "That underlies all other loves; it is more powerful and binding than any earthly passion. Still, I understand you. If you have given your affection, your devotion, your loyalty to anyone on these islands, it does not surprise me in the least that it is to . . . this friend of ours. She does inspire strong feelings. You know, I suppose, that she is a priestess of her own faith?"

"Shh," hissed Eyvind, terrified that the guards would overhear. Whatever he did, he must not put Nessa at any further risk. "Yes, of course I know that."

"I say this only to caution you. Should you survive, there might not be quite the future you envisage when you speak so passionately of your will to live."

"That's not important," Eyvind muttered. "Let us speak no more of this."

"I expect they'll call us soon enough," said Tadhg placidly. "Perhaps there's time for another prayer. Let me see . . ."

"Say the one about the shepherd again," Eyvind whispered.

The soft voice began its flow of fair words anew, weaving a picture of a place where love and peace and beauty walked hand in hand, where hurts were forgotten and wounds salved, where everything was as it should be. It seemed to Eyvind like a sweet bell measuring out the time of shadows.

FOURTEEN

There were whispers in the dark, furtive voices telling of something that must not be known beyond the walls of this shadowy place of captivity. It seemed they believed him asleep, huddled as he was on the straw pallet, his face turned to the wall. But Eyvind was a hunter, and a hunter hears what other men cannot. They were discussing the manner of his death.

Something had changed. Something had happened, and now no formal decision would be handed down, no fitting remarks would bring the hearing to its close. There would be no execution at dawn. Instead, there would be a covert snuffing out, in darkness. Eyvind strained to catch every word, his pulse racing, his heart thumping. He could not move, he could not alert his fellow captive, for it was vital they not realize he was awake.

". . . completely unexpected, and unbelievably inconvenient. What does he think he's doing here?" That voice was Somerled's, and there was an edge to it that Eyvind knew well, and disliked much.

"How many are with him, my lord?"

"The messenger said thirty at least . . . straight on from Silver Bay . . . certainly before dawn."

"Right, my lord. So what do we do now?"

"We can't wait, this must be cleared up before they get here. And cleared up in a way that leaves no adverse impression. You understand me?"

"Yes, my lord." That voice was familiar too: one of those thugs from the knarr, quicker with his fists than with his wits. "You want him finished off quiet-like."

"It's not quite as simple as that," Somerled said. "I'm not asking you to commit murder; that would leave too many unanswered questions. This will be a straightforward case of attempted escape, where your efforts to apprehend the prisoner very unfortunately ended in his demise. Keep it behind closed doors, and don't make too much noise. Send a man up to fetch me when it's over."

"But—my lord, you know the fellow's reputation. He's a Wolfskin, after all. What if he—?" This was a different voice, and tinged with genuine fear.

"If he frightens you so much, bind his hands before you start," Somerled said coolly. "Just make sure you untie them afterward, or it won't look good for you. I don't want it to be said that we beat prisoners here. Now get on with it, will you? There's no saying when our unexpected visitors may arrive, and I need to be sure we receive them in an appropriate manner. You appear hesitant. Do I detect some reluctance to carry out this order? The man's a coward and a traitor. What are you waiting for?"

"My lord, I'm wondering—"

There was the sound of a door closing, then silence. Eyvind waited a moment, senses alert to any sound. It seemed all had gone out, for now at least.

"Eyvind?" The hiss came from the adjoining cell.

"Yes, I heard them." Eyvind was getting to his feet, forcing his cramped limbs to move, wondering what might be done against a whole group of assailants while his feet were still hobbled.

"You must fight them," Brother Tadhg whispered fiercely. "Fight, and survive. There's hope in this somewhere; he senses defeat, or he would not act thus. You can do it, warrior."

"You, bidding me fight?" Eyvind breathed as he clenched and unclenched his fists, stretched his aching shoulders, stepped back from the grilled doorway so he might have some advantage when they struck. "A Christian priest? I would laugh, if I could spare the breath for it."

"You are neither Christian nor a priest," observed Tadhg dryly. "You must fight for me, and for Nessa, and for the truth. You must fight for Somerled. If he kills you, it will lie like a curse on him all his days. Be strong, Wolfskin. I hear them coming."

Eyvind stood very still. His head was clear now, though the light that flared suddenly down the hallway—a torch? a lantern?—seared his eyes. He waited, poised for the moment of attack. The shackled feet could be used to advantage, if he were quick enough. He judged by the steps that there were five or six men. They did not believe him quite as weakened as rumor had suggested, then. It seemed his reputation was not entirely lost. He paced his breathing in readiness, slow, steady, each inhalation a gathering of strength. They would unbar the door, and possibly goad him out with clubs or sticks, and those waiting outside would likely use staves to topple him. Then it would be a beating, savage and quick. They wanted no noise. No evidence. That sounded familiar. Very well, he would make as much noise as he possibly could before they silenced him. If Grim heard him, if Erlend or Holgar recognized his voice, they might come. If Olaf Sveinsson knew bloody murder was taking the place of justice here, surely he would intervene, whatever his fear of Somerled.

The men were coming closer, their attempt at covert approach ludicrously inept. Clearly these were seamen or laborers, not warriors and hunters. Eyvind waited for the hands on the grille, the creak of his cell door opening. But the door that opened was Brother Tadhg's, and the sound that rang out in the silence of the dark prison was that of a blow, and a gasp of pain and shock as the priest was hurled against the stone wall. He heard Tadhg's voice, breathless and uneven, reciting words Eyvind had heard before, though he did not understand them.

"*Pater noster qui es in coelis—*" The prayer broke with another wrenching indrawn breath, then resumed again, threadier now but full of determination. "*—sanctificetur nomen tuum . . . fiat voluntas tua . . . *aagh . . ."

"Stop it!" Eyvind yelled in outrage, fists now gripping the bars of his cell, face pressed to the grille, straining to see. "Stop that at once! Have you lost all shred of decency, that you assault a priest who is guilty of no crime but honesty? Leave that man alone, or in Thor's name I'll have the bars off this cage and make bloody mincemeat of every last one of you!" He rattled the bars, and felt a red heat rising in him, a fierce grimace contorting his features. "It's me you're supposed to kill, you god-forsaken apologies for men, not him! Let him go at once!"

He could not see Tadhg, but he heard the blows. The halting prayer went on, in his own tongue now.

". . . though death overshadow me . . . yet you lead me forth in the darkness . . . you are . . . you are my strength and comfort . . . you . . ."

Odin's bones, they would kill the brother right here before him; he thought he could hear ribs cracking. He could not allow this. Thor must not allow it.

Eyvind threw back his head and roared. He thundered the name of the god in a great outcry of fury and frustration, and under his grip the grilled door began to break from its hinges, half falling outward. He clung to it, struggling to gain steady footing in his shackles. Quick as the slice of a butcher's cleaver, several pairs of hands gripped his arms, closing iron rings about his wrists, joined by a length of chain which fastened him, firmly and neatly, to the grille itself. The last hinge gave; the door fell to the ground with Eyvind sprawled upon it, neatly bound in place, arms held firm by the manacles, face pressed against cold metal. A trap, it had been, a lure to bring him within reach. Clever. Too clever by far for any of these oafs. He thought he knew who had devised it.

"Are you all right?" Eyvind called out, and heard a gasping "Yes" before the first blow fell across his back. He fought as well as he might, twisting and writhing, wrenching at his bonds, flailing up and back with his bound feet. At least they had left the priest now, in order to concentrate on him. There was a kind of pattern in the way they went about it, as if they were under instructions to minimize visible damage while ensuring the result, eventually, would be as Somerled had requested. Somewhere not too far away the prayer went on.

"Thy house is a place where all paths run straight, Lord. If I walk forward in truth and courage, then in the end, that will be my one sure shelter . . ."

A stunning impact on the temple brought the headache back to throbbing life. There seemed to be blood in his eye. The opportunity to do as Brother Tadhg recommended and fight back was somewhat limited, with the wrist bonds holding him face down on the collapsed grille, and the shackles restricting the freedom of his legs. *Fight for Nessa.* Think of her. Think of life and a future. *All paths run straight . . . truth and courage . . .* Fight for her, and fight for truth. And when he could not fight anymore, make noise, a lot of noise, for they'd said someone was coming, someone whose arrival gave Somerled pause, and if he could just hold on long enough . . .

"Thor!" Eyvind yelled. "Thor be my strength! Odin be my guard and shield! Freyr give me the power of your manhood! Beat me, would you, you cowards?" A club caught him a glancing blow on the left ear; his head buzzed as if a swarm of angry bees had lodged behind his eyes. "Somerled!" He shouted with all the power left in his lungs. "Somerled, come down and fight your own battles! Kill me in the darkness, would you? Coward! Call yourself a king? Come down and fight!"

"Help!" Another voice was shouting now. "Help! Murder!" His prayer at an end, the little brother was making his own contribution to the general commotion, cracked ribs or no. "Help! They're killing the Wolfskin!"

"Silence that fellow!" hissed someone, and there was a thud, and the priest's shouting halted abruptly.

"Curse you!" Eyvind gasped, kicking up and back with his two feet together, and hearing a pained grunt as the random blow struck vulnerable flesh. "Curse the lot of you, you piss-weak vermin! Fight like men, damn you! Or do you save your blows solely for holy men and captives in chains? Free me of these shackles and I'll gladly take on the lot of you, and by Thor's hammer, when I'm done there'll be just enough left of you to throw a dog a bone or two for his supper! Let me up, curse you! Somerled! Somerled, come down and face me, come down and face the truth of the oath you once swore! Come down, *brother!*"

"Quick!" someone said sharply. "Give me that hammer! You, shut your big mouth! Nobody's coming to save you, not Thor, not Somerled, not anyone. You're a dirty traitor, and a liar too."

A boot connected with Eyvind's jaw; he felt the blow vibrating through his skull, and a splintering of teeth. Blood filled his mouth; it became impossible to form words. Nonetheless, he went on making noises, since that seemed the only form of resistance left to him. Someone was sitting on his legs, holding them down however hard he strained to free himself.

"Sounds like some crazy wild animal," someone grunted. "Takes them like that, I've heard. Wolfskins, I mean."

"Shut him up, will you?" This one's voice was shaking. "He's giving me the creeps, howling like some mad dog. Where's the cursed hammer? One good blow to the back of the skull should do the trick—ah, here it is—"

There was an instant of silence, in which Eyvind drew a single long breath, and caught a single image in his pain-wracked head. *My hand in yours . . .* Now the blow would fall, and this agony would be over.

There was a crash, and a sudden flood of light as the door at the end of the hallway was thrown abruptly open.

"What in Odin's name do you think you're doing?" The voice was Somerled's, needle-sharp and dangerous. "Get that fellow up at once, and bring him out to the hall. We have at least some modicum of fair play here, one hopes."

"But—" someone spluttered.

"What has happened here?" This was another voice, Olaf Sveinsson's, in which the shock was almost palpable. "Has this man been beaten?"

There was a brief silence, during which Eyvind felt his hands released from the grille. The iron bracelets remained; the heavy chain between them, two handspans long, prevented much in the way of movement.

"He was making trouble," someone mumbled. "Shouting, rattling the bars, crazy Wolfskin stuff."

"But he's tied up." Olaf's tone was cold with disapproval.

"We were told—" the guard began, and Somerled's voice cut in like a lethal blade.

"Had you something to say?"

"Er—no my lord. It's just—what about the priest?"

"You're telling me you've managed to damage him as well? How very careless. Is he dead?"

A groan from somewhere farther down the hallway indicated this was not so. Spitting out blood and shards of broken tooth, Eyvind found his voice. "Let him go. I will face whatever penalty you have decreed. I'm not afraid to die. But let the sentence be carried out in daylight, before the men of the settlement, not furtively here in darkness. And let the priest go free. He means you no harm."

There was another silence. The men hauled Eyvind to his feet. He could hear Brother Tadhg coughing behind him, a wrenching, rasping sound.

"These men will pay the price for their misguided attempt to take the law into their own hands." Somerled's voice was calm and precise. "That was very foolish. Very foolish indeed. The tide of opinion is against you, Eyvind; this is simply a sign of that."

"Why have you come here?" Eyvind asked as the world spun around him, threatening to blur into the blankness of unconsciousness. The faces of his guards had turned pasty white. "Don't tell me you've developed a sudden passion for justice. Or did I finally shout loudly enough to awaken your conscience?"

"Stop trying to be clever," Somerled snapped. "It's never suited you. We have unexpected visitors, and it's become necessary to show them that you have come to no harm in my custody, thus far." He glanced at the guards. "Bring them up!"

The hall blazed with light. For all it was so late, perhaps close to the first predawn brightening of the sky, few had gone to their beds. Ale cups clinked, platters were strewn on the tables, and a litter of mutton bones and crusts of bread showed a repast had been taken with enthusiasm. There were forty or fifty men assembled there, most of the complement of Somerled's household, and a few women as well. The arbiters had returned. They were not seated calmly at their table now, but stood behind it, their expressions ranging from mild surprise to complete disbelief as they stared at the small group of travelers who had entered through the great rear doors and now stood waiting quietly in the middle of the hall. As Eyvind was dragged forward to the place immediately before Somerled's chair, he looked back down the hall and straight into Margaret's furious, dark eyes. Two burly guards flanked her, with hands poised on sword hilts; others stood behind. They were facing outward: her own protective force, then, not some warders set to confine her.

"My lady," Eyvind managed, not understanding at all what was happening, but seeing in her wan features a shadow of something deeply reassuring. It was, he thought, the quality that Ulf had possessed in abundance, and which Somerled had never been able to grasp: the understanding of what was right. He could hear Tadhg's labored breathing; the little brother stood close by him, a guard at his elbow as if he, too, were on trial here.

"These men have been beaten." Margaret's tone was crisp and challenging. "I thought you said Eyvind was being held, awaiting a verdict. He's bleeding. The priest is covered in bruises. Has it come to this, that we set thugs on our prisoners now, instead of observing basic rules of fair play? I am ashamed to see this, ashamed for myself, and ashamed for Ulf, who always sought to carry out his responsibilities in a manner befitting a chieftain of Rogaland. What has come over you? Olaf? Harald? How could you condone such a blatant misuse of authority?"

Feet shuffled; throats were cleared. Somerled had moved up close to Eyvind, in front of the table. He, it seemed, was not afraid to respond.

"My dear, as I said, I did not expect you here, and I do not understand why you have come such a long way tonight, in darkness. It is a taxing ride for a woman; you should rest now, and leave this to the men of the household to settle. It is a sorry affair, scarcely fitting for a lady's ears. I'm sure you are quite exhausted. A private corner, a warm fire . . . In the morning, I'll explain all this. If my men have been a little overzealous, and left the Wolfskin with a bruise or two, it is only their distaste for the treachery he has demonstrated that drove them to it. Please allow me to escort you to your own quarters, my lady, as is appropriate." He stepped forward, smiling.

"Appropriate?" Margaret's tone was icy calm, the very echo of Somerled's own. "I'm not sure we agree on the definition of that word, brother-in-law. Is it appropriate to attack a priest, even one of the Christian persuasion? Do you hear the rasp of that man's breathing? Can you see how hard it is for him to stand upright? Shame on all of you. You have indeed become blind to the ways of justice, which my husband demonstrated so ably, the ways that we all observed at home in Rogaland. What is the Wolfskin's offense? Why is he bound and shackled, he who was ever your most loyal companion? Tell us."

Somerled frowned. "My lady, this is not at all—"

"Appropriate, yes, you told me. I want answers, Somerled. If you will not give them, perhaps Eyvind can tell me himself, if his sojourn in your custody has not taken away his power of speech."

Somerled responded immediately. "Everyone knows what he did. He's a liar and a traitor. Under my laws, a traitor pays with his life. There is no more to be said."

"I see," said Margaret coolly. "And I suppose, in this formal hearing, Eyvind has been allotted his time to speak? What account did he give of himself?"

"He confessed," snapped Somerled. "He confessed to everything. The case is clear-cut. Alas, our old friend's mind has been completely warped by the winter he spent in the custody of these island folk. He's a danger to himself and to all of us. It saddens me to have to tell you this."

Margaret took a step forward, and now Eyvind could see that there was somebody else standing behind her, a slight, dark-cloaked figure bearing some sort of burden in her arms. His scalp prickled; his heart leaped.

"What reason did you have for these actions, Eyvind?" Margaret asked quietly. "You were ever the bravest of warriors, and the truest. My husband held you in high esteem. Why did you try to stop the attack on the Whaleback?"

"It's not necessary that we hear all this rubbish again—" put in Harald Silvertongue angrily.

"Be silent!" The whiplash of Olaf Sveinsson's voice startled them all. "Is not this Lord Ulf's widow? The lady Margaret must be given whatever details she wishes to know. The lady is right; we've been forgetting what is correct here. Speak up, Wolfskin. Perhaps this account will distress you, my lady," he glanced at Margaret, brow furrowed in concern, "but you should hear it."

"Go on, Eyvind." Margaret's voice was calm.

"The attack was wrong," Eyvind said faintly. *Step aside a little. Who is that who stands behind you?* "It was against all the principles of right engagement. The folk of the Whaleback were in mourning. And there was a ring-sworn treaty; Engus intended to keep peace, as Ulf himself did. I only tried to stop an act of barbaric slaughter."

"And?" Margaret was looking at him with something of Somerled's own ferocity in her gaze. It was as if she knew the truth already.

"And . . . and I'm sorry to be the one to tell you this, but it was Somerled who killed your husband. I know this is true, and I have tried to show it, but they say I have no real proof, no true witness. They say I might just as well have done it myself. I'm sorry, my lady, for I have failed here. I have tried to seek justice for Ulf—"

"Nonsense, of course," said Somerled crisply. "The rambling product of a confused mind. Our friend here was always susceptible to female influence. A sorceress caught him in her net. Very sad. He has no case, no witnesses, nothing at all. Ridiculous, the whole effort, and a sorry thing to see, for you are right on one point: this was once the foremost of our warriors, and the truest of friends. Such is the evil these island folk can set in a man's spirit. Weak as they seem, they are still dangerous. We must not forget that. Now, it grows late. Shall we retire, and consider this in the morning?" For all the confidence of his tone, Somerled seemed edgy; Eyvind had learned to read him long ago, and he saw the little twitch in the cheek, the tapping of fingertips against the thigh, the signs of unease. Somerled was nervous. What had they said before in the darkness? Thirty men coming? Somerled had been warned of surprise visitors; it was clearly someone other than Margaret he expected.

"It would be cruel indeed for a brother to kill his brother, so that he could take those things his brother possessed," Margaret said. Her voice was less steady than before, and her face was sickly pale, but she held her head high. "Cruel and unnatural. Should such a crime be committed, it is hard for me to imagine what a just penalty might be for the perpetrator. Such an act is a horror far greater, I believe, than an attempt to stop a misguided attack on a settlement of sleeping folk, who have nothing in their hearts but grief for lost kin, and a will for peace. Do you not think so, you who sit in judgment here?" She turned, looking each of them in the eye: Olaf Sveinsson, Harald Silvertongue, the sea captain, the Wolfskin guards, the men of the court standing motionless around the hall, riveted by the unfolding drama. It was very quiet, so quiet that the rustle of small creatures could be heard in the roof thatch. Last of all, she looked at Somerled. "Do you not think so?" she asked, and her voice was as steady as a rock now, and as hard.

"What I think is immaterial," said Somerled smoothly, "since no such crime is under consideration here, and for all Eyvind's wild accusations, there is not a single unbiased voice that can speak out in support of him."

Margaret smiled. It was a smile to chill the very marrow: the smile on the face of a player as she moves the last piece into place, in anticipation of certain victory. "I see," she said sweetly. "I feel a little faint, brother-in-law. I haven't been well lately. I think I might sit down. A cup of water, maybe. Thank you, Ash," she added as one of her men hurried up with a high-backed chair. She moved aside and seated herself gracefully; it was only those very close, such as Eyvind, who could observe how her hands were shaking. "As you see," Margaret went on, "I have not come alone. This is the lady Nessa, heir to King Engus of the Light Isles. She has traveled here in my safe keeping. Here is your witness, Wolfskin. Here is your voice of truth." Margaret closed her eyes a moment, swaying where she sat. Olaf Sveinsson moved swiftly to fill a cup and set it in her hand.

The cloaked figure moved forward until she stood alone in

the center of the hall, facing Somerled. She slipped the dark, hooded cape from her shoulders. A gasp went up from the crowd, for it seemed an unearthly light clothed her slender person, a light made up of all the subtle colors of the islands: pearl gray, summer sky blue, deep wave green, the pale gold of sand under spring sun, the dark hue of a seal's shining skin. Clad in a shimmering silken gown, her long, brown hair smooth as an otter's pelt, Nessa stood straight and slight before them, her wide, clear gaze meeting Somerled's with no sign of fear. The garland on her head was of finely woven weed, studded with little shells, wound with fern and bracken and the first blush-pink flowers of the season. Eyvind could hear nothing but the beating of his own heart, the joyous, terrified surge of his blood.

"I am Nessa, priestess of the mysteries." The voice was as clear as some sweet chime; the thrill of its power made every nerve quiver, every tongue fall silent. "I am the last of the royal line in the Light Isles. I speak for King Engus and for his kinsmen, cruelly slain as they mourned their dead. I speak for the women and children of our people, held captive in this settlement. I speak for the ancestors, for the ancient powers that dwell in the cairns and the standing stones, for the beings of deep earth and ocean surge; I speak for every creature that inhabits this fair place, and for those who lie slain upon its green fields, their heads sundered from their bodies, their spirits roaming unquiet. I speak for all. What I bear with me is the last, undeniable witness: the voice that must tell deepest truth."

Her slender fingers moved to pluck the dark cloth from the thing she bore in her arms. Before it was yet uncovered, it sounded, shivering. *I am . . . Ulf . . .*

There was another gasp of shock, palpable as a gust of chill wind around the hall. Faces paled; hands moved to make signs of protection. And under cover of the general consternation, Somerled moved. Knife in hand, he lunged toward Nessa with a suddenness that spoke of a Wolfskin's tuition.

The voice came, true, strong, a war trumpet sounding in the heart. *Burn bright! Strike true!* Eyvind scarcely remembered, afterward, how he had done what he did. The leap came almost before the thought, quick as the final spring of the wolf to seize and snap the quarry's neck. He jumped two-footed, bridging the gap before Somerled could lay a hand on her, and with a jerk and a twist brought the king to his knees. A flick of the hands, a sudden sharp tug, and Somerled was drawn back hard against Eyvind's chest with the short chain that joined the Wolfskin's wrists pulled taut around his neck. Eyvind's hands were crossed, his arms holding the iron links tight enough to threaten choking, but not to stop the breath entirely.

"Any of you lays a hand on her, and Somerled dies!" His voice rang out across the hall. "Any of you moves, and I show you how much damage a Wolfskin can do when he sets his mind to it. Now hold your tongues and listen, you blind fools!" He dared to look at Nessa then, where she stood grave and calm not three paces away from him. So close, so close, and it was he who had taught Somerled the trick with the knife and the sudden dash.

"Take what time you need," Eyvind told her quietly, and now he could not stop his voice from shaking. "I won't let them hurt you. I promise."

Nessa nodded, and a tiny, tentative smile curved her mouth, accompanied by the faintest rose-pink blush in the cheeks. It was a smile completely at odds with the solemnity of the strange gathering, where men now stood staring in mingled awe and terror as she drew back the covering fully to reveal the delicate, pale form of the small harp. It was a smile that belonged to someone quite different from the ethereal figure who stood in their midst like a goddess of ancient story. Eyvind's heart stood still. He could not speak, could not summon the slightest response, for love and fear, delight and terror held him frozen in place. Nessa did not seem dissatisfied. Perhaps his eyes spoke for him, for she nodded gravely, the smile gone now, but her gaze warm and true as he had seen it before, when she reached out to him by lamplight. It was only a day ago, a single day, yet it seemed like something from a distant past, as if a whole lifetime had gone by in the span of sunrise to sunrise. Now, locked in this strange embrace, feeling in his own chest each labored breath that Somerled drew, Eyvind could scarcely encompass in his mind the changes that had occurred.

One of Margaret's men stepped forward and unrolled the shining breadth of the wolfskin on the bare earthen floor. Nessa knelt, setting the small harp before her on the skin, and with delicate fingers she touched the little pegs of bone, one, two, three . . . five . . . and the last, which might not be tuned to its true note save in the place where it was called to bear witness. Somerled's body jerked violently as he struggled for freedom. With two hands needed to hold the chain tight, it was not possible for Eyvind to restrain his captive's limbs, and Somerled was a wiry, cunning fighter, well able to extricate himself from awkward situations. Desperation gives a man unnatural strength. Somerled's fingers clawed at the chain. Eyvind pulled his own hands farther across one another; Somerled spluttered, his face turning purple. He writhed anew, straining his body, bracing his legs against the ground in one final effort to topple Eyvind before the harp could be made to speak. Just how long he could maintain this, using the chain alone, Eyvind was unsure. His head was throbbing, his arms ached, and Somerled was struggling in a way that should, he supposed, make him proud of his own teaching all those years ago. He could kill him, of course; that would be easy. It would be too easy.

There was the smallest of sounds across the hall, a low whistle, brief, unobtrusive, a sign well known to any Wolfskin skilled in forest ambush. Eyvind gave a tiny nod, and an instant later a knife flew through the air to land neatly in the hand he had opened in readiness. In the moment of shocked realization, as Somerled took in Grim's self-satisfied grin and the shift in Eyvind's grip, the chain was unhooked, and Somerled was shoved forward until he knelt with his left arm twisted painfully up behind him, and Eyvind's right hand holding the knife at his throat. It had been done in an instant. Nessa looked up, eyes wide in shock.

"It's all right," Eyvind said softly. "Do what must be done." He could see them all now, Grim, Holgar, Erlend, even those who had doubted him, taking up strategic positions around the hall, weapons openly in hand, as if to defy any man who might seek to turn back the tide of events here, now that it had begun to follow the path of truth. Grim could not keep the fierce smile off his bearded countenance; Holgar was nodding approval. Even Erlend had respect in his eyes now, a respect Eyvind had not expected to earn again.

"Sorcery!" hissed Somerled. "Witchcraft! Don't listen to this evil thing!" His words ceased as the knife moved, and a bright drop of blood was seen to trickle down his neck, staining his cream linen scarlet.

"It seems to me," said Olaf Sveinsson, in a voice that blended amazement and respect, fear and wonder, a voice that perhaps reflected what all present had begun to sense in their hearts, "we scarcely need to hear the sound of this instrument, for all of us know our lore, and all of us recognize what it is. One note, one word gave us the voice of our lost chieftain, and we see on the face of our king something that tells a more bitter truth than we could have imagined. Friends, I think we have been blinded by fear and prejudice. I think we have forgotten what kind of men we really are. Let us listen, then, and try to remember what we once knew of justice. Let us listen and weep for our folly."

Somerled writhed in Eyvind's grip. "Fools!" His voice was a strangled whisper. "She binds you all with her dark arts, even as she bound Eyvind and turned him from me! Don't listen, I command you!" The knife scored a fine red line across his neck; he fell silent.

Now it was Harald who spoke, his bluff features flushed with confusion. "If the harp is not what she claims it is, my lord king, then it will not sing, and there's no harm done. But we all know the ancient wisdom of such charms: the tale of Snorri Half-Shoe, who gathered up his son's bones to seek vengeance; the story of the girl who went up Eagle Crag and came back as a voice all gold and white, telling of secret murder and conspiracy. You can only benefit from giving the young lady a hearing, for if this indeed was made from your brother's bones, we all know it can tell only truth. And truth, surely, is what we most sorely need tonight."

Eyvind might have smiled at that, if he could have done. But his hands, one on the knife and one forcing Somerled's arm cruelly up behind him, so that there would not be the slightest risk of harm to her, to Nessa kneeling there so pale, so quiet, so distant and lovely, the hands required all his strength of will; to listen, and breathe, and disregard the pain in one or another part of himself, took all his concentration.

"You won't kill me," Somerled croaked as Nessa turned the last peg. "You don't have it in you. You'd never—"

"He would." It was Margaret who spoke from where she sat, outwardly calm, watching Nessa's fingers on the little bone peg, Nessa's thumb testing the last slender, dark string. "If you laid a hand on her, he'd snuff you out like a candle. I see it in his eyes. And after all, it's not every day one tries to tell the truth, and ends up condemned to death for it." She stood and turned toward the folk assembled there. At the back of the hall, the women of Nessa's people had gathered in a small group, their garments of red and blue and green a note of vibrant color in the lamplight. They held their heads high. Their bruised faces, their shadowed eyes now blazed with pride as their priestess touched her work one last time, then sat back on her heels, waiting. "Let this harp be heard," Margaret said. "It speaks with the voice of Ulf, who was your chieftain. His very bones, his very hair have given it substance. Hear it and weep."

In later times, if a man asked those who were present at Hrossey settlement that night what it was they heard, he would get almost as many different accounts as there were men and women in that hall. There were some who would not tell what the harp had sung to them, and one of these was Margaret, daughter of Thorvald Strong-Arm. Whatever it was she heard, it flooded her face with tears until she put her head in her hands, so others might not witness her grief. Perhaps she heard the words of a young husband driven hard by his vision of a new world, beset by fears of what his brother might do to stop him, a man so desperate to achieve his goal before prophecy overtook him that he had neglected to make time for his wife, planning always to do so one day when there were not so many matters to be attended to, sometime when his settlement was made and his own people and Engus's folk were living the life he wanted so fiercely to make for them. Perhaps, that night, Ulf spoke the words of his heart; perhaps he told Margaret how his admiration and respect for her had blossomed into love, a love which, being a reticent sort of man, he had never been able to put into words. Maybe he told her how much he had longed for a son. Maybe not. Whatever it was the harp sang to Margaret, she kept it to herself.

Others were more forthcoming. It was a terrible tale, Harald Silvertongue related, a tale of fratricide and heinous lust for power, all couched in the most expertly crafted skaldic verses. Now, if a poet could memorize that, it would be a fine piece for recitation on feast days, around the hearth fire. And how wrong they'd been, all of them. Mind you, he'd always had his doubts about Somerled . . .

On some aspects of the tale, all were agreed. There had been a plot, men paid by Ulf's brother to lead others astray, to ambush the chieftain by night on High Island, to bind him with ropes and net, to convey him to his place of cruel execution and above all, to keep their mouths shut afterward. That must have cost Somerled dearly. Still, he had his following, having bought the loyalty of men who were nothing without his favor, and terrified others into silence. He had a persuasive tongue, and a clever way of twisting the facts. They'd all believed the Wolf-skin had been ensorcelled and turned against his own. They'd all believed the island folk were treacherous, murderous savages, expert in the dark arts. But that girl . . . you only had to look at her to see the goodness in her, like a shining light: something more than human, as if a daughter of the goddess Freya walked among them, clad in the very breath of springtime. Besides, this was a bone harp. A bone harp had to tell the truth, everyone knew that.

It was Somerled who had made the knots. It was Somerled who had plugged his brother's mouth with weed, stopping the last cry of truth, and had left him to perish on the cliffs above the dark waters, harried by knife-beaked gulls. Perhaps that part had taken rather longer than Somerled had intended. Ulf had wanted so very badly to live.

As for Eyvind, what he heard was different again. He did not need the story; he knew enough of it already. He felt the deep shudders that ran through Somerled's body, pinned hard against his own; he heard . . . what, exactly? A voice that was neither the speech of a man nor the vibration of strings, a sound that was neither singing nor playing, neither words nor notes but rather something ancient beyond knowing, a presence of ancestral wisdom, like the quiet at the heart of a violent storm, or the turning point where the tide's inward surge becomes outward ebb, or the moment . . . the moment at the end of the exhalation, when life and death are in the balance. It is pause, stillness, waiting. In that moment, he felt the recognition of how precious is life, how wondrous: how foolish a man would be to squander the least instant of such a gift, such an immense and fleeting gift. Eyvind held the knife at his friend's throat; the smallest

movement could rob Somerled of a future, as Somerled had
robbed his brother. Some would think that no more than justice.
But Eyvind heard what he heard, and he looked across at the
woman standing before him, her face pure and pale as moonlight, her strange, wide eyes full of wonder as the song she had
brought to life rang in the air around her, and he knew he was
no arbiter of men's fates, no godlike player of games, dispens-
ing judgment and penalty with a confident hand. These things
were beyond him, they always would be, and he was glad of it.
They were surely beyond any man, however wise.

His head was still hurting; the wonder of this song was not
quite sufficient to drive that away. Other parts of him seemed to
be protesting as well: his jaw, his back, his knees. There was a
certain blurring in his vision, as if the lanterns were somehow
smudged, and bees were buzzing in his ears again. At some
point, he became aware that Grim and Erlend had taken
Somerled from his custody, and relieved him of the knife.
Later, he remembered sitting down on the ground, still shackled, and resting his head on his knees. Closing his eyes: much
better. Then, as the music rose and fell, graceful, terrible, he
thought he could smell a faint scent of spring violets; he
thought there was a soft rustling as of silken cloth, and the
brush of gentle fingers against the swollen and damaged flesh
of his cheek. Under the harp song, he heard a whisper: *I'm so
proud of you, Eyvi. So proud my heart could burst with it.* He
did not open his eyes, lest this be only in his mind. A moment
later the hand withdrew, and it seemed she moved away again.
Only the music remained: the voice of truth, weaving its magic
in the quiet of the crowded hall. And finally, exhausted, aching,
vindicated, Eyvind allowed his tears to flow.

After that, everything seemed to blur into a sort of dream or
nightmare, taking on the unreality the world sometimes does
when one has spent a little too long at the drinking hall. There
was a great roar of a voice from down by the rear doors, shouting, "Where's my brother? What have you done with him? In
Thor's name, I'll skin the lot of you, you godforsaken wretches!
Where is he?" There was no doubting this less than dulcet tone
was Eirik's. Behind it there were other voices now, voices that
did not seem to belong here in the Light Isles, voices of men
farewelled long ago in another spring. The harp was quiet now.

He could not hear Nessa or Margaret or Brother Tadhg. He could not hear Somerled. The manner of the pain in his head suggested it might not be a good idea to open his eyes. But he did, just a slit, to see the broad, hirsute figure of his brother striding toward him down the hall, red-faced and bellowing. Eirik's arm was in a makeshift sling and he had two black eyes.

"Eyvind! Freyr's bollocks, man, what have they done to you? Get these bonds off my brother, you whelps of an evil cur, or I'll show you the edge of this axe double quick! And what in Thor's name is *that?*" Eirik had seen the harp and now fell momentarily quiet.

"Gudbrand! Thorvald! Where are the keys to these shackles?" Olaf Sveinsson asked crisply. "You can release him. I'm sure we have Eyvind's undertaking that he won't leave the settlement until these proceedings are completed. We all need rest before we continue. And we have guests to welcome. Distinguished guests." He glanced toward the rear of the hall, where a large number of men were now entering, men with the salt-stained and weather-beaten look of sea travelers, men with the tall stature and fair complexions of Rogaland. Eyvind knew all of them. They were of the household of Freyrsfjord, and now, coming through the doorway with an air of quiet assurance, there was the broad-shouldered, upright figure of Jarl Magnus himself. Eyvind squinted against the light; knives dug into his skull. A dream, all of it . . . or more than a dream, for perhaps they had actually beaten him to death, down there in the darkness, and this was some vision on the journey beyond. He closed his eyes again, bowing his head, and felt hands on his wrists and ankles, unfastening his bonds. Gudbrand and Thorvald, it seemed, had no difficulty with the sudden change of allegiance required of them. Even so quickly may the balance alter.

Eirik was addressing Olaf now, the roar of his voice barely diminished. "Proceedings? Continue? What proceedings? Are you telling me my brother is accused of some crime?"

Olaf cleared his throat. It takes no little courage to stand up to a Wolfskin when he is in such a temper. "Eyvind has certain charges laid against him. We were deliberating when . . . when events overtook us. We now find ourselves considering charges against the king as well. The one must be weighed—"

"King?" exploded Eirik. "That dark-hearted, devious little

puppet? I can prove your charges in the blink of a mouse's eye-
lid. There's a fellow here, I've brought him with me, will tell
you all about it—the plot to kill Ulf, Somerled's part in it, the
bribes they were paid to set it up and keep silence. This man's
the only one left of them, and scared fit to wet himself. The rest
of the bunch have been picked off one by one. It seems this *king*
of yours didn't trust them not to tell. And he was on to us as
well; ask the priest here, who bears the marks of Somerled's
long arm as Thord and I do. If the Jarl here and his band of in-
trepid voyagers hadn't happened by, we might still be tied up in
some fellow's cowshed. Would you give credence to Somerled's charges against my brother, when I can prove Somerled is
leader here only by virtue of an act of premeditated fratricide?"

"Had you arrived just a little earlier," Olaf said quietly, "you
would have been the bearer of your brother's release from a
sentence of death. As it is, we have already heard the voice of a
witness more powerful than any human tongue. Your man's testimony is hardly required, since Ulf himself has told the truth
here. My lord!" He was speaking to Jarl Magnus now, his voice
taking on a tinge of nervousness. "Welcome to Hrossey! We
had news of your landfall not so long ago. A great surprise.
None dreamed your own seagoing vessel might be ready so
soon, nor that you and your men would think to journey here
but one year after our own voyage. I regret the inadequate welcome, but as you see—"

"I've seen my favorite Wolfskin covered in bruises and
trussed up like a roasting chicken," Magnus observed, "and I
have to say I'm more than a little displeased. You'll have a hard
time convincing me Eyvind's done anything amiss. The lad
hasn't a bad bone in his body. Lady Margaret, it is both pleasure and sadness to see you again; they greeted me as I set foot
on shore with the news of Ulf's death. I'm so sorry, my dear.
And where is Somerled?"

"A little unwell." This was Harald Silvertongue. "Retired to
his own quarters. Holgar and Erlend are keeping an eye on him.
Eyvind did half-slit his throat, after all."

"I see. And I see what stands before us, and believe I recognize its purpose, silent as it is now. We have indeed walked into
strange times here. Poor Ulf. He set out with such hopes, such

dreams. He learned, perhaps, that it is not enough simply to wish that folk might tread a path of amity. In these troubled times, a man without a sword in his hand has no hope of moving forward. Peace is a luxury we cannot afford."

"My lord," Brother Tadhg wheezed, a hand to his ribs, "it is very late, and all have gone long without sleep. Eyvind here is badly hurt and needs the attention of a physician or herbalist, I think. There should be rest for all, before this goes on."

"And you are?"

"My name is Tadhg, a man of Ulster in Erin; but I and several of my kind now dwell nearby on Holy Island, thanks to the kindness of King Engus who ruled in these islands before the coming of your own people. He allowed us freedom to tell our tales and teach of our Christian faith among his own folk. My lord, this lady is Nessa, the niece of that same Engus who was cruelly slain by Somerled's forces. Nessa is the voice of the island people here. It was she who brought this harp to the hall and enabled Ulf's testimony to be heard. And it is she to whom you must speak of the future. In view of what has occurred here, the sudden arrival of yet another complement of voyagers from the east can only give us cause for disquiet."

"Really? Did not Ulf come here in peace?"

"Ulf died," Tadhg said flatly. "It is a long tale, which you should hear before further deliberations occur."

"And does the young lady possess the same excellent grasp of our own tongue as you do, priest?"

"Not as excellent, my lord, but good enough." Nessa's voice was small and clear, delicate and precise. It made everyone go quiet. "I would not expect you to understand so quickly what has happened here, the manner of it, and how much now lies in the balance. We've all gone a long time without sleep, and these men are injured. My lord, your Wolfskin has shown great courage in the most difficult of times. You should hear the tale from myself, and from Lady Margaret, and from Brother Tadhg here, if he is well enough. You should have the story first from us. These other men, they hear Ulf's voice now and say they recognize the truth. But all of them lived in mortal fear of Somerled, and all of them followed him. Dark acts were carried out under his leadership, and what was lost can never be regained. Brother Tadhg is right. The last thing I wanted to see here was another ship full of wheat-fair warriors hung about with the instruments of war. What do you seek in these islands? Power, conquest, dominance, as Somerled did? He burned our king in his own hall, he cut down our young men and imprisoned our women. He took our farms and gave our ancient lands a new name of his own choosing. He sundered the heads of our warriors from their bodies and set them up for birds to peck at. What more is there to take from us, save our belief in ourselves?"

Magnus made no reply. Perhaps he had none. Nessa's words had been a fierce challenge. Into the silence, Margaret spoke.

"A short time for rest, and we must fetch a healer for Eyvind, or—"

"Rona will be here soon," Nessa said, her tone gentler now. "She'll tend to him. Meanwhile, his brother, maybe?"

As she spoke, Eyvind felt the strong grip of Eirik's hands, Eirik's arms hauling him up from the ground, and there was a dog, not Guard, because Guard was surely dead, but another like him, which could only be his own Shadow, dancing about anxiously and jumping up to lick his bruised and bleeding face. Where was Nessa? He could not see her, he wanted to see her . . .

"A short time," Margaret said again. "Decisions must be made soon. My lord Jarl, I'm sure the kitchen can manage a bite to eat for you and your men, you must be weary indeed. It is a trying voyage."

People began to move, to talk among themselves.

"Come on, old fellow," Eirik muttered. "Let's get you out of here. Odin's bones, that so-called friend of yours has a lot to answer for. Wouldn't I like to get my hands on him in a quiet corner . . . and what's all this about throat-slitting?"

Eyvind was incapable of speech. Leaning heavily on his brother's shoulder, with a dizziness in his head that made sensible thought impossible, he managed to open his eyes again, just a crack, and look backward as Eirik led him away. There she was, kneeling on the wolfskin once more, quiet, pale, her graceful hands rewrapping the little harp in its covering of cloth. Its work was done. It would be kept concealed, now, until it could be returned whence it came. By Freyr's manhood, it froze his blood to think where she had had to go, to imagine what she had had to do, to make this thing and bring it here. What courage she had shown, what endurance. How could she be so fragile and yet so strong?

"No, I . . . ," he croaked, and Eirik, somehow understanding, came to a halt, still holding his brother's dead weight propped against one massive shoulder.

She couldn't have heard him. Still, she rose to her feet and walked over, features gravely composed. Her odd, deep eyes, sea-gray shading to darker blue, were troubled, shadowed. For all her display of confidence, Eyvind could tell Nessa was frightened. And she was weary, so weary; he could see the marks of that in the droop of her mouth, the translucent pallor of her cheeks.

". . . will be . . . all right . . ." he managed. "Magnus . . . good man . . ."

"I hope so, Eyvi," she said soberly. "At such times it can be hard to hold on to a vision of the future. Your folk are so strong, strong and determined. And we have so little left to give."

Somehow that hurt him more than any wound, any bruise or battering. It was like a knife straight to the heart. "I'm sorry," he whispered, closing his eyes once more, and he let Eirik lead him away.

People moved about him purposefully, examining his wounds, applying salves, wrapping linen strips around his body. A cup was held to his lips; he drank thirstily. Here in the sleeping chamber shared by the Wolfskins, the light was less bright, a candle only, and the first rays of dawn seeping in down the hallway. Eirik muttered to himself. Grim was quieter, a certain air of satisfaction about him as he readied a pallet, then fetched blankets of best wadmal cloth, far finer than any of them was used to. The cup was offered again. Eyvind sniffed at the contents. Not water this time. They had every intention of rendering him insensible at least until midday, that much was clear. It would not do. It could not be so. His mind dwelt on Nessa's face as he had left her; he saw those clear, courageous eyes which, despite her victory and his own, despite all they had done and all they had endured, had nonetheless held the shadow, not merely of exhaustion, but of defeat. That, he could in no way allow.

He had never been a man of words. He understood there would have to be discussions. He realized Nessa's people would want them gone from these shores, all of them. They could never be accepted here, not after what had been done under Somerled's command. But he knew that Magnus, wise and just chieftain as he was, was also too astute to let slip the chance to secure the use of safe anchorage in such a strategic place, now that he had made the journey for himself and knew it could be done with relative speed. To influence the course of such delicate negotiations was beyond Eyvind's own abilities. Had not Somerled reminded him, this very night, how lacking he was in the skills of weighted argument? It was not he who had won this battle, but Nessa, and the voice she had brought with her. It was Ulf who had defeated Somerled, not a Wolfskin with a talent for killing and no gift at all for words. Still, he was not quite helpless. There was something he could do to start putting it right, something to ease that dark weariness in Nessa's eyes and lift just a little of the burden from her slender shoulders. Perhaps it was all he could do for her, now. She despised them, that was clear. She wanted them gone. Why would there be one rule for Eirik, for Grim and Thord, good men, all of them, and a different rule for himself?

"Odin's bones, Eyvind, lie still, will you? We'll never get this bleeding stopped if you keep bobbing up and down like that. This tooth'll have to come out. Need that fellow with the tongs. Or one of us can do it. Thor's hammer, man, settle down, can't you? You're as twitchy as a brooding hen. Drink that up, don't just hold it."

"No," said Eyvind, and got to his feet. The room reeled, his ears rang with sound, his eyes wanted to close, oh, so much, but he forced them open. "No, not yet. Who's here?"

"What do you mean?"

"Shut the door. Who's here, who's near at hand?"

"Just us," Grim said as Eirik drew the thick, coarse hanging across the doorway. "Just me and Eirik and Thord there. What is it, man? What's eating you?"

"Listen, little brother," said Eirik, planting his bulk in front of the doorway. "I see a look in your eye I recognize, and I don't like it. It suggests to me that rest and recuperation are not exactly foremost in your mind right now. If you think for a moment—"

"I can't stay here. There's something I need to do—"

"Nothing that can't wait," Grim put in firmly.

"Besides," Eirik said, "like it or not, you're under orders to stay here until these legal proceedings are over. Think how it would look if you went rushing off now, guilty or not guilty. Now lie down, drink that up, and shut your big mouth. You're not the only one here who needs sleep, little brother. Whatever it is, now's not the time for it."

"You can't go on, old fellow." Thord's tone was kindly. Thord didn't understand. None of them understood. He had to go on. That was what a Wolfskin did. If it was not the Warfather who had called him to that sudden burst of crazy effort which had saved Nessa, then it was some other deity of equal power, a force which still compelled him forward, weary and damaged as he was. Whatever it was, it spurred him. It drove him. It came to Eyvind, as he lay down obediently on the pallet, that it was his own voice, and a truer one than any that had hitherto commanded his steps. With that knowledge came a clearing of the head, and caution. He made pretense of swallowing the sleeping draft; the woollen blankets soaked up most of it. Now he must wait. Not long: they were all tired. Then he would go and do it, and at least he could show her, before she sent him away, that his own kind was capable of changing if they got the chance. He knew he was not a clever man, but that much, surely, even he could manage.

So it was that a little later, when Eirik and Thord and Grim were sleeping the slumber of deep exhaustion, and the Jarl and his companions were enjoying flatbread and cold mutton by the fire, Eyvind slipped out of the settlement past unattended sentry posts—for what guard need be kept when one's enemy is reduced to a scattering of old women and infants?—and, on a stolen horse, made his way northwestward under the pale, bright sky of a spring morning. By his side ran Shadow. They passed across the borders of King Engus's land, and turned the corner of the hill, that wondrous corner which reveals to the traveler's eye the vast, rising mass of the Whaleback like a great, gray-green sea creature breaching majestically from the western ocean. No smoke rose from the ashes of the hall fire; no clash of battle rang out above the high screams of the gulls. Now he came down the hill and toward the point, and now he could see the line of spears with their strange cargo, stark evidence of the carnage that had defiled this shore so short a time ago. One dawn, one bloody battle, and a whole race of sons and fathers lost. The horse shied; a trembling coursed through its body, and Shadow hung back uneasily. Eyvind dismounted, staying on his feet only by clutching the horse's mane. Gods, he was indeed weakened. He must get a grip on himself. This weariness, these aches and pains were nothing to what others here had endured.

He tied his horse outside the fisherman's hut where, not so long ago, he had confronted Somerled. Somerled. What would happen to him now? The Jarl would decide it according to the penalties of Rogaland, he supposed. There would be a fine paid in ells of wadmal cloth or bags of silver, or they might forbid him to return to the home shore of Freyrsfjord, or to his birth-place in Halogaland. It might all be settled before Eyvind was finished here, for there was much to be done, and only himself to do it.

Eyvind set to with what strength he could summon, noting absently the bracelets of raw flesh around wrists and ankles, the finger that was probably broken, the continuing ache in the jaw. From time to time, blood still trickled in his mouth; he spat, and went on. The line of spears still stood in earth by the point, and on the tidal island the limp forms of Engus's warriors still lay dotted on the grassy slope like some bright flowers of spring-time, vivid in their brave tunics of red and blue and green. There were many birds there, circling above the fallen men, ea-ger for whatever morsel they might scavenge in the hungry times of the nesting season. Eyvind shuddered, remembering Ulf. No time for thinking; it was close to low tide, and he must work quickly. He could not do all that must be done; the rites of farewell, the manner of laying to rest, that was for Nessa and the remnants of her own people to decide. But he could undo this act of sacrilege. He could set things out properly, so that the bodies of the fallen ones lay in some semblance of wholeness. He could cover them until the proper rituals might be enacted. There was enough time, he judged, before the incoming tide washed across the causeway once more, sealing the Whaleback safe from the shore.

The wooden spears were long, and had been thrust in with considerable force. There had been a rage in his people that day. By the time he had wrenched out the first and lowered its pathetic burden to the ground his hands were shaking, and he realized this would be a slower job than he'd thought. A pick or lever of some kind would help, and a bag, for each of these poor, decaying things was part of a man, and must be carried across to the island with a modicum of respect. One could hardly grip them by the hair, as if transporting a carcass for the pot. Eyvind searched inside the darkened corners of the small hut, finding, to his surprise, a pile of fishy-smelling sacks, a shovel or two and a dangerous-looking bar of heavy iron, with a pointed end. Someone, it seemed, had been here with the same intention as himself. Indeed, the longer he stayed on the shore, the more he felt that prickling of the scalp, that shiver of the spine which suggests others are nearby, unseen, watching. Foolish. There was nobody there. The only eyes that observed his labors, his wrenching out of each cruel stake, his careful stowing of their trophies into the waiting sack, were the empty eyes of the slain: brave old man, sturdy warrior, fierce-hearted boy. Their faces held nothing now but the creeping shadow of decay. What they had been, four days since, was wiped away. Even so had Somerled erased these people's future. So quick: as quick as the time it took a lad to swim across the Serpent's Neck and back again, or sweep a winter roof clean of snow.

He came to a spear that had scratches and gouges in the hard earth at its base. Someone had indeed been there before him, and had failed in this work. This one must wait, for now the bags held as much as they could: the remains of six men. Six long shafts of ash lay neatly on the shore. He had laid them close to the water. Perhaps the sea would take them; wood was as scarce as precious amber here, but these, he thought, would never be used for their purpose again, nor taken to form the frame for a cottage roof or warm a man's hearth in the chill of night. They were cursed.

Now came the walk across the narrow pathway between the lovely, many-hued pools of the tide's ebb, fringed by dark fronded weed, strewn with thick, glistening rods of wrack, and dotted with myriad small, scurrying creatures. The sky looked up at him, blue and wide, from the small cups and channels of these ephemeral waterways. He saw Nessa's eyes there, as deep and dazzling as this vision of sky in sea; he saw her little smile.

He walked on over, and up to the place where King Engus's hall had stood.

The work was not easy. There were many men lying here, and women too, and none were familiar to him. Some were whole. He lifted the bones of the king from the ashes of his hall, and laid him down on the sward. The fire had burned hot; there was little left. What song would that harp sing? A wail of grief, a story of loss and waste. A great shout of proud defiance. They had fought on to the last, knowing there was only death in it. The bodies lay in some semblance of peace, each with hands crossed on breast, as Nessa had placed them on that terrible morning when she had sheltered in a secret cove, listening as her folk died there above her. He moved them one by one until the sheltered sward beside the king's hall bore row on row of folk, disposed as gently as his aching arms, his agonized back could manage.

He had worked a long time, had traversed the causeway over and over until all but three of the heads were carried across, when it became apparent to him that he was no longer alone. First it was a lad, surely no more than six or seven, sidling out of a ruined shed to take up the dragging feet of a man Eyvind carried, and help to bear him to his place of rest. The job done, the boy scuttled back to safety; not long after, another child crept out, and another. They had been watching all the time, it seemed, waiting until they could be sure this fearsome-looking warrior with his bloodied face and reeking hands was indeed some kind of friend. And when he returned to the point to gather his final grim harvest, there were women there, those same chalk-faced women of Nessa's household whom he had seen taken captive in this very place as he sat bound and screaming his wrath into Somerled's deaf ears. They were the same women who had walked with bitter pride and bruised faces in Somerled's hall last night, suffering the crude taunts and careless fondling of his own kind. Now, released no doubt on Nessa's demand, their first act had been to return here. Perhaps they, too, had observed him for some time in silence. Now, as he lowered one spear, and two, and three, they moved forward to take up the bloodied contents. One girl hissed at Eyvind, her eyes fierce with hate; another chided her, and somewhere in her speech he heard Nessa's name.

They walked across the causeway in grim procession, dry-eyed, three bearing each a young man's head cradled like some priceless treasure in her arms. Eyvind came behind, head bowed, and after him the old women made their own slow progress, with infants on backs and here and there a tiny, stumbling boy or girl clutching their hands. When they were halfway over, a cry rose into the salt air, a wailing ululation of grief that bristled the hair on his head and set a chill in his blood. Another voice rang out, and another, until the very rocks vibrated with it, and the gulls fell silent before its force. Thus chanting, they crossed to the green field of the Whaleback and formed a ragged circle around the broken bodies of their men. It became apparent to Eyvind, then, that the most difficult part of the morning's work was not his, but theirs. With a song that rose from deepest pain, from a loss beyond the measure of tears, the women of the Whaleback mended the sundered forms of son, husband, father as best they could, setting the ancient hymn of grief spiraling up, up into the pale sky and out across the rock shelves and the waters of the western sea, as if their sorrow might carry to world's end and beyond.

Eyvind stood quiet. Beside him, one of the lads was doing his best to put a brave face on it, but his lip was trembling ominously. Perhaps that was his brother, not so very much older, who lay before him empty-eyed, the neck of his tunic dark with old blood. Eyvind put a hand on the lad's shoulder; a moment later, small fingers crept into his, and the boy gave a sniff, and set his jaw firmly.

"A man can weep, at such times," Eyvind said quietly. "Look at me, after all. And I'm supposed to be a Wolfskin." The boy couldn't understand, of course; none of them could. But by the time the disposal was complete, and the anthem of sorrow died down to a little, mournful melody hummed under the breath by one young woman who rocked and rocked a man's still form in her arms, her eyes squeezed shut so tight it seemed she would never open them on the world again, Eyvind found himself sitting a little farther away, with his back to the remains of a low rock wall, and several children clustered by him as if seeking some kind of shelter in his own massive form. The two lads crouched on either side, and at his feet were a pair of small girls, their pale, translucent skin and long dark hair bringing

Nessa sharply back to his mind. One touched the raw patches on his ankles with small, soft fingers. The other simply squatted there, staring at him round-eyed. A third girl, somewhat older, perched on the wall next to the first lad, and seemed to be trying to ask Eyvind something, but he couldn't understand her, of course. He knew she said *Nessa,* and he nodded at that; he thought she said *Rona,* and he wondered about Rona, since the dog Shadow had returned. Had he heard rightly last night? Had the old woman somehow survived, against the odds? If anyone could do it, she could.

A third lad was scratching the dog behind the ears, talking to it almost as a child would who had not just witnessed so much of death and loss, so much of hatred and cruelty. And the sun was shining; through all the song of anguish, it had cast its light across these green meadows, these strange, lichen-crusted stones, these fair bays and shining waterways in sweet, impartial benison. The season passed, the tide turned. There were children here, children who would one day be young men and women with the same beauty and fire and goodness in their spirits as Nessa, and her young kinsman, Kinart, who now lay here at rest on the hard earth. Shadow pranced forward, planting her feet on Eyvind's shoulders and washing his damaged face with her long, wet tongue. The children laughed, and Eyvind felt a powerful grin stretching his swollen lips. Odin's bones, this tooth really did have to come out.

"To work, now," he told them, rising to his feet with some difficulty. "We must finish and get back before the tide comes up. You'll all have to help me."

Later, a howe would be made in the old manner, of layered stones, and the dead laid to rest within. That would need far greater strength than he could summon now, for all his complement of willing small helpers. But it was important to shield the fallen from the ravages of wind and weather, the careless attention of the passing gulls. The earth would swallow them in its time; that was only as it should be. A simple mound could be laid over them now, a gentle enough blanket to warm their long sleep. All could help with that, all save that one young woman who rocked in place, and would not let go. Her man remained unburied as the shovels rose and fell, as the lads dug, as the girls carried earth with their hands, and the women gathered stones to lay around the edges, to place in spiral and circle, in pattern of blessing and protection. Before it was quite done, they coaxed his fractured body from her clutching arms and laid him by his comrades, and Eyvind spread the soil as softly as he could over the staring eyes and pain-twisted mouth. Who had he been? A fisherman, a shepherd, a young father? He had been loved, that much was sure. When it was done, the woman lay on the ground, her hands thrusting themselves into the earth, her fingers twisting, gripping, and her cry went on, a thin, harsh keening. She would not move, even though the tide had turned and it was time to go.

Finally, with a nod, one of the old women settled in a crouch by her side, and the others moved away, walking in silence now down to the place where the tilt of the Whaleback was lowest. They looked across the causeway to the point, and on the point, now, a group of horsemen waited, the sun touching their weapons to glittering brightness, the stirring breeze fluttering the fringes of their helms and rippling through the thick, shining fur of their strange cloaks. It had not taken Eirik so long, then, to track him down. Thord and Grim flanked his brother, and the fourth man, the one who did not wear a wolf-skin, was Magnus of Freyrsfjord. The women froze in their tracks; the boys whispered to one another, reaching for their little knives.

"It's all right," Eyvind said, trying to reassure them with his tone, his hands. "I'll protect you, I promise. I will make sure no harm comes to any of you. I give you my word." It came to him, as he moved to the front of the line, as he led them forward on the narrow pathway between pools now filling and spilling over, their shawls of weed moving lazily on the flow of the incoming tide, that he could do precisely that. He could guard these folk, he could ensure their farms and their fishing boats were safe, their boundaries secure. He could make it his job to see that these bright-eyed children, who still had laughter somewhere within them after so much terror, grew up strong and brave, wise and glad as their lost fathers and brothers had been. He could teach them to fight. Engus's warriors had fought bravely, but not well enough. An island people needed to learn how to win even when the enemy had greater numbers. They had to know how to prevail by stealth and skill when the invader had superior weapons. He could teach them that. All they needed was time. All they needed was another chance.

"I will protect you," Eyvind said again, and although they could not understand his words it seemed they recognized the meaning, for they followed him across, young women in bright tunics now stained with the marks of their slain men's wounds, children unnaturally quiet, staring at the broad-shouldered figures who sat so still on their horses there where the spears had fringed the shore. The old women walked more steadily, age perhaps giving them a quicker understanding. They reached the shore. The islanders halted close-grouped by the water's edge; memory held them in check here where they had been herded like animals under the goading of the Norsemen's spears. Somerled's hand still stretched like a dark shadow over this place. It was Eyvind who climbed from the flat stones by the causeway, where he had fallen to Grim's hammer blow, up to the higher ground, and stood as straight and tall as he could by Jarl Magnus's horse.

"I'm sorry I disobeyed orders and left the settlement, my lord," he said quietly. "It was necessary. There was a matter to be attended to which could not wait. It is done now, and I will return to face whatever judgment I must. I—" A wave of dizziness caught him; his words faltered.

"Stupid young fool!" growled Eirik, getting down in a hurry and striding over to grip his brother's arm in support. "What in Freyr's name did you think—"

"Eyvind?" Jarl Magnus was gazing across to the Whaleback, his eyes perturbed, his mouth unusually grim. His tone, however, had nothing of censure in it. "Tell me what happened here. Tell me all of it. What is it that Somerled has done, and what must come next?"

Eyvind stared up at him, quite taken aback. The Jarl was asking *him* what to do? Him, Eyvind, who had always been better with his big axe than with his wits?

"This can wait," Eirik snapped. "He's not up to it, my lord—"

"No," Eyvind said. "No, it cannot wait. My lord, there has been a great wrong done here, and we have a chance to make amends, I think. Please hear me out."

Now Grim was bringing up the other horse; with Eirik's help, and a considerable amount of pain, Eyvind managed to scramble up. When he looked back to the shore, the women were moving away, shawls now drawn tight around shoulders or over heads, children shepherded close to their skirts. One of the lads gave a half wave in Eyvind's direction. Eyvind raised a hand in response, and was rewarded with a brief, dazzling grin.

"You've changed, Wolfskin," Magnus observed gravely as they rode away. "Changed so that I would scarcely know you. Still, you're the same lad: fixed straight ahead, true of purpose. Come then, let's have this tale. I see something here that astonishes and saddens me; something that's a great deal deeper than it appears on the surface. Tell us about it, Eyvind. What is it we must do here?"

FIFTEEN

This time he woke slowly. Sensations returned one by one as the cloak of slumber dropped away from him: the pallet soft beneath his aching back, the blankets warm around him, the chamber dim, though there was light seeping in around the fringes of the door hanging, a quality of light that suggested late afternoon and a slow fading to dusk. His jaw still hurt. A cautious exploration with the tongue told him his shattered tooth was gone, and a neat wad of tight-wrapped wool had been plugged in its place. His mouth tasted of some foul herbal concoction. Vaguely, he thought he remembered Rona's face, very stern, as she ordered him to swallow her draft. There had been two dogs by her side, like and like. Guard was alive, then: another small miracle. *Drink,* the old woman had commanded, and he had not needed the language to understand, or to obey. Whatever she had given him, it had flattened him promptly; it seemed he had slept all afternoon.

There were other memories: a ride, during which he had talked a lot and the others had listened in silence, and before that the Whaleback, and those lads with no fathers . . . His hand encountered something soft and warm, and he became aware of a slight weight lying against his body. He raised his head; looked down. His breath caught in his throat. She had fallen asleep there, sitting on a stool by his pallet. Her dark hair fanned shawl-like across him, her head rested on his chest, one small hand pillowed her cheek, and the other lay on the blanket close to his own. Now he scarcely dared move at all, lest he wake her. For it seemed to Eyvind this was another of those moments of enchantment, time out of time, when the world held its breath. All the same, his fingers crept to stroke her hair, to touch her cheek, where the marks of bitter weeping showed red and swollen on the fair skin. There were dark smudges beneath her eyes, and a little sigh in her outward breath. To take away that sorrow, he would give much. He would give his whole life, if that were allowed.

"Eyvi?" Nessa whispered, not opening her eyes.

His hand stilled. Perhaps she had not, after all, been asleep. "You've been crying," was all he seemed to be able to say.

She sat up, wincing as she straightened her cramped limbs. "I must have fallen asleep."

He frowned. "You should have been resting properly. I'm surprised Rona didn't administer a dose to you as well."

Nessa's lips curved. "She did try. I wanted to be here when you woke up. I was worried about you, Eyvi."

He stared at her in amazement. With the weight of her responsibilities, her fears, and her exhaustion, she was worried about *him?*

"Don't be so surprised," Nessa said, looking down at her hands as if suddenly abashed. "You disappeared, after all. And you were so badly injured. Some people were saying you had run away, the same as before. I knew where you had gone, of course. Once they thought to ask me, it was not so hard for them to find you."

"You knew? How?"

She glanced at him under her lashes, eyes bright. "I–I know I hurt you . . . what I said . . . that wasn't fair, and I'm sorry—but I've been so worried, and sad, and then when I saw you . . . I was trying so hard not to cry in front of them all, and . . ." She put her hands up over her face.

"Oh, no, oh, no, don't—" Eyvind moved, his arms enveloping her, holding her close, his cheek against her hair, his heart thumping. "It's all right, it's all right," he murmured, knowing this to be both true and untrue, for the past could never be re-fashioned, but the future, surely, was theirs to make. "Weep all you will, my pearl; you have held back these tears long enough. Let them flow."

For a while Nessa clung to him, and he felt the strangest of feelings flowing through him, as if while he sat here cradling her in his arms his heart were being slowly mended, stitch by stitch, seam by seam, until it would be whole again. At length, she sniffed and wiped a hand across her cheeks, and told him, "I knew where you were because I knew you'd try to make things right for me, for us. That's what you've done all the time. It is no more than the ancestors showed me, though for a while I would not believe them. But you were hurt and sick. I was worried. There's so much in the balance here, so much to be decided. My people depend on me, and I've never done this before, treaties and negotiations, games of power. I'm frightened. I'm fright-ened I may get it wrong, and lose even what little we have left."

She had moved back from his embrace now, but her hands were still in his, small, warm, and sure. Gods, she looked weary. What a burden it was she bore; the whole future of her people rested on her shoulders.

"I hoped it might help, just a little," Eyvind said hesitantly. "What I did this morning, I mean. It seemed important to set it right. But there's no undoing the ill deeds my own people com-mitted here. And I am still a warrior, Nessa, that's what I'm best fit for, and I don't think that will change. I've tried to show you. I've tried to show how I will help, if you'll give me a chance. There were children there this morning, boys and girls of your own folk. They can forgive, they can still smile. They can learn to survive."

Nessa nodded gravely. "I heard the tale of what you did. It was good, Eyvi. It was no less than I expect from you, and will always expect."

"Nessa—"

She looked up at him, brows raised, but he found, this time, he could not put the question into words. Too much depended on the answer.

"What is it you want to ask me?"

He shook his head, looking away, releasing her hand. "I can't. It doesn't matter." But it did, of course; it mattered more than anything. He thrust his feet into his boots, fumbled for a cloak.

"Eyvi?"

When she used that particular tone, he had to look at her. Her expression pierced his heart: the wide, grave eyes, the lips half-smiling, a little hesitant.

"I talked to Rona before, while you were sleeping," she said. "We spoke of many things, yourself included. In particular, we spoke of a promise I made, coming here: a promise given in return for aid with the making of the harp, and its safe delivery to this hall. That was no easy matter, you understand."

"What did you promise?" He forced the question out.

"That I would guard the mysteries as priestess here in the islands. And that I would guide my people as the last of the royal line. Two promises, really. So I was left with a problem. The two do not really go together very well. This was the reason I asked Rona's advice. Promises are not to be broken, not when given so solemnly."

Eyvind was unable to speak.

"I asked Rona, must I choose? And how can I choose, when both vows must be kept? In the preservation of the old secrets lies our people's very being; without that sacred trust, the heart of the islands withers and dies. Yet how can we go on if the royal line falters to an end? How can the Folk endure without true leaders? My child, and only mine, is the heir by blood. Without him, the people have no hope of the future. It is an impossible choice. Surely the wisest woman in the world could not determine what was right."

She paused. Eyvind held his breath.

"Rona laughed," said Nessa. "Then she asked me if you and I hadn't made this choice already?"

He breathed again. "But—" he said, his head reeling.

"Perhaps she knew it from the look in my eyes: from the way I spoke your name. She's a shrewd old woman. She said . . . she said . . ." Nessa faltered suddenly, her cheeks flushing scarlet.

"What did she say?" asked Eyvind gently, as a smile began to curve his mouth, a grin of pure joy in which the pain of bleeding gum and bruised lip were of no account whatever.

"She said, the child I carry now will be a girl, for the mysteries; and the next must be a boy, for the islands. But I don't think I want our son to be a king, Eyvi," Nessa added soberly. "I just want him to have a life of gladness, and purpose, and peace. That's as much as any of us needs."

The turmoil of feeling made it hard to form coherent words. "A child—you are telling me—?"

"Of course, it is much too soon to know such a thing. But Rona seemed quite sure, and she's never been wrong before. I hope this does not displease you, Eyvi. It was somewhat of a shock. Rona will teach her, when she reaches four or five. But I'll be much occupied as well, for it will be necessary for me to do both for a time: to be both priestess and leader. I hope I can be strong enough."

Remembering last night, he had no doubt of that whatever. "You know I will help you," he said, his voice shaking. "All that is in me, I will give you. But you said—your words, last night— what if—?"

"It won't be easy for you. At least you understand that. My people will not forget the slaughter at Ramsbeck, nor the times when Somerled was allowed to act unchecked against us, while your kind stood by. You may spend your whole lifetime atoning for these things, Eyvi. You may never be quite free of the shadow of Somerled's ill deeds, and of your own failure to restrain him. Back home in Rogaland you would probably be some sort of hero, lauded for your bravery, celebrated for your skills in warfare. Most men would not hesitate to sail away on the next tide."

"You do not imagine I would choose—"

"No, Eyvi. I understand what's in your heart, dear one, and I have never doubted your loyalty, not since the day you said sweet things that filled me with confusion." Her hand slipped into his, she laid her head against his shoulder. "I simply want you to know this will be hard for you. Still, you have made a good beginning. They saw you stand against him at the Whale-back. They know you saved my life and Rona's. They know you spoke the truth at risk of harshest penalty. And they watched what you did this morning, and set their own hands to work alongside yours. There is a quality in you that draws folk to follow you. It's like a light, pointing the way forward. It is no won-der they say—" She paused again.

"What, my Bright Star?"

"They give you a name, I cannot translate it into this tongue, but it is an old name, a deep word of the ancestors. It relates to what you wear on your shoulders, and to the hound that follows you so faithfully, and to what you were in your home country. It is somewhat like *dog,* and somewhat like *golden,* and yet it is a name for a man: a man who takes on the garb of the animal to whom he speaks in the night. They know of the skin you wear into battle; they have seen something in you that brings this ancient lore to life, I think. It is a good thing; they will set the highest standard for you, as you do for yourself. Still, I want you to understand how difficult it may be."

"Children, you said. A girl and then a boy. Does this mean you would consider lying with a Wolfskin once more, if the opportunity presented itself?"

"If such a man were my husband," Nessa said with a crooked smile, "the opportunity might present itself quite often, I should think. But he would need to be prepared to stay on these shores: not to heed the call to join a ship and go a-voyaging. He would need to be farmer and fisherman, arbiter and teacher, leader and guardian as well as warrior. He would have to learn how to be a father."

He lifted her hand to his lips; now his own eyes seemed to be full of tears, for the second time today, or perhaps it was the third. He could not form words, but simply bowed his head.

"It's good, I think," Nessa whispered. "It has to be good from now on, doesn't it, if we both try our hardest?"

Then he put his arms around her and held on, feeling her warmth flow into him, feeling her heartbeat against his own, not wanting to move beyond the sweetness of this moment. Still, the shadow was there on the edge of the thought. Somerled. She had said, *Your own failure to restrain him.* That was true. Somerled was his friend, his blood brother, and if it had not been for Somerled, none of this would have happened. There was, therefore, a matter to be attended to before they could move on.

"He asked to see you," Nessa said in a small voice, as if she had read his mind. "Your Jarl Magnus said no, you were to be left sleeping. Rona was here then. She won't let anyone else care for you, says she doesn't trust them. They called her away to tend to Brother Tadhg's injuries. For a holy man, he seems quite prone to trouble."

"Somerled wanted to see me?" Eyvind took a deep breath. Better sooner than later; better now, while he could still summon the will for it. "Where is he? In his own quarters?"

"Are you sure you want to do this?" Nessa asked him gently.

"I owe him this, at least, since we are brothers of a kind," he said. "The chance to speak to me, to explain, perhaps. What comes after will not be for me to determine. Each of us stands accused. Each must face some judgment, and a penalty. And each shares responsibility for the other's offense, I think. That's how it is with brothers. Will you wait here for me? You must rest; I don't like to see you so pale and weary."

"I'm well enough. Go on, then." She stood on tiptoes, and kissed him softly on his swollen lips, a breath of spring, a whisper of promise. "Go now, Eyvi. I'll be waiting when you come back."

Here there were no shackles, no iron grilles. Even the looming presence of Erlend and Holgar, sword and axe at the ready, was no more than Eyvind had encountered when he had faced his friend as a recaptured fugitive. But this well-armed presence did not protect the king now. Instead, it rendered him a prisoner in his own domain.

There was a brief altercation. Eyvind saw the awkwardness in their eyes and heard the hesitation in their voices. Everything had turned around. They had misjudged a comrade. Such an error sat uneasily in a Wolfskin's code of loyalty.

"Let me in," Eyvind said. "And leave the two of us together awhile."

"Alone? That's against orders—"

"Whose orders? Come on, Erlend. I'm completely unarmed. Somerled is in no danger from me, nor I from him. Stand right here by the doorway, if you will. I'll scream for help if I get into trouble, I promise."

Holgar suppressed a snort.

"All the same—" Erlend began, frowning.

"You owe me a favor," Eyvind said quietly. "Come, give me your hand; you, too, Holgar. We must move on from this, all of us. Good. I won't be long."

Somerled was writing. He sat at the small table, an oil lamp to one side, a piece of parchment spread before him. He frowned in concentration as the neat, black script flowed across the pristine surface. His shirt was immaculately clean; above the collar there was a strip of linen tied around his neck. As Eyvind came in he glanced up, his eyes unreadable. The quill ceased its disciplined movement; he laid it down carefully on the table.

"Eyvind." The tone gave nothing away.

"You wanted to see me." Eyvind came forward into the glow of the lamplight. "I'm not sure what to say to you, save to let you know that if you had touched her, I would have killed you. There is no oath in the world that would have stopped me."

"That might have been better," Somerled observed, rising to his feet and moving to the narrow window, where he stood gazing out into the dusk. "A clean ending. Didn't you always prefer that?"

"Must it always be thus?" Eyvind asked him wearily. "That each conversation between us is a kind of battle, a game in which rules are made and broken even as we play? I have not come here for this, Somerled."

"Why did you come?" Somerled's back was still turned, his arms obstinately folded. The stance was familiar; it brought old memories sharply to mind, memories that only made this more difficult.

"I don't know." Eyvind hesitated. "I think, because of . . . duty, obligation. It felt . . . necessary."

"Duty." Somerled's tone was flat. "What duty is that, Eyvind? The duty of a warrior to his chieftain? It cannot be the duty of friend to friend, or brother to brother. That you have already betrayed many times over. You have shown the world quite clearly how little you believe in me." The shoulders were as tense as those of a wild creature poised for flight. He gazed fiercely away.

"Odin's bones, Somerled, I can't talk to you! You don't make sense to me anymore. How can you speak of the duty of brother to brother, when—I don't even know where to begin."

There was a brief silence.

"It was not always thus with the two of us." There was a somewhat different note in Somerled's voice now. He had unfolded his arms and was staring down at his hands; the fingers twisted together.

"I was proud of you once," Eyvind said quietly. "I confess, when first you came to Hammarsby, I resented the task imposed on me. I thought you would never be able to learn anything, and yet at the same time I admired you. You were so quick-witted, so sure of the path you would follow. Then, of course, I discovered that I could teach, and that you could learn. You learned far more than I expected. I think, until the time we left Freyrsfjord and sailed for lands unknown, I still believed that I had succeeded in the task Eirik set me. But I have discovered, between last spring and this, that there was something I did not manage to teach you, and without it the rest was worthless. You always considered me stupid, and I don't suppose that has changed. But it is you whose understanding is lacking, not I. At least I know . . . at least I comprehend—"

"What, Eyvind?" Somerled had half-turned, and there was no trace of scorn in his voice now, no supercilious lift of the brows, no amused quirk of the mouth, only wariness. He stood very still, waiting.

"It is hard to put it into words. The value of a life, I think; I have learned how precious that is, and what it means to take that gift away. I know not a moment must be wasted. And I have learned what love is. If I had been able to teach you those things, your path would have been different. I failed you in that, but I did not let myself see my error until it was too late."

"Oh, dear, my old friend! You make an even worse philosopher than you do a lawman. It simply isn't true."

"What do you mean?" Eyvind asked as Somerled stepped forward from the shadows, his eyes now bright with something new, something indefinable.

"One of these lessons, at least, I did learn at Hammarsby," Somerled said in a voice no stronger than a whisper. "You just never saw it. Even now you are blind to it. That's just as well, perhaps." He cleared his throat. "Eyvind, what will happen here? I find myself weary, and much inclined toward a quick and efficient conclusion. What will Magnus do, do you think?"

"You're asking me? I imagine our offenses will be weighed one against the other. You don't need me to explain the law to you, Somerled. It's common for both men to pay a fine or receive some other penalty: the forfeiture of lands or office, perhaps banishment. It is my honest opinion that your own crime should be judged more heinous than mine. A man does not kill his brother, not even when that brother is a cruel and dangerous tyrant. And Ulf was not that; he was a fine chieftain, a man of honor. I still can't understand why you did it."

"Cannot a man act decisively in order to comply with a foretelling?" Somerled's brows lifted now in familiar fashion. "Indeed, I brought not one but two such prophecies to fruition here. That is an achievement, surely."

"If that's a joke," Eyvind said, his temper growing shorter, "it's a black and bitter one. You cannot be unaware of what you unleashed on the people of these islands."

"Ah." Somerled was by the table now; his long fingers took up the quill, rolling it absently. "The people of the islands. That is the heart of the matter for you, isn't it? Or rather, one particular person. I saw how you looked at her, and she at you with those deceptively pure eyes. What happened to you, Wolfskin? Did you get lonely without your pink and gold whore? Did the lusts of the flesh become too pressing to ignore, out there in the wilderness among those benighted natives? How was she? Did she—"

"Enough." Eyvind controlled his breathing with some difficulty. He forced his tight-clenched fists to relax. "If your intention is to enrage me to the point where I set my hands around your neck and strangle you, you misjudge my self-control. Such summary justice is not sufficient in this case. You must answer to the Jarl and to Nessa's people, not to me. This would be too easy."

"You disappoint me, Eyvind. You would have killed me last night, you said so yourself. Why not now?"

"I am not angry now, only disappointed. I saw so much in you. Now I see only the waste of what you could have been."

"Indeed. So, in your mind, you have judged me already, and found me gravely wanting. Under my own laws the penalty would be no less than I set for you. I have to say, to die quickly and cleanly at your hands would suit me far better than a lengthy hearing and a penalty determined by those who can never hope to understand me. A merciful, efficient end: the least of creatures deserves that. Isn't that what you always maintained?"

"This is not a hunt."

"Maybe not; still, I have the uncomfortable sensation of sitting in a snare, waiting."

Eyvind made no comment.

"These folk are not worth your loyalty, Eyvind," Somerled said, now rolling up the parchment with its tidy, black rows of script and fastening it with a cord. "Nor were they worth the attention Ulf lavished on them. My brother was misguided and soft, two fatal flaws in a leader. He listened too attentively to the opinions of others. The fire that drove him to these shores burned out under an excess of good intentions. Eyvind, these people cannot endure here. Our kind are stronger, abler, in every way fitter to rule. You are blinded by the heat of what you call love. Step back a little and use what intellect you possess. Even you must see that, in time, these islands will be governed by men of Rogaland, and rightly so. The place will be swept clean of these people; it will be as if they had never existed. My only fault, I think, was that I dared to make that decision too early. Now it seems I have been robbed of my chance to achieve the conquest myself. But what I began, others will continue, until the only faces seen on this shore will be those of our own kind. The place provides safe haven for our ships. It is a prime staging post for voyages south and west, and the pickings there are substantial, if travelers' tales are to be believed. This change is inevitable."

He had been wrong, Eyvind thought, to believe Somerled could no longer shock him. "Thor be my witness," he whispered, "I will stand against such an abomination until the last breath leaves my body. These are an ancient people. There is a strength in them that you have not seen, not even though it stood before you in plain view last night. It is in a king's decision to hold firm against an attack he knew he could not counter; it is in a girl's determination to bring the truth before her enemies at risk of her own life. It is in the bruised face and laboring breath of the Christian priest, and the brave smile of a child. You are the one who lacks understanding if you remain blind to that. Odin's bones, Somerled, you must indeed have loathed and resented your brother, that you stole not only his life but also his life's vision. In doing that, you came close to destroying what was here before we touched this shore: a fine, courageous people who had tenanted this land peaceably since time before time. For what? Because you feared the uncertainty of an old woman's auguries, half-seen in a cloud of smoke?"

"Shut your mouth! You understand nothing!" Somerled's voice was shaking, the cloak of indifference quite gone. "Do you think Ulf was the only one with hopes and dreams? I'm sorry I have disappointed you, but unfortunately that seems to be what I do. I tried to be—I tried to—" He faltered to a stop, gazing at Eyvind, his eyes cave-dark, his mouth a tight line.

Suddenly, the desperate child of Hammarsby was there, holding himself rigidly upright, forbidding himself the words that might have revealed too much, forcing back the tears that might have shown his hurt. Eyvind saw that, and heard the words from long ago. *Nobody cares what happens to me.* He felt his heart contract. And yet, he could not see that lonely child without the vision of Engus's ruined hall, and Ulf's bloodless face pressed close to his own, and Nessa's tears. He could not pity that lost boy without feeling the warmth of a child's fingers creeping into his, and seeing the courage in a lad's face as he watched father, brother, kinsman laid in earth.

"The error was not yours, Somerled," Eyvind said quietly, moving to the doorway. "It was mine. I failed to teach you the one lesson you could not do without: how to be a man."

In the moment before he turned and went out, he saw the change on Somerled's face. It was as if a mask, which had hitherto varied only from bloodless calm to mild mockery to scathing disapproval, were now stripped away entirely to show the face that had been present beneath it all along, but skillfully hidden. There was love there, and longing, and self-mockery. There was fierce intelligence and deepest pain. To look on that face too long was to weep hot tears for what might have been. Ducking under the lintel and around the hanging, Eyvind fled.

In the end there was no lengthy deliberation, no drawing out of testimony, and very little in the way of legal arguments. Magnus had, after all, been their chieftain and leader back home in Rogaland, and the expedition to the Light Isles had depended to no small degree on his patronage and approval. Besides, he was himself kinsman to the dead man, Ulf, and the Wolfskin was still a member of his personal guard, having been granted leave only from spring till autumn. He had heard the story, Magnus informed them. Olaf had told him, with Harald filling in the gaps. He had spoken to Margaret and to the foreign princess. He had had a word with the Christian priest. The one voice he had not heard, he informed all those assembled in the hall that evening, was Somerled's. And Somerled now faced a charge of murder. It was reasonable that he be allowed to defend himself. Briefly. They were all tired.

Indeed, he was weary enough himself, Eyvind thought, and he could see the marks of the same exhaustion on many faces gathered in the lamplit hall tonight. Magnus did not believe in the use of shackles, nor in the formal arrangement of arbiters at a table with captives forced to stand before them. This was more like the Thing of Rogaland, with folk grouped by family or faction. Eyvind stood with his brother, Eirik; Thord and Grim had placed themselves close by. Magnus had arranged seats near the hearth for Nessa and Margaret and for Brother Tadhg, and he sat close to them with Olaf Sveinsson standing by his chair. The men from the knarr were no longer present, having seen, perhaps, the wisdom of an unobtrusive return to their duties in Hafnarvagr, followed, with luck, by a quick voyage home with no questions asked.

Eyvind knew that Nessa had not slept yet, save for that brief respite as she sat by his bedside. After he had left Somerled, Eirik had waylaid him with questions, and with arguments about family and duty and plain common sense. He had spoken at length of Hammarsby and of their mother. By the time that was over, Nessa had been in private conference with the Jarl for some time, and Eyvind had not seen her. Rona now stood behind her student, a grim expression on her face; the dogs flanked her like twin guardians from some ancient tale. As for Nessa herself, she was milk-pale, with purple shadows like bruises under her eyes. It seemed to Eyvind she kept herself sitting so straight by an immense effort of will. Let this be short, he prayed. Let it be as short as Somerled himself wished: brief and merciful. There comes a point where one must say, enough. And then, he told himself, he would see she got into bed, and he would tuck the blankets around her, Rona or no Rona, and hold her hand until she fell asleep. What did Eirik know about duty, anyway?

Tonight it was Somerled's turn to stand before the court and be judged. He wore the plainest of black tunics, and his complexion rivaled the bandage at his throat for pallor. There may not have been visible restraints, such as iron rings and chains, but Holgar and Erlend stood watchful at a discreet distance. All bore the marks of a long time without rest. A Wolfskin, however, can endure such privations and still be relied upon to act instantly and effectively when required. Somerled had forgotten that, last night.

"Let us begin," Magnus said, rising to his feet. "There were charges laid against my Wolfskin, Eyvind Hallvardsson, and he has admitted they were true, in terms of fact. I've been given several accounts of what happened that morning at the Whale-back, and I have concluded that Eyvind's actions were entirely justified. The attack was a shocking breach of a ring-sworn treaty. I hope you feel deepest shame, every one of you. What you have done here is unforgivable."

Harald Silvertongue cleared his throat. "The men were obeying Somerled's orders, my lord Jarl. It had been a long winter of inactivity. This cursed place—"

"There comes a point," Magnus said, "when blind obedience must give way to some questioning of conscience, however great one's fear of punishment. Don't get me wrong. I'm as ready as the next man to take decisive action in the field when it's called for, and my Wolfskins don't hesitate to charge forward on my be-half. Thor rewards such courageous deeds. Eyvind here has a reputation as the most daring of all; his axe has tasted its share of blood and will do so again, I dare say. Still, I weigh matters first. I don't pit myself against ill-armed households of fishermen and shepherds. I don't offer a man the hand of friendship only to stick a knife in his back. Tell us what happened to Hakon, Somerled. How is it that my loyal warrior, whom I released with much reluctance from my service, is no longer with us?"

Magnus's tone had remained level and courteous as he asked the sudden, unexpected question. His eyes were iron-hard.

"Hakon was not as loyal as you believed," Somerled said flatly. His face was quite without expression. "He died. There is no more to be said."

It was not quite a confession. Still, a ripple of horror ran through the crowd, and Eirik Hallvardsson was seen to lay a white-knuckled hand on his sword hilt.

"No? Then tell us about your brother. We heard his own voice here, a wondrous thing indeed, which served only to deepen my respect for the lady Nessa and her people. I've heard a more earthly witness as well, thanks to Thord and Eirik, who managed to get the man to this hall, despite being set upon by your hired henchmen. There is, therefore, no doubt at all that you were re-sponsible for Ulf's death, nor that this must be considered against Eyvind's act of disobedience to you. I was ever proud that your

brother was my kinsman; he was a fine man, fierce in his convic-
tions and steadfast of purpose. I feel a great deal less ready to acknowledge my blood bond with you. Still, it should not be
discounted when we weigh crime and penalty. You'd best account
for yourself now, Somerled. This has been a long, weary time.
Under your own new laws, Olaf tells me, the penalty for such a
killing would be death, and the sentence would be carried out at
sunrise tomorrow. I am uncertain as to which set of rules we
should follow here. After all, you are still king of Hrossey."

"My lord—"

"But—"

Eyvind stepped forward in shocked protest. The other voice
that spoke was Margaret's. Jarl Magnus silenced them both
with a curt gesture.

"The charge is proven, Somerled," he said, fixing his gray
eyes on the slender, upright figure in black. Somerled's gaze
was level, impassive. He appeared entirely relaxed. "Have you
anything to offer in mitigation? An explanation for this coldly
premeditated act of slaughter, this abomination that went
against every code of kinship and loyalty? Speak now. Tell us."

Somerled drew a very deep breath and let it out slowly. Perhaps, after all, he was not so relaxed. The little muscle in his
cheek was twitching. "There really seems no point," he said
quietly. "If the charge is proven, why would I make the effort to
deny it? I find I am rather weary and disinclined to legal arguments, and a simple explanation of such a complex matter is
beyond me tonight. I prefer to say nothing."

The hall buzzed with the sound of startled voices. They had
expected something exceptional from this subtle, cunning
wordsmith who had so quickly turned from feared chieftain to
despised brother-killer. They had not anticipated silence.

"We want your explanation!" Eirik called out from amidst
the hubbub. "We deserve that at least! Justify yourself!"

"This is a coward's way!" Thord put in, turning his gap-
toothed grimace on Somerled and raising a bandaged fist. "We
need satisfaction!"

Jarl Magnus lifted a hand, and folk hushed.

"This would be most unwise, Somerled," the Jarl said. "You
cannot sway the guilty verdict, but you have the power to influence the penalty we determine, if you can provide some

words in your own defense. And we know you to be able in such arguments; we have seen you defend many a villain in Rogaland with wit and fluency, and reduce a fine from fifty ells to five, or a year's banishment to a mere purse of scrap silver. There is more in the balance here than that: far more. Do you set such a low value on yourself, that you offer no defense whatever? Don't you understand what the penalty could be?"

Somerled smiled. It was an expression quite without mirth, save for that bitter self-mockery from which Eyvind had earlier turned his gaze. Eyvind's heart thumped. He found he was willing his old friend to speak. Now would be the time, now would be Somerled's chance to turn things around, here where he had the ears of all the court, here where he could show Eirik and Nessa and the Jarl himself that they had been mistaken about him. He could show that another man existed, the one behind the mask, a man who was clever and able, who could learn and grow and be a real king. He could set this right and walk forward on a new path. A fine, a time in exile, these could be easily sustained. All Somerled had to say was, *I was wrong, and I am sorry.*

Somerled shrugged. His eyes passed over Magnus and Nessa and Margaret. His gaze met Eyvind's, and changed. His words fell into the silence like drops of chill water.

"I have nothing to say." He bowed his head and closed his eyes, as if what he had seen in the Wolfskin's face was, at last, too hard to bear.

"Very well," Magnus said heavily. "A man has the right to remain silent, even when to do so is the height of folly. And you know your own laws, I suppose. Under those, a man who kills his kinsman faces summary execution, by what means the arbiters deem appropriate. Such a penalty could only be reversed or mitigated if the circumstances were quite exceptional, and only at the king's request. As the king himself stands guilty here, I suppose that decision would fall to me. I do not like these new rules of yours, King Somerled. I find them somewhat barbaric. Still, it seems entirely appropriate that we adhere to them for a little. Until dawn tomorrow, I think."

There was a mutter of approval, centered on Eirik Hallvardsson and the Wolfskins. Margaret sat with lips pressed tight together; the glow of the lamplight failed to relieve the ghastly pallor of her face. Nessa's eyes were wide and troubled, but the man she watched was not Somerled.

"Death at sunrise," Somerled observed. "It is not so very long to wait. Just don't give me that Christian priest to keep me company. I find him meddlesome and irritating, and I've no wish to spend my last night on earth listening to his pathetic efforts to convert me."

It was courageous. Still, he did not look up.

"My lord—" Margaret's words burst out as if against her better judgment. "This is—it is—"

"You wish to speak, my dear?" Magnus queried. "Please do; you most certainly have the right, as the slain man's widow."

Eyvind saw Nessa reach out and take Margaret's hand in hers; on the other side, Rona had laid her own gnarled hand on the young widow's shoulder.

"I—" Margaret faltered; a shiver seemed to run through her. "It is just that . . . my lord, my husband's murder was a terrible blow. As you said, it was an abomination. There seemed no reason for it, no way it could be justified. It is this, I imagine, that holds his brother silent now."

Somerled's lips curved in the shadow of a smile. Margaret, too, had always been clever at playing games.

"All the same," she went on, her voice now almost under control, "what you propose seems somewhat . . . uncivilized. In Rogaland, a guilty man pays a price, and learns from his error. If the penalty is death, a man has no chance to learn."

Magnus turned to stare at her. His surprise was clear. "You speak on Somerled's behalf?" he asked. "Somerled, who killed your husband?"

Margaret's lips tightened. Her face was sheet-white. "No, my lord," she said. "It simply seems to me that if we follow this king's new laws in determining his penalty, we show ourselves to be exactly what he is: cruel and unjust. We show ourselves to be blind to the value of a human life."

"Ulf would not have wanted death for his brother." It was Tadhg who spoke now, his voice still somewhat breathless. "Your kinsman was keenly interested in the teachings of my own faith, and we spoke long of such matters. He valued the philosophy of forgiveness, and the sanctity of human life. God pardons all sins, even the murder of a brother, if we turn to him.

Ulf would have wanted Somerled to have a chance to seek God's grace, to repent of his wrongdoing. He would have wished that even though he spoke, also, of how much he feared his brother and the havoc that Somerled might wreak if there were no one to check him."

"Tell me," Magnus said, fingering his neatly trimmed beard and frowning, "do you see something in this man that I cannot see? I have known Somerled a long time, since he came to Freyrsfjord as no more than a boy, and proved himself most able in a courtier's arts: poetry, games, law speaking, and even, to an extent, the wielding of sword and bow. A year or two ago, I would have said he was a young man of great potential, who had yet to rise above certain . . . flaws of character, shall we say . . . which held him back. Today, I am not so sure. You speak of learning, Lady Margaret. Perhaps such a man cannot learn. It seems to me entirely just that, having established his own rule of law here, he should himself be subject to it. Would you not wish satisfaction for your husband's cruel death?"

"My lord," said Margaret quietly, "I would wish that the penalty this man pays be appropriate to his wrongdoing. An execution is quick: in its way, merciful. Death is what he wants. It is the easy way out."

Magnus was silent for a time, while low-pitched conversation hummed around the hall. Rona was bringing water for Margaret, watching hawk-eyed as she finished every drop. It must end soon, Eyvind thought. One way or another, they must end it. Somerled stood very still, maintaining his poise, his impassive gaze turned in the direction of Magnus and Olaf. His hands were laced together in front of him. The fingers were tight: the only sign that he was less than perfectly comfortable. In times past, he had considered Margaret a worthy opponent, but he had never liked to concede a point.

"This presents a difficulty," Magnus said. "Still, no problem is without its solution. We have not yet asked the lady Nessa for an opinion. Yet she, of all those present tonight, can most truly pass judgment on what Somerled has done in these islands. It is her own people who have suffered under his brutal rule, her land that has labored under the yoke of his tyranny. She is not only the royal princess of this place, but also a wise woman, able to touch what lies beyond the shadows. That we saw last night, when she conjured my lost kinsman's voice for all to hear. Let us seek her wisdom here, and that of the elder priest-ess, her companion. This decision is, I believe, beyond the reach of our own knowledge. Will you speak, my lady?"

Nessa had been translating in a whisper for Rona. Eyvind's breath caught in his throat as she rose to her feet, now clad not in the strange and wondrous gown of last night but in a plain blue tunic and skirt, the everyday garb of the island women. Her hair was severely plaited down her back; she wore no adornment save the narrow cord that bound it, no jewelry, no finery. Yet she seemed to him entirely lovely, completely wondrous, as if each time he looked on her she had grown in beauty and power.

"My lord, I thank you for your courtesy," Nessa said gravely. "But I can in no way do as you ask. Were this man on trial for the great wrong he has done my people—the slaughter and maim-ing, the abduction of the innocent and helpless, the disregard for the ancestors, whose bones are the deep fabric of the islands—I would indeed pass judgment. I would say to him: go free, for your freedom will be short indeed. The ancient powers of the Light Isles will not allow such a creature of evil to walk long un-scathed on these fair fields, on these bright shores. But the charge Somerled faces tonight is not within any authority of my own people to judge. He answers here only for the murder of his brother, an offense in which both perpetrator and victim are of your people. It is a matter for your law and your judgment."

There was a brief silence. They appeared to have reached an impasse. Somerled folded his arms and shifted his weight from one foot to the other; Nessa's words, it seemed, had penetrated the façade of calm.

"Odin's bones," he snapped, "are we to be here all night? It is plain, is it not, why I instituted new rules to expedite the con-duct of legal hearings. It would be simpler by far—"

"I'm not finished," Nessa said softly, turning her wide gray eyes directly on Somerled's face. There was something there that rendered him instantly silent, something Eyvind thought was ancient, and wise, and extremely dangerous. A chill went up his spine. "I understand the difficulty you face," Nessa went on, "and I will offer you a solution. Sometimes a problem arises that is indeed beyond the scope of man's laws and codes, one that requires a wisdom beyond that of the sagest among us. I do not expect you to understand our own beliefs and observances. No doubt you would find them as hard to comprehend as I do Thor and his war hammer. Were I myself faced with such a dilemma as you have before you, I would seek guidance from the powers of earth and ocean. I would seek answers in the patterns of sun, moon, and stars. I would seek the wisdom that lies in the hidden places, the truth that cries in the voice of the wind. Were I to seek out such guidance tonight, I have no doubt as to what I should be told. There is only one man among you who is qualified to make this decision. He is the one man who saw the truth, and had the courage to lay it before Somerled at risk of his own life. He knows Somerled better than any of you. Ask Eyvind, therefore, to determine the penalty for his friend. The ancestors have made it plain to us from the first that your Wolfskin must play a vital part in the unfolding of this tale. Let him choose."

As Eyvind stood stunned, pride and horror warring within him, and the assembled folk broke into excited talk once more, the sound of Somerled's laughter rang out through the hall, at once bitter, shocked, and genuinely amused.

"By all the gods!" Somerled exclaimed. "The Wolfskin, who never did learn to put more than five runes together and struggled to comprehend the simplest point of law, making the final decision on the life of a king? It's clear the tale you refer to is no heroic saga set out in cunning skaldic verse, but a trifling thing best suited to the drinking halls frequented by such mindless servants of Thor as this fellow you call courageous." He turned to Magnus, his face now blazing with outrage. "He bedded her, of course. That's what this is all about, a simple matter of the lusts of the flesh. An impressionable young woman, a yellow-haired warrior they used to call Little Ox—what do you expect? The girl wants him back between her legs, that's all. She just can't get enough."

Red rage welled in Eyvind's head, blinding and terrible; the voice called in his ear, urging him to action. It would be three long paces to Somerled's side, and a matter of moments to lay hands around his neck, give a strategic squeeze, and make an end to his filthy accusations. Everything in him was screaming, *Forward!* Nessa's eyes were on him, and Rona's, and the Jarl's. He drew a long breath. He held himself very still: as still as a standing stone. The red mist cleared; the voice faded. There was, after all, a choice. If he had once been the mindless servant of Thor whom Somerled described, he was no longer.

It was Rona's voice that rang out now, an old woman's voice, but strong and thrilling. Brother Tadhg provided a prompt translation.

"The wise woman asks Somerled if he has forgotten how much can change from spring to spring? He would be wise to recall it, for in a few seasons' space, the Wolfskin will be the father of kings, while he himself will be no more than a shadow on the edge of memory."

"You astonish me," Magnus said, staring at Rona, who returned his gaze with fierce eyes. "The father of kings? I do not think this can be. I must make it clear to you," he looked at Nessa now, "that Eyvind was given leave to come here only for a short time. I was most reluctant to release him from my service; indeed, it was only through the offices of Somerled himself that I gave his friend permission to accompany him. Eyvind is foremost among my strike force, and an indispensable member of my personal guard. He's the best warrior we have, and a great favorite on the sporting field. He simply cannot stay on here. Indeed, I believed it was the lady Nessa's desire that all of us quit these shores without delay. The events of the past year have given her no cause to trust our kind. For now, I plan to respect her wishes and withdraw my forces, both those of Ulf's ill-fated expedition and my own exploratory voyage. Though I have to say, I believe it is inevitable that others will make their way here wanting to settle, whether by force of arms or peaceably. You will not keep these islands to yourselves much longer, my dear. Nor will you keep my favorite Wolfskin, I think."

Nessa's hands were clutched tightly together; still, her voice was that of a leader, level and considered. "My lord, I thank you for your wisdom in choosing to withdraw your men from the Light Isles. That is a great gain for my people. As to the future, I am not so foolish that I cannot see a time of change is upon us. All I seek is a respite, enough time to prepare. Without that, the wisdom of the ancestors will indeed be lost. My lord, I am not entirely without practicality. Many of our able-bodied men were slain, in the rout at Ramsbeck, in the assault on the Whaleback, or alone and silently while on watch in darkness. Our women and children are strong, but not so strong that they can make up all that was lost. We need help. Your Wolfskin, Eyvind, is prepared to stay and offer us that if you will release him. We had hoped that he would stay." The well-controlled voice cracked. It had been a very long time to remain strong.

"Your problem can be solved another way," Magnus said, and Eyvind remembered that the Jarl himself had always had a fondness for games. "When I allowed my men to journey here with Ulf, some of them were given leave to stay on and settle. Hakon was one. Alas, Hakon is no longer with us. Thord might be persuaded to remain here; I'm told his woman has taken a liking to the place. I dare say one or two other volunteers may be found, provided you're able to guarantee their safety once the rest of us sail. An easy matter, I think. You should get your complement of able-bodied men."

"My lord," Nessa's voice was shaking now, "I don't think I have made myself sufficiently clear. My grasp of your tongue is less than perfect, I know. If one or two men wish to stay on, I will consider them. But it is this warrior, in particular, whom I wish to retain."

Somerled grinned. "As I said," he commented.

"Mmm," mused Magnus with the trace of a smile. "A dilemma, for I, too, wish to retain him. Let's hear what the man himself has to say. Step forward, Eyvind."

He stood before them, his wolfskin on his shoulders, his sword by his side, the beating of his heart now strong and steady. The rage was gone and with it the last traces of uncertainty. He looked at Nessa. "You know what's in my heart," he said. "I have sworn to be guard and protector to your people, and I would do no less for you. It is a lifelong promise. My lord Jarl, I ask to be released from my bond to you and permitted to remain on the islands. You are a fine and fair leader, a model for any man to aspire to. But I must walk on my own path now, and follow the voice within me. Will you let me go?"

"Lifelong promise, huh!" Somerled spat. "Our friend here breaks vows and changes allegiance as often as a courtier changes his shirt. What about his oath of loyalty to me? What about his lifelong vow to Thor? You can't trust him, Nessa. He'll serve you awhile then toss you aside as soon as another great cause takes his fancy. Eyvind is no hero. He's nothing but a big man with a limited capacity for thought and a newfound penchant for attempting what's just a little beyond him. You'd have been much better to stick to killing, old friend. You're so good at that."

"Enough!" Magnus's voice was like a thunderclap; everyone jumped. "I did not give you leave to speak. Well, Eyvind," this in a different tone, "I see a solution here. A test: a test of your ability to carry out the duties this lady seems to envisage for you. We know you are strong and determined. We know you are steadfast and courageous. Now you must show us that you have also learned wisdom."

"What do you mean, my lord?" Even as he spoke, Eyvind realized what was intended. A dark matter indeed: the most perilous of games.

"You must pronounce sentence on Somerled," Magnus said quietly. "Lady Nessa herself set you the task, and I think you must pass the test not simply to satisfy myself and the folk assembled here, but also the lady. If I am content with your judgment I will release you from my service. And I will consider your offense of disobedience to your chieftain fully acquitted. If your decision fails to please me, or the court, or the lady, then you must honor your vow to me and return to Rogaland with my vessel, before next full moon. Once in Freyrsfjord, I would expect at least another five years' service from you. Do you understand me?"

"Yes, my lord."

"Do you need time to consider? This man's life hangs in the balance, after all, and he is your brother, sworn in blood. Such a decision is not made lightly."

"Odin's bones, can we just get on with this?" Somerled's tone was brittle. "I've never known such a tedious, long-winded debate—"

"I need no further time," Eyvind said. His heart was beating hard now, hard and quick, and yet at the same time he felt a curious sort of calm settle over him. There was no need to think about what he would say. The answer was there inside him, arrived complete and unbidden. He turned to face Somerled. "You are indeed my brother," he said quietly. "The marks we bear are witness to that bond, and I have done my best to honor it. You think I have betrayed that promise, I know. But it is not so. I have watched as you made your path through life, as your mind grew ever more cunning, your decisions and your actions harder to understand. I have wondered, often, what it was that drove you, why the craving for recognition burned in you so strongly that it rendered you blind to the consequences of your actions. It seemed you could see no man's pathway but your own. In time I recognized the way you had chosen was wrong; it came to me that you had taken an ill turning a long time ago, that you had wandered almost beyond the reach of the most loyal friend. There was a foretelling—you must remember it—"

"Get on with it, will you?" muttered Somerled.

"It is never too late for a man to go back to that fork in the road and try again," Eyvind said. "Brother Tadhg would tell you it is just a matter of recognizing you were wrong. You haven't learned how to do that, Somerled. Your eyes are still closed to the possibility, but that does not mean you cannot learn. I have not betrayed our oath. That I speak these words tonight, after all that you have done, is proof of my loyalty to that bond."

"What is it you're proposing, to incarcerate me among a gaggle of proselytizing Christians so that I suffer a gradual demise from sheer boredom? Come on, Eyvind. You know how to do this neatly and quickly. I've seen you dispatch numerous victims with the ruthless touch of an expert hunter. Just get it over, will you?" His eyes were shadow-dark; a terror of the unknown looked out from their depths. Eyvind saw that, perhaps for the first time in his life, Somerled had absolutely no idea what to expect from him.

"I would not choose imprisonment," Eyvind said. "There is no place here in the islands where you could be held: no place where your life would be worth more than a scrap of straw from the midden. I would not send you back to Rogaland. There's not one among our countrymen would offer you safe passage. Nor would I weigh your penalty in ells of cloth or pieces of silver, for there's no treasure in the world would buy pardon for what you have done."

"Then," Somerled said with a crooked smile, "there's not much choice, is there? Death at sunrise seems the only remaining option."

"You know," Eyvind said, "I might once have thought that myself. Indeed, I've come very close to administering your punishment by my own hands: as close as a hair's breadth, I think. I've been contemplating courage, Somerled. I've been called courageous tonight, and it warmed my heart to hear it.

But there are far braver folk here." He looked about him: at Nessa's lovely face, now touched by a delicate pink flush in the cheeks; at Margaret's tight lips and ashen pallor; at Rona standing grim and strong, with the dogs by her side. He looked at Brother Tadhg, who bore a strapping around his ribs, and bruises on his face. "Fine people, who have endured far worse than I ever faced, and remained strong and good. I see in their faces the marks of your cruelty, the scars inflicted in your blind quest for power. And I see in them a strength that you could not combat, for all the grip of fear you placed on our own men, so that they obeyed your will, despite themselves. It seems to me you never stopped to think, to consider. It seems to me you never allowed yourself the time for that."

"You hold up girls and old women and weakling priests as models for me?" Somerled raised his brows; his mouth twisted. "This is ridiculous. There is no logic to your reasoning. These folk are nothing. They are the merest of pawns in the struggle for dominance here. They will not last. Our own kind must prevail. You speak of time. It will not be so long before time proves the truth of my words."

Eyvind took a deep breath. "You dismiss the priest as weak. Do you know how he and his kind made their way to this shore?"

Somerled did not reply. His expression changed almost imperceptibly. He had always been very quick at working out puzzles.

"You do know, I see that. But perhaps the Jarl and our newly arrived comrades do not. The brothers came here by sea, in tiny curraghs of skins and wattles. They set out from their home shore with no map but that of the heart, with no certainty of landfall but that which the voice of their god whispered in their ears. They journeyed under the soft light of the stars and the fierce heat of the midday sun. Little enough they carried with them: a water cask, a fishing line, a book of prayers. They floated at the mercy of ocean surge and treacherous current, driven by storm and gale, on a path known only to whale and seal, to gull and serpent, until the tide cast them up on the shore of the Light Isles. They sent up thanks to their god, and made a new life. That is courage, Somerled. It is a shining example to every one of us."

Somerled waited, dark eyes fixed on Eyvind's face.

"I was witness to the sickening sight of your men beating this priest," Eyvind went on. "I heard his voice, steadfast as the blows rained down, calmly reciting the fair words of a prayer. A strong man indeed. Let us see if you can be as strong."

A ripple of excited anticipation ran around the hall. Somerled folded his arms.

"You propose to administer a beating while I compose verses?" he queried in a show of bravado.

"No, my old friend. I would obtain just such a small boat as that which bore Tadhg and his kind safely across the sea from their homeland. I would place in it a water cask and a fishing line. And on the first tide after sunrise, I would set you adrift in this frail craft, on a westerly current into exile. Your path, then, would be determined by ocean and storm, and your destiny placed in the hands of whatever gods might have mercy on you. My hope would be that you learn wisdom and peace as Brother Tadhg did. It seems a fitting penalty."

Somerled's eyes had widened. For a moment, stark horror transformed his face as he recognized the finality in Eyvind's words. Then the mask came down again, and he was once more calm.

Eyvind turned back to Magnus. "This is the sentence I have determined, my lord. I hope you think it satisfactory."

"You know," Magnus observed expansively, "I did think the young lady might be just a little biased when she referred to you as the only man among us capable of making this decision. A Wolfskin, young and impetuous, at the mercy of the fierce call to battle—such a man, surely, could not possess the wisdom required for such an impossible task. I see now that I was wrong. You are still the same man who charged forward against my enemies, a warrior brave to the point of insanity. That determination and that courage still blaze in your eyes. But you've changed. You have become the man these women see in the future of their islands: the father of kings. Your decision pleases me very well. Are all of you in agreement?"

The answering roar of approval made the whole hall shudder. Perhaps they had wanted blood, but there was a satisfaction in this that went beyond that. It was like the working out of an ancient tale, deeply strange and yet somehow inevitable. Surrounded by the clamor of acknowledgment, the pounding of fists on tables, Eyvind looked across and saw Nessa's little smile and the warmth in her eyes, and a moment later he saw her turn suddenly white and crumple at the knees. He reached her side in two long strides, catching her in his arms before anyone else had time to move. His heart was pounding. Surely the gods would not be so cruel, not now, after everything . . .

"Sheer exhaustion," Margaret observed, looking as if she herself were barely staying on her feet. "And she couldn't eat, before. You'd best carry her through to my quarters and I'll tend to her. A very strong girl; she's been through a great deal."

Nessa was feather-light in his arms. She was snow-pale and as limp as a doll, her long hair hanging to the floor as he carried her to the chamber she was sharing with Margaret. Rona followed just behind him, muttering to herself. He laid Nessa down on a pallet and tucked the covers over her. It was necessary, then, to give way to the wise woman, who produced a little vial, uncorked it and released a powerful, pungent odor that made his nose sting and his eyes water. Nessa's eyelids fluttered. She stirred, and opened her eyes. Eyvind hovered, expecting to be banished at any moment from this domain of women, yet quite unable to tear his eyes away from her.

Now Rona was pouring water into a cup and putting it in his hand, gesturing. It was Margaret who spoke.

"You're being given a little time, I think. Not much. I'm overly weary myself, and do not plan on undressing and getting into bed when there's a Wolfskin present. Be quick. There are certain matters still to be attended to, but the two of us won't be long at all."

They left, not without a rather penetrating look from Rona. It was a warning of sorts; he knew he must continue to meet their expectations, that he would be measured and judged for the rest of his life. That was not such a bad thing.

"Did I faint?" Nessa asked as he held the cup to her lips. "I never did that before. Maybe I should have eaten some supper. It's been such a long time, I hardly know if it is night or day."

"Shh," Eyvind said, easing her back to the pillows. "Don't try to talk. You must rest." His thumb lingered by her temple, brushing the soft strands of hair back from her face. She gazed up at him, her eyes slate-dark in the lamplit room.

"You're sad, aren't you?" she whispered. "Sad that you couldn't make him understand."

Eyvind bowed his head, saying nothing. She seemed to see right inside him sometimes, uncovering secrets he had hardly known were hidden there.

"And you're sorry you had to do what you did," Nessa said. "But it was right, Eyvi. You have given him a second chance. A generous gift; he has been less kind in his friendship."

"I don't know. It could be cruel. Such a journey is fraught with peril. It is a voyage across trackless seas. Who knows what landfall may be found before world's end? He wanted death."

"And you gave life. A man such as yourself could make no other choice. Eyvi?"

"Mmm?"

"Margaret will be back soon, and Rona will give you a lec-ture on keeping me awake, and another on not looking after yourself properly."

"Mmm," he said, his fingers stroking her hair where it lay like dark brown silk across her neck and shoulder.

"I wish you could stay here," she said in a small voice.

Eyvind swallowed. "Might I kiss you good-night, do you think?" he ventured. Despite what had been between them, things seemed different now. He felt a certain constraint, almost as if they were starting all over again now that death did not overhang them so closely.

"Certainly not," Nessa said, but she was smiling. "Don't look so crestfallen, Eyvi. You have a jaw that's covered in bruises and swollen like a ripe fruit, and I happen to know you had a tooth pulled earlier today. Such pursuits must wait—"

Her words were lost as he drew her up into his arms again, and touched his lips to hers quite gently, for a kiss, after all, can be as light as a butterfly's wing provided one exercises control. It was only after a moment that her lips parted, and he felt her hands moving against his back and her tongue sliding across his own, jolting his body to instant, painful hardness. The kiss deepened; his fingers slipped inside her tunic to touch the smooth curve of her breast. And then he winced in pain, and Nessa drew away, a little breathless, laughter and concern min-gled in her soft voice.

"I told you. One should not attempt so much so soon. There

will be a time for us; it won't be so long to wait. Will you sleep tonight?"

Between the ache of longing in his body and the consideration of what must be done at dawn, Eyvind thought that unlikely. "I'll try," he told her. "Now close your eyes and rest. Perhaps I should go."

"Oh, no, not yet." Her fingers tightened on his.

"Just a little longer, then. Though I have to say that to be so near, and not to do what I want so badly to do, causes me some discomfort."

Nessa smiled. "Such discomfort is not solely the province of men, believe me. Still, we must not shock Rona. Perhaps you might put one arm around me, above the blankets, and rest your head here by my shoulder. Mmm. That feels very good. Maybe I really can sleep."

In fact, when Rona did return not long after, she had to wake him, and as she ordered him off to the men's quarters there was a smile on her weathered features. Margaret was with her, looking worn out; Ulf's widow would be eager to return home now, Eyvind thought, back to her family in Rogaland. He bent to touch his lips once more to Nessa's pure brow, to her heavy, shadowed eyelids, and very lightly to her mouth. She was fast asleep. *Sleep sweetly, my Bright Star. My hand in yours.* Rona made some further comment, not ungently. He must take steps to learn the language as quickly as he could, so he could talk to her, so he could talk to all of them. He would ask Tadhg to help him.

"Eyvind," Margaret said dryly, "if you're not out of this chamber by the time I count to five, I'll summon your brother to drag you out. Good-night and sleep well. You chose wisely tonight."

"Wisely?" he echoed. "I don't know. I'll probably never know."

"We must be prepared for troubled dreams," said Margaret, "for shadows on the edge of our thoughts. He leaves us that legacy. But we must not let that hold us helpless. Life goes on; we must make of it what we can, I suppose." She sounded so bleak and hopeless, Eyvind was hard-pressed to summon any response at all. He was saved by Rona, who approached with a cup containing a steaming brew which smelled even worse than the reviving herbs. It appeared this draft was meant for Margaret. With great relief, Eyvind slipped from the room and back to the Wolfskins' sleeping chamber, where two men snored on their pallets already and his brother waited, ale cup in hand.

"Sleep," Eirik ordered, pointing to the bed that bore the best woollen blankets and the plumpest pillow. "Now." And suddenly it did not seem so very hard at all to obey.

Nessa thought that was the most difficult moment for Eyvind: the touching of hands to the little boat as it rocked in the shallows, ready to bear Somerled westward on his journey into exile. For herself, she felt the somber mood of the occasion, the dark solemnity of it, yet she knew it was at the same time a cleansing. The weight of grief they all carried on their shoulders must be lightened by this man's departure. It was an ending of sorts, necessary before new beginnings could be made. For Eyvind, it was different. She could look at Somerled's tight, withdrawn features and feel not a shred of doubt, for she saw there a man who simply did not understand the difference between right and wrong. Eyvind saw his friend, a boy for whom he still felt responsible. And she knew that somewhere, deep down, Eyvind doubted his own judgment. Even now, even after all he had done, the strength he had shown, the wisdom and leadership, Eyvind could not see himself as others did. In his own eyes, he would always be no more than a simple warrior, a man who needed time to understand things, an unsubtle thinker lacking in cleverness. He did not read the admiration and wonder in others' eyes—the Jarl's, Margaret's, Olaf's—at how he had changed and what he had become. He did not understand how astonishing was his acceptance by her own people: the speed with which he had begun to establish that difficult bond. He was quite blind to it. That was one of the reasons she loved him.

There was a shadow in his clear, blue eyes that morning. Nonetheless, he held himself tall and straight as always, as if he were part of the monumental slab of rock on which he stood. Although the breeze ruffled his hair and stirred the folds of his tunic, he seemed to Nessa an island of stillness. Just so had she seen him on the shore, long ago, before she had known what kind of man he was: before she had understood that he belonged in the islands. Yet in a way she had known, even then. From that moment, the spirits had whispered in her ear, *He is part of this tale: your tale, and the tale of the Folk. You must hold him fast. Within this warrior's breast beats ancient truth.*

Nessa was the only woman present on the shore. Margaret had declined the Jarl's invitation to attend. It was plain Ulf's widow had reached the point where she could bear no more. They said Somerled had given her a letter before he left the settlement, but nobody knew what was in it. As for Margaret, she had not sought an opportunity to speak with her husband's killer in private. Nessa guessed there was a certain piece of information that Somerled did not know, and she wondered at Margaret's decision not to share it with him, but kept her silence.

She would have preferred not to be here herself, but with an eye to Eyvind's pallor and his grim-set jaw, she had accompanied the small group of men to the chosen place. Not three boat lengths out from this narrow, pebbly stretch of shore, a strong westerly current would seize the curragh and bear it away from the islands. Only the most skilled of sailors might turn the craft and steer it back to land. Her cousin, Kinart, could have done it; Somerled most certainly could not.

It was very quick. Men had worked during the night to place all in readiness; water barrel, fishing gear, and a small, oiled sack of provisions were neatly stowed. There were oars. It was also possible to rig mast and sail. Nessa shivered. The boat was so small. On the shore, Brother Tadhg stood with his wooden cross in his hands, staring out over the choppy waters.

A silence fell. They were waiting for Somerled to step aboard. Nessa had wondered if it would be done without any more words; if now, at the very end, Eyvind and Somerled would have nothing to say to each other. Perhaps there was so much to be said that neither man knew where to start. She could feel Eyvind's grief, even though she did not fully understand it. As for Somerled, he had surprised her this morning. Quiet, calm, dressed in plain, warm clothing, he had walked down between his Wolfskin guards with perfect dignity. Nessa was forced to admit that outwardly he had conducted himself in every way like a king.

"It's time," Magnus said. "You'd best be gone. Have you anything you want to say?"

Somerled looked at him. "Not to you," he said. "But I have a question for Eyvind. I told him I preferred death. I made that quite clear. Of course, I was not offered a choice. Tell me,

Eyvind, what's to stop me from turning the boat around as soon as the current ceases to grip her, and coming back to land? The locals will finish me off then, if Nessa's island spirits don't get to me first. What's to stop me from slitting my wrists with a fishing knife? I'm sure there's one on board somewhere. Or I could simply go out a certain distance, then slip overboard and drown. You'll recall from our boyhood that I'm not the strongest of swimmers. Give me one good reason why I should feel bound to comply with this ridiculous punishment?"

Several people spoke at once.

"Maybe I should go with him—" That was Brother Tadhg, and his words sparked a horrified "No!" from Nessa. Several voices, Eirik's among them, spoke up telling Somerled to hold his tongue and stop stalling for time. But it was Eyvind's response that hushed them. He stepped down from the rock, his face ashen, and walked across until he stood not an arm's length from Somerled.

"Here's your reason," he said, and rolled back his left sleeve to show the long, straight scar on the forearm, sign of their blood bonding. "Give me your hand. I have not forgotten the oath we swore. You urged me to loyalty; now I ask you for pledge of that loyalty. Give me your hand, Somerled."

Somerled pushed back his shirtsleeve. He stared at Eyvind; the dark eyes seemed to devour the blue. Each man clasped the other's left arm. Now one scar overlaid the other, a perfect match.

"Very well," Eyvind said. "Now I want your solemn vow, given in the spirit of the friendship we promised as lads, that you will do all that is in your power to survive this journey. Swear that you will head onward with the courage I know is in you, with all the cleverness and wit and ingenuity you possess, until you make landfall on a new shore. And you must promise that, once there, you will make a new life, and strive to be all that you can be."

He was holding Somerled's gaze with his own, but Nessa knew he could not see what she saw, what made her heart shrink with pity and with sorrow for the two of them. He could not see the love in Somerled's eyes. For her, that moment was a glimpse behind the mask, an insight she would rather not have had. She thought now she knew what was in Somerled's heart: *I would never have been good enough for you, never, no matter how hard I tried, no matter what I achieved. And I can never be the man you are.*

"It's a great deal to ask," Somerled said in a whisper, his mouth curving into a wry half smile. "I don't think I ever required such a demonstration of loyalty from you."

"If I did not have faith in you," Eyvind answered, his own voice scarcely stronger, "I would not ask it. Now swear."

Finally Somerled had run out of words. He jerked his head in an awkward nod and released Eyvind's arm abruptly. As he turned to climb into the curragh, Nessa saw him scrub the back of his hand across one cheek and then the other. A king does not weep, not where people can see him.

"Really," said Brother Tadhg, wading into the water, "really, he should not go alone—"

"Spare me from priestly company, I beg you," Somerled snapped. "I've always much preferred my own. Besides, they're short on translators here, and it's going to take you forever to teach Eyvind the language. Now get on with this, will you?"

Then Eirik and Thord and the other men set their hands to the curragh's stern and pushed, and Somerled took up the oars and, with reasonable competence, began to row out to sea. Nessa moved forward to take Eyvind's hand in hers, and now she could see the tears that were running down his cheeks. A Wolfskin, it seemed, could weep without shame at such a time of loss. They stood watching until the little boat had been out of sight for some time, until the others had already headed up to the place where the horses were tethered, ready for the ride back to the settlement, and the two of them were alone with the wash of the waves and the call of the gulls. Then Eyvind wiped his face with his hand just as Somerled had done, and put his arm around Nessa's shoulders, and they set their steps away from the sea.

She saw Eyvind's sorrow and his doubt and wanted to comfort him with her counsel, with her body. But it was a busy time and privacy was hard to come by. Before Magnus sailed home to Rogaland, he had determined to take stock of what Ulf had begun, and to deploy his own forces in the restoration of what Somerled had destroyed. Nessa made it known as courteously as she could that the Folk would manage quite well with the help they had chosen for themselves: Eyvind and Thord and one or two others. Her argument was strengthened by the arrival, one afternoon in drizzling spring rain, of no less than twenty of her own people, fishermen and farmers from the far outer islands, come to her aid after word had finally reached them of the slaughter of their kinsmen. Most were gray-haired and the rest little more than boys, but that did nothing to dampen the fire of dedication in their eyes, or mute the ring of fierce commitment in their voices as they knelt before her one by one, each offering himself as her warrior. It would have made her weep, once. Now she gave each her hand, and each his own solemn words of recognition and acceptance.

She explained to them all, afterward, who Eyvind was and what he had done. He was her husband, her partner from this day on; their union lacked but the formal ceremony of handfasting, and that would take place when spring was at its peak. She did not add the words of clarification, *When the others are gone,* but this was understood. Eyvind would stand by her side; he would help her lead them. He would teach them what they needed to know to get ready for the new times, when the islands were no longer a place apart from the rest of the world. The lads eyed the golden-haired giant with excited anticipation, scarcely tinged with caution. The older men would take longer to win over, but she did not doubt that they too, in time, would follow the Wolfskin into the jaws of death if he called them there. That thought made Nessa shiver, as if a breath of cold had passed through her. So much change: every day brought something new. The times of long, silent meditation, the nights of communion with the ancestors seemed distant memories, and she grieved for the loss of that utter stillness, that space for setting the spirit at rights. Still, this was her choice. She would be a mother before next winter, so Rona said, though how the wise woman could know was a mystery.

The ships were ready: the *Golden Dragon* proud and sleek at its mooring, the blockish knarr, and Magnus's pride and joy, the new vessel he had named *Lady Hilde,* after his wife. Perhaps he had thought by that to sweeten her toward him in view of yet another departure. This time, she would get him back sooner than she expected. The men were eager to be off. Eyvind would be saying farewell to his brother; Eirik had sorely missed his woman and his young sons, and vowed never to sail so far again. Indeed, he was heard to tell his fellow Wolfskins over the ale cups, he'd a fancy to give up the calling of Thor altogether, and go back to Hammarsby to lend his mother a hand on the farm. At five and twenty, he was getting a little long in the tooth for the finer points of wielding sword, club, and axe. The others greeted this with uproarious laughter, telling him he'd never do it, he wouldn't last one season on the land before he'd be back among them on the longship's prow, sniffing out Danes. But Eyvind told Nessa they were wrong. He knew his brother, and he had seen the longing for home in Eirik's eyes.

There would be others staying in the Light Isles besides Eyvind and Thord. Thord's woman had already made quite a name for herself in Hafnarvagr as a cook. What she could create from the simplest ingredients had grown men lining up with their platters, begging for second helpings. She was a lively girl, admired as much for her saucy manner and outrageous jokes as for her baking. That she had once been a thrall was of no import here.

One afternoon, as Nessa snatched a few moments' quiet on a bench outside the hall, Margaret came to sit beside her. Ulf's widow seemed nervous, twisting a handkerchief between her hands. It was clear she wanted to say something, but she hesitated as if unsure how to begin. Nessa waited, hands resting in her lap. At her feet lay Shadow; Guard was away with Eyvind and Thord, bringing up some timbers that had washed in to the beach.

"I—I wanted to ask you something," Margaret blurted out eventually.

"Of course," said Nessa.

"I can't go home." Margaret's words came out in a rush now, as if she must say them all before her courage failed her. "Everyone expects me to go, but I just can't. Would you let me stay here? I could make myself useful, I can order a household, I know how to keep a reckoning and organize stores. Maybe I could do some of the work I would have done if Ulf hadn't . . . if he hadn't . . . sweet Freya aid me!" She buried her face in her hands. "I just can't do this, it's hopeless, how can I even say it? Oh, please—"

Nessa waited a little. Margaret was not crying; she would not do that in the open, even though there were only the two of them about. But her pose, shoulders drooping, head down, neck exposed beneath the heavy bundle of auburn hair, spoke of a helpless despair.

"Rona says I'm going to have a child at the end of autumn," Nessa said tranquilly. "It was a bit of a surprise. You're the first person I've told, apart from Eyvind."

Margaret gave a choked gurgle that might have been laughter. "A small, yellow-haired warrior? You are full of surprises!"

"Rona says it will be a girl. But I expect there will be little Wolfskins as well, in due course."

There was a long pause.

"My own child will be born far earlier than that," Margaret said in a whisper, "but alas, not soon enough to be called my husband's son. Though no doubt the brat will bear some sort of family resemblance." Her tone was bitter. "You understand why I'm reluctant to return home to Rogaland. How could I begin to break such news to my parents? And yet, I know I am foolish to ask you for help. I expect you can hardly wait to see me gone from this shore. Why would you want to give shelter to Somerled's child?"

"Your child is welcome here, Margaret," said Nessa gently. "He'll be a son of the islands. It will be up to you, as his mother, to foster his growing and teach him what your own parents taught you: strength, forbearance, and generosity. As for yourself, you must earn your place here; that much I ask of all who make the choice to stay."

"Your people must hate me," Margaret said, but there was hope in her voice now. She straightened her back, lifted her head. "After what was done—after the killings—how can they . . . ?"

"As I said, you must earn your place. You'll be watched; you all will. But my people remember how you helped them in the time of the sickness. In due course, I think you will be accepted. And I will value your skills and your friendship, for I never expected to be a leader of men and women, not in this way. My path has changed, and I cannot always face it with courage."

"I fear greatly to have a child," Margaret said in a low voice, "although, for me, that would have come about eventually. It is the prospect of this particular child that disquiets me. He was not conceived in love. I don't know if I can be a good mother to him. I think I may hate him."

"Look at me on the day he is born and tell me that again,"

said Nessa, "and perhaps I may believe it. We are lucky that we have Rona. Why not ask her to seek answers in the fire? She will tell you something of the child, if she can."

Margaret shivered. "I don't think so. I would rather not know. Nessa?"

"Yes?"

"My little maid, Gunhild—might she stay as well? And my men, Bjorn and Ash? They are loyal, all of them. They will not want to leave me."

Nessa frowned. "Gunhild can stay; you'll have need of her. The men must speak to Eyvind. He will decide. Each must plead his own case and show himself worthy. If your faith in them is justified, perhaps we may keep them."

"They are good workers," Margaret said eagerly, "I promise you—"

"As I said, you should speak to Eyvind. It is his choice. I do not set myself up in place of a king here. There are difficult times ahead of us; I intend that we should all face them together. I'll be glad of your help, Margaret." Nessa put out a hand; a moment later, she felt the cold touch of Margaret's fingers, grasping hers. They sat in silence awhile, side by side.

Then Margaret said, "Thank you. Oh gods, I'm going to be sick again."

"It will pass," Nessa said, holding the other girl's head as she doubled over, and wondering how long it might be before this particular malady struck her as well. "I promise you, it will pass."

Magnus was true to his word. The ships had been gathered together at the safe harbor for final repairs. At the second full moon they sailed for Freyrsfjord, and Eyvind waved goodbye to Eirik and to his old comrades, Erlend and Holgar.

It was a strangely assorted company that stood on the hillside above Hafnarvagr, where the sweep of sheltered water spreads out before the dazzled viewer like an ever-changing shawl of lustrous blues and grays and greens all the way across to High Island. In springtime, that stretch of sea is a vessel of light whose loveliness quiets the heart. They watched in silence as the oars dipped and rose, and the fleet moved farther and farther away across the silver of the bay, threading between the isles on the perilous journey back to the home shores of Roga-land. One might have looked at these people, Nessa thought, and wondered what future the islands could have under their care. There was pale, silent Margaret with her woollen shawl hugged around her, and beside her a small, tight circle of pro-tectors: young Gunhild, pink-cheeked and anxious, and the two stalwart guards, Ash and Bjorn. Behind them were two other men of Ulf's household. All had convinced Eyvind of their worth and loyalty. To Nessa's right stood Rona, tall and straight with her iron-gray plait and her shrewd, far-seeing eyes, and be-side her the slight, unassuming figure of Brother Tadhg. Thank all the powers he had not followed his first instinct and jumped into that boat with Somerled. How would they ever have man-aged without this brave, calm little man? On the sloping sward below Nessa, Thord stood with wolfskin on shoulders, a hand lifted in salute as the *Golden Dragon* hoisted her sail to catch the westerly wind. Thord's woman, Zaira, watched the ships pass with a dimpled smile. She had it in her to give, that one; Nessa had seen it. And she loved the place: already, among the island women, Zaira had a wide circle of friends. Even thus, quietly and without any fuss at all, is the torn fabric of commu-nity mended. *Give us time,* Nessa prayed, closing her eyes. *Give us long enough, so this can be.*

Eyvind was not standing alone this time. He had a lad on ei-ther side, and his arms around their shoulders. At his feet the two dogs stood, guardians, companions, messengers—who knew what they were, in truth? Close by, seven of her own men, clad in island colors, sky blue, sea green, blood red, stood in a watchful group. And Grim was there: a surprise defection, this, which had not pleased Magnus at all, but he had made the best of it, seeing this most hard-bitten of warriors would not change his mind again. One of the young men from Sandy Island seemed to be glancing at Gunhild rather often, and Gunhild's pink cheeks were positively glowing. *Time,* Nessa begged again. *It is not so much to ask for.*

"Make time." Rona had come up beside her, and spoke in a manner Nessa had grown used to over the years. Rona could not read minds, exactly; she simply seemed to know things without needing to be told. Maybe that was the Sight, maybe just an old woman's acute powers of observation. "For him, especially. Take him away a while; space and quiet, he needs now. Time to grieve and time to be comforted. You can give him that, and take some for yourself as well."

"But—" Nessa hardly knew where to start, there were so many objections to this. So much to do, so few of them to manage it: stock to be tended, boats repaired, dykes mended so the tender grain, planted almost too late to be guided by the season's rhythm, might not now be mown too early by hungry sheep or wandering cow or foraging hare. They must divide responsibilities and set to work. And she must travel to the outer islands to visit her people there and reassure them. How could she take time?

"He seems strong," Rona said quietly. "Already they gather around him. He will continue to grow; whatever challenges the world sets him, he will meet bravely. But he's still a very young man, Nessa, and he has bid the last of his family farewell today. You, who have lost so much, know how that feels. Take time for each other. Trust us; we'll get on with things until you're ready to come back."

Thus it was that, on a day when the sky was a cloudless warm blue and the sweet grasses of the Light Isles were dotted with flowers of many hues—blush pink, sun yellow, dusky violet—Eyvind and Nessa made their way on foot, each bearing a small pack, up to the west and along the shore near the Whaleback to a place where a burned-out cottage now stood half-rebuilt, and a low opening between stones led to a chamber a little girl had once named the tower in the earth. There they unpacked what they had brought, and Eyvind made a fire where Rona had once baked fish wrapped in weed, while Nessa fetched fresh water and set her provisions neatly at hand. Neither of them spoke much; the frequent meeting of blue eyes and gray, the touch and clasp of hands in passing, the brushing of body against body as they walked said more than any words could signify. In this quiet place there was a whole world of sounds: the wash of waves on the westernmost shore, the high passing cries of seabirds and the closer, reedier voices of pipit and meadowlark, the distant lowing of cattle and the small anxious cries of lambs, all these were part of it, and yet, beneath and beyond the signs of habitation there was an immense silence, a vast, open emptiness in which the mind might drift, searching for answers, and find there were no answers; there was no ending—only a journey to be taken, a pathway to be followed. One could do it well or badly; every man and woman had that choice.

"Well," Eyvind said, sitting back on his heels as the fire settled into a darkly glowing mass crowned with licking flames. "What next?" He looked at her, eyes fire-bright, and she looked back smiling.

"A walk," she told him, reaching out her hand.

"Oh."

"Don't sound so crestfallen. Not very far. Only up to the clifftop, there to the south. Do you remember?"

Eyvind nodded. "You promised," he said. "Or wished, if not promised. You said we'd go there in springtime. Then, it seemed impossible that would ever come to pass, for one reason or another. We are so blessed, I hardly dare look beyond tomorrow, lest it all change before my eyes."

"It will change anyway," Nessa said. "The trick is changing with it, I think. Shall we walk?"

There is a place, just below that highest rise of the cliffs south of the Whaleback, where the narrow pathway spreads into a shallow bowl, a cup in which a man and a woman may sit in safety as if supported by the hand of Bone Mother herself, and look out to the west across the trackless ocean that leads to world's end. Below this small shelter, the cliffs fall away to a rocky shoreline. On this sheer face, generations of birds have nested over the seasons, rearing their young in the teeth of the wind, fighting for space on the narrow ledges, gliding and soaring on their endless journeys to pluck the sea's bounty. Their diving, intricate dance weaves magic about the place; their harsh voices cry an ancient, many-threaded chant of survival.

Nessa and Eyvind sat there as the sun passed to the west; as the bright blue of afternoon began to fade to violet and gray, and the shadows changed. They did not embrace, not yet, for all the tide of longing that had filled them, rising and rising, since the very moment they had left the settlement to set out on this journey. Simply, Eyvind put one arm around Nessa's shoulders, and his other hand laced its fingers in hers. Warmth shared; memories awakened. The sky changed, dimmed; the birds were quieter now.

"I expected too much of him, at the end," Eyvind said, staring out over the darkening sea. "More than any man could give."

"Perhaps he will prove you wrong."

He glanced at her. "You don't believe that, do you?"

Nessa shivered. "I don't know. And I will not look in the fire for that answer. You opened another pathway for him. What happens now is his choice, not yours."

"This was not done cleanly. I should have known better."

"You are a man, not a god. Perhaps time will give you answers. Now, I'm getting cold. And I want to cook supper before it's quite dark. Shall we go?"

"Supper sounds good. But can you better Rona's onion broth?"

Nessa grinned as, hand in hand, they began to pick their way back down the cliff path. "I would not attempt such a feat. But I've an excellent line in flatcakes flavored with dried mushrooms and herbs. The last time I gave you those, you fed them to the dog, I seem to remember. This time I expect better of you."

"I hope not to disappoint you," he said quietly.

Nessa felt a hot blush rise to her cheeks. She realized he was entirely serious. "Unlikely, I should think," she told him, understanding that whatever he achieved, however he was loved and recognized, he would always expect more of himself: would always consider himself in some ways wanting. That was Somerled's doing.

She had not thought it would be possible to eat; the yearning ache in her body and a strange nervousness seemed enough to rob her of any appetite for food. But the walk had changed that. Eyvind stirred up the fire while Nessa shaped the dough she had prepared in the morning, adding a pinch or two of this and that from the depths of her pack. Once the flatcakes were cooking in the iron pan, and Eyvind had set a warm cup of herbal brew between her cold hands, she found she was able to sit quietly, enjoying the savory scent of the mushrooms and the sizzling of hot butter, and look across at him with a smile that banished any awkwardness.

"We have a little longer, this time," she said. "A luxury, to be alone. We must make the most of it."

Eyvind did not smile, but there was a warmth in his eyes, a

steadiness that did not quite conceal the shadow of desire. "So, you intend to take me on many walks?"

"I keep my promises," Nessa told him, lifting flatcakes onto a platter. "Visiting the beach at dawn is one of them. I want you to see the colors. And we must go to the Whaleback, later. I need to stand by the Kin Stone and tell my uncle about you; explain to him, and to the ancestors, what we will do here. I could not do that at the time of the burial rites. It is something for just the two of us."

Eyvind bowed his head. "You honor me in this," he said quietly.

"Yes. But you should understand, it is usual for the royal women of our people to take husbands outside the Folk. Men of Saxony and Dalriada have fathered our kings. Thus the line is kept strong, and kinsmen away from each other's throats."

"Your uncle would not have wished such a husband for you, surely."

"My uncle was a man like your chieftain, Ulf, and like yourself, Eyvi. He judged people by their own worth before he considered their lineage. I must hope our sons grow to be leaders of equal wisdom."

"Sons?"

"If the ancestors will it. A daughter first, though." She laid a hand on her flat belly; as yet there was no sign at all.

"You will keep me very busy, then, with one pastime or another," Eyvind said.

"With one pastime or another," Nessa agreed gravely. They were silent a moment, and then, suddenly, both broke into laughter. He put his food down and moved across to wrap his arms around her; she laid her brow against his shoulder, still chuckling at how foolishly solemn they had become, and felt his hands on her hair, stroking, and his mouth against her temple, not laughing now.

"I don't think I can wait any longer, my dove," he breathed. "But if you are not ready, then—"

"Shh," Nessa said, stepping back. "Damp down the fire, here—" She moved to rake the ashes in, to set the pot to one side. Careful habits are not forgotten, even in such moments. "I see it is almost dark; we must light our lamp and settle for sleep, I think. And it's getting cold. How fortunate I have brought some blankets. Will you come with me, dear one?"

So, leading him by the hand, she made it quite natural as they crept through the low entry into the tower in the earth. Eyvind set the lamp in an alcove; Nessa spread blankets on the earthen floor. Time out of time: each moment a precious gift. His fingers were careful, unfastening the small hooks at the front of her gown. She could feel the warmth of his breath against her cheek; the light touch of his hands through the thin wool of her bodice was somewhere between delight and torment. Her fingers moved to touch the butter-yellow hair where it curled behind his ears. Her heart seemed to be thumping quite hard, doing a wild dance all its own.

"I'm sorry," Eyvind whispered. "My hands have become very clumsy all of a sudden."

"Shall I help?"

It did not take long to unfasten bodice and skirt, to let both slip to the floor, so that she stood before him in her fine-woven shift. She could hardly bear the look in his eyes, and yet she could not tear her gaze away. That a man could feel such need for her was astonishing; it filled her heart with joy and terror, and found something in her own body that strained to meet and answer it.

"Turn around," Eyvind said, and when she obeyed, startled, he untied the ribbon that bound her long plait, and ran his fingers through the dark, silken strands until her hair fell like a soft curtain across her shoulders and down below her waist. Then she undressed him in his turn, an awkward task in view of his height. There was a certain difficulty with the trousers, which had both of them helpless with laughter again. They found a solution quickly, and the laughter ceased, for their long-denied need rose in them fast. Last of all, Eyvind bent to take the hem of Nessa's shift between his fingers, and drew it upward, and she lifted her arms so that the fine garment could be shed entirely, leaving her naked in the lamplight save for the cloak of her long hair.

"My Bright Star," Eyvind said shakily, "I would stand here and simply gaze at you, for such loveliness can surely be found nowhere else in the world. But I find such restraint is beyond me at this moment—will you—?" Nonetheless, he held back, as always demanding of himself more than might be expected of any other man.

She took a step forward, rose on tiptoe and kissed him; the whole length of her body was abruptly against his own, flesh to flesh. Restraint, then, became an impossibility for both of them. They had waited a long time for this, and the urgency of it was no less than last time, when each had felt death hovering near. Eyvind came close, for a little while, to forgetting what Signe had taught him and surrendering himself too early to the flood of desire, the dark urge to completion. But this was Nessa, who had captured his heart and freed his spirit, and he did not forget. So they came together in laughter and longing, and moved together in passionate joy, and in the end, reached together a blinding, shattering moment of fulfillment, which left them weeping and trembling in each other's arms.

"Did I hurt you?" Eyvind whispered, easing his arm so she could rest her head more comfortably on his shoulder, and drawing the blanket up over her.

"You could never hurt me, Eyvi," she breathed against his sweat-dampened skin. "Never. You should not need to ask me such a thing."

They lay awhile in silence then, overwhelmed by what was between them, the fierceness of it, the strength that was both wonder and terror. If such a bond were ever broken, how could one hope to survive it?

The lamp burned steadily. Eyvind fell asleep with his legs entwined in Nessa's and his arm across her, his fingers twisted in her hair. His breathing was slow and peaceful; there would be no dark dreams tonight. Nessa lay wakeful awhile, watching the shadows as they stirred and shivered in the secret space of the ancient cairn. And although the two of them were alone in that deep place, it came to her that they were not truly alone, for through the narrow entry, and again through the tiny opening in the roof, a faint blue light came and went in regular sequence, as if outside in the darkness a dance took place, a ritual of greeting, of welcome. And from the shore, over the endless roar of the western ocean came a sound of voices, wordless, fluid, singing recognition, a hymn of sisterhood telling of a bond deeper than blood. As for the dark voice of the earth, that remained silent, and perhaps would forever. Nessa had made her choice. For everything, there is a price to be paid.

Nessa closed her eyes. Eyvind moved in his sleep, tightening his arm around her; she could feel his heartbeat against her cheek, steady and strong. Later he would wake, and they would laugh and whisper and make magic together in the darkness. It was a miracle, surely, that out of such bitter losses, such depth of sorrow, could come transcendent joy. *Are you strong enough to lose all you have, and still go on?* It seemed she had been, and for that, the ancestors had granted her a gift that was truly beyond price. Smiling, Nessa drifted into sleep.

The little boat bobbed onward across the dark sea, escorted by gulls and seals. Somerled's expression was blank; it told nothing of what was in his mind as the wind and the swell bore him ever farther into the realm where great whales breach and dive in the spray, and long-armed creatures slither and move in the ocean's tides like tangles of creeping sea wrack. On such a journey, a man has time for thinking. There was the exile itself, a sentence cruel in its kindness, a decree both curse and redemption. There was the irony of it, that his long-sought prize had been snatched from him by the very man who had once believed in his vision when all others scoffed in scorn. Somerled's bitter laughter flew up to blend with the harsh voices of the seabirds. Eyvind some kind of leader? The Wolfskin a father of kings? He could no longer say his friend would never surprise him. There was a sort of amusement to be found in that. And there were tears, here where nobody could witness them; he bowed his head and let them fall into the pitiless surge of the ocean, salt on salt. He had loved Eyvind, and Eyvind had betrayed him. He had loved Eyvind, and Eyvind had saved him. Which was the truth?

Westward, ever westward the small boat moved, passing on to the edge of the world. Dusk came, and dolphins danced at the bows. Night came, and stars awoke in a vast blackness of sky, such a sky as can be seen only when a man is alone on a midnight watch. Somerled gazed at them, and waited. What was to be done but wait? Sometime, this voyage would have its ending.

HiSTORiCaL NOTE

Orkney's history exists in the very bone of the islands. Culture overlays culture: Neolithic houses, chambered cairns, and stone circles, Bronze Age burial cists, Iron Age brochs lying cheek by jowl with remnants of later settlement by those elusive and independent people, the Picts, whose most stunning legacy is their symbol stones. After them came the Vikings, and with their arrival, the rapid establishment of a Norse culture in the islands. By A.D. 880 Orkney had become a Norse carldom ruled by Rognvald of More.

The Orkneyinga Saga, written by an Icelandic chronicler around A.D. 1200, tells the story of Norse settlement in Orkney. Prior to that, we have only the archaeological remains and passing references from sources of varying reliability. The *Saga* tells us nothing of the people who lived in the islands prior to the Norse arrival. It is likely they bore the blood of both Iron Age ancestors and more recent Celtic immigrants. The archaeological evidence points to a Pictish-style culture. Their kings owed a token allegiance to the Pictish kings of Caithness, but geographic isolation gave them a certain degree of independence.

So what happened? Did a Viking invasion wipe them out in battle, or did the newcomers arrive gradually, welcoming the opportunity to settle in a place that offered good grazing land and sheltered fishing grounds? The transition to the dominance of Norse blood and Norse ways may have been peaceable, intermarriage eventually causing the absorption of one culture into another. That raises its own set of questions. Can such a change occur without the loss of something precious and irreplaceable: ancestral identity?

Such "gray areas" in history are an irresistible lure for writers of historical fiction. In *Wolfskin* I have not attempted to recreate the history of the first Norse arrival in Orkney. A great deal of the story, not least its magical and folkloric elements, is imagination. I've simply presented one possible picture of how it might have been when the old inhabitants of the isles first encountered these fearsome strangers from the east with their vastly different culture. What might each have thought? Was it ever possible for them to understand one another? How much did each stand to lose?

The Folk, then, are my own creation, as is their king, Engus. But they are based on what we know of Pictish culture in Orkney. I have allowed them their own names for places and landmarks, since most of the current ones are of Norse derivation. Most of the places in this story can be found on a modern map under other titles. The Whaleback, site of Engus's court, is the Brough of Birsay, which does bear the remains of a substantial Pictish settlement overlaid by Viking buildings. Other places on Somerled's map are given the names his own folk bestowed on them, the old Norse names such as Hrossey and Hafnarvagr. The Kin Stone was indeed shattered by a careless hand at some point in its history. The original can be seen in the Museum of Scotland. The Great Stone of Oaths, known as the Odin Stone, is gone now, victim of an overzealous farmer. The greater and lesser stone circles still stand, and close by them you may possibly find the old howe where Eyvind and Nessa sheltered together. You can even walk up to the hollow where they sat and looked out westward, not far from the highest point of Marwick Head. You can take a ferry across to Hoy (High Island) and walk up to the Dwarfie Stane, the rock-cut tomb which so impressed that perceptive chieftain, Ulf.

The Christian brothers and their perilous journeys from Ireland were entirely real. Early monastic settlement in Orkney is well documented; Eynhallow (Holy Island) is their home in *Wolfskin,* but in fact they were scattered in many parts of the islands and had a strong influence on Orcadian culture.

Orkney was only half the inspiration for this story. The other half lay with the ultimate warrior of his time, the berserk. This name probably derives from *berserkir,* bear shirts. Another title for such warriors was *ulfhednar,* wolfskins. Such apparel probably marked their special status as the elite strike force of a king or nobleman.

Paddy Griffith's excellent book, *The Viking Art of War*

(Greenhill Books, 1995), was responsible for sparking off my interest with its insight into the nature of berserks. The common view that such a soldier was a psychotic, shield-chewing oaf who rushed naked into battle sits poorly with his depiction in the saga literature, where he is usually highly respected and, like other Vikings, pops off home to do the seeding, gather the harvest, or father a child in between his military duties. There are references to bands of berserk brothers hired en masse, and others suggesting that hallucinogenic substances or shamanistic practices may have played a part in the berserk's ability to summon an insane, trancelike courage.

Then there was the religious aspect: the berserks were usually followers of Odin, trickiest of gods, and fought in obedience to a vow that would guarantee them glory in the afterlife. In *Wolfskin*, my troop of warriors owes allegiance to Thor, whose straightforward nature makes him more suited for a soldier's god.

Having fixed on berserk warrior as hero, I then found my tale exploring the theme of loyalty and vows. To a man in Viking times a blood oath was deeply binding, as was a promise to a god. To break such an oath was to betray one's honor, to step far beyond the boundaries of acceptable behavior. Eyvind faces a dilemma that tests him to the utmost. In such a case, perhaps only a man of transparent goodness can find a solution that is both compassionate and honorable.

Look for

Foxmask

by Juliet Marillier

Now available from
Tom Doherty Associates

Turn the page for a preview

ONE

. . . if anyone can understand, it will be you; I have always respected your intellect. I had so much to offer here. I could have achieved great things, and in time all would have thanked me for it. Yes, even the Wolfskin. That he has been the one to wrench the possibility from my grasp is bitter indeed . . .

EXCERPT FROM LETTER

The day Thorvald's mother gave him the letter, everything changed. Creidhe was weaving, hands busy on the loom, shuttle flying, a fine web of blue and crimson unfolding before her in perfect pattern, testimony to the skills Aunt Margaret had taught her. So industrious was she, and so quiet, that it seemed she had been forgotten. The bestowal of such a perilous gift as that letter was surely best suited to a moment of complete privacy. Aunt Margaret spoke to her son quietly, in the long room before the hearth. Creidhe could see them through the doorway from the weaving chamber. They did not argue. Voices were seldom raised in this most orderly of households. But Creidhe heard the front door slam open, and she saw Thorvald go down the three steps in a single stride, then vanish across the yard and out over the spring fields as if hunted by demons. She saw the bloodless, driven look on his face. And although she did not know it at the time, that was the moment Thorvald's life, and her own, took a twist and a turn and set off on an entirely different path.

Creidhe knew Thorvald better than anyone. They had been childhood playmates, and they were fast friends. Thorvald had few friends; the fingers of one hand would be more than enough to count them. There were perhaps only two to whom he ever spoke freely, and whom he allowed close: herself, and Sam, the fisherman on whose boat Thorvald sometimes helped. As for

Creidhe, she understood Thorvald well: his black moods, his lengthy silences, his sudden, brilliant schemes and his rare times of openness. She loved him, for all his faults. In her mind there was no doubt that one day they would marry. He wasn't a real cousin, just as Margaret wasn't a real aunt. The tie was one of old friendship, not kinship. If Thorvald hadn't seen yet that he and Creidhe were destined to be together forever, he'd realize some time. It was just a matter of waiting.

The shuttle slowed to a stop. Creidhe stood gazing out the doorway across a landscape dotted with sheep, new lambs at foot. From Aunt Margaret's house you could see all the way to the western ocean, where stark cliffs marked the margin of land and sea. Far off now, there was the small, dark figure of Thorvald, running, running away. Creidhe had seen a terrible change in his eyes.

"Finished?"

Creidhe jumped. Margaret had come up beside her without a sound.

"N-no, but maybe I should go home. Father's due back from Sandy Island, and I should be helping—" Creidhe fell silent. Aunt Margaret had tears in her eyes. Such a phenomenon was astounding. Her aunt was a model of propriety and restraint. She never lost control.

This household, run by Margaret's long-time retainer, Ash, but ordered by Margaret herself, operated to a strict routine, with little allowance for errors. This approach was reflected in Margaret's own appearance. She was a handsome woman of around six-and-thirty, her hair a rich auburn, plaited neatly and pinned up under a snowy lace cap. Her linen gown was ironed into immaculate pleats, her woolen overdress fastened with twin brooches of patterned silver polished to a moon-bright shine. She bore the accoutrements of a good housewife: knife, scissors and keys hanging from a chain. Margaret was capable. Some found her intimidating. She had never remarried after her husband died in the very first year of Norse settlement here in the Light Isles, before Thorvald was born. Creidhe did not find her aunt frightening; there was a bond between them. Creidhe might not be skilled in the arts of a priestess, as her sister Eanna was. She might not be beautiful in the style of the island girls, slender, dark and graceful. But she had other abilities. Young as she was, Creidhe had the best hands for midwifery in Hrossey, and had advanced quickly from assisting the island expert to taking a full share of responsibility. The women valued Creidhe's deft touch and cool head; these made her youth irrelevant. The same clever hands gave her a talent for spinning, weaving and embroidery. Margaret valued that talent, and over the years she had taken pleasure in fostering this buxom, fair-haired niece's skills.

If Thorvald never comes round to marrying me, Creidhe told herself sourly, some other man surely will, just so he can say his wife's the best weaver in Hrossey.

It wasn't as if nobody was interested. Creidhe was never short of partners for dancing. Sam had made her a whalebone comb with sea creatures carved on it. Egil had composed a poem for her and recited it, blushing. Brude had kissed her behind the cowshed when nobody was looking. The problem was, she didn't want sweet-natured Sam or scholarly Egil or handsome Brude with his merry blue eyes. She only wanted Thorvald. Thorvald had eyes dark as night and smooth auburn hair like his mother's. Creidhe loved his cleverness, his wit, the way he could always surprise her. She loved his moments of kindness, rare as they were. She wished, sometimes, that he were a little less aloof; she'd heard other girls call him arrogant, and she didn't like that. He did keep himself to himself; she was lucky to be one of those he considered a friend. Creidhe sighed. Thorvald was taking a long time to realize she could be more than just a friend to him. At sixteen she was a woman, and ready to be married; more than ready, she thought sometimes. If Thorvald didn't wake up to himself soon, her father would start suggesting likely husbands for her, and what could she say then? As her mother's daughter, she must wed and bear children. It could not be long before Eyvind began to apply subtle pressure.

"Creidhe?"

"Oh! Sorry." She'd been daydreaming again. "Are you all right, Aunt Margaret?"

"Well enough." The words belied the red eyes, the tight mouth. "Go on then, if Nessa's expecting you home. This can wait for tomorrow. The design's coming out well, Creidhe. You're quite an artist."

Creidhe blushed. "Thank you, Aunt." She paused. "Aunt Margaret—"

Margaret raised a hand. It was a gesture that said plainly, no questions. Whatever it was that had sent Thorvald out of the house like a man pursued by dark dreams, it was not going to be shared just yet.

"Creidhe," said Margaret as her niece hovered in the doorway, small bundle of belongings in hand, "don't go after Thorvald. Not today. Believe me, he's best left alone a while."

"But—"

"If he wants to tell you, he'll tell you in his own time. Now off home with you. Your father's been away a long while. I expect he'd enjoy some of his daughter's fine cooking, perhaps your roasted mutton and garlic, or the baked cod with leek sauce. Off with you now."

The tone was light, kept carefully so, Creidhe thought. It was her aunt's eyes that gave her away. Thorvald's had held the same shadow.

Sometimes Creidhe did as she was told, and sometimes she didn't. Thorvald was sitting on the ground, his back to a low stone dyke overlooking the western sea. He had his head in his hands, his face concealed. His sleek red hair had escaped its neat ribbon, and the wind whipped the strands like dark fire in the air around his head. He was very still. Behind him in the walled field, sheep bleated and lambs answered. Above in the sky birds fluted songs of spring. Creidhe climbed over the wall and sat down by his side, saying not a word. She had become quite good at this kind of thing.

"Go away, Creidhe!" Thorvald growled after a while. He did not open his eyes.

There was a little boat out in the swell, coming in from fishing. The wind was picking up; the scrap of sail carried the vessel forward on a fast, rocking course southward, perhaps to Hafnarvagr, or some point closer. Creidhe raised a hand in greeting, but they did not see her.

"I mean it, Creidhe," snapped Thorvald. "Go home. Go back to your embroidery."

She took a deep breath and let it out, counting up to ten. It was useful to have wise women in the family; one might not learn the mysteries, for those were secret, but one did at least pick up techniques for staying calm.

"What is it?" she asked him quietly. "What did she give you?"

"I don't want to talk about it. Not to you, not to anyone."

"All right," Creidhe said after a moment. "I understand. When you do want to, I'll be here to listen."

Thorvald balled his hands into tight fists. His eyes were open now, staring out to the west. It seemed to Creidhe that what he saw was not cliffs, gulls, clouds, a wind-stirred ocean, but something quite different and much further away.

Time passed. Father would be home soon; the remark about roast mutton had been true. Such simple pleasures had the power to bring a smile to Eyvind's lips and a light to his eyes that warmed his whole family. It was not so much the good food that did it, as his daughter's thoughtfulness and skill. Creidhe rose to her feet, picking up her bundle.

"Creidhe?"

It was a dark whisper. She stood frozen in place a moment, then sat down again without a sound.

"A letter," Thorvald said. "From my father. She kept it all these years. She never even told me."

Creidhe was at odds to understand the bitterness in his tone. His father had died before he was born, and that was indeed sad, though surely sadder for Margaret than for this son who had never known the father he had lost. From what folk said, Margaret's husband Ulf had been a fine, noble chieftain who had led the first Norse expedition here to the Light Isles. He was a father to be proud of. A letter was good, wasn't it? It seemed not inappropriate that Margaret had saved it until her son was a man.

"From Ulf?" Creidhe asked gently. "I suppose that is distressing; it reminds you of what you might have had. It is a sorrow he was not here to watch you grow up."

"I didn't say it was from my mother's husband, the worthy Ulf Gunnarsson." Thorvald's voice was sharp-edged. "I said it was from my father. The man she tells me was my real father, that is. Here, if you're so interested. Why not find out all about it, since it seems half the island knows already?"

He drew the little roll of parchment from the breast of his tunic and thrust it into her hand. Creidhe was mute. What could he mean? She untied the cord that bound the letter and uncurled it to reveal row on row of neat, black script. It was old, the edges worn, the characters smudged here and there as if by drops of w^ter. There was a pale line all across the outside where the cord had fastened it, as if the small scroll had lain long untouched.

"You know I can't read, Thorvald. What is all this about?"

"I'll tell you what it's all about. It means I'm nobody. Worse than nobody, I'm the son of some evil madman, a crazed killer. Forget Ulf; forget a conception in the respectability of marriage, and the sad demise of my father before I saw the light of day. Ulf was not my father. She kept that from me all these years. And they knew: your father, Nessa, Grim, everyone who came here in those first days. Even that stick of a serving man, Ash, knew the truth and kept quiet about it. A conspiracy of silence." His voice was shaking; he stared fixedly at the ground by his feet. "How could my own mother be so cruel?"

Creidhe was lost for words. She wanted to put an arm around him for comfort, as she would do if this were one of her sisters. But she did not; Thorvald would shake her off the instant she touched him. This news was indeed terrible, if true. What if such a thing had happened to her? Her own father was the center of her world, the warmth at the core of the family. Indeed, sometimes it seemed Eyvind was father to the whole community, guardian and loving protector to them all. To hear your father was not your father would be like the snatching away of everything safe. It would be like sundering the heart from the body. There seemed no way to comfort him.

"You're very quiet," Thorvald said suddenly, turning his head to glare at her. "No ready words of advice? No quick solutions to my problems?" His eyes narrowed; his mouth went tight. "But perhaps you knew this already. Perhaps I am indeed the last to be told the truth about my own heritage. Did you know, Creidhe?" His tone was savage; Creidhe shrank back before it.

"Of course not! How could you think—?"

Thorvald's shoulders sagged. His anger was turned inward again. "That's just it. I don't know what to think anymore."

Who—who was he?" Creidhe ventured. "Was this letter written to you? Where is he?"

"Ask your father. He knows the answers."

"But—"

"Ask Eyvind. He was the one who exiled my father from this shore, so that he never knew he had a son. The letter was to my mother. It says nothing of me. It attempts to explain to her why her lover killed her husband. It tries to justify his murder of his own brother. You see the delightful heritage my lady mother has chosen to make me aware of now I'm deemed to have reached years of maturity?" Thorvald picked up a stone and hurled it out beyond the cliff edge. A cloud of gulls rose, screaming protest. His face was sheet-white, the eyes dark hollows.

"What was his name?" Creidhe asked, playing for time as her mind searched frantically for the right thing to say. In such a situation, there probably was no right thing.

"Somerled." He threw another stone.

"Why don't they speak of such a man? They must all have known him."

"Why don't you ask them, if you're so interested?"

She breathed slowly. "Thorvald?"

"What?"

"Aunt Margaret was wise not to tell you this before. You're grown up now. Couldn't you see this, not as a reversal but a challenge?"

His brows rose in scorn. "What can you mean, Creidhe?"

"You could find out about Somerled. As you said, there must be plenty of people in the islands who knew him back then. Maybe he wasn't as bad as you think. Everyone's got some good in them."

"And what comes after that?" Thorvald snapped. "I jump in a boat and go off looking for him, I suppose?"

The words hung between them as the silence stretched out, giving them a weight Thorvald had not intended. Blue eyes met black; there was recognition in both that this crazy idea was, in a way, entirely logical.

Thorvald rolled the letter up and knotted the cord around it. He put it away and leaned back against the wall, arms hugging his knees, eyes firmly closed. She waited again. At length, not opening his eyes, he said, "I know you're trying to help, Creidhe. But I really do want to be by myself." There was a pause. "Please," he added.

It was not possible to bestow a gesture of affection, a quick hug, a hand-clasp, although Creidhe longed to touch him. "Farewell, Thorvald," she said, and made her way home under darkening skies.

If you enjoyed this book, you won't want to miss. . .

NEW YORK TIMES BESTSELLING AUTHOR

CONSTANCE O'DAY-FLANNERY

0-765-34889-6 • $6.99/$9.99 Can.

Shifting Love

SHIFTING LOVE
CONSTANCE O'DAY-FLANNERY
IN PAPERBACK NOVEMBER 2004

Tor is proud to launch its Paranormal Romance
line with a passionate tale of magic and love
from *New York Times* bestselling author
Contstance O'Day-Flannery.

**"An author of incredible talent and
imagination. She has the magic."**
—*Romantic Times Bookclub*

TOR
www.tor.com